MEN OF LONDON

Volume One
Books 1 – 5

Susan Mac Nicol

www.BOROUGHSPUBLISHINGGROUP.com

LOVE YOU SENSELESS
SIGHT & SINNERS
SUIT YOURSELF
FEAT OF CLAY
CROSS TO BARE

ISBN 978-1-951055-24-0

LOVE YOU SENSELESS

Scorched skin and roast pork. Smells that would forever be etched into his nostrils, scraped onto the walls of his heart and mind like burning tattoos. The best thing to do would be stop smelling anything altogether so that the memory of that night could be buried deep within his psyche, never to see the light of day again. It was his only hope.

Chapter 1

The man in the bed tossed and turned as his body tried to find solace in sleep. His skin glistened with sweat and he mumbled as he thrashed among messy covers. Hands moved in agitation like those of an Italian in conversation, flapping, expressive. The sheets slipped lower on his body as his legs scissored and the covers slid off onto the floor.

He muttered a loud expletive and then gave a sharp cry. The sound echoed through the dark bedroom. His eyes opened and he stilled. For a moment, there was only the sound of his heavy breathing as he struggled to compose himself. Finally, he swung his legs out of bed and stumbled unsteadily to the en-suite bathroom. There was the sound of pissing, a steady stream that went on until the flush of the toilet. Then he made his way back to the bed where he lay, gazing up with pained eyes at the ceiling.

***

Gideon punished the piece of nicotine gum he was chewing with iron jaws. He scowled from inside the kitchen doorway of the restaurant he owned as he watched Eddie Tripp artfully place the last piece of garnish onto the dish he was plating. With a final look at the plate, like a man eyeing out a lover, Eddie picked it up and set it down on the long, heated conveyer belt that ran from one end of the stylishly designed kitchen of the restaurant to the other. The younger man watched it almost reverently as the plate made its way sedately down the belt, out into the serving area, toward hovering waiters who waited ready to pluck it up and serve it to a hopefully satisfied customer. The belt was one of Gideon's indulgences; he had seen the same practice being used in New York when he was on holiday there.

Eddie turned and whistled softly as he prepared the next plate, his hands darting like dragonflies as he skilfully picked up the ingredients to prepare yet another masterpiece. His wavy, dark red hair was held in place by a hair net, something Gideon insisted on when anyone was in the kitchen. The sous-chef had ears that were slightly larger than normal, which Gideon found endearing—why, he had no idea. Ears weren't a big turn-on for him in the usual course of things. The wide smile on Eddie's expressive, freckled face told everyone who saw him that he was enjoying himself. Gideon wanted to kiss the smile off Eddie's face and fulfil his lustful longings to pound the man into the table. He had wanted to do that about two days after the man had joined the staff of Galileo's. The red-headed man appealed to Gideon like no one had in a very long time. He didn't like the feelings Eddie caused in him, something possessive and definitely needy. It had been a little while since he had gotten laid, and craving one of his employees sucked.

"Boss? What's that look for? Is something wrong?" Carmen de Luiz, his secretary, office manager and good friend, placed a soft hand on his arm as she peered at him anxiously out of black-rimmed eyes, her black lips set in a worried curve. Gideon was used to her whole new goth look now and it no longer made him start. Carmen's lips were speckled with what looked like icing sugar and he suspected she'd been sampling the new dessert dish he knew Eddie was working on—pirouettes of raspberry shells with crème fraiche or some such sweetly named concoction. He felt a flare of envy surge through him at the thought Eddie was creating such sweet treats. Another thing blotting that particular employee's copybook.

He shook his head in frustration as he shoved the gum to one side of his mouth. "No, nothing wrong. And if you keep sneaking in to sample Eddie's wares, you're going to get bloody fat." He disregarded Carmen's moue of hurt and carried on. "But does he have to look so damn happy all the time? I swear that man is the fucking reincarnation of the bluebird of happiness." He ran a hand over his own shortly cropped light brown hair in frustration then tugged at his neatly manicured beard.

Carmen shook her head. "Baby, then you must be the reincarnation of the raven of doom." She sniggered as he scowled even deeper. "Giddy, honey, chill out. Eddie loves his job; you should be pleased you have such an asset in your kitchen."

Gideon turned freezing eyes on her. "Firstly, don't call me Giddy. You know I hate it. Secondly, I'm well aware of what an asset I have in my kitchen, thank you. I employed him, remember?" Oh, he knew about Eddie's assets. Those green eyes, that piercing stare, those talented fingers that look like they would play havoc with his dick. He pushed *that* thought out of his mind. "But I don't need to see his face wreathed in merriment every time I look at him. It's bloody unnatural." He scowled. "And I heard he broke another plate this morning? Does that boy think we're made of bloody money?" He chewed frantically on his bland piece of tasteless gum. He wanted a damn cigarette but that wasn't going to happen.

Carmen sighed. "It was just one plate. And he's twenty-four, not a boy. I wish you'd stop calling him that. You're only four years older than him, old timer."

"Well, he looks like a kid. All long limbs and flailing arms and costing me a fortune when he knocks something off or drops it." Gideon's inner bitchiness at not being able to control his feelings for Eddie rushed to the surface.

"Jesus, have you not had any for a while? You're being a real prima donna, even for you. Give the man a break, will you?" Carmen sounded a little pissed off as she marched over to Eddie's side, probably to resume her tasting session, and Gideon knew he'd better back off. A truly riled Carmen was not someone he wanted right now. So he ignored her, glowered and left the kitchen behind to enter the main restaurant.

It seemed as if all was usual, running like a well-oiled machine, but it never hurt to make sure. As the owner he took great pride in making things happen. He'd rather be in the kitchen creating dishes but he knew *that* wasn't on the cards. He looked around, his mood even darker. It was seven o'clock on a chilly September night and the place was packed.

Sarah Townsend, his very capable front of house manager and his right hand as far as the running of Galileo's was concerned, smiled at him as she led a couple to their table. This restaurant in London's Soho district was Gideon's pride and joy. It was also his home, as he occupied the large, roomy two-bedroomed flat above the restaurant. He was proud of his almost penthouse-like abode, furnished with all the mod cons and able to be accessed from inside the restaurant. It also had a private entrance, just the way he liked it.

Galileo's was currently abuzz with patrons. Some sat enjoying cocktails and pints at the highly polished dark oak bar along one side of the restaurant. Others were seated in the table area, an opulent arena of red and bronze décor, heavy wooden tables and the ambience of the Renaissance era. To the left was the huge brass telescope he'd found at an antique store and had cost him almost the price of what he thought a black market kidney would fetch. Indeed, when he'd been told the price he'd thought someone had reached inside and ripped it out. But he'd paid the money because he really wanted it. And what Gideon wanted, Gideon tended to get.

The ceiling was speckled with stars and constellations, a beautiful cosmic frieze that a local artist, Rafael Montero, had done for him. One Gideon had been fucking at the time but who no longer graced his bed due to the fact that said bed had been the scene of Rafael's infidelity with a man Gideon didn't know—some young college student called Richard. Gideon had promptly given Rafael his marching orders. They may have only been together three months but he would never tolerate cheating.

Gideon was lucky that Rafael hadn't been back to try and claim his "masterpiece" out of spite; he could insist it was his creative inspiration and he wanted it back. He wouldn't have put it past his rather fiery Latin ex-lover to have snuck in and whitewashed the mural over.

He watched the tableau before him now—impeccably dressed waiters bearing wine buckets, plates of beautifully prepared food being whisked from the specially created serving area to tables. Customers chatted and relaxed, looking for the most part as if they enjoyed themselves. He breathed a deep satisfied sigh and relaxed.

For a whole twenty seconds.

A loud noise from the kitchen made Gideon turn in consternation and his temper, already short by lack of sleep due to the nightmares that plagued him, flared as he stormed back in.

Christ, has the kid broken something else because by God, if he has, it's coming out of his wages.

There was a shattered mess of porcelain on the floor, and a flustered Eddie knelt trying to clean it up with a dustpan and brush. Carmen stood dabbing at the front of her dress, trying to get what looked like tea out of it with a dish towel.

Gideon spat his gum into the nearby dustbin. “Tripp!” He bellowed. “What the fuck have you broken now? Tripp by name, Tripp by nature, is it?” He’d heard the good-natured ribbing in the kitchen from the other staff about poor Eddie’s klutziness.

Eddie’s face flushed scarlet, an unfortunate side effect of being a fair-skinned redhead. His freckles stood out deeper on his pink face and his sea green eyes held a look of dismay. The rest of the kitchen staff looked on in trepidation.

Gideon’s head-chef, a large Jamaican man named Jerome Sawyer, moved toward him with purpose and Gideon took an instinctive step back. While the two men were both work colleagues and friends, Jerome’s rather fierce glare didn’t bode well for Gideon. He was distracted from Jerome’s intentions by Eddie’s continued rambling.

“I was just cleaning up, Mr. Kent,” he stuttered. “There was a bit of a mishap with the beef stock bowl—”

Gideon scowled. “There seem to be a lot of those. You are a one-man demolition squad. I can’t afford to have you keep breaking stuff—”

“Now see here, Gideon, it wasn’t like that.” Jerome towered over Gideon now, his large, sausage-like fingers resting on Eddie’s shoulder. “I can’t have you thinking it was his fault—”

Jerome’s words were cut off as Carmen’s firm fingers pinched the flesh of Gideon’s right side and he yowled loudly in pain.

Jerome blinked at being rudely interrupted but looked fairly amused.

Eddie’s eyes were wide as he gazed from one person to another. Gideon turned to stare at Carmen angrily. Her face was set, her eyes unfriendly.

“What the hell?” he exclaimed. “What was that for?”

“May I see you outside, please? Thanks, Jerome, but I’ll take care of this one,” she hissed and flounced out of the kitchen, no doubt headed to the small office which they’d agreed was their neutral territory to discuss things out of earshot of staff.

Gideon stared after her then turned to a still red-faced Eddie. Jerome had a large grin plastered over his beaming face.

“Could you clean that up, please?” Gideon demanded, and passed a haughty glare at Jerome, who winked at him.

Bastard. He knows I'm going to get my balls handed to me somehow.

"Yes, Mr Kent," Eddie sighed wearily and bent down to sweep bits of pottery into the bright red dustpan he held.

Gideon couldn't help noticing the tight curve of his arse as he did so and the swell of what looked like a real bubble butt beneath the loose black-and-white-checked catering trousers he wore.

What the hell? Now I'm ogling his backside in public? Jesus, this is too much. I need to get laid...quickly.

He averted his gaze and left then walked into his small but comfortable office on the other side of the kitchen.

Carmen glared at him as she stood with hands on hips, looking fairly miffed. "*I* was the one who knocked that bowl off the counter, Gideon Kent. Not Eddie. So if you're going to garnish anyone's wages you'd better make sure they're mine."

He huffed. "Fine. He can count it as a warning for the next time he *does* break something. It's always good to put the fear of God into the staff." His tone sounded defensive even to him.

Carmen's face softened. "Gideon, you can't keep doing this."

"Doing what?" But he knew.

"Honey, I know more than anyone how frustrated you are at not being able to cook, to be a chef like you were before. I get that. But if you keep harassing Eddie, one day he's going to leave. And that would be a shame because he's one of the best up and coming chefs there is. You know that or you wouldn't have taken him on. But you're being a damn bully to him."

Gideon's stomach tightened at Carmen's words and he felt the old familiar sense of loss, grief and disappointment take over. The kitchen had once been his domain until the tools he needed to perform there had been cruelly taken from him. It was where he should be right now, creating signature dishes and making people's taste buds soar. Instead he was stuck with being a manager and a host. While he enjoyed it, it wasn't where his passion lay.

"Carmen, you're stepping over that boss-employee line," he warned. "Is it my fault I want things to run smoothly?"

Carmen came over and placed her hand, with slightly scary long black fingernails, on his wrist. "You're pissed off because you can't cook and you're taking it out on Eddie because he has what you don't. And baby, there's not much you can do about that yet. You know I believe you'll get those senses back someday. And it would come sooner if you'd talk to someone about that night, tell them the whole story. You never say anything about what you went through to anyone. Not even me." She regarded him shrewdly. "Are you still having nightmares?"

Gideon stiffened. "It's my business. Not anyone else's."

Carmen sighed, her eyes compassionate. "Everybody needs someone to talk to."

He clamped his lips. He wasn't getting sucked into Carmen's ploy to get him to talk about that night, the night he'd rather forget.

She saw that and sighed sadly. "So for now, let Eddie do his job. And what I say to you I say as a friend, not as an employee, so the Gideon 'line' doesn't count."

Gideon's throat was dry and tight. "I see. So I'm simply an arsehole then? Thanks for that."

Carmen sighed. "You are so damn prickly." She kissed his cheek softly. "But you're still a good friend. I'm going to go check everything got cleaned up in the kitchen seeing as how it was my fault. You might want to apologise to Eddie later. Make things up for the future, just in case." With a knowing look she was gone. Gideon didn't even want to think about what her last words might have inferred.

He slumped down into the office chair and stared moodily at the chart for staff leave on the wall. The trouble was…she was right. Ever since the accident six months ago, when the fire in his old home had taken away his sense of smell and taste, left his housemate dead and Gideon injured, he'd been a miserable git whenever he went in the kitchen. The sense of loss at who he had been, an award-winning, much talked-about chef in the city, was sometimes too much to bear.

He rubbed his eyes tiredly and closed them, recalling that night with a sense of dread. The explosion next door due to a gas leak, the fire licking through his shattered lounge, which had shared a wall with the doomed kitchen. Luckily, he'd been thrown away from the blast, away from the flames, but had been pinned by a wooden beam, his skin blistering as the wood smouldered. Hugh had not been so fortunate and had borne the brunt of it. He had lain burning on the floor, as the smell and stench of his roasting flesh had invaded Gideon's nostrils.

He'd woken up in hospital to find he'd sustained second-degree burns to his left side. The injuries had left the skin along his hip and stomach a little thickened and sensitive, although he'd definitely been the lucky one. Hugh and the neighbour were dead. A couple of days later, as he recovered, Gideon had realised his sense of smell and taste had disappeared completely.

The doctors told him his loss of smell was psychological, a condition called anosmia. They'd attributed it to him trying to shut his mind off from the odour of his friend's burning flesh. They said it could come back at any time, that there was nothing physically wrong with him, no blows to the head, no damage to his brain.

He'd hated the clinical diagnosis of a condition that meant the loss of his soul.

The doctor had tried to explain it. "Smell counts toward a person's sense of taste, and the term, *ageusia*, is used to describe your inability to do so. Be patient. You could still get both senses back."

His *condition*. Words that struck terror into his heart, the reason that his whole damn world had fallen apart. Some people with the affliction could taste salt or sweet on their tongue but he wasn't one of them. Everyone had tried to get him to talk to therapists and psychologists but Gideon wasn't made that way. He'd never talked to anyone about the events of that night other than to give some general detail to the police and paramedics. It was his cross to bear, even the montages in his head that woke him, sweating and crying out, in the middle of the night.

"Because what fucking good is a chef who can't taste and smell, eh?" he muttered as he rolled a pen between his fingers. "I'll tell you. No damn good at all. If I can't do it properly, no point doing it in the first place. Just like smoking."

Gideon had been a fairly heavy smoker before the accident and had enjoyed it. Now that the pleasure of inhaling the smoky odour of a cigarette and the woodsy taste of it on his tongue had disappeared, he'd decided there was no point in doing it anymore. Like a martyr, he'd given it up. It had surprised him just how quickly he'd been able to stop—with the help of his gum.

He frowned, gave up on his pity party and lost himself in menus, bookings and details for his accountant. Finally he'd had enough. It was close to eleven p.m. and time to do the rounds to ensure everything was shut down for the night. There was a soft knock on the door and he looked up to see Eddie standing there diffidently, looking ready to leave, his blue wool beanie jammed over his thick red-gold hair, his slightly protuberant ears looking endearingly elf-like. A fleeting thought passed through Gideon's mind that he would make a great Legolas with his fine bone structure and dimpled chin. Albeit with hair the colour of flames and thick enough to run a hand through, long enough on top to wind it around a fist and pull that luscious pink mouth down towards Gideon's—

And there the fuck I go again. God, get a grip.

Gideon groaned inwardly as he regarded Eddie with narrowed eyes, shoving all thought of sexy elves, blow jobs and a naked Eddie Tripp out of his crazy brain.

"Uhmm, Mr. Kent, before she went home earlier, Carmen said that you wanted to see me before I left?" Emerald green eyes stared into Gideon's. Eddie stood firm as he hitched his backpack tighter to his shoulder and met Gideon's gaze unflinchingly.

Gideon tapped the pen on the desk in nervousness at having Eddie so close. Not for the first time he wished he could smell him, see if the man's scent was sweat or cologne, or soap or sweet-scented sugar from the creations he made.

"She did, did she? She can be a really interfering biddy. And how many times have I told you to call me Gideon? Mr. Kent was my dad. And I don't see him here."

He bit his lip as his snark returned in Eddie's presence. It was as if his mouth had no other way to react when Eddie was near.

Eddie seemed to be suppressing a smile. "It's a little difficult to be on first-name terms with a man who's always growling at me," he said, faint amusement in his tone. "I thought perhaps I should keep it professional."

Oh, Eddie bites does he? Not such a whippersnapper after all. I quite like that. The idea of him biting is definitely something I'd like to pursue.

Gideon shifted in the chair, trying to stave off the erection forming in his jeans.

Christ, that would be all I need, physical evidence of how he turns me on. I don't even know if the man is gay or straight and he'd probably deck me. They say redheads have tempers, don't they?

"Yes, well, about that. I'm sorry I growled at you in the kitchen earlier. Carmen told me it was her fault, so…" Gideon shrugged.

Eddie was grinning now, a wide, easy look on him that made Gideon's heart race just a little bit and the dick in his pants harden even more. "Wow. An apology. Thanks, I'll take it." He set his backpack down on Gideon's desk and rummaged around like Mary Poppins, an endearing pout of his lips making Gideon think of that blow job again. "I have something here I wanted to give to you, if I can find the poxy thing—ah, there you are."

He took out what looked to be a bedraggled red napkin, which Gideon knew to be one of the restaurant's special orders, and handed the soiled item to Gideon, who reached out and took it. There was something encased in the napkin and Gideon unfolded it to reveal a delicate pastry covered in icing sugar. No doubt one of the ones Carmen had enjoyed sampling earlier.

He felt a twinge in his chest. "I hope you aren't going to ask me to smell or taste this, because you know I can't, right?" He hadn't meant there to be a sneer in his words but he heard it just the same.

Eddie nodded. "Yes, I know you can't smell it or taste it, we're all aware of that, but I wondered if you'd mind giving me your opinion on the texture. Is it light enough, too heavy, does it melt in the mouth, feel like soggy cardboard…" He shrugged. "I wondered if you'd tell me, that's all."

Gideon placed the pastry on the desk and re-commenced his pen calisthenics. "I suppose I can. Perhaps later."

Eddie's face darkened. "Thanks. I know you'll be honest at least." His tone was testy. He hefted his rucksack onto his shoulder. "Well, if that's all, I'd better be getting home. It's late and I've got a bit of a walk to the tube."

He turned to go and Gideon stood up. "Eddie?"

The younger man turned to face him. "Yes?"

"Have a safe journey home. See you tomorrow."

Eddie smiled that wide smile again, the one that caused Gideon's sleeping heart to slowly stir with wakefulness. "I will. See you then." He turned and left.

Gideon stood there for a while and then sighed. He adjusted himself to get more comfortable then picked the pastry up, removed the napkin and popped it into his mouth. There was no sensation of sweet, no sugary caress to his taste buds, no hint in his mouth of raspberry coulis. He couldn't smell the almonds that would be in the pastry. He'd seen Eddie's recipe in the kitchen. Nothing. He felt the old familiar angst and resentment rear its ugly head as he chewed. It *was* light, flaky and melted in the mouth. There was nothing wrong with the texture. It was perfect.

Gideon swallowed the morsel, his heart tinged with bitterness, then threw the napkin into the waste bin. He gathered up his jacket and went to find Sarah to tell her he'd lock up and she could get the hell home to her family.

Chapter 2

Eddie heaved his rucksack onto his lap as he sat in the squashed confines of the tube and gazed out into the darkened tunnel as the train sped its way home to Kennington, to the small three-bedroomed mid terrace he shared with housemates Leslie and Taylor. Nicknamed Gay Way by Leslie, due to the fact that three gay men lived there, it was cramped, dark and a little mouldy in places but it was home to him now. His childhood home of Diss in Norfolk where his parents still lived was now just a memory. Eddie had his independence, his own small room and he and his housemates came and went as they pleased.

Eddie was lost in thought when a hand squeezed his thigh. Startled, he looked into a pair of red-rimmed, rheumy blue eyes and winced at the sour breath coming his way from a very buff, older man seated next to him.

Great. A fucking pervert who likes hitting on young men.

"Lost in thought, hey?" the pervert murmured. "Now what could a gorgeous young thing like you be thinking about then?"

Eddie politely removed the man's groping hand from his leg and shifted his rucksack over his lap to better protect himself. He'd been in situations like this before and didn't really want any trouble.

"I think that's why they call them thoughts," he said gently. "Because they're quiet and private." He looked away, hoping that the man would get the message. But no, there was his hand again, moving even closer to his crotch. Eddie sighed and tried to move further away but the woman next to him scowled fiercely as he encroached on her territory. Eddie closed his eyes momentarily and thanked God he got off at the next stop.

"It's a shame you hide that lovely hair under a bloody beanie," the man said, his fingers tightening on Eddie's leg. "I'd love to feel it under my fingers while you blow me. How about it? Do you fancy going somewhere with me next stop?"

Eddie stood up swiftly and moved away. "Not one bit," he said politely. "Not interested." The man didn't look pleased but Eddie didn't give a damn.

Why the hell did men hit on him? He didn't think he was all that much of a flamer, not like Leslie, and he didn't broadcast the fact, especially at work. Yet he couldn't go anywhere without being accosted by dirty old men or young bucks who wanted to bend him over and fuck him into next week. It's the bloody hair, he thought gloomily as he waited for the train to stop. *My effing red hair and pale skin that's been the bane of my life. Makes me look like a girl.*

Of course the fact he wore it quite long on top didn't help but he was damned if he'd cut it off just to make himself look less "feminine."

No, Eddie would rather look more like the delectable Gideon Kent, all male and decidedly sexy. He had one helluva of a crush on his boss and had done since he started at Galileo's. Gideon might be a testy bastard but he was testosterone personified with those smoldering chocolate eyes and that neatly trimmed dark golden stubble around his chin and lip. Eddie often found himself wanting to brush his fingers over it then lick that full bottom lip until his boss's stubborn mouth gave way. And joy oh joy, the man was gay too, even if he was off the menu being Eddie's boss. Eddie didn't really think icing the cake in his own bakery was a good idea. That was a clear invitation to trouble.

Even if I do want to rip those form-fitting trousers off his gorgeous butt and slap it. Besides, he'd never be interested in me. He likes them all dark and moody.

Gideon's last rather loud argument with his very volatile Spanish lover had attested to that, and the staff had stood in wide-eyed amazement as Rafael had stormed out of Gideon's office one day a few weeks ago and not been seen since. They had already broken up but it appeared Rafael had been trying to get some money from Gideon. Last Eddie had heard through the scuttlebutt grapevine, Rafael had gone to Spain with a new lover. He hadn't wasted any time, Eddie mused.

The train screeched to a stop and Eddie clambered off and started to make his way home. It was only about a ten-minute walk and he rather enjoyed it. The night air was chill, being September, but it was crisp and refreshing. As he reached the house, climbed the two stairs to the front door and squinted under the dim porch light to see the keyhole to open the door, he heard a frightening screech from inside. He'd just stepped back when someone came barreling out, almost knocking him off the stairs.

The person gave a muttered "Crazy fucker," as he jostled Eddie and then something whipped past Eddie's head. He saw with resignation it was yet another poor telephone directory being lobbed, no doubt, by Leslie.

"Stay the fuck away from me, you double-timing, cock-sucking, arse-dribbling twat!" Leslie's high-pitched voice screamed the invective as Eddie entered the house and found Leslie in a strop, phone in hand, clacking around on high heels, tiny silk shorts and a tight tank top that said he'd just been clubbing. It was after midnight, which was still early in Leslie's world of late-night partying.

"Oh, thank God you're home, Ed," sobbed Leslie as his eyeliner ran down his cheeks in stripes reminiscent of a zebra.

The man would be mortified if he could see himself. Eddie hated being called Ed but he let Leslie get away with it when he was in this state, which had been fairly often in the three months they'd been housemates. Leslie was a very high-maintenance twenty-three-year-old drama queen.

Sighing, Eddie took out a hanky from his jeans pockets. Leslie hurled himself into his arms, and he patted him on the back as the hanky flapped like a peace flag.

"That motherfucking bastard had the gall to suck someone off at the club tonight after he promised me we were exclusive. I saw a text on his phone from the guy. He even gave him his number!" Leslie's body shook with sobs.

Eddie pulled Leslie away from him and dabbed his zebra stripes with his hanky. "It'll be fine, Leslie." No one called Leslie "Les." He would have a conniption bar none if that happened and would probably scratch eyes out with his pointy fingernails. "He was an arsehole who didn't deserve you. You'll find the right one, I promise. Now come on and I'll make you a cup of tea."

Eddie was bone tired and wanted nothing more than to get into bed but he needed to get his friend settled first. He led Leslie over to the couch and plonked him down. While Leslie sniveled into his hanky, Eddie went to the kitchen to put the kettle on. He wondered absently where his other housemate was. Taylor was a bit of an enigma, a man who kept his private life just that, and who worked in a music shop down the road. He was normally home by now and as very good at sorting out Leslie's meltdowns with his no-nonsense attitude and snarky wit. The two men were very close and sometimes Eddie wondered why they weren't a couple. They suited each other. He'd asked Taylor one day and he'd laughed and said Leslie was beautiful but not for him. Not in that way anyway.

Eddie finished making tea and took it into the lounge. He stopped short when he saw Leslie curled up on the sofa fast asleep, looking like a decadent floozy in his heels and red-streaked black hair sprinkled with glitter. Dark, silky bangs hung down over sleeping eyes. Eddie slipped off the stilettos, gathered the blanket from the footstool and covered Leslie with it. He put the steaming tea down on the coffee table in case Leslie woke up and wanted it then wearily went to bed.

Chapter 3

The following morning the kitchen was abuzz when Gideon walked in at around eight, a little more refreshed than he'd been in a while. He'd actually slept through last night with no dreams about burning men. Though the wet dream he *had* experienced had been one he wouldn't mind repeating.

He grinned as he pottered about, making sure everything was okay for the staff meeting. This early morning between eight and eight-thirty was for all the kitchen staff to ensure that the preparation for business breakfasts they offered was all in hand. From nine-thirty onwards, it was the Eggs Benedict Brigade that flocked through the open doors, ready for an early morning caffeine and hollandaise sauce boost.

Eddie was working on one of the stainless steel island tables between the hob and ovens. Gideon couldn't help notice that he looked tired, with dark circles under his eyes. His thick hair was once again caught up in a net on top and the normally short-clipped sides and back were showing signs of soft curls. Gideon felt an overwhelming desire to reach out and see if he pulled it, if it would spring back like a slinky. He masterfully resisted the impulse and waved everyone to pay attention.

"Morning. We have the Sherlock Holmes Appreciation Society in this morning, all twenty of the buggers wanting a hearty meal before they wander down to ogle the film set for the new series. So please look sharp, let's make sure we plate the food up as quickly and possible and get it out there. You all know the drill and I've no doubt you'll all do a sterling job."

He was feeling magnanimous this morning after that rather raunchy dream featuring warm lips around his dick and a cascade of red hair across his groin. In the cold light of day, seeing the man he'd dreamed about, he felt like a pervert and he tried not to catch Eddie's glance as those green eyes appraised him carefully.

"If we do a good job with this lot, they'll more than likely make more bookings, and it's nice turnover for us. Not to mention one of the members has a contact in the film production crew for one of the big TV series and she's promised to try and get their business for us as well. We all know word of mouth is essential in this game."

There was a chorus of agreement and Gideon smiled warmly at his staff. "Right, you all know what to do. In the meantime, there are a few other things I need to talk you about."

The staff meeting went well and twenty minutes later Gideon was back in his office poring about some accounts his book keeper had sent him. He popped a piece of gum in his mouth as he perused them. The business was doing very well and he felt a swell of satisfaction. He was a lucky man to have the team he had. Galileo's reputation for good food, great ambience and excellent service was growing.

He sat back in his chair with a happy sigh. A loud sneeze from the door announced Carmen's arrival. Gideon glanced at his watch. Nine o'clock on the dot. Carmen was only due into work at nine-thirty but was always in early.

"Morning, boss. I see you got Jenna's accounts. They look good, don't they?" She ambled in and sat down in the office chair opposite Gideon. Black lace-up boots thumped onto his desk, followed by thin black legs in tights.

Gideon shook his head ruefully. "You are so damn disrespectful of a man's work place, you know that? I honestly don't want to look up your damn dress so cross your legs."

Carmen snickered. "Wasted on you, my considerable attributes." She crossed her legs to protect her modesty and raised one multi-pierced eyebrow at him. "You'd rather look down Eddie's drawers then?"

Gideon's stomach lurched. "What the hell? What's that supposed to mean?" He swallowed and fumbled with the papers on his desk arranging them into neat piles. His gum chewing got more energised.

Carmen snorted loudly. "Oh come on, I've seen you looking at him with those goo-goo eyes. You fancy him," she drawled slyly.

"Don't you fucking dare spread rumours like that around," Gideon hissed. "Christ, I don't even know if the man is gay—" his voice tailed off at Carmen's not-so-subtle wink and thumbs up in his direction. "Oh. Anyway, I do not have the bloody hots for him." He scowled as fiercely as he could. "How do you know he's gay anyway?"

Carmen flapped a hand. “I know one of his roommates, Leslie. We’ve met at a couple of gay clubs when I do my whole fag-hag thing with my friend Pete. And I’ve seen Eddie there too.”

Gideon felt a flicker of jealousy. “Really? Which club is that?”

“Bon Appétit,” Carmen said with a sly grin. “Why, you going to go down there later, see if you can find him? I can tell you Eddie can dance up a storm. He’s got a lot of really good moves and the guys love him.”

Gideon squashed the feelings rising inside at the thought of Eddie gyrating with the horny guys at the gay club. “Good for him,” he muttered. “He can be as big a dancing queen as he likes on his own time.”

Carmen tut-tutted.

Gideon thought testily it was just as well they’d been friends for the last ten years or else he might have to turn nasty.

“We’re going down there tonight actually,” she said cheerily. “There’s this whole goth night going on and Eddie, Pete and me are heading down there all dressed up to party. It is Friday night, after all, and none of us are working in the morning. Why don’t you join us? Eddie finishes his morning shift at twelve but we’re meeting back here at seven tonight to get dressed. He’s going to need some help getting into the outfit I have planned for him.” She chuckled nastily. “He is going to be so screwed walking a city block with his new goth look.” She leered. “Maybe even literally when the guys at the club get an eyeful of him.”

Gideon was morbidly and desperately curious but refused to rise to the bait. “No, I won’t be going, so you all go and have fun. Not my scene.” He turned his studious attention to the papers on his desk and attempted to ignore Carmen and the comment about Eddie being screwed. The images his mind was conjuring up were not conducive to his sanity. He had a sick feeling in his stomach at the thought of other men eying Eddie out and perhaps getting to first base.

“Well, if you change your mind, I’m sure you’ll still be here at seven tonight.” Her tone grew concerned. “Gideon, you need to get out, have some fun. This restaurant is your life; hell, you even live here,” she gestured vaguely above her head, “but you need to relax a little or you’ll burn out. Let Sarah look after the place on her own occasionally. That’s what you pay her to do and she’s good at it.

Think about it, okay?" She stood up and walked out the door to her own small office next to Gideon's.

Gideon booted up his PC as he busied himself with running his business in the forlorn hope it would take Eddie Tripp off his mind.

***

Around seven o'clock he made his way back from a quick meeting with Sarah and heard giggles and deep masculine laughter from Carmen's office. He'd thought about Carmen's words earlier and decided that perhaps he might have an early night and get upstairs by eight tonight. He wasn't going to Bon Appétit, not on a goth night—Gideon shivered at the thought—but he might start that DVD box set he had of *Game of Thrones*. A night in sounded like a plan. He had plenty in his kitchen to eat and he was sure he could knock up something nutritious if not tasty. He still cooked for himself as it was plain, simple food that didn't need much effort. Eating nowadays for him was a means to end and no longer any form of enjoyment.

He wandered over to Carmen's office, jacket slung over his arm, and stood at the door. He stopped dead, his heart beating like a pacemaker gone wrong and his dick instantly standing to attention at the scene before him. Eddie stood with his back to him, in black skin-tight leather trousers, and Gideon could hardly drag his eyes away. The leather fabric hugged a taut, round backside, clearly defined in its two parts and leaving little to the imagination. His feet were encased in high-heeled, studded boots that made his normal five-foot-five or -six height closer to eye level at Gideon's just over six-foot. Eddie wore a black, silky, skin-tight tank top, showing off well-defined arms and pecs that Gideon didn't even know he had. Eddie tended to wear loose tee shirts and baggy jeans most of the time.

This strongly muscled, very sexy figure was miles away from the Eddie that cooked in the kitchen.

Gideon felt faint.

Eddie's rich red hair was streaked with what looked like black boot polish and he had long gold hoop earrings in both ears. He looked like pure sin on legs and Gideon wanted to sin with him, oh so badly.

Neither Eddie nor Carmen noticed him standing there. Carmen was dressed as usual in her goth fare and she was focused on applying lipstick to Eddie's lips. He was looking distinctly uncomfortable and trying to talk but Carmen was shaking her head.

"Shut it Eddie! This is a very delicate operation. God, you have great lips. I wish mine were like yours," she said enviously. "Yours are all lovely and full and mine are so damned thin."

Gideon had definitely noticed Eddie's almost bee-stung lips with their rich pink hue and lickable appeal before. They haunted his waking dreams.

"Urghh, Carmen, my balls are hurting," Eddie managed to gasp out as he wiggled a bit and tried valiantly to adjust his tight pants. "And my crack is chafing."

Gideon's own balls were hurting at the thought of what lay beneath Eddie's second skin and how he might partake of their particular charms.

"Slave to fashion, darling," Carmen drawled. "You look fucking fantastic and believe me, this outfit is going to get you so fucked." Her voice broke off as she noticed Gideon salivating at the door. "Gideon, doesn't Eddie look fabulous? Leslie chose this outfit for him, and boy, I have to say the man has a good eye. Just as well he's in fashion."

She pulled Eddie around unceremoniously so he faced Gideon. Gideon nearly passed out again from the rush of his entire blood supply to his dick. Eddie was wearing mascara and eye liner, his green eyes amazingly vivid. The black lipstick made his lips poutier and fuller. Gideon wanted to plunge his mouth down on that sensuous mouth and take it until neither of them could breathe. His dick was hard steel and his eyes were drawn to the clearly defined package that was Eddie's obviously very substantial cock. Gideon moved his jacket in front of him to shield the rabid beast that lurked in his chinos.

Eddie's eyes widened as his skin turned from creamy magnolia to blush rose pink and he stared at Gideon like a deer in headlights. If he could have bolted, Gideon thought he might have done so. However it was safe to say Eddie wouldn't be running anywhere in that outfit. With an effort he dragged his eyes back up to meet Eddie's gaze. Gideon swallowed.

Christ, he just noticed I had an instant boner for him.

"Well, say something," Carmen said in irritation. "Isn't he gorgeous? He is so going to pull tonight."

Finally Gideon found his voice. “He looks very nice.” He winced at that statement.

Way to go, Gideon. The guy looks like your personal wet dream and all you can say is nice.

“He smells good too. Our Eddie has a man crush on Adam Levine and he’s wearing his signature scent. Very woodsy and spicy. Delicious.”

Carmen had a habit of describing smells to Gideon. It had taken some getting used to and he appreciated it most of the time but at this point, he was desperate to smell Eddie, taste Eddie, kiss Eddie, hear Eddie groan his name and rip those tight trousers off and fuck Eddie, and Gideon’s remaining three senses were on high alert. He was sure that they had amplified since losing his others.

He got his one wish to hear Eddie, but not in the way he really wanted: *Panting and groaning in ecstasy as I plough him into the mattress.*

“Mr. Kent, I hope you don’t mind us doing this here, but there was no way I could have gotten into these damn trousers without help and these boots take some getting used to. I’m not used to wearing heels and Leslie didn’t bloody tell me that these trousers would be so effing tight and honestly, I can hardly breathe. I think my bollocks have separated.” He ran out of steam and passed a hand over his hair, transferring some of the black goo to his hand. He looked at it helplessly and Carmen clucked like a mother hen. Gideon was speechless. Now he couldn’t stop thinking about Eddie’s bollocks.

“Here you go.” She passed Eddie a couple of tissues. “Wipe it off, that stuff stains if you get it anywhere. Then I think, my gorgeous goth guy, that we’re ready to go. Shall I call a taxi to get there or can you walk on those heels?”

Eddie looked down dubiously at his boots. “It’s only a block. I think I’ll manage as long as I can hang onto you. Thank God this is the West End and no one will look at me twice. Well, not that much anyway.” His face fell. “Shit, where am I going to put my wallet? I’m always getting carded because people don’t think I’m old enough and in these pants there is just no space to even slip a playing card.” His pale freckled face glowered darkly as he bit his bottom lip with slightly crooked white teeth and Gideon thought he’d died and gone to heaven to meet a sinfully alluring angel.

Carmen picked up her small bag and slung it across her shoulder. "No worries, I'll pop it in my bag." Gideon thought faintly that her bag was hardly big enough to stuff a flattened dormouse in but somehow she managed to get Eddie's wallet in.

She grinned. "There we go. All ready to party. I hope you have plenty of condoms with you, Eddie." Eddie huffed as his skin went an even deeper shade of pink. Carmen raised an eyebrow in Gideon's direction. "Sure you don't want to come with us?" Her knowing glance made Gideon push his jacket closer to his traitorous dick.

"No, I'm going to watch *Game of Thrones*." No sooner were the words out than Gideon was mortified.

Way to confirm you are one sad motherfucker with no life. And bloody condoms?

His jealousy rose like a Mexican Wave at the thought of anyone else doing his sexy sous-chef.

Eddie's eyes brightened and he moved toward Gideon, tottering slightly on his heels. "*Game of Thrones*? Which season?"

"Season three. I've finished watching the others already."

Eddie's face fell. "I'd love to watch those. I haven't seen any of them yet and I do want to." He smiled that wide smile. "I have a bit of a thing for Jaime Lannister. He's so damn sexy."

The words were out before Gideon could take them back. "Well, you'll have to come up sometime and watch them with me. And call me Gideon for God's sake. Enough already with the Mr. Kent."

The breath seemed to leave Eddie's body and he regarded Gideon with a little trepidation and a definite hint of interest. "Err, yeah. Sure. We can do that sometime."

Gideon didn't miss Carmen's grin and she turned to pick up her wrap from the back of her chair.

"Well, now you two have a date, I have my own waiting for me. Come on, Eddie, let's go. Pete and Andy are waiting for us. We're going to have a few drinks at the bar across the street before the party."

"It's not a bloody date," Gideon growled. "It's just watching TV."

"You tell yourself that, boss man." Carmen said airily.

Eddie was still staring at Gideon, his gaze heated. Gideon held his breath as green eyes appraised him with needful intent. Then

Carmen punched Eddie on the arm impatiently and the spell was broken.

Eddie blinked and yowled. "Ouch! Yes, by all means let's get off and see if Goth Boy here can make it in these bloody shoes." He stared at Carmen. "And just so you know—any future testicle damage I am billing to you personally." He winked at Gideon and tottered out of the room.

Carmen swished by and patted Gideon on the cheek. "Well done. See, that wasn't so bad, was it?" She gave a throaty chuckle. "What has that jacket ever done to you to deserve that death grip? Are we perhaps having a *hard time*?"

With a cackle of laughter, she left the room leaving Gideon in a state of tumescence he couldn't ever recall experiencing before. He could almost hear the shower beckoning so he could ease his aching dick.

Chapter 4

Two days later and Gideon was still avoiding Eddie. Yes, he'd been in the kitchen to check up on things, managed a few words to Eddie, but Gideon was doing his damndest to try and stay out of his way. The vision of him in his leather trousers and eyeliner still acted as Gideon's aphrodisiac to jerk off to each night, sometimes more than once a day. Eddie's name had become his mantra to regular orgasms and Gideon's hand around his own dick as he stroked and man-handled himself to imagined sounds of Eddie's breathy voice urging Gideon to fuck him harder.

With that in mind, it was very difficult to meet Eddie's eyes and carry on a normal conversation. In truth, Gideon had no idea how he was going to get over this obsession he had. So he tried to ignore it like any man would, hoping the urges would disappear.

It hadn't helped Carmen telling him all about that night and how every man in the nightclub had tried to pick Eddie up. She'd said airily that he had disappeared at one time for a while and she thought he might have got his rocks off with someone. Gideon had the impression she was trying to make him jealous. Worse thing was, it was working. The thought of anyone touching *his* Eddie made Gideon's blood boil.

Gideon muttered loudly as he attempted to un-jam the ancient printer in his office. His patience was at low ebb today after another night of nightmares and very little sleep, and his eyes were sore and gritty from being up since three a.m. He'd tried to huddle with a blanket on the couch and watch crap on telly but nothing had worked, and at five, he'd taken a shower and come down to his office. It was now ten and he was grumpy and irritated. His jaw hurt from chewing so much gum. He really wanted to smoke but knew he wouldn't.

The paper he was trying to get out finally ripped loose and Gideon swore loudly as it tore, leaving half of it in the machine.

"Fucking-arsehole-goddamn-printer," he cursed as he thumped it, causing the paper tray to jump off and hit the floor. "Why do I have to struggle like this?"

"Would you like some help?" An amused voice behind him interrupted his tirade and Gideon's heart leapt like a paper clip being sprung. He turned to see the grinning face of Eddie at the door, in his chef whites, holding a brown paper bag.

"It's fucking stuck," Gideon grumbled. Eddie moved into the office and shooed Gideon away from the recalcitrant office equipment.

"It doesn't help if you swear at it and hit it," he murmured gently. "Sometimes gentle works best." He put his paper bag on the desk and Gideon huffed and watched as Eddie's long fingers nimbly manoeuvred the printer parts around. Finally he gave a soft cry of triumph as a tatty piece of paper was extricated from its bowels.

"Eureka! There you go. All better now." His eyes met Gideon's. "It's pretty old, that thing, isn't it?"

Gideon looked down at the paper in his hand. "Stop being so bloody condescending," he said snarkily. "I would have sorted it eventually."

"Yes, but would the printer have survived the battle?" Eddie's eyes glinted with merriment. "I think it might have come off second best the way you were treating it." He turned back to the machine, checked the paper, pushed a few buttons and Gideon's Chamber of Commerce invitation to their annual banquet slid smoothly out and landed on the floor.

Eddie grinned, picked it up and put the paper tray back into place. "Party time?" He enquired with a wicked smile as he looked at the invite. "*You* at a boring Chamber of Commerce dinner? The mind boggles."

Gideon remembered that he wasn't really talking to Eddie and plucked the invitation out of his hands. "Was there a reason you were in here in my office?" He enquired. "Not that I'm not thankful you fixed that thing," he waved a hand at the printer, "But shouldn't you be in my kitchen cooking?"

Eddie's eyes narrowed. "Wow. Way to put me in my place," he said sarcastically. He picked up the brown bag. "Carmen said you were here at sparrow's fart and probably hadn't eaten. I made you a bacon sandwich."

Gideon was nonplussed. No one had ever brown-bagged a bacon sarnie for him before. "Oh. Thanks. You didn't have to do that."

"No, I didn't," Eddie agreed. "But there you have it. One sandwich."

Gideon nodded and went to sit down behind his desk. His dick was being most uncooperative and seeking attention and he wanted to hide the evidence.

Eddie gave a long-suffering sigh. "How is your *Game of Thrones* marathon coming on? Still watching?"

Gideon remembered with a pang that he'd extended an invite to Eddie the night of his goth party to watch episodes with him. "Oh, yes, still good." He looked up at Eddie. "Uhm, I know I said you should come and watch them with me but you do know that wouldn't really be a good idea if we, you know…" His voice trailed off as Eddie's eyes filled with something that looked like hurt. They darkened as he looked down at the ground then looked up.

"Sure, I know you were just saying that. It doesn't matter." His voice was even but Gideon heard the tremble in it. "I understand the whole 'employer-employee line that can't be crossed' thing." He turned and walked toward the door. "Enjoy the sandwich." Eddie disappeared, leaving Gideon feeling like he'd just kicked a puppy then thrown ice water over it for good measure.

But it isn't a good idea, is it? He's an employee and things could get awkward. It was the right thing to do. No matter how much I want him. He's too bloody tempting and I get the feeling he could see into my soul if he wanted to. I can't have that.

Gideon wondered then why he felt so damn miserable.

***

The kitchen was very busy that night and Eddie had no time to ponder the fact that Gideon hadn't really wanted him to sit and watch films with him. When Gideon had first said that to him, Eddie had told the little warning voice in his head—the one that said employer/employee hook up was a bad idea—to bugger off and leave him be. It wasn't every day a guy got an opportunity like that.

Now though, Eddie felt rather stupid. He'd hoped it had been a genuine invitation and he'd subtly brought the subject up to remind Gideon. Well, now he knew it had all been nothing more than a throw-away comment. Eddie knew Carmen was trying to match-make and to be honest, he hadn't stopped her. If it got him where he wanted to be, i.e. in Gideon's pants, or Gideon in his pants, then he'd have been a happy bunny. Once again though, Eddie had read the signs wrong. He had a penchant for that in his relationships. Reading too much into them then getting his heart broken when he was left alone once again. For a while he'd sworn off dating and men completely but that had proven too much for his libido to handle. He wasn't really a one-night stand man and frantic encounters in bathrooms and cars were not for him. He needed some emotional attachment to have sex with someone.

He sighed deeply as he chopped parsley for his famous pan-seared trout in hazelnut butter. There'd even been a rumour that one of the food critics were here tonight "in mufti" so Eddie wanted to make sure he did his best.

Around him the kitchen was awash with noise, the sounds of cooking food, shouts and jokes, dirty one-liners and pots and pans clanking as the pot washers loaded the industrial dishwashers. Normally Eddie felt a real part of the kitchen but tonight, his heart just wasn't in it. He longed for the next half hour to go quickly so the kitchen would close and he could clean up and get home. He wanted to check on Leslie too, and perhaps share a beer with Taylor.

One of the other chefs, Andrew, nudged his shoulder as he stood plating up food. “Hey, Eddie, what’s up? You’re very quiet tonight.” Andrew was about thirty, happily married with two kids and a willing part of the chef clique. He’d only been at the restaurant about two weeks.

“Oh, just thinking about the story that Max Warrington was supposed to be here tonight.” Eddie picked up chopped herbs and sprinkled it onto the plate of trout. “One of the other foodies that was in the other night told Sarah about it; I think he fancies our Sarah but he’s got no chance, her being married and all. Do you think Max is here?”

Andrew shrugged. “Who knows? Anyway, if he gets your trout dish and that incredible ginger soufflé you make as dessert, we’ll have no worries. Your cooking is awesome, Eddie. He can’t find fault with it.” He smiled cheekily at Eddie, who placed the dinner onto the conveyor belt out to the serving area.

Eddie felt warmth flush his body at the compliment. “Thanks Andy. I’m glad you think so.”

“Yeah, pity the boss can’t taste it though. The poor guy must be really gutted at not being able to cook anymore because of his condition. I mean, he was one of the top guys in the city, wasn’t he? Won all those awards for his food and all. Now he’s just the manager. It must really cut him up.”

The one thing Eddie had learnt about Andrew in their time cooking together was that he was like a freight train. Unstoppable. Eddie tried to tell him not to talk about Gideon’s condition as it was a bit of a sore subject and fairly private, but he couldn’t get a word in edgeways as Andrew rambled on.

“You’re the next gastro star, aren’t you? I saw a piece recently in the local rag enthusing about your smoked salmon coronets and the guy said you were the next young rising chef to hit the scene, maybe even better than the boss. It even said you’d been made an offer by The Next Best Thing to go and chef for them? I bet there was a lot more money involved in that offer than this place, given that it’s Michelin-starred. What are you still doing here then? ”

Throughout Andrew’s rather loud verbal diarrhoea Eddie hadn’t noticed that the kitchen had grown very quiet. He felt a presence behind him and turned to see a dark-faced Gideon glowering at them both. The other staff were staring down at their work stations, trying to avoid being singed by the eruption they thought was no doubt coming.

"Mr. Calloway. Mr Tripp. Do you think the two of you could stop gossiping long enough to do the job you're paid for?" His tone was biting. Eyes almost black glittered with anger and Eddie saw a side to Gideon he'd never seen before. "We have customers waiting, and by my reckoning this kitchen doesn't close for another half an hour."

Andrew was pale, his mouth gaping open with dismay and Eddie thought he probably didn't look any better. He hadn't been able to say a word while Andrew rattled on and now felt a slow-burning temper at Gideon's obvious inclination to think the worst of him, too.

Gideon's glare at him stabbed like a laser beam. "Mr. Tripp, if you feel your talents are better suited elsewhere then please don't let me stop you. I'm quite sure I'd manage to replace you like that." He snapped his fingers and Eddie's fuse burned shorter at that dismissive gesture as Gideon sneered at him. "Please, far be it from me to stand in the way of the next rising young chef on the scene."

There was a collective gasp at Gideon's words as he turned and stormed out of the kitchen. For a few seconds the kitchen was silent. Then there was a complete outburst among the staff.

"Fuck me, I have never seen him that mad," Joao, the diminutive Filipino pot-washer was aghast.

"He was really pissed, wasn't he?" Jerome rubbed flour-coated fingers across his glistening sweaty forehead, leaving a light dusting against his dark face. "I'll have a word with him later, saying you were both doing your jobs, just having a natter. But Andy, you should really have kept your mouth shut about the boss's affliction. You know he doesn't like it being discussed among the staff. It's my fault. I should have stopped you." His tone was a soft warning to Andy and one of censure for himself.

He rolled his eyes at Eddie as if acknowledging it wouldn't have been easy stopping the express train that was Andrew, but it should have been attempted.

Andrew was speechless for once, but Eddie knew the damage was done. His throat was choked with disappointment at Gideon getting on the defensive like that without knowing the full story.

"Jerome, don't worry. You trying to defend us will just piss him off more when he's in one of his moods. It'll all blow over." Eddie loved working with Jerome. He was an institution in the kitchen, having been there for over two years. He was warm, funny and not at all like the Gordon Ramsey bossy-chef persona that television cooking series were so fond of portraying.

"Yes, but he was really mad at you and I'm not having that," Jerome said amiably. "You turned down that bloody job at the fancy restaurant because you like it here and he needs to know that. He's a good man. He'll accept he was in the wrong."

Privately Eddie thought that might be a pipe dream. Whatever bug was up Gideon's arse concerning him, it needed to come out. He nodded at Jerome. "It would be better coming from me. I'll have a word and set things straight with him later, if that's okay? Please, Jerome. Let me handle this."

Jerome sighed deeply then nodded. "But if it all goes pear shaped, I *will* talk to him," he warned.

Eddie accepted that but felt relieved. The last thing he wanted was for Jerome to get into trouble on his behalf. He looked around the kitchen. "Now come on, we'd better all get our arses into gear before he has another hissy fit."

Everyone got back to what they'd been doing before Hurricane Gideon had hit the kitchen. Eddie worked on autopilot, a sour taste in his mouth and his gut churning at Gideon's rudeness.

Chapter 5

Gideon blasted his way into his office like a mini tornado and slammed the door. His hands were trembling and he clenched them at his sides as he paced his office.

Fucking twats! How dare they get off talking about me behind my back! Just a manager, he said. I'll show him just a bloody manager when I fire his arse.

Gideon reached into his desk drawer and took out a quarter-full bottle of Jack Daniels. He opened it and slugged a mouthful.

And Eddie. I thought he was better than that. And what was the business about another job offer? I didn't know about that. If it was that damn good, why didn't he take it? Put me out of my misery seeing him here each day, untouchable when I want him so much.

Although in hindsight, Gideon couldn't recall Eddie actually saying anything while Andrew had mouthed off. He'd been too busy chopping up parsley. Gideon felt a twinge of guilt. He took another few slugs from the bottle and sat down in his high-backed chair, closing his eyes and running a hand over his chin.

Christ, Andrew's words had hurt. Hearing someone actually say it like it was cut him to his core. His future had been destroyed by a quirk of fate that in his eyes had left him less than the man he'd been. The overwhelming desire he'd had to become a "someone," a top-class chef, even more than what he'd been, had all been plucked from him in one foul spark of a faulty gas oven.

Guilt and shame stabbed him again, deeper and more painful. His housemate Hugh, a man he'd only known three weeks, had lost his life in that explosion, as had the woman next door.

I'm a compete prat. I am a fucking selfish bastard. At least I'm alive, even with some scars inside.

He gulped more of the JD, feeling the warmth flood his veins and the familiar buzz start. It was the only way he knew that he was actually imbibing alcohol. Gideon had a plan. Get absolutely shit faced and hopefully fall asleep down here and not have the nightmares.

***

Gideon was woken by a low muttering and some really creative swearing. Finding his head resting cheek-down on his desk, he opened his eyes to peer blearily at a very shapely rear end at eye level at his side, perched on his desk. Said rear end was familiar and the voice was too.

"Bloody arsehole, stupid, self-pitying cretin, miserable excuse of a skin."

Gideon snorted slightly at that last comment, finding it funny in his drunkenness. He reached out and ran his hand over one firm arse cheek, squeezing it tightly through the jeans. The figure stilled and then stood up and turned slowly. Gideon grimaced as he gazed into flinty green eyes.

"Oh. So you're awake then? I've been trying to wake you up for five minutes, you idiot." Eddie frowned. "I told Sarah to go home; I'd take care of you. But you wouldn't open your bloody eyes. I was about to call Carmen and get her to come out here. Thought perhaps she'd have better luck rousing you." He glared at Gideon. "Would you grope Carmen like you did me?"

Gideon raised his head from the desk where it had been resting and shook his head. His brain exploded and he moaned softly. "Not Carmen. Too much trouble. And you're much sexier than Carmen. Don't tell her that though."

Eddie's lips twitched. "You deserve Carmen's wrath." But to Gideon's relief, Eddie put the desk phone back on the hook. He harrumphed and crossed his arms across his chest. Gideon giggled.

"What the hell is so funny?" Eddie sounded pretty pissed off but Gideon was sure he saw the start of a smile.

"You look like one of those preppy guys who used to tell me off in chef school for not following the recipes. All stuck up and holier than thou."

Eddie pursed his lips. "Hmm. Well you need *someone* to tell you what a fool you've been. You finished whatever was in that bottle." He picked up the bottle on the desk and then put it down again. "I need to get you to bed so you can sleep this drunk fit off."

Gideon chuckled, his big head swimming but his little head stirring in his jeans. "Yes, please. That's the best offer I've had all night." He pushed his chair back and tried to stand up but got dizzy. Eddie moved forward and took his arm with a surprisingly strong grip.

"Hold onto my arm and I'll help you upstairs."

Gideon clutched Eddie's arm as they stumbled out of the office and toward the back of the restaurant where the stairs to the flat were. He took advantage of the situation to feel Eddie up, grabbing at his waist, his shoulder, his arse, anywhere he could get traction. He even managed to brush the front of Eddie's groin once with the back of his hand, a gesture causing a sudden hiss from Eddie. Gideon was impressed by what he found there. The man was impressively hard.

He smirked seeing that even in his drunken state he could still give someone a hard-on. He himself didn't do well when he drank, so the swelling he had now pressing against his trousers was bound to disappear. He certainly wouldn't get to first base with Eddie tonight. But he might be able to steal a kiss.

Eddie got him up the small staircase and to his door. It was never locked so Gideon simply opened it and fell in. He stumbled and the room swam. Eddie clucked behind him and switched on the overhead light. Gideon winced at the brightness hitting his tired eyes.

Eddie looked around. "Where's your bedroom?"

Gideon flapped a hand in the vague direction of his room. Eddie helped him get there and then once inside, he steered Gideon to the bed then switched on the bedside light. He regarded him thoughtfully.

"Do you want me to help you undress or can you manage?" His voice was hesitant, his body language cautious. Gideon lay back on his comfy bed, his head on the pillows and waited for the room to stop circling in his brain. He closed his eyes and shut everything out.

"Just the shoes, maybe. The rest is fine." He cautiously cracked open one eye. "It's not the first time I've slept in my clothes."

Eddie nodded and sat on the bed, gently removing Gideon's shoes and then pulling his socks off. His feet twitched as Eddie's hands touched his bare skin. He'd always been ticklish there. His eyes flashed open and he saw Eddie's tongue move slightly to the side of his mouth as he focused on his task.

This feels good, having someone here taking care of me. Very nice. I could get used to this, could get used to him. God, I want that tongue in my mouth…

Eddie's eyes widened and he sat back, his breathing becoming deeper. Gideon had the sneaky feeling he'd said those last thoughts out loud from the look on Eddie's face.

"I want to kiss you." The words were out before he could even think about what he was saying.

Eddie shook his head. "Oh no. That isn't going to happen." He stood up and went to the windows, drawing the curtains and instantly making the room cosier.

"Why not?" Gideon was aggrieved. "Is there something wrong with me?"

Eddie snorted. "Oh, don't get me started on that one, sunshine. I'd be here all night."

Gideon's face fell. "Oh."

I can't blame him. Not after how I behaved today.

He reached out and caught Eddie's hand, holding it tightly and pulling him down onto the bed. Eddie hitched a breath as he plonked down and stared at him with wide eyes.

"Eddie, about what I said today. I'm sorry. I was out of line. It's your business what you do with your job. I had no right to say those things to you." His fingers slowly caressed the warm skin of Eddie's palm. It felt so right.

Eddie exhaled a deep gust of warm air that caressed Gideon's face. He supposed one of the benefits of not being able to smell anything was never having to experience anyone's bad breath. Although, he wagered a bet that Eddie's breath was sweet, like his mouth would be.

Eddie shrugged. "It's all right. You were pissed by what Andy said about you. He shouldn't have really said that, that's your personal business." He watched as Gideon made slow circles on his palm with his thumb.

Gideon noticed his pupils were wide and dark. He chanced a long lingering caress up Eddie's wrist and felt the shiver run through his body. His dick swelled in spite of the drink and he stared at Eddie's mouth, visualising those pink, full lips around him, driving him crazy and making him blow into the sweet, warm cavern that was Eddie's mouth. Eddie was staring back at him, his chest heaving.

Despite his inebriated state, Gideon felt a sense of longing. His mouth ran away with him, his inhibitions at not wanting to get close to anyone disappearing like smoke.

"I wish I could smell you," he whispered longingly. Eddie's eyes darkened. "Smell your sweat and what makes *you*, you. Taste your skin."

Eddie stood up swiftly. "You're drunk and you don't know what you're saying," he said roughly. "I should go. Get some sleep." He turned to go.

Gideon sighed heavily as he closed his eyes. "It's the only way they stop sometimes," he whispered as his head swum. "The only way to forget what happened…" The world went black and he spiralled down thankfully into his darkness.

***

Eddie watched as Gideon fell asleep. He was very confused and his chest was tight with both need and a little apprehension. The man lying on the bed, looking innocent and at the same time like a debauched satyr with his pink lips and long eyelashes resting against a tanned cheek, was an enigma.

One minute he's growling at me, the next he wants to kiss me, taste my skin? How much of that was him talking and how much was the booze?

Eddie sighed as he adjusted himself to try and get his cock under control. He hadn't missed all those sly touches to his body while he'd been helping Gideon up the stairs. The look in Gideon's eyes, a dark, desirous lust, had done nothing to quell the erection and breathlessness he'd felt at the man's roaming hands. If Eddie wasn't a gentleman, he'd be ripping the man's clothes off while he slept and satisfying himself. Instead, he draped the duvet over Gideon's sleeping form. No doubt in the morning he would remember nothing and if he did, he'd be as irritated as all hell that he'd come on to Eddie. It was the way the man seemed to work. Offer with one hand then take away with the other. Eddie wasn't about to make a fool of himself. He brushed Gideon's cheek gently with his hand and smiled in spite of his reservations when the man nuzzled into his palm with a faint, sleepy smile.

"What demons do you have?" Eddie whispered softly. "What makes you scared of sleeping?" Eddie knew the brief story, of course. That Gideon had been injured in a house fire, that his housemate had died and he had been left with no sense of smell or taste. It was one of the first things Carmen had explained when he started working at Galileo's as she put all the employment paperwork together. That and the stern reminder not to gossip about it or ask Gideon about it on pain of death. Even Carmen had seemed frustrated at the lack of knowledge of the events that surrounded that fateful night. It appeared the boss man liked to keep things to himself.

Eddie brushed a hand over Gideon's tousled blond hair. "Sleep well," he murmured. "Try to keep the bogey man out of your head." He turned and left the room, closing the door softly behind him. He padded down the stairs, made sure the alarm was armed before he left, having been given the code by Sarah, then exited into the street, pulling the glass doors closed behind him.

The street was still busy, despite it being just after midnight. This part of the city never slept. Theatre goers, late-night revellers, rent boys and those simply seeking company all milled around in dark corners, along brightly lit streets and alleyways. Eddie sighed again. He'd have to catch a late-night bus home as there were no tubes running. He hated buses with a passion but he didn't fancy the more than two-mile walk at this time of night. He didn't fancy it any time of the day actually.

It was almost one o'clock in the morning when he finally opened the front door to his home. Eddie thanked God he wasn't working today. It would give him plenty of time to catch up on sleep and also not to see Gideon after his drunken entreaty to kiss him. He tried to keep the noise down as he passed the small, darkened lounge and his heart leapt in fright when he heard a noise. Eddie laid his rucksack down on the floor and peered cautiously into the room. Someone sat in the large armchair, and Eddie swore they were talking to themselves. Hardly breathing, he listened, then heard a familiar voice.

"Taylor?" he whispered as he edged into the room. "Is that you?"

It was indeed Taylor, sitting stock-still in the chair, eyes open, a blank look on his face. His mouth whispered words that didn't make sense. Eddie saw his slim hands lying on his thighs, saw his shock of long, dark, curly black hair outlined in the sodium light of the street light outside. It was unnerving to say the least.

"Taylor?" Eddie swallowed as he moved closer. The other man gave no sign of recognition or acknowledgement, simply kept up the strange, stilted words he was speaking under his breath.

"Can't do this. Not going to make it." He stopped and Eddie edged closer. "It's not a fucking fairy tale. No gingerbread house here." His voice was strangled, as if it were coming from a long way away.

Eddie's skin prickled at the words. The words sounded familiar to him somehow but he was tired and he couldn't quite remember where he'd heard them before. Taylor continued his mumbling.

"Need to call Eddie. He'll know what to do." At hearing his name, Eddie moved faster toward Taylor. As he did so, his foot knocked the small side table and something fell with a loud clunk onto the wooden floor. In the dark recess and stillness of the room it was like a rocket going off. His heart beat fiercely and Taylor leapt to his feet, his hand to his chest as he stood up in fright.

"Who's there? Who is it?" The panic in his voice made Eddie reach out a soothing hand and clasp his shoulder which seemed to make Taylor even more jumpy as he stepped backward to fall into the chair with a soft exhalation of air.

"It's okay, Taylor. It's just me, Eddie."

Taylor reached out and switched on the overhead light. The bright light made both of them wince.

"Eddie, what the hell? Did you have to sneak up on me like that?" Taylor's usually soft tone sounded harsher than usual.

Eddie stared at him in confusion. "You were pretty zoned out there," he muttered. "I called your name and you didn't answer. You were, like, in your own little world."

"Oh." Taylor's words were flat. "I must have dozed off then." His café au lait skin coloured slightly.

Eddie shook his head. "You were talking to yourself. Not sleeping. What was all that about?"

Taylor stood up again, his face guarded. "Nothing. I must have been talking in my sleep. I do that sometimes." He tried to move past Eddie but Eddie placed a hand on his arm, stopping him.

"You were awake, your eyes were open. You mentioned my name. Something about asking me something, saying I'd know what to do?"

Taylor shrugged and Eddie saw the lie coming before it was even spoken. Taylor's dark brown eyes were very expressive, unable to hide much. He'd always said that was a legacy of his Mauritian mother and grandparents. "I have no idea. Like I said, I must have been dreaming." He looked at his watch. "You're home later than usual. Everything okay?"

Eddie knew he was trying to change the subject. He was exhausted so he let it go. He'd find out more tomorrow. "Yeah, had to put my crazy–arse, rat-faced boss to bed." He grinned. "He polished off too much JD and needed help getting home."

Taylor smiled slightly. "The crazy-arse boss you have the hots for?" His dark eyebrow quirked. "Did you manage to get him into bed then?"

Eddie chuckled. "Not in the way I'd hoped. I was a true gentleman and left him alone. You'd have been proud of my restraint."

Taylor grinned back, looking more relaxed now the focus wasn't on him. Eddie wondered what he was hiding.

Taylor nodded. "Well, it's late. I think we should both be getting to bed." His lips twisted in a wry smile. "Leslie got home about eleven, a little the worse for wear, but he seems to be over that other tosser that cheated on him. He brought another one home so we have an extra house guest tonight in case you see a stranger lurking about in his skivvies in the morning."

Eddie grimaced. "Thanks for the warning."

Taylor nodded again. "Anytime. Night, Eddie." He brushed past Eddie and left the lounge. Eddie heard the soft tread of footsteps up the carpeted stairs and reached out and switched off the light. Then he tiredly made his way upstairs to bed.

Chapter 6

Eddie was on his hands and knees on his bed, body bent low, one hand clenched in his sheets as someone pounded into him from behind. The incredible sensation of being filled so completely was coupled with a heady mix of animal need as the man above him drove his cock deep into Eddie's body. The scent of warm, sweaty man and the faint hint of some spicy aftershave drifted into Eddie's nostrils as he pushed back, urging the man to fuck him harder.

"You can do it," he gasped, as his arse was slapped by the man's balls, the sound welcoming among the gasps and groans of the man behind. "Christ, you feel good inside me. If I'd known it was going to be this good, I've have waylaid you sooner."

The gasping chuckle of Gideon Kent echoed in Eddie's ears as strong hands pulled Eddie's hips back and his lover sank deeper inside. Eddie moaned as Gideon leaned forward over his back and bit his earlobe, warm breath ghosting his cheek.

"You are such a slut," he whispered and Eddie's balls contracted up further, as he frantically fisted his cock with his free hand and felt the heat rise in his groin. "I love watching you jack yourself, you are so damn hot. I can smell your come, Eddie, and it smells like sweet release." Gideon's breath hitched and he gave a deep groan. "Hell, you make me feel like no one else ever has. When I say, 'come' you come, hear me? We try to do this together."

Eddie could only nod fervently as he felt Gideon tense, his strong thighs tightening as he pushed Eddie's legs further apart to drive deeper, and Eddie thought he might split in two as pleasurable as it was. The sound of Gideon's husky "Come for me," sent an eight-point-zero-sized earthquake tremor through Eddie's body. He cried out as his hand gave one last hearty pull on his aching hard-on and he released warm spunk onto the covers below him. Gideon gave a strangled cry and pulsed inside him, the warmth of semen coating Eddie's arse and thighs then Gideon collapsed on top of him, flattening him, still deep inside his now aching channel. He turned his face to find Gideon's mouth—hot, needy lips that sucked the life out of him and tried to choke him with a desperate tongue.

Eddie kissed back, wanting nothing more than this moment, this man in his body and his lips on his. Somewhere a bell rang and for a minute Eddie thought it might be the sound of his own passion translated to tinkling sleigh bells and fireworks like in the cartoon movies when two people kissed. He smiled at that thought then as the bell got more insistent and irritating, he turned to Gideon only to find he was no longer there. Eddie scowled and reached across to where the annoying bell sound was…

He woke from his dream upright, sweating, sticky with come and tangled in musty-smelling sheets that had seen their fair share of jack-off action lately and needed washing. His hand rested on his mobile phone as it trilled incessantly with his Big Ben alarm. He blinked owlishly for a minute, wondering where he was. As the dream faded, he fell back in a loose heap with a sense of loss.

"A fucking dream," he muttered to himself in irritation. "It was a dream. Definitely not the real thing, you horny twat." He looked down at his stomach and grimaced at the sight of it and his boxer shorts covered in white goo. His nostrils wrinkled at the rank, stale smell in the room and he clambered out of his bed, his legs boneless. He was still in post-orgasmic shock, as Leslie liked to call it.

Eddie glanced angrily at the phone that had awoken him from his sizzling sexcapade. He'd forgotten to turn the alarm off last night and the numerals stared up at him, the time of five a.m. in all their digital splendour imprinted in his head. He cursed and fumbled with the alarm to switch it off. He wrinkled his nose at the smell of himself and took a deep breath. Wow, that had been intense. He'd dreamed about men fucking him or him doing the fucking before but never with such vigour and not with Gideon Kent. This had been the wet dream to beat all others.

Eddie was what he called an "equal-opportunity man," not labelling himself as a top or a bottom but as one who rather gave into the moment and enjoyed whatever was offered. As long as both men got enjoyment out of what they were doing, who cared about labels?

He made his way out of the room to the communal bathroom to pee and clean himself up, clad still in his stained boxers and keeping a wary eye out for Leslie's houseguest—it might be five a.m. and he doubted anyone else would be up but he'd rather play it safe. He wondered idly if that would be what sex with Gideon would be like. He also mused whether he'd ever get the chance to find out. Eddie grinned to himself. If he ever got the chance to kiss the man or more, he thought he'd take it, consequences be damned. He could always go work for The Next Best Thing if Gideon fired him for sexual harassment. Now though, he thought he might just clean up a little, go back to bed as he had the day off and do it all again, only awake this time. That dream had given him enough masturbation material for a good long while.

***

The man who had just featured so prominently in Eddie's wet dream sat shivering and naked on the ledge of his bedroom window, staring out into the early morning traffic below. His eyes were gritty, his head was throbbing and the cold sweat on his body from the early-morning nightmare he'd suffered still lingered. The drink had only deferred it, not taken it away. Gideon passed a trembling hand over his face.

Hell, I should never have drunk all that Jack last night. I'm a bloody idiot.

His gorge rose and he ran to the bathroom, just in time to hawk up bile and sour whiskey into the toilet bowl. He retched again until he was sure there was nothing left but his insides to come up. He leaned his face against the cool porcelain of the toilet bowl.

Pain. Burning pain that bit deep to the bone and made him gag. Smoke, stinging his eyes, suffocating him as the stench of cooking flesh insinuated itself slyly into his nostrils, a smell he knew he'd never forget. Desperation at being pinned beneath a smouldering wooden beam, heat hooking its greedy, invasive fingers into the side of his body, until he retched from the agony. A throat dry and burning that made him try swallow but finding no solace in his parched state. And finally, the shocking stillness of a friend as he lay dead no more than five feet away. Gideon would have wept tears of grief and despair had he any moisture left in his body to do so. Instead all he could do was lie there and watch a dead man burn and hope that it would all soon be over.

Gideon could still see Hugh's empty eye sockets staring at him from a burned, blistered face hardly recognisable as human. He shuddered as he remembered the flames licking at Hugh's body, and the memory of smelling the sickly smell of roasting flesh. He'd prayed Hugh was dead, even though common sense had told him he was, that no one could be burned like that without screaming. He'd been lucky in that the fire truck had not been far away and had reached the house within minutes of the explosion. The fire had been raging then and there'd been no hope for Hugh. Gideon remembered vomiting all over the firefighters after they'd freed him and loaded him onto a stretcher, while he babbled that he was sorry he hadn't been able to save his friend.

Gideon himself had healed well from his ordeal with minimal physical trauma, the skin on his left side from waist to hip simply sensitive from his burns. And while he could no longer smell anything, in some small way he was relieved, as reliving that smell of cooking human flesh might have driven him crazy. It was a double-edged sword, one he lived on the edge of every day. He wanted his senses back desperately, but he wasn't sure he could cope with them if he did regain them.

Gideon eased his aching body from where he sat hunched over the toilet, brushed his teeth then started the shower. Perhaps it might wake him up, make him feel better. He stood in the hot, steaming water of his power shower and a stray thought came to him as he soaped himself down. A vague memory of asking Eddie whether he could kiss him.

That made him groan in mortification.

"You stupid bastard, did you really ask him that?" he muttered to himself as he washed his balls, lingering a little on the thought of whether Eddie had accepted his request. He didn't think so; he thought he'd remember *that.* Eddie's wide, warm mouth beneath his, his tongue slicking against Gideon's, searching the deep recesses of Gideon's mouth, his breath hot and probably sweet from all the pastry tasting he did.

Gideon stroked his dick, softly at first then harder as he imagined running his hands over Eddie's taut chest, pinching the nipples until the man moaned for release. He pictured reaching down to cup the hardness at Eddie's groin then feeling velvety silk steel beneath his fingers. His breath caught as he imagined turning Eddie around as he jerked him off, then sliding his prick between those tight, round cheeks of Eddie's backside and sinking into delicious, smooth heat that would clench around him and drive him crazy.

Gideon closed his eyes and groaned as he tugged his dick harder, faster until he finally came, his semen washing down his stomach to the shower floor. He laid his forehead against the cool, wet walls of the shower and wondered what the hell he was doing.

At least that little sojourn into his fantasies had taken his mind off the nightmare.

Chapter 7

When Gideon arrived at work and found out that it was Eddie's day off, there was a sense of relief that he wouldn't have to face him mixed with a sense of ire that he wouldn't get to see him. Gideon wondered in exasperation when he'd become such a sad and needy arsehole. Sarah eyed him out with some concern when she saw him later that day. Her pretty face clouded over as he walked over to her in the dining area.

"Gideon, what the heck happened to you last night? It's not like you to pass out in your office, sweetie. Eddie was such a honey; he was so worried about you. That young man is a real treasure, you know." She laid a hand on his forehead. "You're a bit clammy. Is it just the booze or are you coming down with something?"

As much as Gideon loved Sarah, this maternal instinct she had for him made him feel uncomfortable. She was ten years older than he was and he'd not had to put up with it for a long time; his mother had died when he was only eleven years old and he hadn't seen his dad in years. Peter Kent travelled extensively as part of a geological survey team and the last time Gideon had seen him had been about four years ago. They'd spoken probably about eighteen months ago for five minutes. They'd tried to Skype and call more, but neither of them were particularly communicative– not that they made much effort.

Despite the headache, his throat still sore throat from retching and the nausea, Gideon smiled at her fondly. "It's just the booze. I was feeling a little down and decided to have a party by myself. Sorry you got involved. And yes, Eddie looked after me. He got me upstairs and into bed."

The knowing glance she sent him made him flush. "Not that way. God, between you and Carmen, there's no damn respite about your indecent curiosity about my sex life."

Sarah laughed, a lovely sound that always helped Gideon feel better. "I promise we're not matchmaking. But Carmen and I can't help seeing the looks you and Eddie give each other now and then. I don't think anyone else has noticed. It's just because we're such fans of you both." She stuck her tongue out at him and he grinned.

"Well, stop it anyway. You know he's staff and as the old saying goes, you don't shit on your own doorstep."

Sarah made a moue of distaste. "You can be so crude." She eyed him out. "When did you last get laid anyway?"

Gideon's mouth dropped open. "Jesus, Sarah, that's none of your business. I can't believe you asked me that." His face was warm and he cast a quick glance around him to check no one had heard.

Her laughter pealed around the rapidly filling restaurant. Patrons looked over at them curiously. "Well, since El Señor left, I haven't seen you serious about anyone. I suppose you're getting your rocks off somehow, maybe blow jobs in the alleyway and quick screws in your room after hours? Then you kick them out so no one sees them?"

Gideon swallowed. While she was right about his current sexual activity, there was no way he was telling her that. "Seriously, Sarah, you need to stop. This is *so* not a conversation I want to have with you." He turned and walked over to the tills to check on the employees and the registers. "Now perhaps you can make yourself useful and check on those bookings for tonight for that doctor's birthday. I think we're expecting a party of twenty and I'd like to make sure it's all sorted."

Sarah saluted him with a giggle. "Aye-aye, Captain, my Captain."

Gideon threw her a warning glance which only made her giggle more. He shook his head in amusement. He loved the two women in his life but oh boy, they were a handful. He sniggered. Well, Sarah was definitely more than a handful. Her husband had been known to espouse the delights of his wife's bosom, something that made Gideon fairly uncomfortable but that he accepted as the straight man's right. He felt the same about dicks. And arses. And smiling, full lips like Eddie Tripp's…

He gave himself a mental shake and went to work greeting patrons and showing them to their tables. It was a part of the job he enjoyed, chatting and meeting people. It took his mind off the fact that he should really be in the kitchen.

It was around eight p.m. when Michael Fortescue walked in. Gideon felt a sense of unease. He hadn't seen Michael since before the fire. They'd had a three-month relationship about eight months ago. Michael had been the one to break it off, citing he needed something "less prosaic" and to be honest, Gideon hadn't been that cut up about it. They'd had some sexual chemistry to begin with but not much else. Then Michael had tried to get back together when his last relationship had fizzled out and Gideon had said no. He wasn't a rebound catch. That conversation hadn't gone well and Michael had been bitter about it.

Gideon pushed the unease down deep and went over to greet him. He smiled at Michael and his partner, a young twenty-something with platinum blond hair, long lashes and dressed like a Calvin Klein model. Michael looked at Gideon with a faint sneer. He looked Gideon's attire up and down—his simple Burton Brothers suit of dark grey, with pale blue button-down shirt and striped dark green and navy tie.

Michael's lip curled. "Gideon. Good evening. I see your dress sense hasn't changed. Still playing it safe."

And that was the reason Gideon hadn't minded breaking up. Michael was a snob, a social climber. Gideon wasn't.

He smiled pleasantly at his customer. "Yes, I'm still as prosaic as ever. Can I show you and your companion to a table? Any preference? Over by the window or in the corner where you can be more private?"

Michael's pale blue eyes regarded him icily. "Somewhere quiet please. Daniel and I enjoy our privacy."

Gideon nodded and swept up two menus from the nearby table. "Very well. Follow me; I have just the spot."

The two men followed him over to a quiet, dimly lit section of Galileo's, to a table in an alcove, set for two, with fresh flowers and candles. Behind the alcove, people waited to be seated in the bar area. Gideon got them settled and handed them the menus.

"There you go, gentlemen. I shall have your waiter come over in about five minutes, give you time to check out the menu."

"You have a new chef, I believe," Michael said idly but Gideon didn't miss the glint in his eye. "I was so sorry to hear about your accident and your...*unfortunate* circumstances. That must be very difficult for you, not being able to cook anymore. From what I remember, it was a passion of yours." His hands smoothed the table cloth and Gideon wanted to brain him with the silver candle holder.

He took a deep breath. “Thank you. Yes, we have a couple of new chefs. I can guarantee the food will be excellent.”

“I hear one of them, your sous-chef, is reputed to be even better than you were.” Michael perused the menu idly but the edge in his voice was evident. “They say he’s on his way to the top. Is he here tonight?”

Gideon willed his racing heart to calm down. “No, I’m afraid Eddie isn’t working tonight. But Jerome is top of his game and I’m sure the food will be to your liking. Now if you’ll excuse me, I need to check on something.” Gideon noticed the confused glances Daniel was giving him and Michael and he felt a little sorry for him. He obviously didn’t know he and Michael had a history.

Michael smiled at Daniel even as he addressed Gideon. “How does it work not being able to smell or taste anything? I can’t imagine losing two of your senses like that. It must be quite a challenge. I’d hate it. So you can’t smell my new Paco Rabanne fragrance then?” He waved his wrist in Gideon’s direction. Gideon’s nostrils flared instinctively but there was nothing. “And to go through what you did, with your friend burning to death—are you seeing someone for therapy? If not I can recommend someone if you like.” His smile didn’t reach his eyes.

Gideon felt a little dizzy as a panic attack threatened. He hadn’t had one in months and now it was all getting a bit too much. He tried to take quick, deep breaths to stop the wooliness growing in his head.

“I’m fine, thank you Michael.” His tone was sarcastic. “Gratified at your concern, seeing as how you didn’t bother to contact me at all at the time. Anyway, I think you’ve had your say. I hope you both enjoy your meal.” He nodded and saw Daniel frown and lean over and whisper to his companion as Gideon turned and walked back to his office. He took deep, cleansing breaths each step, but the tingling sensation in his fingers worsened, his mouth was dry and he was sweating. He needed to stave this off. He couldn’t afford an attack now.

In his office he made it to his chair and sat down in it, the feeling of dread seeping through his bones and causing his hands to shake.

“Please, not now,” he whispered. “Not now. Fight this, you weak bastard. Fight it.”

“Gideon, here. Drink this.” Gideon jumped as a glass of water was pressed into his hand. He took it and drank it numbly. Eddie stood there, his eyes shadowed, one warm hand slowly stroking Gideon’s arms, calming him like a rider would calm a horse. That slow, tender caress centred him as he drank thirstily now and finished the water. He put it down on the desk and stared at Eddie.

“I didn’t think you were working tonight,” he said hoarsely. “What are you doing here?”

“I needed to drop something off for Andrew as it’s his day off tomorrow. Some tickets for a show tomorrow night that I promised him. I can’t make it so he took them.” Eddie scowled. “I saw that prick talking to you and you didn’t look too well. I heard most of what he said.” He looked shame faced. “I wasn’t spying, honest; I was in the alcove behind their table—”

Gideon waved a hand at him tiredly. “It doesn’t matter. You’re right—he is a prick.” He was feeling more balanced now, Eddie’s calming presence helping.

“And you’re not a weak bastard,” Eddie said fiercely. “From what I heard you went through hell and anyone would have a few issues.”

Gideon loved the protectiveness emanating from that sexy body. It had been a long time since anyone had cared enough about him in that way.

Eddie stared at him worriedly. “I thought you looked agitated. My mum suffers from panic attacks; you had the same look.”

Gideon snorted. “Thanks.” There was an almost comfortable silence.

“Why couldn’t you make your show?” Gideon asked Eddie softly.

Eddie looked embarrassed. “I have to help a friend. My roommate Leslie needs a plus one for an event he’s going to, it’s important to him. So I said I’d go with him.”

Gideon’s jealousy rose to the fore. “Are you and this friend—together—then?”

Eddie looked shocked. “Good God, no. Leslie is not a fuck buddy.”

Gideon’s dick rose at that comment. “So where are you going then?”

Eddie looked a little gloomy. "Some damned fashion show. Leslie is a trainee buyer for an independent fashion house and this is his chance to sparkle with the boss *and* say a huge Fuck You to his ex." He sighed. "I have to wear a tux and clean up nicely." He shrugged. "Not my ideal date but I'll get free food and help him out."

"You do that a lot," Gideon murmured. "Help people out. This is the third time you've come to my rescue. My knight in shining armour." He knew he was taking this down a route he really didn't want to go—*shouldn't* go—but he couldn't help it. Eddie was special.

"I like you," Eddie said simply. "Something tells me you could do with a bit of looking after."

Gideon felt the air shift and change around him, the sexual tension evident. It wasn't only his dick that was enjoying this. He really liked Eddie too.

"Are you feeling better then?" Eddie moved over to stand behind Gideon as he sat. Slowly, almost reverently, he began to rub Gideon's shoulders, his fingers digging into the knots and muscles. Gideon gave a soft moan and leaned back into his hands. It felt so good to have hands on him, to have somebody care about him. Eddie seemed to be a very tactile person.

Eddie hadn't finished talking. "Oh and by the way? That dickhead's Paco Rabanne fragrance? He obviously emptied the bottle on himself and it was all wrong for him. He smelt like a rancid kipper."

Gideon snorted with sudden laughter, his shoulders shaking with mirth at the dry words. He looked back to see Eddie looking down at him, a strange expression on his face. Before Gideon knew it, there was nothing but the closeness of Eddie's face and his mouth taking Gideon's in a deep, possessive, upside-down kiss, his tongue pushing its way into Gideon's mouth as the action targeted Gideon's needy dick to the point of pure hedonism. Gideon sighed into Eddie's mouth as he opened his own, his tongue finding Eddie's. That sweet mouth left his suddenly and Gideon groaned, needing more of it..Eddie swivelled the chair around and sat down, straddling Gideon, locking his fingers into Gideon's hair and taking his mouth again. Gideon thought he would burst from pleasure. His arms snaked out, gripping Eddie's arse and pulling them closer together.

Eddie was now sitting directly on his dick, those tight buttocks of his grinding against him and there was no way *that* could be continued right here, right now. Anyone could come into the office and find them dry humping each other. As much as Gideon wanted Eddie, this wasn't the right place. He managed to extract his swollen and bitten lips from Eddie's suction to make a feeble protest.

"Eddie, this isn't right. Anyone can come in and I don't want them to find us like this."

Eddie's eyes were black, his erection hard against Gideon's stomach, virtually pushing through the fabric of his jeans. He moved back to stare at Gideon through unfocused eyes. His lips were pink and wet and Gideon shivered with need.

God, he is so mine. I want him so badly. What the hell is this man doing to me?

"Okay. Where then?" Eddie said huskily and it went straight to Gideon's dick.

"Later, after everyone leaves. Come back to the restaurant before close up and go upstairs to my flat. I'll see you there when I'm done."

Eddie nodded then leaned forward and swiped his tongue sexily over Gideon's bottom lip. Gideon was already ready to explode. He pushed Eddie off his lap and stood up, breathing heavily.

"God, you are something else. If you touch me again I'll blow and I can't have that. Leave it for later. Think about what I'm going to do to you."

Fuck I hope he wants me inside him. But either way, he can have me.

"You want inside me, Gideon?" Eddie's voice was low, sensual. "I don't mind either way. Whatever you want."

The man is a mind reader as well as being the sexiest man on earth.

"Oh Jesus, Eddie. Please go." Gideon's voice wavered. "Let me finish up here and I'll see you later."

Green eyes blazed bright. "That you will." With one last, smouldering look at him, Eddie turned and walked out of the office. Gideon tried to calm his pulse down to just a potential heart attack instead of total brain annihilation. He didn't think he had any blood left to spare; it was all in his groin. Finally he managed to get his libido under control and took a tiny sip—well, a gulp—of the second bottle of JD he had in his drawer. It wasn't the brightest thing to do given his overindulgence last night, but he needed to calm down. In another few hours, he would be alone, in his room, with Eddie, both of them naked and horny and that alone was enough to induce another panic attack of a different kind.

Chapter 8

Eddie walked out of Galileo's in a state of complete meltdown. Not only had he just kissed his boss, he'd also promised to let him fuck him later. While this had been high on his list of "Things to Do with Gideon" he wasn't sure he was really ready for it.

"You are a horny bastard," he muttered to himself as he made his way home on the tube, his denim jacket placed strategically on his lap to conceal the problem rearing its literal head in his groin. Eddie felt rather confused actually. He'd never been as aggressively sexual before as he had been with Gideon earlier. Something in the man brought out his inner dominant beast and strangely enough, Gideon, a man he'd have imagined was a complete alpha male in the sack, had gone with the flow.

"Huh," he muttered as he sat on the tube as it wound itself around dirty corners and dimly lit concrete walls. "Who would have figured *that* of either of us?"

The woman across the aisle from him gave him a tentative smile as she juggled with various parcels on her ample lap. He nodded his head back at her. Mr. Perv, the man who had grabbed his leg the other day and asked him to go with him, sat two seats down. Eddie hunkered down, trying to make himself invisible. It didn't work. Mr. Perv caught his eye and stood up to come sit beside him. Eddie hadn't realised just how wide the man was. Of course it could have been the bulky suede jacket he wore. He looked like a damn wrestler.

Eddie moved further away and studiously ignored him. The man licked his lips lasciviously and Eddie took out his iPhone and put in his earbuds. Irritation at being so dismissed emanated from the man but Eddie didn't give a fuck. He wanted to get home, beat off, relieve some of the tension he felt then go back for more later.

When he got off at his stop Mr. Perv did too. Eddie knew it wasn't his normal stop and he kept a wary eye on the man. He seemed harmless enough, following the same route but not too close. Eddie sighed.

I'm just being paranoid. The poor sod's probably just on his way to a friend or something. Maybe a local peep show. He grinned. With music blaring in his ears, he hummed softly to the tune as he made his way home in the darkness. The route was sparsely populated, and Eddie was nearly home.

He relaxed as the sight of the house came into view and was so wrapped up in his music that when something shoved him with great force into the nearby alley, he could only shout out in panic and turn to see who or what had pushed him. His head rocked sideways due to a violent slap across his cheek and his earbuds were pulled from his ears as his phone went slamming to the ground.

Mr. Perv stood before him, his face a mask of fury as he pushed Eddie back against the wall, pinning his arms to his sides. Eddie felt fear at that moment that he'd never experienced before. He was fairly scrappy when it came to a fight but he didn't think he stood a chance against this man. He remembered his father always telling him to stand up to bullies, get on the defensive so he gave it a try.

"What do you think you're doing, you arsehole?" he spat at the man as loud as he could. "Let me the fuck go, Gigantor." Eddie tried to bring his arms up but the man grinned nastily and pinned them above his head with one meaty, sweaty hand.

Shit, this guy was really strong.

Eddie's heart beat faster and he felt sick.

Mr. Perv smiled at him and it was a dreadful sight. "You're a cock tease," he whispered, rancid breath wafting into Eddie's face. "A little cocksucker, and that's exactly what you are going to do right now. And I'm going to make sure you don't get any clever ideas and use those teeth of yours while you're down there." He reached into the pocket of his bulky jacket with his free hand and drew out a switchblade, which sprung to life with a glint of steel.

"This will be in my hand while you suck me, little boy, and if I think for one minute that you are going to me harm, I will slice you like a chicken fillet." He gestured downward. "Now get on your knees, unzip me and do what little cocksuckers do best."

Eddie's body was frozen and his eyes darted around, desperately trying to find some help. His throat clenched and he looked into the implacable eyes of his captor, seeing no mercy. Mr. Perv released Eddie's hands and slowly, deliberately, he forced Eddie to his knees. His hand pushed down on Eddie's shoulder and Eddie bit his lip, trying to stop from crying out at the iron grip. He didn't want the man to have that satisfaction. Eddie pushed back, his hands trying to find a place to hit, to stop what was happening, but the man had at least ninety pounds on him. He landed one punch against the man's chest, but he winced when it seemed to hit steel.

His attacker laughed then punched Eddie on the side of his cheek, causing a ringing in his ears. The skin opened and his head spun. Through splitting pain, he tried feebly to hit back but his hand again hit the taut flesh of the man's stomach. Mr. Perv fumbled with his trousers and a large, purple cock sprung up in front of Eddie's face. It was pushed toward Eddie's mouth and he pressed his lips together.

He stared up at the man, whose lips were coated in spittle. The hand on his shoulder grew tighter as lust flared in his attacker's eyes.

Eddie snarled. "I am not putting that in my mouth, you fucker. You can slice me all you want." Brave words and Eddie just hoped that they wouldn't be his last. The knife wandered slowly down to his cheek and was drawn across the skin. Eddie hissed in pain as his skin parted and he felt the warmth of blood on his flesh. Now he was more scared despite his bravado.

"I have no problem marking you, boy," the voice above him growled. "Make you look not so pretty anymore." The knife made its way toward one of his eyes. Eddie swallowed and closed his eyes as Mr. Perv chuckled. "Maybe I should take one of these beautiful green marbles you have and keep it with me as a reminder that you sucked my cock? I can look at it when I jack off and remember what you used to look like." The tip of the knife was pressed into his eye and Eddie tried to draw his head back, away from the weapon.

Then all hell broke loose. A fearsome and unworldly shriek rent the air as something launched itself at Mr. Perv's back, knocking the blade from his hand to clatter on the pavement. A pale hand raised a sharp-heeled shoe with three inch stiletto heels, repeatedly slamming into Mr. Perv's head and face.

Eddie's attacker cried out in anger and shock and tried to rid of himself from what Eddie now saw was a spitting Leslie, all one hundred and twenty pounds of him, clinging to the man like a limpet and using a shoe as his weapon of choice.

"Get off me, you little wanker," Mr. Perv yelled as he tried to rid himself of his burden. "Stupid git, get off me!" He stumbled around in circles as he tried to pluck Leslie off his back, his trousers around his ankles.

"Motherfucking arsehole prick," Leslie screeched at the top of his voice as he wielded his shoe with malevolent intent. "Hurt my friend, you bastard? We'll show you. Taylor, I'm gonna get off then you smack him, baby. Right across the head." Leslie made a quick dismount off the man and landed gracefully on the street, black stockings under his tight shorts now the worse for wear and definitely laddered.

A thwack sound split the air and Eddie watched in amazement as his would-be molester fell face down onto the pavement. Eddie looked up to see a grim-faced Taylor holding what looked like a rubber truncheon.

"Eddie, are you okay?" Taylor said anxiously as Leslie danced around the fallen man with a cackle of glee. "Did we get here in time? You have blood on your face."

Taylor helped Eddie to his feet. Then he leaned over and checked the now supine man on the pavement. Eddie saw him heave a sigh of relief.

"He's breathing, just dazed. I'll keep an eye on him so he doesn't get up." He waved what Eddie could now see was definitely a truncheon. "I never thought I'd get the chance to hit someone with one of these. Pretty cool."

Eddie's mind was whirling. Leslie was fussing over him, clucking his tongue as he saw the cut on one of Eddie's cheeks and the split on the other.

Eddie winced. "I'm okay, Taylor. Just a little damaged. Arsehole didn't get what he wanted. But how the hell did you know I was here? Did you see me?" He looked wildly around, realising that there was no way he could be seen from across the street where the house was.

Leslie waved a manicured hand. "We were at home. Taylor just knew you were in trouble. Like the time I got really plastered and those guys were going to drag me down to that gangbang and he found me and got me home? Remember? Taylor said he had a feeling you needed help. He is so damn amazing." He glanced down at his legs and frowned. "Fuck, look at these damn stockings. They're bloody ruined." He kicked the man lying prone on the pavement. "They cost me twenty quid, you bastard!"

The wail of sirens split the air and Eddie's mouth gaped open. "You called the police?"

"Damn right we did, honey," Leslie crowed. "Just before we ran over here, Taylor dialled a mate of his on the force and told them we had a mugging in the alley."

The whole evening had become a little surreal to Eddie and he grabbed Taylor. His legs were shaking and seemed no longer capable of supporting him.

"I don't want you guys getting into trouble for me, maybe you should split—"

Taylor shook his head and gripped Eddie's arm. "No, we should be fine. I mean, Leslie whipped this guy's arse with a shoe, I got in a good smack, we'll say you did the same and he went down. There's three of us. And his cock is out and there's a knife that will have his prints all over it. I dare say the police will make the right connections and cart his sorry effing arse off to jail."

Eddie stared at him. Taylor looked like a force to be reckoned with as he stood there, his features set and a look of complete determination on his face. Eddie's legs gave way and he would have tumbled to the ground had Taylor and Leslie not been holding him up.

"Just hold out a little while longer," Taylor said softly. "Then we'll get you home and sort you out."

Eddie nodded gratefully. An hour and a half later, he was seated in the old, worn armchair in the small lounge, with a cup of chamomile tea pressed into his shaking hand by an insistent Leslie. He would have preferred a shot of brandy but Leslie had glowered at him and bit out something about chamomile being better than booze in this situation. Eddie had refused hospital treatment for his damaged face and instead Leslie had patched him up using the home first aid kit.

The police had come and gone, taken statements, carted the now fully conscious Mr. Perv off in handcuffs and told the three of them to be ready for more enquiries if needed. Leslie had simply explained that he'd been on his way home from a club night and seen what was happening. He'd called Taylor to come and help and bring his trusty truncheon. It had helped that Taylor had seemed to know one of the policemen, Sergeant Shaun Grant, who had arrived on the scene and been very supportive. He'd even given Taylor's hand a squeeze when he'd left. From the look in his eyes, he'd wanted to do more.

The truncheon had apparently been a gift from said Sgt Grant to Taylor as part of a self-defence class he'd undertaken. Once this had been explained and confirmed by the policeman, and Leslie had butted in and gone on and on about the virtues of the implement, being virtuous about the fact it was a better self-defence tool than a knife or a gun, the policeman had wearily agreed and taken it away as "evidence."

"So Taylor, how did you know I was in trouble?" Eddie sipped his tea under Leslie's gimlet eye and tried to keep his distaste at the dishwater taste from showing on his face. His cheek stung where it had split open and he swore his ear was still faintly ringing.

Taylor sat next to Leslie on the worn couch. He sighed and ran a hand over his curly dark hair and stretched his slim body as if he were tired. "I sense things. See them sometimes." He stopped as if he expected Leslie and Eddie to burst into disbelieving laughter. When they didn't he carried on. "My mother had it too. She could sense things, before they happened."

"Like premonitions?" Leslie said in awe, his big blue eyes wide. Eddie loved Leslie's deep blue eyes, fringed with sooty back lashes, and thought they were his best feature.

Taylor nodded. "Yeah, sort of. I've been able to do it since I was a kid." He cleared his throat uncomfortably. "I don't tell many people about it because they think I'm a freak. Or ask me if I can tell them the lotto numbers for a Friday night. It doesn't work that way. It's pretty random."

"Wow." Eddie was impressed. He was quite into that kind of thing anyway so hearing someone who could actually do cool stuff like this was quite a win for him. "So how do you see things, is it like a movie, does it play out in your head?"

Taylor shook his head. "No. I catch glimpses of stuff, images, just fleeting random things, and I feel things and just know. Like with you"—he waved at Leslie—"I saw these guys holding you between them, saying they were going to fuck you and just knew they were up to no good. I saw the club logo and that's when I came down and dragged you out." He scowled. "You shouldn't have been in that state anyway, Leslie. It's too easy to let people get to you when you're drunk like that."

Leslie had the grace to look abashed. "I know, baby. Normally I have someone watching my back when I get like that but he'd disappeared somewhere, probably for a quickie in the bathroom and I lost it for a minute."

Taylor nodded. "Well, you need to be more careful. Make sure you have me or Eddie here looking out for you next time. We won't let you down."

Leslie reached out and laid a soft hand on Taylor's arm. "Thanks, sweetie. I promise I'll be more careful."

"So what did you see about me then?" Eddie asked curiously.

Taylor shrugged. "I just felt—unsettled, I guess. I kept having this flashback of that alleyway and I knew it because I see it every day. I saw you on your knees," he stopped, looking grim, "And I didn't get the feeling it was voluntary. So I told Leslie about it and being the prima donna he is," he grinned at Leslie who grinned back, "He was on the phone calling 999 then running across here with me hot on his heels."

"You should have seen him, Eddie." Leslie shivered. "It was fucking spooky. He just stood there, all zoned out and kept saying, 'Eddie's in trouble.' His eyes were all blank like there was no one home. And he was pointing to the alley and saying shit like, 'He's over there, the guy's going to cut him.'" Leslie harrumphed. "Well, I just *had* to do something. He was *very* convincing."

Eddie grinned despite the chill running down his spine. "And if it had been a false alarm and Taylor was just messing with you or wrong?"

Leslie waved a hand. "Oh well, better safe than sorry I say. I could have made some excuse up to the boys in blue if there'd been nothing there. But as it turned out, you weren't wrong, were you, Tay?" He grinned. "Tay here is a regular old psychic."

"Is that what happened the other night?" Eddie asked quietly. "When I found you in here, all creeped out, talking about gingerbread and fairy tales?"

Taylor nodded. "Yeah. I didn't see that much of that, just had this feeling someone you knew was in trouble. But I don't remember much about it. Maybe it's sorted itself out." He sounded hopeful. "It normally only happens with people I'm close to, or have some kind of connection with."

"Gingerbread and fairy tales rings a bell somehow but I can't remember where." Eddie sat back, exhausted. "That's quite a gift, Taylor. Or I guess a curse depending on how you look at it."

Taylor's face darkened. "You could say that. It's something I have to live with. I have no choice." He looked up, his eyes panicked. "Promise me you won't tell anyone about this thing I have. You guys are my friends, so it was bound to come out sooner or later. Please don't tell anyone else."

Eddie shook his head gently even though his head was splitting. "We won't tell anyone, promise."

Taylor's face cleared, the look of relief evident.

Eddie leaned forward and touched Taylor's hand. "I for one am glad of your talent. You've saved us both now, and I'd hate to think what might have happened if you hadn't got your talent. It's truly incredible and you need to tell me more about it. But right now, I am so fucking tired." His heart thumped suddenly and he shot forward, his eyes wide. "Hell, I was supposed to go meet Gid—" he swallowed his words, not wanting to tell his friends he was going to a booty call with his boss. Leslie's plucked brows arched.

"Meet Gideon, were you going to say? Have you finally managed to get in that man's pants?"

Eddie flushed. "We had a moment earlier. I said I'd go back after close up and—" his voice tailed off at Leslie's grin.

"You were going to get laid, sweetheart!" Leslie crowed. "Oh how fortune has smiled upon our little Eddie."

"Shut up," Eddie growled. He touched his face gingerly. "I can't go over there looking like this. I'm a mess. Plus I honestly don't think I have it in me to have wild animal sex tonight."

"Oh, you definitely don't have it in you, *yet*," Leslie purred, his eyes sparkling. Taylor chuckled. Eddie cast a withering glance at his amused friends.

"Can it, you pervert. I'd better call him, tell him to take a rain check." He felt a pang of regret but he knew he wasn't in any mood to go across town and have Gideon see him all vulnerable and weak. He still felt ashamed that a pint-size man in heels had been the one to help rescue him.

"Did you say *rim* check?" Leslie said slyly and Taylor spluttered with laughter.

Eddie's mouth tugged. "Shut it you." He patted his pocket for his phone. "Shit, I forgot that asshole broke my phone. Did one of you pick it up at all?"

Taylor nodded and stood up to fetch his jacket. "Yeah, I got it. It's knackered though." He reached in the pocket and drew out Eddie's smashed and sorry looking mobile.

Eddie heaved a sigh. "Great. I'll have to try and call the restaurant directly and see if I can get hold of him or leave a message on the office phone. It's late so I doubt anyone will answer. I had his mobile number in there," he waved gloomily at the stricken phone. "And I'm not on shift tomorrow; it's my day off so I won't see him." Another thought struck him. "Shit, we're going to that dinner of yours tomorrow night, Leslie."

"Oh darling, it doesn't matter if you don't want to go and you'd rather see your man." Leslie's eyes shadowed though and there was no way Eddie was going to let him down after what he'd done for him tonight.

He shook his head firmly. "Uh-uh. I'm going with you and we are going to dance up a storm and show that miserable ex of yours exactly what he's missing." Leslie smiled, a sight that lit up the room. "Just give me a few hours' sleep and a shower and I'll be good to go."

He's not my man anyway. Not yet at least.

Eddie called the restaurant with Taylor's mobile—he'd been gracious enough to let Eddie use it in case he needed anything—and got the answering machine. It was almost midnight so he guessed Gideon might be upstairs in his flat already. He left a message saying something had happened and he needed to sort it out, and left Taylor's number, and that he'd see Gideon the day after tomorrow.

Then a battered and slightly emotional Eddie dragged himself wearily off to bed.

He was rudely woken up by the shrill tones of the house phone lying on his bedside table. Blearily, Eddie peered at his bedside clock and winced. It was two a.m., for God's sake. Even if it were Gideon, this was not the time to be waking a man up.

"Hello?" he barked roughly into the phone.

A soft breathing was all that could be heard. Eddie squinted his eyes as if doing so would make him hear better. Daft he knew but it was a habit he had. "Hello, who is this?"

"It's me, cuz," was the faint reply.

"Luke? Do you know what fucking time it is?" Eddie's cousin Luke was seven years younger than him, a mix of geeky Tobey Maguire meets Dylan O'Brien. He was also Eddie's best friend despite their age gap. He'd been the one person Eddie had really regretted leaving behind when he left Norfolk. Luke was a little highly strung and given to mood swings.

"Yeah, I know. I just—" Luke's whispered voice cut off and Eddie sat up, his senses on alert.

"Cuzbuster, is everything okay?" The old nickname bought back memories of the two of them drinking beer by the seashore, covered in sand as they got rather merry and then went for midnight dips in the freezing sea. The fact Eddie was supposed to be the mature one and he still let Luke drink alcohol at his tender age sometimes made him feel guilty. He also felt bad that he'd only been home twice in the past three months to visit his family and Luke in particular.

"Yeah, everything's fine, Red. I just wanted to hear your voice." Luke's voice was soft, and Eddie squinted more.

"It's pretty late, man. Have you been drinking? Is this a drunk-man call like those ones we used to pull when I was home?"

He and Luke had often made prank calls to people when they'd had a little too much to drink and had nothing better to do.

Luke's quiet laugh echoed in his year. "No, idiot. I just couldn't sleep and thought maybe you'd still be awake. I know you work some late shifts sometime."

"Okay, well this wasn't one of them. I was dreaming about giving some guy a really great blow job and you woke me up." Eddie grinned despite his initial ire at having his sleep disturbed.

This was Luke after all. "How are things back home? Everything all right?"

There was silence then Luke replied. "Yeah, there's some stuff going on that maybe you can help me with but it can wait until you visit. You are planning on coming home soon, aren't you?"

"I thought I'd try get home for Halloween. I know you like that time of year and we can have some fun at the village bonfire. You know how we love messing about and scaring the kids to death."

"Oh, I thought it might be sooner than that. Never mind." Luke sounded tired and Eddie frowned.

"You don't sound yourself, Luke. What's going on, sunshine?"

Luke's tone sounded forced. "Nothing that can't wait until next month. I'll make sure we have the best pumpkins ready to carve for the competition. You know how Mum and Dad think we design the best ones for the fete. We can't let them down." There was a rustling, like newspaper, or the pages of a book. "Anyway I'll go and let you get back to sleep. I'll call you soon, unless you call me first."

"Okay, yeah, I'll give you a ring soon. Oh and give a kiss to Rachel for me. Tell her I'll see her soon too." Rachel was Luke's girlfriend. They'd been going out for four months now and while Eddie hadn't got to know her that well before he'd left, he'd liked the seventeen-year-old brunette.

"Erm, sure, I'll do that. Listen, I'd better go. Speak soon, Red." The phone went dead and Eddie laid it back on the bed side table. He felt a little unsettled as if something was wrong but he couldn't put his finger on it. As he snuggled down under his duvet to try and get back to sleep, he decided to try get back home a little sooner than planned. It sounded like Luke needed him.

Chapter 9

Gideon stormed across the restaurant floor wishing he could hit something to rid himself of the temper bubbling inside him. He felt like a fool, a stupid,"I should have known better" fool. He'd rushed around like a crazy man last night in preparation for Eddie's visit. He'd closed up the restaurant in record time; had a shower, shaved and put on his best pair of jeans—the ones with thc buttons, as there was something about a man unbuttoning them slowly that did things to him. His tee shirt had been just right, hugging his body and the contours of the muscles he had, and he was ready and raring to go. And then the little wanker hadn't even bothered to show up. Gideon had sat up drinking wine until two a.m., even though he'd known Eddie was a no show. He hadn't even called and Gideon hadn't got his number. He'd gone to bed horny, jerked off and fallen into an uneasy sleep, populated by images of fire, burning bodies and angels bearing Eddie's face cackling as they flew around in the skies taunting him.

Eddie wasn't on the duty roster today and there'd still been no sign of him, telephonically or otherwise. Gideon should have known better. He should have stuck to his original instinct of not mixing business and pleasure. Well, he wouldn't be making that mistake again. He chomped down fiercely on his piece of gum wishing it was Eddie he was chewing out. He plucked at the rubber band on his wrist, drawing it away then letting it go to leave a stinging mark on his skin. It was one way to manage the panic attacks that sometimes threatened. He hadn't had to use one for a while but lately…things were different.

Carmen laid a hand on his arm as he stalked past her. "Hey, Gideon, you all right?" her black eyes were concerned. "You look pissed off and as if you haven't slept again."

"I'm fine," Gideon snapped. "Just have a lot on my mind. I'm going to the kitchen to speak to Jerome. If you see Sarah can you tell her that I've arranged for the Goodwins to go on table four? They're the one with that hyperactive kid and that's the best place to put them so he doesn't disrupt the other diners."

"Sure, honey. I'll tell her." Gideon felt Carmen's eyes on him as he entered the kitchen. The staff waved and smiled at him and not wanting to be churlish, he managed a grin and a few words. Jerome was busy at the stove with scallops and what looked like strips of juicy, thick pork belly. He turned as Gideon tapped him on the shoulder and his face split into a huge toothy grin.

"Gideon! Good to see you here, my friend. What's up?" He turned back to the sizzling dish on the stove. Gideon's chest tightened at the easy demeanour of the man cooking, taking it so for granted that he could smell the aromas in the kitchen, the energising scents of herbs, spices and meats, taste them in the back of the throat, taste buds watering and ready to consume the delights that were offered.

Gideon's hand clenched as he replied. "I was asked by one of the patrons if you'd like to go out to the front—table eleven? He said he loved your spinach roulade so much he'd like to pay his compliments." Gideon's stomach plummeted. There'd been a time when *he'd* been the one going out to greet satisfied patrons but he'd never begrudge Jerome his moment of glory.

Jerome beamed as he wafted the spatula he clutched in a big hand around in front of Gideon's face. A blob of something flew off and hit Gideon's cheek and he raised a finger and wiped it off, then instinctively put it in his mouth the clean off. It was wet, warm—and that was it. He had no idea what he'd just eaten. He picked up a dishcloth and wiped whatever it had been off his cheek. He dropped the cloth down next to him on the surface idly as his mind raced.

Jerome nodded. "Well, that's a lovely surprise. Sure, let me finish up here and then I'll pop over to table eleven." He turned to his still cooking dish and poked it around a bit. Gideon watched him for a minute, seeing the tantalising brown of the scallops as they seared, appreciating the pale gold hue of the butter as they cooked.

Jerome turned with a faint scowl on his face and then sniffed loudly. "What the hell is that smell?" Suddenly the kitchen was rent by the sound of the smoke alarm, a shrill, irritating beep. People glanced around wildly, trying to detect the problem. Jerome's eyes darted to Gideon's side and they widened. "Shit, Gideon, the dishtowel is burning."

Gideon's face turned towards the source of Jerome's concern and saw the dishtowel smouldering, starting to smoke and flame. Bile and panic rising in his throat, he reached out quickly and plucked it from where it lay, still on the stovetop plate that no doubt had still been hot. He dropped it hastily into the kitchen sink, which was still full of sudsy water. The fiery dishtowel fizzled out.

Gideon's body flushed with heat that firstly he had been so careless and that secondly, he hadn't smelt the dishcloth burning. He gazed down at the wet dishcloth with eyes that didn't really see and Jerome laid a meaty hand on his. Gideon looked up to see a pair of brown eyes regarding him compassionately. He thought they might be seeing directly into his withered soul. One of the kitchen staff was flapping another large dishtowel at the offending and still trilling smoke alarm in an effort to stop it. Finally the kitchen was silent.

Jerome gazed at Gideon, his eyes soft. "Nothing we can't fix, boss. Dishtowels are a dime a dozen in this kitchen. And thank God for smoke detectors. It's not the first time we've had that happen."

Gideon nodded. He felt sick. What if he'd done that at home? He could have caused a fire, burnt the restaurant down, hurt people. Bile rose in his throat and he nodded jerkily. Then he turned and got out of the kitchen as fast as he could. He walked blindly to his office and sat behind his desk, staring blankly around his office. And *that* in a nutshell was the reason why he didn't work in a kitchen anymore. He was fucking useless. Tears pricked at the back of his eyes and he blinked them away fiercely. A noise at the door made him look up.

Carmen smiled at him. "Sarah says thanks for the heads up. She says the Goodwins are all settled and little Jeremiah is under control with the colouring books and Lego kit you left for him. That was a sweet gesture."

"Yes, well it distracts him and keeps him busy. He's a nice kid, just a little manic." Gideon chewed rapidly as he picked up a sheaf of papers not wanting to see the expression of what he thought was pity in Carmen's eyes. No doubt by now she'd have heard of his stupid fuck-up in the kitchen. "I've got some paperwork to sort out so I'll be out on the floor in a minute."

"Okie-dokie, honey. Oh by the way, remember I'm leaving a little earlier today from my shift. You okayed it last week. I said to Eddie I'd pick up his tux on my home and drop it off at his place. He's only a few blocks away from me and it saves him coming in today on his day off. I tried to call Eddie today to remind him but I can't get through. It goes straight to voice mail." She grinned. "And I'm not in tomorrow, remember. Day off."

Gideon remembered then that Eddie was accompanying his "friend" to some fancy dinner. "Oh yes," he muttered. "Far be it for Eddie to make it back this way for any reason. Or call anyone." He winced even as he said the words.

I sound like a bloody teenager being stood up on prom night.

Carmen wandered into the office, looking all innocent but Gideon knew her too well. She was a piranha, with teeth that were able to dig under his skin and make him bleed with her concern.

"Sounding a little peeved there, G? Is everything all right in paradise?" Her brows rose in query.

"Everything's fine. I'm here, you're here, what could possibly be wrong?" Bitterness leaked out of his mouth like toxic waste. "Now be off with you and leave me alone. I've got work to do." He pulled the pile of paperwork toward him with intent and ignored Carmen.

She sighed heavily. "Fine. I shall leave you to get on with whatever you're not doing. And Gideon?"

He looked up at her in exasperation. "What?"

"Cut yourself some slack. Please." She disappeared. Gideon let out a breath and leaned back in his chair.

Concentrate, Gideon. Forget Eddie, getting laid and anything else. Just focus on work. It's all you need to do right now.

***

The following morning Gideon knew Eddie was on a double shift. He deliberately stayed away from the kitchen, not wanting to hear any discussions or scuttlebutt about his burning dishcloth affair. He still flushed every time he thought about it. It was a particularly busy day, and the restaurant was a chaotic amount of people in and out the doors. It was close to six that evening when he finally had a break and went out to the back alley for some fresh air. He missed the act of smoking, of coming out here with the other smokers and shooting the breeze. He'd tried to join them and simply enjoy their company but the sight of them all so obviously enjoying their smoke break pissed him off a little. So now he and his packet of gum stood outside. He was about to throw his current piece away in the dumpster when he heard a low cough. He turned to see Eddie standing there, smiling at him. Immediately Gideon scowled and his fingers nervously moved to his rubber band. He fingered it, noticing Eddie's face, the cut on his cheek, and the bruising. He felt a twinge of concern, wondering what had happened but he was in too bad a mood to simply ask about it like a caring person would. Instead he went on the attack.

"Had a really good time last night then? Have a little bit of trouble in the bathroom—didn't you want to give it up?" he said scathingly.

Eddie's eyes widened. "What? No, nothing like that." He flushed pinkly. "What the hell do you mean by that anyway?" His smile had disappeared.

Gideon shrugged. "Looks like you had to fight them off, or maybe made the wrong move." He knew he was being a total prick but his ire was seething and wanted out. "The sight of you in a tux too good to resist then? Like those damn leathers you had on the other night. Nothing says 'I'm available' like those ones did." He flicked his gum into the bin then snapped the band against his wrist, uttering a slight hiss of pain at the sting.

Eddie stepped toward him, his body taut. "What the fuck is wrong with you? Why are you being such an arsehole?" His voice was tight.

"It's in my nature, Eddie. I don't like being stood up. It brings out the nasty in me." He saw Eddie about to speak and shook his head. "I'm not interested in why you didn't come back. I guess you found something better to do. And so have I. It was probably for the best anyway. It'd never have worked. So maybe I should thank you for not coming around for a fucking."

Eddie swallowed, his green eyes filled with hurt and confusion. "Gideon, I—"

Gideon swept past him and went back into the restaurant. He'd said his bit although he felt sick. He'd never set out before to hurt someone deliberately like he'd just done to Eddie.

Christ, what the hell is wrong with me? Have I just completely lost it?

He was still wondering that when he finally went to bed that night with a stinging wrist, his gut churning, his head aching, and with a sense of self-hatred he'd never felt before.

Chapter 10

The following morning didn't start all that well for Gideon. He'd had a really bad night and ended up puking into the toilet after a particularly bad dream.

"You fucking selfish prick. What the hell is wrong with you?"

Gideon glanced up in amazement at a spitting mad Carmen, who stood with hands on hips in front of him halfway down the steps as he cleaned the beer lines in the quiet, dimly lit basement of Galileo's.

He frowned. "Hell, it's a good thing we're friends, Carmen, or I might have to fire your arse for spouting off at me like that. What the hell is your problem?" He rubbed his wrist, noting absently that he hadn't put the band on after his shower.

Carmen glowered. "What bug is up your arse that you had to say those things to Eddie yesterday? He didn't deserve it. Did he actually get to tell you what happened the night he missed your booty call, Gideon? Did you at least let him explain what went down?"

Gideon stood up, wincing as his back complained from being hunched down. "I know enough. He—"

"You know nothing!" Gideon was amazed to see Carmen's eyes glittering with tears. "Someone attacked him, Gideon. Tried to force him on his knees to give them a blow job then smacked him around. If it hadn't been for his friends seeing what was going on, he might have been badly hurt. The man had a knife at Eddie's face, for God's sake."

Gideon's body went cold. His heart threatened to plummet to his stomach and join the acid coiling around his innards. "What?"

"Oh, very good comeback, arsehole." Carmen clattered down to the bottom of the steps and stood in front of him. "He was all shook up and his phone was smashed when he was attacked. So he didn't have your mobile number. He left a message on the phone in the office. But I bet you didn't check, did you?"

Gideon hadn't checked the messages in fact. It was one of those jobs he was terrible at doing. He could only stand there and listen to both the self-recriminations flooding his brain and Carmen spouting off. His fingers tingled and he tried taking deep breaths to calm himself down.

I can do this. I don't need a fucking rubber band.

Carmen's face was a picture of disappointment. At Gideon.

"He tried to tell us he'd fallen and hit a wall, but you know me, I have ways of ferreting out the truth. He's absolutely bloody miserable about what you said to him."

Gideon stood, hearing Carmen but not listening to her words. The shame he felt at mouthing off and causing Eddie's distress on top of what he'd already suffered mortified him. He could only watch Carmen's mouth move while he figured out how to make this better.

Finally Carmen ran out of steam. She stood, bosom heaving, as she glared at him again.

Gideon sank down onto the cold stone bench in the cellar and buried his face in his hands. Then he looked up at his friend. "I'll apologise to him," he said huskily. "Is he still here?"

She nodded. "Yes. He's knocking off at five. You'd better find him and make this right, G. He's a bit of a mess. The police had to re-interview him because the man who attacked him said he paid for the blow job, and then Eddie tried to rob *him*. I don't think it will stick but being painted as a rent boy isn't helping."

Gideon closed his eyes. "I promise I'll make this right," he agreed quietly. "No matter what. Can you please do me a favour and get him to my office somehow? I have the feeling if I ask him he'll just refuse. I don't want to do anything in front of the others either."

Carmen narrowed her eyes. "I'll think of something." She turned and walked up the stairs, turning back to look at him gently. "You need help, Gideon. This isn't you, this bad-tempered bastard. You need to talk to someone about the accident and the nightmares. Before you have a breakdown, honey. Please say you will at least consider it."

Gideon huffed a breath. "I don't need—"

"Yes, you do," Carmen said, her face wreathed in sympathy. "It needs to be addressed." She went up the stairs and didn't look back. Gideon finished what he was doing in silence, his body numb as he went through the motions. His hands were freezing, his mind dull. Finally he ascended the stairs, switched off the light and made his way through the restaurant to his office. He was an autopilot, stopping to talk to one or two of the regulars, chatting to Sarah and complimenting some of the waitstaff scurrying about. Eventually he walked into his office to see Eddie bent over the printer once more.

He turned as Gideon came in. Gideon closed the door and locked it. His heart lurched at the sight of the bruise on Eddie's face, and the thin red line of the cut on his cheek. Eddie's normally beautiful and pale skin was marked with brutality and Gideon felt a seething of hatred for the man who had done it.

Eddie regarded him expressionlessly. "Carmen said you were busy and the printer was acting up. I seem to be the fix it man for some reason. But it looks fine to me." His eyebrows rose. "Why is the door locked?"

"Because I owe you an apology and I wanted to do this privately without an interruption." Gideon perched his arse on the corner of his desk as he looked at Eddie with resolve. He wanted to lean over and kiss the damage on Eddie's face but wasn't sure he had that right. He'd probably get smacked but he thought it would be worth it. Definitely worth it, he mused.

Eddie's lips curled. "I think it's a bit late for that. You had your say. Now if you don't mind, I need to get back to work." He moved past Gideon and Gideon caught his upper arm.

Eddie yanked it away, his face angry. "Let me alone," he warned. "You know what they say about red heads and tempers? Well they were talking about me when my gander is up. Don't fucking mess with me."

Gideon might have been feeling like the world's shittiest arsehole but he still thought Eddie was absolutely adorable. His pale, marked face was flushed with colour, freckles standing out across the bridge of his nose. His green eyes were like chips of green bottle glass, and his biceps had felt like steel when Gideon had grabbed him. He still wanted to kiss the crap out of this man. He also knew he had to say his piece quickly.

"I need to tell you how sorry I am," Gideon murmured. "I was a complete dipshit. You didn't deserve what I said and I didn't mean it. I have no idea how to make you believe me. If you want me on my knees apologising, I'll do it. Whatever you need me to do to make this better, just ask."

"According to you I'm the one on my knees." Eddie's voice was acidic. "And the

police thought so too. It took everything we had to convince them I wasn't a prostitute. Oh, wait, I forget. You didn't know about my brush with a molester did you, the night I was supposed to meet you?" His voice shook.

Gideon swallowed. "I heard about it from Carmen. In no uncertain terms, let me tell you." Thoughts of kissing Eddie fled from his head at the disgusted expression on Eddie's face.

"Yes, well. Carmen's a good friend." Eddie's tone was uncompromising, leaving Gideon in no doubt that *he* wasn't. "I see what you think of me now though, and in all honesty, we should simply leave it there. Thanks for the apology."

He turned, unlocked the door and marched out of the office.

***

Two days later Gideon could bear it no longer. He was a nervous wreck. He was hyper sensitive to Eddie's presence—watching him stride across the floor of the restaurant from stock room to kitchen, seeing him go into the kitchen staff room to change before catching his train home and catching sight of his studious frame hard at work every time Gideon went into the kitchen. Eddie did his best to ignore him too, but Gideon knew he was watching him. He'd felt Eddie's eyes on his back and when he turned around, they'd be elsewhere.

Eddie must have the quickest damn reflexes, Gideon mused darkly. He was like some bloody sneaky ginger-haired tomcat that spat and clawed and then simply affected an air of disdain as if a person wasn't there. Gideon snorted. Typical cat. He was a dog man himself.

It was driving him completely crazy and there was no way he wanted this friction between them. So Gideon did what any red-blooded man needing to fix things in a non-relationship would do. He waylaid Eddie in the staff room one night late after work, when all of the rest of the kitchen employees were gone.

Eddie's habit was generally to be the last one to leave. He'd disappear to get out of his smelly kitchen clobber into comfortable jeans and sweatshirt and then wrap his old suede jacket round his lithe body before he hot-footed it for his train. It was easy enough for Gideon to wait and then make sure no one else was in there before sneaking in behind him and locking the door.

I don't give a damn what anyone thinks. This is my bloody restaurant and they can deal with me if they don't like it.

At the click of the door closing, Eddie turned in surprise and his face darkened when he saw Gideon standing there, trying to look as contrite as possible. He even fixed a smile on his face in the hope Eddie might feel more susceptible to his charms.

"Gideon? What are you doing here?" His voice was husky and Gideon heard a slight wariness.

"It's my restaurant. I can be here if I want to."

Oh, so damn smooth, you stupid tosser.

Gideon wanted to kick himself for that airy reply. "We have some unfinished business, Eddie." No sooner were *those* words out than Gideon wanted to claw them back.

Way to phrase that one, Kent. It sounds like you expect him to fall to his knees and give you that blow job you always wanted.

Eddie's eyes narrowed, a flush rising on the pale cheeks and he took a step forward, fists clenched. "Honestly? *Unfinished business?*"

Gideon winced. "That didn't quite come out the way I wanted it to. I meant we need to talk. A bit more. If that's all right with you." He was gabbling now and perhaps he should shut his mouth.

Eddie regarded him with suspicion. "I thought we'd said what we had to already."

"No, you said what *you* had to say then walked away. You didn't give me a chance to explain more."

He moved closer to Eddie. Eddie watched him carefully, his lips trembling. Gideon sensed he was a little on edge, uncertain of where this was going. So he did something that completely surprised them both. He took Eddie's face gently between his hands and kissed him. Tentatively, slowly, brushing his lips against Eddie's cool ones, trying to impart the apology and guilt he felt in that one single caress of lips on lips. He braced himself for a punch, for Eddie to shift away. Instead Eddie sighed, warm breath on Gideon's face and Gideon had to physically hold himself back from pulling Eddie into him, taking his mouth violently and thrusting his own hardness against what he knew would be reciprocated. Gideon laid his forehead against Eddie's as his thumbs traced Eddie's jaw.

"I'm so sorry for what happened to you," he whispered raggedly. "I'm glad you had friends to come to your rescue. I couldn't bear the thought of you being hurt." He pulled back then placed a gentle kiss next to the cut on Eddie's cheek.

Eddie was still, his eyes staring into Gideon's with an intensity that made his groin ache and his heart beat faster.

Gideon moved away a little. “I’m sorry I was such a bastard.” He brushed a stray strand of hair from Eddie’s eyes, relieved that Eddie hadn’t pushed him away. He had a feeling he would have, had the situation been reversed.

“What is this, G?” Eddie asked quietly. “This thing we have…” His hands slowly moved to Gideon’s shirt and he smoothed the fabric idly over his chest, causing turmoil in Gideon’s body. He loved the diminutive of his name reduced to one single letter by this man who played havoc with his emotions.

“I have no idea,” Gideon confessed. “I’ve never felt this way for someone before. Thought about anyone like I do you.”

Eddie smiled and Gideon’s world instantly got to be a better place. “Ditto.”

He traced Gideon’s lips with his finger tips and then pressed his mouth to his, harder and more possessive than the original kiss had been. Eddie licked along Gideon’s lower lip and pushed into his mouth, eager, greedy.

Gideon was lost. He’d dreamed of this for so long, this crush he had on this flame-haired, sexy man. Now that he had him in his arms, he never wanted to let go. It was crazy, groin-tinglingly over the top, “are you fucking mad” bat-shit confusing, but it was all Gideon needed and wanted right now. He gripped Eddie’s round, tight arse cheeks, pulling him against his front and Eddie whimpered in his mouth as he ground himself against Gideon, his hardness pressing into his own.

That whimper sent shades of vibrant colour to Gideon’s closed eyes, a surge of heat to his already throbbing dick, and his body shivered with pure animal need at the hard-muscled strength of the man in his arms. The man who was currently trying to reach Gideon’s tonsils with his searching tongue and whose warm fingers trailed licks of fire down Gideon’s spine and skin. Somewhere along the line, Gideon’s shirt had come unbuttoned, his trousers had been unzipped and now a hand stroked his hardened prick through the thin fabric of his cotton boxers.

Gideon could no longer think straight. The world suddenly seemed a smaller place, shrunk to a universe of two people, skin to skin—somehow Eddie’s shirt was also rucked up under his armpits—and as Gideon fought desperately to absorb Eddie into his body using his own backside as an instrument to draw him in, the fact he couldn't smell or taste this man was eclipsed by the fact that he could *feel* him in every cell in his body.

Under Gideon's fingertips, beneath his loose trousers, the skin of Eddie's arse was dimpled with goose bumps. His hair was soft against Gideon's face, the stubble that coated Eddie's chin and upper lip grazed Gideon's cheek and jaw. The noises Eddie was making as he kissed the crap out of Gideon were a turn-on beyond belief. Gideon's remaining senses ran riot, the sensory overload making him dizzy with need.

He needed to breathe, so he pulled his lips away from where they were being devoured, then pulled back to see Eddie's swollen pink mouth and glittering green eyes regarding him with a lustful fervour that he made no effort to mask. Gideon felt a sense of egotistical pride in causing that type of reaction in the man panting before him.

"Eddie, let's slow this down," he gasped, needing to get some sense into his head even though his body was screaming for more. "This is work and we can't really do this here. Not everything I want to do to you anyway."

Eddie drew a shuddering breath. "Is this another rain check? Because I have to tell you, that whole idea sucks." His lips curled in a wolfish grin. "As do I."

He knelt down before Gideon, red hair tousled, cheeks pink and without any hesitation, he pushed Gideon's trousers and underwear down to his knees then engulfed Gideon's dick in a hot, wet mouth. All Gideon's sanity departed in a rush of blood to the very organ currently being assaulted with loving and desperate care.

"Oh-my-fucking-God," he managed to get out before losing the power of speech completely and splaying his hands in Eddie's hair, pushing his mouth deeper onto his dick in the hope that maybe that way they may both be better assimilated into each other. Because, really, he wanted to wear Eddie like a second skin. There was no way he was stopping now. Half of the patrons of Galileo's could have walked in to find Eddie blowing him and he would simply have ignored them all.

He watched Eddie's mouth around his prick, that decadent, fat-lipped mouth bobbing up and down on him like a ship at sea. Eddie raised his eyes to look at him, eyes that were half hidden behind swathes of flame-coloured hair to match the fire in his eyes, and

Gideon felt the incredible pressure in his balls, the flood of fluid into his prick, and he cried out loudly as he filled Eddie's tempting mouth with the warm wash of his seed. His body shuddered and jerked like a man with a fever, and he gripped Eddie's head tighter. He stood, trembling, his legs boneless limbs, as Eddie stood up, a wide grin on his face and his own cock pushing out of his black-and-white-checked trousers like a Big Top circus tent-pole.

"My turn," he whispered, voice sultry, and Gideon stared as his fingers were raised to Eddie's mouth. Eddie took his time sucking each one of them in turn then licking Gideon's palm until it was wet. Gideon's breath deepened as his hand was pushed southwards and Eddie's intent was perfectly clear.

Gideon growled softly as he pulled Eddie's pants down onto lean, pale-skinned hips and wrapped his hand around Eddie's cock. "How do you like it—slow, hard, fast? Tell me, Eddie." He began jerking him off to soft moans from Eddie's punished pink lips.

"Just like that," Eddie hissed as he once again found Gideon's mouth and proceeded to ravage it again. Time seemed to cease in the office, and Gideon's only focus was the hot flesh in his hand, the slickness of fluid coating his fingers and palm, the groans and pants from the man thrusting his tongue in his mouth and his own breathlessness as Eddie tensed against him and wet, sticky come cascaded over his hand and wrist. Eddie collapsed against him, his mouth tickling Gideon's neck.

"Oh God," he breathed into Gideon's ear. "That was pretty fucking awesome, I have to tell you. Your hands are magic."

They stared at each other and Gideon ran a hand through Eddie's sweating hair. "I'm glad you're okay," he murmured. "The thought of that bastard touching you, forcing you to do things to him—I want to bloody kill him myself. Are you sure it's safe now for you out there now?"

Eddie reached up and caressed his cheek gently. "He's in custody. I'm sure he's not daft enough to come after me again." He pressed soft lips to Gideon's and he closed his eyes, revelling in the feeling.

"I just wish I could taste you," he whispered to Eddie. "Smell you. You have no idea how much I miss it."

Eddie sighed gently. "You can feel and hear me, G. Right here, right now. Feel my fingers in your hair, my mouth on yours, feel my body against you. Hear my breath and my voice. Concentrate on those senses instead." He pressed himself closer. Gideon's breath hitched at the sensation of warm, hard man. "You can see me. Watch my face when you make me feel so good."

Gideon groaned and found Eddie's mouth again, bruising his lips in his intensity to absorb the man. A sudden hard knock at the locked door bought them to their senses and they moved apart quickly.

"Eddie, are you in there? Why's the door locked? You're going to miss your train if you don't hurry up."

"Christ, is she still here?" Gideon said in a panic. "Don't any of my staff go home on time?"

Sarah's voice sounded amused and Gideon couldn't help wondering just how much she knew of his infatuation for Eddie. He knew she and Carmen were good work friends and he was sure that his crush wouldn't have gone unspoken about when the two women got together.

"Just a minute," he called out as he hastily tucked himself away and watched Eddie do the same. He motioned around the room with his hand. "Does it smell of sex in here?" he hissed. Eddie sniffed then grimaced. "Yeah, pretty much reeks of it. Have you any air freshener?"

"No, I don't have bloody air freshener, what does this look like, a damn hotel?" Gideon gazed about him, wild eyed.

Eddie sighed. "*And* he's back. Mr. Fucking Grumpy." His eyes darted around the room. "Wait. Someone keeps deodorant in here, I think." He opened a desk drawer and picked up a can of Lynx Dry Twist spray. He sprayed it liberally around the room.

Gideon hissed at Eddie. "Open the door and try and act like we haven't just—well, done what we just did."

"You mean the blow job and jerk-off?" Eddie said drily as he unlocked the door. "I have no problem not sharing that."

Sarah marched in and the wicked smile she gave made his heart beat faster with panic.

"Having a little bit of a sweat problem in here, lads?" Her grin was knowing. "You need to watch that." She fanned herself. "Boy, it's hot in here."

Gideon regarded her warily. "Eddie and I were just…talking." He knew it was a lame excuse and from Eddie's soft snigger, he did too.

Sarah chuckled. "Of course you were." Her eyes glinted mischievously. "I just thought I should remind Eddie about his train. Plus I still have your credit card in my bag from lunchtime when I paid the suppliers. I needed to give it back before you left and I thought I might find you both in here." She handed over Gideon's credit card with a smirk.

He scowled as he put it in his trouser pocket.

Eddie moved toward the door and Gideon tried to catch his eye. Eddie nodded at him but there was a knowing glint in his eye. "See you later, boss. I've got a train to catch." He disappeared out the door. Gideon was left with Sarah who was all but sniggering.

"So," she drawled. "You and Eddie, huh? Who would have guessed?" Her face clearly showed that she definitely would have guessed.

Gideon scowled again. He seemed to be doing that a lot lately and he really needed to stop it before he got lines on his face. "What's between Eddie and me is none of your business, nosey parker," he said loftily.

Sarah pursed her lips. "Oh, indeed, boss man." She turned with a giggle and disappeared out the door. Gideon heaved a sigh of relief.

Well that all hadn't gone too badly. He was back on an even keel with Eddie and had released some of the sexual tension he'd had. Gideon still wasn't sure that this thing with Eddie was a good idea but he didn't think it could be avoided. The chemistry between them was too intense. Gideon felt a prickle of unease down his spine. The feelings he harboured for his red-haired chef seemed to be more than sexual attraction. When he'd been kissing Eddie, he'd felt very at home in the man's mouth and holding him in his arms. It had almost felt like home.

Chapter 11

Eddie was flying high in the kitchen the next day. He buzzed around it like a darting dragonfly, feeling the goofy smile on his face as he worked. He'd only broken two glasses and Jerome had given him the evil eye for a while, but then he'd relented on seeing Eddie in a better mood. Instead he'd merely warned him airily that if he broke anything else today he'd shove his fist down Eddie's throat. Eddie had simply nodded and agreed that was fine.

The day passed swiftly, Eddie's shift coming to an end all too soon at six o'clock. He'd hoped to manage to see Gideon again, to find out whether they could get together that night, but so far Jerome had kept him so busy, there'd been no time. Gideon had come into the kitchen once or twice, glancing at Eddie, almost as if reassuring himself that Eddie was still there. Eddie liked that feeling; the one that said someone cared about him enough to be a little possessive. Each time he saw Gideon's lithe frame and broad shoulders in view, his nether regions tingled and his skin prickled with longing.

Eddie had it bad.

He felt his new mobile vibrate in his pocket. It was a message from his cousin Luke.

Hi Red. Hw r thngs with u?

Eddie texted back. He had a real dislike of text speak, probably because he'd had one very strict and anal retentive English teacher in college who had constantly lectured on the correct use of language. She had despised the whole shortened text and email speech, saying it made students lazy and unable to spell. Eddie tended to agree with her but he'd never told her that. She would have hauled him to the front of the class with a smirk and embarrassed the shit out of him.

Good thanks. What are you up to?

There was a delay then ***Ok. U stll cmg back 31st?***

Eddie remembered he'd told Luke he'd be home for Halloween.

Think so. Going to try.

Gd. Need to tlk. Spk then.

Okay. See you soon. Tell Rachel hi.

Eddie popped his phone back in his pocket. He frowned. Luke was certainly being very attentive. Twice in one week he'd contacted

Eddie when normally the little git had to be forced to keep in touch. Something was up and when he got home he'd find out what.

He finished cleaning up and said goodbye to his colleagues then made his way to the change room. He'd just changed into jeans and a comfy tee shirt and was busy stuffing his dirty whites into his rucksack when he heard a cough behind him. He turned to see Carmen grinning at him.

"Did you two kiss and make up then?" she asked.

Eddie's face warmed. "Yes, I guess we did."

Carmen flapped a hand. "About damn time, you two stubborn arseholes." She came closer. "So everything is okay now between you two? No more miserable Eddie and grumpy Gideon?"

Eddie sniggered. "No, no more Mr. GG." He frowned and rummaged around in his pocket. He drew out his phone and looked at Carmen. "Do me a favour and give me Gideon's mobile number. I just got this new phone yesterday and I need to put all the numbers back in."

Carmen reached over and plucked the phone from Eddie's hand. "Let me pop it in for you now." She deftly pressed the buttons as Eddie watched then handed it back to him with a satisfied smirk. "There you go. It's filed under 'Booty Call.'"

Eddie chuckled. "Really, that's the best you could do?" He put his phone back in his pocket and hefted his bag onto his shoulder. "I'll give him a call later then."

Carmen's face softened. "I'm glad about you and the boss. He needs someone right now. He won't talk about that night of the fire to anyone and he bottles it all up inside. The fact he had to give up cooking—that killed him. It festers inside him and he needs to move on. Maybe you can make him see that."

"I'm not sure we're there yet," Eddie said quietly. "I mean, I like the guy but I doubt he's ready to share his man angst with me yet. Hell, I don't even know what's going on. This could just be all about sex. But I'll let him know if he needs to talk, I'll be there."

He moved toward the door. He wanted to pop by and see if Gideon was in his office before he left and whether he had plans for the night. It was Friday after all. "I'll see you Monday then, as I'm on late tomorrow and you don't work Saturdays. Enjoy the weekend." He left Carmen behind and sauntered down to Gideon's office. The man wasn't in there or in the restaurant. Eddie sighed.

Okay, well I'll give him a call later. I don't want to be too needy or I might scare him off.

His ride on the tube was coupled with both anxiety and a little bit of fear. Eddie found himself studying the people around him, assessing who might be a threat and who might be giving him the eye. He hated that he felt this insecure. When he got to his stop and stepped onto the platform, he glanced behind him to make sure no one was following him. The walk home was fraught with dangerous possibilities; every alleyway, every homeless bum knocking into him, every person that was big and beefy looked like a threat. He was very glad when he reached the front gate to his home and made his way inside. He closed the door behind him with a sigh of relief and plopped his backpack onto the floor in the entrance.

When he walked into the kitchen he found Leslie with a spatula in hand, earbuds in and dancing around the kitchen as he cooked pasta. His flatmate looked relaxed in a pair of low-hanging blue sweatpants and an oversized tee shirt with the words, "Sperm whales blow and so do I" written all over the back. Eddie choked back a laugh and tapped Leslie on the shoulder. Leslie shrieked and the spatula went flying across the kitchen to land on the floor.

"Oh my God, you scared the fuck out of me," Leslie hissed as he pulled his buds out of his ears. Eddie heard the tinny sounds of Lady Gaga blaring out of them.

Eddie peered into the boiling pots on the stove. Billows of fragrant steam blew into his face and he smelt the tantalising aroma of garlic and basil. He felt a pang at the fact that he took it for granted he could smell it. He knew that if he too were to lose his sense of smell and taste, part of who he was as a chef would be irretrievably lost.

"Smells great," he remarked. "Are you expecting company? There seems to be lot of it."

Leslie bent down to retrieve his spatula and shook his head. His wavy black hair bobbed on his head, coifed as it was into thick, elegant curls. "No, it's just you, me and Taylor. He should be home soon. That damn music shop he works at is making him work double shifts this week because one of the guys is sick. As if they don't get their pound of flesh from him anyway." He busied himself lifting pan lids and stirring what looked to Eddie like a ragout of creamy chicken and mushrooms.

Eddie stared at Leslie in disbelief. "It's Friday night. Shouldn't you be getting ready to go out partying instead of being Momma Bear Cook?"

Leslie huffed as he turned to stare Eddie down, his blue eyes ringed with mascara. "Even we party animals like a night off now and then, you know. And I thought after all the action this week with you being attacked and nearly violated, we should have a home-cooked meal, drink some beer and chill out together. I didn't think you had plans." The unspoken *You never have plans anyway* wasn't lost on Eddie. Leslie looked at Eddie anxiously. "Oh God, you *did* have plans, didn't you? I'm going to have to eat this whole damn pot of chicken stroganoff by myself. Then I'll put on twenty pounds, get fat and no one will look at me twice. I'll end my years as a fat, frumpy old maid with no man to share it with because he can't get near my dick for the fat rolls." Leslie's tirade of words only stopped because Eddie placed a firm finger on his glossy lips to shut him up.

"It's fine. I had no plans yet so eating in sounds good to me. I just need a shower first." Thoughts of what he might do in the shower thinking of Gideon made him smile.

Leslie's gazed at him curiously. "You seem in a really good mood these days, Eddie…" His voice trailed off and he looked at Eddie with wide eyes. "Oh my God, you totally had sex with your boss, didn't you? I think I can smell the pheromones seeping out of your body." He tapped the side of his nose with the spatula, leaving a small glob of cream on it. "You know this proboscis of mine is a fine tuning fork, boyfriend. And this nose is telling me you got laid. Was it that gorgeous boss of yours?"

Leslie's nose was indeed a marvel of the modern world. There wasn't a man alive who could wear a cheap eau de cologne around him and hope to pass it off as anything other than what it was.

Eddie reached over and scooped the glob from Leslie's nose with the tip of his finger. He wiped it on the dishtowel. "I gave him a blow job and he jacked me off in his office yesterday. So I guess that constitutes sex." He smiled. "And honestly, proboscis?"

Leslie squealed and hugged Eddie, warm arms wrapping themselves around his waist as he plastered kisses on Eddie's cheek.

"Awesome. I'm so glad. You two seem to have been dithering about it for ages." He unpeeled himself from Eddie and turned his attention back to the simmering contents of the pot. "You'll have to tell me and Taylor all about it when we eat. I'm dying for all the details." He waved his spatula. "Now shoo. Off you go and get yourself all cleaned up before supper."

Eddie rolled his eyes but went to do as he was told.

An hour later he was lying on his bed, still wet and clad in nothing but a towel when his phone rang. He peered at the screen. *Booty Call.*

Eddie felt the grin split his face as he answered. "Hi, Gideon."

"You knew it was me? You have me programmed in your phone?" Gideon sounded surprised but pleased. Eddie snorted. He wasn't about to tell him about his call sign.

"Of course I have your number." He noticed the flirty tone of his voice and cringed.

Way to be cool, Eddie. Tip the man off just how much you want him.

"I'm sorry I didn't get to see you before you left. Carmen said you came looking for me." A deep sigh echoed down the phone. "Some kid locked himself in the bathroom in a strop and I had to coax him out using only my incredible charm and the promise of a free knickerbocker glory when he finally deigned to come out."

Eddie chuckled. "A knickerbocker glory would entice anyone out of seclusion. It's one of my favourite puddings."

"That's good to know when I want to tempt you." Gideon fell silent.

"What are you up to tonight then?" Eddie thought he'd better fill the awkward silence. He almost heard Gideon shrug through the phone.

"Not much. I'm lying down flicking through TV channels, debating whether to go back downstairs and catch up on some paperwork. What are you doing?"

"I'm about to have dinner with my housemates. One of them cooked this whole pasta thing. I just got out of the shower."

"Out of the shower, hey?" Gideon's voice sounded much more interested in that titbit. "What, so you're naked then?"

Eddie's chest thumped and his cock slowly tented the towel. "Not quite. I'm in a towel." His hand moved slowly down to caress himself through the fabric of the thin bath sheet. He couldn't help a slight gasp escaping his lips as he did so. On the other side of the phone he heard the noise of someone moving around, the rustle of clothes or bed coverings.

"So you're all alone then?" Gideon's voice was husky and the sound of it sent a shiver through Eddie's body. He swallowed as he stroked himself.

"Yeah, it's just me and this rapidly rising problem I seem to have."

Gideon's chuckled stirred Eddie's cock harder and he couldn't help a slight moan as his hands brushed the tip and sent a surge of electricity through his groin.

"Are you doing what I think you're doing?" Gideon whispered down the phone. "Because if you are, it is so damned hot."

"I dunno. Are you doing something that side that *I* should know about?" Eddie stroked himself languorously as he lay back on the pillows, hugging his phone to his chin and ear and letting the towel fall to the side as he took himself in his hand. He was already wet and slick under his fingers, and just knowing Gideon was listening to him and knowing he was getting off was a complete turn-on.

"I'm lying naked on my bed, touching myself and wishing you were here to suck my dick. Then I could fuck you." Gideon's throaty growl made Eddie's buttocks clench together and he swore he felt the pressure of a cockhead at his entrance, so intense was the image of seeing Gideon behind him, ready to enter him.

"Crikey, you don't waste any time, do you?" he gasped, as his hands gripped firmer and he stroked harder at the thought of Gideon taking him.

"No time to waste," was the equally gasping retort. "Just thinking about bending you over and pushing inside you makes me want to come."

"Oh fuck." Eddie had no doubt if he saw himself in the mirror now, he'd see a wild-eyed, messy-haired man with pink cheeks and a purple cock, manically fisting himself as he tried desperately to make his sensations last.

Mental note: get a mirror installed so next time I do this I can watch. That would be bloody incredible. Better still, get Gideon here with me so we can watch ourselves rut like rabbits.

That idea made Eddie even hornier. He heard Gideon's low groans.

"God, Eddie, what you do to me. Want you, just can't stop thinking about you and that tight arse of yours… Want inside you so bad."

"Hell, you say the sexiest things." Eddie's legs tensed, his thighs straining with the effort of prolonging the orgasm that threatened. He didn't want to stop pumping his cock, yet at the same time, he wanted this experience to last longer. He was in agony deciding what to do. Finally he stopped his strokes and gripped the base of his shaft tightly as he tried to slow things down. "Tell me how you'd do it—how would you fuck me?"

Gideon's strangled voice gave confirmation the fact that he was in as delicate a place as Eddie. "I'd put you on your stomach, use my tongue and my fingers, eat your hole until you were ready, put my fingers inside you to open you up and then my dick would pound your gorgeous arse into the mattress."

Hearing those words, Eddie had no place to go but up. As his hands went back to their frenzied fisting of his cock, his balls drew up in his groin, his body stiffened like the onset of super rigour mortis and he cried out loudly as plumes of wet, warm semen shot out of him and covered his hand, wrist and stomach with come.

Eddie chanted, "Oh God, oh God," over and over again like a prayer. The phone fell onto the bed and he scrambled to pick it up desperately, not wanting to miss the sounds of Gideon's climax. He pressed the phone back to his ear with shaking hands as his still-shuddering body collapsed back on the bed.

There was a loud explosion of noise over the phone, something that sounded like a cross between a roar and a snort and he heard Gideon moaning softly, words he couldn't make out. Eddie listened for a while and then when his heart had finally calmed down and he could breathe properly again he spoke into the phone.

"G? You there?"

There was a shuffling noise and then Gideon's deep voice resonated down the phone, breathy and relaxed. "Yeah, I'm here. Hell, that was something. I haven't come like that in ages. Nearly blew my damn balls off."

Eddie felt a sense of pride in being able to engineer such a response. "Well, let me tell you, it was pretty explosive this side too. Now I have to have another shower or the proboscis downstairs will be all over me."

"Proboscis?" Gideon sounded out of breath.

"My flatmate can smell something at a thousand paces. He's the Svengali of scents."

"Oh. I see."

Eddie felt a prickle of unease at the suddenly flat tone of Gideon's voice. He mentally kicked himself for bringing up the sensitive subject of smell. He babbled on.

"Anyway, that was a lot of fun. Pity you weren't here so we can act out some of those fantasies you have."

"I'd like that." The smile was back in Gideon's voice. "If you didn't have plans with your housemates, I'd ask you to get your butt over here so we could do that." His voice was hopeful and Eddie sighed in disappointment.

"I'd love to, but after the attack the other night, Leslie's on this whole mother-hen thing and he's cooked and we're waiting for Taylor to get home so we can relax together. I can't let them down."

"I understand. No problem then." There was silence. Eddie wondered what the right thing was to say to your boss after you'd given him a blow job then had phone sex with him. He didn't think *that* would be in the *Dummies, Get your Boss to Like You* book, should such a thing exist. He bit back a chuckle.

"Uhmm, I checked your shift schedule earlier and you're off tomorrow night it looks like. Do you want to go out with me, watch a film or something?" Gideon sounded shy, unsure and Eddie's heart melted.

Gideon actually checked my schedule?

"Yeah, sure. We can go watch that new Spider-Man movie if you like?"

Hell, way to tell the man I'm a dork and a geek. Spider Man, for God's sake. I could have chosen something a little more cerebral like one of those highbrow independent films at the Ritzy.

"Spider Man sounds good. I like super hero films. Great escapism."

Eddie was relieved Gideon was apparently as big a geek as he was. "Okay. That's a date then." Eddie squirmed. A date? Was that what it was?

Gideon gave a quiet laugh. "Yeah, it's a date. I'll see you around tomorrow anyway, but tomorrow night is ours."

"Cool. I'll see you tomorrow then."

"Eddie?"

"Yes?"

"Are you really okay after that arsehole hurt you? Because if not, I have a baseball bat and I'm not afraid to use it to beat him to a pulp when he gets loose."

Eddie was touched by the concern in Gideon's tone. "I'm okay, honest. I'm a bit warier now than I was but that's probably a good thing, right? Being more careful when out and about."

"Just watch out for yourself. See you tomorrow." The line went dead and Eddie placed his phone on his bedside table with a smile. Then he gazed down at his belly and sighed heavily. It was definitely time for another shower.

***

When he finally made it down to dinner it was to see Leslie and Taylor both seated in the kitchen, at the breakfast bar. Leslie raised one manicured eyebrow at him as he entered.

"Glad you could join us, honey. Two showers in one night? What gives?"

Eddie scowled. "Wow, nothing gets past you, does it?" He nodded at Taylor. "Hey there. You're looking tired, man. The business giving you the runaround?" He went over to one of the pots and dipped his finger in to sample the sauce. Leslie harrumphed loudly but made no move to stop him.

Taylor shifted on the bar stool. "It's been pretty busy with Greg not being there. The shop has been manic this week too, with all the festivals and promotions going on and people wanting to buy music and guitars and shit." His dark eyes were shadowed. "I haven't been sleeping all that well either. I think I need me some of Leslie's chamomile tea tonight." His long, coffee-coloured fingers twisted what looked like a set of rosary beads as he stared down at them with vacant eyes. He looked washed out, his normally warm brown eyes dull, his dark skin paler than usual. His face bore a haunted look.

Eddie walked over and clasped his shoulder gently. "You know if anything's worrying you, you have me and Leslie to talk to, right?" He decided to take the bull by the horns. "If there's anything weird going on in your life, like, you know, that psychic stuff you do, well, we might not understand it all but we can listen 'kay?"

Leslie nodded his head in fervent agreement. "Oh yes. You know I like to think of myself as quite a spiritual being, Taylor, so if there's anything you want to share, you go ahead."

Taylor smiled. "Thanks, guys. I know it must seem a little out there, me being like this and saying strange stuff sometimes, but I appreciate the concern. There's nothing anyone can do at the moment; it's just something I have to deal with myself."

Eddie noticed Taylor backtracked a little when he saw Leslie looking displeased at that comment.

"I mean, I know I have you two and you'll be the first ones I come to if I need to talk." He grinned, looking more like the old Taylor. "Maybe I just need to get laid. It's been a couple of days and the itch needs scratching."

Eddie raised an eyebrow. "I've heard stories about you and that music shop you work in. Sounds to me like there's no shortage of guys wanting to help you out in the storeroom or behind the alleyway." He had heard a few rumours about Taylor's propensity to casual jerk-offs and blowjobs, but the man never brought anyone home.

Taylor shrugged and grinned. "I never said I was a saint, Eddie. And I do work in the music industry after all." He chuckled. "Now what say we give this chicken dish Leslie cooked a go and see if it tastes as good as it smells?"

The trio were soon tucking into plates of steaming and very tasty chicken and pasta, and Eddie ate until he thought he would burst. He loved his time here at his home with these two men. He didn't think he could get better flatmates. He was only listening with half an ear when he heard the word "gingerbread." He flicked a glance to Taylor who was sitting deathly still, his eyes unfocused and his hands still in his lap. He kept muttering one word over and over again.

Gingerbread.

Leslie looked at Eddie, concern on his face.

"He's zoned out again," he murmured. "Another psychic guy I know said we should just leave him to get over it because if we interrupt him mid zone he could die. Or the spirit thingy that he's with could escape and roam our world forever."

Eddie glared at him. "Some comfort you are. That sounds like a lot of cock and bull to me."

Leslie shrugged. "'Swhat he said. So let's just clear up the dishes and maybe by the time we're finished he'll be back with us."

Eddie didn't like the idea of leaving Taylor in whatever world he currently inhabited but he didn't think they had a choice. Personally he still wasn't sure what the whole "psychic" thing was all about and it was outside of his comfort zone. But he'd been saved by it first-hand so he had to give it some value.

"So you had phone sex with your man, hey?" Leslie said casually as he washed the dishes and stacked them in the rack for Eddie to dry.

Eddie stared at him, feeling his face light up like a lighthouse beacon. "What?"

"I passed your room and couldn't help overhearing you." Leslie grinned. "It sounded like quite a session."

"You mean you stuck your ear to my door and listened," Eddie said acerbically. "My door was shut."

Leslie was unrepentant. "It's been a few days since I got any. I was in need myself and yours did just as good."

Eddie gazed at him in disbelief. "You wanked off to *me* jerking off? Hell, that's just not on."

Leslie flashed him a sly grin. "Live with it, girlfriend. You got yours, I got mine." He fluttered his eye lashes and mimed jerking off. "Oh God, oh God…" He laughed loudly as Eddie flushed scarlet and snapped the dishcloth at him. He dodged around the kitchen, trying to avoid Eddie's slaps and finally the two of them came to rest, out of breath, in front of the sink again. Eddie glanced at Taylor and saw him blink and take a deep breath. He went over and knelt beside him.

"Are you okay? You left us for a little while."

Taylor nodded, a dazed expression on his face. "Yeah, I'm okay." He looked around the room in apprehension. "I didn't do anything silly, did I? Sometimes I do funny things when I'm like that…"

"No," Eddie reassured his friend. "You just sat there and said the word gingerbread over and over again." His subconscious said he knew the significance of that word but for the life of him he couldn't recall why. "Taylor, are you sure you're okay when this happens?"

His friend gave a tight smile. "I've fucking lived with it all my life, Eddie. Well, since I was about five years old and can remember it. Believe me, I'm fine. This was mild compared to sometimes." A flash of pain shone in his eyes and Eddie wondered what else Taylor had seen when he was in his dream world.

"I don't remember much about this trance," Taylor murmured softly. "I just keep hearing some man saying stuff about gingerbread, and he sounds so lost and alone and scared. But I can't see him. But he knows you, Eddie." Taylor's voice strengthened. "And you know him. This is something to do with you. That's all I can get at this time."

Eddie's skin crawled with apprehension. He wasn't sure what the significance of it all was but he'd hazard a guess it wasn't anything good. His mother had a saying. "I feel it in my water, son," she'd say when she had an inkling something was wrong. And Eddie felt something in his water right now.

"Do you think it has something to do with that bloke who manhandled me the other day? Perhaps it's some sort of delayed reaction to that event…"

Taylor passed a hand over his eyes. "I don't know. I suppose it could be. But what the hell does gingerbread have to do with it?"

Eddie pursed his lips. "Perhaps the guy has an obsession with it," he said helpfully. "Maybe they'll get to his flat and find he has a shrine to gingerbread or something. Or maybe he kidnapped someone who was a baker and makes gingerbread houses." Again there was that flicker of something at the back of his mind that niggled at him.

Taylor snorted. "Oh that's funny," he smiled. "A shrine to gingerbread. I doubt that's it but it's a good story." Eddie was pleased he'd made Taylor feel a little better.

Leslie snickered at the conversation then pressed a cup of his "every solace known to man" chamomile tea into Taylor's hand. "Drink this," he commanded. "It'll do you good. Then we're going to watch *Priscilla* again and I want no arguments."

He flounced off and Eddie and Taylor looked at each other and groaned. They were about to be subject to *Priscilla Queen of the Desert*—again—and then no doubt *To Wong Fu* would follow. It was definitely time to have more than just a few beers and inure themselves against the charms of Terence Stamp and Patrick Swayze in drag.

Chapter 12

Gideon watched the closing credits of the Spider-Man film and winced. Sitting in these awful cinema seats really wasn't good for his back. He ached everywhere and needed to stretch his legs. He chewed his gum and looked over at Eddie who sat still clutching his nearly empty carton of popcorn and staring starstruck at the screen. The one thing Gideon did appreciate about his loss of smell was that his nostrils weren't assailed by the stench of popcorn. He hated the bloody stuff. Eddie, however, was a popcorn fiend and the carton he held was his second one.

"What a great movie," Eddie breathed reverently. "And there's something about a bloke in tight Lycra that really gets me going. But that Dane de Haan…" his voice trailed off and he looked at Gideon. "He's just gorgeous."

"Which one was he?" Gideon asked. He knew who played Spider-Man but that was the extent of his spidery senses.

Eddie stared at him wide eyed as he stood up, clutching his carton of popcorn to his chest as if he'd defend it with his life. "The guy who plays the Green Goblin."

"Oh." Gideon looked at Eddie curiously, feeling a pang of jealousy. "You like 'em cute and with floppy hair?"

Eddie grinned, put on his jacket then turned to walk down the stairs toward the exit. Gideon watched his backside contemplatively, wondering whether he'd be partaking of it later. He'd thought about kissing Eddie during the film but as they were in the middle of the seating and there were kids in the audience, he'd decided against offending anyone's sensibilities. It was definitely happening the minute he got him alone, though.

As they walked out, Eddie dropped his popcorn box into the bin and reached over to cup Gideon's face in cold hands. He kissed him long and hard right there on the steps of the cinema, causing Gideon to stand at immediate attention. He moved his gum to one side of his mouth and thought he really needed to think about giving it up now. It got in the way at awkward moments. Then Eddie released him.

"I like them cute and with floppy hair, yes. But I also like them all macho and growly with amazing lips and beautiful hazel eyes. I like them moody and difficult and challenging. Sound familiar?"

Gideon stared into mocking green eyes and lost his breath. He truly had no idea what it was about Eddie that affected him the way it did. He'd been with plenty of men in his time, but none had ever clutched at Gideon's heartstrings and made them sing the way Eddie did. He tried to keep it light.

"Well, if I find one of those, I'll be sure to send him your way. The only one around at the moment is a drop-dead sexy restaurant owner with a definite yen to ravage a young chef he knows."

Eddie's eyes darkened and Gideon could swear *he* growled. The sound sent a surge of electricity to his dick.

"Then I guess we'd better introduce them, see what happens." He leaned in and whispered in Gideon's ear. "I want to make out with you in a taxi, so damn the tube; we're taking an easy ride home. Call for one. The sooner the better."

Gideon nodded and found himself in the street hailing a taxi. He spat his gum into a rubbish bin and when a taxi stopped, they clambered in. Even before the directions back to Gideon's were given and the taxi had pulled off, Eddie's hands were burrowing under Gideon's jacket, under his lumberjack shirt and finding the bare skin of his ribs. Eddie's mouth nibbled at his ear and the side of his throat and Gideon found it difficult to breathe. That became even more of a trial when Eddie's mouth closed over his and Gideon was subjected to an exploration of his mouth that would have made a dentist squirm with its intimacy. Gideon was *so* definitely not calling the shots tonight. He wondered with a shiver if he ever would.

"You taste so good, of coffee and gum," Eddie murmured as his tongue slid into Gideon's ear. "You're forever chewing that stuff. Don't you ever get tired of it? Doesn't your jaw ache?"

"The only time my jaw will be aching will be when I'm sucking you off," Gideon managed to gasp out between kisses. Eddie's body trembled in his arms and his kisses became even fiercer. Gideon saw the taxi man regarding them in the rearview mirror and he hoped the guy was tolerant of men making out in his vehicle.

It was all he could do to scrabble around in his pockets and find the money he needed to pay the man when they reached his flat. Eddie's hands were still all over him and Gideon felt quite faint. At this rate he didn't think he'd make it upstairs to the bedroom. Visions of bending Eddie over the buffet counter sprung to mind and he groaned.

Unhygienic, a potential Health and Safety fine of alarming proportions and so not what I want tonight to be about. I don't want fumbling in the office or stolen kisses in a theatre complex. I want him in my warm bed, with the lights down low, soft sheets under our bodies and—oh my God, I want bloody romantic.

What the hell is all that about?

Finally they were inside the restaurant and Gideon was trying to pry Eddie's hands from his body.

"Eddie, I need to switch the alarm off. Or we'll have the damn security company around in a jiffy. Jesus, take your hands out of my pants so I can—for God's sake. Please let me punch the code in before you do that." His dick was rock hard in his pants and he shifted uncomfortably.

He was able to disarm the alarm despite the groping of his groin and he finally managed to get space between him and Eddie. "Right. Let's go upstairs and take a deep breath so I can think and not blow a gasket before we even get properly busy. Maybe have a drink first." He cast a wry glance at an unabashed Eddie. "You are not good for my sanity, you know that?"

He propelled Eddie ahead of him across the restaurant and up the stairs to his flat. He armed the alarm again, forever hopeful he wouldn't have to disarm it later if Eddie decided to leave. Gideon had hoped that he would stay the night, wake up with him in the morning rather than disappear once the evening was done.

He opened the door and pushed Eddie inside. "You've been here before so I imagine you know where everything is—kitchen, bathroom. Do you want a drink? I have wine, beer, vodka…"

Eddie nodded. "Vodka and Coke please."

Gideon grimaced at that choice. Eddie followed him into his compact open plan kitchen, and then made Eddie his drink. He filled it with ice, gave it to Eddie and opened the tab to his beer.

Eddie grinned at him wickedly. "Dine me, wine me then fuck me? Is that the plan for tonight, G?"

Just the mere thought of being inside Eddie, having him beneath him on his bed, surrounded by his heat and with his mouth on his, caused Gideon to shiver and his dick to strain against the zipper of his jeans. He was so ready to have this man in his bed and if truth be told, in his life.

That thought scared the shit out of him.

Gideon was all too aware just how fast he was falling. He put his beer down on the kitchen counter, and took Eddie's drink from his hand. Eddie's lips were parted slightly, his eyes darkened and his gaze focused on Gideon's face. He swallowed and Gideon saw his Adam's apple bob up and down.

"You are a damned tease," he murmured softly as his hands framed Eddie's face, the slight feel of stubble under his fingers an aphrodisiac. He leaned in and pressed his lips to Eddie's, and the sound that came out of Eddie's mouth was the most erotic thing Gideon had ever heard. It flooded his senses with want.

"You need to get undressed," he growled as his hands began ripping Eddie's shirt from his shoulders. All thoughts of the calm before the storm had ceased. "I want you naked on my bed, right fucking now."

Eddie's lithe frame was a portrait of decadence as Gideon set to the task of stripping him. His body was taut lines, muscles that rippled beneath the surface of pale, freckled skin the colour of cream and just as smooth. It was hidden curves and crevices, and the V-line of his hips made Gideon's mouth water. He wanted to lick it, feel that skin beneath his lips. He might not be able to taste the man but by God he could feel him. Feel that warmth and desire that was causing Eddie's breath to get deeper with each uncovering of his body. Finally Gideon had him naked in front of him; Eddie's long, thick prick was swollen, already wet. It was a work of pure art. Gideon reached out a finger and dipped a tip into the slit, scooping up the wetness there and then raised it to his lips. It was warm, thick and for a brief moment he despaired that he couldn't taste anything of the man that was Eddie Tripp. Then he lost all sense of reason as the man who had Gideon in knots reached down and released Gideon's own needy prick into his warm hands.

"God, that feels good," Gideon managed to get out of a throat that was clogged with desire. "I wish I could smell you. I don't even know what you taste like." He heard the yearning in his voice and felt the tug at his chest.

Eddie moved forward and ran a hand across Gideon's jaw, his fingers warm and calloused. "You can feel me, and hear me, G," he whispered back as his hands undid Gideon's trousers and he began the task of undressing him. "Every bit of me is yours. There's no place you can't go, nothing you can't do to me."

Gideon's breath hitched at those words, his heart beating faster. Eddie pushed Gideon's trousers and briefs down his hips and they fell to his ankles. He stepped out of them as Eddie then pulled his shirt over his head. Gideon was naked now and Eddie stepped back to look at him, his nostrils flaring, his eyes darkened with desire. "And look at you. You're gorgeous. Just perfect."

He trailed his hands down Gideon's hips, brushed them against his hairy thighs, and Eddie's wrist fleetingly brushed his prick. Gideon hissed and closed his eyes in pleasure.

Eddie carried on with his words of torture. "I love the hair on your body. I want to run my fingers through it, taste it. I want to take your cock in my mouth and suck you, feel you come. Then I want you inside me, need you there. I need you to fuck me, G."

Gideon could take no more of the erotic talk. His cock was straining upward, his balls felt as if they were going to burst with the power of Eddie's words alone. Green eyes met dusky brown and Gideon pulled Eddie to him in a fierce embrace and took his mouth with all the feeling he had inside him.

Eddie moaned against his lips as Gideon all but pushed him through to his bedroom. The beside-the-bed lights threw off a soft, warm glow, shadowing the walls with their entwined figures, an erotic display of male need and strength. Gideon threw Eddie onto the bed as Eddie chuckled sexily, the sound targeting Gideon's cock like sonar.

Eddie lay back on the cotton duvet, his hands moving up over his head as he licked his lips and looked up at Gideon standing by the bed. Eddie spread his legs wide and Gideon felt dizzy at the delicacy now being displayed just for him. The man before him looked like a decadent red-headed, cream-skinned angel, his tight bum cheeks, that rosy, puckered hole and the thatch of reddish-blond hair between his legs taunting Gideon.

"Is this what you want?" Eddie said teasingly. He moved one hand and dragged it lightly down his cock. "Or this?" He moved his finger suggestively down toward his arse and Gideon growled as he leapt onto the bed and stilled the man's hand, clenching it tightly in his own.

"Christ, how does someone that looks like an angel manage to sound so damn dirty and sexy?" He shifted to kneel beside the man splayed before him. "You know you drive me crazy, right? Totally, batshit crazy." Gideon pulled Eddie to him and once again, the two men's bodies merged, cocks rubbing together, skin to skin, both desperately seeking the other's touch. Hot tongues slicked against each other, teeth grazing lips, mewls of satisfaction echoing from both of their lips as they rolled and tussled on the bed, sweat and semen holding them together like the glue of sex.

***

Eddie was lost in the sensation of having Gideon's tongue in his mouth, his lips against his, his body pressing him into the bed as if he wanted to imprint him into the very fabric itself. Eddie wasn't generally a really dirty talker in bed, but Gideon brought out the wild animal in him, the side that said to hell with everything and let this man take him with all the energy and power that he had. His arsehole was actually clenching at the thought and all he could think of was having that steely rod of flesh inside him, pounding him hard until he came, and nothing else was going to assuage that burning need he had. If Eddie was the angel, Gideon was the devil, his hard, masculine body the torment, and the only release would be having the pleasure of being finally fucked by the man he'd desired for a long time.

Eddie cried out softly as Gideon's fingers found his hole and caressed the skin around it. He pushed himself toward Gideon's seeking fingers and Gideon laughed quietly.

"Steady on, tiger. Let me at least get you a little lubed up. I don't intend going in dry." Nimble fingers stroked at Eddie's entrance, sunk deep down inside him until he wanted to scream from the pleasure of the feeling. He closed his eyes, revelling in the scent and taste of the man on top of him, hearing his soft sighs and grunts, and when he heard the rip of the condom packet Eddie nearly came undone. Soft light flooded behind his eyelids as he gasped at feeling Gideon seat himself at his hole, pushing tentatively. Yet Eddie could feel Gideon's restrained urge to plunge inside him in the tautness of his biceps as Eddie hung on for the ride.

"Okay there?" was the whispered entreaty in his ear and Eddie shivered as he pushed his hips toward Gideon's, the need to merge with this man a primal instinct.

"Just do it," Eddie gasped as he clutched at Gideon's arse and propelled him deeper inside. "Please, G. Need to feel you more. Oh my God…" his words were cut off by the deep intake of air he took as Gideon pushed fully inside him, hot silk and steel forged together to make a weapon Eddie wanted to feel pierce him deeper and harder. Their lips clung together, tongues greedy and grasping as both men moved together, bodies synchronised like athletes at their prime, slick, rhythmic movements that would no doubt have won gold at the Olympics. In between air breaks, Gideon's breathing was harsh, his warm, peppermint-and-coffee-fragranced breath like a soft caress against Eddie's cheek.

"God, you feel so dammed good," Gideon whispered, "I feel like I could live inside you, you know that? You were made for my cock."

Eddie chuckled in between finding his breath. "You say the sweetest things. I like having you home."

The soft laughter that rumbled through Gideon's chest made Eddie flush with heat and pleasure. It had been too long since he had heard this man sound happy. The sensation of flying and dizziness assailed Eddie's brain as he gasped, feeling his own climax building. The rub of his cock against Gideon's hard belly seemed to be all he needed to release the pressure he felt building his balls. Just to make sure, he reached down and stroked himself.

Oh yes, I am definitely there. That feels so good...

"I am so ready..." Gideon grunted and Eddie fisted himself faster as his head swum and his body tensed, his balls pulling up as he came, hot semen spurting from the end of his dick to splatter between the two bodies that were slick with sweat and fluids. His cry of triumph as he arched up and tightened himself around Gideon's cock was obviously all it took for Gideon to throw back his head, his neck muscles corded tightly, and let out a loud groan of ecstasy as he climaxed. Eddie's body still shuddered with the aftershocks of his orgasm, and from the slight tremors rocking Gideon's body. He felt the same. Finally Gideon collapsed on top of him, nuzzling Eddie's sweaty neck and slowly licking a trail from his jawline to his ear. Gideon seemed to have fascination with his ears, a part of himself Eddie had never really liked because he thought they were too big. Eddie's cock stirred and Gideon groaned.

Eddie grinned. "I'm younger than you, remember? My cock doesn't take much encouragement to get hard. So maybe you should stop that and get that off me so you can recover, old man." He waited with bated breath for Gideon's reaction to his teasing.

Gideon pushed himself up over Eddie, his eyes indignant as he opened his mouth to say something biting. Then he smiled down at Eddie and leaned down and kissed him tenderly.

"You little bastard. I see the way things are. You're going to give me hell, aren't you?" He leveraged himself to the side of the bed onto his back, pulling off the spent condom and dropping it beside the bed. They lay there, chests still heaving, staring up at the ceiling. Eddie wasn't sure whether to move over and cuddle or stay his side of the bed. He had no idea—now that the urge for each other had been fulfilled—whether this was simply a one-off and he needed to leave, or whether he was welcome to stay. He knew which one he wanted.

His decision was made for him as Gideon reached out and drew him closer, into his shoulder, so that Eddie's head was on Gideon's chest.

"Sleep," he said gruffly as he pulled the covers around them. "We can get up early and clean up, take a shower. I hope you don't bloody snore. That's a deal breaker."

Eddie snuggled into his lover's broad chest, his heart leaping at the fact he wasn't being kicked out. "I might, a little. I hope you don't fart. *That's* a definite deal breaker."

Gideon's low chuckle reverberated against Eddie's cheek. "Everybody farts in bed, sunshine. This isn't a romance novel."

Eddie's nose twitched. "Well, at last give a man some warning so he can hold his breath." His eyes closed as the steady thrum of Gideon's heartbeat in his ear. "And no molesting me when I sleep. I want to be awake for anything you want to do me." He looked up at Gideon with a leer and a hopeful glance.

"Oh you'll be awake," Gideon agreed quietly, his eyes soft and Eddie flushed with heat at the need in those eyes. "I'm no necrophiliac. I want my prey to be alive and kicking when I molest them."

"Good," Eddie murmured sleepily, already half asleep. "I guess that's our list of demands done then. Now let's get some shuteye. You wore me out."

As he slipped into the warm darkness of slumber, he heard Gideon's soft words, said with affection.

"There's plenty more where that came from."

Eddie fell asleep with a smile on his face knowing there were more nights like tonight to come.

Chapter 13

Eddie was on cloud nine for the next two weeks. He floated through the kitchen at work, leaving himself open to taunts and teasing from his fellow workers about the constant smile on his face and how it got there. He and Gideon saw each other often and it was no secret at the restaurant. Eddie had thought Gideon would be closed-mouthed about their relationship but instead, the man seemed to be proud of the fact he was bedding Eddie.

He took his staff's good-natured ribbing in his stride and grinned when they made ribald comments. Eddie also melted each time Gideon's eyes met his across the kitchen—a place he'd taken to coming more often that he had in the past. Those smouldering, possessive glances had led to bedroom calisthenics most nights in Gideon's flat and Eddie was definitely feeling well exercised.

The euphoria ended Wednesday midday when he came in to work a half-hour early for his shift and found the restaurant in an uproar. It wasn't opening time yet, but staff were anxiously scurrying about, avoiding conversation, seemingly harassed. As he walked in, he saw quick glances darted in his direction and tight smiles. Perturbed, he went to Gideon's office to see what was going on. The door was locked. He listened and heard the faint low sound of someone talking inside. He knocked.

"G, are you in there?" He sniffed. There was the faint smell of burning plastic and something else lingering in the air. Smoke, and something chemical.

There was no reply to his question so he tried again. "Why is the door locked? Is everything all right?"

"Just go away, Eddie. I'm fine." The fierce growl from behind the door certainly didn't give Eddie any confidence that things were all right or that Gideon was fine.

"What's going on?" He knocked again, louder this time. "Gideon, for God's sake let me in."

"Go away!" was the shouted retort. "I'm not in the mood for company right now. Just leave me the hell alone."

Eddie's throat constricted and he swallowed.

He won't even talk to me? What the hell is wrong with him? I thought…

His thoughts tailed off. Yes, he'd thought perhaps they were a bit more than they were, not just fuck buddies, but perhaps that had all been a mistake.

Perhaps I read too much into this whole thing. Fuck. I always do this. I always get too close and get hurt.

He remembered Simon. He had pissed off and left as soon as Eddie started mentioning going on holiday together. And Lewis—he'd point-blank laughed in his face and told him that he was just a "pleasant distraction" as he went back to his older boyfriend. Eddie knew he was probably overreacting, but given the state of his past love life, he thought he had the right to feel a little paranoid.

A gentle hand on his shoulder made him start and he turned in surprise to see Carmen smiling at him in sympathy.

"Eddie, come on. You know there's no use talking to him in this mood. I had hoped as it was you…" she sighed deeply. "Never mind. Come get a coffee and I'll fill you in. It's been a bloody nightmare this morning."

Eddie stole one more glance at the locked door. "Please talk to me, Gideon," he pleaded but there was no response. His heart heavy, he followed Carmen into her office where she had her own coffee machine. He perched his backside on the corner of Carmen's small desk as she busied herself with making drinks. She made him a latte with the coffee pods and handed it to him.

"There you go." She made her own then sat down in her rather wonky typist's chair and looked at Eddie.

"This morning, that bloody printer on the table behind Gideon's desk shorted out. It's an old damn thing and I've been trying to get him to replace it for ages. It shocked him the one time but he said he'd fixed it." She made a moue. "Apparently not. There must have been some faulty wiring. Gideon was sitting in his office reading some financial accounts. The whole thing burst into flames and was merrily burning away. He didn't smell a thing. It was a bit like a repeat of the whole kitchen dishtowel episode, but worse. It was only Andy coming past his office to get to his shift and smelling the fucking thing that alerted anyone. There wasn't so much smoke then. He rushed in and alerted Gideon and then found the fire extinguisher. The darned thing was blazing away by then. He managed to put out the fire."

Eddie's heart sank at Carmen's story. He knew Gideon would not have taken the event lightly.

"What happened then?" he asked softly. "Isn't there a smoke detector in his office?"

Carmen shrugged her shoulders. "It didn't go off. Then Gideon lost it. He was ranting and raving about how he could have burned down his restaurant and killed everyone. We tried to tell him that wouldn't have happened but he wouldn't listen. Stubborn bastard." Her eyes darkened. "He went bat shit is more like it. He threw what was left of the printer against the wall, kicked his chair over and shoved everything off his desk, including his PC." Her voice faltered. "Then in front of everyone he had a panic attack."

Eddie closed his eyes in regret. His proud lover would not have taken kindly to everyone seeing him have a meltdown.

Carmen carried on in a slightly shaking voice. "I managed to get him settled but it was bloody scary seeing him like that. Hyperventilating, as white as a sheet and then he blacked out. I've seen it before but never that bad."

Eddie reached over and took her cold hand. "They can be pretty frightening to watch. My mum has them, so I know." He took a deep sigh. "So now my stupid boyfriend has locked himself in his office and refuses to talk to anyone? Figures."

Carmen smiled slightly. "Boyfriend? Does Gideon know that?"

Eddie flushed. He'd shot his mouth off too soon. The term had just slipped out. It was how he thought of Gideon, though. They hadn't just shared sex; they'd been to films, dinner, a concert or two and even taken a sail down the Thames on a dinner boat. He'd liked the idea of calling him boyfriend but he wasn't sure how Gideon felt about it.

"It's better than *fuck buddy*." He rolled his eyes. "And no, G doesn't know I use that term around him and don't you tell him. I don't want to scare him off forever."

“You really like him, don’t you?” Carmen said gently as she sipped her coffee. “He likes you too, I can see. I’ve never seen him with anyone else like he is with you.”

“Yeah, well.” Eddie felt a lump in his throat despite Carmen’s words. “He told me to leave him the hell alone; he doesn’t want to talk to anyone. I don’t know where that leaves me.”

Carmen squeezed his hand. “He’ll come around soon. We just need to let him simmer down.” Her face was worried. “He really needs to talk to someone about the attacks and his moods. I thought he was going to see someone after the last conversation I had with him, but that doesn’t seem to have happened.” Her face lit up. “You need to talk to him about it too.”

Eddie sighed gloomily. “I have. I’ve been a real pest, trying to push him into it over the past few weeks. I even went so far as to call my doctor and get a card for a recommended therapist. Gideon said he’d call him but I don’t think he has yet. He has these nightmares and wakes up in a cold sweat. I think I’m slowly convincing him to get help; he just has to take that first step.” Eddie loved sleeping with Gideon in his bed but the occasional nightmares were something else. “We talk about it a little more now though which is a good sign. So he’s caving slowly to pressure. I just hope he comes around soon before he bursts a blood vessel.”

***

Gideon sat behind his desk in his locked office, his hands tapping out an agitated tattoo on his desk. He’d managed to salvage most of the items he’d swept off it in his temper earlier but his PC was never going to work again. It was irrevocably screwed. He’d kicked it into the corner intending to take it to the local recycling centre and he supposed he’d have to buy a new one now. He scowled fiercely. *And a new fucking printer.* Andy had been diplomatic enough to remove the offensive item from his office after putting out the fire. It was just as well, as Gideon thought he’d still be kicking the crap out of it.

He stared moodily into space, chewing his gum as he’d really craved a smoke, and trying to ignore the guilt sitting heavily in his chest at sending Eddie away. He’d heard the hurt in his voice as he’d pleaded with Gideon to talk to him.

I just can’t yet, he thought desperately. *I need to get this blackness out of me, let it drain away like oil-stained water. I’m no use to you like this.*

Gideon had no doubt that his feelings for Eddie, even in just such a short time, were not simply a matter of lust. Eddie was peace to Gideon's war, his warmth to Gideon's chill. Even Rafael hadn't come this close. Gideon realised that now. Eddie was funny, quirky, cute, and when he was in the sack, he was a different person. Demanding, aggressive and so damn sexy. Someone Gideon was falling in love with. That was why he needed a little space right now.

He was also ashamed to admit that he was envious of Eddie in the kitchen. He'd spent more time in there the past two weeks. Seeing Eddie's skills and his incredible ability to create dishes that Gideon thought looked sublime had highlighted Gideon's own insecurities about no longer being what he was. He'd received a phone call earlier today–before the printer episode—from a mainstream newspaper wanting to feature Eddie in their "Culinary London" insert special as their featured chef. Of course Gideon had said yes—not only was it good for Eddie's career it was good for Galileo's as well—but it still rankled. That should have been him in the papers. Thinking like that shamed him deeply.

Lost in his thoughts, he didn't notice someone standing before him. He looked up, startled, into a sea of emerald green that regarded him evenly. His temper flared.

"How did you get in?" he demanded as he stood up to face Eddie. He glanced at the open door.

"Jerome helped. Apparently this office used to be a large storeroom and he still has a key." Eddie moved around closer to Gideon. "Please don't give him any grief. We were all worried about you."

Gideon noticed Eddie seemed hesitant to touch him and his heart tightened.

Was that what it's come to? He feels he can't touch me in case I have a hissy fit?

"Very MacGyver-like of you," Gideon said quietly.

Eddie turned back and closed the door. "Do you want to talk about it?" He regarded Gideon with both affection and a little wariness.

Gideon shook his head. "I'm sure you've heard everything there is to hear from Carmen or Andy or anyone else that happened to see the sorry event of this morning." His tone was scathing.

Eddie's face darkened. "Gideon. It happened. There's really no need to get all bent out of shape over it. Luckily someone smelt it and got it under control…" His voice tailed off and he stared at Gideon uncertainly.

Gideon felt the shame and frustration building in his chest and stomach and he fisted his hands. "So it's no big deal, is it? The fact I couldn't smell burning behind me which could have led to me torching this place, myself and let's not forget the other people in this building? The fact that the smoke detector that I only had tested about a week ago and was working fine *didn't* work because of whatever fucking reason—who knows with those bloody things. I think that's a pretty big deal, Eddie." He was close to shouting now in his agitation.

Eddie's eyes widened. "Calm down. You don't need another panic attack—"

Gideon saw Eddie clamp his lips shut and a look of chagrin cross his face. He seemed to realise he'd poked the bear for a second time. Gideon leapt on that bandwagon like a trumpeter playing a march for an approaching army.

"Oh and of course then I have to go all *emo* and have an attack that everyone in here saw and Carmen had to help calm me down. Just the sort of thing an employer needs his employees to see." His chest heaving, Gideon kicked the piece of debris on the floor that still remained as evidence of his transgression. It looked like part of his computer.

"Oh for Christ's sake, you're a fucking human being. No one thinks any less of you for what happened or for you having thrown a bit of a wobbly." Eddie's voice was heated. "The only person blaming himself here is you. And perhaps if you'd talked to someone professional about what happened to you in that fire six months ago, you'd be dealing with things better."

Gideon stared at the flushed face of his lover, at the glittering green eyes staring back at him with passion and a little trepidation, perhaps at being so bold.

The gauntlet had been thrown and it was up to Gideon to pick it up. He moved closer to Eddie, invading his personal space, and Eddie's nostrils flared. He leaned into Eddie's face and spat the words he wanted to say out. "Have you ever smelt someone burning to death? Ever had a smouldering beam fall on you, pinning you to the floor while your skin scorched?"

Eddie's face whitened but to his credit he held his ground, staring at Gideon's face like a man seeking a revelation. "Hugh might have been dead when the wall fell on him and cracked his skull wide open, but he was on fire." Gideon's voice was hoarse as he recalled the event of that night. He'd never said this to anyone before. "I couldn't get to him, I wasn't even *sure* he was already dead at that point. I thought he had to be because he wasn't screaming while he burnt. But someone *was* screaming and that someone was me. I screamed for someone to help him, to stop him charcoaling like some sort of pig roast at a BBQ." Gideon's chest was heaving now, his voice stuttered and heavy. "Eventually I couldn't scream anymore because of the smoke."

Eddie reached out to touch his shoulder and Gideon shook it off. The wounded expression in Eddie's eyes cut Gideon to the core but he was on a roll now. All the things he'd never said to anyone came vomiting out of him like a kid on a fairground ride who'd eaten too much cotton candy. "All I could feel was the pain in my side as I burnt, and hear the crackling of his flesh as it cooked. It's true you know. It sounds just like a roast in the oven, spitting and sizzling. Smells like it too." Gideon felt his face contort with remembered disgust at the overwhelming smell of cooked meat.

Eddie's face was a mask of horror and despair. He opened his mouth to speak but Gideon put a strong hand over his mouth. "This is my turn to speak. You want me to share? This is me sharing while you shut up."

Eddie took a step back and his hand grabbed at the desk as if looking for support. His face was milk white, his lips trembled and his eyes resembled someone who'd seen something from a nightmare. They showed dark, deep depths of pain and regret for Gideon.

"I was the lucky one. My burns were only second degree because they got to me in plenty of time. But Hugh looked like one of those crispy critters you see in CSI, all scrunched up and black and red." His head swam with the visions of Hugh's horribly mutilated body. "The firemen were there very quickly, thank God. They managed to get me out before the smoke got to me too much or the flames did too much damage. I woke up in hospital looking like a fucking mummy, with bandages everywhere." He shuddered at the memory of that pain. "But I was the lucky one, I recovered well. And then I discovered I'd lost the ability to smell anything. I can't even distinguish between salty and sweet like some people can. Nothing. " His voice faltered. It was strange how that little fact had been the proverbial straw that broke the camel's back. A man was dead; Gideon had been grievously injured; yet this singular fact and the loss of what he saw as his passion for his culinary art had broken him.

A wave of dizziness swept over him and he passed a hand over his eyes, rubbing at them like a child. Eddie moved forward, his face determined, and strong arms encircled Gideon as he pulled him into a ferocious embrace. Gideon tried to pull away but Eddie wasn't having it.

"Fucking let me hold you, G," he snarled. "You need me, you arsehole. You know you do. Stop fighting me."

Gideon *did* need Eddie's strength. He needed Eddie's arms around him, keeping him safe and grounded. He wanted Eddie's voice in his ear, his breath on his mouth, his skin against his. He just simply wanted Eddie. He sunk into Eddie's hard body, collapsing like a black hole as his arms slid around his lover's waist and he clung on like a drowning mouse to a reed.

All the frustrations he'd held in for so long, all the pain and disappointments, all the fear and self-hatred flooded to the surface and the floodgates opened as Gideon cried hot tears. Eddie's deep voice in his ear soothed him, murmured words of support and affection. Gideon wept for his dead friend, for the loss of his calling, for the nights spent waking up covered in sweat as he relived the event. Finally he was spent and he remained plastered against Eddie's broad chest, while strong hands stroked his back and hair and told him everything was going to be all right.

And for once, Gideon believed that it might be so.

He sniffed, hiccupped and finally loosened himself from Eddie's hold to rummage in his desk drawer for tissues. He wiped his eyes then blew his nose, wincing at the fact he sounded like a wheezing elephant. Eddie's eyes never left him. Gideon took a deep shuddering breath then gave a wan smile.

"Sorry you had to see that meltdown. I must look a mess."

Eddie's eyes shone with a teasing light. "Not to me. You look very dashing with your pink nose and cheeks."

Gideon scowled. "Idiot." But there was no heat in his tone. Instead he felt a growing love for the man who studied him now with such concern.

What if he doesn't feel the same? What if this is just temporary to him?

Eddie perched on the side of the desk, his long legs splayed out in front of him as he crossed his arms. "I have to ask. The fact you lost your sense of smell. Was that because you got trauma to the head?"

Gideon shook his head. "No. The doctors can find no physical cause. They say it's psychological, that I subconsciously block out smell because of what I smelt that night and my brain is protecting me from reliving it. They call it a conversion disorder." He shrugged. "Because my sense of smell is gone, so is my sense of taste. It's a common thing apparently."

Eddie stood up excitedly. "But that's great!"

Gideon frowned. "In what Eddie-universe is that news 'great'?"

"It means that if it's all in your head then maybe you can get it back. It means that there's hope."

Gideon stared at him. "You think I haven't tried? I stood in a kitchen once chopping garlic and onions, mixing curry pastes, using every spice and herb I could find, to try and electroshock my brain into smelling something again. I told myself I could, that nothing else mattered but getting that sense back. I've tried all manner of things to try and tell my damned head that I want to smell again but it's having none of it." He gave a defeated sigh. "The doctors say there is no magic way to do it. That one day I could simply wake up and it will be back as soon as my brain lets go of whatever is holding me back."

Eddie was still excited. "I still say it's hopeful. And there were a couple of things you didn't have back then that you have now."

"Oh yes?" Gideon knew the answer to one of them but wanted to hear Eddie say it. "And those are?"

Eddie moved forward and cupped Gideon's face. He laid his forehead against his. "One of them was the ability to talk about this whole thing and stop being so macho." He grinned. "The other thing is me."

"Now how did I know you were going to say that?" Gideon murmured as his lips brushed Eddie's.

Eddie smirked. "Well now that big stick up your arse is out, and you've shared your story with someone, maybe you can stop being so uptight. And perhaps then something good might happen." He stepped back from Gideon and narrowed his eyes. "I need you to promise me something. It's important to me."

Gideon heaved a sigh. He should have known Eddie would have demands. "Go on then. What am I to sign my soul away to now?"

"I want you to talk to someone professional, tell them what you just told me. They might help you more than you know."

"I was going to call—" Gideon's heated retort was cut off by a hard kiss from Eddie, a kiss that made his head reel and his dick swell.

"No negotiations," Eddie whispered against Gideon's mouth. "I won't ask for anything else. Just this one thing. Please, Gideon. It's just talking to someone."

Gideon heard the pleading in Eddie's tone and sighed. He knew it was way overdue and if it made Eddie happy…

"Fine," he grumbled." I'll do it. I still have that card you gave me, that guy in Enfield who specialises in this sort of thing. I'll give him a call."

Eddie's face lit up like a lighthouse beacon. "Really? Thank you, that means a lot to me."

Gideon laid a hand on Eddie's cheek. "*You* mean a lot to me," he muttered softly.

Christ, my big tough boss image has now been tarnished forever. This damn man has made me soft.

But the joy on Eddie's face at his promise was enough to light up the Taj Mahal and the moon at the same time. Gideon didn't think he'd ever been responsible for such a look of happiness on someone's face before. He found he liked the feeling and wanted to do it more often. For Eddie.

The sudden glint in Eddie's eyes and low growl that emanated from his throat should have warned Gideon what was about to happen. He found himself being propelled back against the scorched wall of his office and kissed to death. To be honest it wasn't a bad way to go, and the way in which he was being manhandled was doing wonderful things to his cock and his body; for a moment there he thought he'd already entered Nirvana. As a greedy, slippery tongue invaded his mouth and Gideon lost all sense of rational thought, he could swear he heard bells ringing.

The ringing bells unfortunately weren't some sort of "happy ever after" cartoon event but instead was Eddie's mobile.

Gideon wondered as he unglued his mouth from his lover's, why anyone would choose to have a tone that sounded like Gothic bells from a horror movie. Eddie moved away reluctantly and took his mobile from his jeans pocket.

"Sorry. That's my dad's ringtone. I need to get this one." He moved away and answered and Gideon busied himself with readjusting, trying to quell the rising erection in his pants into some sort of modicum of decency.

"Dad? Hi. How are things?" Eddie wandered around the room as he talked. Gideon watched him. Eddie frowned deeply.

"Really? Well you know Luke. He likes to have his alone time. Perhaps he's gone over to Greg's place or maybe Randy…oh, you've called them and he's not there?" His frown deepened. "Well, yeah, I'll try and give him a call. If he's ignoring everyone else, he'll probably take mine. You know how he is." He was quiet as he listened and Gideon saw the worried glance at him. "Well, I was intending coming home for Halloween in a couple of weeks' time. I got the time off already. I told Luke I'd see him then." Again he listened. Gideon sat down in his office chair and glanced at some paperwork. The prospect of stock and re-ordering didn't really take his fancy at this time and he sighed as he pushed it away.

Maybe I'll take the afternoon off. See if Eddie has time off and we can go watch movies and make out upstairs. Although I actually think he was due on shift five minutes ago. Jerome is going to damn kill me for making him late.

"Yeah, okay Dad. I'll try calling him. Speak later." Eddie hung up and stared at Gideon.

"It's my little cousin, Luke. He's seventeen and he's disappeared. No one's seen him since yesterday. I just need to make this call if it's okay?" He glanced at his watch and his eyes widened. "Shit! Then I'll need to get to work before Jerome comes in with a butcher's knife and slaughters the pair of us. You know what he's like with tardiness." He dialled a number.

Gideon did indeed know. He'd seen many an unfortunate victim of Jerome's wrath quiver in fear at the sight of the hulk-like chef storming upon them like the vengeance of Godzilla. It was sight that entertained him but one that he didn't want to be on the receiving end of—boss or not.

He nodded at Eddie. "Go ahead, make it quick. If he comes looking for you, I'll stall him off and protect your virtue." He grinned as Eddie fluttered his eyelashes at him girlishly.

"My hero," he simpered then stopped as someone obviously answered the phone on the other side. "Luke? What the fuck, mate. I've had my dad on the line asking me where you are and your mum is going crazy 'cause she didn't know where you were." His eyes narrowed. "Are you okay? You sound a bit funny. Have you been crying? Is everything all right?" His fierce protectiveness for his cousin entranced Gideon who not so long ago had been subject to it himself. "You have a cold? Okay…" His voice drawled off in uncertainty. "Where the hell are you, anyway, and why haven't you called your mum?"

There was a pause as Eddie listened and then scowled. "Well, okay then. Have fun. Just don't bloody do that again. It scares the living shit out of everyone and it's damn inconsiderate." He nodded at the phone. "Yeah, yeah. Just call her, okay? My battery is going flat and I have to go to work now so don't let me find out later that you didn't. And tell that mate of yours next time to have some sort of radio with him when he plans on going out on the river. You never know what can happen out there."

Gideon chuckled quietly at Eddie's parental tone and wondered idly if one day their kids might be hearing it. His heart lurched.

Jesus where the fuck did that *thought come from?*

"Well, I'll give you a call later when I get home. It will be a late one." He caught Gideon's eyes and winked. "Nah, I have something I need to do later with my boss. He's a damn slave driver and works me hard. Very hard. The man doesn't know the meaning of taking it easy. He's a real ball breaker."

Gideon's erection had been subsiding but now leapt to full mast again at the sly innuendo in Eddie's voice. Eddie gave him a cheerful but naughty grin. "Right, we'll speak later. And Luke, be careful with that cold. It's chilly out there on the water. Later, mate."

He put his phone back in his pocket and looked at Gideon. "He went off with a friend on a barge on the Broads yesterday and they apparently got stuck somewhere. He says he had no mobile reception and they've only just managed to get the boat started again and on their way home."

He didn't sound sure and Gideon raised an eyebrow. "You sound as if you don't believe him."

Eddie huffed. "He just sounded a bit weird. But then he always—"

The two of them jumped a foot when a loud bang echoed through the room and an angry voice belted out, "Eddie, you might be the boss' favourite but I need your arse in my kitchen right now! Don't make me come in and get you because you know I will!"

Jerome's Jamaican lilt always sounded more pronounced when he was pissed off, and Gideon hastily shooed Eddie toward the closed door.

"Get off with you before he comes in and beats the hell out of me and you both. He'll bitch-slap me just as much as he will you. He's no respecter of hierarchy when it comes to his kitchen."

Eddie leaned and stole a quick kiss. "I'll see you later then?"

"Count on it. Now go!" Gideon watched in apprehension as Eddie opened the door and slid past the man mountain standing outside it. Jerome's face was threatening but the wink he threw at Gideon made him feel better. Jerome just narrowly missed slapping the back of Eddie's head as he darted past, ducking as he did so. Jerome growled loudly.

"Eddie, my boy, you are playing with fire. Get your little arse to work right now before I have this man fire you."

Eddie's laughter echoed down the hall as he dashed away and Gideon acknowledged Jerome with a smile. The big man grinned at him warmly.

"Boss, everything okay?"

Gideon nodded. "More than okay, Jerome. Thanks."

Jerome nodded and Gideon noted the expression of satisfaction on his face when he next spoke. "That little tyke is good for you, I think. He makes you laugh and smile. It's been too long since I've seen that." He gave a wide smile and turned and disappeared in the direction of Eddie. Gideon laughed to himself.

Eddie was certainly that. The man had chipped away at the scars of Gideon's heart and found the living flesh beneath. Gideon would be forever thankful. He sat down at his desk and opened his desk drawer. He took out a small business card and sighed. He'd promised to talk to someone, so he might as well make the call now and get an appointment. He grinned. Eddie could show his appreciation for his efforts later. After all, Gideon thought he deserved a reward for doing what he was told.

***

Three days later, Gideon beside him, Eddie sat in the waiting room of Martin Wingmore, the therapist recommended by one of Gideon's doctors. Eddie had insisted on accompanying him—firstly, to make sure Gideon actually went and secondly, as moral support for his lover. Gideon had not been convinced the appointment was a good idea, but Eddie had slowly chipped away all resistance. Personally, he thought Gideon had got so sick of all the constant hints over the past few weeks: the YouTube link videos in his inbox depicting stories of people who'd had therapy and "survived" and random *Keep Calm and Go to Therapy* posts on Gideon's Facebook wall. Eddie had made two posts which Gideon had promptly deleted with a frown. But the message had been received loud and clear.

Gideon fidgeted in his chair, looking nervous.

Eddie reached over and took his hand. "G, stop being so damn twitchy. All you're going to do is talk to the guy. He isn't going to bite you." His tone went lower. "I might do that, when we get home, if you're a good boy and take all your medicine…"

Gideon's eyes darkened and a pink tongue came out to lick his bottom lip. "Eddie, not here for God's sake. That's all I need, having a boner when I go in to see the psychologist."

His words were stern but his face was affectionate and his voice warm and like thick honey. When Gideon got turned on, his voice thickened and roughened.

"Much as I like that idea though, save it for later." He gave a quick glance around the waiting room, taking in the bookshelves and the leather furniture, the potted plants and abstract paintings on the walls.

Eddie was sure one of them was a picture of an elephant with an erection, with a dwarf riding on his back. Gideon had spluttered with laughter when Eddie had innocently blinked his eyes and imparted that little gem of wisdom. It had gone a long way to calming Gideon down though and he'd relaxed a little more after that.

Gideon started as the inner office door opened and a portly, bespectacled man with a kind smile appeared.

"Mr. Trent?" He stepped forward and held out a hand to Gideon. "I'm Martin Wingmore."

Gideon stood and shook his hand. "Pleased to meet you, Mr. Wingmore."

The man laughed. "Call me Martin, please. I'm pretty informal and seeing as how you're going to telling me some personal things about yourself, I think that's the best approach, don't you? Like friends although…not."

He grinned widely and Eddie warmed to him. He could see Gideon relaxing too. He stood up beside him, one hand resting loosely on Gideon's waist, the other entwined with Gideon's hand.

Martin extended his hand again and Eddie took it. "And you must be Eddie. I think I have you to thank for getting your man here, don't I? Gideon and I spoke a little while on the phone and I think your name might have been mentioned a couple of times."

Eddie felt a swell of pleasure that Gideon had told the man about him and that Gideon was considered "his man."

"His man" looked a little embarrassed at the conversation and Eddie chuckled. "I did sort of have to do some convincing but he's here now." Martin gestured to the door, indicating Gideon should enter his office.

Eddie squeezed Gideon's hand. "Go get 'em, tiger," he murmured softly. "I'll be waiting here when you come out." The look of gratitude and affection he got from those honey-coloured eyes made Eddie's heart bounce like a ping pong ball in his chest.

Gideon squeezed his hand back. "See you later." He followed Martin into the office and the door closed, leaving Eddie standing outside. He sighed and sat down, idly browsing through the magazines on the side table. Picking up one called *Psychology Today*, Eddie began reading while he waited for his lover to bear his soul.

Chapter 14

Eddie was woken very early in the morning by the steady sound of his mobile going off. He opened one eye sleepily, and saw Gideon's sleeping face only a few inches from his. He smiled softly and tried to extricate himself from the strong tug of Gideon's arms around his waist. The last week had been sheer bliss, going to sleep with this man and waking up in his arms. Eddie rather liked the fact that he appeared to be a sleeping balm for his lover. Not to mention the fact that he was getting regular sex.

Gideon had also made more appointments with Martin, once a week, and the arrangement seemed to agree with him. He and Eddie had talked a little about his first session and now Gideon seemed less troubled, more at ease with life. He'd even stopped chewing gum as much, saying he was more relaxed and didn't need it anymore.

Eddie was quite pleased, because as much as he appreciated Gideon giving up smoking, the taste of the nicotine gum didn't really turn him on. He preferred the taste of Gideon's mouth virgin and sweet.

Eddie had his own guilt to tackle, worrying about abandoning his housemates who hardly saw him anymore. The only saving grace were the regular pub nights when they all got together and either got drunk or talked about Leslie's current man squeeze.

Gideon muttered as Eddie got free and swung his legs over the side of the bed. He picked up his mobile off the charger and peered at it blearily. His spine chilled as he answered. At this time of the morning, three a.m., he didn't think it was good news.

"Leslie? Is everything okay?"

Leslie's voice babbled loudly in his ear. "No, it's not fucking okay. Taylor's gone all weird again and I can't get him to wake up. He's just sitting there in the hallway in his skivvies. Eddie, you have to come home, he keeps saying your name over and over again…" Leslie sounded frantic with worry and Eddie clambered off the bed and held the phone to his chin with his shoulder as he tried to pull on his jeans.

"Slow down, Leslie. Is he hurt, or just in one of his zone-out freaky things?"

"It's a fucking MAJOR zone-out freaky thing, Eddie." Leslie sounded like he was on the verge of crying. "He went to bed about midnight and I woke up when I thought I heard someone moving around. It was Taylor but he looked so damned scary, his eyes were all blank and he had this look on his face. Like he was possessed or something." Leslie's voice rose to a shriek. "Oh my God, you don't think he is, do you? Possessed like the chick from *The Ring*? Oh my God, Eddie what if something's going to come crawling along the top of the wall, oh Jesus, I can't cope with this." There was a wail on the other side of the phone and Eddie felt a shiver of fear run through his body at his friend's distress.

"Leslie? Are you still there? Tell me what the hell is happening. I'm on my way over there now."

By now Gideon was awake and looking at Eddie with concern.

"What's going on?" he said huskily.

"Leslie is freaking out because Taylor's had one of his fits." Eddie placed the phone down on the bed as he pulled on a tee shirt. The squawking noise from the phone continued and he grimaced as he picked it up again.

"Leslie, I'm on my way. Just hold out."

"Oh gawd, hurry up. I'll try and make it through until you get here. I need to get me some salt. Make it quick!"

The phone went dead. Eddie frowned at the cryptic salt comment as he threw his mobile on the bed as he finished getting dressed. Gideon looked puzzled as he sat up in bed, the sheet falling to his waist. Even in his worried state Eddie could appreciate the sight of broad shoulders and a tight stomach.

"Your roommate? What, is he having like, an epileptic fit?" Gideon swung onto his feet and began dragging on clothes.

Eddie looked at him. "What are you doing?"

"I'm going with you." Gideon's tone was firm. "There are no taxis, no tubes so you're going to need a car to get to Kennington at this time of this morning. And I happen to have one."

Eddie hadn't even known Gideon had a car. "Okay, thanks. I appreciate that." He thrust his feet into trainers, not even bothering to put on socks. In a few minutes they were both ready. Eddie tucked his phone into his jeans pocket and followed Gideon down the stairs as they made their way to the back entrance of the restaurant. Outside, the night air was cold and crisp.

"She's over here." Gideon walked over to small garage about fifty feet from the restaurant. Eddie had seen the building many times when he went to empty rubbish and shoo away drunks, but he'd never realised it belonged to Gideon. Gideon took out a bunch of keys and unlocked the steel roller door, pushing it up as his arms flexed and his biceps bulged. Another sight Eddie appreciated. The door was rusty and made a terrible groaning noise as it gradually opened to reveal a dark space. He could see the faint outline of a car.

Eddie stepped inside, squinting to try and see what it was. "How many times have you opened that damn door? It's like something out of a horror story, that noise." Something scuttled in the darkness and Eddie moved closer to Gideon.

Gideon shrugged. "The last time I had Ellie out was about two months ago when I went to Liverpool for a convention."

Eddie stared at him in disbelief. "You called your car Ellie?"

In the darkness Eddie saw the gleam of teeth. "After my mother. Ellie is a real lady. So was my mum."

Eddie hadn't ever heard Gideon mention his parents. He knew vaguely from Carmen that his father was still alive but off on some godforsaken mission somewhere as part of some organisation, but that was about it. Even Carmen knew very little. From the word "was," Eddie gathered Gideon's mother was dead.

"Oh. I'm sorry about your mum."

Gideon was quiet as he stumbled over to the wall and gave a small groan of relief. There was a click and then the garage flooded with bright light. Eddie winced as his eyeballs had self-ignited and then his jaw dropped. In the middle of the space, a sleek, cherry-red MX 5 Roadster Coupe sat gleaming. Eddie moved quickly toward the car and lovingly ran his hands over the hood.

"Oh, wow, Gideon. She's beautiful." He peered inside. "And automatic too. That must make her a bit special."

Gideon gave a loving glance towards his car. "Yes. I bought her about five months ago, just after the accident. I wanted an automatic because I'm a lazy git." He chuckled as he unlocked the car and it beeped. "Climb in. We have somewhere to be, don't we?"

Eddie needed no further invite. He opened the door, sat down and was soon inspecting the interior as Gideon strapped himself in.

"Seatbelt, Eddie, before we go anywhere." Gideon's admonishing tone made Eddie smile as he reached and clipped the belt across his chest. He fiddled with all the dials and the radio like a kid. He loved cars, but although he had a driver's licence, he'd never owned one. He'd driven his parents' cars if he needed to, as insurance and upkeep had been way too expensive for him to afford.

Gideon started the engine, which purred as if she'd only been driven yesterday, and he slowly reversed out of the garage, across the gravel drive and turned into the darkened street. Traffic was still fairly busy even at this time of night.

"Don't you want to shut the garage door?" Eddie asked in surprise. "Someone may steal something."

Gideon shrugged. "There's nothing in there worth stealing, only this baby." He patted the dash affectionately then leaned over and switched on the radio to Radio 1 and the bass sounds of dub step music filled the car. Not something Eddie was partial to but Gideon seemed to be enjoying it.

"So this friend of yours that's gone rogue. What's his story?" Gideon manoeuvred the little car through the streets with all the experience of a seasoned London driver. Aggressive, defensive and confident. Eddie found it a real turn-on and wondered if Gideon had ever made out in his car.

Well, there's always a first time if not.

Eddie didn't really want to get into the nitty-gritty of what Taylor was as he was sure Gideon wasn't particularly fanciful. He knew it would have to happen once they got to his house but perhaps he could postpone the explanation until then with a little dross.

"Leslie is a bit of a character, a real flamer and proud of it. He's a bit highly strung so just be wary when you see him. He might try to launch himself at you, wrap his legs around your waist, you know. He's very demonstrative."

Eddie giggled at the expression on Gideon's face. He didn't look particularly convinced of Leslie's good points. Leslie *was* an acquired taste, no doubt.

Gideon expertly moved the car around a slow-moving truck and sped down the road.

"Okayyy. What about zoned-out freak? The one who has the fits?"

Eddie blew out his cheeks. "Taylor has these…episodes." His voice trailed off and he cleared his throat.

Gideon glared at him in exasperation. “And? Is he on medication?”

Eddie sighed. “It’s not the sort of thing you can take medication for.” He fiddled with his seatbelt, aware of Gideon’s rising impatience beside him. The car seemed to pick up speed and Eddie glanced at the speedometer. He was sure Gideon shouldn’t be doing eighty miles an hour in the centre of London. The man was apparently something of a speed merchant.

Isn’t he worried about speeding tickets?

“Fuck, Eddie, you’re more evasive than a politician on Twenty Questions. What the hell’s wrong with him then?” Gideon growled as he narrowly avoided hitting a rubbish bin on the side of the road. Eddie’s backside clenched at that close call.

Oh, just cut to the chase before he kills us.

“Taylor is a psychic. He sees things. It’s how he saved me when that bloke attacked me in the alley and he did the same for Leslie. He’s the real deal. I’ve seen it myself.”

A loud snort of disbelief and a bark of laughter was Gideon’s response. “Oh come on. You believe in that shit?”

“Yes,” Eddie said quietly as he stared at Gideon’s profile. “I told you. He knew I was in trouble that night. There was no way he could see what was happening. Leslie was there too, for everything.”

Gideon flashed a thoughtful look but didn’t say anything. There was silence for a while and Eddie breathed a sigh of relief, hoping his friends were all right, when he saw they were only a few minutes away from his house.

“So Taylor saw this stuff happening to you and that’s how you were rescued?” Gideon said. “I thought they came by and saw you.”

Eddie felt a little uncomfortable. “No, that’s not what went down. It’s what we told the police because they’d never have believed us. If Taylor and Leslie hadn’t come over when they did because Taylor had his vision, that guy would have stuck his cock in my mouth or worse.” He shivered.

Gideon hissed a breath and his hands clenched angrily on the steering wheel. “Bastard. I still want to cut his nuts off for putting you through that.”

Eddie reached out and ruffled his hair affectionately. “I like that you want to do that to him for me.” He stopped and pointed. “That’s my house on the corner, the one with the green door and the lights on. You can park behind that old Rover, that's Mr. Coolidge's parking and he's away in Thailand or something." He grimaced. "He likes the lady-boys. They go in and out of his flat all the time. He tried to get Leslie to visit him one time and Leslie slapped him with a piece of fish."

Gideon guffawed and Eddie laughed. "No, honestly. He was on his way home late with a piece of prime cod from Sainsbury's and Mr. Coolidge groped him. The man got slapped around the face with a wet fish for his troubles. He was not a very happy bunny."

Gideon and Eddie were both giggling now as Gideon pulled up and switched off the engine. Gideon held his sides as tears fell down his face. Eddie loved this side of him.

"I think I might like this Leslie of yours," Gideon spluttered. "Come on. Let's go see what's going on with your crazy friends."

Eddie stared at him as he got out of the car. "That's it? You're not going to give me any more grief over the whole visionary thing?"

Gideon came around the car and pulled him into a hug. "Babe, he saved you. Doesn't matter how but you say he did. That's all I need to know. I need to thank them both. Now come on. I want to meet this fish-slapping man and the mysterious psychic."

Eddie didn't have to wait long. As if there was some rotating beacon on his head attracting drama queens, no sooner had he stepped onto the front porch and made to open the door than it opened from within and a bundle of long limbs and muscled flesh launched itself into his arms.

"Oh God, Eddie, thank God you're here. Taylor is so damn out of it and I just don't know what to do." Leslie's arms hugged him close as he buried his face in Eddie's shoulder. "Hmm, you smell nice. Is that Davidoff? You dog, you. Here you tell me you can't afford the good stuff—"

Eddie reached out a hand with difficulty as Leslie was squeezing him like a melon being fitted for a fruit salad. He was vaguely amused at the sight of Gideon watching with wide eyes as the hurricane that was Leslie latched himself onto Eddie like a leech.

"Leslie, sweetheart, calm down and focus. If you let me go, I can introduce you to Gideon and we can see what we can do to get Taylor sorted." With a testy huff of breath, Leslie released Eddie and swung his eyes slowly in Gideon's direction. Gideon flushed as

Leslie appraised him from top to bottom, with a definite focus on his package. Leslie licked his lips as he regarded Gideon's groin and Eddie choked back a laugh at Gideon's obvious discomfort at being so blatantly inspected.

"Well, Eddie, he's a bit of all right indeed. I can see why you got all bent out of shape when he—"

Eddie leaned forward and placed a hand over Leslie's mouth. Blue eyes regarded in him mock hurt.

"Enough." Eddie said firmly. Gideon didn't need to know how much Eddie had moped because of their little argument earlier on the relationship. "Now if you've finished scoping out my boyfriend, we have more important things to attend to. Like a possessed friend." Leslie's eyes widened and Eddie could have kicked himself.

Boyfriend? Shit, he hadn't meant that to come out. What the hell would Gideon think about that?

He tried to cast an inconspicuous look at Gideon to see what the reaction was to that word. Strangely enough, Gideon didn't look all that fazed, but looked rather thoughtfully at Eddie.

He swallowed. "Come on. Let's do this." He and Gideon followed Leslie into the house. The expression on Gideon's face as he took in Leslie's choice of attire was precious. Eddie sniggered. He guessed Gideon wasn't used to seeing someone sashaying—because Leslie sashayed, he never walked—in tight black trousers that left nothing to the imagination, an oversized pink tee shirt sparkled with sequins and a pair of blue Papa Smurf slippers. They were Leslie's "comfort" clothes.

The lounge was dimly lit, and he saw the figure of Taylor lying on the couch. He was muttering softly to himself.

"He paced for hours. I managed to get him into the lounge and he sat down eventually." Leslie said quietly as he sunk deftly to the floor like a long-legged, graceful giraffe. "I tried to get some chamomile tea down him but he wouldn't drink it. Before, he was pacing around the place like a wild man. He was going on about gingerbread again, and kept saying your name. So I called you." He shrugged and glanced over at Gideon. "Sorry to disturb the whole love nest thing you two have going on but I really needed your help." His tone was wry but Eddie heard the worry in it.

He reached over and hugged his friend. “No love nest comes between you, me and a friend in need,” he said. He frowned. “What the heck is that on the floor?”

There was a large circle of fine white crystals in the middle of the living room. Leslie looked a little guilty. “It’s a ring of salt. You know, when you watch *Buffy*, they always protect themselves from demons and stuff by staying in the salt. I was sitting in the circle until you got here.”

His tone was defiant and Eddie wanted to giggle loudly at the thought of Leslie in his Smurf slippers sitting inside a ring of salt. From the look on Gideon’s face, the man was having difficulty controlling his laughter too.

Eddie nodded solemnly. “That was quick thinking, Batman. Always a good idea to protect oneself by salt.”

Leslie gave him a quick smile as if to say, “Thanks, I knew you’d get it,” then turned to look at Taylor. “Tay? Eddie’s here, sweetie. Can you maybe wake up and tell him what the problem is?”

Eddie shivered at the blank look in Taylor’s eyes as he stared at the far wall. His face was slack, his dark eyes expressionless. His lips moved and Eddie could hear him saying, “The gingerbread house. He’s there. He’s in trouble. The trees are staring at him and he’s so scared. So scared….”

Gideon frowned and knelt down beside him. “Eddie, maybe if you talk to him he might recognise your voice and come out of it. Keep talking to him and maybe you can get through.”

Eddie nodded. He cleared his throat and reached over to squeeze Taylor’s shoulder. His friend’s body was rigid like marble and he was cold. Eddie shivered. “Tay, it’s Eddie. Leslie said you’ve been calling me? Well, I’m here now. What do you want to tell me?”

For a minute, Eddie thought he’d get no response. Then slowly, like a puppet being controlled by invisible strings, Taylor turned his head to stare at Eddie with those unseeing eyes. The sight was chilling and Eddie gasped then felt Gideon’s warm hand on his back.

“Keep talking,” he whispered as he rubbed circles on Eddie’s skin. “You’re getting a reaction. I know it’s damn spooky but I think he heard you.”

Leslie’s eyes were focused on the two of them, his gaze soft and longing. He watched the slow circles Gideon was making with eyes that seemed to envy them.

Eddie tried again. “Taylor, talk to me, mate. I know something’s up, so tell me what it is. I can’t help you if I don’t know what the problem is.”

Taylor’s eyes darkened and Eddie thanked God at least something had provoked a response. Taylor’s voice was anguished when he spoke again.

“He’s so cold, Eddie. He’s in the gingerbread house, and the trees scare him. They shiver and shake and bend over. He doesn’t know what else to do, he needs to do this. He’s so alone, God, he’s so alone…”

Eddie felt the first stirrings of recognition in Taylor’s words. There was something about the trees and the gingerbread house that conjured up an old memory, one he thought was from his childhood. But he just couldn’t quite get it.

Frustrated, he reached out and clasped Taylor’s face between his now chilled hands, trying to ground him, make him explain. As he did so, a sudden dark feeling swept through him. He cried out loudly as the sensation burrowed into his being and flushed his body and mind with pain, guilt, sorrow and anger and fear. It overwhelmed him, swooped in like an eagle plucking its prey from the depths of a cold sea, leaving him trembling.

He vaguely heard Gideon’s exclamation of panic and Leslie’s frantic entreaties to “come back, Eddie, you arsehole.” An image of an old shed and the forbidding vision of tall, dark trees speared his consciousness like an old movie scene, gaunt in its appearance. It was only a brief flash, but with a sudden burst of clarity, Eddie remembered.

He reeled back from Taylor, into Gideon’s warm and strong arms as his lover pulled him to his chest, the fear in his eyes evident. Eddie gasped and buried his face into Gideon’s chest as he took a heaving breath.

“Jesus, what the hell happened? You just went blank and scared the shit out of me!” Gideon’s voice trembled with fear and apprehension. Eddie nodded against his man’s beating heart.

“I know the place Taylor is talking about. I saw it. It’s an old shed back home, a few miles from my house, set deep in the woods. Luke and I used to play there when we were kids. He always called it the gingerbread house, after Hansel and Gretel, and we used to pretend the witch lived there and was going to eat us.” He took another deep breath. "Something's wrong with Luke. I can feel it. That's what Taylor's being trying to tell me. Luke is in trouble." He scrambled to his feet. "I have to call him, find out if he's okay. We'll take it from there."

Eddie pulled out his phone and started scrolling through his contacts.

***

Gideon took a deep breath. When Eddie had gone all pale and quiet and looked zoned out, Gideon's heart had clenched and he'd gone cold. He didn't really believe in all this clap trap of Taylor being able to have visions but Eddie did and that was what mattered. And that "boyfriend" comment—he hated to admit it but he'd gone all warm and fuzzy inside thinking that was how Eddie thought of him. Gideon rather liked the idea. He'd had the man in his bed for the past few weeks and was definitely taken with him. He thought he might even want to keep him, and wasn't that a turn up for the books? Eddie was a definite nightmare deterrent, something Gideon was ever thankful for. He'd known peace for the first time in a long time.

Taylor was now lying quiet on the couch, his face softened and his body more relaxed. It was as if he knew his job was done. Leslie bent down and smoothed dark curls off his forehead as he murmured sweet nothings to his friend, all the time casting anxious glances at Eddie and Gideon. Eddie sat at the dining table, on his phone, looking pale but decidedly better than when he'd all gone spaced out.

"Luke's not answering; it's just going to voice mail. I need to call his mum." He dialled another number, his face anxious. His face lit up as someone obviously answered their phone.

"Aunt Claire? It's Eddie. Yes I know what time it is but this couldn't wait. I'm so sorry to wake you up. "

There was a squawking noise from the other side and Gideon grimaced. They didn't sound very happy being woken up at four in the morning. He moved over to stand beside Eddie, placing a hand on his shoulder.

"No, this isn't another drunk prank call. And I only did that a couple of times." Eddie's voice was aggrieved. Gideon grinned despite the situation at the thought of his man placing rambling drunken calls to his family. "Can you please do me a favour? Can you tell me if Luke's home? He's not answering his phone."

More squawking and Eddie's face brightened. "Oh, he is? Are you sure?" He hesitated. "Can you do me a really big favour? Can you check his place, make sure he's there for me? I've just had this bad feeling about him…" His voice trailed off and he rolled his eyes, looking as cute as hell to Gideon. Leslie was watching them both as if he were at a tennis match, his eyes flitting from Gideon to Eddie and back. Taylor was quiet now, seemingly sleeping and Gideon envied him.

Eddie's voice got louder. "Please, Aunt Claire. He's just in the guest cottage, please can you wander down and check and see he's okay?" He huffed and scowled at his phone as he mouthed, "She can be such a pain in the arse. I don't know how poor Luke puts up with her."

"She's his mum," Gideon said with a grin. "You put up with a lot when it's your mother."

Eddie frowned. "Well, she finally said she'd check. Luke lives in the little guest annexe just off the house. He came home at ten p.m. apparently. She saw his car pull in." He waited, tapping his other hand impatiently on the wooden table. The constant noise was driving Gideon crazy. He reached out and stroked Eddie's cheek tenderly.

"Stop that. I hate repetitive sounds like that. It makes me want to scream."

Eddie smiled wanly. "Sorry. It's just something I do when I'm nervous or worried." He leaned forward and planted a soft kiss on Gideon's cheek.

Leslie let out a deep sigh. "Oh my God, you two are so damn cute together. Just fucking adorable." His voice sounded like he'd just seen Cinderella with her prince. "I hope one day I'll find someone like you have, Eddie. Nobody seems to want me." His voice was sad.

Gideon wasn't sure what to say. "I'm sure one day you'll find that special someone."

Leslie gazed at him with sad, puppy-dog eyes.

Gideon coughed uncomfortably, feeling he needed to say more to this pixie-like young man with eyes like skies of cerulean blue. "I mean, you're a nice-looking guy and very sweet, any man would be glad to have you at his side."

Eddie flashed a beaming, approving smile at him, one that turned Gideon's insides to jelly and gave him an instant boner. The man had that effect on him when he so clearly showed his feelings. It was something Gideon wasn't used to doing but was getting easier with Eddie in his life.

Leslie certainly looked happier with his words. "Ooh, Eddie, you need to keep this one. He's adorable." He looked hopeful. "Do you have a brother and does he swing my way?"

Gideon stared at him. "Err, no, I don't have a brother."

Leslie sighed. "Pity." He looked at Eddie. "Jesus, how far is your cousin's flat? Barbados? Haven't they checked he's there yet?"

Eddie frowned. "There's a lot of noise and I can hear Aunt Claire saying something. And I think that's my Uncle Dave in the background. Hello? Hello?" He shouted into the phone and waited impatiently. He made to start tapping his fingers again but a glare from Gideon stayed his fingers.

Eddie's face whitened. "Aunt Claire. He's not there? You found what? Oh God, please don't say that." His voice tailed to a whisper and the stunned look on his face and tightening of his shoulders made Gideon apprehensive.

Eddie looked up at Gideon. "He's not there. They found a note in his room, a suicide note. Oh God, Luke, what the hell have you done?"

Gideon reached over and took the phone from Eddie's trembling fingers. He spoke into it as he placed a warm and comforting hand on his boyfriend's back.

"This is Gideon, I'm a friend of Eddie's." He didn't want to mistakenly out Eddie to his other family members by saying he was the boyfriend, although from what he knew of Eddie it wasn't something he hid. "What does the note say?"

Eddie's aunt's voice trembled as she replied. "He says he's sorry but he can't bear the guilt anymore and he's very confused about things. He wants us not to worry, says he's going somewhere better." Her voice finally cracked. "Oh my God, where is my boy?"

Gideon closed his eyes at the anguish in that tone. "Ma'am, I'm going to put Eddie back on the phone. He thinks he knows where your son might be." He handed the phone to Eddie who nodded.

"That's what Taylor's been trying to tell me. The old shed."

Gideon nodded. "I might not believe in this stuff, but we have no other options at the moment. Tell your aunt to go to that old place, and check it out. It's worth the shot isn't it?"

Eddie nodded in stunned silence then lifted the phone to his ear. "Aunt Claire? Listen to me. You and Uncle Dave need to go the old Watson place in the woods down the road. The old shed there where Luke and I used to play. I think he might be there."

His voice rose slightly. "I just have a feeling, that's all. If he's not home, then he has to be somewhere else and he hasn't taken his car, you said. Please, just get Uncle Dave to shoot out there now. We've got nothing to lose—except Luke."

Those final words seemed to end the debate and Eddie closed in his eyes in a gesture of relief. His body relaxed and Gideon felt a swell of tenderness that his normally confident chef looked so vulnerable.

"Good, tell him to make it quick. And phone me the minute you hear anything. As soon as I hear from you, I'll be travelling up there to see what the hell Luke is playing at." His lips set in a mutinous line, one Gideon recognised well. "The boss owes me some time off so I'm sure he'll agree to me taking it." His eyes sought Gideon's, defiant.

Gideon chuckled softly at Eddie's fierceness, despite the circumstances. "Take all the time you need. I'm going with you anyway."

Eddie's face lit up and a smile split his face. Gideon loved the fact he could please him just by something simple like being there for him.

"You are? That's great, thanks."

Leslie sighed, a deep, heartfelt one that echoed in the room. "Just beautiful," he murmured to himself as he stroked Taylor's sleeping cheek.

Gideon swore the man had tears in his eyes. Uncomfortable, he wandered to the window to gaze into the darkness beyond. Eddie paced around the room, muttering, and Gideon finally lost patience with his agitation and scowled as he moved toward him. Eddie looked up in surprise as he was pulled into a bear hug.

"For God's sake," Gideon grumbled. "Stop bouncing up and down like a cat in a cage. It's driving me crazy." His hands stroked down Eddie's spine and Eddie shivered. He melted against his body, his mouth seeking Gideon's throat as he trailed soft kisses along his skin.

"I thought you liked it when I bounced up and down," he said wickedly and Gideon's face flushed as Leslie gave a cackle.

"Oh touché, Eddie. Great comeback on that one." Leslie's eyes gleamed. "The thought of you two doing it like that makes me really hot." His face became hopeful. "Maybe one day I can be a voyeur?" He giggled at the glares he got from both Gideon and Eddie in return. "Or maybe not…" His voice trailed off and he turned his attention once again to the dozing Taylor.

Eddie was still jittery and Gideon led him to the couch and made him sit down, seating himself beside him. "You need to be patient," he said softly. "I know it's scary but we need to have faith that they'll find Luke and he'll be okay."

Eddie nodded, his face pale. "I don't know what would drive him to try and kill himself," he said, his voice trembling. "I mean, I should have been there for him; I knew he wanted to talk to me."

"Don't go blaming yourself," Gideon said gruffly. "You're not responsible for your cousin's actions. All you can do is be there for him when they find him." Privately he felt a little unsure about a positive outcome but he needed to keep Eddie's spirits up.

Eddie sighed, his eyes closing. He looked exhausted. "I hope they call back soon." Gideon held him and felt Eddie's body slowly relax as he fell into sleep. He looked over at Leslie, who was watching them.

"How's Taylor?" he asked quietly, not wanting to wake Eddie. "Is he okay, do you think?"

Leslie leaned back and stretched. "He seems fine. Sleeping at least, just like your man." His mouth split in a huge yawn. "I'm knackered myself but there's no way I'll fall asleep." He gestured at Eddie. "You really like my mate, huh? Eddie's good people. You'd better treat him right or you'll feel the sharp end of my longest and thinnest stiletto heels in your balls."

Said balls scrunched up at that threat. "I've no intention of treating Ed badly," Gideon said with a scowl. "He's a grown man. He can take care of himself without some heel-wearing diva doing it for him."

Leslie flapped a hand airily. "Oh make no mistake about this diva, girlfriend. I've been known to hurt the balls of bigger men than you, Gideon Trent, and you really should heed my warning." His dark eyes flashed and Gideon felt a slight sense of unease.

This slight, effeminate man was a little more than he looked if that glint in his eye was anything to go by.

Leslie smirked. "You do know he hates being called Ed?" he murmured. "He says it makes him sound like a donkey."

Gideon blinked. "A donkey?" he said faintly.

Leslie's long lashes fluttered in amusement around darkened, sleep-deprived eyes. "The donkey from the TV series *Mister Ed*?" He shook his head soulfully at what must have been Gideon's blank and mystified look. "Oh Giddy, you have led a sheltered life. I feel sorry for your arse not having the delight that is *Mister Ed*." His smile grew wider. "I'll have to tell Eddie to educate you somewhat."

Gideon glared at him. His own eyes were gritty and sore from the lack of sleep and Leslie was seriously not helping. "First, don't call me bloody Giddy. I hate it. Secondly, Mister Ed was actually a horse. And you can keep that show to yourself, thanks very much." He grimaced. "It's bad enough I have to sit and watch *Flog It!* with Eddie because he has this unholy fascination with all things antique and he gets off watching other people selling their crap."

Leslie's eyes widened. "Really? He was a horse? I could have sworn he was an ass." He giggled then grinned. "Wow, you can be quite grouchy, can't you? I don't think Eddie relieves your tension enough." He winked. "Dr. Leslie proposes a lot more blow jobs for you to get rid of that sexual frustration you have."

Gideon opened his mouth to retort that he was getting blown quite regularly fuck you very much but spotted the wicked glint in Leslie's eyes and stopped. "Well, at least *I'm* getting some," he finally said loftily.

Leslie cackled and waved long fingers in his direction. "Get you, all snarky and quick-witted."

In spite of Leslie's comment, Gideon saw the sudden flash of pain in his eyes which made Gideon feel like a heel. He pressed his lips together lest he put his foot in it again. Eddie had told him all about Leslie's abortive relationships and how his friend thought he'd never find Mr. Right.

"I'm sorry. I shouldn't have said that," he muttered. "Blame the fact it's the middle of the bloody morning and I need more sleep. I can be a bastard when I'm tired."

Leslie shrugged. “No worries.” He reached out and brushed his hand against the sleeping Taylor’s cheek. “When you’re right, you’re right.” He glanced over at Gideon, who shifted uncomfortably. “I wish I had something like what you and Eddie have. It looks pretty special to me.”

Gideon looked over at the slumbering Eddie. “I’m not sure about special, but I like the guy.”

Leslie cocked his head like a curious parrot. “You do, don’t you? I can see it on your face when you look at him. My Eddie has gone and got himself a big, bad protector.” Despite the apparent snarkiness of the words, Gideon heard the approval in Leslie’s voice. He felt a little uneasy about Leslie’s words. When he had stooped to wearing his emotions on his face?

It was all a bit confusing. To the point where, when he heard Eddie’s voice and saw his face, his heart leapt in his chest like a salmon in mid-stream. Waking up to warm man in his bed, seeing Eddie’s softly snoring face only inches from his…

Knowing he’s all mine.

His stomach clenched.

Fuck. He was in so deep in such a short time; it was like something out of a penny dreadful.

“You know, I can hear the wheel spinning from here.” Leslie’s amused voice cut into Gideon’s panicked thoughts like a tinkling bell. “That hamster seems to be peddling mighty fast.”

Gideon stared frostily at Leslie. “What the hell are you talking about?"

Leslie chuckled. “Taylor might be the real psychic here but I have a few talents of my own.” He frowned, his mouth pursing into an adorable pout.

Even Gideon appreciated a twinky pout.

“You were standing there wondering what the hell was happening and how you got so invested in Eddie so fast. It was written all over your face.” His own face softened. “I’m glad for both of you, so don’t fight it, Gideon. Eddie thinks the world of you.”

A sleepy voice interrupted. “Eddie is now awake and wondering what the hell the two of you arc talking about.”

Gideon turned to see Eddie’s still-unfocused eyes staring at him with some trepidation. “Leslie, what the heck have you been saying to Gideon? He looks like the axe is about to fall. The whole deer-in-the-headlights thing."

"Oh, nothing. We were just passing the time." Leslie looked at the clock on the wall and frowned. "Talking of which, when the fuck are your auntie and uncle going to call back? They should have found your cousin by now surely."

Eddie's face darkened. "Unless there's a problem and they had to call the police, or an ambulance," he said softly, the fear in his eyes causing Gideon's chest to tighten. He walked over to his boyfriend and sat down beside him, drawing him into his arms.

"Don't assume the worst," he murmured. "If they haven't called in another fifteen minutes, we'll call them back for an update."

Eddie reached up and captured Gideon's mouth in a tender kiss that made him wish they were alone so he could visit more upon Eddie's person than just his lips. Eddie's breath was warm, slightly stale with the faint taste of mint. When he finally released Gideon's mouth, Gideon gazed into green eyes that promised so much.

"Thanks for doing this with me," Eddie whispered. He gently brushed a strand of hair from Gideon's cheek and looked over Leslie who was misty eyed.

Eddie grinned. "Please don't start bawling, Leslie. I think Gideon might run for the hills if you did."

As Leslie sniffed and blinked back obvious tears, Eddie's phone rang. Eddie's face whitened and he looked at the innocent item lying on the side table as if it might grow teeth and rip him to shreds. He reached out with trembling hands and picked it up, as Gideon laid a comforting hand against his back.

"Hello? Aunt Claire?" A squawk on the other end of the phone answered his enquiry.

Taylor started suddenly and sat up with an exhale of air and a look of panic in his eyes. "What's going on, guys?" His voice was throaty, almost raw, and he grimaced and cleared his throat. "Is everything okay?"

Leslie reached out a hand and patted Taylor's shoulder. "It's all under control, Tay. You had one of your turns then fell asleep. Now we're about to find out what's going on." His voice shook a little but he smiled at Taylor who still looked bemused. "Eddie's just on the phone to his family to check on his cousin, Luke, who decided he'd had enough of life." He smiled softly at the panicked expression on Taylor's face. "Don't worry. We're on the case."

Eddie's face was tight as he listened to the conversation, and Gideon continued reassuring him with slight strokes to his back. Finally Eddie's shoulders relaxed and he closed his eyes as a look of relief crossed his face.

"Luke's all right," he said, his voice trembling. "He took pills but they managed to get to him in time. He's on his way to the hospital now." Anxious eyes gazed over at Gideon. "Can we go see him, Gideon? Will you drive me up there?" At Gideon's firm nod, Eddie's face softened and he spoke back into his mobile. "Yes, I'm on my way up to see the stupid bastard. I'll find out what's going on, Aunt Claire, I promise. Even if I have to string him up by the balls and torture it out of him." His face was fierce and Gideon's heart stuttered with affection at the look of determination on his man's face.

"We'll go up there in a few hours once we've both gotten some sleep," he said quietly. He forestalled Eddie's protest. "We're both knackered, Eddie. There's no point me driving when I'm tired. We want to get there in one piece."

Eddie's face was mutinous. "But I want to see Luke," he muttered as he passed a hand over tired, swollen eyes. Gideon hid a smile. His lover sounded like a sulky child. He nodded. "And we will. But first we're going to catch some shut-eye. Where's your room?"

He raised an enquiring eyebrow.

Eddie scowled. "Fine. Have it your way. Browbeat the exhausted, traumatised person into submission. Let him worry about his favourite cousin languishing in a hospital room with no one to wake up to." He waited, no doubt hoping Gideon would feel guilty and have a change of heart. Gideon continued gazing at him patiently.

Taylor snorted tiredly. "Looks like you've met your match, Eddie, my friend. I like this one. He doesn't take your crap." He stood up and stretched as Eddie regarded him with narrowed eyes.

"You're supposed to be on my side."

Taylor shrugged. "I agree with Gideon. At least I think this is Gideon. We haven't been formally introduced." He grinned tiredly and Gideon nodded. "Pleased to meet you. Now, Edster, have you seen yourself? You look like crap. I'm glad your cousin is okay. Maybe you should take your man off to bed and go and get some sleep. I'm going to do the same." He reached out and touched Leslie's cheek tenderly. "You've been so busy taking care of me and no one's been looking after you. So if you want to come and sleep with me and cuddle, I'm game. You can tell me what I've been up to." He yawned and smiled at them all. "Goodnight you lot. Eddie, if I don't see you before you leave, stay safe and call me when you get to Norfolk. Let me know how Luke's doing." He nodded at Gideon. "Take care of my friend, please. You're good for him. And he's definitely good for you. Maybe he can chase those nightmares away for good." He winked. "And I have a feeling you'll be cooking again in no time."

Gideon's jaw dropped. How the hell did he know about all this? He supposed Eddie had told him. And that comment about cooking? Was he talking metaphorically—in the bedroom cooking, or something else?

Taylor turned and left. Leslie watched him fondly then turned to Eddie and Gideon.

"A man doesn't get an offer to cuddle often so I'm going to take advantage of it." He reached over and gave Eddie a huge hug. Then he turned to Gideon and reached out his arms. Gideon scowled. "I'm not the hugging type—umff." His words were cut off as Leslie enveloped him in a clutch than nearly cut off his air supply. It was like being tackled by an octopus. A very nice, firm-bodied and warm octopus. Gideon felt guilty at even thinking the thought. Resigned to his fate, he let Leslie finish his embrace and step back. The younger man's eyes were shiny.

"You two take care of each other, and Eddie, call me too when you get to Norfolk. G'night." He disappeared into the hallway. Gideon looked at Eddie.

"Are he and Taylor, uhm, you know? Doing the dirty together?"

Eddie chuckled tiredly. "Not that I know of. They have this rather strange relationship and often sleep in each other's beds but I don't think they've fucked each other. Taylor's a bit of a player although he's never brought anyone home here. And I was too busy mooning over you to give a damn what they were up to."

Gideon felt warmth flush his body and he reached out his arms. Eddie came into them willingly. He turned his face up for a kiss and

Gideon obliged. Warm male in his arms, soft lips on his with a hint of stubble, a tongue that delved into the far reaches of his mouth and made him breathless. Gideon knew, not for the first time, he was a goner, well and truly fallen. His body responded to Eddie's passionate kiss and he pressed his hips against his boyfriend's, needing him, wanting him but not sure if Eddie was in the mood. When Eddie's hands found his jeans zipper and pulled it down to reach inside and stroke Gideon's upright and straining cock, he had his answer.

"Don't start something you don't intend to finish," Gideon growled in pleasure at Eddie's firm, hot strokes on his prick, and his hips pushed toward Eddie's in anticipation. Eddie's eyes opened in mock surprise, their green depths drawing Gideon in.

"Them's fighting words." His fingers grew stronger and Gideon hitched a breath as the sensations overwhelmed him. "I thought you deserved a little reward for being so nice to me and agreeing to take me home. But I can always leave it for another day…."

His hand left Gideon's cock and Gideon snarled. "Don't you fucking dare."

He gasped in relief as Eddie's hand resumed its teasing on his prick and his warm breath huffed against Gideon's throat. Eddie's mouth made warm trails down Gideon's overheated skin, tongue flicking at the sweat, drinking him in, and Gideon gasped. "Christ, just keep that up. I'm not going to last long. What the hell do you do to me anyway? I'm like a horny teenager when you're around."

Eddie nipped on Gideon's shoulder, biting through the fabric and making Gideon hiss in both pain and pleasure. "I just want you," he murmured. "A lot. Can't you feel?" He took Gideon's hand with his free hand and dragged it down to his crotch. "You have a choice. You can either jack me off now with you or you can give me a blow job when we go to bed. Which one is it going to be?"

He didn't wait for a reply. The fingers on Gideon's cock gave one final tug and Eddie whispered into his ear, "Come for me. I want to see you let loose."

Gideon's breath left him at those erotically charged words and his balls crept up into his groin. He grunted and groaned with the force of his orgasm. It shot through his cock, covering Eddie's hand with stickiness and leaving Gideon boneless. "Good Christ, Eddie," he rasped. "Are you trying to bloody kill me?"

Eddie chuckled. “I guess it’s going to be a BJ then.” He removed his hand from Gideon’s sticky cock and wiped it on his jeans. Gideon collapsed against the wall, his now spent prick peeking out of his jeans. Eddie tut-tutted and tucked him away, pulling the zip up and giving him a cheeky grin. He unzipped his own chinos and softly palmed what looked to Gideon like a very impressive erection.

“Come on, big guy. Little Eddie’s waiting for you to wrap those sexy lips around him and blow him to kingdom come. That’ll make me sleep and then we’ll be ready for the drive home.”

He disappeared into the hallway leaving Gideon still a little unsteady. Their sex life was very good, incredible, in fact, but when Eddie took charge like that, and whispered dirty things into his ear, it turned Gideon on no end. Eddie had a definite dominant streak and Gideon? Well, Gideon was quite happy to play along, something he thought he’d never do with another man.

As he walked the dark hallway toward Eddie’s room, a rush of delight assailing him at the thought he’d soon have Eddie’s lovely cock in his mouth, giving him pleasure and making him come so he could swallow every last drop, Gideon wondered not for the first time how this would all end. He knew he wanted Eddie around for a long time to come but he had no idea whether Eddie felt the same way. As he entered the bedroom and saw Eddie lying on the bed stark naked, his glistening cock already in hand as he stroked himself, Gideon told himself those thoughts could wait. Right now, he had something better to do.

Chapter 15

The drive late the following morning to Eddie's hometown of Diss was without incident and they made it in good time. There had been a few stops along the way for the usual coffee breaks but by the time midday rolled around, Eddie and Gideon were walking into the hospital. Eddie managed to catch a glimpse of his sleeping cousin and placed a soft kiss on his forehead with the whispered promise to come back later. Luke's stomach had been pumped and the nurse—a large, stern-looking woman Eddie found rather scary—had told them he was doing well but would probably be away with the fairies for a while.

It didn't take long for them to track down Eddie's aunt and uncle. They were sitting in the cafeteria looking tired and drained. Claire rushed over to her nephew, enveloping him in a fierce hug. She threw a questioning glance at Gideon. Claire was a tiny woman, five-foot-and-a-bit with a petite frame and dark blonde hair streaked with grey. Her husband Dave, though, was a mountain; he'd played rugby in his earlier years and it showed in his stock frame and muscled legs and arms. His bald head shone in the glare of the harsh hospital lighting.

Eddie turned to introduce Gideon to his aunt and uncle. "This is my boyfriend, Gideon. He owns the restaurant I chef in. Gideon, Aunt Claire and Uncle Dave."

Hands were shaken, appraisals made, Dave's keen blue eyes assessing Gideon and obviously approving as he gave a little nod to Eddie. There was the faint trace of an approving grin on his face despite the circumstances. Soon they were seated at the cafeteria table over steaming cups of tasteless coffee in plastic cups.

"So what happened?" Eddie was itching to find out what had driven Luke to try and kill himself. "I know he was bit off lately but I thought maybe he'd had a row with Rachel and needed a referee."

Claire glanced at her husband then at Eddie. "He broke up with Rachel two months ago." Eddie's eyes widened. "I had no idea! The couple of times I spoke to him, he never mentioned it. God, what happened?"

Dave gave a great sigh. "We don't know. Luke simply said it was over and wouldn't tell us why. I spoke to Rachel's parents and all they told me was that Luke had decided it wasn't working and he needed to be on his own. Rachel was upset but they'd only been going out four months so I expect she'll get over it soon enough. She's young and sweet."

Eddie was flabbergasted. Luke wasn't the sort to cut and run. Something momentous must have happened to make him hurt Rachel like that. Eddie had thought they were really good together.

I just have to talk to him.

He stood up. "I'm going to go and see whether he's awake," he said. "If not I'll bloody pinch the shit out of him secretly so that scary nurse doesn't see me. He really needs to tell us what the hell is going on in that damned head of his."

"Do you want me to come with you?" Gideon asked softly. Eddie shook his head.

"I'll be fine, thanks. He may tell me more if it's just me. Of course, you might want to speak to him first," he looked at Claire and Dave, "so shall I let you do that before I get hold of him?"

Dave shook his head. "If anyone can get into his head and find out what's been going on, it's you, Edster. You and Luke have been as close as brothers in the past and he'll talk to you. God knows we tried to. You go ahead. We'll stop by in a little while."

Eddie nodded and turned to his boyfriend. "Okay. I'll see you later, baby." He leaned down and kissed Gideon on the lips then turned and walked down the corridor. A few minutes later he was sitting by his cousin's bedside, debating which part of him to pinch into wakefulness, when Luke stirred and his eyes opened. They were unfocused and drowsy but lit up when he saw Eddie sitting at his bedside.

"Eddie." His voice was husky, no doubt from the tube that had been forced down his throat to pump out his stomach contents. "I knew you'd come."

Eddie leaned over and clasped Luke's cold hand. "You know it, cuz. I just wish you'd waited for me before doing something stupid. I'm really glad you're all right. Everyone was worried about you."

Luke's eyes filled with tears. "I'm so sorry, Eddie. I really fucked up, didn't I. Mum and Dad must be so damn mad with me." He sniffled and tears ran down his pale cheeks as he struggled up in bed. Eddie stood up and gently pushed him down back against the pillows.

"Don't be so bloody daft. Your mum and dad are just pleased you're safe. A little bewildered as to why you'd want to do such a damn foolish thing, as we all are, but just happy you're still with us."

Eddie sat back down, gently stroking Luke's hand and waiting until the younger man had recovered before pressing on. His stomach churned with guilt and he had something he needed to say before it ripped him apart. The words came out like a flood. "I knew you were upset about something, but I never thought you'd take something this far. I thought it was maybe a problem with Rachel; that you'd had an argument, but nothing serious enough to try and kill yourself. If I'd known how desperate you were, I'd have been here sooner. Honest, Luke. You have to believe me. I was so damn busy with my own life I wasn't there for you. But I'm here now and I want to help, Luke."

Luke's eyes had widened at Eddie's verbal diarrhoea and his red-rimmed blue eyes looked panicked. He opened his mouth to say something and Eddie rushed ahead.

"I promise I'll stick around until you feel better and we can deal with whatever is on your mind—"

There was a slight snort from the doorway and Eddie turned to see Gideon standing there, arms crossed against his chest as he leaned against the door frame. Even in Eddie's state he could still appreciate the broad chest and sexy grin of his lover.

Gideon moved into the room. "Eddie, sweetheart, you've terrified your poor cousin from the looks of it. The man can't get a word in edgeways with you spouting off like a water fountain." He leaned down and kissed Eddie's lips which were beginning to pout at Gideon's words.

The kiss was warm and gentle and Eddie closed his eyes in pleasure. He knew he'd said he could do this on his own but he was really glad Gideon was with him. When the pressure of Gideon's mouth disappeared, Eddie opened his eyes. He found Gideon arranging his tall frame in a small visitor's chair.

"I wanted to be here with you," he murmured quietly. "Just pretend I'm not here."

Luke's eyes were completely focused on him and Eddie, an expression of both yearning and despair etched across his elfin face.

"Wow, Eddie. You have a real boyfriend." His whispered words made Eddie fidget.

"Oi, you. What do you mean a *real boyfriend*?" His tone was teasing. He knew his track record hadn't been all that good in the past. He'd not really counted Seb, the lanky skater boy, Daniel the two-timing bitch and Jasper, the crazy vegetarian as real boyfriends. Fuck buddies to start, with the hope that things might develop into a lasting relationship, but none of them had made it further.

Gideon smirked at him.

Eddie scowled and sat down on the bed next to Luke. "And stop distracting me. You and me, we have some talking to do. Maybe not right now but when you're feeling better."

He was being a lot more patient than he felt, as he was desperate to find out what had prompted Luke's actions.

Luke swallowed and leaned back against the pillows, closing his eyes "I just lost it, Edster. I had a really shitty couple of weeks and I did something I'm not proud of and…" His voice tailed off. "It all got too much."

Eddie reached over and caressed his cousin's cheek. "Nothing you could have done or found out would have been enough to do what you did. I know you're a good person—"

"I'm a fucking shitty person!" Luke's voice grew stronger and the look of disgust on his face threw Eddie. Luke's eyes were dark, his mouth twisted into an ugly grimace. "I made someone hurt themselves because I was a bastard, a fucking coward. If I'd had more damn guts Francis wouldn't be lying in a hospital with his wrists slashed. I deserve to be here."

His voice cracked and his slight frame shook with sobs as he cried, tears of anguish coursing down his cheeks. Eddie stared at him in stupefaction. Gideon leaned forward and spoke quietly, his voice steady, calming.

"Luke, you're seventeen years old. We do stupid things at that age." He gave a dry laugh. "Hell, we do stupid things at my age. Ask Eddie. He'll tell you I can be a complete arsehole myself." His soft, self-deprecating grin at Eddie seemed to soothe Luke, who took a shuddering breath. "But whatever you did, you can fix it, make it right. You don't deserve to die for being stupid." He reached out and took Luke's hand in his. Eddie swallowed, his throat constricting at the tenderness on Gideon's face for someone he didn't even know.

"You need to talk to your cousin, tell him what happened. Eddie's a good listener. If you want me to leave, I will." He stood up to go but Luke pulled him back down.

"No, stay. I don't mind you being here." He looked down at the white sheet, his hands plucking invisible threads as his chest heaved with emotion. When he looked up at Eddie, his face was bleak.

"Eddie, you knew you were gay when you were really young, didn't you? I remember you telling me about the time you saw Dennis Manning naked in the locker room after a rugby game when you were only thirteen. You said you got such a boner at his naked arse and the look of his package that you had to jack off in the bathroom." Luke smiled faintly and Eddie now knew where this was going. His face flushed as Gideon looked over at him, and Eddie could see he was trying to withhold his laughter.

Eddie shifted uncomfortably. "I don't think I *quite* put it that way, Luke," he began, knowing that was exactly how he'd put it. The sight of the very manly Dennis in all his rosy glory after just coming out the shower had given him an erection that had threatened to poke his teammates' eyes out. Luckily he'd had a pile of dirty towels in his arms at the time and managed to hide his arousal until he could sort it out five minutes later.

Gideon chuckled, a sexy sound that turned Eddie's bones to mush. "I'm having a bit of a problem visualising you playing rugby, Eddie. You're not exactly built for rugger."

Eddie glared at him. "I was only in thc tcam a fcw wccks. The coach told me I was better suited for other sports like running, as I had some co-ordination problems." He heard the agitation in his voice. "I only smacked into the guys a few time when I was running with the ball. It wasn't my fault they all got in the bloody way."

Gideon's shoulders shook with silent laughter and even Luke had a wide smile on his face. For a moment, it was as if everything was all right with the world and Eddie was happy to be the brunt of the amusement if it made his cousin smile and forget for a while.

Gideon snorted. "Hell, I can just see you, all adorably klutzy on the field. God, you are so damn cute."

"Yeah, well, let's see how cute I can be when you beg me to suck you off," Eddic said accrbically. "Then we'll see how klutzy I can be when I miss your dick with my mouth."

Gideon was giggling now and didn't Eddie think *that* was adorable. His man *didn't* giggle.

Finally both Luke and Gideon stopped sniggering and Eddie sat in mock injury next to his boyfriend who still had a leer on his face. Luke looked slightly better, having more colour in face as he gripped the covers and smoothed his fingers over the fabric.

"We got sidetracked, sorry," Eddie said softly. "I guess we should hear the rest of your story."

Luke nodded. "You can probably guess where it's going," he murmured. His bright blue eyes gazed over at Eddie, weariness in their depths. "I'm bisexual, gay, whatever. I've been…seeing this guy from college. We've got together a few times." He sighed heavily. "I had to break up with Rachel. She didn't take it too well." His face darkened. "Francis and I really clicked together, and she found me kissing him in my room when we were studying. I didn't want to cheat on her, but the sex—what we had was nothing like what Francis and I had. That was explosive." His face coloured pink. "Well, you two know what that's like. It just felt so much better being with a guy."

Eddie nodded. "No argument from me there. So when did you discover this whole 'I like men better' thing?"

"The last year I've just felt…unsettled, not sure why I didn't want to make out with girls as much as I used to. That's why I started going out with Rachel. I thought maybe it would solve my problem." He shrugged. "It didn't. There's this guy, Francis, and he was really sweet, so gentle and clever." He looked stricken. "He was going through a rough time. His mum and dad died a year ago in a car accident and he lives now with his uncle. He was still cut up about it; he was very close to his folks. We used to get together after school, go for coffee, hang out. He was helping me with my trigonometry, because I'm pants at it." His voice choked up. "I didn't want anyone to know about us so we kept it a secret. I wanted to find out if it was the real me before I told my folks or you. Maybe it was just a phase, maybe I just wanted to experiment."

Gideon nodded, his eyes compassionate. "I can understand that. It can a very confusing time, finding out your sexual identity. You needed time to process things, make sure you were comfortable before you told anyone else."

Luke nodded, his eyes dull. "But I fucked it up. I came out into the courtyard at school one day a couple of weeks ago and these guys were harassing Francis. They had his backpack and they were calling him names. Ugly names. Telling him he was a queer boy, and that he liked to suck cock. He saw me, and his eyes lit up. He thought I was going to help him." His voice broke. "But I didn't. I walked away and let them torment him. I didn't want to out myself. I thought they'd just pick on him then let him go." He heaved a breath and tears welled in his eyes. Eddie moved forward and laid a comforting arm around Luke's shaking shoulders.

Gideon's face was grim. Whether it was at Luke's actions or the homophobic taunts of the other boys, Eddie didn't know. He hoped the latter.

Luke's words came in between halting breaths. "They beat him up when he tried to fight back. He knew he didn't stand a chance again them but still he tried. My Francis, who'd never thrown a punch in his life managed to get home, and when I tried calling him later to tell him I was sorry, he wouldn't talk to me."

Luke's voice was flat. "I tried for two days to see him, tell him I'd fucked up and I could understand why he hated me. I stopped calling him. He was better off without me anyway." The pain in his voice made Eddie's heart ache. "I took a few days out, disappeared by myself to the old abandoned barge on the river." He looked at Eddie guiltily. "I wasn't with anyone when you called me that day. I'd been drinking and thinking about jumping into the river. Your call made me think twice."

He fiddled with the seam in the blanket. "Then the next thing I knew a few days ago, I heard Francis had been taken to hospital. He tried to slash his wrists. He left a note for his uncle saying he couldn't cope with everything, the bullying, me not being there for him. But he also said he forgave me for walking away, he understood. That was the worst part. I didn't deserve forgiveness." Luke was sobbing again.

Eddie let out a shocked gasp and Gideon's face grew grimmer.

"The doctor said he hadn't cut too deep, that he was lucky. He did it the wrong way."

The dead look on Luke's face hit at Eddie's heart, making his chest tight and leaving his throat dry as tears prickled behind his eyes. He pulled Luke into his arms as the younger man dissolved into heart-wrenching sobs. His eyes met Gideon's across Luke's dark brown head and the look of understanding and love in Gideon's beautiful brown eyes was Eddie's undoing. Emotional as he was holding his weeping cousin, Eddie realised something.

I am so *in love with him. God, what the hell do I do now? What if he doesn't feel the same way? He might look at me that way but it hasn't been that long and this man has dug into my soul and I'm damned if I know what to do about it.*

He tried to forget the turmoil circling like an eagle in his head and concentrate on the man in his arms. "Luke, honey, it's going to be all right. Francis is still alive and so are you. The two of you will get a chance to talk this out. You have to believe that. Maybe I can go and see him, say hello from you. Is he still here in the hospital, or has he been discharged?"

Eddie's shuddering breaths started to abate. "He…he's still here. In a ward above." He grasped at Eddie's shoulder. "You have to go and see him for me. Tell him he deserves better than me, that he can find someone else who will treat him like he deserves. He's really special, Ed. You have to make him see that."

"You can tell me yourself, Luke," a soft voice said from the doorway. "We've both been bloody idiots."

***

Gideon turned from his soft stroking of Luke's hand and saw an ethereal, blond young man, pale and wan with light black spectacles on his nose. His thin wrists were covered in bandages. Luke made a sound that was part cry, part sob and Eddie stepped back as the youth moved over to Eddie's side and laid long fingers on his arm. Gideon assumed this was Francis from the tender look he gave Luke.

"You stupid sod," the blond whispered. "Why did you have to go and pull a Francis? You always have to one-up me."

Luke's arms reached out as they embraced.

Francis kissed Luke's lips gently. "We're a couple of selfish wankers, aren't we? Causing our families such trouble." The gentle kiss grew into something a little more heated and Eddie moved away to Gideon's side, feeling like a voyeur.

This is my little cousin making out with his boyfriend for God's sake.

Francis turned to look at them both. "Thanks so much for what you did," he whispered, his eyes tearful. "He's alive and so am I and that's all that really matters. Our folks are going to help us get through this." He ran thin fingers through Luke's straggly hair as Luke gazed at him with adoration. "We'll be fine, love."

"Maybe we should leave them alone," Eddie murmured. "I think they need to clear the air."

Gideon nodded, seeing his boyfriend's eyes suspiciously bright and his heartstrings tugged even more at his sensitive lover's emotional capacity to feel.

"Yeah, let's go grab coffee," he whispered back. His lips found Eddie's neck as he pressed butterfly kisses to the skin. "I feel like just being alone with you for a little while, appreciating what I have. You also need to call Taylor and Leslie or they'll be pissed as hell."

Minutes later they were sitting in the hospital garden, the sun shining down on them as they sipped bad coffee from polystyrene cups. Eddie had made his phone calls to the friends waiting for news and promised to be home soon.

Gideon gazed out with unseeing eyes across the neatly kept lawn and the beds of roses that edged the garden. "I can't imagine how two young men must have felt to get to that depth of despair that they think the world will be a better place without them." He shook his head in bemusement. "Those two will need a lot of support to get through this. At least they have each other it would seem."

"Yep." Eddie smiled at him, a soft, knowing smile." You were great with Luke. I saw another side to my man in there."

Gideon cocked an eyebrow. "Oh, so I have another official title besides the boyfriend now? I'm your *man*?"

Eddie nodded vigorously. "Oh yes. You're definitely mine."

Gideon couldn't suppress a shudder that ran from the tips of his toes to the top of his head at those confident, possessive words. He saw the heat in Eddie's eyes and the slow lick of his lips and he wished that they were anywhere other than in a public place. He wanted to get on his knees and give thanks to the sexy human being that was Eddie Tripp. And while he was on his knees…

Eddie chuckled. "God, you've become so damn transparent. I can see the lust in your eyes. This is a hospital for God's sake. Control yourself." His teasing tone lingered seductively. "Although if you wanted to put on a doctor's gown and play probe the patient with your sexy doctor tool, this patient wouldn't object." His wicked grin and dirty words made Gideon's cock take flight and press to get out of his jeans. He moved to try and accommodate his swelling erection.

"You are a damned tease. You wait until I get you home. I'll show you Doctor Gideon."

Eddie laughed. "As if that's a damn threat. You've got me in a state of anticipation now." He palmed his groin suggestively.

Gideon ignored the blatant gesture. If he didn't he'd be coming in his pants. "Talking of home, how long do you want to stay here? I know you'll want to see that Luke is really okay, although from what I saw earlier he's got a fighting chance at getting over this. As will Francis. I guess the news about him being gay still has to be broken to your aunt and uncle though and I'm guessing that you'll want to be there when Luke does that." He'd already spoken to both Sarah and Carmen who were running his restaurant in his absence. He was itching to get back but knew Eddie would stay behind on his own if he did. So he'd resigned himself to a short unplanned holiday in Norfolk so he could be with him. Carmen had gloatingly told him that he was hooked like a carp and Gideon had used a couple of choice words to tell her what he thought of that statement. It hadn't fazed her in the least.

Eddie's face softened. "You see, that's why I lo-like you. You know me so well." His skin grew rosier and his freckles stood out. Gideon heard the hitch in his voice as he corrected himself and decided not to go there yet.

Best leave that for when all this drama is over. We have enough on our plates at the moment without contending with the L word.

It still gave Gideon a warm and fuzzy feeling that Eddie might feel that way about him.

The fact Gideon still had some issues of his own to resolve didn't escape him. He wasn't wearing rose-tinted glasses but he'd definitely come a long way since meeting Eddie. If two young men could cheat death and still end up together, he was damn sure he could get over his own frailties and make sure it didn't adversely affect their relationship. Nightmares and insecurities about his lost sense be damned; with Eddie's warm body wrapped around him keeping him grounded, Gideon thought the nightmares deserved a rallying "fuck you" to their face. The therapy wasn't doing a bad job of helping either, even though he's begrudged the time and effort. As for the lost of smell and taste, he'd realised seeing Luke and Francis that simply being alive and having someone to care was enough.

***

Three days later, the journey home was filled with sadness, hope and expectation. Hope that the two young men would find their feet now their parents knew about them. Hope that said parents would support them on their journey to acceptance. Sadness because Eddie had to leave Luke behind: but with the promise of another trip to see them in the near future. Expectation because both Eddie and Gideon were as horny as goats since they didn't have sex at Eddie's parents' house.

The walls of the new-build home that Eddie's family lived in were so thin and Eddie and Gideon so vocal that it simply wasn't worth taking the chance on being heard calling for God in the middle of the night. So there had been the rather abortive attempt at mutual blowjobs in the carport behind Uncle Dave's car while the rest of the family were sleeping late one night. It was far enough from the house for no one to hear the swearing and entreaties to the God of fucking. However, some old dear had been highly vocal in her assertion to her husband that there were effing cats out in the courtyard making an effing noise and Gideon and Eddie had barely contained their sniggers. They had both managed to achieve their objective but it was slightly tarnished by the bucket of water thrown over them in the throes of their passion. They had also managed one fairly successful, highly contorted session in Gideon's car, which had led to Eddie pulling a muscle in his arse and Gideon bruising his hip on the gear stick. All in all, it had been interesting sex but not conducted with quite the finesse they were used to.

Gideon had enjoyed meeting Eddie's folks, Chloe and Frank, and had a great appreciation now for how Eddie had come to be. Frank was warm, rough-spoken, with twinkling eyes and he obviously adored his son. Chloe was quirky, rather scary in some ways but one of the most liberal women Gideon had ever met. Even he had blushed when she'd started chatting about gay man sex and the vagaries of rim jobs and blow jobs. Eddie had gone scarlet in embarrassment and gazed at his mother like Chicken Little expecting the sky to fall. It wasn't an experience Gideon wished to experience again anytime soon. While he and Eddie had enjoyed their time there they were both glad to get back on the road home.

They finally got to Gideon's apartment around nine p.m. Eddie's parents had insisted on taking them to a seafood restaurant in the town, one that had a good reputation if Frank was to be believed. Eddie had worked there as a sous-chef in his early start into the food business and the manager still waxed lyrical about his chef talent. It hadn't been a patch on Galileo's in Gideon's opinion but then nothing measured up to his restaurant. It had been a replete but tired couple of men that had finally boarded Ellie for the trip home. They were both glad to walk through the doors into Gideon's flat.

Gideon was in the wet room shower washing off the dirt and grime of the day when he felt a lithe form press itself against his back. The familiar presence of a hard-on indicated it was a man with definite needs and the slow swirl of a warm tongue in his ear made him shiver in delight.

Strong hands ran themselves down his flanks and then reached over to grasp his cock in a firm grip. He smiled and leaned back against Eddie as water ran down their bodies.

"Couldn't wait, sexy?" He teased as his hands reached back and drew Eddie's lips down for a kiss. Eddie's erection slid between his arse cheeks as he pressed himself closer. Gideon's body prickled with need, with want and he turned to face his boyfriend. Eddie's face was pink from the warm water and steam, his freckles standing out starkly against his pale, smooth skin. His deep red hair was plastered to his head like wet, richly coloured silk and some of it fell forward, obscuring eyes that looked at Gideon with such affection and lust.

"I want to be inside you." Eddie's whispered words sent a shiver down Gideon's spine and sent an immediate signal to his already hardened cock to stand up further and take notice. Eddie loved to top him when he was in the mood, and it was an experience and a half. He had a latent instinct to be a bossy and dominating brat when he took control and Gideon loved every minute of that side of his lover. He swiped his tongue lasciviously across Eddie's wet lips and grinned.

"Then do it. You don't need to ask. Take what you want. I'm all yours." The words had never been truer for Gideon. He was definitely no longer a free man, and while his heart wanted to make that very clear to Eddie, his head told him to go slow. He didn't want to ruin this thing they had by jumping the gun.

Eddie growled and bit Gideon's earlobe as his hands reached for the ever-present packet of lube in the shower tray. Gideon heard the rip of the packet and then words from his lips fell like explosive bullets into the steam of the shower. He didn't even know he was going to say them until they were in the air, lingering there like soft droplets of misty liquid.

"Forget the condom. I want this bare."

Eddie stilled behind him and Gideon closed his eyes and swallowed. They'd always used condoms but tonight, he wanted to feel Eddie and *only* him.

"Uhmm, Gideon, that's a new play rule." Eddie sounded unsure although there was a definite hint of excitement in his tone. "I know we're clean because we've talked about it but are you sure?" His hard-on pushed against Gideon's arse, needy and more excited than ever and Gideon nodded.

"I'm sure, if you are. I want to feel skin inside me, not latex. I want to feel Eddie." His soft words seemed to inflame Eddie and Gideon gasped as rough fingers breached him, fingers that were slick with lube, and his arse was delightfully filled. Eddie breathed heavily against the back of Gideon's neck. Gideon leaned forward and bent his knees to accommodate his shorter lover, splaying his hands against the shower wall. Eddie pushed eager fingers inside him, and Gideon rocked back in pleasure, fucking himself on them.

"Eddie, I don't need all the arse play. Just get yourself inside me. Please."

The feeling of Eddie sliding into him with his bare cock, his wet skin against his arse was like Nirvana. Gideon cried out at the sensation of hot, silky flesh impaling him as Eddie began moving with deep strokes, gripping Gideon's hips so tightly he knew he'd have bruises there. The sound of wet flesh slapping his, the intimacy of having his man deep inside him, as he grunted in pleasure and licked Gideon's skin, made Gideon's head swim as the sensations deepened. Eddie got rougher and Gideon closed his eyes and revelled in the moment. The hiss of the water, the heat of the shower steam, the groans of his lover, the sensation of being filled and wanted—it made Gideon feel like they were the only two people that mattered, that this was a moment of deep significance.

"Oh God, you feel so amazing," Eddie groaned as his cock pounded Gideon. "I know you always feel good but fuck, this is too good to bear much longer." He bit down on Gideon's shoulder and Gideon hissed with pain. "I am going to come in your arse, no barriers, that's just…" His voice tailed off as he gave a loud groan and Gideon felt the pulsing of his cock in his sensitive channel as Eddie emptied himself. The mere thought of Eddie's come inside of him made Gideon dizzy and he took one hand off the wall and fisted his cock desperately. It didn't take long and he thought he'd have come without even touching himself, the eroticism of the whole beautiful act he and Eddie were performing enough to make him orgasm. He cried out loudly as he climaxed, clenching around Eddie. His boyfriend moaned softly at the sensation of Gideon's muscles clasping his spent cock. Gideon's chest was heaving as he spurted against the shower wall and over his belly. His legs threatened to give way. The water continued to flow, showering them with warm jets, washing away the sweat and the semen from their bodies. Gideon felt a sense of loss at that. He wanted Eddie's come inside him, wanted to feel for that little bit longer Eddie's claiming of his body.

Eddie chuckled behind him as he drew out. Gideon turned to see him lean against the back shower wall, his emerald eyes with their wet, sandy lashes gazing at Gideon with a look that couldn't be mistaken. Gideon's breath stopped at that look. It was possession, lust, desire…and love.

Decision made, Gideon reached over and framed Eddie's face in his hands, leaning his forehead against his as his chest tightened at the words he was about to say.

"I love you, Eddie Tripp," he whispered. "I truly do."

Eddie's eyes widened and for a moment, Gideon had a heart-wrenching fear that he'd said the wrong thing. Then Eddie's wide mouth curved in a huge smile and his mouth found Gideon's and took possession of that too. When he finally released a gasping and breathless Gideon, his eyes were bright. They were also wet, but Gideon gave him the benefit of the doubt, pretending that it was the spray from the shower.

"I love you too," Eddie murmured. "I've never fallen so damn hard for someone in my whole life. This is it for me. *You* are it for me."

Gideon laughed in relief. "Thank God for that," he said as he reached over to turn off the water. "I thought maybe I'd moved too fast, spoiled things—"

Eddie shook his head as he drew back the screen and stepped past Gideon to get a towel. "No, that was just the perfect moment. Baring your soul after we did it bareback? I think that's a commitment to each other." He grinned as he vigorously towelled his hair dry before wrapping the towel around his waist. Gideon stepped out and did the same, marvelling at the feeling in his chest. *I just told another man I loved him. I've never said that before. It feels good. I should have done it sooner.*

"I meant it," he said quietly as he watched Eddie brush his unruly curls back. "I know it's not been long, but it just seems right, this connection you and I have. I want to see where it goes."

Eddie's face softened. "I do too. Let's just wallow in this moment before we start second guessing ourselves." His face grew mischievous. "I suggest we order something in, eat ourselves silly, then go back to bed and have more raunchy sex. How's that for a plan?"

Gideon certainly had no problem with that. "My choice of takeaway tonight," he said. "Last time you ordered that god-awful Thai stuff that looked like shit and had no redeeming qualities whatsoever. I fancy some good old-fashioned pizza. Extra olives and mushrooms. Deal?"

"Deal," Eddie agreed as he wandered out of the bathroom. Gideon watched his slim hips and pert backside disappear and grinned at himself in the mirror. This being in love thing wasn't so bad after all. For the first time in a very long time Gideon Kent was truly happy.

Chapter 16

A week later, Eddie was busy in the restaurant kitchen cleaning up. He'd volunteered to do the whole kitchen clean down himself as he was staying over again anyway and everyone else was going to some late night concert. Suddenly a pair of warm hands covered his eyes. The perfume was familiar and he grinned.

"Carmen, honey," he drawled, crumpling up the tea towel he held and throwing it in the laundry basket. "What are you still doing here so late? I thought everyone had gone home already."

The hands left his eyes and he turned around. Carmen stood there, her dark kohl-lined eyes gazing at him and the smirk on her face reminding him of a Cheshire cat.

"What? That look normally means trouble for me. What's up?"

"Oh, nothing." Carmen shook black clad shoulders. "I was just wondering how you and lover boy are doing now that you've proclaimed undying love for each other."

Eddie flushed. "Carmen," he growled. "I told you that in confidence."

Well, he'd declared it to her in a drunken, happy haze more like it, when the two of them had gone bar hopping to find the best Tequila Sunrise in London. He shuddered at the memory of going home to his own place, on one of those rare nights he did, to have a very unsympathetic Leslie put him to bed after Eddie had vomited all over his prized Christian Louboutins.

Carmen laughed, a raucous sound that sounded like a flock of cawing crows. "Honey, the staff are all clubbing together to buy you a thank-you present. We now have a boss who smiles every day, is a lot more relaxed, actually joins in at some of the socials because you're there and he's not the miserable git he used to be." She prodded Eddie's chest with a purple-tipped finger. "And that, my friend, is all *your* doing. You have been the best thing to happen to him since ever." Her tone was affectionate and there was no doubt that she meant every word she said from the look on her face.

Eddie felt warmth flush his face and a strange feeling of complete and utter satisfaction flood his body.

He nodded. "Gideon *is* a different man. He still has nightmares now but they aren't as extreme. He's still seeing his therapist, Martin, but he thinks he's doing so well, that there might only be a couple more sessions. He's sleeping better, and he hasn't had a panic attack since coming back from Norfolk." He flushed. "We're talking about moving in together but I'm not sure I'm ready for that yet."

Carmen smiled at him. "You're crazy about him, Eddie, and he you. It makes sense to stay together."

Eddie smirked "Well, you give a man hip-wrenching, mind-blowing sex and he's yours to keep forever. I know exactly how to keep my man interested."

Carmen rolled her eyes at him. "I've no doubt the two of you are heating up the sheets if that moaning the other night from his office was anything to go by. The whole damn staff knew what you two were doing."

Eddie swallowed as his face grew hotter. "We weren't doing anything," he blustered, knowing she wouldn't believe him–truth be told, neither would he. If it was the night he was thinking about, the night Gideon had taken him over his desk in a big bad boss-and-employee role play in which they'd gotten very invested. He was surprised the whole of London hadn't heard his screams of delight as Gideon 'disciplined' him. "And besides, it was after hours. No one should have been here."

No sooner were the words out than he wished he'd kept his mouth shut.

Carmen cackled again. "Busted!" she yelled, brandishing her plum-coloured fingertips at him. "It so happens me and Jerome were here, as well Andy. We'd been to the club down the road and came back to pick up Andy's train ticket home which he'd left here in his work clothes." She winked wickedly. "Jerome was tickled pink and Andy—well, he was just mortified. I had to give him a double brandy to calm his nerves." The glint in her eye belied the tall story.

Eddie scowled. "Well, they should be so lucky to have a boyfriend with a huge dick and an overwhelming desire for his young and extremely sexy boyfriend." He crossed his arms across his chest smugly as he gained momentum. "Perhaps we should be putting on a show and charging for this activity if everyone's going to start listening to us and pretending it's the latest episode of *Porn Star for Hire*."

Carmen's eyes widened in glee as she looked behind Eddie.

"Gideon's there, isn't he?" Eddie said resignedly. Carmen burst into peals of laughter as Gideon's smoky voice echoed in Eddie's ears, causing his toes to curl and his trousers to grow tight.

"Wow, Eddie, go giving away all our secrets, why don't you." Gideon's sexy drawl never failed to turn Eddie on. Gideon moved up behind his boyfriend and put his arms around his upper arms, pinning them to his side. "Maybe we should show Carmen here how we do the whole rope tying-up thing and how you beg me to bend you over and—"

Carmen let out a screech. "Oh God, someone pour bleach in my ears. That, I don't need to hear. I'm going home." She turned to Gideon. "That spreadsheet you wanted is finally finished. I had to recreate it from scratch." She flapped a hand at him. "Your new PC will be delivered in the morning, by the way. Do you think you might like to look after this one and not go all ape shit on it?"

Gideon scowled. "I suppose I might be able to do that."

Carmen sniggered. "I'll send you the bill, boss man." She grinned and reached over to give each of them a smacking kiss. "See you Thursday, boys. I have the next two days off. See you!" Carmen disappeared, leaving Eddie still captured in Gideon's arms. He didn't mind at all, he admitted to himself. There was nowhere else he'd rather be.

Gideon leaned in and nibbled his earlobe, then dragged his wet tongue down Eddie's neck. Eddie closed his eyes and shivered. Goose bumps flourished on his pale skin.

"I never get tired of doing this to you," Gideon murmured. "Making you shiver, seeing your skin all bumpy because of what I do to you. Do you have any idea what a turn-on it is to see it?"

"I can feel it," Eddie said huskily as he tilted his head to one side, giving Gideon better access to his skin. "That thing in your pants needs some TLC from the feel of it."

Gideon released him and pulled Eddie around to take his mouth in a bruising kiss that left Eddie weak kneed and wilting. He wrapped his arms around Gideon's neck as he pushed his hips against Gideon's groin. For a while there was no other sound besides lips wetly smacking together, low moans and groans and the occasional rusting of clothing as each man found his way to warm skin and leaking cocks. Hands wrapped around each other, they kissed slow and deeply and when Eddie came in Gideon's hand with a shudder and a muffled expletive, Gideon wasn't far behind. They stood, breathless and sticky and Gideon's nose wrinkled.

"Ugh. God, this room honks of us both. Sweat and jizz. Someone should bottle it."

The words didn't factor at first and then Eddie stilled, his heart literally missing a beat as he took a deep breath at the import of Gideon's words. He'd heard them but still couldn't believe it.

"What did you say?" He moved away from Gideon and tucked his limp cock back into his chef trousers. Gideon was doing the same but he looked a little confused.

"What? I said we reeked—" His voice tailed off and his eyes widened. His nostrils flared and a look of stupefaction crossed his face. Eddie couldn't stop the grin from splitting his face in half, couldn't stop his eyes stinging with sudden tears of hope and thankfulness. The same look of wonder that Eddie thought was on his face was now reflected on his lover's.

"Eddie, I can smell us." Gideon's voice was awed, whispering the words as if by doing so he hoped no one could take this incredible moment away. His eyes darkened, suspiciously wet and to Eddie, he looked…radiant. His hands were shaking as he tucked in his shirt and Eddie danced over to him in glee.

"Wow, that's awesome news. Can you still smell it? Can you smell anything else, like my aftershave or food odours?"

Gideon shook his head in a daze. "I could smell our come and your sweat—" He sniffed the air experimentally like a dog "—and I can sort of smell something spicy. It's very faint but it's there." He seemed to finally realise the breakthrough he'd just had. "Jesus, my sense of smell is coming back. Martin said it could happen, that at any time I might get it back as my brain allowed me to sense it." His face shadowed. "God, what happens if I start cooking again and can't stand the smell of meat cooking? What if I have a flashback, or a panic attack?" His voice caught and he moved towards Eddie, holding out his arms.

Eddie reached over and wrapped Gideon in his instead. "Gideon, love, stop second guessing the whole thing. It's just one milestone. Let's not get too ahead of ourselves and think of the bad stuff."

He looked around the room and felt a thrill of satisfaction when he spied a packet of chewing gum sitting on the kitchen counter top.

He opened the packet and popped a piece of gum into his mouth and started chewing.

Gideon's eyebrows waggled and he looked at Eddie with confusion. "What the hell are you doing? You don't eat gum normally."

Eddie kept chewing and motioned for Gideon to wait. Finally he finished and with a grimace, he took it out of his mouth and threw it into the nearby bin. "Ugh. I'll never understand how you can chew that muck. It's awful."

Then he bounded back to Gideon as he watched in bemusement and latched onto his mouth. "Can you taste me?" he whispered into Gideon's mouth. "Please tell me you can." His lips sought Gideon's urgently and Gideon's mouth opened as their tongues met and slicked against each other. When Eddie drew back, Gideon was looking at him with eyes that drank him in, the expression of joy and relief on his face giving Eddie his answer.

"It's faint," Gideon said breathlessly, "but I taste peppermint. I can taste you, Eddie." His voice trembled with emotion. "Jesus…" Eddie's eyes pricked with hot tears at the wonder in Gideon's tone.

"It's a start," Eddie reached up, wrapping arms around Gideon's neck and resting his forehead against Gideon's. "Let's hope it gets better. But you know what?" He kissed Gideon tenderly. "Even if this is all it is, then I'm happy for you. God, I'm happy for me. Now all that expensive aftershave I wear won't be for nothing. My man can appreciate it now."

Gideon gave a choked chuckle and bear-hugged Eddie until he thought he might pass out from lack of air. They stood together like that for a while before Gideon reluctantly pulled away and wiped his eyes with his sleeve. He tried to do it nonchalantly but Eddie knew he was having trouble suppressing tears. His tough man was just a softy deep inside.

"I guess we should finish up here, and then we're going to celebrate with a bottle of the best champagne and go to bed." Gideon's eyebrows rose suggestively. "I'd like the chance to get up close and personal with that aftershave of yours. Maybe with other things as well." He slapped Eddie's backside hard and Eddie yowled.

Gideon grinned. "Come on, gorgeous. Let's get this place spick and span and then I'll steal a bottle from the cellar. I might even let you pour it over me and lick it all off." And with that parting shot that made Eddie's cock stand up and take immediate attention, he grabbed a cloth and a bottle of spray cleaner and with a jaunty spring in his step, he disappeared over to the far counter to wipe down the counter. Eddie watched him go with a grin then picked up his own cloth.

Way to go. That man will be the death of me with his throwaway comments.

Eddie knew that Gideon's high would soon disappear as his logical mind came to terms with what had happened. Getting his sense of smell back was a huge step and Eddie hoped it would continue to get better. The fact Gideon was already worrying about his senses bringing back memories of his ordeal in the fire was troubling. Eddie hoped that it would all work out. But he knew that no matter what lay ahead for them both, he wasn't going anywhere. Gideon was stuck with him and whatever they were going through, it would be together. As he watched his boyfriend whistling as he polished and cleaned, Eddie thanked God for whatever it was had brought them both to this place.

The fact he loved the man senseless was certainly a step in the right direction. The fact he was loved back—that was a definite plus in his book.

SIGHT AND SINNERS

Chapter 1

The man Taylor was blowing definitely didn't know how the hell to keep quiet. Taylor's lips were wrapped around his dick, while above him a man stood, panting and moaning, turning the air blue with his curses. Taylor stopped what he was doing, making the blowjob recipient groan in dismay as he glared at the sweaty face above him.

"For Christ's sake, Georgie, can you stop it with the fucking porn noises?" He glanced around him nervously. "This is where I work, damn it, and if anyone hears you they'll come outside to see what all the fuss is about."

Georgie's wide eyes cast a quick glance around the deserted alleyway behind 'Music Mayhem' where Taylor was employed, then looked down at Taylor kneeling between his legs.

"Sorry, mate, it's just that you're so damn good at this and it's been a while."

Taylor felt a surge of pride at that praise and went back to what he'd been doing. A few minutes later, he'd successfully made Georgie blow his load, while keeping the ruckus to a few grunts and sighs. Taylor had been jacked off by Georgie's rough hands, and watched as the satisfied thirty-year-old bricklayer went back to the building site he worked at. Taylor rubbed his mouth, still tasting *eau de* hunky builder and sighed. He and Georgie were a long-standing arrangement, buddies even to the point of sharing a few beers after work, but Taylor was really getting fed up of the casual sexual encounters. He wanted something else. A Gideon and Eddie relationship perhaps.

Oh yes, that would be an idea. I could stop all this damn nonsense in cold alleyways.

Taylor gave another deep sigh, made sure he had no stray spunk on his clothing and opened the back alley door to get back to work.

Sometimes life sucked.

***

Blood and faeces. They were pungent smells that ripped into his nostrils and made his eyes water. The soft light of the dimly lit room cast shadows, gargoyles looming on red speckled walls. Somewhere in the room, a clock did what it was made to do. *Tick. Tick. Tick.* The air was heavy with the scent of death, redolent with grief and pain. It sucked the breath out of his body, leaving him helpless, useless.

Taylor screamed, gut-wrenching sounds that pierced through the heaviness of the air of his bedroom, as he fought his way out of the hell he found himself in. His hands grasped at bed covers that were already creased and wet with sweat and as his eyes snapped open in panic and despair. He took a deep, shuddering breath and shot upright in bed.

It was a chilly February night and although the window was open to let cool air in, the room was stuffy and smelled stale. Taylor thudded back against the wall and shivered as his naked back hit the peeling plaster, causing goose bumps to form on his clammy skin.

His bedroom door was flung open and a warm, male-scented bundle leapt onto his bed, wiry arms reaching for him to pull him close against a silky chest.

"Oh my God, Tay, you fucking scared me to death with that scream of yours!" Taylor's housemate, Leslie, gazed at him in horror from eyes still crusted in sleep and hollowed with dark shadows. The last few nights had been keeping Leslie awake as well, as he came to Taylor's aid when the nightmares hit with the force of an Acme sledgehammer raining down upon Taylor's head.

"What the hell is going on, sweetie? Where are these horrible dreams coming from?" Leslie's dark eyes framed with long lashes regarded Taylor with concern and fear. Taylor shuddered as Leslie's fingers combed themselves though his sticky, wet hair and the closeness of his slim body gave solace to Taylor's shaking form.

"The fuck I know, *chéri.*" Taylor heaved a deep breath. His French roots were buried deep and he didn't have a good grasp of the language apart from schoolboy-type phrases when he and his family had travelled to Provence for family holidays. His father had insisted on English at home despite his Mauritian-born mother speaking French. "It's the third time this week, different each time but still the same, you know?"

Leslie stared at him blankly. Taylor sighed and shifted in the bed, grimacing at the boxers stuck in the crack of his backside and groin. He reached down to pull them out and stop the constriction currently threatening to dissect his balls in half. Leslie let him go and sat back, his blue silk pyjama-clad body curling like a cat against the wall. Despite his emotional state, Taylor let out a soft chuckle. Even in the hot, humid nights, Leslie looked like a courtesan ready to please a prince. His innate sense of "good fashion or death" existed even when he slept. Leslie had always said if he died in his sleep, he wanted to go out with a sense of style.

"I mean, it's the same scene—the blood, the despair—but each time the dream shows me the whole thing from a different angle. It will stop soon, like it always does. It's just the whole initial phase thing of someone's death that affects me."

Not for the first time Taylor cursed his abilities, abilities that had plagued him since he was five years old. This whole "psychic" element of his psyche was really started to piss him off. He hadn't asked for it and he as sure as fuck didn't really want it.

But if I hadn't got this ability, I wouldn't have been able to help Eddie find Luke. Luke would have died.

Some months ago, using his abilities, Taylor had managed to help his ex-housemate, Eddie, prevent his younger cousin from dying from a suicide attempt.

"But you normally only feel this sort of thing if you're close to someone, Tay; that's how you say it works." Leslie's voice trembled. "So it must be someone you know, or somebody they are close to." His eyes widened. "Oh God, it can't be Eddie or Gideon, can it? Please tell me they're okay." He bounced on the bed in agitation, his dark black bangs falling over his face, obscuring cobalt blue eyes. "Could it be your dad?"

Taylor reached out and stayed his friend's anxious movements. "No, Leslie, it's none of them." Eddie had moved in a month ago with his boyfriend, Gideon, into the flat above the restaurant Gideon owned in Soho. "The lads are probably rutting like rabbits even as we speak."

Leslie gave a small giggle and Taylor smiled tiredly.

"As for my dad…" His face twisted. "I'm not that close to him anymore since mum died and he remarried. The last time I spoke to him was about two months ago." He shrugged. He'd intended going home to Bristol for Christmas but his father had told him he and Meg were going on a skiing holiday. So Taylor had spent the festive season with his friends instead.

He leaned back and reached over for his packet of cigarettes on the nightstand. He didn't miss Leslie's gimlet-eyed stare but he ignored it. He lit one up and took a deep, satisfying drag, making sure he didn't blow smoke anywhere near Leslie. He knew he'd get smacked if he did.

"You do know those things are going to kill you, right?" Leslie's voice was disapproving.

Taylor shrugged. "Something will one day. We never know when it's going to hit." Even to his own ears, his voice was bitter. Lately Taylor had been so taken over by his psychic abilities that his tiredness and the constant drain on his energies was beginning to defeat him. It was why he'd started smoking again after two years of abstinence. He had no idea why he was so in tune with the dead and the dying lately, but it seemed he was on high alert, that all the psychic karma in the fucking universe was raining down on his head.

Leslie's beautiful face darkened. "Stop it. I know you've had some really tough nights recently, but you need to suck it up. Something out there"—he waved a pale, long-fingered hand—"is going on with someone you know and that's why you're all tuning-forky."

Taylor took another drag of his cigarette and blew a lazy smoke ring in the air. It wafted toward Leslie. Taylor flapped it away in a panic.

"I have no idea who it can be though. Yes, I need to be pretty aware of someone before it affects me like this but everyone I know—small circle though that may be—is fit and healthy and I haven't got a clue who's in trouble."

He sucked the last bit of life out of his cigarette then stabbed it into the ashtray on the table. He leaned back against the wall and closed his eyes, his weariness soaking into his body.

Leslie regarded him thoughtfully. "How long has it been since you had any?"

Taylor opened one eye to look at his friend. "Are you talking anal sex, blow jobs, frotting, hand jobs, rimming …be more specific, Leslie." His tone was amused.

Leslie bounced on the bed, his eyes wide and his hands flapping in true Leslie style. "I mean, if you'd had a one-night stand, or a back-alley quickie…" He pursed his lips in that adorable pouty way he had and Taylor was entranced at the sight. "And I mean a back alley behind a building, not your back alley…although that works as well. Maybe it might be one of those guys you're feeling?"

Taylor had to admit the thought had crossed his mind. What he hadn't wanted to admit was that a casual encounter could affect him this way, as that would mean his abilities were more vulnerable now. He needed significant emotional closeness to pick up on the vibrations and emotions of a person, or something or someone affecting that person. But if what Leslie was suggesting was true, it meant that last night's frantic blow job behind the music store with Georgie, the quick, messy sex last week in the toilet stall of a club down the road, and the urgent mutual hand job in a car two weeks ago might all be related to what he now felt. And Taylor wasn't sure he could cope with that amount of mental and emotional stress.

He drew back the covers to his bed. "I'm too tired to think about it now. Come on, get in," he murmured. "I could do with someone beside me tonight." Not for the first time he wondered why he and Leslie had never taken their nightly cuddles and comforts any further. Sure, they'd shared a couple of hot kisses and jerked each other off once or twice, but neither of them had any inclination to pursue a real relationship. They were simply good friends. Leslie slid into the bed beside Taylor, the silk of his pyjamas a sensual touch against Taylor's bare back, his body warmth welcome. He pulled the covers over them as Leslie snuggled in behind him.

"Watch what you do with that thing," Taylor muttered. "I don't know where it's been."

Leslie chuckled softly. "And I'm not going to tell you," he retorted. "Suffice it to say lately it hasn't seen much action, so honestly? I can't promise I won't ravish you while you sleep."

"Well, slip it in quietly," Taylor said sleepily as his eyes shut. "And make sure you stick a sleeve on it before you do. I don't want to get pregnant."

Leslie's sweet laugh echoed in his ears as he fell asleep.

Chapter 2

Draven swore loudly and threw the mug he was holding across the room. It flew through the air like a cricket ball to a batsman and came to a stop when it hit the wall. Dark fluid spun out of it like an explosion of crap from a baby and the mug shattered into shards, which spiralled down to the floor. He watched the mayhem he'd caused as his hands clenched at his sides and his lips curled.

"Fucking stupid bastard," he growled. He paced around the room resembling a tawny cougar ready to spring: lithe, taut and infinitely dangerous.

He ran a hand through his hair and swore again. "Fucker. I can't believe he did this to me." His gut churned with pangs of guilt at thinking about what might be the reason for his recall. But if it was what he thought, it honestly hadn't been a big deal in his eyes—certainly not enough to be kicked off this case.

He picked up the piece of paper currently residing innocently on the kitchen table and tore it in two with one vicious action. Then he did it again and let the pieces flutter to the floor. He kicked the pieces and then stomped on them for good measure. He'd printed the email purely so he could abuse it. When his temper tantrum was spent and he had his breathing under control, Draven whirled around to pick up his mobile. He jabbed numbers into the phone as if it was being punished then narrowed his eyes as he waited for the person on the other side to pick up.

"Clay Mortimer here." The drawled tones of the man on the other side only inflamed Draven more. He felt his face go puce and he looked at his phone as if were a mortal enemy before raising it to his ear again. He went onto the offensive in his usual Draven way.

"You traitorous sack of shit. How the fuck could you do this to me, you arsehole?"

"Ah, Draven." The voice sounded amused and Draven bit his bottom lip to keep from spitting at the phone in fury. "I thought I'd be hearing from you. Got my email, did you?"

"You took me off the damn case, Clay. You're recalling me to London and letting that simpering twat Jeremy Flaherty take over from me. This was my case, and I should be the one to finish it."

Draven glared out across the waters of the Adriatic, the crystal blue sea no panacea at the moment to his anger. The city of Dubrovnik had been his home now for nearly a month, and the case he was working on for Mortimer Investigations on the outskirts of London was almost over. It had been a difficult decision to leave his younger brother Jude behind in the hospital for any length of time but it wasn't as if he'd know Draven was gone anyway. Draven was on tenterhooks every time his phone rang, thinking it might be news about Jude's condition. For better or worse, he wasn't sure which news he dreaded the most.

That thought didn't make him feel better and the sinking, hollow feeling in his stomach hadn't dissipated. Draven had hoped his anger would feel more righteous than it was. He'd tried to rationalise it, but the truth was he had fucked up. Badly. And now he was paying the price.

"You have to let me finish this one, Clay. I am so close to getting the bastard who stole the blueprints; I just need another week. I can do this, I promise. The fact Ian is involved…"

Clay's cool voice interrupted his ramblings. "That would be Ian Ramsey, our informant? The man you've been sleeping with and who now threatens to compromise this whole case that we've been working on for over six months?"

Draven growled again. "I haven't been sleeping with him. I've been fucking him. There's a difference. We're just bed buddies." He tried once again to rationalise it. "And it was only three times. It's not like I'm going to ask the guy to marry me and bear my children, for Christ's sake."

"As entertaining as the idea of you in a suit swearing fidelity and allegiance to one man is, Draven, the fact remains that this man, this informant, is a delicate asset and not one I need compromised in any way. If the powers that be in government found out you two had a relationship, purely carnal or not, it would undermine this agency's credibility, and no one, I repeat, no one, fucks with the credibility of my agency." Clay's voice was hardened steel and even Draven baulked. "Am I making myself quite clear?"

Draven scowled and mouthed "Fuck you" at his phone.

And fuck you, Ian, you miserable, smarmy little git for being so damn fuckable.

The irony of that inner thought didn't escape Draven and he snarled quietly.

"Ahh, you're still there then? I recognise that rather nasty sound. There are return air tickets to London downstairs at the reception desk. You leave tomorrow. Jeremy will arrive tonight and you can debrief him." Clay's voice was dry. "And by debrief him, Draven, I mean update him on the case, not yank his pants down and stick your dick in him like you did with Ian. Although I have to say, I'm not sure Jeremy swings your way so it would be one helluva surprise to him if you did."

To add fuel to Draven's fury, Clay Mortimer snorted in amusement.

His temper rose again. "You are so fucking funny, you know that, Clay? Fine. I'll tell all to good old Jeremy when he gets here but he isn't going to get the job done like I would and you know it. I screwed up with Ian but that doesn't affect my ability to do my job."

There was silence on the other end of the phone and for a minute Draven thought he might be given a reprieve. Then he heard a deep sigh.

"Draven, you are one of my best operatives. You're tough, driven and highly motivated. But you have this self-destructive flaw to screw things up and think with your dick. Ian Ramsey is, as we speak, trying to get a better deal for himself by saying he was sexually harassed by the man who was supposed to be watching and helping him—that would be you, by the way—to get the information we need to prove that Kyle Enterprises is stealing government secrets." He coughed. "He has video footage of the two of you going at it like weasels. He said you seduced him into sex to keep him sweet and on our side."

Draven's jaw dropped and his hands grew clammy.

That fucking handsome, sexy little tosser. He stitched me over. How the fuck did I lose my focus like that? And, weasels? I obviously need to work on my technique.

But he knew. It had been Ian's charm, his sparkling blue eyes and oh-so kissable mouth, that tight arse and flat abs encased in denim and tight tank tops that had sent the blood rushing to Draven's groin and led him to bend Ian over the couch, the balcony and the private casino table at the swanky Christo Club.

"Furthermore, I've had to eat humble pie and grovel a bit and you know that never goes down well with me. I've managed to salvage the situation and made him some promises I'm going to have to keep, but you fucked this one up. He played you, Draven. Like a bloody harp."

Draven stared blindly out into the falling twilight of the early February evening. He felt cold and more than a little sick to his stomach at the colossal mess-up he'd made because of a piece of arse. He couldn't justify his lapse in judgement any longer.

"Draven, are you there?"

God, does he actually sound worried about me? Jude, it looks like Clay does have a heart after all.

Draven had been one of Clay's men for the past six years and he'd been a great support to Draven, especially after the tragedy—the car accident that had killed Draven's parents and left his little brother in a coma. His boss had picked up a drunken and almost senseless Draven from the bars and pavements with monotonous regularity. However, friendship and compassion notwithstanding, Clay had blood like ice water when it came to business, and now Draven had let him down. A true blue British cock-up, no less.

"Yes, I'm here," he said quietly. "I'll be back in London tomorrow and you can haul me over the coals again then."

Clay's voice softened. "Draven, you fucked up. It happens. That doesn't detract from the fact that you've had more successes than failures and you're the best man on my team. Come home and we can find you another assignment." There was a low chuckle. "Maybe I can find you a woman to work with; then I don't have to worry about that dick of yours getting into trouble." He sniggered and Draven growled softly. "Come by the office tomorrow afternoon before you go home. We can talk then. And say hello to Jude for me when you see him. Tell him his Uncle Clay is thinking about him." His voice was warm with concern and Draven blinked, his throat tight.

The line went dead. Draven laid his phone down on the kitchen table and went to the fridge. He took out a bottle of Stolichnaya vodka and fetched a glass from the cupboard. Then he made his way out to the balcony and sat down to gaze with unseeing eyes across the ocean.

May as well finish the bottle so I don't waste it now I'm going home.

The fact the bottle was half full had not escaped him. He only hoped that he'd be sober enough to fly home the next morning without puking his guts out into a paper bag.

Chapter 3

Taylor sipped his rum and Coke and sighed as he gazed around the restaurant. Galileo's was one of his favourite places to eat, mainly because the sous-chef was one of his two best friends here in London. Eddie Tripp had been a housemate until he'd moved out and moved in with his new boyfriend, the owner of Galileo's. Gideon Kent was an acquired taste: a rather growly, sarcastic individual with a rather tragic incident in his past. Yet in Eddie's hands the man was putty. Genuinely slippery and completely mouldable goo. Taylor appreciated Eddie's choice. Gideon was very tasty indeed if you looked past the scowling.

The restaurant was frenetic, testament to the great service and exceptional food. Taylor had come here to celebrate the end of the nightmares that had plagued him recently. They'd ceased about two days ago, and while he wasn't sleeping well, he *was* sleeping. He hadn't yet found out who had come to a grim end or how but he knew he would sooner or later.

He'd wanted Leslie to come with him but Leslie had apparently got a hot date. Taylor just hoped the guy had stamina, as Leslie had spent the day anticipating what he would do to him. His friend could be extremely creative.

Taylor watched as a man entered the venue and stared around fiercely. He was definitely worth looking at, he mused idly. Broad shoulders, blond hair, a rather curvy arse and a pair of strong legs currently encased in black chinos. He was shown to a table near the window and Taylor tried not to be too obvious as he watched the front of house manager attend to her customer's needs.

I'd like to attend to his needs. I'm sure he would make me very needy too. God, why don't gay guys wear a button or something so we know whether it's worth pursuing?

Taylor smirked and watched the sexy stranger pick up his menu. As he did, he lifted his eyes. They met Taylor's, and for a minute Taylor lost his breath. Mr. Mysterious had eyes as dark as grey slate, with straight brows and the longest, sexiest eyelashes Taylor had ever seen. The two men stared at each other for a moment, the other man's gaze challenging and open, his eyebrows raised quizzically until finally Taylor dropped his glance. He looked down quickly at his plate of spaghetti Alfredo as if he'd discovered the Holy Grail in it. For some reason, that confident, sexy stare had unnerved him like no other. He thought the man looked rather familiar, but recognition eluded him.

Taylor fiddled with his fork, twirling some pasta onto it and raising it to his mouth. As he did so, he couldn't help notice that Mr. Mysterious was still staring at him, his gaze hooded. Taylor shovelled the food into his mouth then licked sauce off his lips. Twice. The man watching him tensed slightly then looked away as a waitress approached his side with a drink.

What the hell? I feel like I know him. And he seemed a little rattled at my lip licking. At least that worked. Perhaps he does *bat for my team.*

That idea made him smirk. He risked another quick glance over at the man as he sipped his drink. Blond and hunky had now got his food and was eating it in quick, economical bites as if he expected it to run away and he needed to eat it before it did. There was nothing sloppy about it, just focused, structured movements of his knife and fork. He ate what looked like a rather large steak, putting in between full, pink lips. He didn't look Taylor's way again.

Taylor appraised him idly and ran his tongue wetly around the rim of the glass, just in case he looked up. He had it on good authority that the move was a guaranteed show starter when he did it. He heard a gentle cough to his left side and glanced over. Gideon Kent stood there, his handsome face amused and his hazel eyes glinting in the dimmed light of the wall sconces.

"Seen something you like, Taylor?" His deep voice echoed softly in the quiet of the alcove where Taylor sat. Gideon looked immaculate in his dark blue tailored business suit, coupled with a pale blue button-down that hugged his muscular chest. If Gideon wasn't spoken for, Taylor would definitely have made a play for him. As it was, he felt guilty for lusting after the man when he was in a relationship with his best friend.

He waved a hand airily. "I was admiring the view, yeah. Wondering if he played on my team and whether I should go over and buy him a drink."

Gideon snorted. "Good luck with that. He might be on our side but Draven Samuels is a difficult bugger. Comes in here regularly and always tips the staff very well. But he's not an easy man to get to know."

"Draven? Unusual name. I like it." Taylor stared over at the man on the far side who was sipping what looked like Coke. "Funny thing is, I think I've met him before but I just can't put my finger on where."

Gideon turned and ran a critical eye around his restaurant before turning his attention back to Taylor. "Well, make whatever play you like but I don't want to find you in the bathroom stalls together."

Taylor opened his mouth to deny that he did that and Gideon laughed. "Remember who sleeps in my bed, Taylor. Eddie loves post-fuck conversation and he's told me a few stories. Not that it's any of my business; I just don't want jizz messing up my clean bathrooms." His nostrils flared and a small smile softened his lips. He sniffed once, a look of pure satisfaction on his face.

"I like the aftershave. Maybe Draven would like it too."

A light went on in Taylor's brain. He remembered Gideon had lost his sense of smell and taste in a bad fire some months back. Recently he'd begun to be able to smell again and Eddie had been as excited as all hell about that fact. You'd have thought he discovered the cure for all the afflictions of the human condition.

Gideon laughed and motioned toward the empty plate as Taylor eyed him with narrowed eyes. "Looks like you enjoyed your food. I'll ask Eddie to send you out an Italian coffee, on the house. I know that's what you usually have to finish off a meal." He checked his watch. "Gotta go. I might be the boss but I can't be seen to be slacking off. Say hi to that crazy roommate of yours. I'll tell Eddie you say hi." He grinned fondly. "The man is causing havoc in the kitchen tonight. He's broken two plates already."

He waved and disappeared into the busy hive of the restaurant. Taylor hadn't even had time to thank him for the free drink. Sighing, he looked over at the mysterious Draven Samuels. He was absorbed in some sort of pudding, poking at it with a fierce scowl that looked as if he thought it might bite him. Taylor choked back a laugh. Well, at least he knew the man's name now. He grinned wickedly. He'd take the bull by the horns and go over there, buy the man a drink. Perhaps he could seal the deal on this one; he just had to make his move. Taylor licked the rim of his glass again and smiled.

***

Draven prodded at his mocha latte ice cream dish and scowled. It wasn't the pudding, dribbled with some sort of delicious honey sauce and peppered with pecan nut chips that were causing his ire. No, it was a honey of another sort. It was the man across the room who'd licked his lips like some sort of porn star then ran his pink tongue around the rim of his glass. Draven wanted desperately to feel that tongue circling another kind of rim. But now he'd remembered where he'd seen the younger man before, and there was no fucking way on God's green earth that he was pursuing his initial instinct to take the man home and screw the lip-licking crap out of him.

When he'd first laid eyes on him, his dick had reared to attention like a meerkat popping out of its hole. The man had every attribute that pushed Draven's "want it, have to have it" buttons. A little younger than him, with light, coffee-coloured skin, thick, curly black hair down to his shoulders, what looked like a trim and wiry physique under a tight red polo shirt, well-muscled arms that led to fingers that could definitely strum what they liked, and lips beneath a hint of dark stubble—those damn lips again—that would look just as good sucking his cock as they did licking sauce off. He'd seen Gideon wander over to him and have a conversation and then watched as Brown Eyes went back to trying to be sexy. He was succeeding if the steel in Draven's chinos was anything to go by.

He attacked his dessert with gusto, lamenting each time he stabbed the spoon into the goo that was melting in his bowl that he wouldn't get to take the man home tonight.

"Has that pudding offended you in any way?" The enquiry was delivered in an amused, warm tone. Draven knew who it was before he looked up. He schooled his face to show the required expression of diffidence and disinterest. The man from the table with the beautiful lips stood before him, a slight smile on his face, but Draven noticed the hands fidgeting at his sides. Brown Eyes wasn't as confident as he made himself out to be.

"I'm sorry. Did you say something?" He stared at the younger man, trying to convey the fact he wasn't interested even when he knew it was a lie. He'd felt the same thing the first time they'd met as well.

Warm, dark caramel eyes stared into his appraisingly. "Well, the way you were stabbing it, I thought it might have disagreed with something you said. You don't strike me as the kind of man who'd take kindly to being argued with."

Draven set his spoon down and leaned back in his chair. The man's smile faltered a little but he held Draven's gaze.

"I don't think we know each other well enough for you to make that assumption," Draven said sharply. "Anyway, is there something I can do for you?" He stared at the other man.

"I was going to ask if you wanted a drink." The man held out a hand. "My name's Taylor, by the way. Taylor Abelard."

Draven nodded. "I know who you are. And no, thanks. I have a drink." He held up his empty glass and waggled it then set it down and picked up his spoon.

"We've met before? Where? I thought you looked familiar but I couldn't remember where from…" Taylor's voice trailed off as Draven deliberately went back to eating the last remnants of his ice cream. He ignored Taylor's sharp, indrawn breath as he was deliberately dismissed.

"Aren't you going to at least answer my question? I'm sorry if I offended you offering you a drink but…" Taylor's voice was husky with anger.

Draven ignored him and continued eating, yet still the man didn't get the hint and move away. Instead, one slim hand reached down and plucked the spoon from between his fingers. Draven looked up, startled, as Taylor smiled and held the spoon away.

"You're quite rude, aren't you?" Taylor said conversationally. "You could just have said no thanks, politely."

"No thanks. Now piss off." Draven growled and reached for his spoon.

Taylor shook his head, his face set. "Oh no, you're not getting this back until you tell me where we met and why you're being such an arsehole."

Draven looked around the restaurant. "I'll just get the waitress to bring me another." He knew he was being childish, but his frustration at not following through on his desire and his knowledge of what this man did to people was like acid in his stomach.

"Fucker." Taylor said quietly, and at that insult, Draven looked up, his fists clenching. No one called him names like that, especially not beautiful men with kissable lips and the look of a dark angel.

"Give me back my fucking spoon." He made a move to rise out of his seat and Taylor moved forward, his hips just below the level of Draven's mouth and he swallowed at the sight of that silky groin. Taylor was wearing a pair of drawstring pants made out of some sort of soft, black material. Draven wanted to pull the knotted cord at his waist with his teeth and watch them slide off slim hips to the floor. The outline of Taylor's crotch was visible beneath the fabric, tantalisingly close.

"Just tell me where you know me from and I'll leave," Taylor said curtly. Draven could see from the implacable set of his shoulders and the hardened eyes that he'd have no peace until he told Taylor what he wanted to know.

"We met at an investigation a year ago, when Bobby Meredith went missing. Remember him?" Draven said bitingly. "Little kid with strawberry-blond hair, six years old, who was found in pieces under an oak tree in a field in Sussex."

He watched as Taylor's café au lait skin paled and he thought Taylor might pass out from the sick look on his face.

"Bobby?" Taylor said haltingly, and Draven watched his Adam's apple bob in his throat as he swallowed. "Yes, I remember Bobby…" His voice tailed off and he paled even more. Draven felt a spurt of satisfaction at being able to shake the man's composure. "You were consulted on that case to help 'find' him."

Taylor's body was trembling and he had a haunted look in his eyes as Draven continued. "His parents were friends of your parents, if I remember, and they thought you could use your *powers* to help. You used to babysit the kid from what I recall." He spat the word "powers" out with the derision he felt. "I was helping a friend of mine in the force do a psych profile for the guy we thought took him, and that was when we met. There in the field over the remains of Bobby Meredith. You were looking at part of his left leg when you passed out, if I recall." He had no idea where his viciousness came from and he knew it was totally out of line but at those last words, Taylor gave a strangled cry and spiralled senseless to the floor.

***

"Taylor? Honey, come on back, okay? It's Eddie. Come on bud. Wake up."

Groggily Taylor opened his eyes to stare into a pair of bright green ones that regarded him with concern. Eddie's face was pale, and his freckles stood out like raindrops on a pavement.

"There's my lad," Eddie crooned as he brushed a hand through Taylor's hair, lifting sweat-drenched strands from his cheek. "I thought you were never going to wake up."

Taylor struggled to a sitting position as Eddie helped him up. "I passed out?" he said faintly. "God, I'm sorry, I didn't mean to make you worry—"

He was in Gideon's office, seated in the big armchair in the corner of the room. There was a ring of worried faces surrounding him: Eddie, peering at him anxiously, Gideon regarding him with a concerned frown and…Draven-fucking-Samuels. He stood there with a scowl on his face.

But there was something else too. Guilt.

Taylor's temper rose at the fact that this man had caused such a reaction in him with a few choice words. Little Bobby's case was one that still resonated with Taylor, and hearing Draven speak so disparagingly of a little boy who had suffered horribly had cut him to the core. The scenes of Bobby's death and the bond he'd had with the child when he'd been asked to help find him still gave him nightmares.

"You motherfucker," he swore quietly as he gazed gimlet-eyed at the blond man. "What the hell are you still doing here? I'd have thought you'd have cut and run as soon as I hit the deck. You should have. Because when I get up I'm going to punch you in the damn face."

Taylor's legs still felt weak, so as tough as his threat might have sounded, he wasn't yet ready to play it out. Eddie turned slowly to Draven and stared at him frostily. Taylor knew him to usually be an easy-going man, but when his red-headed temper flared, no one was safe.

"What the fuck did you do to him?" Eddie demanded as he moved closer to Draven. "Tay, you want me to smack him for you?"

Gideon snorted and laid a hand on his boyfriend's arm. "Love, no one's smacking the patrons of my restaurant," he said in amusement. "Although if I find out Draven needs a good whack, I'm sure we can come to some arrangement outside." His brown eyes stared at Draven thoughtfully. "What did you do to Taylor to make him fall down like that? He looked like a puppet with the strings cut. I saw him pole axe from across the restaurant."

Taylor stood up, wobbling a bit as Eddie steadied him. "It was something he said that brought back a memory I'd rather forget," he said quietly. The fight had disappeared from him and all he wanted to do was get home and curl up into a ball, preferably with a bottle of something, and try and forget the world for a bit. "I'll be all right, Gideon. "

For the first time Draven spoke. "I'm sorry. I didn't mean to make you faint. I shouldn't have said what I did."

"You bastard," Taylor spat bitterly. "You think you can remind me about one of the worst events of my life and not have it affect me? You remembered all too well what it did to me the last time we met."

He'd remembered who Draven was now. He'd met him at the scene when they'd found Bobby's body. Well, where *he'd* found Bobby's body and helped apprehend a child killer. He'd been called in to help the family trace their missing child, and he'd succeeded. It hadn't been made common knowledge that it was his abilities that had done that. The police force was still wary of telling the general public that a psychic was assisting them in their enquiries and had succeeded where they hadn't.

The area where Bobby had been dumped had been a wooded area deep in a forest, and when Taylor had spotted the boy's dismembered limb lying in a bush of something with red berries, he'd thrown up then promptly passed out. The psychic energy and painful emotion emanating from the scene had been tremendous. Draven had been standing near the limb, a look of horror and pain on his face as he gazed down at what had once been a vibrant little boy.

The events after that hadn't been much better. When he'd come to, Taylor had heard the sneering comment from Draven about people abusing others and leading them on to try and make themselves heroes, and good old-fashioned investigative police work won out every time rather than these "frauds" who played havoc with grieving people's emotions. He'd had no doubt the nasty comments were directed at him.

"And just to set the records straight—*I* was the one who found Bobby and helped them get the guy who did it. The police kept it quiet and let the public think it was them because, well, because they didn't want people to know a *fraud* had done what they couldn't so far." He spat the word out and watched Draven's face pale. "I'm sure they would have found Bobby eventually. My mate Rick is a damn good copper and he'd have succeeded. But knowing I do what I do—he decided it was worth the chance. And I was more than happy to stay out of the limelight."

Gideon and Eddie's faces were a mixture of horror and anger as they gazed at Draven. They knew first hand of Taylor's propensity to "see" things.

"He's genuine," Eddie burst out vehemently. "I can vouch for that. I've been on the receiving end of his so-called 'fraudish' abilities."

"I said I was sorry." Draven's voice was even. "I don't believe in all this hocus-pocus crap so it's difficult to believe. Back then I saw you as someone just feasting off the grief of a family desperate to know what had happened to their kid. I didn't know."

"Yes, well, maybe next time you shouldn't let your mouth run away with you." Taylor was drained. He turned to Gideon and Eddie. "I need to go home. I'm knackered. Thanks for looking out for me, guys." He clapped Eddie on the arm and moved toward the door.

Gideon stopped him. "I'll run you home. I don't want you passing out again." He raised a finger at Taylor's protest. "No buts. Let's get your gear together—it's at reception—and go. Babe, I'll see you later." He grinned as he stared at Eddie. "And please don't beat up Draven when I'm gone. He might have been an arsehole but he's a paying customer." He cast a quick glance over at Draven then leaned over and gave Eddie a deep, loving kiss. Despite his bad mood and tiredness, Taylor smiled. He never tired of watching these two together. They'd been seeing each other for over six months now, and while Taylor missed his old housemate, he knew that Eddie belonged here with Gideon.

He moved toward the door, intent on collecting his belongings and getting the hell out of there, when Draven reached out a hand and gripped his shirtsleeve. Taylor glared at him.

"Take your damn hand off me. Aren't you scared you'll catch something?"

Draven growled but removed his hand. "I just wanted to say I hope you feel better. But hey." He waved a hand. "Feel free to leave."

"I intend to," Taylor growled back.

God this man makes me want to punch him.

He followed Gideon out the door.

***

Draven stood, a little nonplussed at all the fuss he'd caused and shot a quick look at Eddie when the man gave an exasperated puff. His dark red hair was sticking up on his head like a parrot's crest, probably because he'd taken off the chef's cap he had tucked in the front of his rather mucky apron. He regarded Draven with a look of dislike in his green eyes.

"So, you make a habit of being a bitch then?" His eyebrows cocked and he folded his wiry arms across an equally wiry chest. Draven could see the attraction of the man. He was a feisty little bantam ready to do battle.

Draven held back a weary chuckle. Telling the man that *would* probably earn him a beatdown. "Taylor's lucky to have you on his side. I guess before the glove hits the ground and you challenge me to a duel, I should get going myself. I still need to settle the bill. Everything happened a bit fast and I didn't get the chance."

Eddie waved a hand. "You're damn right you'll settle up. You're lucky I'm not charging you a surcharge for all the fuss tonight."

Draven smirked. "I thought this was Gideon's place? Aren't you just the chef?" The careless words were out before he could pull them back and he took an instinctive step back as Eddie's face darkened and he moved toward him.

"You truly are a bastard, aren't you?" Eddie poked a long boned finger at Draven's chest. "Just a warning. Don't cause Taylor any more grief. He's been through enough lately, what with all the damn nightmares and stuff," he broke off and sniffed. "Not that you'd care anyway. Now I hear a bus or something with your name on it. Time to go."

Draven got the impression Eddie would have preferred him to be under the bus instead of in it. He was hustled out of the office then Eddie closed the door behind him.

"You know where the pay desk is. Have a nice rest of your night, arsehole." He turned and strode off toward the kitchen, leaving Draven to pick up the pieces of his night.

Later that night as he drank whisky from a grimy tumbler, Draven had the strangest feeling that he'd be seeing Taylor Abelard again. Where that certainty came from, he didn't know. When he got into bed that night, he jacked off to the thought of caramel eyes and warm lips and pale tanned skin that writhed against his in sweat and passion.

Christ, the damned man had certainly left a lasting impression.

Chapter 4

A week later, Taylor sat at the dining room table and stared at the newspaper with a feeling of disbelief. He'd just showered and come down to have a plate of granola before leaving for work.

How can they be having a service for Drew? I didn't even know *he was dead.*

Now, though, the nightmares and events of the past few weeks now made terrible sense.

He swallowed bile as he finished reading the notice.

There will be a funeral service for Drew Whittaker on Friday 12th March at 09h00 at the Waltham Abbey Church. Donations please requested in lieu of flowers to The Suicide Prevention Fund set up in his name *www.Inmemoryofdrew.co.uk.* Thank you for being a friend of Drew. We hope his memory lives on in all of *your hearts.*

Taylor closed his eyes as the sick feeling in his stomach threatened to overtake him. He fought it off and took a couple of deep, calming breaths. Drew's smiling face leapt up off the page. He and Drew went way back. They'd been occasional fuck buddies, mutual 'blow jobbees,' and had been jerking each other off for over a year off and on in the small hotel behind the music store. Drew was also a married man with two kids, whom he adored—or *had been* a married man, in any event. Taylor had never felt quite comfortable with being the "bit on the side" when the man had a wife at home, but Drew had assured that if not him, then it would be someone else. And he had really liked Taylor. That like had been reciprocated.

In his mid-forties, Drew had been a man so far in the closet that it would have taken him a week to get out of it. He'd been unrepentant about his need for younger men to give him the satisfaction he needed. Taylor and he had met at a grocery store and Taylor had instantly recognised the hunger in the other man's eyes when they'd stood at the vegetable stall talking about the best melons to buy. One thing had led to another, there'd been a quick BJ in the customer bathroom—Taylor on his knees taking Drew's big cock in his mouth and turning the man into a slush puppy—and the two of them had fallen into a comfortable rhythm of quick fucks and encounters to satisfy them both.

It had been no hardship for Taylor. Drew was a handsome man, slim and pumped from working out in his home gym, and Taylor had appreciated his considerable assets, especially when the man was pounding his arse. He'd also been a warm and generous lover and Taylor had even once thought that if Drew had been out of the closet, and not already attached, he might have considered a man like him permanently in his life. And now he was dead.

Taylor hadn't seen him since the last very tasty suck off about three weeks ago. He'd thought nothing of it; Drew was a businessman who travelled all over the world and there was no commitment between the two of them to meet up with any regularity. That was what mobiles were made for. Insta-fuck was a new buzzword in Drew's dictionary and Taylor had enjoyed being part of the conversation.

He stared dismally out of the window in the street beyond. He'd have to make a plan to go the memorial service. Drew deserved that much. At least he'd found the source of his nightmares. He still smelt the blood and shit in his nostrils, and felt the desperation permeating the air. He reached over and powered up the small netbook he kept on the table. With grim determination he began the search for local stories. Ten minutes later he found the news article.

Police were called in yesterday to the home of Drew Whittaker, 42, after neighbours reported hearing a loud noise. Mr. Whittaker was found dead in his study, at his home in Waltham Abbey, from what appears to be a self-inflicted gunshot wound. His wife and children were not in the house at the time but were told of his death and are currently being comforted by relatives.

A wealthy entrepreneur, Mr. Whittaker was well known in the city. His position as CEO and owner of his multimillion pound company, 'Whittcon Enterprises,' which specialised in the manufacture of computer chips for the digital market, was cemented in respect and admiration from his peers in the industry.

Foul play is not suspected. Investigations into Mr. Whittaker's death are continuing.

Taylor gave a shuddering sigh and leaned back in the rickety dining chair. He felt a sense of helplessness that he hadn't been there to soothe Drew with any demons he'd had. He'd never even known what he did for a living. There might have been no promises between them but Drew had still been a friend of sorts. His throat ached and he tried to hold back the hot tears that threatened to fall from eyes that felt gritty and sore.

"God, Drew," he murmured as he closed the laptop. "What the hell happened to make you so desperate? Surely there was someone you could have talked to? I would have listened."

He stood up and picked up his jacket and shrugged into it. Time to go to work before he was late and his boss Jemima gave him a tongue-lashing. The music store was her pride and joy and she relied on her employees to hold the same passion for it that she did. 'Music Mayhem' was a place that Taylor really enjoyed working and he had no desire to jeopardise his position by being late. With a heavy heart, Taylor left the house and made his way to the tube station.

That night, after a day from hell at the office, he was glad to make it home and collapse into the dilapidated armchair in the lounge. Leslie wasn't home yet and Taylor was glad of the peace and quiet. He closed his eyes and laid his head back against the chair. He had a smoke then lit up another one. When he was done, he got the air freshener out and opened the windows.

He'd been relaxing for about half an hour when he heard the front door open and a whirlwind hit the entrance hall as keys were thrown onto the small table. There was the tread of footsteps and a waft of expensive masculine eau de cologne assailed his nostrils. Leslie was home.

"Tay? Baby, are you home?" Leslie appeared in the doorway. His trim, lithe body was clothed in very tight black and white plaid trousers, a form-fitting white button-down shirt, currently rolled up to his elbows, and his black matching jacket slung over his shoulder. A silver scarf was wrapped around his elegant neck. Taylor bet he was the epitome of office chic at the fashion house he worked as a trainee buyer, and he could only but envy Leslie's casual yet innate sense of dress style. Leslie, however, was not as conservative when it came to his time off, with his high heels, makeup, thongs and myriad of bright and striking clothes.

"I'm here," Taylor said wearily and sat up, running a hand through his curls and wondering whether the top of his head resembled a bird's nest in the making.

Blue lasers fixed on his face, a patrician nose sniffed the air in suspicion and then a worried frown crossed Leslie's beautiful features. Taylor was glad he'd been distracted from the stale cigarette smoke.

"Honey, have you been crying? Your eyes are all red and puffy, and you're as pale as my mum's tea. And we know all she does is dunk the tea bag in once and drink tea-flavoured dish water." He shivered, his face disgusted. He sat on the chair arm and laid a warm hand on Taylor's back. "What happened?"

Taylor sighed. He should have known he wouldn't get away with much when it came to Leslie.

"I had some bad news this morning and I had a shitty day. I sold something for less than I should have and had to make it up, and Jemima crapped all over me for it. Then I dropped a whole tray of drinks I was making on my tea round at lunch time, and coming home the tube was packed and some random guy goosed me." He closed his eyes at the gentle strokes of Leslie's hand on his back. "I wouldn't have minded, but he was dirty and smelly and I had to spend the whole journey with my nose in his armpit. And not in any way I normally like."

Leslie tut-tutted as he stroked Taylor's hair from his face. "Oh fuck. That does sound like a shit day." His eyes met Taylor's. "What was the bad news?"

Taylor swallowed. "Remember the nightmares and the blood? Well, I know who it was now. A friend called Drew. He shot himself."

Leslie gasped, his blue eyes wide. "Oh my God, sweetie, that's bloody awful." He scooted onto Taylor's lap as he sat in the chair and hugged him like a limpet. Taylor was grateful for the closeness even if he was being squeezed to death.

"What kind of friend was he? Were you two close?"

Taylor shook his head tiredly. "He was a fuck buddy. A good guy though, and he didn't deserve whatever he went through. I don't know why he did it."

Leslie's eyes clouded. "Baby, I'm so sorry. But at least it explains the visions you were having. That must be a relief, that you know what they were."

Taylor's throat clenched. "Until the next time when someone close to me dies or I see the pain of someone close to them as they die? I'm fucking fed up with this whole curse of being psychic. I wish I was just bloody normal."

Leslie pressed soft lips to his temple. "But you're not, sweetie," he said softly. "You're my Taylor and my hero. And a lot of other people's too. I don't claim to understand what you do, but you've helped people. Like me, and Eddie. And that little boy." In one of his darkest down moments, Taylor had told Leslie the story of little Bobby Meredith and they'd cried together over that tragic tale. "So you need to suck it up and put on your big-boy pants." He wrapped his arms around Taylor's neck and gave him another smacking kiss on his cheek. "I know just the thing to cheer you up. Chamomile tea. I'll go make you a cup."

He scrambled off Taylor's lap and sashayed his way into the kitchen. Taylor heard the soft tones of a song by Lady Gaga, Leslie's personal lady crush, being sung in a melodic tenor voice as Leslie rattled cups and filled the kettle. Taylor grinned wearily. Chamomile tea was the remedy for all the ills of the world according to his roommate, and just for once, he wished that the magic brew could take away the pain he felt at a friend's untimely death.

***

A week later, on a cold and grey Wednesday afternoon, Taylor stood quietly at the back of the beautiful church in Waltham Abbey. He'd been lucky to get the day off work, promising Jemima that he'd make up the time. He was dressed in a sombre grey suit, feeling as uncomfortable as all hell. It was an outfit outside of his comfort zone, being more used to chinos, jeans and sweat shirts. Leslie had tsk-tsked and told him to get a grip when he'd complained the suit was tight across his shoulders and restricted his movement. When he'd continued whinging, Taylor had gotten a glare from his friend and an admonition that "someone was fucking dead, and Taylor could play nice in a suit for a little while."

He watched the people milling around as they talked softly and occasionally gestured to the coffin that sat at the front of the wide, ornate chapel. It was covered in myriad types of flowers and looking for all the world like a display at the Chelsea Flower Show. Taylor himself wanted a Viking funeral. He'd actually written it into his will two years ago, although the solicitor writing it had coughed gently and told him he didn't think the UK condoned putting someone on an old wooden barge and setting them on fire on the Thames. Taylor had growled that it was his effing funeral and the powers that be could go screw themselves. And so the clause had stayed.

Writing a will at the tender age of twenty-two had been something that had raised eyebrows in the conservative offices of Lester, Mark and Abelard, where Taylor's father worked as one of the partners. Taylor, however, had seen enough death through both his and his mother's eyes and he knew that when the Grim Reaper came calling there was fuck all anyone could do it about it. He might not have a lot to leave anyone other than his collection of antique cigarette boxes and a pile of choice porn magazines, but he was damned if he was leaving what he did have to the State. He knew Eddie and Leslie would make good use of the magazines, the pages of which were already rather stuck together.

Taylor's chest tightened as he watched a pretty, dark-haired woman he knew to be Drew's wife place her hand on the coffin. Taylor had seen the pictures of Catherine, Drew's wife, when he'd taken them out his wallet to show him.

Drew had been proud of his family; there had been no doubt about that. The love for his wife and children had shown in his eyes.

Another older man, probably Catherine's father, put a comforting hand on her shoulder. She was crying silently, her face grief stricken. This close to home, Taylor realised exactly what he'd done. He'd fucked and been fucked by a man who was already spoken for to another. His stomach churned with guilt. Drew *had* explained that he'd no other choice; he had needs he didn't want to share with his family and the occasional bout with Taylor was his way of unwinding.

At the time, Taylor had understood. But now, in the cold light of day, when said man lay cold in a coffin, and Taylor saw the grief of the family, he wondered whether he'd done the right thing in being there for Drew so others hadn't needed to be. He was glad that wherever Drew was, he wasn't in the church today. Taylor couldn't sense him, for which he was relieved. He felt it more at the time of the event, not afterwards. His mother had felt more than him, to the point of almost being haunted by past presences. It was probably what had caused her heart to give out at the relatively young age of forty-nine.

"Are you friend or family?" The gentle tones of a woman echoed breathily in his ear. Startled, Taylor turned to see a tiny, white-haired woman, in about her seventies, regarding him with bright, bird-like eyes. She was dressed in dark blue dress, a white shawl draped casually around her shoulders.

"Uhm, I was just a friend," he stammered.

She nodded sadly. "Yes, Drew was a popular man; he had a lot of friends. That's why it doesn't make any sense that he did what he did. I still don't understand …" Her voice tailed off, her face whitewashed with grief. She lifted a soft, white hand to Taylor to shake. "I'm Lavinia Whittaker. Drew was my grandson."

Taylor shook her hand and wished the ground would open and swallow him up with the lie he was living. "Taylor Abelard, ma'am."

"How did you know him?" Lavinia asked, head cocked to one side like a little sparrow.

"He used to come into the music shop where I work." Taylor was glad that at least that was the truth. "He had a thing for a group called 'In Vitro,' an alternative group, and I used to keep the new releases for him to collect."

Lavinia grimaced. "I think I heard that playing in his car one day. Dreadful noise it was, all screeching and percussion. It made my ears weep blood." Her hand flapped and she looked quite disgusted. But there was a soft smile on her face—a memory perhaps of better days when her grandson was alive?

Taylor chuckled, liking the older woman. "It's not my taste either. I never quite saw what *he* saw in it. But he enjoyed it so I helped him find the albums he wanted." He shrugged. "It didn't take a lot to make him happy." No sooner had he said the words than he wanted to withdraw them.

It sounds too intimate, like I really knew him well. I need to be careful. I don't want his memories tarnished by a slip of the tongue. I have no idea if anyone knew about his other life.

Lavinia regarded him thoughtfully but said nothing. Instead she looked over at the woman still weeping at the front of the chapel, her face bleak and white. "Catherine has taken his death very badly. She was always very dependent on him and now she's a poor lost soul." She gave a deep sigh. "I hope her father can help her through this with the children. I've never seen someone so distraught."

Shame permeated Taylor's very soul. Soft strains of music filled the air and people began filling into the church.

"The ceremony's starting," Taylor said quietly. "Can I show you to your seat, Mrs. Whittaker?"

Lavinia laughed, a tinkling sound that made Taylor smile. "Oh, my dear, call me Lavinia, please. And yes, I'd love a handsome young man like you to escort me to my seat." She held out a thin, fragile arm and Taylor took it as he gently supported her to the front of the church pews. He helped her into the seat closest to the aisle and then turned to leave. She reached out and grasped his arm, her eyes slightly wet.

"He was a good man, one of the best. I'm glad he has friends here. I hope wherever he is now, he's at peace."

Taylor clasped her hand, thin and frail, between his dark ones. "I think he is, Lavinia. That's all we can hope for."

He turned and made his way to the back of the room, away from the family and the true friends that were Drew's. The ceremony was beautiful, heart wrenching and not over soon enough for him. It was with a sigh of relief that he finally went outdoors, found a shady spot under a huge oak tree and lit up a cigarette. He knew he'd promised himself to cut down or stop altogether but today? That wasn't going to happen.

"Those things will kill you, you know." The hated voice drawled in his left ear and Taylor swung around in shock to meet the deep, grey eyes of Draven Samuels.

"What the hell are you doing here?" Taylor growled. "Are you stalking me?"

Draven's face darkened. "Don't flatter yourself." He raised a hand and flapped the spiralling smoke from Taylor's cigarette away with disgust. Taylor blew a smoke ring in his direction in defiance and the man glowered.

"You are such a damn child." He regarded Taylor evenly. "I worked with Drew for a while. What's your excuse to be here?"

Taylor wasn't going to *ever* tell this man the real extent of his and Drew's relationship. "We were friends. He used to come into the music shop I work in." He noticed that Draven filled out a suit really well. Dark charcoal wool, suited to the chilly autumn days, with a pale blue shirt, which stretched across his chest and defined a body that was strong and toned. His blond hair was ruffled in the slight breeze and his face seemed paler than usual.

"No one should be here. It was too damn early for him to go. Stupid bastard."

Taylor's mouth dropped at the fact that a man who'd just died was being vilified. Draven squinted. "What? Are you into the whole 'don't speak ill of the dead' thing,' being in your profession?"

Taylor's temper rose with every word coming out of Draven's mouth but he wasn't prepared to make a scene at a man's funeral.

"You are a real shit." He blew another smoke ring toward Draven, noting with satisfaction as it hit his face and Draven's nostrils flared. "I don't talk to dead people, arsehole. That's not how it works."

Draven said nothing, just stared at Taylor with flat eyes. Taylor ignored him, watching the people walk out of the chapel and mill around, comforting each other. He caught Lavinia's eye and she waved. He waved back at her and blew her a kiss.

"You know Drew's grandmother?" Draven looked surly at that fact.

Taylor nodded airily. "Oh yes, we go way back. She's a lovely lady."

"Huh. I never heard her talk about you. Small world, isn't it, that we keep bumping into one another?" Draven's eyes were piercing and observing him with keen interest. And in their depths was a definite spark of interest. Taylor had seen that look often enough to recognise it for what it was. Lust. Desire.

Oh really? Mr. High and Mighty Samuels isn't above a bit of slap and tickle then with someone he doesn't really like. Interesting.

Taylor filed it away for future use. He shifted on his feet, thrusting his hands into his pockets and drawing attention to the front of his groin as the material tightened. Draven's eyes flicked down and his face grew still. His tongue came out and he licked his lips, and the sight of that pink muscle and the wetness of Draven's bottom lip turned Taylor's insides to mush as his cock began its inexorable rise upward.

Damn, that whole hands-in-pockets thing has bloody backfired on me.

He took his hands out of his pockets as nonchalantly as possible and pulled his jacket over as far as he could to hide the rise of the Titanic under his boxers. Draven raised one very sexy eyebrow and smirked. Taylor wanted to slap it off his face. There was something about this man that made him want to get violent.

"So…" Draven drawled. "How does it work?"

Taylor was taken aback. "How does what work?" At first he thought Draven was talking about his cock but no. That couldn't be it.

"The whole 'I see dead people' thing. How does that work for you?"

Taylor tried to count to five to counter the fury welling up inside him. "I told you I don't see, talk or communicate with dead people." He said between gritted teeth. "I simply feel energies and see places in my mind where they might have been. And it's not just dead people I feel. It's the emotions of people close to me and who I have a connection with." He huffed. "So you needn't worry, because you'll never be one of them."

Draven chuckled sardonically. "Oh I think we have a connection all right." He motioned to Taylor's crotch. "Just not in the same way."

Taylor was dumbfounded. "Are you hitting on me at a bloody funeral?" he snarled. "You don't find that just a little bit sick?"

Draven shook his head. “Drew’s gone,” he said quietly and now Taylor could clearly see sadness in his eyes. “I knew him well enough to know that while he didn’t want to live, he’d have no problem with the ones who did carrying on. He had a favourite quote: ‘The life of the dead is placed in the memory of the living.’ It’s by Marcus Cicero. He’d expect us to remember who he was and the good times, not the one at the end who chose to take his own life.” His eyes grew far away. “Some of us don’t have that choice; we’re still in limbo.”

Taylor had the distinct feeling Draven was talking about something or someone else other than Drew. He also felt like a fraud. He hadn’t really known Drew to the extent that he could take a favourite quote of his and tell someone about it. Draven had been closer to him than he’d ever been.

Suddenly the secluded copse of trees where Taylor had chosen to come for an illicit cigarette closed in on him. He needed to get away, away from the other man’s knowing eyes and the breathless attraction he felt for a man who didn’t even like him and considered him with contempt.

“I need to leave,” he blurted and turned to go back to the car park, back to his car so he could get home and feel cleaner, to hide away and forget he’d ever come here today.

“You were one of his regulars, weren’t you?” Draven’s quiet voice made him stop. He closed his eyes in mortification but didn’t turn around because he didn’t want this man to see the shame on his face.

Draven kept speaking, his voice low, “I knew about Drew’s proclivities and you’re just his type.” He stopped and Taylor stood stock still, not wanting to turn and see more contempt on Draven’s face. “He was a noble man but in the end, he chose to leave this way instead of facing up to whatever it was made him do it.” There was a short silence and Taylor took a step forward to leave. Draven’s quiet voice stopped him.

“I think he was being blackmailed about it. Just a feeling I have.”

At those shocking words, Taylor *did* turn around and instead of seeing disgust in Draven’s eyes, all he saw was sympathy. He still needed to vent, though.

"Blackmailed for being queer? How do you get to that conclusion? And what the fuck do you know about me? The first time we met, you said I was a fraud. The second time around, you said the same thing. Now I'm a prostitute, a 'regular'? Well, fuck you, Draven Samuels." Taylor felt his eyes prickle with hot tears as emotions took him over and he continued his tirade with a cracking voice.

"I cared about Drew, and I'm really sorry that he's dead. I came here because I felt his death, his pain and I wanted to say goodbye and do the decent thing. Not something you'd understand." He felt a familiar lightness in his head and the panic that came with it. There were emotions running high at the funeral and he was picking up on them in his own heightened state.

I can't pass out again; I just can't be so damn weak. Damn this bloody gift, damn it to hell.

The world went black and once again in Draven Samuel's presence, Taylor slid to the ground.

***

Draven cursed as the limp body of the younger man fell like a tree. He had just enough time to catch Taylor before he hit the hard, cold, pebbled surface. He heard a shout from over at the chapel and running feet. As he knelt down, laying Taylor flat and cradling him in his arms, one of Drew's other friends, Jim Carstairs, came running over, his face pale.

"My God, is he all right?" The man looked panicked at having yet another incident to manage. As if a funeral wasn't enough for one day.

Draven nodded. "He fainted, that's all. He's a bit overwrought. I'll take care of him. You get back to the family, Jim. Taylor here will be fine."

Relief crossed the man's face. "Oh, if you're sure, Draven. I'll tell Lavinia he's okay; she was worried about him. She says to bring him back to the house for the get-together." He turned and walked back to the chapel.

Draven looked down at the man who seemed to make a habit of fainting on him. He didn't think he'd been responsible for this one. It had seemed for a moment as if Taylor had gone somewhere, the pain in his eyes evident, and then simply shut off like a candle being blown out.

He patted Taylor's face gently, worrying about his pallor. He couldn't help but notice that the man wasn't as lightweight as he looked, that beneath that coffee-coloured skin was a man of substance, muscles taut and firm. And up close, he was even more beautiful that Draven had imagined. Long, dark lashes lying against smooth skin, full lips that were currently slightly open and very kissable, and curling hair that was the deep, rich black colour of ripe earth. A faint smattering of stubble beneath the classic lines of his nose and around his chin made Draven want to run his face against it. He looked like a decadent gypsy prince.

And isn't that fucking poetic. Get a bloody grip.

Draven scowled and continued his efforts to get Taylor to wakefulness. Finally, after a tap that had probably been a tad too hard, Taylor groaned and opened his eyes and Draven fell into them. Taylor's eyes were the colour of rich, baked toffee, with an emerald circle around the pupil, bleeding into the iris like emerald starbursts. The spell was broken when Taylor opened his mouth.

"What the fuck? What are you doing to me? Let me go." He started to rise and push Draven away.

Draven chuckled. "Calm down, your bloody virtue is safe, I swear. You fainted. Again. I'm going to start thinking it's me that has this effect on you."

"You wish." Taylor struggled to a seated position and looked around with dazed eyes. "Where's everybody gone?"

"Probably back to Lavinia's for the wake or whatever they call it. She said I should bring you there when you'd woken up."

Taylor shook his head vehemently. "I'm not going anywhere. I don't belong there. You can leave me and go on your own."

He rose, a little unsteady. Draven held his arm as they both got to their feet.

Taylor was pale. "Thanks for not letting me conk my head on the ground," he said grudgingly. "That would have been all I needed, a concussion." He dusted off his suit and grimaced. Draven still held onto him and Taylor looked over at him angrily. "I'm fine. You can let me go."

Draven didn't *want* to let him go. The nearness of the man, the scent of his cologne, and the warmth of his body heat all added up to a sudden spike of want. Draven couldn't stop himself. He leaned over and crushed his needy lips over Taylor's soft, full mouth, revelling when it opened and Draven could get his tongue in there to taste the man. Taylor tasted of smoke and need and sin. When Draven finally drew back, his heart was beating as if he'd just run a marathon. He expected to be slapped or punched but nothing was forthcoming.

Instead, Taylor watched him with an expression of pure confusion and yes…there was definitely need and desire in those dark eyes. "I thought you didn't even like me," he murmured, his lips glistening.

Draven cocked his head. "I don't."

The next action gave voice to the lie in his soul as he pulled Taylor closer to him and took his mouth again greedily, like a drowning man gasps for air, and Taylor melted against him, his arms wrapping around his neck and holding onto Draven as if he was a life buoy.

When they finally pulled apart, both men looked at each other with eyes that asked a myriad of questions.

"This is crazy," whispered Taylor. "I…" His face darkened and he shot a look at Draven that made his body chill. "Oh, I see where this is going. I'm a 'regular' so you think you can take me home and fuck me? That I'm a cheap piece of arse? Well, screw you." His eyes glittered and before Draven could get a word in to refute that accusation, Taylor raised his arm and the next thing Draven knew, he was being catapulted backward by a fierce punch to his chin. As he staggered back and fell on his arse, Taylor loomed above him, the fire of a thousand flames in his eyes.

"I hope I never set eyes on you again, you bastard. Stay away from me." He turned and stormed toward the car park, leaving Draven fingering his aching chin and wondering what the hell had just happened.

A few hours later, after fielding some anxious enquiries from the people at the after funeral gathering about his bruised jaw, and eating more cake than he'd ever wanted to, Draven made his weary way to the Royal Hospital. It was one of his weekly visits on his way home to Charing Cross and while it distressed him every time he went, he couldn't miss visiting his little brother. He walked into the long-term care unit at the hospital and the nurse behind the desk greeted him warmly.

"Draven, it's good to see you again. How have you been?" Nurse Anita Richards was a stalwart in the unit, one of the long-standing devotees on the ward. She had looked after Jude since he was admitted nearly three years ago. She tut-tutted as she fingered the red bruise on his jaw. "Ran into something, did we? Or was that something obtained in the course of that secret job you do?" She clucked and Draven smiled faintly.

"No, someone got in a strop and decked me one. Not my finest moment. And it's fine, really. Nothing I haven't had before. How's Jude?"

Anita eyed him with compassion. "He's the same, as always. We're keeping him comfortable and fairly healthy despite the circumstances. Go on in."

Draven entered the quiet private room his brother "slept" in. His heart ached not for the first time at the sight of that pale, lifeless body, thin and wasted, eyelids taped down. Around Jude's slight frame, the machines that currently kept him alive and breathing whirred and pumped and whistled in a symphony of simulated living.

Draven sat down in the chair beside his brother and laid a hand against his cool cheek. Jude's light blond hair was wispy but well cared for, and his skin dry and pale despite the moisturiser that was constantly applied. He was a spectre of the lively, laughing boy he'd once been. His mother and father had always joked that Jude and Draven were carbon copies despite the age difference. They'd even sounded the same.

Draven's heart broke every time he saw him. "Hi, baby brother. I'm here, ready to read another story to you. We finished the other one last time, didn't we? Today we have…" he reached across and took the book off the metal side table, "*Christine*." He wrinkled his nose in distaste. Jude had adored Stephen King novels, and although a psychotic car hadn't been something Draven had ever wanted to read about, it had been one of Jude's favourite books.

Just over three years ago, Jude had been injured in the same accident that had killed Draven's parents. Jude had sustained severe head trauma when the out-of-control truck had careened into their car. Jude had been fifteen at the time, just two months short of his sixteenth birthday. Draven had been in the Ukraine on a case for Mortimer Investigations, ready to come back to the UK. It was the case where he'd met Drew Whittaker and his company, Whittcon.

Draven had rushed back to dead parents and a brother who the doctors told him was in a permanent vegetative state with no discernible brain activity and unable to breathe on his own. The machines keeping him alive were the thin line between life and death for Jude and one that Draven had never quite managed to sever. That line was all he had left of his family. He felt the guilt every day at not being there for them, at being on business at the time his whole family had been wiped out.

Sometimes, in his darkest moments, he wished he'd been in the car with them.

The only silver lining in the whole tragic tale was that his parents had left Draven a very substantial amount of money in both life insurance and wise investments. Every penny Draven had from that went to keeping Jude on these machines, and would continue to do so.

Doctor Frederick had talked about switching them off but Draven just couldn't do it. Not while there might be hope, something he clung to even though the doctors had told him quietly that there was none.

He opened the book and smiled at Anita when she came in to check Jude's airway, change his position to prevent bedsores, replace the tape on his eyes keeping his corneas healthy, physiotherapy, checking his catheter and other waste bags and several other functions that kept Jude comfortable and relatively healthy.

"He seems to be doing okay. Thanks for the cup of tea, by the way."

The nurse smiled gently. "You know we love to look after you, Draven. You look tired. You should get some more sleep. You'll have Sister Alison on your case if you don't."

The retort on Draven's lips that he'd get more sleep when he was dead didn't seem right under current circumstances. Instead he inclined his head.

"I'll do my best. I wouldn't want to upset Ally. She'd probably put me over her knee."

Anita nodded and left the room with a whish of starched white uniform.

Draven sipped his tea and sat there, watching, touching and talking, pretending that one day, Jude would open his eyes and everything would be all right in Draven's world once again.

He got home around about eight o'clock, exhausted, emotionally drained and feeling the effects of the punch to his jaw. Taylor had quite a right hook on him and was stronger than he looked.

After pouring himself a whisky, Draven slumped down into the easy chair in the lounge in his small but cosy two-bedroomed terrace house and stared at the wall while he sipped his drink. A picture of happier times of him, Jude and their parents laughing on a beach somewhere hung there.

"Evening, guys," he murmured softly. "Is it okay to tell you all about my day?" It was something he did when he felt down, feeling that perhaps somewhere, they might be listening. "Where the hell do I begin? I went to the funeral of a well-respected business colleague. Then, I saved a man from bashing his head in, kissed said man, who's the most annoying and volatile man I've ever met, and got punched in the face by… yep, you guessed it, the same man. Who's sexy as hell, I have to say. Then I had yet another conversation with your doctor, Jude." He frowned at the memories of the conversation about possibly turning off Jude's life support. "I just wasn't in the mood to discuss his thoughts tonight. I like Doctor Frederick but he can get all rational and sympathetic and that makes me feel even worse."

Jude's brain damage was so severe that it was a miracle he existed at all. His neural activity was virtually nil, and while Draven understood all the terms they threw at him, having done extensive research himself to try and find a miracle cure, he knew that a minimal Glasgow coma scale of three was a very bad thing.

Since the accident Jude had never opened his eyes, made a sound, moved by himself or given any indication that there was anyone still inside his damaged body.

"I know they have your best interests at heart and they all think there's no hope and I'm holding on because I'm a selfish prat…" his voice trailed off as he choked up, "but Jude, you're all I have left now." He waved helpless hands in the air. "I can't do this on my own. How the fuck do they expect me to make that kind of decision? How does anyone *do* that?"

Draven didn't cry often, yet thinking about his brother no longer being around made his heartache and his eyes prickle. He sat, sipping his drink, then poured another one until he could think unpleasant thoughts no more and retired to bed.

It was the best place to be at times like these.

Chapter 5

Taylor sat in Galileo's at his corner table and picked at his plate of chicken wings. It was a quiet Tuesday night and he'd come there straight from work. The events of the week before had been on his mind and he'd spent the weekend mulling them over, having come to the conclusion that even if Draven Samuels was an arsehole, perhaps Taylor had misjudged the hot kiss at the funeral. Taylor had never punched another man before and he felt really bad about it. He'd once hit a pervert with a truncheon to save a friend, but in his book, that didn't count as anything to feel guilty about. So he'd tracked down Draven's telephone number via Gideon. Gideon, being the soul of discretion, had called Draven first to ask if it was okay to pass his number on. Taylor guessed he'd been happy with that from the smirk on Gideon's face as he'd handed it over, with Eddie grinning like a Cheshire cat behind him.

"What?" Taylor had said in irritation. "I just want to apologise to the guy for planting him one. Take that damn smug look off your face."

The conversation with Draven had been short and sweet. A quick "Hello, this is Taylor, I'm sorry for hitting you, I think I might have overreacted," was blurted out in a vomit of words, followed by silence on the other end of the phone.

"Ermm, okay," had been Draven's response, drawled out rather uncertainly. Then he'd spoiled the whole 'Taylor–being-the-bigger-man thing' by asking cheekily,' "Does this mean I get to kiss you again?"

Taylor's jaw had dropped and instead of telling the man to sod off, the next words out of his traitorous mouth had been "Would you like to have a drink with me at Galileo's tomorrow night?"

No sooner had he said the words than he'd been mortified. To his surprise, Draven had chuckled sexily, causing Taylor's nether regions to react in a way he didn't think boded well for said drink, and said he'd see him there at eight p.m. Tuesday night. Taylor had put the phone down feeling very unsure about what he'd just agreed to.

Now he sat, waiting for Draven to arrive. He'd been outside for a couple of smokes already, to fight of the nervousness. Once or twice he'd thought about eating up his snack and bolting out of the restaurant. He'd just made up his mind to settle up at the front desk and take the coward's way out when a familiar scent of woodsy cologne hit his nostrils and a deep voice said,"Evening."

Taylor swallowed the half-chewed piece of chicken he'd been busy with. It burnt as it went down his throat and he grimaced.

Shit. That's going to give me heartburn.

"Errm, evening. Please," he motioned at the empty seat across from him, "take a seat."

Draven did so, his usual scowl for Taylor replaced with one of the most charming grins Taylor had ever been the recipient of. His stomach clenched and his black Levi's grew tighter. The other man was dressed in an open–neck, deep wine-coloured shirt with long sleeves. It hugged his torso like a wetsuit, revealing a body that had definitely seen its share of gym work. Taylor had already noticed the rather chic-looking grey chinos plastered to the man's long, lean legs and the way they clung to his arse like a second skin. He wondered faintly if Draven knew how damn sexy he looked. That thought was confirmed when the waiter came over to take a drink order and deliver menus and Draven gave him a five-hundred-watt smile that seemed to make the teenager—well, he was eighteen at least—almost cream his pants and return the smile. The waiter fell over himself in his effort to impress Taylor's dinner partner and Draven fed off it like an incubus. Taylor scowled and played moodily with the stem of his empty wine glass.

Draven finished his drink order—a whisky on the rocks—and raised an eyebrow at him. "Not a fan of whisky then?"

Taylor frowned.

“You seemed to disapprove of my choice of beverage from that frown on your face.” Draven’s eyes glinted with amusement.

Taylor stared at him loftily. “I have nothing against whisky.”

Draven’s lips quirked.

Taylor ignored him as he turned to address the star struck waiter. “I’ll have a rum and Coke please. Make sure it’s white rum. I don’t like the dark stuff. Bacardi would be fine if you have it.”

Jim—Taylor had now seen the tag on the waiter’s jacket—nodded but continued to smile at Draven who winked at him. Taylor’s blood began to boil.

You’re my *fucking dinner date, you moron. And Twinkie— you keep your paws off him.*

Where this sudden possessive instinct had come from, Taylor didn’t know. He just knew that if Jim Boy didn’t stop ogling Draven, he was going to have his eyes poked out with Taylor’s fork.

I am going to fork you up, Jimmy, my lad.

He sniggered at that random thought and Draven pursed his lips, the amusement on his face plain to see.

”I’m glad to see you’re in a better frame of mind than the other day.” He poured a glass of water from the jug on the table. “You pack quite a powerful punch.” He sipped the drink, his eyes regarding Taylor.

Taylor flushed as he fiddled with the cream napkin on the table. “Yes, I’m sorry about that. It was probably uncalled for and I suppose I should apologise.”

Draven leaned back in his chair. “I wasn’t looking for an easy lay,” he said softly. “I just really wanted to kiss you. I can’t explain it either but there you go.”

“I wasn’t really at my best,” Taylor muttered. “You caught me off guard with knowing what Drew got up to in his ‘secret’ life.” His tone sounded bitter even to him. “I was fine with what he was doing with me when he was alive, then I saw his wife and kids and…” His voice tailed off. “I felt like a slut.”

Draven leaned forward and placed a warm, firm hand on top of Taylor’s, stilling his fidgeting. “Drew thought very highly of you,” he murmured.” “He never told me the name but he did tell me about his beautiful, chocolate-skinned young man and I just knew it was you when I saw you at the funeral. You really made him feel special and he was very fond of you in his own way." He sighed and his thumb continued stroking Taylor's hand.

Taylor was holding his breath because having Draven doing that unconscious caressing was causing him to have one very extreme reaction in his trousers, not to mention the constriction in his chest that made breathing difficult. His mouth was dry, his skin warm and prickling with heat and Taylor wondered why the hell he was feeling this way toward a man he'd only met a few times.

"Drew would never have left his wife. And he said the times he spent with you made him feel whole. So whatever you're thinking of yourself, slutty certainly isn't a word I'd use." Draven grinned. "And he was right anyway. You *are* beautiful." His brow furrowed. "I know I've expressed some opinions about you in the past, and I still feel the same way to a point. I can't believe in things I can't see, and anyone that makes a living out of these so-called feelings and crap…well, it's just difficult to get to grips with."

Taylor pulled his hand away. He was still in shock at Draven calling him 'beautiful.' The warm glow that suffused his body from head to toe at that comment was still heating him up. "I don't make a living out of anything I've done," he said curtly. "I do it because they need me, not because they pay me." He laughed sharply. "Believe me, if I did I wouldn't be working in a music store nine hours a day, six days a week, and eating ramen noodles and tomato soup."

Jim arrived with the drinks and they fell silent as he busied himself with fussing over getting a coaster for Draven while he simply placed Taylor's drink on the tablecloth. With a smile and a promise, the young waiter disappeared.

"He is so hot for you," Taylor grumbled. "Doesn't he realise we're here together?"

Draven raised a sardonic eyebrow. "Oh? Are we 'together' then?" His lips quirked and he raised his whisky to them and Taylor watched as those full, pink lips wrapped themselves on the rim of the glass as he drunk. He swallowed.

"Well, we are here having dinner, so I guess that counts as being together. Don't get too full of yourself. This isn't a date; I just wanted to buy the man I hit a drink."

Draven nodded, his eyes sparkling. He acknowledged the comment with a tilt of his head. "Of course. Not a date."

Taylor bit back a rude retort as Jim appeared once again to take their meal orders. Taylor was surprised that the waiter didn't feel the waves of dislike emanating from him. Jim managed to brush Draven's shoulder with his hand every time he moved, leaned in to listen to Draven place his order like a man about to deliver a passionate kiss and finally bestowed a dazzling smile on him as he helped Draven tuck his napkin on his lap. Taylor's eyes narrowed.

Oh really? You needed to go there? *God, I need a smoke.* He glanced longingly at the pack on the table next to his lighter.

As Jim flounced off, Taylor glared at the table, wishing it would burst into flames and follow the young waiter like a table tornado, reducing him to a pile of ashes.

"Fuck. That is one mean look you are giving this table," Draven laughed. "I'm glad it's not directed at me. I'd be worried." He reached out and slowly traced his thumb across Taylor's bottom lip, his eyes dark and sultry. "There's only one man I want to kiss here. And it isn't Jimmy over there. And to be honest, kissing isn't the only thing I want to do to you."

The heated look in his eyes melted Taylor's reservations about anything this man might want to do to him or with him. He knew Draven wasn't very accepting of what he did but he seemed to be willing to listen at least. And at the moment, Taylor couldn't care less. He hadn't been laid in a while, the man was mesmerising, and sex was sex. He'd take what he could get and if that made him the slut hc thought he was, so be it.

Out of the corner of his eye, he saw Jimmy approaching their table with a basket of bread.

I think it's time to give this little upstart some competition.

***

Taylor leaned into Draven and ran a hand down the clean-shaven cheek, hearing him hiss at the touch. Jimmy stood before them, a look of sad, resigned surprise on his face.

"And what exactly *is* it that you want to do to me, Draven?" Taylor drawled, licking his lips and seeing Draven's pupils dilate in sheer satisfaction.

Oh yes, Jimmy lad, take notes. I'm the one doing that to him, not you. So piss off and leave us alone.

"God, you are one teasing little bastard." Draven's voice was husky and he shifted in his chair. Taylor smirked at the fact that he didn't even seem to see Jimmy at his side. "I guess my reply would be, what don't I want to do with you, Taylor? Perhaps we should leave and find out just how far we can get." Draven smirked back. "Do you think we'd make it to my car or will I be fucking you right here on this table?"

Jimmy gave a plaintive squeak and scurried off like a frightened rabbit. Taylor stared into grey eyes that held so many promises, and he knew he was irretrievably snared. Jimmy's impression of a scared cottontail had nothing on Taylor's desire for this man to possess him in any way he wanted, to hold him down, take him and use him.

The two men couldn't get out of Galileo's fast enough. Taylor left money to cover the drinks even as they argued over *who* would do it, and he hoped Gideon would forgive him for deserting their post before their food arrived. He *had* given Sarah on the front desk a rather garbled explanation about a family emergency as he'd exited the restaurant and "sorry for the mess up." Once on the pavement, he and Draven looked at each other.

"My place," Draven commanded. "Closer and more private. Get in the car." He waved towards an expensive-looking Honda Civic parked in a bay a few places down from the restaurant. He clicked a remote from his pocket and the car beeped. Draven slid into the driver seat, as Taylor slid in beside him, and they both fumbled with seatbelts.

Taylor tried to distract himself from the fact he was going home with this man to be fucked into oblivion. "Nice car," he said lamely. "How did you manage the parking space? They're like, really rare around here."

"I have a special permit in the window to park places I want to. No one messes with it. And the car is a tourer. Suits my work. Space and comfort all in one." Draven started the car and pulled out at a speed Taylor was sure wasn't legal.

"Where are we going?" He wondered if he should tell someone, perhaps Gideon, where he was off to in case Draven turned out to be a raving killer. Although Taylor was sure Gideon wouldn't let a man who was a little crazy into his cherished restaurant. He was reputed to be a good judge of character. Taylor grinned inwardly. But then Giddy *did* like Eddie…his thoughts randomly buzzed in his head like anxious dragonflies trying to escape a net. Draven's voice interrupted his musings.

"Charing Cross. I have a house there."

"Oh. Nice area. I'm in Kennington myself. Roebury Avenue." Taylor sat back and closed his eyes, willing the drive to finish before Draven killed them both. His fists clenched at his sides, his erection slowly deflating. He'd always hated fast cars and speed, ever since a close friend had died in a fiery ball after hitting an embankment speeding. Taylor had experienced it, felt Michael's agony and fear, and been incapacitated for the best part of the day. Now he felt as if he was reliving that event and the emotional toll was rising.

Draven drove like he seemed to live his life. No nonsense, take charge, efficient and fast. Risky, and on a knife's edge. He didn't seem to notice Taylor, sick feeling in his stomach, gripping the leather seats with white knuckles, bracing his feet in the foot well, his body rigid with expectation and panic each time the car slew around a corner, or stopped sharply to meet the needs of a red traffic light. Taylor concentrated on his breathing.

In, out. In, out. In, out.

He was just starting to get the hang of this ride from hell when Draven shouted out a fierce expletive and the car shot out, going even faster. Taylor heard a screech of metal brakes. He couldn't help it. He shrieked like a girl and turned to Draven in fury.

"Hell, do you have to drive like a bloody maniac? You almost hit that guy!"

Draven turned to look at him in surprise and Taylor felt faint. "Look at the road. Please. Look at the damn road, not at me. Oh hell. I'm going to be sick. Stop the car. Stop the effing car."

Draven swore loudly. "Just hold on, I need to find somewhere to stop. Good Christ, what is it with you whenever we're together?"

A few seconds later, he'd pulled over under a streetlight in what appeared to (thankfully) be a fairly deserted road for London, and Taylor unclipped the belt, staggered out the car and was promptly sick into the rubbish bin attached to the light. When he'd finished hacking up the contents of his stomach, he stood up, dizzy and still nauseous.

Draven's eyes glinted in the dim light but his face looked worried. "Taylor, are you all right?"

"Oh, I'm just peachy fine, fuck you very much," Taylor spat in fury. "Who the hell taught you to drive? Stirling-fucking-Moss?" He held tight to the lamppost. “Oh wait; he’s dead, isn’t he. Well, one day you might join him if you keep driving like that!”

Draven rolled his eyes, which didn’t help Taylor’s temper. “Christ, you are such a prima donna. I knew this was a bad idea.”

“A bad idea?” Taylor was hyperventilating now. “You’re a bad idea. This whole bloody thing is a bad idea. I think you need to take me home.” He patted his pockets, looking for a cigarette and groaning loudly when he realised he must have left them at the restaurant in his hurry to get out.

Draven moved forward, a look of resolve on his face. “No.”

Taylor glared at him. “No? What do you mean, no? Who died and make you God?”

“Taylor, you’re upset. My home is about five minutes away. Let’s get back in the car, and you can calm down at my place. You can wash your face and brush your teeth.” He gripped Taylor’s arm, “Maybe have a shower and just chill out for a while.” His face grew anxious. “Shit, do you need a paper bag? You’re breathing very hard.”

“And I’m not even coming,” Taylor growled. “And that’s not going to be on the cards either when we get to your place.”

Draven shrugged but there was a hint of a smile on his face. “Fine. Let’s just get there and you can stop going all kamikaze on my arse and perhaps we can salvage just a little of this night. What do you say?”

Taylor said nothing, just stormed off to the car, ripped the door open and plonked into the passenger seat. His mouth tasted like crap, his breathing had gone back to normal, and his body felt like it had been through a fast spin cycle in a wash machine. He glowered at the dashboard as Draven got in the car and buckled up.

“Go slow,” Taylor muttered. “I don’t like fast. Brings back bad memories.”

Draven’s eyes widened. “Shit, why didn’t you tell me you’d been in an accident before? I wouldn’t have driven like I did.” He grimaced as he started the car and pulled out, very slowly and painstakingly. “With the work I do, we’re all taught defensive driving and do advanced speed courses. I sometimes forget other people aren’t used to it.”

“I haven’t been in an accident. It was someone else that died.” Taylor was suddenly very tired and all he wanted was to sleep.

"I see." Draven's voice was quiet. "I'll go slower, I promise."

Taylor was woken what seemed just like a few minutes later by a soft voice in his ear.

"Taylor, we're here. Come on. Let's get inside."

Taylor yawned and stretched and clambered sleepily out of the car. They were in a quiet neighbourhood among a row of pretty terraced houses, and Draven climbed the few stairs to one at the end. He rattled some keys and the door opened.

"Come on in. Welcome to Chez Samuels." He disappeared inside as Taylor followed into the dimly lit hallway. A light was switched on and he winced as the brightness hit his eyes. He looked around. It was small, cosy, masculine. Minimally furnished, with a lounge at one side, a kitchen on the other and what looked like a cloakroom. Decorated in deep shades of aubergine, white and bronze, the whole house looked elegant and classic. Very unlike Taylor's little bedroom with peeling wallpaper, a broken faucet at the small basin and frayed carpets covered in various stains. He loved his home with Leslie but this one was in a whole new league. He groaned at that thought. *Leslie.* He hadn't called him to let him know he wasn't coming home tonight. Leslie would have a full diva queen strop if Taylor didn't let him know. He pulled out his mobile and sent off a quick text.

Won't be home tonight. Pulled and ready to rock and roll.

That should please his roommate–even if it wasn't strictly true. He had no intention anymore of putting out for the man in the next room despite the hot and heavy breathing action in the restaurant. The vomiting and making a fool of himself yet again had put paid to that idea.

He went into the kitchen and Draven turned to him and passed him a toothbrush still in the packaging.

"Here, the bigger bathroom is upstairs if you want to brush your teeth. Feel free to shower if you fancy. I can give you a pair of sweats and a tee shirt. I'll leave them in the upstairs bathroom."

"Way to tell me my breath smells," Taylor muttered sulkily.

Draven grinned. "Wow, aren't you just a ball of sunshine." He turned to the large pink pig cookie jar on his counter top. "Freud, what do you think? Shall we adopt him?"

Taylor looked at the pig jar in suspicion. "You named your biscuit jar after a psychoanalyst who was obsessed with sex? And really, who names their containers like that?"

Draven frowned. "Freud wasn't obsessed with it. He was an advocate of psychosexual development."

Taylor looked at him blankly. "There's a difference?" He chuckled as Draven stared him down. "Okay. I'm off to give these stinky teeth a brush. Uhm, I don't suppose you have any cigarettes here, do you? I'd love a smoke later…" His voice tailed as Draven raised an eyebrow. Taylor sighed in resignation. "Fine," he huffed. "I'll do without. Just don't blame me if I get all cranky."

That poxy eyebrow lifted even further and Taylor wanted to smack the face that owned it. But that was what had got him here in the first place.

Upstairs in the bathroom, after seeing the luxurious wet room, Taylor decided to have a shower. He was sticky and sweaty and noticed he had spots of sick down his front.

"Way to go, Tay," he muttered as he shed his clothes and started the shower. "How can any man resist you in this state?"

He brushed his teeth, stepped into the shower and lathered himself up. Hot, steaming water had always had a restorative effect on him, making him feel better, washing away the emotions of the day and making his soul cleaner. He revelled in the smell of warm, orangey citrus shower gel, and hummed to himself as he washed his hair. He thought he heard a noise behind him and peeked out the curtain, but all he saw was fresh clothes laid out on the chair on the other side of the bathroom. Despite his resolve not to put out, Taylor felt a slight sense of pique that Draven hadn't even attempted to get in the shower with him.

Finally he turned off the water, wrapped a towel around his waist and went into the adjacent bedroom to change. This was obviously Draven's room. Dark, deep shades of blue matched with white and lime green, giving the room a rather nautical flair. A clock shaped like a ship's rudder ticked quietly on a far wall and here and there were small items of a nautical nature: a ship in full sail, a lighthouse and a pair of nautical rope doorstops lying carelessly on the floor. Taylor changed quickly, towelling his unruly hair dry then putting the towel back in the bathroom. When he stepped out into the hallway, he started at seeing Draven waiting outside.

"Everything fit okay?" Draven said softly.

Taylor nodded. "The trousers are a little long but they're fine. Thanks."

Draven eye-fucked him from his toes, up the length of his body and then finally came to rest on his lips. The air of desire emanating from the man was disturbing and playing havoc with Taylor's decision not to fulfil their earlier intentions. He knew *that* bloody mindedness had been nothing but wishful thinking.

His cock inflated slowly in his sweatpants like a rising periscope. He stood stock still as Draven inspected him. The air around them seemed to thicken and warm, much like Taylor's dick. He knew Draven noticed the tenting in the front and his teeth showed in a wide, predatory smile. That smile made Taylor's blood tingle, his backside clench, and his mouth want to latch onto Draven's like a Bengal tiger on a succulent morsel of dinner.

"I like the tattoo," Draven murmured, waving a hand at the intricate pattern on Taylor's inside left wrist. It was a pattern of thin, finely drawn vine leaves, winding up along a central stem from the wrist to the crook of Taylor's elbow. He'd had it done about four years ago when he and a previous boyfriend had decided to be adventurous. Taylor hadn't wanted any garish colours, so he'd stuck with the soft grey and black tones.

Draven stepped forward and in one quick move, he slid his hands beneath the loose tee shirt and pulled Taylor toward him. Taylor gasped as his own groin met one equally as hard and the warm, strong hands on his skin sent shivers through his body. '*All thoughts of resistance are futile*' was the first thought that went through his mind.

God, I sound like someone from Star Trek. I need to get a bloody grip.

He loved the feeling of someone taking control of him, someone tough and sexy leading the way. He ached for a man strong enough to see what he needed, and not hold back giving it to him. He didn't want to take it too far but being held down, dominated, needed—that turned him on like nothing else in the world. He'd tried it before in his relationships—the few he'd had that had lasted more than a few weeks. The ones where his lovers hadn't left him quickly because he was a freak when he had his "episodes," as one taunting lover had put it, but never been quite satisfied. His partners had either been too rough or not rough enough.

"You smell like sex and spice," Draven growled as his mouth slid down Taylor's neck and he licked the skin like said tiger. "You drive me fucking mad, you know that. I don't know how you do this to me. Why I want you so damn much."

Taylor closed his eyes as the assault on his neck and jawline continued. He couldn't speak. Hot lips grazed his skin, biting, nibbling and then finally, when he thought he'd go mad from the constant contact, Draven's mouth found his and Taylor's knees buckled. Draven's arm around his waist was the only thing holding him up, he was sure. Never before had he been kissed like this, ravenous, hard, unrelenting as lips and tongue filled him, tasted him, sucked him in and swallowed him whole. When a hand reached into the waistband of his sweats and gripped his cock, Taylor cried out, the sound seeming to inflame Draven more as he stroked him harder and faster, sliding fingers and palm over the slippery essence that coated his dick and making Taylor's senses overload. He pulled his mouth away from the rapacious one that was devouring it.

"Draven, please. You're going to make me come like this," he gasped, as the hand pulled up, released, and stroked down even harder.

Draven's eyes were black, his lips red and swollen, a slight tinge of blood where Taylor had bitten him. "Then come," he demanded and slid another hand round to stroke Taylor's arse cheeks, pulling them apart and grazing his fingers over his hole. Taylor bucked in Draven's arms, his balls tightening, his cock feeling impossibly hard as he climaxed, wet streams of musky come covering Draven's hand, his arm and the inside of the once-clean sweatpants. Draven held onto his dick until he was spent, all the time pushing against Taylor's hole and even inserting a finger at his moment of climax.

"God, love to feel you tighten around my finger like that," Draven panted. "Just think about what it will feel like when I have my cock inside you. Oh God, you feel so damn good,"

He pushed his groin against Taylor, rutting against him then shuddered, and Taylor buried his hands in Draven's hair, holding him tight as his own orgasm took him. Finally they were still, standing in the hallway and supporting each other. Taylor with his sweatpants covered in come and Draven with a huge wet spot in front of his usual immaculate trousers.

"Oh, God, that was pretty awesome," Taylor muttered as he leaned his forehead against Draven's sweaty one. "Why the hell did I have a shower if you intended doing that?"

Draven chuckled." "Because you reeked of sick and no matter how much I wanted to kiss you, that wasn't going to happen the way your breath smelt." He moved back and swatted Taylor's arse. "Now I guess we clean up and maybe we can progress to round two."

"Round two?" Taylor said faintly.

Oh God, all my dreams have come true.

That predatory look crossed Draven's face again. "Oh yes. I want to be buried deep inside that pert arse of yours and I'm intending on doing that just as soon we can." He shivered. "I'm not sure how long I can hold out though. I need to clean us both up then we can start again. In bed this time if that's all right with you?" He leaned in and ran his tongue across Taylor's lips, then bit his earlobe. "So let's get rid of this sticky mess then we can get dirty again."

He disappeared into the bathroom. Taylor stood there, horny again and confused. This had all happened very quickly. For two men who supposedly didn't really like each other, they were doing a damn good job of concealing it. He also wondered mutinously if he looked like a bottom because Draven sure as hell seemed to think so. Never mind that he swung both ways and could just as easily be buried in Draven's tight arse. He might like being manhandled but he liked to do a bit of his own too. He heard a slight noise behind him and turned. It had sounded like a faint whisper or a swish of something soft against a wall. He frowned, seeing nothing there to explain the noise. The noise came again, slightly louder this time but he still couldn't make it out. He waited patiently, then, no longer hearing it, he went into the bathroom.

***

Draven stared at his swollen, bitten lips and sleepy, satisfied eyes in the mirror. He peered closer, as if expecting to see someone else there. His clothes lay in a heap on the floor.

That little session in the hallway had been explosive, and Draven had actually come in his pants, something he didn't do often. Taylor was so damn sexy, with that tight body, coffee-coloured skin and lips that begged to be ravished. He grunted.

Ravished? What the hell am I, some lead in a bloody romance novel?

He grinned at himself in the mirror as he swooped warm water up from the basin on the cloth and cleaned himself.

God, I am so fucked. I have never felt this strongly about anyone before. Let alone a damned professed psychic.

In getting to know the younger man who was now in his bathroom, Draven's instincts had already told him Taylor Abelard was no charlatan, no fraud out to make a quick buck. He'd checked with his friends in the investigative services and they'd heard a little about the "kid with the weird ability to sense scary crap," as one of them had put it, but Taylor had never been paid for any of those services. And according to those sources, he'd quite a good track record in helping the local police at the Lambeth Police Station—one sergeant in particular, a man called Rick Grant, someone with whom Taylor seemed to have a personal connection.

Draven couldn't deny that a little bit of the jealous green man in him wondered just how good friends they actually were.

He saw Taylor behind him, his eyes dark and smoky, his lips puffy and well kissed. His eyes travelled down Draven's body in frank appreciation, lingering on the curve of his arse. Draven loved that appraisal. He turned around and beckoned to the basin. "There's a wash cloth in there if you want to clean up a little. I'm done." He waggled his eyebrows. "I'll see you in bed."

"You do know it's only just gone ten p.m.," Taylor observed drily. "Old man."

Draven snapped the wet washcloth against Taylor's backside.

Taylor jumped and swore. "Bastard. That stung."

He glared at Draven and Draven looked at the pale pink welt against the soft caramel skin. "Count yourself lucky it was only a wash cloth." His voice was husky and he was already growing hard again. "I have other implements that can make much sexier marks on that gorgeous skin of yours."

Taylor's eyes grew wide as his gaze flicked to Draven's growing erection, the desire in his eyes evident.

I see you in there, my sexy sub. I can see right into your damn soul.

Draven wasn't big into the BDSM scene but he liked being adventurous and using some of the sex toys on offer. It was finding someone else willing to do so that was sometimes the problem.

Draven caressed Taylor's arm. "I'll kiss your boo-boo better when we get to bed if you like? Lick it better, even."

"Boo-boo?" The husky tone of Taylor's voice turned Draven on even more. "I take the old man comment back. You're actually a kid."

Draven smiled wickedly. "Believe me, sexy, what I'm going to do to you tonight will never make any programme under the watershed. That will be strictly triple-X rated."

He bounced out of the bathroom toward the bedroom, laughing softly at the complete lack of noise coming from the bathroom.

Hell, this was becoming fun.

In his bedroom, he turned back the covers, adjusted the lighting and made sure the condoms and lube were in his side drawer where he normally kept those and other more extreme implements should anyone choose to play. He was pretty sure Taylor would make a beautiful playmate. He got under the covers and gave a sigh of satisfaction. There was still no noise from the bathroom and he called out.

"Taylor? I'm lonely here. Get your arse into bed."

There was nothing. No response. Frowning, he clambered out of bed and went into the bathroom.

"What's taking so long—"" His voice cut off at the sight of Taylor sitting naked on the floor, arms huddled around his knees, a blank look in his eyes. He was shivering, his skin covered in goose bumps; Draven wasn't sure if it was from the cold or something else.

"What's happening? Did you slip?"

Taylor continued to stare blankly into space, and Draven reached up and took a fluffy towel off the rack. He draped it over Taylor's shoulders as he tried to get him to stand up.

"I don't know what's going on, but you need to come out of here and into the bedroom where it's warmer, 'kay? Come with me. Get up, that's right." Slowly he lifted Taylor to a standing position and then led him into the bedroom.

Taylor was mumbling quietly now, words that Draven couldn't make out. He managed to get Taylor on his side on the sheet then pulled the covers over him. Still Taylor stared into blank space.

Draven felt a prickle of fear down his spine. Taylor's eyes were vacant, glassy. He had no idea what to do other than let him get over whatever it was he was doing. He got into bed behind the shivering man.

"I'm here, just relax and sleep. I don't know what you're going through but I'm here." He leaned back and switched off the light. "I'm here for you. Sleep now." He wrapped strong arms around the chilled form and stroked Taylor's hair softly. All thoughts of sex had gone, and all Draven had left was a fierce desire to protect the man in his bed. After a while, the sound of deep breathing echoed in the still room. Draven leaned over, careful not to disturb Taylor and saw long eyelashes framed against pale cheeks. He felt a sense of relief as he lay back and pulled the covers up over them both again. Perhaps in the morning he could explain what the hell had happened.

Chapter 6

Draven awoke to an empty bed and silence. He blinked sleepily and sat up in bed, the sheets falling to his waist. The house was still; outside he heard the distant sounds of children playing. He swung his legs from the bed and sat there, rubbing his eyes. He picked up his phone and squinted at the display. Eight a.m. Christ, he'd slept in for a change. Normally at between five and six-thirty without fail he'd be waking up and padding through to the kitchen to make his first cup of black coffee. He stood, stretched, yawned, pulled on a pair of old sleeping shorts and went in search of Taylor. He hoped he was still here and hadn't slipped out like a thief in the night. He was disappointed. The house was empty of another human presence.

Draven swore. "Fuck. That little bastard."

His pique at last night's date and sex partner running out on him caused him to storm into the kitchen and grab for the kettle. He frowned. The kettle was still hot, which meant Taylor couldn't have left all that long ago. He cursed again and reached into the cupboard for a mug. He started as cold hands wrapped themselves around his naked waist and the cup dropped just short of falling to the floor as he managed to keep his grip.

"Did you miss me then?" Taylor sounded like he was smiling, although his voice sounded a little…lost? Draven couldn't stop the sudden pounding of his heart, both from fright and from—something else.

"I thought you'd bailed on me," he said, his tone surly as he busied himself making coffee, not even bothering to turn around. The low, husky chuckle made his skin tingle.

"I heard what you called me." Fingers made light trails against Draven's spine and he shivered. "I needed a smoke. Had to rush out to that corner shop and buy some." Smoky breath blew against the back of his neck and Draven's needy skin rose in goose bumps. Soft kisses dotted the puckered skin, making him groan softly as he closed his eyes and leaned back into the hard frame behind him.

"You know those things will kill you. Have you ever tried giving them up?"

Great, here he was with a sexy guy kissing his shoulder and caressing his stomach and all Draven could think to talk about were his lover's smoking habits. The National Health Service would *love* him. Maybe they'd make him their poster boy.

"I did for a while. Then crap happened and I started again." Draven sensed the shrug. "We all have to die some way, right?" Taylor's voice was uncertain and his fingers ceased their soft stroking of Draven's midsection.

Draven's lower section was pretty needy, too, and the shorts he had on were no barrier to his rising cock, which was currently pressed against the hard surface of the kitchen counter. Draven shifted, trying to get some release. He didn't want to turn around, wanted to stay here all day with those fingers touching him, that unique scent of Taylor drifting into his nostrils, his breath warm and not unpleasantly fragranced. Draven didn't mind a man's cigarette breath; he found it quite a turn-on actually. And now he'd definitely *lost* any chance of being the spokesperson for the anti-smoking bods.

"That doesn't mean we have to give it help," he murmured and let out a gasp as a wet tongue slid into his ear then gently bit his ear lobe.

"Stop preaching. I get enough of that from Leslie. You're supposed to humour me."

Taylor's hand had now found Draven's cock, although admittedly it hadn't been hiding very well, and his fingers slid into the shorts with an easy move. He grasped the hardened, heated flesh that was trying to get out. Draven gave up all thoughts of making coffee or trying to make the world a safer place for non-smokers and yielded to that hand, pressing his arse back against Taylor's groin, finding him as hard as he was.

Both men were panting, small groans of satisfaction, need rumbling up for chests that were tight from lust and want. Taylor's breath on his ear and cheek was an aphrodisiac; his slight moans and throaty noises making Draven want him even more.

There was not much finesse in this early morning jerk-off; just strong fingers wrapping themselves around his engorged and slippery dick, stroking, pulling and gripping until Draven's balls shot up into his groin like steel marbles and he cried out, a soft, sharp expletive that shattered the earthy silence of the kitchen as he jetted hot, viscous fluid into his shorts, onto Taylor's hand and his own stomach. He leaned back against Taylor, legs weak with the force of his orgasm, and soft lips found his in an awkward embrace that left Draven even weaker. He even thought he mewled like a kitten as Taylor's wicked tongue sank into his mouth, teeth clicking against teeth. Soft stubble left a burning sensation on his chin.

Finally they released each other and Taylor stepped back, allowing Draven to turn around and see him for the first time. There had been something so utterly hot about not yet seeing the man with his hands around his cock, simply taking what he wanted, giving what was needed.

Taylor stood, soft smile on his roughened, pink lips, eyes as dark as black holes, dressed in Draven's too-long sweats and an old Iron Maiden tee shirt. Those strong arms that had wrapped themselves around his waist were covered in faint, dark hair. His hair was wind- swept, curling in tendrils across his face, a face that regarded Draven with a mixture of satisfaction and apprehension.

There was something else too, a sense of unease emanating from the man. Draven wondered if the early morning hand job had been some sort of penance for something.

"You did something for me and I zoned out last night, and didn't get a chance to give you anything back, so…" Taylor lifted his shoulders in a Gallic gesture that Draven had seen on waiters in fancy French restaurants. An expressive shrug. He also felt a sense of disquiet that Taylor seemed to be able to read his mind.

"I didn't do it to get something in return," he said quietly, conscious of the sticky mess in his shorts and that he'd need another shower or at the bare minimum, a clean-up. "And yes, I was rather worried about you last night. I couldn't get you to wake up, or whatever."

Taylor's eyes narrowed. "It happens sometimes, you just have to let it run its course." He moved over to the cupboard and took another cup out. He switched the kettle on again and took Draven's mug from him. "Let me make this while you clean up."

Draven stared at him then glanced down at the bulge in Taylor's pants. "I can sort that out for you if you like," he said softly, but Taylor shook his head.

"No, I'm okay. Thanks anyway. I need to be off soon, back home." He gestured to Draven's busily whirring tumble dryer. "Hope you don't mind but I got up early and washed the vomit out of my clothes. I popped them in to dry, so they shouldn't be too long now."

The drying cycle was nearly over and Draven knew that particular one took two hours. "You must have been up early to wash them and get them in the dryer," he said, with a keen look at Taylor. "What time did you get up?"

Taylor busied himself spooning coffee into cups. "I woke up about three a.m., couldn't sleep so got up." He sounded tired and disheartened, his mood changing like the sun disappearing behind a cloud.

Draven reached out and grasped Taylor's wrist, his thumb caressing the tattoo. "What happened last night? One minute you were fine, the next you were in a kind of coma on the bathroom floor. Is that how it happens…these visions of yours?"

Draven knew how it worked on the television when people had psychic abilities. They either went all blank and white marble-eyed and spoke in funny voices, or their damn heads twisted around on their shoulders—something he found exceptionally creepy. He hid his face every time he saw a scene like that. Others simply went all Zen-like and creepy and he thought Taylor might fit into *that* category if that was what had happened last night.

Taylor gave a curt laugh as he poured water into the cups and then went to Draven's fridge to look for milk. The man looked really at home here. "Sort of. It's a bit like an out-of-body experience. You know you're around somewhere but you can't do much to communicate to the outside world.

"I knew you were there, by the way. Thanks for just getting me into bed and holding me. That was the right thing to do." He finished making the coffee, stirred both cups a few times then handed one mug to Draven. Draven took it, cradling his hands around the steaming coffee-fragranced manna from heaven. He took a sip and gave a satisfied sigh.

"God, that's good. I needed that." He glanced at Taylor. "So what did you hear or see in that sexy head of yours last night?" Knowing he'd probably get another punch to the jaw if he mentioned anything about Taylor seeing dead people, he tried to rein back the natural instinct he had to ask. He might be slowly and grudgingly accepting that perhaps Taylor did have something special now he was getting to know the man, but that didn't mean he understood any of it.

Taylor's eyes became wary. "Nothing, really." Draven knew he was lying. He was trained to spot them and this was definitely a liar in front of him. "I sometimes remember, and sometimes not. This is one I can't recall."

He sipped his coffee and Draven could see that in Taylor's mind, the questions were over. But he hadn't finished. Draven's co-workers didn't call him "The Inquisitor" for nothing.

"You're lying," he observed and drank his coffee, keeping his eyes focused on Taylor's face, which, predictably, grew mutinous and dark.

"I'm not fucking lying." Taylor slammed his coffee cup down on the counter, causing it to slosh over. Draven raised an eyebrow at the temper tantrum. He watched as Taylor went to the dryer and opened the door, stopping it mid cycle.

"It hasn't finished the cycle yet," Draven observed mildly.

"It's fine. They're dry enough for me to go home." Curt words were snapped at him like wet towels and Draven sighed.

"Taylor, come on, for God's sake. You scared me last night. One minute I'm expecting the blow job and fuck from heaven, the next I have a comatose man in my bed. Surely you know I'd be curious about what went down last night. And it wasn't you. "He tried to joke about it in the hope Taylor might lighten up. Instead he got a face full of angry man, a man like a spitting tiger cub, all claws and teeth.

"I gave you what you wanted earlier," he snarled. "I'm sorry I didn't manage to come to bed last night so you could fuck my arse, but I had stuff in my head to deal with, you tosser."

Taylor's teeth were bared, his hands balled in fists at his sides, but Draven saw the panic in his eyes. The man looked fraught, outwardly composed, but inside he was a damned mess.

Draven knew how to deal with this side of Taylor Abelard. He took hold of Taylor's arms and pushed him backward, towards the wall, pinning him there. Draven's hands tightened like steel bands on the other man's wrists, pushing them up above his head. Taylor tried desperately to break free but Draven knew his heart wasn't really in it despite the fire in his eyes. He'd seen the submissive side to this man, the man who ached for someone to take control. If ever there was a time to bring that side out, then this was it. Perhaps it would mean no more pissed-off psychic for a while.

"Let me go." Taylor's teeth grated between thin lips and Draven smiled. This seemed to inflame Taylor more as he struggled harder to break free.

"Nuh-huh. You, my friend, are going to listen to me instead of getting all pissy." His own body pressed against Taylor's and the flare of need in Taylor's eyes told him everything he wanted to know. Draven held his wrists, loosening his grip so as not to leave bruises. He brought his lips close to Taylor's, hearing him draw a shuddering breath, his cock stiff against Draven's rapidly hardening one.

"Something is worrying you. You went strange last night and whatever it was, it's unsettled you. You need to tell me about it so I can help you deal with it."

Taylor's amazing eyes stared into his and Draven's heart stuttered at the pain in them.

"I can't tell you," he whispered brokenly. "I don't really understand it all but I don't think it's good news."

Draven's spine tingled like an ice cube had been drawn down bare skin. Taylor bit his bottom lip and Draven wanted to kiss it. There was something about this man that definitely brought out the protective streak in him.

"Tell me," he whispered gently, relaxing his hold on Taylor's wrists. He knew Taylor wouldn't try and get free.

"I only dream, have visions about people close to me who have died or who may be in danger. Last night…." His voice shook and he closed his eyes.

"What about last night? Tell me," Draven demanded.

Taylor's eyes opened. "I dreamt about you." His voice was shaking. Draven leaned in, his lips brushing Taylor's cheek and he tightened his grip, wanting to make Taylor feel just how alive he was.

"I'm not dead, as you can see and feel. Nothing's going to happen to me. Although I'm glad you care just a little bit about something happening to me. There's hope for us yet."

Despite his tone of affected nonchalance, Draven couldn't help feeling a frisson of fear in his stomach. He supposed ruefully that was a definite sign that he was beginning to believe in Taylor and the voices in his head.

Taylor stared into his eyes with pupils as black as lava stones. "I heard your voice, or what sounded like your voice. You were asking me to let you go, to free you. You sounded so sad, and yet so yearning. I felt you all around me when you spoke, could smell your aftershave, feel you."

His voice grew fiercer. "I'm tired of this whole thing. Tired of feeling fucking scared and worried about what I see, tired of seeing people I know die horribly in my head, seeing mutilated kids in fields and smelling the blood. Oh God, Draven, when I smell things…" his voice tailed off and he closed his eyes in apparent exhaustion. "I just want it to stop. I want to be normal. I don't want anything to happen to you even if you are a pain in the arse." His breath hitched and Draven let go of his wrists and pulled him against him, wrapping broad arms around him. For a moment he held the firm body in his arms and listened to Taylor's soft breathing as he pressed his face against Draven's chest.

"Listen. Nothing is going to happen to me. I'm too bloody mean to die." Taylor's body tensed in his arms and Draven held him tighter. "And you know what they say? Only the good die young. And I am nowhere near good. Well, unless you count good at sex, of course. I'm pretty good at that, I have to say." He was warmed by Taylor's slight chuckle and snort. "So promise me you'll stop bottling it all inside and tell me how you feel."

He stopped as the enormity of those words drenched him like a cold shower.

Oh. My. Fucking. God. Since when did I become the sensible one in this relationship? I need to check I haven't grown girly parts.

Draven wasn't quite sure whether it was the thought of growing lady's bits or the fact he considered himself to be in a relationship that made his heart thump like a jackhammer.

God, we haven't even had proper sex yet.

These thoughts whirled around in his confused head and it was only when he felt Taylor shift beneath him, grinding his groin against his own erection that he came back down to earth.

He swallowed as Taylor lifted his head and gave him a searing hot glance from beneath sooty, wet-fringed lashes.

"Do you *want* to have proper sex?" The husky timbre of his voice went straight to Draven's cock, which perked up even more at those words.

"Oh. Did I say that out loud?"

Taylor nodded, amusement in his eyes. "You did, yes." His lips brushed Draven's, causing a jolt of electricity down his spine, and once again Draven wondered who had the power in this relationship.

Taylor leaned in and whispered, "Do you want to go back to bed and fuck me?"

"Is that a trick question?" Draven growled, releasing Taylor's wrists and then rubbing them gently. Taylor watched the slow movements of Draven's fingers on his skin as Draven traced the path of one of the vines on his wrist.

"Much as I'd like to take you up on the kind offer, I have to be at work in an hour or so for a meeting." Draven had never hated his job as much as he did now with a willing man in his arms and a raging boner. "So I'm afraid the proper sex thing will have to wait."

He brought Taylor's wrist up to his lips and kissed it lingeringly. Taylor's eyes watched every move. "So the plan is now I get in the shower… alone," he said decisively, even if he didn't want it to be that way. Taylor would be too much of a distraction and he'd never make it out of the shower. "Then I can get cleaned up and get to work before my damn boss fires my arse. He's not too happy with me at the moment anyway so I can't chance my luck. And you… you can stay as long as you want, and just lock up when you go.

Chuck the key back inside through the mailbox. Do you have to be at work?" He raised an eyebrow and Taylor shook his head.

"I called in and took a personal day. I have some things to do today and I haven't had a day off in forever so they can do without me. My boss wasn't too chuffed about that either but she can go to hell. I'm never sick and I'm always there." His beautiful face contorted into a fierce tiger-cub frown and Draven thought it was adorable. "It's been a rough week and I need some me time."

Draven reached over and drew him in for a long, sexy kiss that made his own toes curl and the boner he was sporting even harder. He'd have a bit of work to do in the shower before he got out. Finally he pulled away, leaving Taylor with wet lips and dazed eyes.

"Right, I'm off to shower." He turned and walked toward the stairs. He turned back, a slight fluttering in his stomach preceding his next words. He had a visit planned, as usual, to the hospital to see Jude. He hadn't been as often lately due to work and personal commitments and he felt as guilty as hell.

"Errm, I have somewhere to be after work for an hour or two then I'll call you later. Don't phone me; I won't have my phone on where I'm going." Curiosity flitted across Taylor's face but Draven wasn't ready to tell him about Jude. Not yet. "And remember, nothing bad is going to happen to me." He winked at Taylor. "Keep that thought about the proper sex bit. I'll hold you to that later."

He felt Taylor's eyes on him as he walked up the stairs to the bathroom, and for once in his life, he prayed to whatever entities resided above and below that he could keep that promise.

Chapter 7

Taylor had no idea how he made it through the next few weeks without physically combusting. The spark that had ignited between him and Draven had become a raging furnace and neither of them seemed able to keep their hands off one another. He had no idea what this thing between them was. Taylor was disparaging of the whole “love at first sight” thing but he had to admit he hadn’t felt this strongly before about a man who, in truth, he barely knew.

Taylor had been relieved that whatever the vision was that he’d had that night he’d first slept with Draven hadn’t come to anything. He still heard the voice sometimes, soft yet yearning, but he’d learned to simply accept it as he did with others. It was more difficult to do, though. The *faux* Draven (because if he imagined it to be the real one he’d go bat-shit crazy) had felt helpless, and the yearning to be somewhere else had been all encompassing.

Their days consisted of each of them at their respective jobs, keeping in touch with texts and quick phone calls. The nights—they were what held Taylor together. Long, passionate evenings into the early mornings, volatile sex and steamy shower sessions that left them both spent and exhausted. Most of the time they spent at Draven’s house, as it was more private than having Leslie coming home, sometimes with a friend of his own. Taylor was feeling a little guilty about neglecting his friend.

Now, on one of his rare days off, he got up around eleven a.m. and stumbled tiredly into the small shower. After drying himself, he put on old tracksuit pants and a tee shirt that he grabbed from the wash hamper. It was close to one p.m. when, after checking his texts and emails—Leslie had texted him earlier from work saying he was staying the night at a friend’s—and fixing himself a snack of peanut butter and jam sandwiches, he was seated comfortably in the old armchair with the remote, selecting a Netflix film called *Going Down in La-La Land.* He thought it sounded good enough to keep him occupied, and perhaps he might even engage in a little under-the-cover action later to relieve the permanent sexual tension he had.

Taylor woke up hours later, dry mouthed and needing to pee. He struggled out of the chair, wincing at the tired muscles and dried come on his stomach and took his trip to the bathroom. He rinsed his mouth out with breath-freshener, cleaned himself up, and loped tiredly back into the lounge. The afternoon sun shone in through grimy windows and Taylor thought not for the first time that he really needed to get around to cleaning them sometime.

After pottering around and doing some much needed housework he settled in to watch some television, glancing at his watch and wondering when Draven might call. It was close to eight-thirty p.m. when his mobile finally rang. His stomach dipped at the thought it was Draven. It wasn't him on the phone but he smiled when he saw who it was.

"Eddie, my man. What's up?" If he hadn't had the caller ID he'd still know who it was from the sounds of the kitchen in the background. Men's voices, the clutter of utensils and whir of whatever culinary machines made those sort of noises. Taylor wasn't big on the whole cooking thing.

"I should be asking you the same question." Eddie laughed. "How are things going with Mr. Blond and Grouchy? Are you still getting laid regularly?

Taylor smiled. "I can't keep up with him; the man is insatiable. But I'm enjoying his company." He wandered into the kitchen and took out a beer, uncapping it and taking a deep drink.

"Is he still being so bloody secretive about where he goes when you can't get in touch with him?" Eddie sniffed. "Are you sure he hasn't got another boyfriend somewhere, Tay? You know how I worry about you…"

"No, I don't think that's it," Taylor muttered. "He's hiding something, that's for sure but I don't think it's another man. The guy couldn't possibly do what he does with me and have a bit on the side, believe me. He'd have to have the stamina of Superman."

Taylor felt a twinge of discomfort at his own words. He'd been there, been the bit on the side and who knew just how much sex Drew had been getting with his wife before coming to Taylor? He supposed he shouldn't really make such wild assumptions.

"Have you asked him? You know, talked instead of just screwing each other's brains out?" Eddie sounded worried.

"Yeah, we talk. A little anyway, but it's more physical at this stage I think. He's a tough guy to get to know, but I really like him. He's a real softy inside; it's one of the things I like about him."

"Really? You mean that whole douche-bag thing he has going for him isn't the real Draven? Wow, miracles never cease." Eddie's teasing lifted Taylor's spirits a little. He also felt the need to defend his new lover.

"Oh, when you get to know him a bit better, I guess he's not such a bad bloke." Taylor tried to change the topic away from his sex life. "Anyway, if I recall Gideon used to be a douche bag too before you got your hands on him."

There was a loud snort from the other side. "Oh yeah, too true." Eddie's tone turned wicked. "You just need to train them then they become a little more bearable." His voice got louder and Taylor grinned as he realised Gideon had probably just walked into the kitchen. "I mean, what's the point of having a man if they don't toe the line and let you show them who's boss?" There was a yowl from the phone. "Ow, baby, that hurt. Really, you need to remember we're not in the bedroom now—you need to have some self-restraint. Ow!"

Taylor chuckled loudly as Gideon came onto the phone. "Tay? My man is having a sudden crisis this side; he says he'll call you later. I need to take him home and make sure he knows who's the boss." His voice was amused and loving and Taylor felt a pang as he realised how lucky Eddie was.

Will I ever have that someone who talks about me like he really cares? Is it going to be Draven or is that just a one-time thing?

The phone was obviously grabbed away as Eddie reappeared, breathing fairly heavily. "Damn bully. I'm back. Anyway, where were we? Oh yeah, I was asking you about your love life. Don't let the grass grow, yadda, yadda. And have fun, Tay." His voice grew serious. "Don't let him hurt you. He doesn't sound like the type of guy who's into relationships so make sure you don't get in too deep unless you know it's going somewhere. I did some checking on this guy and he's a bit of a player." Taylor had no illusions that Gideon had been Eddie's information source.

"So was I, Eddie," Taylor said softly. "I might not have brought a lot of guys home to the house when we stayed together but, believe me, I've had my fair share of casual sex." He remembered Drew and the warm light in his eyes as they'd lain in bed together. That hadn't really been casual to him.

"Thanks for worrying but I'll be fine. This thing with Draven isn't really serious. I'm not sure where it's going. Just a bit of fun really." He'd say anything to put Eddie's mind out of protective mode. He was tired of having everyone see him as someone who needed babying. Leslie had said much the same thing as Eddie.

He heard a noise at the kitchen door and turned swiftly to see Draven standing there, his face blank but with a strange look in his eyes. Taylor's heart leapt as he motioned to him to come in. Draven nodded and moved into the small space, crossing his arms across his chest and regarding Taylor evenly.

Taylor swallowed, feeling strangely guilty at his last words about Draven being a bit of fun. "Listen, Eddie, I need to go. Draven's just arrived, so I'll call you later in the week, okay? Maybe we can make a plan to go out for a beer, you, me and Leslie. Like old times."

"No worries. I'll speak to you soon. Oh, and Taylor?" Eddie's voice lowered to a whisper. "Fuck his brains out." The line went dead and Taylor laid his phone down on the side table and looked up to stare at Draven.

"Do you always leave your front door open?" Draven asked quietly. "Anyone could have come in. I did knock but you were occupied." For the first time Taylor noticed the brown folder under his arm.

Taylor shrugged. "You know I don't lock it when I'm home. It's not a bad neighbourhood. Maybe I should start, seeing as how just anyone could walk in." He smiled, meaning it as a tease, but Draven's jaw tightened and he cricked his head from side to side as if loosening tight muscles.

Taylor swallowed. "I wasn't expecting you to come over in person. I thought you were going to call first, like usual. Did you get your business sorted out, you know, the stuff you do after work?" Taylor didn't want to be nosy but it was a habit that was hard to break.

Draven nodded, rather curtly Taylor thought. "Yes."

He said no more but Taylor saw an expression cross his face, something sad and rather unsettling. He looked at Taylor, a wary expression in his eyes.

"Sorry, I didn't mean to walk in on your private conversation. I don't want to interrupt if you have plans." He uncrossed his arms and took hold of the folder in his left hand. "I should go. Maybe this was a mistake coming here unannounced."

Taylor frowned. He didn't want Draven to leave. "I told you that's not a problem. I come over to yours without always calling first."

Draven drew a breath. "I guess. Is it all right then if I stay?"

"Yeah, of course. I'll get you a drink. Beer?"

Draven nodded and Taylor fetched a San Miguel from the small fridge.

Draven scowled slightly. "So that was Eddie? What was he doing? Checking out what my intentions were toward you? Finding out how much *fun* you were having with me?" There was a slight bite to Draven's words and Taylor's stomach plummeted.

"So you heard the last part of my conversation then?"

Draven didn't reply but the way his nostrils flared told Taylor he definitely had.

"It's the only way to keep him off my back." Taylor explained, fairly lamely he thought. "He's not sure you're the right person for me to get involved with, and telling him that will make him worry less."

"Whatever. You're right. It's nothing serious, anyway, I agree. Too early for that. It's just a bit of fun." Hearing his words repeated back at him in that flat tone made Taylor feel like a heel. He also didn't like the fact that Draven thought "fun" was the key word for their budding relationship either.

"Draven, I…"

"I had another reason for coming around to see you." Draven ignored him and moved over to the couch and sat down, placing the folder on the scarred wooden table in between the chairs. "I wondered if you could help me with a case I'm working on." He raised that sardonic eyebrow at Taylor's sudden intake of breath.

"What? You thought I wouldn't be able to get past my own inhibitions about what you do and see if there's any truth in what you say you do?"

"Well, yeah, it's a bit surprising." Taylor shuffled forward, suddenly conscious he was in old sweatpants and a grubby tee shirt while Draven was immaculate in a green polo shirt which showed off muscled, blond-haired arms and an impressive set of pectoral muscles. His trendy black jeans looked as if they'd been poured onto him.

Way to impress a man, Taylor, looking like some of hippy guy in a coffee-stained tee.

He slumped next to Draven and ran a hand through the tangled curls of his hair. Draven's eyes followed that movement closely and there was a sudden longing in his eyes that was hard to ignore. Then his face settled back into the blank mask again.

"I'm a businessman. I'll use any tools I need to get what I want and finish the job."

Taylor wasn't sure he liked being called a "tool." He'd been called it in other situations where it had a different meaning but somehow, this dispassionate assessment of what he did seemed worse.

"You do know I'm not something you can just pull out of a fucking cupboard and turn on, don't you?" he said acerbically. "That's not the way this works. I don't even know if I can connect with anything without something emotional binding me to them."

Draven's grey eyes assessed him thoughtfully. "You are emotionally involved," he said. He picked up the folder and waved it. "This is about Drew."

Taylor's heart stopped then stuttered to a slow start again. "Drew?" he whispered. "What about him?"

"I told you I thought someone was blackmailing him about his affairs with men and that was what drove him to kill himself. Now I know that was the case after reviewing the police file. I think he was protecting his family. And I know about protecting family and what you'll do to make sure they survive in this world." Draven's voice was steely. "Now are you going to help me, or not?"

Taylor's first question came out of his mouth without him even realising it. "What do you mean, protecting family? Are yours in danger? Is that where you were tonight?" He leaned forward in concern and hope that perhaps he'd finally get some answers about Draven's secrecy. He laid a hand on Draven's leg, feeling the man tense.

"I don't think that's anything I want to get into with someone who sees me as 'just a bit of fun'," Draven remarked silkily. "Let's just focus on this, shall we?"

He opened the folder and Taylor saw various documents and photographs spill out. He was still stung by Draven's last remark but he had a feeling this wasn't the time to pursue it. He'd try and explain more about what he meant later, when Draven didn't have such a bug up his arse.

"There aren't any pictures of Drew in there are there?" he muttered. "You know, after he killed himself." He definitely wasn't up to seeing one of his lover's heads blown apart at the seams. He really didn't want to pass out again or be sick or anything else around this prickly man.

Draven nodded. "There are, but they're in a separate envelope and you don't need to see them. I'm not that cruel." He indicated to a white A4 envelope splayed across the table. "The thing I really wanted to show you was this."

He handed over a white piece of notepaper with a scrawl on it, a scrawl that Taylor was achingly familiar with.

"It's a copy of the suicide note Drew wrote to his wife, Catherine. I wondered if you could read it, see if you can get any sort of vibe out of it, or whatever it is that you get." Taylor hesitated, not wanting to take the paper. He was scared of what he might see and experience. Draven saw his reluctance.

"It's all right if you don't want to do this," he said evenly. "I'd understand. I've seen what happens to you when you do your thing. I don't want you hurt."

Taylor drew a deep breath. "It's fine. I can do this." He reached out and took the paper from Draven. Almost immediately he felt a sense of suffocation, of grief and emotions that threatened to overwhelm his senses. His vision blurred, his heart sped up and his skin felt clammy. He shook his head, trying to get rid of the sensations invading his body. Through a dim haze, he heard Draven calling his name in panic.

Flashes of light and dark went through his head, blurs of scenes as if they were something out a film, sped up and indistinct, fragments of events that only lasted seconds and made Taylor sick to his stomach with anguish. He heard a man sobbing, felt the warmth of tears down his face, tasted the salt in his mouth and felt cold metal in his right hand. In his vision, he saw a dark-haired woman moving over to Drew, her hands outreached toward him. She seemed familiar. Taylor was falling, falling into an abyss of despair and sorrow and as the cold metal touched the side of his head, the woman screamed.

"Drew, oh God, no. Drew!"

The world went dark.

***

Once again Draven sat with Taylor's jerking body in his arms, holding the man with all the care he could summon as he passed through whatever it was he saw. Draven hoped he would come out unscathed. When he'd asked Taylor to touch the paper, he'd never been prepared for a reaction like this. Taylor had gone white, his lips pinched and bloodless, a low keening noise coming out of his mouth like a soul in torment. His eyes had darkened to an unseeing black, a travesty of their usually warm brown, and his body had shivered and trembled.

Draven had tried to pull him back but could only watch helplessly as Taylor shuddered and mumbled and his hands had fidgeted incessantly, bunching up into his tee shirt, exposing his belly and at one time he'd drawn his fingers down the skin, leaving deep scratch marks and blood in their wake. Draven had managed to pull those restless hands away before he could do any more damage and now he sat, heart pounding with fear and shame at having put Taylor through this.

There was no doubt what he was seeing was real. How the whole psychic thing happened he had no idea, but this? This wasn't the natural order of things. This was outside of that. And Draven was both scared and awed by Taylor's abilities.

All the ire he'd felt on Taylor's careless comment to his friend that Draven wasn't anything serious disappeared for the time being by watching this man in the throes of what looked like great sorrow and discomfort.

He managed to get Taylor to the couch and held him tightly, willing him to relax and murmuring soothing platitudes. It was a good fifteen minutes before Taylor's body calmed down and he fell into a deep sleep. Draven slipped off his shoes, got up carefully, easing his aching back, taking care not to wake the sleeping man, although it looked like he was out for the count. He rummaged in Taylor's bedroom for a blanket then came back and lay down on the opposite side of the couch. He pulled the senseless man between his legs, his back against Draven's stomach, head resting on Draven's chest. Draven covered them with the duvet and closed his eyes wearily.

I seem to be making a habit of this. God help me, but there is something about this man that draws me into his orbit and I am going to get burned.

He was dozing when he heard a door open noisily and he came alert instantly. Taylor was still asleep, and Draven's arm was tingling with pins and needles. The light was switched on and he saw a tall, slim, dark-haired man staring down at him with an expression of wariness.

"Who the fuck are you?" The younger man's voice seemed to awaken something in Taylor and he mumbled and opened his eyes. The dark-haired man in high heels and tiny shorts—Draven had to blink twice just to make sure he wasn't in some horny fantasy dream—rushed over and knelt down beside them. He reached out a slim hand and pushed back the duvet, then glared at Draven before falling over the prostate form of Taylor.

Draven oomphed at the press of both bodies weighing him down.

Taylor grumbled and tried to sit up. "I'm okay, Leslie. Give me some space, you freak."

Draven's balls sprang back to life. He heaved a sigh of relief.

"Freak?" Leslie's voice was indignant. Strangely enough, his voice was deeper than Draven would expect from someone dressed like he was. He'd expected a high-pitched girly tone. "You bastard, you're the damn freak. What did this arsehole make you do?"

"Nothing that I didn't want to," mumbled Taylor as he tried to sit up and blinked the sleep out of his eyes. He frowned at Leslie's arm across his waist. "We're working on a case together." He frowned. "I thought you were staying out tonight?"

Leslie's shrugged slim shoulders. "Didn't work out." His eyes narrowed. "So this is Draven…the investigator guy you're fucking?"

"Yes, that would be me." Draven drawled, trying to keep some semblance of dignity even as he was trapped beneath two warm male bodies. In another situation that would have been just the kind of setup he might have appreciated. "Perhaps you can both bloody get off me so I take a pee? My bladder is bursting." He'd been putting it off long enough trying not to wake Taylor up.

Leslie huffed but backed off, allowing Taylor to scramble to his feet. He still looked a little shell-shocked but had more colour than when Draven had technically put him to bed.

"You stayed with me again." His voice was soft, wondering.

Draven grimaced as his bladder threatened to blow. "Of course I did, you idiot. Now can you show me where the damn bathroom is before I wet myself?"

At a vague wave in the direction of the room on the left of the kitchen, Draven hastily made his way to the small toilet and locked the door. He gave a huge gasp of pleasure as his bladder voided itself. Five minutes later he was back in the lounge where Taylor stood, back to him, facing the window and Leslie sat perched on the table, shoes off, rubbing his feet.

Draven cleared his throat and the two men turned to look at him. Taylor's eyes were dulled, dark circles under them but Draven thought he had never looked sexier being so vulnerable. He wanted to wrap this man in a cocoon and never let him go.

"Taylor, are you up to talking about it or should I wait for tomorrow? I know you saw something but I don't want to push you." The last thing in the world Draven wanted was to leave. He wanted to find out from Taylor what had happened, perhaps even get to explore his comment about this being just "fun." It rankled still that that was perhaps how Taylor saw this whole thing.

Leslie glared at him. "Of course it can wait. The man is obviously distressed."

"Leslie." Taylor's voice was firm. "Draven is staying and we're going to my room so we can talk about what I saw. This is important and I need to remember it now while it's still fresh." He bent down and kissed Leslie on his red-streaked black hair. Leslie grunted but reached up and touched Taylor's cheek as if comforting himself.

"You yell if you need me." He cast a suspicious look at Draven. "Don't let *him* wear you out."

Taylor seemed to choke back a laugh. "I promise I won't. Well, he can wear me out only in the ways that matter, anyway." He reached out a hand to Draven as he picked up his duvet. "Come on. We can chat in my room. I have a lot to tell you."

Draven just had time to snatch up the folder and contents before he was pulled along to the bedroom. He followed Taylor in as he closed the door and then found himself the recipient of a mind-blowing, toe-curling kiss as Taylor grabbed his shirt, ground his lips against his and proceeded to mine the inside of his mouth.

The folder dropped to the floor and Draven didn't give a fuck. He'd never been so thoroughly excavated. As a hungry, wet tongue entwined with his and small gasps of breath escaped both of their mouths, Draven felt a sense of belonging. Of ownership and being owned. It was the strangest sensation to realise that fact as warm hands crept into his shirt and caressed skin that was set on fire. Taylor pushed him backward onto the bed, straddling him, dark curls falling down across his face, eyes shining with feverish intensity and mouth red and swollen from kisses.

"Thank you for staying with me," he breathed against Draven's ear as he trailed a hot tongue down skin that suddenly felt too tight for his body. Draven tingled with every sense he had. "I'm sorry this relationship seems to always end in me passing out and you having to rescue me."

"Relationship?" Draven gasped as hands unbuckled his trousers and Taylor's palm bore down on the erection that was about to erupt from his pants. "I thought you said this was only a bit of fun." He uttered a deep groan as warm lips mouthed his highly sensitive cock through the black briefs he wore. His hands clenched into Taylor's hair.

"I lied. I told you, I just want them to stop pestering me about things and thinking I can't take care of myself. I'm a big boy. I know what I want. And fuck, I want you so badly. In me. Now. The talk can wait."

Those words drilled directly down into Draven's dick. His balls were tucked tight in his groin and he shuddered.

"Christ, Taylor. I am going to come right now if you keep saying things like that to me." He lifted his hips as Taylor tugged on his trousers and shuffled back to pull them down with his briefs. He licked his lips, his eyes feasting on Draven, naked from the waist down, the biggest erection Draven thought he'd ever had begging for attention. Thick, swollen, leaking and rosy and Draven was very proud of it.

Taylor reached up and pulled off his shirt in one sexy move, revealing a torso that was almost hairless, just a faint dark treasure trail down to the a groin that definitely was ready for action from the tenting of the sweatpants.

Draven's eyes followed him as he stood up above him, on the bed, and slid his pants down his legs. Taylor stepped out of them and gave them a careless kick with his foot. The pants landed in a puddle on the floor. Draven lost his breath at the sight of so much male magnificence standing above him, that beautiful purple cock that thrust proudly from wiry black curls. Heavy balls hung below his groin, and Taylor gave a wicked grin and shimmied his hips, causing both cock and balls to move decadently. Draven's mouth watered at the sight.

He reached over and gripped Taylor, pulling him forward. Taylor gave a breathy sigh and fell to his knees. All that beauty and sexiness got closer and Draven wanted to taste it so badly. He shuffled up the bed backward, toward the wall, and pulled Taylor's hips toward him. Taylor's pupils were blown, his chest heaving, lips pouty and wet and Draven leaned forward and engulfed that beautiful prick in his mouth, wrapping his tongue around it, licking and sucking and hearing Taylor's grunts and moans as he paid undivided attention to that swollen part of him that needed release. Draven loved feasting on cock, loved the slickness and heat in his mouth, the taste of it, the burn at the back of his throat when he deep throated.

Taylor moaned in displeasure when Draven released him.

"God, don't stop. Please don't stop." His voice was ragged, his body almost vibrating with need.

Draven smiled wolfishly. "Don't worry. I have no intention of stopping. Just needed some air before I tell you to fuck my mouth."

Taylor gasped, eyes widening and Draven pulled him even closer. "Let me see you lose it. Then you can ride me, because, honey, I think that would be the most beautiful sight in the world. You riding my cock."

Taylor groaned and rammed his dick into Draven's mouth. Draven held Taylor's eyes as it disappeared deep inside his willing lips. Taylor's eyes were mirrors of hazy ecstasy as he pumped in and out of Draven's needy mouth, his movements getting more erratic as he gasped and moaned his way to orgasm. Draven alternated between closing his eyes to appreciate what he had in his mouth to opening them to see Taylor above him, looking down with those dark eyes and wet lips. For a minute, Draven didn't think he'd make it long enough to have that ride he was promised. He gripped the base of his cock with one hand, willing it not to explode before he was inside Taylor.

His other hand slid between Taylor's firm cheeks, as he sought the opening he wanted. Taylor moaned as Draven slid a finger inside, slick with his own fluids. He had the lube ready but for now, he thought this was all that was needed to open Taylor up.

"Oh, God, that's it, just fuck me with your fingers," Taylor whimpered. "So damn good."

It took a while but finally there was a rhythm, Taylor pushing into his mouth while Draven fucked his arse as he pushed away and out. It wasn't perfect but it didn't matter. Draven now had three fingers in Taylor's hole as he impaled himself with each thrust backward.

Taylor gave a grunt, then a loud cry and his cock swelled in Draven's mouth as warm come flooded his tongue, slid down his throat and Taylor pressed hands against the wall for support as he slowly stopped thrusting. For a while, there was only the sound of Taylor panting, and Draven's lip smacking as he relished Taylor's essence. Draven was quite content to lie there, one hand on Taylor's hips, the other still tightly gripping his engorged cock.

Taylor leaned down and kissed him, mouth still hungry and Draven knew the best was still to come.

"Get yourself ready for me," he whispered. "I want to see you do it."

Taylor nodded and reached over him. There was the sound of a drawer opening, some activity and then Draven watched while Taylor opened the lube and spread it on his fingers. Then he nearly came as Taylor reached around himself and with a wicked smile, he began to prep his hole for Draven.

"I don't think I need much," he murmured. "You seem to have made quite a good job of doing it while I was otherwise engaged."

He threw the tube down and opened the condom, rolling it out on Draven's cock, grinning as his fingers slyly caressed the tip and the sides as he did so.

"Taylor, can it," Draven growled, trying hard to keep himself from flying into orbit. "Just get on."

"Say please," Taylor whispered as he positioned himself above Draven with a smirk.

"Please, baby."

Taylor moaned softly as he lowered himself down and when Draven found his needy cock enmeshed in the tight, hot embrace of Taylor's body, he wanted to howl like a wolf. The sight of this beautiful, coffee-coloured man with the wild eyes and even wilder hair riding him like a mustang was enough to make him wonder how he'd ever survived without it. The feeling of his cock being slickly and expertly manipulated inside Taylor and the soft, panting of the man driving him out of his mind were like nirvana. He never wanted it to end.

Emotions swelled in his chest as Taylor smiled down at him, already semi-hard again and Draven reached over and gripped Taylor's cock as he performed the most graceful and erotic ballet on Draven that he'd ever experienced.

Time was not something to be measured now, but rather luxuriated in, embraced and absorbed like the treasure it was, each minute special, unique and each essence and smell something to be revelled in. Draven came inside Taylor with an explosion of desire, affection and passion, his body a slave to the man who held it in his thrall and who was slowly doing the same to his heart.

Taylor climaxed again too, hot streams of semen streaming across Draven's stomach and chest as finally, the performance was over and the actors took their bows off each other.

They lay together afterwards, limbs entwined, both wet and sweaty with the smell of sex. Taylor's hands gently strayed across Draven's chest, fingers gentle and soothing. He felt as if he'd been dipped in a vat of thick honey, his arms and legs barely moving and the taste in his mouth of both Taylor and his kisses sweet and sticky.

"Do you believe me when I told you I don't just see you as a bit of fun?" Taylor nibbled at Draven's nipple, causing him to shiver in delight.

"So wasn't what we did here tonight fun then?" Draven smiled as Taylor huffed in exasperation.

"You know what I mean. Don't be bloody obtuse."

"Big word, small fry," Draven chuckled as Taylor pinched the skin at his waist. "Ouch. Yes, I think I believe you. I still can't believe we've gone from disliking each other to having mad passionate sex nearly every night."

"Believe it," Taylor whispered as his hands drifted lower toward Draven's groin. "And from the feel of it, you're ready to go again…"

Draven shook his head and stayed Taylor's wandering hands. Much as he wanted to make love again, he wanted to hear about Taylor's visions more.

"Oh no, you don't. We said we were going to talk and then you ravaged me. So now we get to have that conversation."

Taylor pouted and Draven was smitten all over again. The man was adorable.

"Fine." He sat up, covers falling from his waist, and sat cross-legged on the bed, splendid in his nakedness. He was so relaxed about his body. Draven sat up, making sure his nether regions were hidden from Taylor's prying eyes and squinted as Taylor leaned over to light a cigarette taken from a pack in the bedside drawer.

Draven sighed heavily. "So stereotypical. Smoking after sex? Really?"

Taylor shrugged as he took a deep drag and made sure to blow the smoke away from Draven. "So sue me. If I have to tell this damn story, I need a cigarette." He narrowed his eyes. "But this is an 'I'll tell you mine, you tell me yours' situation. Afterward, I want to hear about your family and what makes you want to protect them."

He raised an eyebrow as Draven visibly squirmed at that statement. "There's no negotiation. Either you let me into your private life just a little…hell, you know enough about mine…or I stay *schtum* about what I saw in my vision."

Draven could see Taylor wouldn't be dissuaded. And it would be good to share something about Jude with someone who wasn't a doctor, a nurse or a pro-lifer.

"Agreed. You first."

The tip of the cigarette glowed red in the light of the room as Taylor took a drag. "I felt him in that room he died in. Drew was sitting at the desk. He was crying."

Draven felt a chill. The suicide note had shown traces of salt and other chemicals associated with tears but that was something Taylor wouldn't have known. However it was a pretty reasonable assumption to make. The man *had* killed himself for God's sake.

"He was writing the note and the tears were falling on it. He had to keep wiping them away so he could keep writing. It's why there were smudges in the ink. I noticed it when I read the note. Some parts were blurred." Taylor's voice was distant. Draven thought it was hard to believe that only half an hour ago they'd been in the throes of sexual passion. "It isn't all that clear; I've filled in some of the gaps myself. But they feel right. For whatever reason, I saw more than I usually do this time. It was more…like a jerky black-and-white film, with missing scenes. That hasn't happened before."

He took a deep breath. "He had a note with him, some typewritten thing. I couldn't see it, but he kept saying, 'Why would anyone do this? Who cares if I'm seeing men that they would do this to me?' He wrote the note, saying he was sorry, but it was better this way than destroying his family any more. Then he burnt the other note in the dustbin. He took the gun out of the drawer. He kept in the right-hand side. He was right handed, so I guess that made sense."

Taylor went quiet and Draven thought he'd gone to sleep or into one of his fugues. He leaned forward to check and started when Taylor started speaking again. "He toyed with the gun a while, looking at it, smelling it, as if he wanted to remember what it felt like. He was so unhappy, so tormented. Whatever it was, he felt the only way out was dying. I can't imagine how desperate he must have been."

Draven leaned forward and touched a hand to Taylor's cheek.

Taylor's voice was taut. "He said goodbye to everyone he loved, then he just raised the gun and shot himself." Taylor shivered, a full-body shudder, and Draven pulled him into his arms.

Taylor's voice was muffled as he pressed his face into Draven's shoulder. "But someone was with him just before he pulled the trigger. A woman."

Draven went still. "There was no one with him when he died, according to the family. He was alone. His wife says she got home a little while later and found the body."

Taylor sat up. "There was someone there, I saw and heard her. She shouted out 'No, Drew, no' just as he shot himself. She sounded …panicked, so damned shocked. Then everything went black. I think it was his wife, but I only saw the back of her."

Draven sat back, feeling bone tired. "You didn't get a chance to read the note before you went all *Red Lights* on me. He basically said that he'd brought shame upon his family by being with men and he didn't want them to suffer. So he thought the best thing was to take himself out of the equation."

"He killed himself because someone found about his bisexuality?" Taylor's hands waved in the air. "That's no damn reason; he could have talked about to his wife, his family, not killed himself."

"There was more." Draven knew this was inevitable but he still dreaded the fallout it would cause with Taylor. "Someone had videos of him fucking other men. Not just that, there was other stuff as well, more kinky shit. It was all over the internet. They threatened to make it public if he didn't pay up. It all seemed to take place at some club called Dive Bomb out in Sussex somewhere."

Taylor's body went still. "He asked me to go there with him once," he said quietly. "I looked it up and didn't quite fancy the whole scene. A little much for me. I declined. Just as well or I'd be all over the internet too, wouldn't I?" He giggled slightly hysterically and Draven held him tighter. "I have to ask, was there anything you saw where he was fucking me or the other way around?"

Draven kissed Taylor's raven curls. "No. Don't you think I would have told you that fact first? There was nothing involving you. I'm glad you didn't go to that BDSM club though. You'd definitely be in the film, the latest porn star to hit the news. And I only want you to be my porn star. No one else's."

They were both silent, thinking about the cruelty of someone driving a decent man to kill himself. Draven had a story to finish.

"So he told his family about it all, the whole truth and then shot himself. He decided it was the only way for his family to move on. He knew it might go public afterward anyway; they might do it out of spite for not giving over the money. He thought with him dead the scandal would die a quicker death. He was CEO of a huge multinational company after all, worth millions. He even left instructions in his will for a new CEO and Management Board to run the company in his absence."

"And now we have a mystery on our hands," Taylor said softly. "And I only hope I'm going to be able to help you figure it out. This gift I have…it's not an exact science, you know, but it's all we seem to have."

Draven ran fingers through soft hair, and smiled as he placed a kiss on the top of Taylor's head.

"You're amazing at this stuff. No one who has seen what you can do could doubt you know, least of all me. I was an arsehole, I admit it. I didn't believe in you, but now I do."

Taylor grimaced. "You don't have to flatter me for sex. I'll do you for free." But he shot a quick smile at Draven as he swung his legs out of bed. "I need to take a piss. Don't go far."

He disappeared out of the bedroom and appeared back a few minutes later. He climbed into bed and Draven grumbled.

"Christ, you're frozen. Come here, let me warm you up."

They snuggled back up under the duvet and Draven was half asleep when Taylor spoke sleepily.

"So this woman I saw. Do you think it was the wife?"

Draven opened a groggy eye. "I dunno. Maybe the wife was lying. Would you recognise the voice if you heard it? Or her appearance from the back?"

"I think so." Taylor's voice was uncertain. "Definitely the voice anyway."

"Well, maybe we'll take a trip to Drew's house. Pay our respects to the family. We might get lucky and you might recognise who she is." He was aware of Taylor's body stiffening beside him.

"I don't want to see them. I have no place there," he muttered stubbornly.

Draven sighed. "It's for Drew, Taylor. We're trying to solve a murder, because to me that's what this is. Someone drove him to kill himself and in my book that's murder."

Taylor huffed quietly. "You sound like that guy in *Hart to Hart*. The factotum guy who travels around with them." He put on a terrible accent. "I take care of both of them…which ain't easy; 'cause when they met it was murder." He pronounced it *moi-der* like the man in the TV show, and Draven groaned theatrically. He noticed Taylor didn't object to going anymore though. He must have really liked Drew.

"God, not only are you reminding me of bad American TV shows, you really mangled that accent. Go to sleep, Tay. I'll see about getting us in to see the family in the morning. Then if you're a good boy to me," he made the words as suggestive as he could, "I'll take you to an early dinner."

Taylor cuddled up against him with a chuckle and Draven felt the prod of a semi-hard erection in his back.

"'Kay. Sleep tight. If you fancy taking advantage me in the middle of the night, just wake me up."

Draven smiled in the darkness. "I'll bear that in mind. G'night."

He lay for a while listening to Taylor fall asleep and the sound of his steady breathing. He was relieved that Taylor seemed to have forgotten all about Draven spilling his guts out about his throwaway family comment.

Perhaps for the time being, that was the better option. The more Draven told people about Jude, the more likelihood they'd have an opinion on what he should be doing. Just like Doctor Frederick at the hospital. For a while longer, Jude was his and no one else's. The decision he needed to make was buried deep inside him and for the moment, he didn't want it letting out to take root and bear fruit.

Chapter 8

The following morning, Taylor woke around eight and watched Draven sleep. His dark blond hair was mussed, his lips twitching in some dream, and his hands curled into the duvet as if in the throes of a pleasurable dream. Hands that had caressed Taylor, driven him crazy with want and finally ended up releasing him from the pent-up sexual frustration he'd had.

The memory of their rather energetic and raunchy love-making session echoed in Taylor's mind, his body still sore from being so fully taken and possessed. He reached out a hand and touched Draven's cheek and was rewarded by the glint of sleepy grey eyes as Draven awoke. For a moment both men stared at each other, dark chocolate meeting stormy seas and for a moment, the world ceased. It was as if somewhere, somehow, they were the only two people on earth.

Then the spell was broken by a loud knock at the door.

"Taylor. Get your debauched arse out of bed. There's a phone call for you." Leslie's voice reverberated through the door and Draven grinned, his face mischievous.

"He's got your number, Mr. Debauched. I still have a beautiful memory of you riding my cock as if I were a thoroughbred stallion."

He sat up in bed, the duvet falling to his waist and revealing a semi hard-on in the process.

Taylor flushed as he got out of bed. “Yes, well, I was a little horny last night.” He pulled on a pair of shorts, not missing Draven’s interested glance at the fact they were rather tight and clingy and showed everything off to best advantage.

“Taylor, are you in there? The person said he’d call back in five minutes. Get off that man and get dressed.” Leslie’s voice was amused with a hint of impatience and Draven chuckled.

“He sounds like a real peach,” he remarked as he swung his leg out of bed and padded naked to the door. “Maybe I should surprise him.”

Before Taylor could object, Draven had opened the door and stood there revealed in all his glory to a wide-eyed Leslie, who looked as if he had been about to knock. He was dressed in plum-coloured silk pyjamas that clung to his slim frame.

“You were looking for Taylor?” Draven drawled lazily, his cock bobbing as he scratched his balls.

Leslie smiled widely and looked pointedly down at Draven’s groin. “I don’t blame him for being distracted with *that* at his beck and call,” he said silkily. “I can see why he likes you so much.” His eyebrows rose in a question. “Is there room for one more when you guys play next?”

Taylor sniggered, both at Draven’s look at Leslie’s calm reaction to him being naked and at the look of discomfort that crossed his face at the question. Taylor knew Leslie was joking—he had a specific aversion to threesomes or more and for Leslie, a free-minded spirit, he was considered quite a prude on the subject. Taylor had often been on the receiving side of Leslie’s lectures about love making being between two people and another person simply making things complicated. Taylor himself had no such aversion and had been a willing participant in such situations before. He waited now to see what Draven would say.

Draven cast a quick glance at Taylor, who kept his face blank. “Uhm, I’m not sure that’s a good idea,” he said carefully, with another glance at Taylor. “I mean, I’d really prefer to have Tay to myself, nothing against you, but I think, you know, sex is between two people.”

Leslie gave a loud squeal of pleasure and wrapped arms around Draven's neck. His cock was pressed against cool silk and it twitched at the friction of being accosted by what seemed like an octopus.

"Good for you, Tay. You found another believer." He pulled away and then licked his lips lasciviously. "And what a believer he is. Hung like a fucking rhinoceros."

Taylor laughed as he pulled Draven into the bedroom. "I'm pretty pleased too. Now you'd better get dressed," he motioned at Draven then turned to Leslie. "Any idea who it was on the phone?"

Leslie shrugged. "He was from work, wondering whether you were going on in today. Chris something or the other."

Taylor frowned. "I'm on a few days' leave this week, he should know that. I'll give work a call in a minute, remind them I've got the time off. Draven and I have some plans today."

Leslie grinned. "Do they involve you two locking yourselves in the bedroom and rutting like rabbits?"

Taylor shook his head, smiling at that thought because, honestly, he liked the sound of that. "No, you idiot. We have to go visit someone for the case Draven's working on." He waved at Leslie. "Now be gone with you so we can get dressed. I think you've seen enough of my guy for one day."

He smiled politely at his friend, pulled Draven back into the room and closed the door firmly. There was a snort of laughter from the other side.

"You two are so going back to bed and doing the bunny thing. I just know it!"

Draven raised an eyebrow as he stood there, still magnificently nude. "Is he right?"

Taylor snickered. "Much as I fancy that idea, no." He opened the scratched and pitted door of his small wardrobe and took out a threadbare but clean towel. "We're going to shower and go and do this thing with Drew's family." He handed the towel to Draven who wrapped it around his waist. It covered his private bits but left little to the imagination. As Draven had already been revealed in all his glory, Taylor didn't think he'd mind a little more "flasher" activity. "The bathroom is at the end of the hall. Take a shower and I'll be in after you. Then we can get this whole visit out of the way."

Draven reached out a hand and caressed Taylor's jawline gently. "Are you okay with this? You're not going to have another meltdown, are you? Because I don't think I want to see you lose it again."

Taylor's eyes softened. "I'll be fine. It's just listening to her voice and seeing if she's the same woman as in my dream, right? As long as I don't touch anything while I'm there, it'll be okay. That seems to be when these things spark it off."

Draven opened the door and peered out into the corridor, looking for the all clear. "Feel free to join me in the shower if you like," he said mischievously as he padded barefoot down the hallway.

Taylor chuckled. "Not likely. The shower barely fits one person, let alone two doing the vertical hump. Maybe we can try that out at your place."

"I heard that!" came a sing-song voice from Leslie's bedroom. "Dirty bastards, the two of you." His comment was followed by a loud snigger and Taylor rolled his eyes. He loved his friend but he was like a damn jackdaw, all cheeky, bright-eyed and inquisitive.

He grabbed another towel and followed Draven down into the bathroom. He might not be able to fit into the shower, but there was nothing to stop him lusting after the man while he was naked with water running down his body.

***

An hour later they were in Draven's car, on their way to Drew's home on Crooked Mile in Waltham Abbey. Draven said he'd been there a couple of times before when he worked with Drew on the ultra-secretive case he'd had when he'd helped him with his business espionage issue. Taylor was dying to hear that story but Draven was very close-mouthed about it. Like he was about a *lot* of things about himself, Taylor had to admit. Thinking about that, he shot a glance at Draven as he drove. He wanted to ask about his ultimatum on "I'll tell you mine, you tell me yours" but wasn't sure whether he wanted to chance any fallout when the man was driving.

Draven turned and smiled at him. "You okay there? Is my driving up to scratch?" His voice was teasing.

Taylor grinned. "Yeah. I don't think I'll be puking my guts out anytime soon."

Capable fingers threaded the wheel as Draven manoeuvred his way around a large farm trailer.

He seems in a really good mood. I guess now is as good a time as any to ask.

"Draven, I still didn't get my wish to find out what it is that makes you need to protect your family. You promised me the story and I'm holding you to it."

He groaned inwardly as Draven's fingers clenched on the wheel and hastened to qualify his statement. "I mean, I don't want to pry but I'd like to share. You know stuff about me that I've never told anyone before. Hell, you've watched me pass out a few times and be sick in a street bin. You've definitely seen me at my worst."

The silence echoed in the car and finally Draven turned and glanced at him. There was a slight frown on his face coupled with a look of sorrow in his eyes. Then his gaze shifted back to the front.

"It's nothing dramatic, Taylor. Just a family tragedy that means I have a decision to make in the near future. One I really don't want to make." He scowled and Taylor laid a hand on his leg.

"Then tell me about it and maybe I can help."

Draven frowned darkly. "It's not something you can help with. Why all the curiosity about my situation, anyway?"

Taylor sighed heavily. Draven's mood seemed to have changed within seconds, going from the playful demeanour of before to a moody individual hell-bent on keeping secrets.

"Fine, don't worry about it. It'll keep, I guess, until you're willing to tell me. Far be it from me to force anything out of you."

He stared forward, fingers tapping nervously on his jeans-clad leg. They drove in silence, the air in the car thick with tension. The busy road ahead looked like a ribbon of motorcars, exhaust pipes belching plumes of smoke, trucks whizzing past with no care as to the speed limit and endless paths of concrete and tarmac in view.

Finally Draven sighed and reached out and stayed his hand. "Three years ago my parents were killed in a car accident."

Taylor swallowed. "I'm sorry, Draven. That must have been really tough to get through." He didn't really know what else to say. There was a deep quiet in the car before Draven spoke again.

"My little brother Jude was in the car with them. He survived." He gave a sharp laugh with no discernible trace of amusement that Taylor could hear. "If you can call it that. He's been in a coma ever since they pulled him out of the wreck. He was just heading for his sixteenth birthday."

His voice was flat, tired and dispirited. Taylor had heard men's voices that sounded like that before. Like the day Bobby Meredith's father found out his son would never be coming home. It chilled Taylor, made him remember all the voices he'd heard in his head and the sad sounds of their dying. He shivered, a full-body tremor that shook him to his core.

"Where is he?" he asked quietly. "In a hospital somewhere? Is that where you go when you turn your phone off?"

Draven was still, eyes focused on the country road ahead. They'd left the main road behind and were meandering down country lanes filled with picturesque houses and chocolate-box fields and greens. Far ahead in front, Taylor saw the back of what looked like a Bentley from the looks of the badge. This area was obviously fairly affluent.

"He's in the Royal." Draven finally answered. "And yes, I spend a fair amount of time there with him."

"How bad is he?" Taylor shifted in his seat and pressed down on Draven's leg, hoping the touch brought comfort. Draven overtook the Bentley rather adroitly and Taylor held his breath. From the driver-side window, a silver-haired man glared at them as they whizzed past smoothly.

"He's not good. Very low on the coma scale to the point of being…" Draven's voice caught. "Let's just say every time I go in there it's possible it might be the last time I see him."

Taylor pulled in a breath in horror. "That really sucks." He couldn't imagine being faced with such a terrible burden. Something niggled in the back of his brain, that little second sense that told him perhaps he'd felt something about Draven's pain already; that somehow he'd known. Draven's next growled words made him forget that train of thought.

"It's a nightmare, a cosmic fucking joke that someone like Jude could be like he was…he was always so lively and fun and now…" His broad shoulders shrugged. "I live in hope that one day things will get better, but it's getting to the stage where I can't really be positive about it anymore." His face tightened. "The worse thing about it is not knowing if he's in pain, if there's anything of my little brother still living inside that body. It rips my heart out every time I see him."

"I'd like to meet him," Taylor murmured. "Maybe one day you'll take me there to visit."

Draven didn't answer, but started to slow the car down. "This is it," he muttered. "Drew's place. Fancy isn't it?"

Taylor filed away the fact that he hadn't agreed to take him to see his brother, but let it go. There was time enough to pursue it later. At least he knew a little more about where Draven went at nights when he didn't answer his phone. He felt sick at what Draven was going through and even worse for the young man in the hospital bed with what seemed like little chance of recovery. Taylor's heart ached for them both but especially for his lover being left to pick up the pieces.

Taylor just wished Draven would let him help.

His sympathy at Draven's plight was temporarily forgotten as he saw the house and felt a spark of surprise at its opulence. It could be seen set back from the road, a huge mansion of pale grey cobblestone set in what looked like a national park, with a sweeping driveway up which they now drove, through opened wrought-iron metal gates. The front door stood above a set above of regal steps, about twenty feet in width, with a stone balustrade either side.

Draven pulled up, turned off the engine and undid his seat belt.

"Wow," Taylor exclaimed softly. "That is something. Makes my place look like a hovel." He climbed out of the car and followed Draven, who was already striding toward the steps. Draven turned to look behind him, one eyebrow raised.

"Come on then. Let's see who's at home. I did call earlier to make sure Catherine was in today. I didn't tell her to expect us. I like the element of surprise."

"So do I," Taylor remarked drily as he followed him up the stairs. "So don't think I've forgotten about your story and meeting your brother. I'll make sure to follow that up sometime."

Draven turned back and stared at him with a strange look then smiled slightly and dipped his head in acknowledgement. He rang the bell and from inside, a there was a loud chiming sound. Taylor's stomach plunged to his feet and he willed the sick feeling he had in his gut away.

There is no fucking way on this earth that you are going to pass out in front of him again. So suck it the fuck up you big baby and fight it.

There was no doubt that some of the emotions he'd originally felt around Drew's death were present in his head, simmering bubbles of agitation and grief. He and Drew might have been occasional lovers but there was no doubt that Taylor had been very fond of him. He sometimes caught Draven watching him carefully when he talked about him. Taylor could see the curiosity in his eyes, the question there as to whether Taylor had felt more for Drew beyond being a fuck buddy. Well, the answer was yes, but it had been more of a fondness for another human being and not the overwhelming passion Taylor seemed to have for the man currently standing next to him.

There was no point in taunting himself with what-ifs, Taylor thought sadly. Perhaps in another life, he and Drew might have meant more to each other. But now they'd never know.

He took his hands out of his pockets to run fingers through his hair and just as quickly shoved them back in, not wanting to chance a reaction to the emotions running through the house, or accidentally touch anything.

Maybe I need to get myself a pair of gloves. A sexy pair of leather ones that I can tease Draven's dick with.

He swallowed a chuckle at that thought even as his dick stirred in his pants. Draven frowned and rang the bell again. Then he knocked loudly using the brass handle fixed to the door. He stepped back and surveyed the surroundings, his keen slate eyes narrowing.

"I know someone's home. I saw them in one of the upstairs rooms when we got out of the car."

Taylor was impressed. "Wow. You can take the investigator out of the city but you can't take the investigator out of the man. Are you always so observant?"

Draven grinned wolfishly. "I had noticed that slight boner in your pants. What the hell were you thinking about to put that there?"

Taylor's mouth fell open. "You…what? Honestly?" He took a quick look down at his groin. Yes, he wasn't particularly soft but he didn't think anyone would have noticed his semi hard-on.

Draven snorted softly in laughter. "I tend to notice everything about you, Taylor. I really think…"

What Draven thought was cut off as the door opened and a man's voice said, "Yes? Can I help you?"

Taylor thought he'd stepped out into the pages of a detective novel written by Agatha Christie, one of his favourite authors. It was the man he'd seen at the funeral. He looked like the archetypical butler, grey hair, regal bearing, dressed in a white shirt and a black suit. His rather bushy eyebrows were raised, and he had a rather querulous expression on his face.

Draven stepped forward. "My name is Draven Samuels and I was a friend of Drew's. This is my friend, Taylor Abelard. He also knew Drew. We're here to pay our respects to Catherine and see how she is. I did call ahead and told someone I'd be stopping by and to expect us."

Taylor opened his mouth to say something about that outright lie then shut it. A sneaking pride suffused his body at the effortless way his lover lied so smoothly and confidently. Then he thought about possibly being on the receiving end of Draven's lying mastery one day and his admiration turned to apprehension.

The man at the door sighed heavily. "Well, please do come in. No one told me we were expecting visitors. Catherine's been a bit distraught today and my daughter isn't very good at dealing with things."

Draven nodded. "I'm sorry. Would you prefer we came back another time then?"

God, Draven is so charming, even when he's suggesting something he doesn't really want to do.

Not the butler, Catherine's father. He shook his head. "No, don't worry. To be honest, I'd be glad of the male company. Being surrounded by a bunch of hysterical females gives me somewhat of a headache. My wife and daughter have been a bit of a trial." He beckoned to Draven to enter. Taylor followed close behind, feeling empathy for Catherine at the same time he felt the start of dislike for the man currently showing them in.

The woman lost a husband, for God's sake. The man could have a little bit of patience, surely?

From the flaring of Draven's nostrils, Taylor thought he felt the same way. He fidgeted, trying to suppress the emotions that coated him like soft ash, settling on his skin and making him itch. To distract himself, he stared around the palatial entrance hall, with marbled floors, fancy, ornate light fittings and a long flight of stairs that seemed to lead up to the next level. It was plush, luxurious and so unlike the Drew he'd known that he felt a little gobsmacked. His Drew had been happy to eat takeout from Chinese-labelled containers, lie on the wet spot and listen to music on his iPhone while lolling on the lumpy hotel couch. This all seemed too extravagant for the man and Taylor guessed more of the house décor was to do with Catherine's needs, not Drew's.

"Are you okay?" Draven said quietly. "Not going to weird out on me, are you?"

Taylor shook his head. "As long as I keep my hands in my pockets, I'll be fine. It's a little overwhelming, but I'm managing."

Draven regarded him with a concerned look then turned back as the man at his side extended a hand.

"Jack Threadcourt. As I said, I'm Catherine's dad."

Draven shook his hand. "Glad to meet you, sir. I'm really sorry about Drew. He was a good man."

Jack's face darkened. "I thought he was. Then we found about his other, ahem…preferences. I wouldn't have minded if he'd come clean and told us he was gay and had some rather dubious habits. Instead he chose to cheat on my daughter then killed himself when someone found out. I think that was the coward's way out."

He turned and walked toward one of the rooms off the entrance hall. "Let me see if I can find Catherine. She was sleeping in the lounge while my wife watched over her. If you two gentleman would like to wait in the conservatory, I'll let her know you're here. It's that room over there." He waved a hand in the direction of a sun-drenched room to his right and strode off.

Taylor's knees threatened to give way at that. His old insecurity about him being a slut and pandering to Drew's needs reared to the fore. And yes, Drew might have had other options than pulling the trigger but who knew what was in the mind of a man who had had a deep, dark secret of the kind he had.

Draven moved over to his side, his presence a comfort, and gave Taylor's arm a slight squeeze. "You didn't encourage him and you are not a slut." Draven's whispered words were a balm to Taylor's soul. "So take that panicked look off your face and man up."

Taylor gave him a grateful glance.

How the hell does he do that? Can he read my damn mind? God, how weird would that be, both of us being special.

Draven grasped his elbow and led him over to the waiting room. They both sat down on plush seats made of some very expensive-looking fabric and waited.

***

Draven watched Taylor closely. He knew the man well enough by now to see the constant fidgeting, the slight frown marking that expressive face, the full lips pressed together as Taylor tried to suppress whatever it was he was feeling. He could see Taylor was uncomfortable being in Drew's house; not just for the emotions he seemed to be picking up, but for the fact that he felt like a thief in the night stealing another man away from his family, even if only for sex and companionship. Not for the first time, Draven wondered exactly how close Drew and Taylor had been. To hear Taylor say it, they'd been occasional fuck buddies, albeit fond of each other and that was it. However, Taylor's reactions seemed to indicate more than that. Draven felt a prickle of jealousy and he quelled it, admonishing himself internally for being jealous of a dead man.

They both started as a loud wail echoed from a room on the other side of the house, somewhere in the bowels of the mansion. It was a cry rent with grief and pain.

"No, Daddy. I can't do this anymore. Tell them to leave, tell them to go. Please." The sound dissolved into heart-rending sobs. Draven shivered when he heard it—even more so when he saw Taylor's reaction to the sound. Taylor went ghostly white, his dark eyes shadowing and his hands incessantly moving in his pockets. The agitated stare levelled at Draven told him everything he needed to know. This must be the woman whose voice Taylor had heard in his vision—Drew's wife, Catherine.

He moved closer to his lover, reaching out to touch an arm that felt like whipcord, taut and immovable. It was as if Taylor was set in granite. Draven felt a sense of unease at the small movements of Taylor's bloodless lips, as if he was chanting a prayer or incanting something to ward off evil spirits. He gripped Taylor's chin firmly, forcing him to look at him.

"That's the woman's voice you heard?" he murmured as Taylor nodded jerkily and then closed his eyes, his face stilling. Draven cursed softly as he recognised all the signs of one of Taylor's classic meltdowns. He expected the man to fall unconscious to the floor at any minute.

"Taylor." He shook him hard; gripping his arm, leaving what he was sure would be bruises. He needed to stop what was happening. "Look at me. Look at me!"

Taylor's eyes opened, revealing panicked dark orbs and Draven leaned into him. "You are going to be fine. Go outside and get some fresh air. I'll finish up here and then our job is done. You hear me? You did it, baby. Now go," He pushed Taylor toward the entrance. "Wait for me outside. I'll be there soon. And for God's sake don't faint and fall down the stairs. Hold onto the rail, you hear me?"

Once again Taylor nodded as ragged breaths forced out of his body. He turned and fled the house, opening the front door and slamming it shut behind him just as Jack Threadcourt made his way toward Draven across the entrance hall. His face was wearied, lips pinched and Draven thought he was seeing yet another man at the end of his tether.

Jack raised his hands apologetically. He stopped and glanced at the front door with a slight frown. "I'm sorry, Mr. Samuels. Catherine's really not up to visitors at the moment. I'm sure you heard that outburst." He sighed. "My wife is sitting with her now, but honestly, I think it would be best if you left and tried another day. Perhaps give it a few days then call ahead again. It will save you wasting your time coming here."

Draven nodded and extended a hand to shake Jack's. "I completely understand, Mr. Threadcourt. It's a terrible situation and I have no desire to make it worse for any of you." He waved at the front door. "Taylor wasn't feeling too well—a little emotional himself, I think—so I sent him out to get some air. I'll definitely call again and see if we can come by. Thank you for trying anyway."

Jack led the way to the door and opened it. Taylor sat on the steps of the house smoking, and Draven felt a surge of relief that he looked better; his colour was back and his eyes weren't as tortured as they had been. As the door opened, he stood up and stared uncertainly at Jack.

"Thank you for letting us in, Mr. Threadcourt," Taylor said softly as he extended his hand. "We appreciate you trying to let us see her and I'm sorry if we upset her."

Jack sighed as he shook the offered hand. "Don't worry. It's been a really tough time for her, and I'm just pleased she has people who care about her."

Draven placed a hand on the small of Taylor's back. He wanted to make sure he didn't have sort of turn and fall down the broad steps. Taylor smiled at him gently.

Draven nodded. "Thank you, sir. I'll be in touch soon."

A few minutes later both of them were seated in the car watching the door at the top of the stairs shut with finality.

Taylor shifted in the seat as he pulled his seat belt on and regarded Draven with a slight look of amusement. "Baby?"

"What?" asked Draven distractedly as he too put his belt on and started the car.

"Back there, in the house. You called me 'baby'."

Draven frowned. "Did I? Oh." There was silence as he pulled off and drove down the winding drive toward the open gates. He felt a little embarrassed. "Shouldn't I have? I mean, it just slipped out. It's okay if you don't want me to call you that, I won't do it again..."

"Draven." Taylor laid a warm hand on his leg and squeezed. "It's fine. Don't get all wiggy about it. I just didn't expect it from you, that's all."

Draven nodded slowly. "Okay. So I'm not in trouble?"

Taylor leaned over and cast a soft kiss on Draven's stubbled cheek. It tingled. "No. I rather liked it actually."

Draven scowled. He had a warm feeling in his stomach and wasn't quite sure about it. "That whole damn emotional episode, and the only thing you remember is that I called you 'baby'? Are you going soft on me, Abelard?"

Taylor chuckled, a dirty, low sound that went straight to Draven's groin. "I think the one thing I'm not around you, *Samuels*, is soft."

Draven stared at him.

Taylor grinned then his face sobered. "So...we've established that the voice I heard in the study, when Drew shot himself, was the wife. The wife who said she wasn't in the house at the time. What the hell do we do with that information?"

Draven shook his head. "Not us. Clay, my boss, can deal with this. We're going to go see him right now, pass on this information and he can take it further." He felt a shiver of apprehension at that. *This* story would take some telling.

"Your boss at Mortimer Investigations?" Taylor's eyes widened. "*The* Mortimer in the title?"

"The one and only. Clay will know exactly what needs to be done. He and Drew were sort of friends too, and business partners in a case I worked on. Clay was the one who originally uncovered the whole blackmail scenario. He knew something really bad had to happen for Drew to do what he did and he went digging. He moves in some…rather murky circles." Draven took a deep breath. "It will be a difficult job convincing him how we got the proof, but I'll give it a damned good try." His voice was grim. "He's pretty open-minded, so I hope it won't be too difficult. But you're coming with me. I might need you to do a demonstration."

Taylor's jaw dropped. His voice was disbelieving when he spoke. "You're taking me with you to your boss's office while you tell him a psychic guy…one that you're sleeping with… has evidence that contradicts the current state of events… gathered through solid police work I guess…and he needs to investigate something based on said crazy guy's input?" His voice rose. "And what do you mean, 'a demonstration'?"

Draven winced. Put like that it sounded crazy, and based on his last cock-up with Ian the Informant, he knew he was on shaky ground with Clay. Thinking about that, he hoped like hell Clay wouldn't bring it up in front of Taylor. Nothing like having the guy you're currently in bed with hearing about a past indiscretion and you sticking your dick where it didn't belong.

"I mean I might need you to show Clay what you can do." He ignored Taylor's exasperated snort and forged ahead. "It might not come to that, but I want to make sure I can convince him."

"Yeah, I'm sure he's going to listen to the likes of me. I'm sure you made your views about me well known back in the days when you thought I was a fraud." Taylor raised one sardonic eyebrow. "He probably thinks you've been cock whipped and you'll say anything to keep me sweet so you can continue to get some."

Draven felt his face flush. "Cock whipped?" he said haltingly. "What the hell are you talking about?"

Taylor smirked. "Well, I can't say pussy whipped because I don't have a…"

"Tay, I get it. Please don't even finish that sentence." Draven glared at an unrepentant Taylor. He thought his lover had certainly recovered from his little episode given the leer he had on his face. It made Draven want to pull the car over behind the hawthorn bushes growing on the side of the road and fuck him senseless. He manfully suppressed that impulse and rolled his eyes instead. "Now shut up a minute while I figure out how the hell I'm going to sell this to him."

He ignored Taylor's adorable pout and again reined in his desire to have his way with him. An hour and a half later, as he parked in front of the offices of Mortimer Investigations, in the rather pretty and scenic business park of Wembley, he still wasn't quite sure how he'd tackle the affair.

Taylor clambered out of the car. He'd been quiet on the way through, leaving Draven to figure things out and finally got bored and watched a film on his mobile phone. Draven could tell he was nervous.

"Are you sure this is a good idea, Draven?" Taylor asked hesitatingly. "I mean, this guy might think I'm a damn nutter, and maybe you might be putting your job at risk if he thinks you're one too. Maybe we should…"

Draven effectively shut him up by pulling Taylor toward him and sealing his mouth with his lips. Taylor gave a breathy moan and dissolved against Draven like a melting slab of Cadbury's. When Draven let him go, his lips were pink and swollen from the force of his kiss.

Draven grinned. "Now that you look truly fucked, let's go meet my boss."

He jauntily sped across the grass, blithely ignoring the No Treading On the Grass signs that were perched in fields of lush green, and made his way to the glassed entrance. He chuckled quietly as he saw Taylor make the longer way around using the path, the long-suffering expression on his face priceless.

Draven entered the building and smiled at the receptionist. "Hi, Shelley. How are you this afternoon?"

The pretty blonde woman behind the desk waved at Draven as Taylor came in behind him. Her eyes skipped Draven and alighted on Draven's man like a woman about to take a bite of a delicious chocolate-covered cherry. Draven thought she'd start drooling soon.

Shelly sat up, pushed her already perky boobs out and gave Taylor the full wattage of her smile. Draven felt a prickle of jealousy at the blatant come-hither action. She'd never done that to him and she didn't even know he was gay.

"Hi, Draven. Good to see you, it's been a while. And who is this gorgeous fellow then?" Her eyes lapped Taylor up, her interest obvious. "Wow, I'd like to get to know *you*. Are you going to be working with Draven?" Her tone was hopeful.

"He's with me, yes." Draven growled as he made his way to the lift and pushed the button with a short, stabbing action.

Let her take that comment any way she wants. Taylor is mine.

"I'm taking him to meet Clay. We have some business to discuss."

He didn't miss Taylor's smirk as he joined him at the lift after bestowing a dazzling, white-toothed smile at the receptionist. Draven saw her almost swoon in her chair and he fiercely jabbed the button again.

"Careful, Draven. I might even start to think you care about me," Taylor teased *sotto voce* as the lift doors opened and Draven propelled him inside. As the door closed, Draven pushed him back against the lift wall, pressing himself against an obviously amused Taylor.

"I don't like it when people come onto you," he muttered sulkily, his hands gripping Taylor's hips. "You're mine."

He hadn't meant to make such a statement but he couldn't help it. He was possessive by nature, he knew that, but he didn't want to scare Taylor off completely by being too Neanderthal.

However, knowing Taylor's propensity for being dominated now and then, he thought it might not go down too badly. He was right. Taylor's eyes darkened, a wet, pink tongue coming out to lick his lips unconsciously. A soft, peppermint-scented outtake of breath caressed Draven's skin.

Draven groaned as his cock sprang to life in his jeans. He stepped away quickly and adjusted himself. "Christ, stop that. Clay will notice. He notices everything."

Taylor laughed softly. "You started it, Mr. Caveman. Now you've got me hard. Do you think Clay will notice that too?"

Draven couldn't resist a look at Taylor's all-too-tight black jeans, losing his breath at the sight of the hard ridge lying left of the fabric.

"He can't possibly miss it." His voice was husky and he wondered whether they could delay seeing Clay for ten minutes while he resolved both of their problems in the fancy executive bathroom, for which he had a key card. His plan was thwarted as the lift doors opened and Clay Mortimer stood there, all one-hundred-and-eighty-odd pounds of muscle, tanned skin, black silver-grey streaked hair and attitude.

"Draven…and friend." Clay's voice was like warm honey, deep and melodious, unless it was busy ripping Draven a new one, which to be honest, was quite often. "What the hell are you doing here? I didn't expect to see you until next week. I was on my way out for a burger." A slight panic coated his voice with his next words. "Is everything okay with Jude?"

Draven nodded. "Jude's fine. That's not why I'm here."

Clay's eyes narrowed, and green eyes observed Draven carefully. Draven groaned inwardly as they dropped slightly toward Draven's nether regions, then across to Taylor's, and then swung back up to him. His lips lifted slightly and Draven saw the amusement behind the cool facade.

"Been practising those weasel techniques, Dray?"

Draven pushed past his boss, out onto the landing. "Fuck. You," he expostulated as Taylor's jaw gaped open at that earthy retort. "It's urgent, and I need to speak to you, so maybe your McDonald's burger can wait." Clay had a habit of buying a Big Tasty almost every day. It was one of his "little pleasures," as he told everyone.

How Clay still managed to look so good, and keep the physique he had from his days as an SAS operative many years ago, Draven had no idea. Clay said that gym, hot sex and tequila were his secrets to maintaining his figure.

Draven walked into Clay's office at the end of the corridor. A fairly large space, with big picture windows looking out onto the green behind, it was filled with bookshelves, wall maps, and a wooden desk stood at one end, with two chairs in front.

Draven stood, staring out at the pond and fountain in the garden below. He was slightly nervous if truth be told. He'd worked with Clay for six years and always found the man to be fair, tough and supportive when it counted. Now Taylor was involved, he felt a little out of depth. Bluster and defensive techniques normally worked for him but today, he needed Clay to listen and accept what he was about to tell him. Clay and Taylor wandered into the office, Taylor looking very ill at ease, Clay simply striding to his chair and settling in comfortably as if he didn't have a care in the world. Draven mused wryly that telling his superior to fuck off probably hadn't been the best thing he could have done.

"Sooo, Dray." Clay swung his feet on top of his mahogany polished desk and sent a missile launch of green eyes his way. "You seem a little pissed off. Still smarting about that whole incident with Ian and me pulling you off the case? I thought you'd have gotten over that." He smirked, casting a sly glance at Taylor who was standing awkwardly at the window next to Draven.

Draven cut that one off at the pass. "Never mind Ian. That's old news." He ignored Taylor's speculative glance as he sat down in the chair in front of the huge desk. He motioned to Taylor to sit beside him in the other chair and Taylor shook his head.

"I'll stand, thanks." Draven noticed Taylor's Adam's apple bob as he swallowed, saw his clenching of fists and nervous licks of his lips.

He sighed. "Babe, stop looking like the guillotine's going to fall. It's going to be okay, I promise."

Clay's eyes widened, his dark eyebrows rising. "Babe? Well, well, well. What happened to the old animosity you felt for Mr. Abelard? This is a turn up for the books."

Draven took a deep breath, suppressing the impulse to snarl. "Clay, that's kind of what we're here to talk about."

Clay's eyebrows lifted further. "Your love life? Isn't that what got you into trouble in Dubrovnik? Putting your dick where it wasn't supposed to go?" He chuckled softly, but cast a softer glance at Taylor, as if commiserating. Taylor smiled uneasily.

Draven closed his eyes and counted to ten. "Clay, please let's forget that whole dick matter. And yes, Taylor and I are an item, okay? Now that's out of the way, do you want to me tell you some breaking news about Drew Whittaker's death?"

Clay stilled and moved his feet to the floor, then leaned forward, his whole demeanour changing. "Drew's death? Are you going to tell me it wasn't a suicide after all?"

Draven shook his head. "No, it was suicide. It's just that we have reason to believe that someone was with him when he pulled the trigger." He didn't miss Taylor's flinch at those words. "His wife lied when she said she wasn't home when it happened. She was there, right in the room with him. That makes me wonder why she lied, what she's covering up. Where there's smoke there's fire. You taught me that."

That wasn't the only thing Clay had taught Draven in the past. He was a mentor of note—if mentoring meant you learnt about 101 ways to kill a man, conduct covert operations and surveillance and be a sneaky bastard.

"I figured I'd tell you, and you could perhaps follow up on it. His wife is a basket case at the moment, and I guess she'd crack if you pushed her."

Taylor's indrawn breath made Draven realise that sounded callous, but he and Clay lived in a very different world than his lover. Sometimes nice wasn't an option when you were looking for the truth. He glanced at him and inclined his head slightly.

"I know that sounds cruel, Tay. But sometimes it's all you have to work with."

"I remember." Taylor said quietly. "You forget I've seen you at work."

Draven winced. Their encounter and his words at the site of little Bobby Meredith's body dump had come back to haunt him. "Yeah, so I was an arsehole then." He smiled, trying to reassure Taylor he wasn't any longer.

Clay laughed softly. "I like this one, Draven. He has balls. And I've never heard you admit you were an arsehole before to anyone." He nodded his head at Taylor in acknowledgement. "Well done, son. You seemed to have calmed the savage beast."

Taylor's face showed the sign of a slight grin and Draven felt a prickle of annoyance. "Can we stop the buddy bonding on my behalf please, and focus?" Both men swung their eyes to him. "There is a slight hitch with this information, though."

Taylor tensed, his arms wrapping around his chest, as he turned to look out of the window.

Clay's forehead creased. "Spill it. What's wrong with the information?" He was all matter of fact now, face set, voice harder, a man demanding answers and explanations. Clay Mortimer was a man Draven would never cross. Firstly, from a sense of sheer respect for him, and secondly, because he'd be hunted down like an animal and have his balls fed to him like culinary delicacies.

Draven took another deep breath as he prepared to speak.

"Because the information came from me." Taylor's voice echoed in the sudden stillness. "And it's not exactly reliable in any way you'd expect." Draven looked over at him. His lover's face was resolved, his arms unfolded and hanging by his sides as he regarded Clay with a stare of brown eyes that said he was about to have his say.

"You know who I am, obviously. So you know what I'm supposedly capable of. I have no doubt you have a dossier on me somewhere in here." He waved a hand around the room. "And Draven has seen what I can do first hand. I think I've made a believer out of him and I imagine you realise that's a fucking miracle based on his past impression of me."

Clay snorted but said nothing as he watched Taylor thoughtfully, his hands steepled together under his chin, elbows on his desk. Draven felt a prickle of guilt at Taylor's words.

"So we're here to tell you that I had a vision of Catherine Whittaker being present at the exact same time Drew shot himself. She cried out his name and I saw the back of her. She had nothing to do with the shooting, but she was there. We went back to the house and I confirmed the voice that I heard in the study was hers. I didn't get to see her, well, except from the funeral, and I only caught a glimpse of her then but the voice…it was her." His tone was challenging and Draven let out a breath, not realising he'd been holding it in. Clay was nodding sagely.

"Uh-huh." He stared at Draven. "And based on this…vision of your boyfriend's, you want me to investigate further, speak to the wife, accuse her of lying and see what comes out of it?"

Draven coughed uncomfortably. "Yeah. Basically." Inside, he was glowing at the term "boyfriend."

Simmer down, Draven. This isn't the time for warm and fuzzy. Hardened investigator, remember? Especially in front of Clay. You already slipped up calling Tay "babe."

Clay's green eyes glittered, his lips pursed. Then he shrugged. "Okay."

Draven felt as if he'd entered the Twilight Zone.

It couldn't possibly be that fucking easy.

Taylor looked gobsmacked too. He turned to stare at Draven.

"That's it?" Draven demanded. "You're going to just accept it like that?" He snapped his fingers. Clay leaned back in his chair, looking very relaxed for a man who'd just been told that his operative's psychic boyfriend had important news to share that he'd gleaned from a vision.

"Sure," he drawled, eyes shining with suppressed amusement. "You forget, Draven, when you used to mouth off about this young man, I didn't really agree with you. Just let you rant. I've seen Mr. Abelard's file, spoken to people who've been on the receiving end of his abilities—fairly senior people who aren't generally very receptive about such things. They vouched for him all those years ago in the Bobby Meredith case. And so have others where your young man's abilities have been useful." He shrugged. "So I can afford to give him the benefit of the doubt in this one."

"You've been talking to my friend Rick Grant," Taylor mused slowly, regarding Clay narrowly. "And probably Rick's uncle, a police detective called Tate Williams. Rick says he's always been very supportive of what I do." A fond look crossed his face.

At the mention of the names, Clay's face closed up and his lips thinned. Draven recognised that tell as being something Clay wouldn't talk about and he wondered what he was trying to hide. He also wondered who the hell Rick Grant was and whether he was the one causing the sappy look on Taylor's face. He'd heard of Tate Williams; everyone in law enforcement had heard of him. He was a dyed-in-the-wool police officer who'd been forced to take early retirement after a horrific shooting. He'd been shot by a vengeful ex-con three times on his way home from his local gym and was lucky to have survived.

"Perhaps," Clay murmured diffidently. "We move in the same circles." He waved a hand. "Anyway, just be glad I haven't put you through the mill on this one." He smirked. "I bet Dray here had you all primed and ready to blast away to give me some sort of 'demonstration' to prove your worth?"

Draven's face flushed and Clay cackled loudly. "God, will you look at him. I can't believe you would have staged something like that for me."

Taylor laughed softly and Draven glared at him. "I didn't think you'd be this receptive. I thought…"

A mobile rang shrilly from the confines of Clay's trouser pocket and he held up a hand, forestalling Draven's words.

"I need to take this," he said quickly and stood up and walked over the window as he answered the phone. "Hey, baby. I've been waiting for your call. What did the doctor say?"

A man's voice could be heard from the other side and Draven grinned at Taylor's look of disbelief as he mouthed the word "Baby?"

As long as Draven had known Clay, the one Achilles heel he knew he possessed was the man in his life. No one knew who he was as Clay was as cagey as all hell about it. Draven wouldn't pry either. Clay's private life was his own. Clay was a kitten where *he* was concerned—soft and playful. Each time Draven heard him on the phone to him, Draven marvelled at the change in the man.

Whoever the man was on the other end of the phone, he was lucky to have the devotion and the heart of a man like Clay Mortimer.

Draven stood up and walked over to Taylor, whispering in his ear. "What, you think you're the only one that gets called that?"

"I just never expected it from him, that's all. Hell, we gay guys need our own damn county. Gaymanshire, or something like that." Taylor sniggered and Draven sighed.

"Funny man. But it's not a bad idea. It beats having to figure out whether the guy sitting next to me swings my way or not."

"Yeah, well, you don't need to worry about that anymore do you?" Taylor said silkily.

"Depends," Draven said airily. "On who and what Rick Grant is to you."

Taylor's breath hitched and he looked a little apprehensive. "No one you need worry about," he said, his hands running through his hair. "Rick and I used to have a thing but that was over a while ago." He smirked. "I'd like to hear that stray dick story sometime too. Anyway, are we exclusive? It's not something we've talked about, is it?"

Draven's stomach clenched. Taylor was right. They hadn't discussed their current situation and perhaps he was reading more into it than Taylor was. He felt a twinge of pique at that thought, that he might be more invested.

I never thought I'd have this worry, he thought as he clenched his fingers. *I'm normally the one backing off.*

Taylor opened his mouth to say something, a slight look of worry on his face. At that moment, Clay turned around and strode over to them. Taylor's mouth closed but he glanced at Draven curiously.

Draven wondered what he'd been about to say.

"Where were we?" Clay muttered, his tone distracted and his face pinched. Whatever news he'd received didn't seem good. "Oh yes. You were both just leaving so I can get home. With my McDonald's."

Draven stared at him. "So that's it then? Are you going to speak to Catherine Whittaker and see what comes of it?"

"I said I would, didn't I?" Clay scowled. "Your boyfriend there seems convinced so I'll give him the benefit of the doubt. Once." He smiled wolfishly at Taylor, who blinked. "If it all turns out to be complete bullshit, I'll get my gun out and shoot the two of you." His voice was grim as he went to his desk and started moving papers, looking for something. Draven saw Taylor blanch beneath his coffee-coloured skin.

"Stop being so fucking melodramatic, Clay," he muttered. "We'll let you get off then. You will call me, let me know how it all turns out?"

Clay turned distractedly. "What? Oh, yes. I'll call you if I have anything to say." He held up a bunch of keys in triumph. "Bloody things always get lost under the damn paperwork." His expression changed as he regarded Draven carefully. "I meant to ask, are things still the same with Jude? Have you made any decision yet?"

Draven's body stiffened. "No." His tone was clipped. "I wish the fuck everyone would let me be on this. Taylor's the only one who doesn't seem to push me on it. And that's the way I want it to stay. It's not his worry. It's my problem to deal with."

Taylor shifted on his feet and glanced down at the floor as he frowned.

Clay sighed. "Not pushing, Dray. Just concerned. Sorry I brought it up. Give him a kiss from me when you see him next." His eyes shadowed as he glanced at Taylor then back at Draven. "I know it's not easy, son. Just go with your gut. That always stood me in good stead when I was in the service. Follow your instincts."

He motioned at them both impatiently. “Now, be gone, the two of you. I have somewhere I need to be.” His voice was pained and Draven knew him well enough to know the man was hurting.

He looked at Taylor and shrugged. “I think we’ve overstayed our welcome. I suppose I should get you home and then get home myself. It’s been a long day.”

Taylor’s eyes narrowed and Draven thought he looked a little pissed off. He wondered fleetingly what he’d said wrong. Again. “Clay, thanks for the chat. I’ll expect to hear from you soon.”

Clay was looking at his mobile intently and he didn’t even look up as he waved a hand. “Yep. See you guys.”

Summarily dismissed, Draven led the way out of the office, Taylor behind him. Taylor was quiet as they took the lift down and walked to the car. It was a very different journey from the one up to the office. When they were in the vehicle with seat belts on and Draven had started the car, he sighed and looked at Taylor.

“Out with it,” he said quietly. “What’s bugging you?”

Taylor’s lips pressed together mutinously. “Never mind,” he said shortly. “It doesn’t really matter. Just take me home.”

“Something’s upset you, Tay.” Draven felt the need to push.

“I’m fine, really.” Draven could see Taylor was anything but fine as he leaned his head against the seat rest and closed his eyes, as if shutting out all possibility of conversation.

“I think that went well, considering,” he murmured, hoping that he’d draw Taylor out.

“Uh-huh.”

“Clay’s good at manipulating people, getting them to paint themselves into a corner. If anyone can get to the truth, that man can.”

“Okay.”

Draven felt the prickle of irritation down his spine at the monosyllabic replies. He tried valiantly one last time.

“I mean, there must have been a reason for her to lie, and while it won’t bring Drew back, maybe it has some bearing on his suicide. Maybe she knows something about the blackmailer.”

“Yep.”

Draven exploded as he weaved in and out of traffic, taking care not to drive too fast. “Christ, Taylor, I’m trying to make conversation here. What the hell is wrong with you?”

Taylor's eyes opened and flashed dark lasers of anger at him.

"Excuse me if I don't feel too chatty. I'm not sure we're on the same page here. Do you know the reason I don't push you on the subject of your brother?" His jaw clenched. "Because I don't seem to really have a say in anything about it. One, I only found out about it today even though I've been asking you what's up for weeks. Two, I asked you to take me to see him and you ignored me. Three, based on one and two, you've given me the bare bones of that tragedy but I doubt you'll let me in to share it with you so we can talk about the *decision* you have to make, whatever the fuck that means. It's 'not my worry,' after all."

He folded his arms across his chest, hugging himself. Emotion vibrated from his lean body like a taut violin string being plucked.

Draven's eyes widened at Taylor's growing anger as his fingers clenched on the steering wheel. He barked back. "Maybe I don't solicit your advice because we might not be 'exclusive' as you reminded me. Maybe the story is more for someone who means to stick around, not someone who thinks this thing we have is just 'fun.' Maybe I'm just another 'regular.'"

No sooner had the words left his mouth, he regretted them. A sick feeling welled in his stomach.

Way to go, you prick. God, that must be just about the worst thing you could have said to him.

Taylor's eyes widened and his face paled. "I was joking back there about the whole exclusive thing, Draven. I didn't think we had to talk about it to realise…" His voice cut off and he closed his eyes, his face suddenly weary. The defeat in his face worried Draven more than if Taylor had hit him again. Something he'd probably not blame him for. "You know what, just take me home. That dinner you promised me tonight will have to wait."

Draven felt another twinge of guilt at the thought he'd forgotten his promise to take Taylor out.

"Taylor, I'm sorry. I shouldn't have said that."

Taylor's lips thinned and he stared out the front window of the car, ignoring Draven. His fingers were curled into tight fists.

"I don't want to talk. Just fucking take me home." His tone was tight and controlled.

Draven heard the warning in Taylor's voice and decided to let it go. For now.

They drove in awkward silence the rest of the way home. Draven stopped outside Taylor's house and switched off the engine, and Taylor clipped off his seatbelt and was out the car before the engine had even stopped purring.

"Thanks for the day trip," he said flatly from outside the open car door. "Are you going to go see your brother tonight?"

Draven hesitated then nodded. "Yes. I'll probably grab something to eat and shower first though. Visiting hours are later." His mouth went dry. "Tay, I…"

"I hope it all goes all right with him. G'night, Draven. I'll see you around." Taylor closed the door with an air of finality and strode toward his front door. Draven could only watch helplessly as he disappeared inside.

***

Taylor got home and slumped straight into the easy chair in the lounge. He bit his fingernails as he sat in the semi darkness, with only the faint glow of a new fish tank lighting up the room. He shook his head in bemusement.

When the hell did that get there? Shows you just how much I've been home lately. Not.

He knew it had to be Leslie's and he grinned faintly at the thought despite the turmoil in his gut and the ache in his chest.

Every pet that Leslie had brought into the house to date had either died or "disappeared." The pet goldfish, Rollo—a gift from an old flame who'd won it at a fun fair coconut shy competition—had been found floating belly up in his bowl one morning. Leslie had shrieked the place down, seemingly overcome with grief. Then there had been the pet spider that he'd "adopted" when it was found in the bathtub. Taylor and Eddie were in favour of flushing it down the toilet. Leslie however had decided it deserved mercy and had kept in a shoebox in his room for the princely time of a whole two days before it had mysteriously "disappeared."

Given the fact that Eddie hadn't seemed too concerned at the possibility of a spider lurking around the house (and him being very afraid of said arachnids) and wearing a satisfied smirk during the frantic search of couches, cushions and cupboards, Taylor had a feeling it had been relegated to the great unknown somewhere, probably a sewer. And then there had been the bird Leslie found in his room, with a broken wing. Gloria Gaynor had been nursed back to health, staying the longest out of all Leslie's guests, until one day, in a fit of sheer indulgence, Leslie had perched her on the windowsill to watch her brothers and sisters enjoy the great outdoors, and she'd promptly flown away. He'd been devastated and it had taken half a dozen cups of chamomile tea for Taylor to calm him down. Not to mention Taylor's promise of a new pair of Ted Baker heels that Leslie had his eye on, something he could ill afford at the time.

Taylor huffed and regarded the colourful fish in the tank with jaundiced eyes. The minute Draven had uttered the words "It's not his worry. It's my problem to deal with," Taylor's temper had flared. Already under some stress from the morning's emotional meeting at the Threadcourts' house, coupled with meeting Draven's boss for the first time, his already fragile psyche had been on high alert. Hearing Draven so brazenly declare he didn't think Taylor needed to be involved in his affairs had really given him the hump. Then taking that throwaway comment about being exclusive out of context, and the barb about being a "regular"—well, that had really been the final straw.

He'd never thought a chest could hurt so much, as his had tightened and his heart had thumped out of control. So now he sat grumpily ensconced in the worn chair, eating his fingers and wondering what to do next. There was no way he was going to call Draven any time soon. The bastard had gone too far.

If he wants me, he can come and find me. I'm not making the first move again. And when he does, he's going to pay for those words. My mission is going to be to drive him crazy. The man won't know what's hit him. Let him see what he's missing when he's being a prick.

The thought of getting his own back on Draven soothed the turmoil in his soul and he closed his eyes and leaned back. He was bone tired.

Taylor dreamt. Not the blood-soaked nightmares of the past but something that felt even a little more disturbing in that it soaked into his bones and sent tiny tendrils of insidious emotions into his psyche. What disturbed him more was that those tendrils were infused with hope. His normal visions of dismembered children, desperate people with violence in their souls and those who simply latched onto him like leeches intent on sucking him dry were long gone. Instead, there was softness, eagerness, a whisper in his mind that it was time to go, time to move on and a gentle urging to make him listen. Focus. Warmth enveloped him instead of the cold dread he was used to, and wrapped comforting arms around his still body, beguiling him with the promise of an ending of something that had dragged on far too long. In his sleep, Taylor smiled softly then nodded as the voice told him that he had to help.

When he woke up, he was crying. Silent tears rolled down his cheeks; his breath was heavy, his chest aching from something that felt like both loss and relief. He sat up in bed, reaching wondering fingers to his cheeks to feel the slick wetness on his face. Taylor drew a shuddering breath as he reached for his shirt and wiped his eyes. He could still hear the echo of the words in his head, resonating in the cold, dark room.

Save me. Tell him to let me go.

Chapter 9

The hospital was silent as Draven sat beside his brother's bedside in the critical care ward. An overhead light above him flickered, and Draven, in his morbid frame of mind, wondered whether someone, somewhere was dying and the flickering light was a reflection of the ebb and flow of life.

He sighed and passed a hand over tired, strained eyes. He heard the soft murmuring from people at the nurse's station just outside the ward, and saw quiet purposefulness in the movements of the personnel on call as they moved around. It was late at night and only a few visitors still lingered in the corridors. He'd come straight from his time with Taylor, needing to see his brother.

He shifted in his uncomfortable chair and lifted his arms above his head, stretching. Jude slept on, his body still, his face never changing. Draven has helped the nurses move him, rub his skeletal limbs and he'd been horrified to see the worsening state of his brother's body. Doctor Frederick had quietly assured him that everything was being done, but before Draven's eyes, his little brother was wasting away before him.

He reached out and touched a stringy, greasy piece of hair that fell across Jude's pale brow. "Hey, there, little bro," he whispered. "Can you hear me?" He asked that question a half a dozen times in the hours he visited Jude. He'd never had a response, no inkling that Jude heard him at all. "I met someone. His name is Taylor. I think you'd like him. He reminds me of you, a little. He's also damn cheeky, causes me grey hairs and doesn't listen to a word I say. I also think I cocked up any hope of a relationship tonight." He laughed softly but there was tinge of despair in it. "We have this thing going, though, and guess what? He's a damn psychic. Yep, you never thought you'd hear your big brother confess to that one, huh?"

He gently stroked Jude's thin arm. The skin was warm, soft, and Draven's eyes prickled. The only thing he had left of him was the feel of his brother's flesh beneath his fingertips. It was the only indication he had that his brother was still there. It was scant comfort when he remembered how active Jude had been as a kid. He'd always been trouble, always enterprising, sometimes to the point of disobedience and devilry. At the time Draven had seen it as rebelling, as flouting Draven's authority when he'd been left to babysit Jude. Now, Draven wanted that back more than anything in the world. He continued stroking Jude's arm.

"I miss you, sweetheart. Every fucking day I miss you, your smile, and your voice. I miss those crazy impersonations you used to do of Pepé Le Pew and Bart Simpson. I miss you singing Bruce Springsteen tunes and playing air guitar." His voice cracked and tears were now rolling freely down his face. "I miss our stupid ice cream challenges to see which one of us got a brain freeze first. God, I miss everything, Jude. I just…"

His voice could no longer express everything he missed, everything that had been taken away from them both, but mostly, from a young boy who would never become a young man. "Christ, I don't know what to do…I don't know."

His nose was streaming now, as he sobbed, bowing his head to sniffle against Jude's side, where the respirator puffed and breathed for him, making his thin chest rise and fall. Draven had never felt such agony, such finality. He knew he was nearing the end of the road with Jude. That fact, coupled with the thought of knowing that he had to make the decision that would break his heart and leave him shattered and torn, made him want to close his eyes, hug his knees to his chest and hibernate in a dark place.

The enormity of the task ahead of him swept through him like cold Siberian air, chilling his bones to the marrow and making him wonder if his heart would ever beat again.

There was a swell of air beside him, like a bubble of warmth and he looked up, eyes red, and blurred, thinking someone was beside him. His scalp prickled and his hair stirred, as if someone had passed by and touched him. There was no one there and he knew it was his own longing and desperation that was creating these illusions.

"Are you there, Jude?" he whispered. "Can you hear me? I wish you could tell me what you want, tell me whether you're in pain. That damn doctor of yours says you aren't but what the hell do they know? They aren't you. They aren't stuck in this fucking bed, wasting away, so how can they say that?" He used the sleeve of his long-sleeved shirt to wipe his eyes and grabbed a box of tissues from the bedside table to blow his nose. "I want to do the right thing, little brother. I want to make sure I do what's best for you and I don't know what that is."

His body shuddered and he sniffed again, trying to clear his blocked nose. "Taylor's the only person keeping me sane at the moment and God knows I don't tell him much about this whole thing. He doesn't understand that I don't want to mess him up; he's going through enough stuff of his own what with all the shitty deaths he sees and the feelings he has to live with. How can I lay this on him as well? I don't even understand it all myself."

Draven remembered a conversation he'd had with Taylor. They'd been huddled in bed, warm under the covers and talk had turned to what Taylor did and how. Draven had tucked stray strands of hair behind his lover's ears as they talked.

"I've never believed in this whole life after death before and to me, this is such a reach to believe that there's something else out there, after we leave this world. I still can't process it."

Taylor had sighed tiredly. "It's strange for me too. Yes, I know I feel things, see things, but that's a world removed from what just happened. I guess if I believe in feeling the spirits or energy of people who've died and I can feel their pain, see their last moments, it's not such a huge stretch to believe that people go somewhere else when they die. Energy, soul, spirit, whatever it is. It's not for *us* to figure out, Draven. It's ours to either accept or not. It's about taking a leap of faith."

He'd wrapped warm arms around Draven's waist. Draven had leaned back into him, as Taylor nuzzled his neck, smelling his man's fragrance and revelling in it. "It doesn't matter where *it* is. To every person, it might be a different place, or a world, or a realm we don't even know about. To people who believe in heaven, that's their place, I suppose. It's wherever anyone wants to go when they leave this world."

Those words still haunted him.

"Draven?" The quiet voice behind him made him start and he turned swiftly to see calm, brown eyes regarding him with compassion. Sister Alison Maduna was a fixture in this ward and her quiet, competent presence was always welcoming to all, but especially to Draven. He'd sobbed against her ample bosom more times than he'd like to admit, as she patted his back and treated him like the mother he'd lost. The reassuring West African nurse had been there for him through the past three years of hell and Draven didn't know what he'd have done without her.

"I thought you were off duty tonight," he croaked as he tried valiantly to dry his eyes and compose himself. She moved over to him and patted his shoulder, her warm hands on his body giving him comfort.

"No, I changed shifts with Julia. She had a family emergency so I took her shift." She pulled over another chair with a scrape of legs against the tiled floor and set her ample buttocks down beside him. "How are you doing, baby?"

Draven waved a hand. "As you can see, I'm fine." His voice was muffled, as his he struggled to breathe through his stuffed nose.

She smiled. "Having a bad night, huh? Is our little man giving you grief, back chatting perhaps?" She reached over and tenderly stroked Jude's cheek. "Hey, you little rapscallion, stop making your brother cry. He's supposed to be a big bad ass and I come in and find him in tears? Shame on you, baby. Shame on you."

Her teasing tone to his still brother made Draven smile wanly. "Yeah, I wish, Ally. I'd take that, you know? Take anything he wanted to give me." His voice broke again but this time the tears stayed away. Draven had cried enough tonight.

Alison cuffed his jaw line gently with large, warm fingers. "I know. I wish that too. You've been so brave through this, honey. I wish I could do more for you, you know? I wish I could wave a magic wand and make this all go away. Bring him back."

Her voice was sad and the unspoken words lay between them like a freight train about to plunge off a mountain.

And you know that's the one thing I can't do.

She sat with Draven, both of them lost in their own thoughts. Draven took comfort in having this woman by his side, the one constant in Jude's situation the whole time he'd been there. They had become friends of a kind inside these antiseptic walls of both grief and joy.

Finally she stood up and placed a soft kiss on the top of his head. She went to Jude and did the same then the nurse checked the leads and wires keeping his brother alive, ran a critical eye over his body and checked the chart at the foot of the bed. When she had finally finished she turned to Draven, who'd been watching the activity with weary eyes.

"There. He's comfortable enough. Aren't you, honey?" Her hands caressed Jude's arm. "Maybe you should go home, get some sleep, Draven. It's been a long night."

Draven shook his head. "No, I'm staying here tonight. I'll sleep in the chair."

Alison nodded. "I know when your mind's made up, you can't be swayed. I'll get one of the night nurses to bring you a blanket and a cup of coffee. Have you eaten?"

"Not hungry. I had a sandwich earlier." The sandwich had been two tasteless pieces of bread with pale slices of anaemic ham and soggy tomato between them.

Alison tut-tutted. "I know your idea of food, Draven, and it scares me. I'll see if I can get you something a little more substantial. It was chicken and vegetables tonight and I have to say, it wasn't too shabby." She grinned. "I had some myself so it must have been okay. I'll be back in a while."

Alison disappeared out of the room. Draven sighed and got comfortable in the chair where he'd probably spend the night.

Best get hunkered down. Tonight I'm here for the long haul.

He thought of Taylor, who was probably not even in bed yet. His heart ached but he couldn't bring himself to call him. Not yet. He was still too raw inside and he needed a little time to get his head right. He was no good to anyone at the moment, least of all himself.

***

One week later and Draven was feeling the effects of not seeing Taylor. He missed the man like a limb that had been removed. The night he'd come home from visiting Jude, he'd had a call in the early hours of the next morning. He'd been sent on another assignment out of the country by Clay, on an assignment that had been "urgent and life threatening," with the fate of the nation hanging in the balance. Clay could often be rather drama ridden himself. Draven had been handed an itinerary, a plane ticket to Lithuania and a grinning admonishment from his boss to keep his dick in his pants this time. Draven had texted Taylor from the airport to let him know he was going away for a while but there had been no response. His subsequent texts and phone calls had been ignored, apart from one text that Taylor had sent back after Draven's last one, the day before he arrived back in the UK.

Tay, I'm back in London tomorrow. Can I see you to talk?

Taylor's response had been short. *Call me. We'll see.*

Draven had scowled at that terse reply, not being a man to chase after what he wanted but the fact Taylor was willing to perhaps get together had made him feel a little better. Of course, his innate sense of bloody-mindedness made him wonder if he *would* call his lover.

Taylor isn't the only stubborn bastard.

The case in Lithuania had been fairly straightforward, and the young hacker genius who operated out there, who had been stealing millions from a state-based charity in Russia—ostensibly based out there to help refugees—had been given an ultimatum.

Work for us or go to prison. That had basically been Draven's brief. The youngster, only twenty-three years old, had talents that Mortimer Investigations would find extremely useful. The money he'd stolen and amassed in an offshore bank account had been returned to the charity who had only been too relieved that it had found its way back to worry about pursuing justice for the hacker. Tomas Pavlis had vehemently defended his theft, telling Draven with glittering blue eyes that the funds were not being used for the purpose for which they were intended and Russian human rights violations made it his mission to relieve them of their funds.

It had taken some doing but Draven had managed to convince Tomas that now they'd tracked him down, handing the young hacker over to the Russian authorities had not been in anyone's best interests and his skills would be better suited to working with Mortimer Investigations. Tomas had grudgingly seen the light and left with Draven to London on a business class ticket. Draven had been glad to deposit the rather feisty and argumentative young man into the clutches of Draven's boss once they'd arrived in London.

The first thing he'd done when arriving back in England was visit Jude. He'd had daily reports from then nurses on how he was doing, the words "No change" being most of what was conveyed. Draven had an irrational fear that something would happen to Jude when he was out of the country and the nursing staff were used to his paranoia. Clay was a ready conduit to how his brother was faring, as he visited often too.

Draven had also given into temptation and called Taylor after he'd seen Jude. Taylor had sounded tired, and a little cool, but he'd agreed to meet Draven at Galileo's for dinner that night. Not only did Draven want to mend bridges but he also had other news to impart, news that he hoped might take some of the weight of Drew's death off Taylor's shoulders and make him feel better about the whole affair.

"Sitting on your own? Is Taylor late?" came the drawl from behind him. Draven turned to see Gideon, immaculately dressed as ever, smiling at him. Luckily he didn't have Eddie with him. Gideon's redheaded lover wasn't particularly enamoured of Draven. He always seemed very keen on sticking a skewer or some other kitchen implement in Draven's flesh.

"Only by a few minutes. We agreed eight p.m., it's just a few minutes past." For a moment, Draven felt a surge of panic that Taylor had decided not to come after all.

"Speak of the devil…" Gideon murmured, his eyes glinting with amusement. Draven followed the direction of his friend's eyes and held his breath on seeing Taylor. His lover (at least he hoped he still was) looked as sexy as hell. He wore tight-fitting black chinos, a deep red shirt open to the chest, and his wayward curls were swept back behind his ears. He looked like something out of *Pirates of the*

Caribbean, wild and untamed, dark eyes observing Draven closely as he approached the table.

"Wow, someone has got it bad," teased Gideon. "Might I suggest you shut your mouth a little? I doubt he's going to put his dick in it right here and now."

"Fuck off," Draven growled, even as he tried to control the rising urge in his pants. "I hate you sometimes. Haven't you got a restaurant to run?"

Gideon sniggered. "He does look *very* tempting…" he drawled. "If I didn't have a jealous red head waiting for me, I might have a taste myself."

Draven knew he was joking but that still didn't stop him from snarling. "He's mine. You can't bloody have him."

Gideon tut-tutted. "Possessive to the last. Now you know how I feel about Eddie. I seem to remember you laughing at me one time and telling me that I was like a rabid dog pissing on his territory. It's not so funny when the shoe's on the other foot, eh?"

He leaned in close as Taylor got to the table and glanced at them both uncertainly. "Don't fuck it up," Gideon mouthed in his ear. "This one's a keeper."

He straightened up and pulled out Taylor's chair, waving for him to sit down.

"Taylor, welcome. Draven here was starting to worry you'd changed your mind." Draven glared at him.

Gideon ignored the laser-like stare. "Can I get you a drink?" he asked Taylor.

Taylor sat down and stared between them, looking a little confused. "Uhm, a Corona please."

Gideon waved an expansive hand and gave a mini bow. "Coming up. I'll bring you another whisky, Dray. I'll send someone over to take your food order later." He turned and walked away then turned back as if he'd forgotten something. "Oh, and Taylor, Eddie said he'd cut off your balls if you didn't say hello to him while you were here. He's going to pop out later and say hi."

He sauntered off and Draven rolled his eyes. "Great," he muttered. "As long as he doesn't come out with a damn meat cleaver, I'll be fine."

"What?" Taylor said, perplexed.

"Nothing." Draven finished off the dregs of his whisky. "It's just your buddy Eddie seems to have it in for me."

Taylor smirked slightly and Draven was glad to see it. It meant Taylor perhaps wasn't so mad at him if he could do that sexy movement with his mouth.

"And I always thought Eddie liked arseholes," Taylor murmured slyly. "Just goes to show you that people can still surprise you."

Draven leaned forward across the table, ignoring that quip. "I tried to tell you I was sorry for what I said," he growled. "But every text or phone call went unanswered, and you damn well ignored me."

Taylor shrugged, and Draven's eyes were drawn to the way Taylor's body made that simple gesture look like full-blown seduction. The man had an unconscious beauty that made Draven want to rip the red shirt off his beautiful shoulders and fuck him across the table. His dick still hadn't quiet subsided from his earlier sighting and that thought brought it alive again like the beast of Frankenstein, electricity surging through flesh and blood rising into places he'd forgotten he had. It had been too long since he'd gotten laid.

While in Lithuania, he'd been to a couple of secret gay bars frequented by people in the know, and been hit on by numerous men, but he'd not taken one of them up on their offers. For some frustrating reason, he'd thought of Taylor every time a man's fingers had brushed his crotch, or squeezed his arse, or as one man had done, stuck his tongue in his ear as if giving him an aural clean.

He had gone back to his hotel room horny and frustrated and jacked off to the memory of Taylor riding his cock like a beautiful wild horse, all sleek skin and lithe muscle. That alone had been the extent of his sexual endeavours in the past week. Now the man in his fantasies regarded him with liquid brown eyes as his hands idly stroked the silky edges of the shirt lying across his chest. Every so often they'd pause and dwell on the caramel-coloured skin beneath, as Taylor's delicate fingertips caressed his own flesh and Draven's eyes were drawn to those movements like a starving dog to a meaty bone.

He finally managed to pull his eyes away to look up and saw Taylor staring at him in amusement, his eyes darkened. He licked his lips, pink tongue wetting full, luscious lips, another gesture that sent

Draven's cock into a tailspin. There was no mistaking the look of avarice in Taylor's eyes or the intent in the movements he made.

The little bastard is doing it deliberately. He's trying to drive me fucking crazy.

Draven admitted it was working.

"So, your little trip to Lithuania. Did it all go well?" Taylor smiled at the waitress placing his beer on the table and she grinned at him as she gave Draven his whisky. Taylor picked up the bottle, wrapping lips around the top, lime and all, and then with his tongue, he pushed the lime deeply into the bottle. Draven had never seen that particular trick performed before but the thought of that lucky bottleneck enjoying that gifted tongue in Taylor's mouth was making his groin ache. Taylor lifted the bottle, exposing the smooth column of his throat and the Adam's apple that bobbed as he drank down his first taste of beer. He made a small noise of contentment, similar to the one Draven had heard before when he was fucking him, and he leaned back in his chair, trying to get more comfortable. He took a slug of his drink and was not surprised to see he'd drank nearly half of it when he put the drink down. Taylor's eyes glinted when he saw what was left and he lowered his bottle with a satisfied sigh.

"Nothing like the first beer of the day," he murmured. "*You* must have been thirsty." He waved at the whisky. "Anyway, where was I? Oh, yes, your business trip. Meet anyone special out there?"

"No," Draven rumbled. "It wasn't that sort of trip. Purely business."

Taylor raised an eyebrow. "I thought you had a habit of mixing business with pleasure?"

Draven's face tightened. "It was just business. Are you going to bust my chops all night or are we going to enjoy dinner like two normal people without the sarcasm and jibes?"

Taylor opened his mouth to answer but a tornado chose that moment to approach their table and attack Draven's dinner date. Eddie Tripp beamed as he dragged Taylor to his feet and enveloped him in a lanky-armed bear hug. A noisy, smacking kiss was delivered to Taylor's lips, a kiss that left what looked like traces of flour on Taylor's mouth.

"Tay, you're looking good, my friend. Oops, sorry, got some stuff on your face." Eddie licked his fingers and wiped the offending smear from Taylor's mouth. "There, got it. So how have you been?"

He turned to look at Draven and tough as he was, the malevolent stare focused on him turned Draven's blood to ice. Eddie looked like Maleficent, albeit with red hair and green piercing eyes.

"I see you two are still together then. The rumour mill is right for once." He turned around and his fingers poked Draven in the chest. "I hope you're treating him right because you know if you don't, I'm coming after you."

Draven was speechless.

How the hell does Gideon sleep at night with this feisty virago in his bed? He must have one eye open when he does.

Taylor was laughing quietly. "Eddie, baby, it's fine, honest. Draven and I are here having dinner, that's all. No need to get all snarky with him."

Draven knew Eddie wasn't too fond of him after the incident in which he'd made Taylor pass out in the restaurant, but he thought he'd have gotten over it by now. He was glad Taylor was defending him though.

"Hmm." Eddie didn't look convinced. "Is he treating you okay, though, is what I want to know."

Taylor looked at Draven. "I'm not sure yet. It's still under advisement."

He shrugged and Draven felt a prickle of unease that he wasn't out of the woods yet. He watched mesmerised as Taylor's lips once again ran around the rim of his bottle and he looked at Draven from eyes that definitely promised…something. Draven wasn't quite sure what it was.

"Well, you know where to find me if you need back-up," Eddie muttered. He made to move away then turned around again and Draven saw the evil glint in his green eyes. "Oh, by the way, did Markie call you? You know, that guy we met in the bar the other night that you gave your number to?"

Draven's chest tightened. It was difficult to act nonchalant when the slow burn of jealousy inflamed him. He pressed his lips together, waiting to see what Taylor's reply was.

Taylor nodded. "Yeah, he did, the next day. He asked me to go with him to the Nickelback concert next week." He set his drink down idly, tracing a pattern on the frosty outside of the bottle. Draven saw it looked like a set of balls and a penis. He glared at Taylor whose lips held the trace of a slow smile as his eyes focused on his circling finger.

"And?" Eddie demanded impatiently. "Christ, it's like pulling teeth with you."

"I told him it depends." Taylor's eyes lifted to meet Draven's and he was under no illusions that it depended on him and what would happen next. Whether things got better and Taylor forgave him for his outburst.

Eddie snorted. "Good. It always helps to keep your options open." He cast a fiery glance at Draven, who stared back. "Anyway, let me go before the boss fires my arse." He grinned and Draven couldn't help noticing that it really was a rather attractive one, making the man seem much more approachable. "Then I'd have to convince him to give my job back somehow."

"I doubt you'd have any problem convincing 'the boss' to take you back," Taylor remarked with a laugh.

Eddie chuckled. "Probably not. Have a good evening, Tay. I'll call you tomorrow." He gave his friend's shoulder a tight squeeze with an evil glare in Draven's direction and a warning to "treat Taylor like something precious" or he'd kick his arse. He narrowly avoided knocking into a waiter passing by with a plate full of food. Taylor sniggered and stared after him fondly.

"He's really protective of you, isn't he?" Draven said softly. "It doesn't bode well for me if I put a foot wrong, but I'm glad someone has your back." He desperately wanted to ask Taylor if he intended going to the Nickelback concert with Markie but didn't want to come across too desperate. He'd try another tactic.

"So you like Nickelback then? I didn't know that. I enjoy their music as well. Chad Kroeger is pretty much a genius."

Taylor nodded. Draven couldn't help thinking he looked rather amused.

"Yes, I love their music. Rock and roll and all that angst-fuelled testosterone in the music. It's just good, dirty fun to listen to. Maybe we should take in a concert together sometime."

Draven couldn't help himself. "Yeah? So you don't want to go with that other guy then?"

Taylor laughed softly and the sound sent chills down Draven's back and made his cock push against his trousers.

"No, Dray, I don't want to go with Markie. I'd rather go with you."

Those words gave Draven hope that things were about to take a turn for the better.

He was still feeling that warm glow of hope when they got back to Draven's house after a very innuendo-laden and hasty dinner and Taylor began ripping his clothes off the moment the door shut behind them. Draven took that as a sign that he'd been forgiven, which had been hinted at earlier with the constant teasing activity in the restaurant as Taylor made love with his mouth to some sort of chocolate dessert and his toes had kept creeping up to rub Draven's balls under the table. He'd also not wanted to spoil Taylor's unexpected good mood by telling him the latest news on Drew's death. Having his balls rubbed was a far better plan.

Draven was happy to oblige now in getting his kit off but he was determined that there was only one way this evening was going to go down. Once they were both naked, he took charge and heaved a protesting, but chuckling Taylor onto his shoulder in a fireman's lift, and stalked into the bedroom. Taylor was thrown onto the bed as Draven followed him, crawling toward him on hands and knees like a hunting leopard.

He lowered his body on top of the struggling Taylor, pinning his hands above his head with one strong hand, and grinding his ready cock against Taylor's own hardness. The struggling ceased and instead, a whimper of need escaped the man pinioned beneath him.

"God, Draven, you feel so good," Taylor gasped, his voice husky. "Please, it's been too long. I need to feel you in me."

Draven laughed sharply, but he also felt the overwhelming desire to plunge his very needy cock into the hot, slick depths of his lover.

"You have been a cock tease all night and now it's my turn," he growled. "Licking your lips and touching yourself, and those damn toes of yours are about to get what they deserve."

His mouth found Taylor's, ravenous and greedy, and Draven got lost in the movement of Taylor's lips on his and the slick tongue that delved into the deepest recesses of Draven's willing mouth. Cocks rubbed together, legs twined like vines, as both men tried hard to absorb each other, feel each other and taste each other. Finally Draven lifted glazed eyes to gaze down into Taylor's, eyes blown and wide, lips swollen and wet from kisses.

"Keep your hands above your head," he demanded as he slowly worked his way down Taylor's body, worshipping the wriggling, panting man under his control. "You don't touch yourself or anything else. You're mine to do with what I want."

"But I need…" Taylor whined as his hands fisted the pillows and his hips arched up toward Draven's heated body. Draven bit the skin of his hip, the soft, smooth flesh like that of a ripe peach beneath his teeth. Taylor cried out sharply, his body bucking and Draven bit him again, softer this time, then licked the skin languorously.

"Behave," he said hoarsely, his own prick so hard that his groin was ready to blow. "I'm running the show. Lie back and enjoy."

Taylor moaned and the sound went straight to Draven's dick. He moved down the warm, spicy-scented skin, licking, nibbling, biting, loving the mewls and soft sobs as Taylor writhed on the bed. Finally he got where he wanted to be. He rubbed his stubbled cheek against a hardened, wet prick then licked the tip of it, rolling his tongue around the glans and finding that little hidden spot beneath.

"Oh God, Dray," Taylor said brokenly. "Please, please. I need to come. Want you inside me."

Draven ignored him and instead, lifted Taylor's legs up toward his chest. He lost his breath at the sight of Taylor's dusky pucker, all ready for him, inviting him in. He reached up and spat on his fingers, then slowly rubbed that little hole and saw Taylor fall apart. His legs tensed, his hands forgetting they were supposed to be above his head and he tried to grab his already slippery cock. His groans were enough to make Draven erupt. He grasped the base of his prick desperately, willing it to last, then bent over Taylor, almost folding him in half. He put his hands back where they were supposed to be. "If you want me to fuck you," Draven whispered, "you'll know what's good for you. Don't move your hands again."

Taylor nodded, his eyes wild, his chest heaving and Draven gave him a deep, dirty kiss then went back to his teasing. Slowly, deliberately, he took Taylor's foot in his hand and sucked his toes into his mouth. He had no idea whether this was one of Taylor's erogenous zones but he wanted to find out. He wasn't disappointed.

Taylor let out a howl at the first heavy suck of his toes, as Draven pulled them into his mouth, licking the firm flesh and sucking them with relish. They tasted earthy, spicy and uniquely Taylor. His fingers massaged the balls of Taylor's feet as he sucked and then he did the same to the other one. He thought with a sense of triumph that Taylor definitely had a thing for having his feet touched.

"Draven, oh fuck, Dray. Please, I need you to stop that, need you to fuck me. I'm begging you, please."

Draven didn't think he could last much longer himself. He reached for the lube and condom on the bedside table and in one of the quickest moves he'd ever made, the lube-covered condom was sheathing his cock and Taylor's hole was wet and slick as Draven rolled his fingers around that sensitive and pulsing area. Taylor was gripping the pillow above his head, eyes dark and wide, mouth pleading with Draven to hurry up.

"This isn't going to be one of those easy, tender, times, Tay," Draven warned as he pushed into Taylor. "This is going to be a rough ride. I need you too much. So damn much…"

He grunted as he filled the condom and Taylor, sinking into that little bit of heaven as if he belonged there. Taylor cried out, his muscles clenching around Draven as they found their rhythm and in between messy, sloppy kisses and murmured endearments, both men worked together as one.

It was about slick, hot flesh covered in lube and sweat, the sounds of sex echoing in the warm air, bodies pistoning and driving, arching and twisting and the feel of Taylor's hands on Draven's body, neither of them caring now about the old rule.

As Draven gasped and felt his balls constrict and as the first hot jets of fluid filled the condom and Taylor, he knew with absolute finality that this was where he belonged. With this man, in this man, and as part of this man and there was no way on God's green earth he was ever going to let him go.

His climax reached and spent, he heard Taylor's loud gasp of completion as his belly grew warm with Taylor's come and the scent of musk and sweat filled the air. Draven collapsed on the sticky, wet stomach of his lover. He sought Taylor's mouth and kissed him gently, not the rough, rude action born of desire or lust like before but rather the soft, passionate kiss of possession and affection.

"Mine," he whispered against Taylor's lips. "You are mine."

Taylor nodded, eyes sleepy. "Yours," he agreed. "Definitely."

Draven wanted to ask Taylor what had changed, why he'd been so forgiving and not given up on him, as they'd yet to speak about it. He didn't want to spoil the moment though, so instead he played big spoon to Taylor's little one, wrapping protective arms around the man in his arms, listening to his soft breathing as he fell asleep.

The feel of Taylor's warm arse against his groin and stomach made him feel complete.

Never felt like this before, must be something in the damn water, were his last thoughts before he drifted off into slumber.

***

The following Sunday morning they sat in the lounge, eating marmalade toast and drinking coffee. Draven thought with a pang of longing that it was all very domesticated. He'd missed having this sort of relationship, the one where you woke up to the same man each morning and took pleasure in the way they liked the sugar in their coffee and saw the adorable frown as they perused the morning newspapers. He'd watched his mother and father as a child; seen their warmth and affection. He'd never really thought he'd want that, but since meeting Taylor it seemed to have become a need in his life. His job hadn't really allowed for it is the past, and he'd been too much of a player anyway but Taylor had put some things into perspective.

He grinned as Taylor's eyes travelled the newspaper, watched his lips part when he read something interesting, all the while taking bites of his toast which left crumbs on his mouth. His hair curled around his face, framing his smooth skin like a puddle of black ink.

Draven chuckled. "God, you look cute when you read the papers. Your nose scrunches up like a rabbit."

Taylor mock glared at him. "Comparing me to soft and cuddly animals isn't going to get you laid any time soon," he declared loftily. "I'd suggest you watch what you say."

"Yeah, yeah. You want this body far too badly to limit your partaking of it," Draven retorted, waving a hand languidly down his body. "You know you can't resist it."

Taylor stuck his tongue out at him and went back to reading his paper, a small smile on his face. Draven didn't want to disturb his wellbeing but there was no easy way and no good time to impart the information he had sitting in his head.

"Tay?"

Taylor looked up. "Hmm?"

"I spoke to Clay yesterday. It was the wife. She was the one in the room when Drew shot himself."

Taylor paled and he set the newspaper down on the table. "It was Catherine? But why, why didn't she stop him, what happened?"

Draven sat down next to Taylor and laid a warm hand on his. "While I was away, Clay went around to see her with one of his friends, some hotshot psychologist who knows just how to get under your skin. Believe me, I know. I've met her. Between them, they pushed Catherine into a place she'd never have known how to leave. They got the whole story. She was the one blackmailing him. She thought it might make him see the 'error of his ways' when it came to his alternative lifestyle." Draven grimaced in distaste. "She'd had enough of his antics and decided she wanted to teach him a lesson."

"She blackmailed her own husband?" Taylor looked ill. "What the fuck did she expect he'd do? Just sit back and let it ride?" He stood up and moved around the lounge in agitation. Draven watched him.

"She said she didn't mean for it to go so far. She'd had someone following him and they'd seen him go into the club. She had him take pictures and then used those to mess with his head.

"That night she got home early and found him in the study." Draven's voice tailed off. "Her story is he literally pulled the trigger as she saw him and she couldn't stop it. Clay said she was completely hysterical and they had to send for a paramedic to come and calm her down." He took a deep breath. "She's in some fancy sanatorium at the moment awaiting some doctor to tell the police whether anything further should be done. After all, she didn't pull the trigger."

Taylor's face was white. "No. But she drove him to it. If she hadn't been such a fucking bitch, he wouldn't be dead. How do you do that to someone you love, for God's sake? Blackmail them, drive them to suicide?" His hands were shaking, his breath laboured. Draven moved over to him quickly.

"Baby, breathe. Come on. Deep in, out, in, out…breathe for me, Taylor." He held his lover tight against his chest as the shudders lessened and then, when he was sure Taylor seemed better, he stepped back slightly and regarded him. "It's over, Tay. You helped

Drew by getting the truth out. It won't change the fact he's dead but at least it's over now."

"It'll never be over. Not for me. I hear his death every time I close my eyes, see his blood coat those walls sometimes when I fall asleep. Nothing's ever over, Draven. Death isn't always the end."

Draven had no idea what to say to that, so he simply held Taylor close, feeling the beat of his heart against his own chest and the warmth that soaked into his skin from his boyfriend's body. Finally Taylor heaved a deep sigh. He looked up at Draven, his dark eyes shadowed.

"Sorry. That was probably a bit more intense that I meant to be. I just hope Drew's at peace wherever he is now. He deserved that much at least."

He moved over to the couch and slumped down, biting his fingernails. He looked a little lost and Draven couldn't stand it. He took a deep breath. "I'm going to the hospital this afternoon. Would you like to come with me to visit Jude?"

Taylor looked up him, face lightening "Are you sure?" he asked hesitantly. "Because I'd love to if you are."

Draven nodded, even as his heart beat faster. Jude's plight had been his cross to bear, for not being there to protect his brother, or make his world right and bring him back. He was trying to share because he knew if he didn't, he'd lose Taylor one day as well. "I think it's about time you met the other man in my life," he murmured. "So if we leave just after twelve, we won't be in the nurse's way at lunchtime and I won't have the smell of hospital food clogging my nostrils."

"Okay." Taylor looked uncertain. "Erm, I'm normally okay in hospitals, although I can tend to space out now and then if there's too much going on. I know I need some emotional connection to see stuff but hospitals are a bit of an unknown." He stood up and walked over to Draven, laying a hand on his shoulder. "So I'll try not to pass out on you or anything, but it might be a scenario we have to face."

Draven was mystified. "Then why the hell do you want to go in there, if it makes you uncomfortable?"

Taylor brushed warm lips across his. "Because it's something I want to share with you," he said simply. "It eats at you and I want to be there for you."

Draven's chest warmed and he pulled Taylor against him and hugged him fiercely. "Thanks," he said gruffly. "Just please try hold it together, though. I hate seeing you all whacked out." He released his lover and started clearing away the breakfast dishes. "Let me get rid of these and then I have some work to do in the study for a while. Can you entertain yourself while I'm gone?"

Taylor smirked. "You have a 48-inch TV, an X-Box and the latest *Grand Theft Auto*. I'm pretty sure I'll be fine."

***

Draven felt strangely out of sorts later on that day as he entered the hospital lobby with Taylor. It was only the second time he'd been to the hospital to see Jude with someone. The first time had been with Clay. His boss had been with him when Draven had gotten the call telling him about the tragedy. If he hadn't been there, Draven knew he would have fallen apart. He remembered that call vividly, and he shivered now at remembering being told his whole family had just been ripped away from him.

Clay had been supportive but tenacious, like a dog humping his leg, until Draven gave in and took him to visit Jude at the hospital. From that point on, Jude had two frequent visitors. Draven knew that Clay had some personal issues of his own in the mysterious man that took up a lot of his time, but he'd always managed to pay a visit to the young man lying prone in a hospital bed.

Draven turned to look at Taylor, who followed behind him. Taylor had seemed hesitant to enter the hospital and Draven wondered if he was feeling any vibes or having visions. He cocked an eyebrow at his boyfriend. "Are you okay? You've been very quiet on the way over here."

In truth, Taylor had hardly said a word. It was as if he'd been psychically building himself up to be here, in the slight movement of his lips, the deep breathing and the nervous twitching of his fingers as he picked at the seam on his worn jeans. He'd smoked numerous cigarettes earlier on in the garden and then glared at the packet in disgust afterward and said he was giving up. The packet had been thrown unceremoniously in the garbage bin and Draven wondered just how long Taylor would hold out.

Taylor gave a faint smile. "I'm all right. I just don't like hospitals much. Reminds me of when my mum died." He seemed to anticipate Draven's heated response of "You didn't have to come if it upset you" with a wave of his hand. "Before you go all postal on me, I want to be here. And no, I'm not tuned in to anything at the moment, so you don't need to worry." He frowned slightly. "Although there's something not quite right, but I can't really put my finger on it. It's as if it's there but not there, if you know what I mean."

Draven stared at him. He had no idea at all what that meant. Sometimes his lover said the weirdest things. He nodded absently. "Uh-huh. Come on. Let's do this then."

Five minutes later he was standing outside Jude's partially open door, his chest tight as he took a deep breath.

Taylor rubbed his back gently. "I'm here with you," he said simply. "Come on." He pushed Draven softly into the room. Draven saw Sister Alison fiddling with the transparent lines leading into Jude's body and she gave a wide, white smile when she saw Draven.

"Draven. Lovely to see you, sweetie. Jude, your brother's here, honey. And he's brought a very tasty young man with him." She grinned at Draven, winking at him and giving him a secret thumbs up. "Now we know who's been keeping your brother company." Her brows furrowed as she looked behind Draven.

Draven smiled and reached out and touched his brother's cheek. It was warmer than usual and he caressed the pale skin. "Hi little bro, I bought someone to meet you." He turned to introduce Taylor and his heart almost stuttered to a stop. Taylor was white, his hands held loosely at his sides, his eyes blank. He resembled a wax mannequin at Madam Tussauds.

Draven wasn't even sure he could see the rise and fall of Taylor's chest.

"Taylor?" He swiftly moved to Taylor's side and touched his arm. "What's wrong?"

Alison was beside him now, her face racked in concern. She stared at Draven in confusion. "Is he all right? I saw him behind you when you came in and he…just…well, he just stopped dead."

A feeling of dread assailed Draven. "Alison, I can't really explain, but he has these turns now and then. I'll get him sat down, and I'm sure he'll be okay in a minute. Can I ask you to get him a Coke or something? Sometimes his blood sugar gets a bit low…" His voice trailed off and he knew Alison wasn't buying the story, nurse as she was. Her eyes narrowed but to his relief she simply nodded.

"Yes, I'll get him something. You get him settled there in that easy chair. I'll be back in a little while."

The sister left the room and Draven took hold of Taylor's unresisting body. "Come and sit down, Tay." He managed to get his lover seated in the chair as Taylor's eyes still gazed unseeingly into the distance. It was as if there was no one home, just the shell of a body left in the wake of whatever had lived in there before. Draven's spine prickled with fear.

"Taylor, please, baby. Where the hell are you?" He ran a hand through his hair, leaving it messy and rumpled. "I knew this was a bad idea to bring you into a hospital with dying and sick people. I just knew it…" He continued to stare helplessly at the man in the chair, as he sat down next to him in another seat and placed one hand on his thigh, and the other on Jude's hand in the bed. His hands trembled.

Hopefully both of the men in my life can feel me and know I'm here for them. Christ, what the hell do I do now?

***

Taylor was aware of Draven beside him, aware of the fear and panic on his face but he was powerless to do or say anything. Instead, all he could do was gaze in wonder into the dark, azure blue of *somewhere*, God knew where, as a slight and blond figure stood outlined against the backdrop of deep blue, rich and vibrant colour that assailed Taylor's vision like a starlit night.

"Hello, Taylor," Jude said as he stepped forward. "I've been waiting for you."

"How…how is this possible?" Taylor croaked, his voice dry with both awe and fear. "Where are we?"

Jude's slim shoulders shrugged. "We call it Earthlight. It's a kind of in-between place, it's the only way I can describe it."

Taylor gazed around him in wonder. "Maybe I should have asked *what* it is?"

Dark grey eyes exactly like Draven's stared at him. The young man looked to be in his early teens and Taylor knew Jude had been fifteen going on sixteen when he'd had his car accident. He was almost a carbon copy of a young Draven, although much slimmer built.

"It's just a place people like me come to. People who can't move on, because something is holding them back. It's a sort of holding pen, I suppose." He smiled and Taylor saw Draven in that soft lift of the lips. His eyes strayed toward his brother with a glance of affection. Taylor followed them and saw Draven sitting, eyes closed, a look of defeat on his face, as he talked to someone, probably trying to bring Taylor back. Taylor's heart clenched at the look of sadness he wore.

"My brother loves me, I know that," Jude said quietly. "He feels guilty that he was the only one who lived, and he feels he should have been the one to die instead of me and Mum and Dad." His face was anguished. "He tells me this when he visits and I want to reach out and tell him he's wrong, he needs to live his life and stop beating himself up over everything. But I can't." Taylor heard the desperation in his tone. "You have to help him and me, Taylor. You need to tell him to let me go so both of us can move on." His eyes observed the machines and the fluids keeping him alive. "I've come to terms with the fact I'm dead. He needs to do that now too."

Taylor shook his head. "It will destroy him," he said quietly. "I can't tell him what he should do."

"No, you can't," Jude said. "But *I* can. It's my life, whatever that may mean," he snorted grimly, "and I want to leave here and be with my folks. I've heard him talk about you, and what you can do and I knew the only way I could get through to him was through you. I've waited so long to see you. I tried reaching out to you but it just wasn't enough. His grief and his guilt blocked me and I wasn't strong enough to get through to you being so far away."

His voice dropped. "I'm tired, Taylor," he whispered. "Tired of being in a halfway house kept alive by machinery. It's comfortable enough, here, I suppose, and I'm not alone but I miss my parents." His voice shook. "They're waiting for me to move on, but I can't. I love my brother dearly, but he needs to let go of me. Only you can make him see that's what he has to do."

Taylor's eyes were burning, filling with bitter tears. "I don't think he'll listen," he murmured, his throat closing up with the lump in it. "He loves you so much, Jude."

Jude smiled sadly. "You know there's that old cheesy saying about if you love someone, let them go? Speak to Draven for me. You're the only one who can. My brother loves you, you know. He might have a tough time showing you or believing it himself sometimes, but he does. I can hear it in his voice when he says your name." His eyes glistened with tears.

"Tell him he can take comfort that there is another side to life and one day, he'll be here with us. It's not goodbye, just *au revoir*." He grinned faintly. "If he needs any convincing that you've spoken to me and you weren't hallucinating, tell him this." He hesitated then spoke softly. "'Our brothers and sisters are there with us from the dawn of our personal stories to the inevitable dusk.' It's a quote made by an author called Susan Scarf Merrell. He enjoyed reading her books and he was really drawn to this quote. He used to say it to me all the time. Remind him I'll always be there for him. Tell him I love him." His face softened. "And tell him Pudsey says hello."

Jude's voice and figure grew fainter. Taylor blinked past the tears in his eyes, both from the fact Jude was in pain and the fact that he believed Draven loved him, and watched the form shimmer. His head swum, his skin prickled and then as the last vestiges of deep blue and Jude faded away, he closed his eyes and fell into darkness.

Chapter 10

There isn't really a Hallmark greeting card to advise a current boyfriend that his comatose younger brother has been in contact with your psychic other half and requested that his life support system be switched off.

Taylor wished there was.

It would make talking to Draven *so* much easier. Even as he knew the complete incongruity and craziness of sharing this, he was thinking how best to approach the subject with the man who now sat broodingly beside him in the car, hands clenched on the wheel, a look of ferocious calm on his bruised face.

It was Taylor's fault that his lover looked as damaged as he did. In coming around from his zone-out, Taylor had flailed so wildly that he'd ended up hitting Draven in the face. He now sported a rather nasty-looking bruise under his eye, which no doubt was going to turn black.

Looking at the silent man beside him, then at the dark grey rain outside, Taylor knew that Draven's current taciturnity had been fear over the fact that once again Taylor had zoned out. The look of helplessness in those slate grey eyes as he'd stared at Taylor doing the crazy chicken dance with thrashing limbs had been sobering.

Afterwards, Draven had made like the proverbial bad-tempered bear and growled that he was "damn sick of all this shit." He'd said his goodbyes to Jude and stormed off to the car, Taylor stumbling unsteadily behind him. As they drove back toward Draven's house, thoughts circled in Taylor's head like hungry sharks all waiting to get a piece of him.

"I'm sorry I hit you," he muttered quietly. "When we get to your place, you should put some ice on that eye. Maybe even some arnica ointment if you have some. If you don't, I'll walk down to that corner chemist and get you some. That always helped me, my mum used to swear by it…"

"Taylor, it's fine." Draven sounded tired but his earlier ire seemed to have dissipated. "Don't worry. You couldn't help yourself." His one hand left the steering wheel and he gingerly touched the swelling under his eye. "It's not my first black eye, you know."

"Yes, but it's the first one from me," Taylor grumbled.

Draven snorted softly and Taylor was relieved to see the corners of his mouth lift up. "I hope that isn't saying there might be more to come?"

Taylor reached over and shoved his arm half-heartedly. "I bloody well hope there aren't."

Draven smiled, but it didn't reach his eyes. He concentrated on driving through the gentle drizzle, squinting slightly. Taylor knew he must have questions.

"Don't you want to know what happened back there?" he asked softly.

Draven shook his head, lips pressed together. "Not now. I can't talk about that shit and focus on getting home safely. I hate driving in the rain. So I'd rather you not tell me now. When we get back to my place…" he heaved a deep sigh. "Maybe then." He glanced at Taylor, almost nervously but said nothing more. Taylor nodded and leaned back against the headrest, shutting his eyes. The next thing he knew he was being shaken awake.

"Tay? We're home. Come on. It's pouring fucking cats and dogs now. I need a drink."

Taylor nodded sleepily and clambered out of the car, following Draven as he dashed for the front door. Once inside, Draven disappeared into the kitchen as Taylor shook the wet from his hair and grimaced.

"Uggh. I wasn't made for wet weather. I should be somewhere warm and dry, where the sun shines all day and I can work on a tan. This shitty weather is not for me."

Draven came through bearing two large glasses of red wine. He handed one to Taylor. "You and me both. I'm not crazy about sun-tanning; I burn too easily but you…" He appraised Taylor. "You're dark enough with that skin tone. Works for me anyway. I like you just the way you are." He padded through to the lounge in stocking feet and plonked himself down in an easy chair.

Taylor followed, feeling warmth at Draven's words. He divested himself of his boots and jacket as he did. "Just the way I am, hey? Perhaps less clothes?" He waggled his eyebrows cheekily, bringing a reluctant grin to Draven's pale face. The bruise around his eye was beginning to darken and Taylor felt guilty at being the cause.

"That'll work too. Maybe later. Right now you need to tell me what the hell went down in that hospital room." Draven's eyes searched Taylor's face as he fell, loose limbed, onto the couch, and draped his feet over the end of the arm. He took a slurp of his drink and then placed the glass on the side table. Draven watched him unwaveringly as he sipped his wine.

Taylor cleared his throat. "You need to listen to me, okay? This isn't going to be easy. Hell, it took me by surprise and I've lived with this sort of thing all my life. I need you to be open minded and not fly off at the deep end—"

Draven interrupted him impatiently. "Taylor, just tell me, blabbermouth. I'm sure I can cope with whatever it is. I'm a big boy."

Despite the confident words, Taylor heard the fear. He tried to inject some levity in the hope it might soothe Draven. "I know that; hell, I've had you up my arse, so I'm very personally acquainted with how big you are."

"Tay," Draven growled.

Taylor sighed. "Fine. There isn't an easy way to say this so I'm just going to say it." He took a deep breath. "I saw Jude. He's in some in-between place and he really wants to move on, to be with your folks. He told me to ask you to please let him go. He wants you to switch off the life support."

Draven's face whitened and the stem of his wineglass shattered in his fingers. The bulb of the glass fell to the floor, causing what looked a pool of blood to land on the pale carpet. Taylor sat up and stared at the fluid dripping from Draven's fingers.

"Dray, you're bleeding. Here, let me get a cloth." He started to rise from the couch but Draven stood up in one cat like movement and pushed him back onto the couch.

"Sit the fuck down." He prodded Taylor in the chest with one hard finger, and Taylor watched, mesmerised, as small globules of blood landed on his Iron Maiden tee shirt. "What the hell do you mean, you saw Jude? I thought you said you didn't see dead people?"

Draven's face was thunderous, his eyes glinting with both suppressed anger and what looked a lot to Taylor like sheer panic. He looked up at Draven, trying to figure out what to say next without causing further injury to what was already a frightened and hurting soul.

"I don't normally, so I can't explain it. Maybe it's because Jude is in this place between living and dead, I don't know. I've never come across this before. But it was him, Draven. I talked to him."

The prodding stopped and Draven stood back, his body taut. "The fuck you say. My little brother wants me to kill him?"

Taylor held Draven's gaze. "He's already dead, Draven," he said steadily, swallowing the bile in his throat. "The machines keep him alive, nothing else. He's come to terms with that and wants you to do the same."

Draven stalked like a caged tiger around the room. He stopped and pointed a finger at Taylor. "He's all I have left in the world, and you want me to stop what's keeping him alive?"

Taylor's heart ached at the words that Jude was all Draven had but he knew the man was shocked. "It's not what *I* want, Draven. This isn't about me."

Draven laughed harshly. "How am I supposed to deal with this? It's all getting too damn much. Sometimes I wish I'd never met you, that I didn't know you talk to dead people and tell people things they don't want to hear."

Taylor swallowed. "I'm sorry you feel that way." His throat was dry, his stomach roiling at Draven's harsh words. "I'm just a messenger, believe me, it's no fucking fun for me either. I didn't ask for this gift, I was cursed with it, and sometimes it seems more heartache than it's worth."

"I don't need this shit," Draven spat. "I don't need to know my comatose brother is talking to my lover and telling him he needs to die to be happy. I just…"

His voice tailed off and Taylor's heart ached at the bleak look on Draven's face.

"I'm sorry," he said helplessly as he stood up and moved toward Draven, hoping to touch him, comfort him. "I can only tell you what I see and hear."

"Well, I didn't fucking ask for it!" Draven snarled.

Taylor's temper flared. "I'm sorry that I'm not able to switch it on and off like a fucking light switch, Dray, just to stop you hurting. I'm just passing on a message from a boy that thinks you're holding onto him for your own needs, not his."

The words echoed in the air and Taylor wished he hadn't said them. Draven's hand rose like a blur toward his face and he closed his eyes, waiting for the slap or the punch that he thought was coming. When nothing happened, he opened his eyes to see Draven staring at him then at his upraised hand with haunted eyes. The desolation on his face wrenched at Taylor's chest.

"I was going to hit you," Draven whispered, his voice agonised. "Christ, I was going to bloody slap you."

"But you didn't," Taylor said, his voice shaking. "You stopped. So it doesn't count."

Draven's face was bleak. "It counts to me. Intent is as good as doing it."

Taylor shook his head vehemently. "Don't talk such crap. It's the action that counts. We all have impulses, which bring out our bad side. It's not acting on them that makes us the better man."

Draven turned and strode over to the front door. He opened it and beckoned Taylor over. "You need to leave."

Taylor stared at him. “Leave? Draven, this isn’t going to go away when I do. I *spoke* to Jude. He asked me to tell you to let him move on. He even quoted some damn line from a book from some author, Susan Scart Milly someone or other, about brothers and sisters. He said it was your favourite quote.”

Draven’s eyes flinched at that, as if recognising the quote, and Taylor took hope and pressed on. “He wants to be with your folks, wants to be at peace. You can’t deny him that.”

“Leave.” Draven’s tone was uncompromising, his shoulders ramrod straight, his face unrelenting. “I should never have gotten involved with you. All you do is confuse people with your bloody so-called psychic crap and I want no more part of it. “

Taylor’s heart broke and his eyes prickled with tears. “Honestly? That’s your answer to all this, to bury your damn head in the sand and push everyone away who gets close to you?” He shook his head. “I’m just the messenger, Draven. I always have been. I can’t distort the truth or tell lies, and I thought you’d realised that. Obviously I was wrong.”

Eyes blinded with hot tears, he fumbled for his shoes and slid his feet into them. “Fine. You want me gone. I’ll go. But I’m warning you. Don’t call me again with apologies until you’ve got your head right.” He shrugged into his jacket and fastened it with shaking hands. Draven still stood as still as someone frozen in time in an old film clip.

Taylor tried to calm his racing heart, and the sobs that threatened to well up. It had been an emotional day and he hated himself for feeling so vulnerable.

He walked to the still-opened door and as he reached the step outside, he turned back to look at Draven, whose face was set, his lips pinched.

“I’m going to say this once, so listen. I know I shouldn’t have but I really care for you.” Taylor swallowed as the lump in his throat grew bigger and his chest grew tighter. “I know it’s only been a short while but I thought we had something starting. It looks like it’s one-sided.

“In case we don’t see each other again, I thought you should know. Perhaps one day when you sit down and think about everything I’ve told you, you’ll realise I never meant to hurt you, I just wanted to help." Tears were rolling down his cheeks now. "I hope you think about things, Dray. For your and Jude's sake."

Draven continued to stare at him through eyes that seemed carved out of obsidian.

Taylor tried to smile but wasn't sure he'd pulled it off. "Jude told me something else. He said to tell you Pudsey said hello. I hope whatever or whoever that is, it brings you comfort. Goodbye, Draven."

Taylor turned away and walked down the stone steps to the pavement and didn't take another glance backward. His eyes were so filled with hot tears it was unlikely he'd have seen anything anyway. He wanted to get home to his place, to Leslie, who would cuddle and mother him, make him feel loved and wrap him in blankets and hold him tight. Then he wanted to fall into darkness and sleep the pain away.

***

Draven closed the door behind Taylor's departing figure and moved to the kitchen. He was numb, confused, his chest ached with pain he'd never experienced before, and his hand hurt like shit from where he'd cut it. Drops of blood spattered the carpet in neat lines, and he ignored that as he reached the kitchen sink and washed away the blood that caked his fingers. Like an automaton, he pulled out the first aid box from the cupboard under the sink, put plaster on the cut then took a bottle of carpet cleaner and a rag back into the lounge and hallway to try to repair the damage he'd done on the carpet. For some minutes he busied himself with cleaning up the mess, scrubbing the blood away and trying to forget the past few hours had ever happened.

Finally, he dropped the blood-soaked cloth in the laundry basket then stood stock still in the kitchen as his stomach tensed and his hands shook. With eyes as gritty as a beach full of sand, he took deep breaths to stave off the panic that threatened as random thoughts flooded his brain.

Dear God, I nearly hit Taylor.

I told him to leave, that I didn't want him. I hurt him so badly. Those tears, God, he looked shattered. He said he cares for me. Does he love me? If he did, he probably doesn't anymore.

Hell, I love him so damn much.

Fuck, my comatose brother wants me to switch off his life support and let him go.

"What the fuck kind of karma is this then?" Draven shouted into the empty kitchen. His hands clenched at his sides. "Have I been such an arsehole in a past life that I get to make these kinds of decisions? I didn't fucking ask for this."

He sank to his knees on the kitchen floor, head bowed as tears overcame him. The sense of loss at Taylor's departure; the keen agony of knowing that he'd been telling the truth when he said he'd spoken to Jude; the fact he'd actually raised his hand to Taylor in his pain—all this came surging into his head and he swore loudly, profanity echoing in the still kitchen.

"Fuck you, Jude, fuck you, Taylor and fuck you, Draven bloody Samuels for your pig headedness."

The outburst didn't make him feel any better. He moved and sat back against the kitchen cupboard, arms wrapped about his body, trying to make sense of it all. When he finally looked up, the accusing eyes of Freud, the cookie jar, on the counter opposite him seemed to stare right into his soul. Draven stared at the overly large eyes of the pig and whispered to it brokenly.

"I didn't mean to send Taylor away. I think I just panicked. He knew the quote, the one Jude and I used to say to each other. No one alive knows that. It was our secret quote." He sniffed and wiped his running nose with his shirt sleeve.

"And he knew about Pudsey. Only Jude could have told him about that stupid cat; I've never mentioned him." He smiled through his tears as he gazed into what now looked like the eyes of a more sympathetic pig.

"We found Pudsey in the shed, all mauled and broken. We fixed him up and stole food and stuff from the kitchen because Mum didn't like cats. When he was better, Jude snuck him into his room. I told him if Mum and Dad found him, they'd make him get rid of him, but he was adamant. So we kept him hidden for about three weeks until we came down to the kitchen one night looking for midnight snacks and found our folks waiting for us.

"They'd known about the damn cat for weeks and were waiting for us to come clean." Draven laughed sadly. "They gave us a real bollocking but when it came down to it, they let us keep him. He died of old age years ago."

Freud looked on wisely, a beneficent smile on his ceramic face. He didn't seem too worried about the demise of the cat and Draven scowled.

"He was a damn good cat so take that look off your face." He groaned. "Dear heavens, I'm talking to a damn cookie jar again. I'm really losing my mind. Taylor would laugh himself silly at that."

His voice tailed off as he realised he probably had no Taylor anymore. He struggled to his feet and picked up his phone, cold tendrils of fear winding themselves through his skin and up his spine. "I fucked up, Freud. Big-time. I need to call him, tell him to come back. Do you think he'll listen to me? God, I can't lose Taylor too. I love him, even if I can't tell him that yet."

He dialled Taylor's number and listened anxiously at the ring tone. No one picked up and finally it went to Taylor's voice mail.

Hi, you've reached Taylor. Leave me a message and I'll get back to you.

"Taylor, it's me. I, uhmm, I'm sorry, I was upset and I took it out on you. Again. Please call me, Tay. I'm so damned fucked up I'm talking to my cookie jar and believe me, that pig isn't a great conversationalist. I know you were telling the truth. I believe in you. You said you cared about me, and that's," his voice choked, "That's good to know." He winced as he said those words.

Good to know? Way to go, Draven.

"Anyway, call me back when you get this message. I have something to tell you too. In person. Bye."

He put his mobile down on the kitchen top and glanced at Freud. The pig stared back.

"I can't do this without him," Draven murmured. "I can't help Jude the way he wants me to if Taylor isn't with me. I need him. I'm not strong enough. Not on my own."

He left the kitchen and went to the hall cupboard. He pulled out an old blanket and went back into the lounge. There, he switched on the television for background noise and settled himself on the couch, mobile beside him. He wanted to be able to answer his phone straight away if Taylor rang back.

Draping the blanket over his chilled body, Draven sat and watched the rain pummel down outside and run down the windowpanes like escaping sperm. He tried not to think about what the future held.

He called Clay, needing to hear a familiar voice. If he'd thought that Clay would be sympathetic to his plight, he was wrong.

"Shit, Draven, you what?" Clay exclaimed. "Christ, are all your brains in your dick and when you come, you lose them? You and I both know that man is the best thing that ever happened to you. We've talked about it often enough."

Draven curled his fingers in both anger and guilt. "I called him to apologise and he's not picking up," he growled. "What am I supposed to do? Kidnap the guy and hold him prisoner until he gives in?"

There was silence on the other end of the phone. Then Clay sighed. "I guess it doesn't work for everyone," he muttered and Draven's jaw dropped.

"What? You mean you've actually done that? I was bloody kidding, you psycho."

"What? Oh. Of course." Clay's voice sounded hesitant, unusual for a man who had a rod of steel in his back and the balls and principles to match. "I was joking too."

Draven wasn't quite so sure but he didn't push it. There was time enough to find out more about that cryptic statement later. Right now, he had a man to win back.

Clay continued. "Well, all I can say is keep wearing him down and hope he'll come around. I mean, he's right, Dray. If that's what Jude wants, maybe you need to listen."

Draven shook his head in wonderment. "You believe him when he says he talked to my brother? I thought this whole thing might have been a bridge too far even for you. I never thought I'd see the day when solid, earth-based Clay Mortimer fell into the hole that is Alice in Wonderland and believes someone actually speaks to people on another plane of existence."

Clay sounded sad when he next spoke. "Not everything can be explained in science. If you'd read the reports from some of the people Taylor has helped with his gift, and when you've been where I have trying to stop someone you love going the opposite way and killing them…" He stopped, seeming aware that he'd revealed too much. "Anyway, I have an open mind. You need to keep one too. For both your and Jude's sake. I love that boy, Draven. But if he's suffering or wants to move on, I rather think that's his prerogative, don't you?"

"I thought you said you tried to stop someone killing themselves," Draven remarked quietly, reading between the lines not written. "Isn't that their choice too?"

"No you fucker, it is not." Clay growled. "This person is alive, walking around and in possession of all their faculties. They need help. Your brother is not one of those people, no matter how you want to sugar coat it.

"I can't tell you what to do about Jude, Dray. But I can tell you that you need to work on getting Taylor back if you love him. Don't let him go." There was an element of pain in Clay's voice and Draven very much wanted to pry, but he knew Clay. The man wouldn't spill his guts without extreme pressure and now was not the time.

So he thanked his friend, mentor and boss for his advice and went back to staring at the pig.

Chapter 11

Four days later and Draven was going out of his mind. Taylor still hadn't called back. It was a grim reminder of the last time Draven had been an arsehole, only this time, he wasn't so sure that it was going to be fixed. His texts and calls were going unanswered. Draven knew there was only one thing he could do. Face the dragons in their den and call on some support that hopefully wouldn't punch him in the face.

It was why he found himself in Galileo's that evening, hopping from foot to foot in anxiety and apprehension by the reception desk, as he waited for Eddie Tripp to make his appearance.

Gideon had been sympathetic to his plight but told him in no uncertain terms that Eddie was pretty mad with him and he'd better watch his right hook. Then he arranged for his boyfriend to take time out from the kitchen to meet with Draven. There was added fuel to the best friend fire, apparently, as Leslie, too, was at the restaurant on a blind date. Draven hoped fervently that he didn't have to face them both down. He didn't think he'd survive it.

Alas, his hopes were dashed when he saw the pair striding toward him, one whose piercing green eyes were fixed firmly on his face with an expression of murder, the other dressed to kill in a simple but elegant suit worn with stiletto heels.

Draven blinked as the Avenging Furies made their way toward him. He was a man who dealt with corporate spies, bad men and all manner of crazy and dangerous people, but the two best friends of the man he loved were making him wet his pants. He took a deep breath and told himself to man up.

In the distance, he saw Gideon smoothly intercept them both, laying a firm hand on Eddie's shoulder until some of the tenseness disappeared. He gave his lover a soft kiss and then waved them on their way with a wicked stare at Draven. Draven's insides quailed as he came face to face with hostility—and in Leslie's case, a man bag held in such a way that it looked as if it was about to meet Draven's head.

He gulped. "Evening, Eddie. Leslie. Thanks for seeing me."

Eddie's eyes glinted. "Thank Gideon. If it was up to me I'd be sticking my size eleven up your arse."

Draven's eyebrows lifted. He blamed the next sentence on the fact he was nervous. "Size eleven, hey? Gideon must be pleased…" His voice tailed off at the shift of Eddie's body closer to him. "I mean, thanks. For not sticking your shoes up my backside."

"The evening is still young." Leslie's modulated tones belied the look of violence in his eyes. "I'd say size eleven followed by a size ten." He waggled a high-heeled shoe on the bottom of a very shapely ankle at Draven, who winced.

Gideon appeared like a wraith at Draven's side, seeming to be barely holding back a grin. "Now come on, guys. Play nice. Draven here is eating humble pie and having the courage to come and face you two. I can't say I'd do the same in his shoes. I know you both better. Eddie, babe, give the man a break. Leslie, my little barracuda, stop scaring the man. Hear Draven out." He pressed Draven's shoulder in a comforting gesture. "I have a kitchen to be in. I suggest you use my office for a bit of privacy. Good luck." Gideon grinned and left them alone.

Leslie sniffed. "Office sounds good. Come on, follow me."

He sashayed off, Eddie and Draven following behind him. Soon they were safely ensconced in an office that smelt of sweat and cologne, and Draven was sure he smelt sex odours. He wasn't about to say anything though.

"Soooo," Leslie chirped, his dark blue eyes narrowed. "You said you needed our help. Why should we help you when you've done nothing but hurt Taylor? He's a complete damn wreck at the moment."

There was a noise behind the slightly opened connecting door to what looked like a storage room on the far side of the office. Eddie's eyes darted in its direction before coming back to rest on Draven, as he crossed his arms across a tight, muscled chest and scowled.

Draven had a speech all prepared on how they could perhaps convince his ex-lover that he was sorry, that they should meet face to face and that he'd been a prick and needed to see him, but seeing the concern and affection on their faces for their friend left him speechless. Instead, he went with his heart.

"You shouldn't really. I mean, I'm a tough guy to like, but he said he cared about me and that's all I've got left. I've got something difficult to do at the hospital, and the only way I think I can face it is with Taylor by my side." He swallowed. "I was a bastard and I told him to leave, but I didn't mean it because, Christ, I really want the guy in my life and I don't know what I'd do if he never came back."

Eddie's scowl lessened. "We heard about your brother. Sorry, but we dragged the whole story out of Taylor. He needed to talk about it." His tone softened. "I'm sorry you have to go through that with a family member. I have no idea how that feels. It's a really tough decision to make and I wouldn't wish it on anyone."

Leslie nodded. "I can't even imagine how I'd feel. I have two sisters and an older brother and I'd hate to be in that situation. That's why we said we'd speak to you. Extenuating circumstances and all that crap." He waved a slim, pale hand. "Anyhoo, back to Tay."

He moved closer to Draven, his full-lipped pink mouth coming so close Draven had a sudden panic he was about to be kissed. Not that it would be hardship because Leslie was damn sexy with his pouty lips and black bangs, but Draven had only one man's mouth in mind when he thought of kissing the hell out of someone, and it wasn't Leslie. Instead, Leslie invaded his personal space and leaned in to whisper in Draven's ear.

"You need to really tell him how you feel, right now. He needs to hear it." Then Leslie moved away. Draven stared at him in confusion.

"I just told you how I feel about him."

Leslie just faked a yawn and cast a meaningful glance toward the open door. Eddie was smiling softly and all of a sudden Draven thought he knew what was going on. His heart filled with hope and he nodded slowly.

"I'm not very good with words, more of an action man," he ignored Leslie's snort, "but I'll try." His throat was dry and he watched as Leslie and Eddie quietly exited the office with a nod of approval his way. Draven walked over and locked the door. He knew he'd only get one chance to do this right.

"I sat at home talking to Freud, my pig and realised something. That pig isn't much of a talker but he's a good listener. I told him how much I cared about a certain person, and that I'd driven him away. I told him how I'd fucked up and I'd do anything to get him back because I didn't think I could make it without him."

He walked quietly to the door and hesitated. Taking a deep breath, he pushed the door open to reveal Taylor standing behind it, surrounded by towels and napkins stacked neatly on shelves. His eyes widened as Draven came closer. He looked tired, his eyes rimmed with dark circles and his usual coffee-coloured skin paler than usual.

He was wearing one of Draven's old hoodies, with the words "Live and Let Live" written across it. It had been one Draven had lent him when they'd been caught in the rain one day and Taylor had needed something warm. Of course, the subsequent undressing and pulling off wet clothes had led to hot sex in the shower and it was a memory Draven cherished.

Draven's heart stuttered in his chest at the thought Taylor still wore his clothes. "I said to Freud that I needed him. Like I need breath in my body to live, like water to a man dying of thirst."

Taylor's eyes flickered and his breath hitched. His fingers were fidgeting at his sides as his dark eyes watched Draven move closer.

"And do you know what that damn pig said to me? He said to me, 'Draven, you're an idiot and if you don't go after that man and convince him that you want him, that you need him, then you'll have lost something precious.' So I decided that's exactly what I'd do."

Draven stood as close as he could to Taylor, closing his eyes to the warm male body heat emanating from him. He opened them to see the rise and fall of his chest and the widening of his eyes as Draven reached out and gently drew his fingers along lips he wanted so badly to kiss.

So he did. He pulled Taylor out of the storage room and into the office, gripping hips that were familiar to him.

His lips brushed Taylor's, softly at first then more possessively as Taylor sighed. Draven's tongue flicked across Taylor's mouth, willing him to open and let him in. When Taylor's lips parted and his arms wrapped around Draven's neck to pull him closer and he ground his hips against Draven's own hardness, Draven wanted to weep with relief. It was like coming home to a warm hearth, to a familiar place where you could be safe and happy.

That place was Taylor Abelard.

Taylor was murmuring something under his breath, words that sounded like "stupid bastard" and "look what you've been missing," and then his words were totally swallowed up as Draven took his mouth completely and tried to consume him.

Finally, they drew apart, panting and dishevelled, and Draven pulled Taylor into a hug that left no doubt as to his desire and need for him.

"I'm sorry," he whispered into Taylor's ear. "I'll spend the rest of my life making it up to you if you'll let me, but please, please don't let me alone again like this past week. It just wasn't the same waking up without you beside me."

Taylor chuckled softly. "You can be quite the poet, you know that? I never thought I'd hear the rough, macho Draven Samuels talking so sweet." He frowned. "There is one thing I need to know though."

"Name it," said Draven as he nuzzled Taylor's neck, breathing in his man's scent and tracing a path of wet down the side of his neck with his tongue.

"What the hell is it with you and this pig? I mean, am I going to be the piggy in the middle in this relationship or what, because getting between a man and his pig can be really serious—" His words were cut off by Draven's mouth taking possession of his once again plus the fact that Draven has just slid his hands into Taylor's sweatpants and palmed a very hardened cock.

"Oh, God," Taylor moaned as Draven closed his hand around it and began sliding his fingers along the slick shaft. "That feels, unggh, I missed your hands on me. Don't stop, or I might have to tell Freud you don't follow through on your promises…."

Draven chuckled as he slid another hand around to Taylor's arse to slide it over the firm cheeks and into his crack, meandering down to his hole. He slid his finger gently across the pucker, causing Taylor to buck in his arms and his cock to push into Draven's hand.

"Shhh. Forget the damn pig. Just enjoy yourself. I'm going to make you come so hard your balls will think they've exploded."

Taylor groaned, his hands reaching down into Draven's pants. Draven pushed them away. As much as he wanted to feel Taylor's hands on him, this wasn't *for* him. This was for Taylor.

"I'm fine, honey, just close your eyes and concentrate on me jacking you off. Focus on me doing this." He slid one finger inside Taylor, loving the moan that came out of his mouth and catching it with his lips. Taylor vibrated against him like a tuning fork and his breathy pants soon turned into gasps as his hips shuddered and hands clenched Draven anywhere they could find a grasp.

"Fuck, Draven, it's been too long. Oh sweet hell…" He warbled as Draven thrust yet another finger inside him, fucking him hard and deep. "That's it, I'm done." Warm fluid spurted over Draven's fingers and palm as Taylor's hole clenched around his fingers and his body shivered and quivered like a man being Tasered.

Draven held him close, breathing in the smell of sex and Taylor and wanting nothing more than this moment to last much longer.

Finally a small voice spoke up from where it nestled against Draven's shoulder. "I think the pig would approve."

Draven laughed out loud. He felt as if he'd been sleeping and just woken up from a dark dream. He leaned back and tucked Taylor's spent cock back into his underwear and arranged his sweatpants to be decent. His own hard-on clamoured for attention, but he thought that perhaps later he might be lucky enough to manage that situation with the help of the man now standing loose limbed before him, eyes softened and lips swollen.

Draven leaned his forehead against Taylor's as he brushed sweaty locks of black hair away from his cheeks. "I don't deserve you, but I'll work on it."

Taylor reached up and framed his face in hands that shook slightly. "I won't argue with that, you stubborn bastard. However, I'm no angel either and we're going to have to work at this thing." His face grew serious. "What I can't have is you chucking me out every time you get angry. I don't think I've got it in me to forgive you again." His eyes were solemn, his face earnest.

Draven nodded. "Fair enough. I don't think I've got it in me to face Eddie and Leslie one more time. I truly think they might hurt me if I go off the rails again. Those mates of yours are a great deterrent."

Taylor grinned smugly. "They're like Rottweilers that I let out when I need someone to be hunted down. They know how to maim and leave no evidence, so beware." He looked down at Draven's groin and licked his lips suggestively. "That looks painful. Do you want to go home and I'll take care of it? Maybe a little ride and drive?"

Draven's cock lurched. Taylor's ride and drives were lusty, loud affairs that consisted of Taylor pounding into him from behind while operating Draven's cock like a gear stick.

He nodded. "I'm not going to refuse an offer like that. God, it drives me crazy just thinking about it."

"Then let's get out of here," Taylor said decisively. "I think we've tainted this office enough with my spunk. Time to taint your bedroom with yours." He turned to leave and Draven grasped him by the arm.

"Tay? I have an appointment next week to see Doctor Frederick. To talk about Jude's wishes. Will you be there with me?" He'd never known his voice could sound so needy. "I know I need to let him go, if that's what he wants. I've thought about it and I guess it's time."

Taylor's face softened. "Of course I'll be there." He took Draven's hand and clasped it tightly. "I'd never let you do anything like that on your own. We'll talk to the doctors and then take it from there."

He pulled Draven to him, warm arms circling his body protectively. Draven fell into the embrace like a drowning man clutching at a life raft. He heard the beat of Taylor's heart in his ear, smelt the warm, living essence of him and heard the love in his voice. This was where he belonged, his future, and it was time to set the past free.

Chapter 12

Taylor sat beside Draven in the quiet hospital room, surrounded by silence. It was strange; he felt Jude's presence but the young man hadn't attempted to make any form of contact with him. Last time the energy Taylor had felt and tapped into had been overwhelming. Now there was only a sweet serenity and an air of watchfulness. It was as if Jude knew what was about to happen and was waiting with bated breath to see how it all turned out.

Draven had been worried for Taylor when they'd first entered the room, thinking he was going to pass out again. When nothing had happened, he'd looked relieved but still, his lover's white face and the grim set to his lips made Taylor's heart ache.

Draven was mute and still, unseeing eyes observing his little brother with an air of both despair and fear. Taylor held tight to his cold hand, rubbing his own warm fingers across Draven's skin, hoping to instil some comfort into what was going to be the most difficult decision Draven had ever faced.

"That nice doctor said he'd give you as much time as you needed," Taylor said softly as he stroked the back of Draven's hand. "He seems like a good enough guy. And that nurse is really lovely. She has a real sweet spot for Jude, from the looks of it. Has she looked after him since he got here?"

Draven nodded absently, eyes still focused on the still form before them.

"Yes. Ally's been a rock, for both of us. I think that woman has seen me cry more than anyone else ever has." He bit his bottom lip nervously, gnawing on it until the skin tore and a small drop of blood blossomed on his pale lips.

Taylor's heart stuttered and his throat tightened. Just for Draven to admit those moments of weakness was an indication of the stress he was under. The man was vulnerable, hurting and Taylor just wanted to fix everything. Yet all he could do was be there for him. He reached over and took a tissue out of the box on the bedside table. He handed it to Draven, who patted his bleeding lip, then looked at the stain with an air of bewilderment.

Draven cleared his throat and looked at Taylor. "So, you seem okay this time. No passing out and me having to watch you come around like a chump." He swallowed, and his fingers fidgeted in Taylor's hands.

"Can you, you know, feel him at all?" His other hand reached out and smoothed limp hair from Jude's cheeks, and his face shadowed. He blinked furiously.

Taylor's own helplessness made itself felt in the sudden prickling in his eyes. He sniffed and tried to keep the tears at bay, much as Draven was doing. "I know he's around, but I don't feel him strongly. He feels…settled. Peaceful."

"Do you think he knows?" Draven's choked voice was barely audible. His eyes closed and when he opened them Taylor saw the wetness and the grief reflected in them. Draven was trembling, and Taylor grasped his hand tighter.

"I think he does. I think he knows that his big brother is about to help him go to somewhere he wants to be. With his family—and Pudsey." Taylor lost his voice for a minute as he held back the tears. He took a deep breath.

"You're doing the right thing, baby. I promise."

"It doesn't feel like it," Draven whispered, his tone agonised. "It feels like I'm abandoning him. I have this fucking hole in my heart that he fills and I don't know how I'm going to close it up, Tay. It just isn't right." His voice rose. "I don't think I can do this."

He stood up suddenly, leaving Taylor startled. "I definitely can't do this. Go out there and tell Frederick I've changed my mind." Relief flitted across his face as he stared at Taylor. "This isn't going to happen."

Taylor's stomach lurched as he stood up to intercept his boyfriend. "Dray," he began, and then felt his head swim. He watched through hazy eyes as Draven grew fainter and blurrier and his last conscious image was of Draven's panicked face and arms coming toward him. Then there was only blue.

"Hello, Taylor," Jude said as he stood outlined against the backdrop of what looked like cerulean skies. "It looks like my brother is having a crisis of faith." His gentle smile was affectionate. "This is really tough for him." His voice wavered. "I love him so much and seeing him going through this? It's killing me." He gave a slight watery sniff and a thin chuckle.

"You're all I have to convince him. I'm sorry I'm putting you through this and making contact again. I have no choice."

"I know." Taylor moved toward the younger man. "But it's the toughest thing he's ever had to do."

Jude nodded. "I know. And I wish I could see him for myself, see him, tell him face to face. But this," he waved a hand around him, "this doesn't work that way. It's a miracle I can communicate with you and one I'm really thankful for. Who knew my brother would fall in love with a psychic? It was obviously meant to be."

"What do you want me to tell him?" Taylor leaned forward and touched Jude's cheek. It was warm, vibrant and a world apart from the emaciated figure in the bed in the hospital ward. "What can I tell him to make it better for him?"

Jude shook his head sadly. "There's no easy way to do this. All I can give you is my assurance that this is what I want and need and that one day, I'll see him again. I can't give you a magic talisman or a message from Mum and Dad to convince him I'm real to you because I can't see them yet. All I have is my words, for you to deliver back to him."

Taylor gave a shuddering sigh. "I can only try." He grimaced. "I don't want to stay here with you too long, because he's stressed out enough as it is. This won't be helping him. I need to go back to him."

Jude nodded and reached out a slim hand to caress Taylor's hair. "Tell him you saw me, that this is still what I want and that I love him. He's been so good looking after me, and trying to keep me, but he has to let me go." His eyes flooded with tears.

"He has you now, Taylor, to help him through. He needs the living in his life, not the dead. Tell him he needs to finish that model aeroplane he was building that's still in his cupboard. He was building it for me and when this happened, he stopped. Tell him to go that rock concert of Maroon 5 he always wanted to take me to." Jude sniggered. "He has a real thing for Adam Levine and all his tattoos. I'm sure he used to lick the music magazines I found in his room, the ones that had Adam on the cover. The pages were always slightly buckled and used."

Taylor's eyes widened. "My man has good taste. Adam Levine is damn hot."

The two men grinned at each other and then Jude's face grew serious. "Tell him to do all the things he wanted to do with me, with you. Don't let this destroy him. Please."

Taylor nodded. "I'll do my best." He hesitated, and reached out to touch Jude's arm. "You'll be okay then? I don't even profess to know how this all works, or what it means. My mind is too overwhelmed with everything. But for Draven's sake I need to know myself you're going to be okay when he does what he has to do."

Jude smiled at him. "I'll be fine, honestly."

And Taylor believed him. He didn't know how, or why, but he knew that Jude was telling the truth.

This whole speaking-with-the-almost-dead thing had really thrown him for a loop. His brain hurt and all he wanted to do was get back to Draven. Although the thought of convincing him to switch Jude off made his insides quail, he knew deep inside that it was the right choice for Draven to make.

Jude reached over and laid warm lips on Taylor's forehead. "I'm glad he's got you." His voice choked up. "Take care of my big brother, Taylor. See you on the other side one day." His voice grew fainter and his figure blurred and shimmered and when Taylor blinked his eyes, he was staring up once again into anxious, red-rimmed, silver-grey eyes. The man behind them was pale, his mouth tight, but his face softened as Taylor stared at him from the chair in the corner where Draven had obviously placed him.

"Tay, you there?" Draven's voice was choked. "Christ, I'm getting fucking sick of this. I never know whether you're going to come back to me."

Taylor tried to blink the fuzziness from his eyes and sat up gingerly. "I'll always come back to you," he murmured. "Right now, I'd love some water. I feel like puking." He retched and Draven hurriedly picked up a glass from the side table and went over to the small corner basin to fill it up. He came back and presented it to Taylor.

"Thanks." Taylor took deep gulps and the dizziness and disorientation he'd felt on coming back into the real world lessened.

Draven perched beside him on the chair arm and stroked stray curls of hair back behind his ears. "Will I ever get used to that?" he asked quietly. "Seeing you drift off somewhere else? Thank God I was there to catch you again or else you'd have found yourself on the floor. Can't you do this sort of thing when you're sitting down, or sleeping?" Draven was trying to be cheery but the sorrow in his eyes belied his attempt.

Taylor gave a soft chuckle. “I wish I could tell you I could. I guess we’ll just have to make sure you’ll always be around, won’t we?”

They looked at each other steadfastly and then Draven sighed. It was a deep, heart-wrenching sigh and Taylor wished he could lift the burden of Draven’s decision from him and throw it into a deep, dark hole.

“You saw him.” It wasn’t a question.

Taylor nodded. “Yes. And he says switching the machinery is the right decision for him. He’s tired. He wants to go home, wherever that is.” He snorted, weary. “I’m not even going to go down the route again of trying to figure out where it is when I go. For all I know it could be a huge white hotel in the middle of somewhere with room service, good wine, a hot tub and a naked man with a six pack and a huge dick servicing my every desire.”

Draven raised an eyebrow, a slight grin on his face. “*That’s* your idea of heaven?”

Taylor shrugged. “Absolutely. I can live with that.”

The sheer absurdity of his statement had both men staring at each other then bursting into a fit of chuckles. Taylor was glad he’d been able to lift Draven’s spirits just a little. When the chuckles subsided, Taylor stood up and went over to hug Draven, holding him tightly.

“I didn’t know you built model aeroplanes,” he murmured into Draven’s ear. Draven stiffened and Taylor carried on, his voice teasing. “I also didn’t know you had a crush on the very sexy Adam Levine. We share that, by the way.”

Draven turned and it was as if a light was finally going on his head. His eyes shone with tears and his face, while still etched with grief, was full of wonder. “He really was with you, wasn’t he?”

Taylor frowned as Draven rushed ahead. “I mean I know you said he was, and I believed you, but hearing you say those things…it just makes it more real, you know? I never doubted you, Tay; I just needed to really understand that this was what he wanted…”

Taylor’s lips stopped Draven’s words midway as he kissed him, and they breathed into each other’s mouths as tongues and lips came together. Taylor’s hands slid around Draven’s waist as he pressed closer. The kiss was long, deep, and in it, Taylor tried to convey every iota of feeling and love he had for the man in his arms. When it was over, they stood clinched together as if they were the last two people standing on a shattered earth.

"It's time, isn't it?" Draven said finally, his voice muffled against Taylor's ear, buried in his curls.

"Yes, baby. I think so." Taylor moved away and tugged Draven toward the bed. "Sit down. Talk to your brother; tell him everything you want to get out of your soul. I'll go find Doctor Frederick and tell him you're ready." He pushed Draven into the chair at the side of the bed and placed a soft kiss on the top of his head and then disappeared out of the door.

***

Draven sat still in the chair, taking deep breaths as he readied himself for what was to come. He wasn't ready. He was nowhere near fucking ready for this momentous decision but he knew deep inside that it was the right thing to do.

"I hope you can hear me, little brother," he murmured softly. "I'm glad you and Taylor got a chance to meet. He's an incredible individual and I know, little brother that I am properly in love for the first time in my life. He means the world to me." He chuckled as he stroked Jude's pale hand. "The man might get ideas above his station and he's already an arrogant little shit. Him knowing I'm that much crazy about him would just give him carte blanche to make my life a constant fest of smug 'I know you love me' crap."

His voice faltered. "He tells me this is what you need and I trust him, more than anyone I've ever known. And you obviously trust him too to tell him about my Adam Levine crush. I'd kick your arse if you were here now for letting that cat out of the bag."

His eyes were hot with tears and he let them roll down his cheeks. "I love you, little brother. I tried to do right by you, and maybe I was selfish keeping you around, but not having you around like you used to be these last few years broke my heart. Maybe we were both just waiting for Taylor to come along so I get this chance to do this. I need him, Jude. I thank God every day I wake to him for coming into my life."

There was a noise at the door and Draven turned to see Taylor standing there, eyes awash with tears and a look on his face that promised the world to Draven. Doctor Frederick stood beside Taylor, face wreathed in sympathy, Sister Alison behind him. Her round face was warm and a welcome sight to Draven.

Doctor Frederick moved into the room and regarded Draven compassionately. "Taylor says you're ready for the machine to be switched off, Draven. I'm sorry to have to ask this at a time like this but there's a form I need you to sign before I can do that." He shrugged apologetically. "The perils of a bureaucracy and a 'cover the hospital's arse' mentality, I'm afraid."

Draven couldn't find any words so he nodded mutely. Taylor moved over to him and his dark brown eyes regarded him lovingly. "I'm here, love. Right beside you. If you're sure…" his voice trailed off. Alison bustled past the doctor into the room and clasped Draven's hands in hers.

"Baby, you are so damn brave. I don't know what made you decide you were ready, maybe it was this gorgeous man standing next to you, but it's the right decision. I've never wanted to push you into it; it's something you've had to figure out for yourself." She handed him a worn clipboard and Draven didn't even read it. He simply looked for the place he was supposed to sign and through eyes blurred with tears, he scribbled his signature and handed the board back to Alison. He though he saw the shine of tears in her eyes as he did so.

Alison laid the clipboard down and enveloped him into a hug that was warm and maternal. Her hands stroked his back as he burrowed into her massive bosom, his tears soaking her uniform as she consoled him with soft sounds of comfort.

He smelt Taylor before he felt him, his warm, spicy masculine scent like home as he stepped behind Draven and wrapped his long arms around his back. Draven luxuriated in being sandwiched between his lover and a woman who had comforted him more times than he could count over the years.

Doctor Frederick cleared his throat as he fiddled at the tubes and lines coming out of Jude's frail body. "Draven, do you want to say anything else before I do this?"

Draven sniffed and nodded, extricating himself from the octopus tentacles of the people who held him. "Yes." He moved over to Jude and brushed the limp hair off his forehead.

"Goodbye, buddy. I love you so damn much. I hope when you see Mum and Dad you tell them I love them too and one day I hope to see you all again." He felt the closing of his throat and the bittersweet wrench in his chest.

"I'll take Taylor to see Maroon 5 and I promise you I'll finish building that aeroplane and fly it for you when it's done. Rest in peace, Jude. I love you."

By now he was a wreck, body shuddering and jerking with sobs and Taylor reached out and drew him in, his voice thick when he spoke.

"God, babe, come here. I've got you."

Draven collapsed into protective arms, and a broad chest that promised familiarity and strength. The two of them clung to each other and Draven vaguely heard Alison crooning something to Jude over the bed and the doctor's quiet voice as he asked to help him.

Draven didn't want to—God, he really didn't want to see his brother slip away, watch as the machines keeping Jude alive were switched off and he simply stopped existing at all. Yet he knew he *had* to or he would never forgive himself. He burrowed into Taylor like a mole and let Taylor's strong arms and whispered comforts strengthen him. Watching Doctor Fredrick switch off the machines, Draven reached for thoughts of he and Jude catching frogs, swimming in the river and hunting tadpoles; sweet memories of the awed look on his twelve-year-old brother's face when he said a girl had kissed him for the first time.

It seemed like forever but was only a few minutes. The sounds of life support gradually ceased along with it the rise and fall of Jude's chest. Draven's eyes were strangely dry and as Taylor's arms tightened around him, he wondered bemusedly when it would all hit him. When the world would stop turning and the grief in his chest would stop hurting. Behind him he heard sniffles and the loud blowing of a nose. Alison was feeling Jude's departure as strongly as he was from the sounds of it.

Fredrick looked at Draven with sad eyes. "It's over," he said simply. "He didn't suffer. I thought you might like to be with him. Alison will have someone come in soon to take care of him. I'm sorry for your loss, Mr. Samuels." He pressed Draven's arm tightly and left the room.

Draven managed to pull himself from Taylor and walked unsteadily to the bed. Jude looked no different than before; he was still pale and frail. Draven liked to think he saw the beginnings of a slight smile on his face but he thought that might simply be wishful thinking.

"He's been gone a long time, Draven," Alison said, her tone soft. "Now he's gone home, where he belongs."

Draven nodded and placed a kiss on Jude's cool forehead. "She'll take good care of you, little one," he whispered. "I have to go now. But one day I know we'll see each other again."

For a while he and Taylor sat there with Jude as Draven held his hand and came to terms with the fact his brother was truly gone. The doctor came in about an hour later and said gently they needed to move Jude and Draven winced but nodded. Taylor held his hand, squeezing it gently as they stood up.

He kissed Jude again then turned to the hovering form of Taylor waiting anxiously behind him. "I guess there's nothing else I can do here. Take me home, Tay. I just want to go to bed and cuddle up with you and not think about anything else." The numb feeling in his chest lessened a bit at Taylor's warm smile and concern.

"I can do that. Come on then, let's get you home. Maybe we need to use an old friend's remedy for feeling stressed or down. Chamomile tea. Leslie swears by it."

Draven grimaced. "Not so sure I like that idea. A stiff whiskey sounds like a better bet."

He gave one last lingering look at the young boy in the bed behind him.

Alison reached out and hugged him. "You look after yourself, Draven honey. I know you won't be around much anymore but don't be a stranger. Pop in and see me now and then and let me know how you're doing."

Draven kissed her plump cheek tenderly. "I promise I will. You don't get rid of me that easy." He swallowed. "Alison, you won't let anyone touch him, or anything, will you? I need to arrange the funeral, it will be a cremation, but I don't want him getting cut or anything like that."

Alison laid a large finger on his mouth. "Hush, young man. I promise you nothing is going to happen to that sweet boy. I will take real good care of him for you until you're ready to take him away from here." She looked at Taylor. "You make sure you look after this man, you hear? He's very special to all of us."

"He's very special to me too, Alison," Taylor murmured. "I promise I'll take care of him."

She narrowed her eyes at him. “You are special too. I can sense it. I know you have the gift. My ancestors had the same thing. It passed me by but I still recognise it when I see it. If that helped these two sort things out, then I’m really grateful to you. And if you ever see that young scamp again,” she waved at the still figure in the bed, “you make sure and tell him Nurse Ally misses him but she’s glad he’s at peace.”

Taylor’s eyes welled up and Draven reached over and slid his finger under a tear that threatened to drop.

“I will,” Taylor said. “I doubt I’ll see him again but if I do, I will.” He sniffed and wiped his sleeve under his nose.

She nodded in satisfaction. “Then get off home, the two of you and get some rest. Draven, you take care of this young man. He’s a keeper.”

Draven glanced at Taylor, who held his gaze. That look seemed to say everything Draven was feeling and he was warmed knowing that Taylor seemed to feel the same way about him.

Taylor leaned in and whispered in his ear. “I heard what you said to Jude. I really liked it all, apart from that bit about being an arrogant little shit.” He pouted.

Despite the feeling of grief in his heart, Draven couldn’t stop a soft laugh at the adorable man before him and he pressed a swift kiss to his lips. “I meant every word of it. But we can talk about this later. Come on, let’s get out of here.”

He pulled Taylor by the hand and together, they left Jude’s room and the hospital behind.

Chapter 13

Taylor kept his hand on Draven's leg the whole drive home. Draven was pale and quiet, and while Taylor wanted to simply take him in his arms and never let go, he knew his lover needed time. Time to process that he would no longer make the journey home from the hospital again. Time to realise he would no longer see his brother each week, or read stories to him. Draven needed space to properly grieve now that the thin and fragile thread biding the brothers together had been severed.

Since they'd left the silent hospital ward where Jude lay, Draven hadn't said a word. He'd walked with Taylor to the car, gotten in, adjusted his seatbelt and started the car. He'd looked calm but Taylor sensed the churning roils of emotion beneath the façade. He'd not been disposed to talk himself much anyway, given what had just happened. He hadn't known Jude long but even in such a short time, he felt a sense of loss and regret. He could only imagine how Draven felt.

Taylor stared out of the window, watching the scenery and London buildings flash by.

Draven cleared his throat now and then and Taylor saw the bob of his Adam's apple as he swallowed, his hands clenching sporadically at the wheel. Taylor simply tightened his grip on Draven's leg, letting him know he was there for him.

Finally, as they neared home and Draven pulled into park, he spoke. His voice was tight, barely controlled. "Thanks for being there with me."

Taylor nodded. "Of course. Where else would I be?" He squeezed Draven's leg gently.

The car stopped and they got out and made their way up the few stairs to Draven's front door. As they went inside, it was as if all of Draven's control went. His shoulders shuddered and he gasped, deep, wrenching breaths of sheer grief, as tears streamed down his face, and he reached out blindly for Taylor. He gathered Draven to him, wrapping arms around that tried to comfort and console, as tears of his own trickled down his cheeks at his lover's distress.

"If it was the right thing to do, why do I feel so damn empty?" Draven's face, wet with tears, was pressed against Taylor's shoulder. Taylor hugged him close, wondering what to say.

"You spent the best part of three years looking after him," he murmured softly even as his heart ached at Draven's pain. "You were his big brother, and you loved him. I could tell that he adored you too. This was the hardest part for him as well, knowing you would be upset but still keeping his wish."

Draven's voice was muffled by Taylor's shirt when he spoke again. "I couldn't have done this without you by my side, you know that, right? You…" he swallowed and looked up at Taylor, his eyes red rimmed and swollen—still he was the most beautiful man Taylor had ever seen. "You make things better, in every way. I don't tell you that enough." His hand came up to caress Taylor's cheek and he felt warmth in his chest at the look in Draven's eyes. For a moment he was breathless. No man had ever looked at him like that before. He didn't want to jinx the moment by reading more into it that was warranted so he smiled instead and placed a gentle kiss on Draven's cool lips, moving away swiftly lest he make a fool of himself.

"Thank you. I feel the same way about you." He released his grip on Draven. "Are you hungry, babe? I can make us pasta if you like, if you don't mind me rummaging in your kitchen for scraps to use. I know you don't tend to have much in there, so I guess I need to be careful when I open the damn fridge that something doesn't grab me and try and pull me in, a rogue bit of mould that's gone mutant." He was aware he was rambling but he was still overwhelmed at the look he'd seen in Draven's eyes and the way he himself felt about the man standing in front of him with a quizzical expression on his face.

He wanted to say the words "I love you" so badly, let out the feelings that dwelt deep in his heart. But he felt raw, as if by saying them right at this minute among Draven's pain that it would cheapen them. Instead, Taylor ignored the impulse and reached down to take out a saucepan from the kitchen cupboard under the sink. "I suppose I'll have to get creative; maybe I can find a new use for out-of-date yoghurt and slightly green potatoes…"

"Taylor." Draven smiled and leaned over to place a finger on his lips. Taylor stopped midway between the action of placing the saucepan on the stove top and turning on the burner.

Draven took it from him and placed it on the top of the kitchen island. Then he reached out, tugged at Taylor's hips and drew him into his body, pressing Taylor back against the island and taking his willing mouth in a punishing yet completely earth-shattering kiss that made his toes tingle and his balls ache. His arse clenched in delight as Draven's hands moved behind him and grasped it tightly as he ground his groin against him. His mouth was being assaulted by a man who knew no boundaries with lips that bruised his with the intensity of the kiss. Food forgotten, they clutched each other eagerly, soft sighs of pleasure and moans of content echoing through the still kitchen.

Finally Draven let him go, and Taylor blinked, disoriented at the loss of his lover's mouth.

"What spooked you?" Draven whispered. "What did you see in my face or eyes that made you all flustered?"

Taylor flushed at the fact he'd been so transparent. "Nothing, I just wanted to do something nice for you…" his voice trailed away at Draven's raised eyebrow, something, which made the man even sexier than usual. The sight of that eyebrow above slate-grey eyes caused Taylor's pulse to quicken and his mouth to dry.

"Tay, tell me." Draven brushed his lips across Taylor's throat and he moaned, the sound embarrassing him with its sense of need.

"I, I…you just drive me damn crazy and I love you. But this isn't the time to tell you, you just came back from the hospital after losing your brother again and I don't want to confuse you or say something to upset you…"

He groaned as warm lips found the pulse in his throat and kissed it gently, like the slow tickle of a butterfly as its fluttered its satin wings against skin. The longing he had to be both possessed by Draven and possess him in turn, mind, body and soul, was bubbling below heated skin and he feared he might explode if he didn't let it loose.

"I can see it in your eyes," Draven murmured, "just as you can see it in mine. Shall I go first? Tell you how I feel about you? How you've taken my heart and made it feel something I've never had before? How the sight of your body makes me hard, makes me want to rip your clothes off and take you?"

Taylor was rock hard in his jeans now as he closed his eyes and gave into the sensations Draven was causing as he pressed close to his body. "Shall I tell you that you're the only man I ever want to wake up to, to kiss, to make love to?" Draven's voice deepened. "I *know* what just happened, and what I lost. I also know what I gained. A beautiful, funny, sexy, infuriating, incredible human being with a talent only the gods could give. You are something very special indeed, Taylor Abelard. And *that's* why I love you."

The words "I love you" were there, in the kitchen, in Taylor's ears, cemented in his heart and the world stopped. With trembling fingers, he traced the contours of Draven's face, marvelling at the joy filling his soul and warming him from top to bottom.

Draven's eyes darkened and he captured Taylor's lips in yet another rough and passionate kiss. Taylor surrendered absolutely, closing his eyes and rejoicing in the simple fact that Draven loved him. And damn the rest of world and its tragedies, its harsh reality and its blurred lines of imaginations and dreams and its ability to intrude in the moments that counted. *This—this* was the moment that Taylor knew deep in his bones and his heart that had been meant to be, a moment where he felt loved, special, and was someone's rock, the person they depended on as much as he did them.

Draven relaxed in his arms, his eager, questing lips on his, and the feel of both his solidity and vulnerability pressed against Taylor's body. In the warmth that followed as contentment and passion flooded Taylor's body, he swore he heard a young man's chuckle as warm fingers brushed his face and said goodbye.

Six months later…

Draven fidgeted as he sat at the intimate, candlelit table in a secluded alcove of Galileo's. His fingers drummed a nervous beat on the table as he watched Taylor make his way back from the bathroom. The small box in his pocket knocked against his hip each time he moved as it made its presence known.

The box and its contents had been foremost in Draven's mind this past week, ever since he'd picked it up from the jeweller. He smiled as Taylor sat down opposite him, dark eyes shining in the candlelight, black hair outlined in the dim light like a halo around Taylor's head. Not for the first time Draven marvelled at the being that was his lover and hopefully, soon to be something else.

"Sorry about that," Taylor grimaced as he leaned over and brushed long, graceful fingers over Draven's tapping fingers. "I think that beer went right through me. I'm peeing like a bloody racehorse at a competition."

Draven shook his head in amusement. "Thanks for that image. I plan this whole romantic dinner and all I can think of now is a bloody horse peeing in a bloody bucket."

Taylor chuckled. "I don't know how they actually do it, it's just one of those sayings you hear." He gazed around the restaurant. "Have you seen the dessert menu yet? I really fancy that chocolate thingy they had on the Specials board when we came in. Eddie's really proud of that one; I think it's called 'Sublime Chocolate Overdose' or something like that…" His voice tailed off as Draven reached over and placed a finger on his lips, effectively stopping him mid flow. Taylor's eyes widened.

Draven smiled at him. "I have something I need to say to you, and I need to do it now before I lose my nerve." He removed his finger and reached into his pocket.

Taylor blinked in confusion. "Uhmm, yeah sure. What is it?" His face grew worried. "Everything is okay, isn't it? This isn't an 'I'm breaking up with you' occasion, is it? Because I am *so* not ready for that conversation…just so you know. I mean, I've just moved in."

Taylor had indeed moved in with Draven, giving up the house he shared with Leslie. Despite his nervousness at what he was about to do, the panicked look on Taylor's face made Draven grin. "No, babe, definitely not that."

His heart was racing now, his throat dry and his stomach in knots. He stood up then knelt down at Taylor's side. He'd debated with himself how he wanted this to go down and had decided on doing it the old-fashioned way. The expression on Taylor's face was a mix of surprise, hope and panic.

The noise in the restaurant seemed to diminish in Draven's ears as he took a deep breath and threw caution to the wind. He'd practiced this speech in the mirror so many times and yet—now he was here, before Taylor, and his well-rehearsed words were forgotten.

"Taylor, I hope you don't think this is too soon, but I think we've been through quite a lot together, and I know how *I* feel, and know how *you* feel, we say it enough to each other." Taylor gazed at him with eyes that seemed to drink him in. His lips parted and

Draven wanted to kiss them and tell him that way what he was trying to ask. He cleared his throat.

"There's no other man I want to share my life with, and fuck, this sounds so damn mushy and sentimental, but I don't know how else to say it." He took a deep breath, seeing the bright, sudden, sheen in Taylor's brown eyes and the slight flaring of his nostrils. "I love you, and I want it to be real." He tripped over himself to amend that last comment. "I mean, it's real, of course it is, but I want it to be even more than that. Taylor Abelard," he brought out the small box that his nerveless fingers had been clenched around in his pocket, "Will you do me the honour of marrying me? Being my husband one day when you're ready?" Taylor's quick, indrawn breath made Draven's stomach clench in fear. "I mean, only if you're ready, I don't want to rush into this if you don't feel it's the right time…"

This time, it was his mouth that was stopped by long, warm fingers as Taylor pushed his chair back and with his other hand, drew Draven up off his knees. Draven stood, slightly unsure of what the answer was going to be.

He got it soon enough as Taylor pulled him into a kiss that curled his toes, made his cock reach for the heavens and sent a tingle through his body, right into his very marrow.

Lips that tasted faintly of citrus and rocket from the salad Taylor had eaten, lips that were so sweet and welcoming that they drew Draven into them like a moth intent on suicide by flying into light and heat. Taylor had finally stopped smoking completely and his mouth was all the sweeter for it. The world stopped as Draven's eyes closed and all he could feel was Taylor's warmth and love flooding his soul. Finally he was released and vaguely heard a clapping sound in the distance as his senses returned to normal.

Taylor pressed his forehead against Draven's and exhaled a sweet breath against his skin. "God, you know how to make a man feel special. That was like something out of a rom-com. And yes, my beautiful lover, I would love to be your husband. Nothing could make me happier."

The restaurant patrons were on their feet, clapping and smiling at the spectacle unfolding before them. Taylor watched with hooded eyes as Draven's unsteady fingers opened the box and took out the palladium ring he'd had specially designed. It was a simple band of smooth metal, with two diamonds embedded into the middle.

Draven gently slid it onto Taylor's finger. He felt a sense of satisfaction. It fit perfectly. He took out its twin and slid it onto his own finger then lifted his eyes to gaze at Taylor.

"Now it's official." Out of the corner of his eye, Gideon and Eddie standing together, watching. They came over and hugged them, Gideon clapping Draven on his back as he grinned widely.

"Bloody well done, Draven. That took some guts, my friend." He slid a sly sideways glance at Eddie. "Maybe you've started a trend…who knows?"

Eddie's fair face flushed with pleasure as he reached out and pulled Taylor into a bear hug. "Yeah, you never know…Taylor, congratulations, mate. So pleased for you both."

Draven flinched as long, muscled freckled arms headed his way and was pleasantly surprised when Eddie pulled him for a hug too. "You make him so damn happy," Eddie whispered in Draven's ear. "I guess my original impression of you wasn't all that accurate. That makes me really glad."

Gideon waved over a passing waiter as the restaurant got back to normal and guests sat back down with friendly glances their way and the occasional "Well done to you" nod.

"Brent, bring us a bottle of the good champers for these guys. I think they've earned it, don't you?"

Brent nodded, his shaggy head of blond hair falling around his face as he grinned. "I think so, boss. Be right back." He sidled past the tables as he made his way to thc bar.

Gideon raised a knowing eyebrow at Eddie. "I think we've outstayed our welcome," he smirked. "Let's let the lovebirds be alone."

Eddie grinned, his freckled face warm with affection. "Congrats again, guys. It couldn't happen to a nicer couple." He cast a scorching glance at Gideon who gave a heated look of his own back. Draven wondered whether there might be another wedding on the cards soon.

Eddie saw his look and smiled widely. "Now we just have to find Leslie a mate and the three of us will all be paired off." He patted Taylor on the arm then disappeared with a smiling Gideon.

Draven saw the fleeting look of guilt cross Taylor's face. It had worried his fiancé—how right it felt being able to call Taylor that—

that Leslie had been left alone now that both Eddie and Taylor were gone to pastures new.

To put Taylor's worries to rest, Draven had made sure he did everything he could with his and Clay's connections to get Leslie an affordable studio flat in Kennington, not far from where the house was. Thanks to a generous boss, who seemed to adore the ground Leslie walked on, he had even got an increase in salary to help him settle in on his own. He reached out a hand and caressed Taylor's cheek.

"Tay, babe, Leslie will be fine. He's a spitfire of a soul and if anyone can look after himself, that man can. And just think how excited he's going to be when he hears he has a wedding to fit us out for. The man is going to wet himself."

Taylor nodded and looked back at him with more love than Draven knew what to do with. He wanted nothing more than to take him home, throw him onto the bed and make love to him until he forgot his own name.

He wanted to taste Taylor, feel his skin against his own and marvel at the man who'd just agreed to be his husband. Instead, he sat down and motioned to Taylor to do the same, and watched as Brent poured glasses of champagne for them then disappeared like a wraith, leaving them in peace.

Taylor raised his glass. "To my fiancé. Good health, good loving and great sex. And may there continue to be lots of that." He chuckled.

Draven inclined his head and raised his glass, to clink it against Taylor's. "To my sexy fiancé, definitely to the good sex and even more loving." They drank deeply then toasts done, they set their glasses down on the table.

Taylor quirked a brow.

"I don't know about you, but I'm as horny as fuck and I really want to get you home to bed. What say we drink this champagne quickly then get home?"

Draven couldn't agree more with that plan. He reached over and took the bottle and topped up their glasses. "I love a man who knows what he wants. Home it is."

The smouldering look Taylor gave him made Draven begrudge even the time it took to finish the bottle until the two of them were giggling like school boys and touching each other at a pace that was about to get them kicked out for public lewdness.

Later, as Draven watched the lean, muscled form of his lover ride him as if there was no tomorrow, his skin shining with sweat and that wicked mouth devouring his, he took time to close his eyes and simply bask in the joy that suffused his heart at having such a man in his life.

As Taylor leaned down to whisper words of love in his ear, kissing Draven's heated flesh, Draven knew that somewhere, not too far away, Jude was happy for him. His heart still ached at what he'd lost but was overfilled with love at what he'd found.

With Taylor in his life, he'd come full circle from being alone to being complete and he had the feeling that life would never be quite the same again.

SUIT YOURSELF

Chapter 1

"That dickwad is so overrated. I hate him. I hope his arse rots and his hole closes up." Leslie Scott scowled as he bit his bottom lip in a fit of pique. He glared at the trim figure on the catwalk mincing along the raised platform.

Beside him, Eddie Tripp snorted in laughter. "Hell, Leslie, I'd hate to be one of your exes. Simon might have been a bit of a douche cheating on you like he did, but even he doesn't deserve that fate worse than death. *My* arse is twitching just thinking about it."

Eddie and Leslie sat at the front of the audience at a swanky London fashion event. Working at a local fashion house providing exclusive men and women's suits, Leslie had been invited to see the latest designs gracing the catwalk. Eddie hadn't particularly wanted to be here at the Mystique Hotel extravaganza on a rare Saturday off, but Leslie had batted his eyelashes and opened his baby blues wide, knowing that Eddie would be powerless to resist.

Gideon, Eddie's boyfriend, had shaken his head at Eddie's capitulation and grinned. "God, Eddie, babe, you are so damn easy…" He'd forestalled Eddie's indignant squawk that he was *so* not with a fierce kiss. Leslie loved seeing his fiery friend rendered speechless even though his heart gave a lurch at the two men being so comfortable together. Leslie really wanted a relationship like theirs.

He narrowed his eyes at the ex-boyfriend now strutting along the catwalk in the posh confines of the Bella Ballroom. Simon Hooper looked as if butter wouldn't melt in his mouth with his platinum-streaked, stylishly coiffed blond hair and pink, full lips, but Leslie had seen that mouth in action on another man's cock and seen Simon's ugly side when he'd been caught out in mid-blow. That pretty mouth could say some fairly hurtful things, like, "Well, I wasn't getting what I needed from yours." That comment had really stung.

"Yes, well, just because he's a model and has everyone fawning over him like he's the next best thing to Michael J Willett means fuck-all to me. The man's a bitch." Leslie huffed and waggled perfectly manicured fingers in Eddie's direction.

Eddie grinned. "You look even better than him, honest. I mean…" He paused and stared hard at Simon currently sashaying away from them. He wore a tailored, ruffled pink shirt and tight, plaid green and brown designer trousers emblazoned with the flamboyant Tracy Trey's signature label of a rainbow-coloured chameleon on the pocket. "No one can fault those trousers you have on, and those shoes. You look like a prince, whereas he looks like the frog. A bloody Amazon rainforest frog at that, wearing all those colours." Eddie winced. "I mean, multi-coloured *plaid* trousers? Come on."

Leslie's heart warmed at Eddie's obvious sincerity and he had to admit he probably simpered a little. "Well, I do try my best." He looked down at his black, silky, clinging long-sleeved shirt and tight, sexy bronze silk pants complete with his favourite pair of comfortable heels, a pair of Jimmy Choo peep-toe pumps, just his style. They were slightly scuffed but he'd not said no to them when one of the diva female models had thrown them aside after a fashion show he'd attended and asked him casually if he wanted them. A starving wolf attacking a hunk of premium quality meat had nothing on Leslie as he dove to get them. He'd hissed like a striking salamander at another woman trying to do the same thing. He'd been gratified when she'd backed off.

The only thing irritating him about his outfit was his thong. It just wasn't behaving properly, riding up his backside and into his crack. Leslie didn't mind fingers or tongues doing that, but an errant piece of a fabric was simply a no-no.

Eddie chuckled as Leslie turned out a well-waxed leg and admired the shoe on his slim ankle. "God, you are such a narcissist…"

"Am not," Leslie declared indignantly. "Can I help it that I like good stuff and classy wear? And that it looks great on me?" He huffed and pretended to glower at Eddie from between his lashes. "I can't help it. I have high standards."

"Yeah, you can be a right snob," Eddie retorted. Then seeing the scowl forming on Leslie's face, he grinned. "But I love you anyway." He nudged Leslie's arm with a gangly elbow. "That guy over there can't take his eyes off you. He's been eying you up since we got here."

Leslie's head whipped round so fast he thought he'd given himself whiplash. An admirer was always welcome in his current state of sexual drought. "Who would that—oh, *him*. That's Charlie." His lips curled in derision and he scoffed. "I wouldn't touch him with my pretty eight-inch bargepole. He's into abusing his boyfriends. I know one of his last ones, Sandy, ended up in hospital with a broken nose when that prick over there," he gestured to the thickset, dark-haired man currently looking at Leslie as if he wanted to lick him all over, "took exception to the way he was looking at another bloke. Sandy insisted he wasn't checking him out, but it didn't stop Charlie." He spat the name out, and Eddie reached up to wipe a small bit of spit off his face with a grimace. "He smashed poor Sandy's face into a door frame. He had to have surgery to fix it, 'cos he's an actor."

Eddie's pale face darkened. "Hell, what a fucking bully. Did anyone report him to the police for it?" His green eyes narrowed as he threw Charlie a look, one Charlie obviously saw as he turned to look at the crowd behind him then looked back at Eddie in bafflement, mixed with a little bit of panic.

"No, Sandy wouldn't do it. He just stopped seeing him. The bastard got off scot free." The unfairness of it made Leslie's blood heat. He hated bullies and men who took out their frustrations on someone else. "However, Sandy's new boyfriend, Alex, did corner Charlie in a bathroom a while ago and they had a 'chat.'" He frowned. "I don't know what Alex said to him but there have been no more beatings that I know of. Alex is a bouncer at a nightclub, so I don't think I'd want to mess with him."

Eddie nodded in satisfaction. "Glad someone put him straight." He chuckled. "In a manner of speaking." He threw Leslie a fond glance. "There was something wrong with one of your last statements, Leslie."

Leslie was puzzled. "What statement?"

"Eight inches?" Eddie laughed loudly as Leslie's face heated up. "I've seen it and I'm not sure that's true—"

Leslie pinched Eddie's arm, causing him to yowl in pain. "Shut up. It's my fantasy and you have no right to cast aspersions on it." He grinned back at his friend. "Besides, maybe it's grown since the last time you saw it. I might be going through a growth spurt, you know. I am only twenty-three."

Eddie guffawed. "Yeah, right, you tell yourself that." They both fell quiet as the crowd around started clapping and the auditorium exploded with a spate of quick-paced and rather loud trance music as Tracy Trey walked onto the catwalk with his models. Leslie started clapping with them. Tracy might be a little eccentric, and his plaid wear didn't appeal to Leslie in the least, but he was sheer fucking genius when it came to underwear and sexy corsets, one of his little pleasures. He owned quite a few items with the chameleon logo.

The noise finally died down, and as Tracy Trey strode off the stage, people started to get up and leave. Leslie sighed and stood up. "Come on. I guess you're anxious to get back to that lovely man of yours and fuck his brains out. Or cook something, depending on how you two spend your leisure time."

Eddie pursed his lips as they joined the throng of people leaving the venue, making their way to the exit in front. "Well, in my opinion, there's a way to do both at the same time. One of my favourite pastimes is making my world-renowned double chocolate mousse then smearing it all over Gideon's dick. Then sucking it off. Delicious…" He waggled his eyebrows and Leslie felt his own dick rise at the image of his two friends getting it on in that way.

"Oh," he said enviously. "I imagine that would be a lot of fun. Not that I haven't done something similar before myself, but I've never really had someone *special* to do it with like you…" His voice trailed off and he knew he sounded a little wistful.

Leslie's relationships tended not to last too long. He was honest with himself. He was rather high maintenance and boyfriends either tended to use him as a one-night fuck or got tired of the whole overwhelming Leslie persona and went on to someone easier to be with. Someone more malleable and not as fiery.

They exited the hotel into the chill grey of a January Saturday afternoon. Leslie shivered and wrapped his warm pea coat tighter around his frame.

Eddie's face softened. "Honey, you are a complete catch for the right guy. So far you just haven't found him. You will, though. You're beautiful inside *and* out, and these arseholes you date never seem to realise that." He reached out an arm and hugged Leslie close.

Leslie snuggled into his friend, enjoying this rare PDA. He breathed in Eddie's scent, feeling safe and cherished. "Yes, well, they never stick around long enough. It's all wham, bang, fuck off, Leslie," he muttered against Eddie's shoulder.

Eddie released him and planted a soft kiss on his forehead. "More fool them," he murmured softly. "There's a guy out there for you, I promise. You know I said you were a prince in there? Well, you gotta kiss a lot of frogs before you find him."

He hugged Leslie again then stood back. "Now I'd better get back home, before Gideon finds someone else to lick chocolate off."

Leslie snorted. "That'll be the day. That man adores you. You know that, you shameless hussy."

His friend's facial expression changed to one that Leslie called 'Giddy Goofy.' Dreamy, with a carnal glint to the eyes. In his fanciful moments, Leslie thought perhaps that description sounded like a delicious recipe.

"Yeah, well, I guess it's mutual." He turned to lope down the pavement, waving as he made his way to the tube station across the road. "Speak to you later, Leslie. Thanks for the afternoon and the company."

"No, thank *you*," Leslie called after him. "For putting up with me and a bloody fashion show."

Eddie shot him a wide grin across his shoulder and crossed the street, striding toward home and no doubt Gideon.

Chapter 2

Leslie watched his friend depart and heaved a sigh. "And there we have it," he muttered. "Alone again."

He started walking, clutching his coat around his shoulders, his underwear still uncomfortable. He'd change it when he got home and throw this beastly thong out. His small but comfortable flat wasn't far, one of the reasons he'd chosen it. It was close to the Mystique Hotel where most of their company fashion events were held. It was also close to his job at Debussy Fashion in Hackney, where he worked as a trainee fabric buyer and general factotum to his rather high-powered and sometimes scary as hell boss, Laverne Debussy-Smith.

Leslie had been living in his new home for three months, ever since both of his previous housemates had moved out of the Kennington house they'd shared. Eddie had of course moved in with Gideon to the palatial flat above their restaurant, Galileo's, and Taylor had moved in his with his fiancé, Draven. Both his housemates had been apologetic about the turn of events and deserting Leslie, but he'd been philosophical about it.

"I knew it would happen one day," he'd sighed when they'd taken turns staring at him with anxious eyes. "I'm really happy for you guys. You deserve this. It's about time I moved my arse and found somewhere closer to work anyway with the amount of time I'm spending there recently. Gives me an excuse to find a nifty flat and put my stamp on it."

Just before Taylor had moved out, they'd given their notice. Taylor's boyfriend Draven had found Leslie somewhere suitable to live, for which he was grateful. He was certainly paying less than he'd expected and suspected Draven had pulled someone's strings. Also, thanks to an unexpected but decent raise from Laverne when hearing of his predicament, Leslie had been able to afford the compact (euphemism for tiny box room, he thought) studio flat in Shoreditch.

Five minutes into his walk home, he passed work and on a sudden impulse, he decided he'd pop in and see if anything was going on. Often there were spare pieces of sample fabric and clothing items left over in the staff recycle bin for them to take home. Leslie desperately wanted a piece of frilly lace for a fancy dress party he was attending soon. He was going as Adam Ant and needed lacy cuffs sewn onto on his royal blue jacket. Perhaps he might get lucky going into the office when there were not too many eagle-eyed and needy employees around.

He made a quick stop for a coffee at the small café next to work and, as he left, he waved cheekily at the construction workers working on the scaffolding above the café. There was one burly young soul called Frankie whom he rather liked and who always wolf-whistled when he walked past. He wasn't there today but Leslie waved anyway. There were a few hoots and comments and he waggled his arse in return.

Normally he wouldn't have been so flamboyantly camp in the vicinity of what he imagined was mostly a heterosexual encamp—apart from Frankie, who'd made his desire to have Leslie known—but they'd been working there for months and he'd gotten to know them. He was still on the fence about taking Frankie up on his offer. The guy seemed very sweet but a bit innocent. Leslie rather liked them a little more experienced, even older.

Laverne made it a habit to send coffee and cake over to them every now and then to keep them sweet. She was philosophical about the noise and dust that swept through their own offices. "At least if I keep them a bit happy, they're happy to return the favour," she'd said one night. "The other evening, I had an important gentleman from Japan here and they stopped twenty minutes earlier with all the drilling and stuff so I could have my meeting in peace. They scratch my arse, I scratch theirs with treats. It works well."

The lobby of the quaint old office building was quiet, with only the elderly concierge sitting behind the worn, scratched desk as he read his copy of *The Sun*. Stuck on Page 3, Leslie noticed with a grin. The man waved at Leslie, who walked over to the old lift, the one that still had the pull-down metal gate, which creaked ominously as it travelled to the third floor.

"Afternoon, young Larry. You do know it's a weekend, don't you?" He scowled. "Not that them lot next door care. Bloody noisy gits, the lot of them. Why they have to work on a weekend, I don't know."

Leslie sighed as he waved hello. Sid's constant moans at the workforce next door could get a little wearing. "Yes, Sid, I do. I'm just here to check something out."

The concierge insisted on calling him Larry. No amount of conversation to explain that his name was actually Leslie had ever got Sid any closer to remembering it. It was easier to simply accept the name change even though Leslie hated it. It reminded him of a game called Larry the Lounge Lizard his older brother Nathan had used to play years ago.

"Well, beware. The cleaners are working up on your floor, and you know what that young Adrian is like. Bloody handsy little bastard, wasn't he, at the last Christmas party? If I recall, he was all over you like bloody ants on a picnic blanket."

Leslie paused. He did indeed remember that night when Laverne had needed to extricate Adrian's tongue from Leslie's mouth and his greedy fingers from his crotch. Leslie had been a little under the weather that night and his reflexes at fending off unwanted attention had been somewhat impaired. The words 'voracious octopus' sprung to mind.

"Oh, thanks for the warning. I'll do my best to avoid him." Leslie pressed the button for the lift and waited. When it opened, he stepped inside and listened to the sound of cheesy music as the lift arrived at the third floor.

Leslie waited for the doors to open then peered cautiously out into the corridor. It was empty. He tried to tiptoe quietly down the corridor so as to not to attract anyone's attention, and he breathed a sigh of relief when he got to the main office unscathed. He slipped in and closed the door behind him, locking it for good measure. Let Bad Breath Adrian try and get through that, he thought with a smirk. As he turned, someone loomed in front of him and he shrieked like a cat being disembowelled. His heart pounded and he pressed himself back against the door, wondering for an instant if Adrian had found him after all.

"Leslie, dear, really?" Laverne Debussy-Smith's husky voice sounded pained. "My fucking ears are now ringing like the bells of Notre Dame."

"Well, jeez Louise, forgive me for thinking someone was about to murder me," retorted Leslie snarkily, bearing in mind this *was* his boss and trying to tone it down just a bit.

Laverne's Adam's apple bobbed up and down as she drawled, "What are you doing here, anyway? On the scrounge again?" Her words belied the affectionate glance she directed at him as Leslie huffed.

Laverne Debussy-Smith was a law unto herself. She was owner and founder of the company, as well as being a talented clothing designer. Her own suit label, simply titled 'Debussy,' was highly prized, made for both women and men. Leslie had one in his closet but doubted he could ever afford another.

Laverne was also a man who'd been born Lenny James, but decided that Laverne was definitely more fun in the office. The man behind the woman was just as treasured by the staff.

"Ha-ha. If you must know, I was coming in to check that delivery for Monday. The suit for that guy in Waterloo, the one who spent a bloody fortune on it. Oliver somebody or the other." Leslie felt gratified that he'd remembered the delivery he was supposed to do and could use it as an excuse. Laverne's comment about scrounging had rather wounded him, even if it *was* true.

Laverne nodded and Leslie didn't like the glint in her aqua eyes. It looked…cunning. That could be a bad sign of things to come, knowing her. He moved away from the door, going toward the open-plan office, and, coincidentally, the recycle bin.

"Not so fast, my little bit of sex on legs." Laverne's tone became playful and sexy and Leslie's stomach plummeted. He just knew he wasn't going to be investigating the bin for his lace anytime soon from the sound of it. Slowly, he turned to face the woman dressed in a form-hugging, deep blue tailored pants suit, mock breasts pushing up the stressed fabric. Leslie wondered idly if it was screaming for release as the mounds pressed against it like sponge being forced through the fabric tear of a stuffed animal. A ripple of apprehension flooded his body. Laverne's favours came in two distinct flavours. One was the innocuous, 'Could you make me a cup of tea, darling?' to 'Could you just rip your first born from your womb and give it to me?' There was no in-between in Leslie's opinion. Perhaps he was being a bit of a drama queen but these ad hoc requests always made him nervous.

"What?" He sighed resignedly. "What do you need?"

Laverne's handsome, square-jawed face beamed at him from under a wig of silver-blonde thick hair and Leslie thought not for the first time that Lenny made rather a lovely woman. Tall, broad-shouldered, statuesque, and beautifully dressed no matter what, Laverne was a force to be reckoned with and Leslie would do anything for her.

"Well, this must be divine intervention." Laverne prowled her way across to Leslie, who took a deep breath. More than once he'd been embraced between the twin peaks that made up Laverne's chest and every time had been a pretty suffocating experience. However, this time he was given a reprieve.

"The client called and said Monday was no longer good for him, so could I please see whether I could get anyone out there today. I was going to call Charlie and see if he could do it, but now you're here in person, my sweet lad, I rather think Mr. Brown can be all yours."

Leslie raised a perfectly plucked eyebrow. "Really? His name is Oliver Brown? That's pretty bleh. I think I'd die from self-boredom with a name like that." He was relieved at the extent of the favour though. It sounded innocuous enough.

Laverne frowned. "Now, now, don't be a bitch. I mean, what's so great about the name Leslie Scott?"

Leslie spluttered. "Leslie *Tiberius* Scott, if you please."

Laverne stared at him then broke out into great guffaws of laughter that definitely made her the man she was beneath the armour. "Oh my God, Leslie, my little chicken. Tiberius? That is not a name I would associate with a gorgeous Tinkerbell like you. The name Tiberius conjures up hunky Captain James T. Kirk." She licked her lips lasciviously.

Leslie wanted to swear and tell Laverne he was not Tinkerbell, but this was Laverne. And she *had* said gorgeous. Instead, he clenched his teeth and took the comment on the chin.

"Well, at least it's pretty unusual. Not like Oliver Brown."

Laverne must have picked up on the slight hurt in his voice because she sailed over to him and enveloped him in her bosom. It looked like Leslie wasn't getting off scot free tonight.

"Leslie. When I call you Tinkerbell, I mean that I see beauty, grace, and a warm-hearted, beautiful soul. I see big blue eyes, pale skin and black hair that'd make a man's heart melt. I don't see a man who is a fairy, or unable to stand up for himself. You, Leslie Tiberius Scott, are a wonderful human being and that's why I call you Tinkerbell."

Somewhat mollified, Leslie managed to extricate himself from Laverne's clutches. His hair was mussed from being held so close, but for once, he didn't mind the unruly state of it.

"Well, that's okay then. It's just everyone thinks I'm this slim twink who can't say boo to a goose, and I promise you, I have my moments." He recalled one moment fondly when he'd attacked a man while wearing his high heels then proceeded to bash said dickhead with the end of them. Eddie had been the unfortunate victim that night of the man's unwelcome advances, but between them, Leslie and Taylor had saved the day.

"I have no doubt of that." Lavern's lips twitched as if holding back a smile and then she was back to business. "So, you'll take Mr. Brown's suit to him then, this afternoon? You can take the car. It's not too far away and I think he said he had off-road parking." She waggled a large finger at him. "Mr. Brown is my best customer. You treat him right." She winked. "And I'm really interested to know what the man behind the sexy voice looks like. I've never met him myself."

Leslie sighed. He and the thong could do this. "Fine. I'll be on my best behaviour, I promise. Let me get the suit from the Arbour and I'll load it in the car." He looked at her hopefully. "I want to change, too." He looked down at his glad rags. "These aren't particularly *suitable* for delivering a suit." He snorted at his own wit.

Laverne rolled her eyes. "There are some spec suits in the back, change into one of those. I've no doubt I'll ever see it again." Spec or specimen suits were ones that Laverne had made but were deigned not good enough for sale even though in Leslie's eyes they were perfect.

Leslie batted his eyelashes. "You mean I get to keep it? Oh, Laverne. You doll. I don't suppose you have spare underwear anywhere, do you?" He wriggled uncomfortably. "This damn string is chafing my backside."

Laverne shook her head. "No, sweets, I don't have any Andrew Christians or fancy thongs lying around. You'll either have to go commando or wear the one you have on. Now be off with you, urchin. Post haste. The Arbour awaits."

The Arbour was the room where all the suits that were already made were stored. It was nothing more than a very large, high-ceilinged and airy room with rails and hangers around the walls and a large olive tree in the centre, hence the name. Laverne was fond of olive trees and this one was close to eight feet, set into glistening white pebbles in an enclosure set into the laminated floor. It was looked after as if it were a precious baby. They'd even held office picnics around its spreading branches.

"I hope the car has petrol," Leslie grumbled as he turned the knob to go out to the door, forgetting he'd locked it. He turned the key impatiently and yanked the door open.

"It's all fuelled up," Laverne promised. "Thank you, Leslie, I owe you one. Be careful how you go now and bring the car back safely." Her tone held a warning. The last time Leslie had used a company asset he'd put the wrong fuel in it and had to call out the Automobile Association to rescue him. The cost had not gone down well with the rather tight-fisted Laverne.

It was on the tip of Leslie's tongue to say he'd take payment of some French lace in return for having his Saturday afternoon stuffed up, but he thought the better of it. He'd have a look in the bin when he brought the car back later and hopefully by then he'd be alone to rummage. Rather let Laverne think she had a debt to pay. Perhaps he could get a Friday off sometime soon and go to Brighton for the weekend. He had a good friend down there who'd be happy to take him out on the town.

Laverne's voice interrupted his musings.

"Text me when you're done and let you know you've made it out of the house alive. I mean, you never know, he might decide to keep you. I would."

At first, Leslie felt a twinge of unease at that thought; then random images of being tied up like an old-school heroine and ravaged by a handsome stranger flitted through his mind.

Hmm, actually that doesn't sound so bad.

Agreeing that he would text Laverne when he was done, and happy he had something to do this afternoon instead of being home alone (and how sad was that), Leslie whistled as he strutted down the corridor to the Arbour, keeping an anxious eye out for pervy Adrian.

He'd go and see the boringly named Mr. Brown, deliver his suit and then—who knew. Perhaps he'd take himself off to a club tonight and dance the night away. He might even meet someone and go home or be taken home for some heart-stopping, sweaty sex. Of course, waking up with the man tomorrow still in his bed would be a bonus. Cuddling was one of Leslie's favourite pastimes and he didn't get to do it often enough.

He changed into a rather nifty suit and a tailored shirt, and grimaced at the fact he'd have to keep the thong on. He wasn't visiting a customer with his balls hanging out. He found himself a pair of much more comfortable and more respectable shoes to wear; they just happened to be a pair of Armani Loafers.

He whistled as he put them on. His Choos and the rest of his own outfit were popped in a bag and held close, not wanting to let them out of his sight. He grinned when he remembered his boss's comment about not getting it back. She knew him so well. Some of his best outfits were 'borrowed.'

Chapter 3

The customer's house resided in a cul-de-sac in the middle of the respectable area of Waterloo. Bare-branched trees jutted starkly up from the pavement, which framed clusters of bungalows and double-storey houses set back from the road. They all appeared to have the requisite postage stamp front gardens.

Leslie parked on the wide kerb—a real bonus in his book as he was used to parking on busy streets with double yellow lines (and getting tickets)—unfolded his legs out of the little red Ford Ka he'd borrowed from work, and stood to observe the place with a jaded eye.

It was a seemingly palatial but grubby white-painted house with an ornate wooden front door, which was set with a bevelled paned glass window. A weed-strewn driveway led up to the house, and the gardens surrounding the place looked overgrown and unloved. In its heyday, it must have been quite something. Now, in its current state, even the house seemed to match the name 'Brown.' Ordinary, boring, and *so* totally lacking in originality. A tickle of guilt passed through his slender frame as he thought perhaps Eddie and Taylor might have a point when they called him a snob. He shook that off with the thought that *he* still preferred to say he had high standards.

He felt a twinge of sympathy for the poor, neglected camellia valiantly fighting its way up from what looked like a clump of thistles. He was rather partial to camellias, having once had an older lover who'd filled a bathtub with the pink blooms and champagne and seduced Leslie into it with one sexy strip of his clothing and a promise of an earth-shattering blowjob. Said lover was now deceased, unfortunately, having had a heart attack when his wife confronted him with the evidence of his various *off-piste* affairs with young men. However, Leslie still thought fondly of Ralphie at moments like these.

He tut-tutted as he opened his boot and removed the enclosed grey suit, giving it a loving caress as he folded it gently over his left forearm.

"There we go, sweetie. I'm not sure why someone who lives in an unkempt house like this needs a suit like you. You're far too lovely for a place like this. I hope he takes care of you."

He picked up his leather business folder and secured it under his other arm. Taking a deep breath, he adjusted his thong, which had once again ridden up between his cheeks. He strode confidently up to the front door, narrowly avoiding what looked like dog crap on a paving stone covered with dead grass as he did. He stopped and frowned down at the offending item.

"You dare get one bit of your smelly self on my Armani loafers and you are toast," he hissed at what he now saw was simply a clump of dried mud. Delicately avoiding all other ground-strewn landmines, he managed to get to the front door. He shook his head at seeing there was only a broken bell with wires hanging out looking sorry for itself, and he raised a hand—neither of which was truly free—to try and knock on the door as hard as he could.

He waited.

The inside of the house was silent. There was no scuffling down what he imagined were worn stairs, no clatter of shoes across laminated floors and no welcoming opening of the door to greet him. He frowned and knocked again, louder this time. His folder slipped from where it was secured under his arm and he quickly tightened his arm to hold it in place.

"Hello? Mr. Brown, are you home? My name is Leslie Scott and I'm here with your new suit," he announced grandly.

He wriggled his backside uncomfortably—that damn thong, what the hell was wrong with it—and scowled as he raised a hand to knock again. As he did so, the door opened. A man's face peered out of him, half hidden. It was dark inside but what Leslie could see of the face looked rather tasty. That was the first surprise of this visit.

A shock of shaggy, honey-blond hair hung over Mr. Brown's forehead, and his tanned skin, neat beard and stubble and one wide amber eye all mingled together to make Leslie feel much better about his customer delivery. Mr. Brown also looked a little familiar.

Leslie gave the man what he knew was a dazzling smile, as he'd been praised for it more than once, and indicated the suit hanging across his right arm.

"Mr. Brown? I'm from Debussy Fashion. I'm here to deliver the suit you ordered."

The man looked a little taken aback, but the door didn't open any wider. "Oh, I see." His well-modulated voice sounded a little strained. "Ermm, perhaps you could hand it over to me?" An arm covered in the faintest blond hair and ending in long, slender fingers with well-kept nails reached out of the door, clearly intent on Leslie pressing the suit into his hand.

The whole thing reminded Leslie of YouTube videos of Salad Fingers, something he was addicted to. He shook his head vehemently. "I really need to come in and get the delivery receipt signed, plus you might like to try it on before I leave, make sure it fits?"

The door wobbled to and fro as Mr. Brown indicated his refusal of such a kind offer. "Oh no, I won't be trying it on. There's really no need for that. Do you really need to come in?" His voice seemed hopeful that the answer would be no.

Leslie sighed. He was starting to think he didn't really want to go in there with a man who seemed a little, well, strange, but he knew Laverne would have a hissy fit if he didn't. "I'm afraid I do need the paperwork signed, yes. I won't take up much of your time, I promise."

There was silence and Leslie shuffled from one designer-clad foot to the other in impatience. It was rather chilly outside and his steadily rising nipples chafed underneath his snugly tailored shirt. Finally, Mr. Brown conceded defeat as the door opened wider and a hand swung behind him, bidding Leslie to enter.

Despite his coat, Leslie shivered as he stepped inside. It was lighter now, and he could see the faint glow of lamps from a room to his left. The air was warm and fragranced with sandalwood. He stood with the suit still draped over his arm and raised an enquiring eyebrow as Mr. Brown remained mute in the small entrance hall.

Now that he was closer, Leslie took stock of the man.

His first impressions had been correct: the man *was* attractive. A couple of years older than him, he guessed, and a little taller, his customer had broad shoulders that were encased in a snug-fitting long sleeved dark green shirt. His narrow, tapered waist was evident in his loose chinos, with legs that were muscular and well defined. Mr. Brown's dark blond hair was long, shoulder-length strands falling like a curtain over the right side of his face, obscuring the full view. His square chin and cheeks were covered in thick, light blond stubble and one eye gazed at him curiously and with a modicum of trepidation. Leslie had to say, he approved, but he wished he could see the man's face properly. He was sure he knew him from somewhere.

"Do I know you?" he asked contemplatively. "Perhaps you've been into the business in person and I've seen you there?"

Leslie didn't imagine the shutter coming down on his customer's face as he turned away and motioned Leslie into the lounge on the side of the hallway.

"I doubt it. I haven't been to the fashion house, I'm afraid. Please, come into the lounge and you can leave the suit there. You said you had paperwork to sign?" His tone indicated that he wanted to get this ordeal over as soon as possible.

"Yes, just the delivery receipt. It's in my folder. Where would you like me to put the suit?" He stopped dead and stared wide-eyed around the inside of the lounge. Clearly, appearances were indeed deceiving. The interior was beautifully and tastefully decorated in shades of cream and amber, splashes of colour populating the eye-catching overall canvas of the room in the form of a multitude of cushions on the large buttermilk-coloured couch. Bright, rainbow-coloured paintings reminiscent of Matisse dotted the walls. Plants were in abundance, green foliage spreading wide and welcoming arms; Leslie felt as if he was in some alternate tropical resort. He expected a bird of paradise or a toucan to whizz past his head at any moment.

"Fuck me. This room is bloody gorgeous," he exclaimed then winced as he realised he'd just sworn in front of a client. Laverne would have his balls if she found out. "Err, I'm sorry about the language, I—"

Oliver Brown gave a quiet laugh and waved a hand around the room. "No worries. I've heard the word before, believe me." His tone was dry. "I'm glad you like it. It's my little bit of fantasy living."

Leslie nodded. "Well, it works for me. Uhmm, where do you want me to put the suit?"

Oliver motioned to the back of the couch. "Just lay it across there, and I'll get that paperwork signed for you. Let me go get a pen. I have one in the kitchen." He disappeared out into the hallway again while Leslie laid the suit down reverently, not feeling too bad about its new home now he'd met the man and seen inside his house. He placed his cherished leather folder on the side table as he took another chance to inspect the room, marvelling at the décor—until something distracted him, something that was easily done as he had the attention span of a two-year-old.

"This fucking thong," he cursed loudly as he reached a hand down into the back of his suit pants and tried to remove the stringed offender from his chafing crack. He was so busy with his bout of arse calisthenics that it was only when he heard a polite cough that he looked up to see a flushed, yet slightly amused half-face observing him. Oliver Brown's dark eye—why on earth had Leslie ever thought that name was boring?—obviously found something funny. Or perhaps he was turned on? There was a hungry look in his eye.

Leslie huffed as his face went pink both with the exertion and the embarrassment of being caught with his own hands down his trousers.

"Is everything all right?" Oliver enquired, his face politely schooled. Leslie waved one airy hand, still fidgeting with the other.

"Oh yes, just having a bit of trouble; I seem to have the wrong thong on." Oliver's eyebrow rose ever so slightly and Leslie hastened to explain.

"I mean it's mine, of course, God knows I wouldn't wear anyone else's—but I have one that I thought I'd gotten rid of for exactly this reason and obviously I hadn't. I think this is the *one*!" He ran out of steam at the precise moment when the problem item resolved itself—for now—and he stood looking at Oliver, unsure what else to say. Gamely, he removed his hand out of the back of his pants.

Oliver nodded wisely. "Ah, thongs. Nasty little hobbits, they are." An uncanny mimicry of Gollum left those beautiful full lips and sounded like the real thing.

Leslie blinked. "Wow. That was a damn good impression."

Oliver shrugged modestly. “A talent, I guess. Not that it will do me any good.” His voice was bitter and Leslie suddenly had a burning desire to know what this man’s story was—not to mention seeing his whole face.

Being constantly confronted with half a man’s visage was strangely disquieting in a *Phantom of the Opera* way. He’d noticed that Oliver was careful to keep the hidden side away as much as possible and that where evident, his hair was artfully draped over it. The tantalising knowledge that Leslie was sure he’d seen this man before also was playing havoc with his natural curiosity.

Leslie realised he was staring when Oliver waggled a hand in front of his face and addressed him. “Hello, anyone in there? Could I have the paperwork I need to sign please?”

He sounded a little testy. Leslie reached out for the pen in a bit of a panic that he’d been caught drooling over a client and as he did, his quick action knocked it out of Oliver’s hand. It went flying across the floor and rolled under the couch.

Oliver sighed with exasperation. “Great. Let me get that for you, shall I?”

He placed his hand on the arm of the couch, and bent down to retrieve the pen. As he did so, his shirt rode up above his waist, exposing the small of his back and Leslie really couldn’t help checking it out.

Oliver’s honey-hued skin was smooth and the tautness of his chinos enhanced his rounded arse. Leslie nodded in appreciation then, as he saw something he really hadn’t expected to see, his jaw dropped and a flash of recognition rushed through his body.

Mouth before brain. “Oh my God, I’d know that tramp stamp anywhere. I’ve seen it often enough. You’re Nicky Starr, the porn actor.”

Pen in hand as he straightened, Oliver Brown turned around slowly. His hand unconsciously arranged his hair across the right side of his face. But it was the look on what could be seen of that face that shook Leslie. Composed of panic and anger, but mostly quiet resignation.

They gazed at each other in silence until Leslie blurted out what was on his mind as he tended to do when he was nervous.

“Sorry about the tramp stamp comment.”

Leslie seemed to be apologising to this man a lot. "But that tattoo is pretty unique, so I knew it was you. I know it's been a couple of years since you made any new movies, but it all clicked in my brain when I saw it. You look quite different now what with the long hair and beard."

The tattoo was indeed one of a kind from what Leslie knew. Beautifully detailed and imaginatively drawn, the two-inch-tall image of Yggdrasil, the tree of life, had captured Leslie's eye as he'd watched the man before him perform in more porn sessions that he could remember.

Nicky Starr had been his hero and his man crush (along with others of course, but Nicky had been his favourite). Now the man who'd given him a lot of wet dreams and masturbation material was standing before him.

Leslie continued gushing. "You've been gone, what, nearly two years? I was devastated when you retired. I mean, you're so young…" His voice trailed off as he realised Oliver Brown really didn't seem happy at all that he'd been discovered.

Oliver moved away and turned to look out of the window. His hands trembled. "Are you going to call the newspapers? The radio station perhaps, tell them they have an ex-porn star in their midst?" His voice was rough. "Get your moment of fame by telling everyone where I've been hiding out?"

Leslie stared at him in horror and more than a little growing fury that he was being accused of something so underhanded. "What? No, of course not. Why would I do that?"

Oliver shrugged but still didn't turn around. "Everybody does." His tone was flat but Leslie saw his shoulders stiffen. The man looked as if he was barely holding it together.

"Well, I'm not everybody. So don't taint me with the brush that other arseholes use." He knew that last comment didn't really make much sense but he was upset.

Oliver turned slowly, his tone a little less hostile when he spoke. "I'm sorry. Sometimes it's not easy for me to trust people."

"Yeah, well, I know that feeling," Leslie muttered. "I had a boyfriend who cheated on me for weeks until I found him with his mouth wrapped around a stranger's cock. So I'm a little wary myself." He warmed to his subject. "And this one time, there was this party I went to, where I got a bit drunk, and some of the guys I thought were my friends, decided I'd be good for a gang bang. Luckily a real friend of mine saw I was in trouble and helped me out. But that could have been one nasty night."

Oliver blinked. "You seem to have led quite an eventful life," he murmured, but his face was more relaxed now.

"Not like yours, though." Leslie waved his hands around like a puppet on a string. "I mean, you had it all, hot guys to screw, the high life, all those great parties and then one day you just disappeared. Nobody knew where you'd gone. I nearly cried when you stopped making films. You were one of my all-time favourites."

Oliver's face darkened and a look of intense sadness washed across his golden skin like a gentle wave. "Sometimes we don't have a choice," he said quietly. "I'm not particularly newsworthy any more, but I want my privacy."

Leslie's heart ached and he moved closer to Oliver. He took a deep breath and laid a hand on his arm. "Not being forward or anything, and I know you're a customer and all, but you look like you could use a friend, or maybe a hug."

Panic flared in Oliver's face and he stepped back. "That won't be necessary."

For a moment the two men stared at each other and Leslie felt the spark that flared between them. Oliver was definitely attracted to him—that much was obvious from the look in his eye and the quick glances at Leslie's lips, where Leslie's groin was enjoying the attention, too, as his dick inflated.

Damn thong, it feels like a bloody boa constrictor has my dick. But fuckity fuck. What I can see of this man is simply beautiful. And knowing I've seen him and *his cock in all their glory isn't helping.*

Leslie's discomfort and porn action reminiscences were forgotten as Oliver moved closer and held out his hand, silently indicating the pen and miming a writing action.

Leslie blinked at it and then with a shrug, he picked up his folder and took out the delivery document. He handed it to Oliver who didn't even read it, simply scribbled a signature across the bottom and handed it back.

"Thank you for delivering my suit," he said, his voice strained. "I appreciate that you came all this way out to do it."

The dismissive tone hurt Leslie, who was simply trying to be nice to someone who looked like he needed a shoulder to cry on.

He decided to throw caution to the wind and ignore the vibes of 'Please leave now' that emanated from his customer. It had worked for him before. He was used to people giving in from the force of his obstinacy and 'I'm here, so you'd better get used to me' personality.

"Where did you disappear to, anyway? The newspapers just said you'd retired due to personal reasons. I searched the Internet for months looking for news on you, but I never found anything. Well, apart from a small article that you'd recently had a bike accident but were recovering well. I was going to send you flowers but I couldn't find out where you lived, or which hospital you were in. I rang your agent but they wouldn't tell me anything either."

He ran out of steam and felt a sense of disquiet at declaring himself to be a stalker of note. Oh, God. Perhaps Oliver would have him arrested now and he'd have to spend the night in a smelly cell filled with sexual deviants who'd see him as some sort of twinky glory hole. That thought caused goose bumps to form on his skin and he shivered. Sometimes his overactive imagination was his own worst enemy.

"You've gone very pale," Oliver said cautiously. "Are you okay?"

Leslie was gratified that Oliver had noticed his predicament. "Just wondering how I'd fight off all the bears that wanted to do me in prison," he explained, seeing Oliver's eyes widen in surprise. "I mean, I'm not bad looking, and I doubt I'd last long in there."

Oliver blinked. The man seemed at a loss for words.

"Because it might have sounded like I was, you know, stalking you," Leslie gabbled. "I wasn't really. I was just worried about you. I'd hate to be arrested for caring about someone."

Oliver found his voice and Leslie was pleased to see the start of what looked like a grin on his half face. "I won't be calling the police, I promise. Well, unless it's one of those stripper grams with a night stick."

Leslie snorted then raised a hand to his mouth, mortified. "Oh, God, sorry. I don't usually do that. I think it's just you bringing out the snort in me."

Oliver definitely grinned now, a wide, easy sight that made Leslie's heart speed up and his toes curl. "It was a pretty adorable snort."

Leslie's cock swelled at the compliment and the fact Oliver thought it had been 'adorable.' The thong took its revenge by wrapping silky fingers around him and squeezing. He winced. He wanted nothing more than to take off his trousers and remove the damn thing, but he had a distinct feeling that would definitely get him arrested. Manfully he ignored his restricted nether regions.

"Glad you liked it. I'm sure I have a few more left in me in case you want to hear them?" He cocked his head enquiringly. "You just have to say something else funny."

Oliver's face relaxed. He seemed to be getting over his earlier mood of 'Fuck off out of my house.'

"You're an unusual man, Leslie. I've never met anyone quite like you."

Leslie's face warmed. "I suppose there are worse things to be called than unusual. Thanks." His hands grew animated. "My all-time favourite was that scene where you were the country gentleman and you found that gypsy lad stealing apples from your orchard. *Fruity Encounter* I think it was called. The way you managed that situation was classic. I wished I was that wicked gypsy."

He fondly remembered jacking off to that scene over and over again as the gypsy lad was ravished to within an inch of his life and enjoyed every minute of it. It had been hot, dirty and as sexy as hell. Oliver was a pretty impressive guy down below.

Oliver nodded. "That was me and Leo Loving," he mused, his face pinking delightfully with the recollection. "He was beautiful, inside and out. He's directing his own films now. Serious films too, not porn. He's done really well for himself."

"Oh, he's wonderful," Leslie gushed. "And I remember you and Gregori Golovin. You two had such great on-screen chemistry. Weren't you both an item at some time? Whatever happened to him?"

Oliver's face darkened. "I haven't seen him in a long time. And we're definitely no longer any sort of 'item.'"

From the look on Oliver's face, Leslie knew he'd struck a nerve. He hastened to fix his faux pas. "So why did you stop? Why aren't you doing something else? You had the talent and contacts to do anything you wanted."

The other man turned to face the picture window and gazed out into the garden. Leslie moved up behind him. He had a suspicion he was wearing Oliver Brown down.

"Honestly, Oliver, you look like you could use someone to talk to," he murmured softly, growing more confident to the point of resting a hand on Oliver's shoulder. "And I'm a good listener."

He waited with bated breath for his hand to be shoved off Oliver's shoulder and to be told to go to hell, but all he heard was a deep sigh, a heart-wrenching one that made his soul weep. It was not short of despair.

When Oliver turned, Leslie moved backwards and watched in apprehension as Oliver drew back the shock of hair covering the right side of face. Leslie's horrified gasp sounded loud in the stillness that followed.

Oliver spoke, his tone weary. "You did ask."

A deep, jagged scar marred the tanned skin of Oliver's face. It was about an inch in width, tapering down from the hairline at his forehead to the bottom of his jaw.

While it was healed and a dark pink in colour, it cast a heavy pall on the beauty of his face; his partial beard covered some of it. Various small pockmarks decorated his cheek and jawline like flecks of silver and his right eye drooped slightly on the outside corner. It gave him a strangely oriental look.

"Oh. My. God," Leslie stammered. "What the fuck happened to you?" He couldn't help feeling a spurt of horror in his stomach that one of his heroes should be so tarnished.

Oliver let his hair fall back across his disfigurement. "Motorbike accident."

"Wow. That must have really hurt. I had no idea…" Leslie's voice tailed off. He really didn't know how to express what he was feeling right now. "I can see why you wear your hair over it..." He bit his lips, seeing the look of derision crossing Oliver's features. He had the sinking feeling his reaction had been what Oliver had expected. Now he'd got it, his earlier seemingly more approachable demeanour soured.

"I was stupid and this was the result." Oliver said curtly. "And afterward no one wanted to fuck or be fucked by me so I was washed up in the porn industry. Apparently they were all squeamish about seeing *this* face in the throes of passion, along with the other scars on my body." His bitter tone bled into the room with the acidity of snake venom.

"So now you know. Don't worry. I'm used to it by now. It's why I don't go out much. I can't stand the pity and disgust in people's faces if my hair blows the wrong way."

"I'm not disgusted," Leslie managed to blurt out. "It was just a bit of a shock. I mean, you were so beautiful…"

Again he knew he'd said the wrong thing by the way Oliver's face hardened and the shutters came down again.

"Yes, because having a scar on my face really changes who I am inside," he spat out. His eyes were both angry and disappointed. "I think the freak show is over now. You should leave."

Leslie tried to smooth things over. "Surely you could have stayed in the industry? Perhaps they could have just shot different camera angles, or left your face out of the shots?"

From the black look on Oliver's face, his efforts had backfired. "What the hell? You mean I should have laid down on the bed or whatever and let some guy screw me from behind all the time so no one gets to see my face?" Oliver was scathing.

Leslie's face flushed and he wanted to crawl into a deep, dark hole. That hadn't been the most intelligent thing he'd ever said, he supposed. But he *had* only been trying to help.

"Thank you for delivering my suit, Mr. Scott." Oliver waved toward the front door. "Have a safe journey home or back to the office, or wherever you're going."

Leslie hurried over to the table, picked up his folder and tucked it under his arm. He felt a little sick at how the day had ended when it had started so promisingly. Perhaps he'd send a Jacqui Lawson *Sorry I was such a prat* greeting card later to the man. He didn't know whether that category existed, but in his opinion, it should. He might have to email Jacqui and tell her about his new idea.

"I'm sorry if I offended you in any way. I didn't mean to," he said softly as he opened the door then turned to look at Oliver. "I'm really glad I met you and found out that you're all right. I was really worried about you disappearing like that. I hope you stay well and uhmm, enjoy the suit."

Oliver's face remained impassive although his jaw twitched, and his fingers clenched and unclenched by his side. With one last smile, which Leslie hoped conveyed his apologies once again, he left the house, closing the door gently behind him.

Chapter 4

Oliver slumped against the closed door, his weary sigh echoing in the now quiet entrance.

Why the fuck did I do that?

His regret at having shown his damaged face to that beautiful, exotic specimen of manhood that was Leslie Scott made his stomach roil and his face heat up in embarrassment.

It was a weakness born of loneliness, his inner voice chided.

I push everyone away from me, don't get involved, and then all it takes for me to renege on the promise I made to myself is a black-haired, blue-eyed, incredibly fragranced creature that makes my heart beat faster. A man I wanted to drag into the bedroom to make our own porn movie. My personal fantasy come to life.

In truth, at the first sight of seeing Leslie Scott on his doorstep, Oliver's heart had leapt like a floundering fish and his rather neglected cock had come to life and made its sad presence known.

For a man who'd once made his living with his dick, Oliver certainly wasn't earning any pennies now. His sexual relations with other men were reduced to the occasional discreet escort from an agency he used, plus an occasional fuck with an old friend, Maxwell Lewis, an air steward who visited when he flew into London on one of his whistle-stop stay-overs.

Max was fun, drop-dead gorgeous and rather kinky, and Oliver enjoyed his company. Max was now on a busier overseas route flying in and out of Heathrow, so opportunities to hook up were few and far between.

Oliver was a bit of a hermit. If he had to go out, he'd go to places where the public wouldn't recognise him, or where it was dark. His small circle of friends, who kept his situation private, was his first choice. Then there was this house—both his haven and his prison, a place where he could hide away without the paparazzi and nosey parkers.

His London apartment was known to everyone, so it was currently hired out to some socialite who was regularly in the news. Going to gay clubs to dance and meet people was out of the question; the chances were someone would recognise him and the whole sorry story would have to be told over and over again.

Then Leslie Scott had inveigled his way into Oliver's staid and boring existence. Looking like an exotic bird with his deep blue eyes, fashionably dressed plumage—*that suit he'd worn had been amazing, the lithe body in it even more so*—and a slender, trim-toned body of the type that Oliver hungered after.

Leslie's attempts at trying to cheer Oliver up had been heart-warming and unexpected; his reaction at seeing Oliver's scars for the first time, however, wasn't. Oliver had seen the pity and horror in those sapphire eyes. Leslie hadn't really deserved the contempt Oliver had thrown at him, but he was tired of people's disgust and commiserations.

I fucked up my face and body not my brain, or my personality. I'm still the same person inside.

Thinking of that reminded him of Gregori. Leslie's careless question had cut deep. It had hurt having the love of your life walk out on you *again* after seeing you for the first time in the hospital looking less than pretty.

Oliver's mobile rung, and wearily, he pushed himself off the back of the door and went to the dining room to see who was calling.

He smiled slightly when he saw who it was. "Afternoon, Katie," he said. "How goes it with you?"

A loud, angry, southern U.S. twang assaulted his eardrums. He winced.

"Don't you 'Afternoon, Katie' me, you bastard. Where the hell are you? You're supposed to be here at Fidalgo's, having afternoon tea with me. I've been waiting an hour. Are you on your way?"

Oliver's skin prickled with unease. "No, I'm, er, I'm still at home." Shit. He'd forgotten all about this *tea party*. His best friend went quiet. That was when Oliver knew he was *really* in trouble.

Katie Elizabeth Fotheringham was a force of nature—the offspring of a tornado mated with a tsunami—wrapped in a statuesque, busty, and *in your face* package of Southern belle and old English money.

"You're still at home, leaving me here to sit on my own, looking like some poor girl a fella just jilted at the altar?" Her accent was more pronounced now, a sure sign she was getting fired up for the finale, which was to dress Oliver down fiercely with a side order of *fuck you*.

"I got a bit sidetracked, I had this delivery—" Oliver's ear nearly bled at the shriek that emanated from the phone. He'd deliberately left out the word 'suit' as he knew what Katie would say. And he certainly wasn't going to tell her about the hot piece of tail he'd just met. She'd never give up convincing him to 'go for it.'

"Oliver, you didn't. Another damned suit? Honey child, what on earth are you doing? You have a whole room full of new suits you've never even worn."

Oliver blushed. It was true; he was what Katie laughing called *a closet suitaholic*. He craved suits. He'd worn them extensively as Nicky Starr when he'd modelled in his past life, and taken great pleasure in feeling the fabric against his skin; selecting a tie and cufflinks to go with his chosen attire and strutting out on the town feeling like a million dollars. Oliver Brown knew how to wear a suit, certainly but Nicky Starr…he'd been a connoisseur, a veritable fashion plate. Women and men had drooled over him and his fashion choices.

Oliver sighed in regret. Those days were over now, but still he kept to his tradition of ordering a new suit every month, sometimes more. He figured he had the money, heaps of it, sitting in the bank, so why not indulge in his collecting hobby?

"It's a new Debussy, I just had to have it…" his voice tailed off at the exasperated expletive on the other side of the phone.

"Ollie, honey, get your sexy ass down here right now or I might just have to disown you. I refuse to sit here looking like Lady Leftalone. I'll wait for you and order you a salad. That at least won't get cold while I sit here and twiddle my thumbs."

The phone clicked off and Oliver gazed at it and heaved another sigh. It was only ten minutes by tube to see Katie. Oliver enjoyed travelling the tubes where no one cared about each other, where it was all strangers with a complete disinterest for one's fellow man.

Sometimes when he was really lonely, Oliver would hop on one and travel as far as he could then come back again.

He huffed angrily at that reminder of just how pathetic he'd become and stalked through to the bedroom to change. He'd better get his arse into gear and make his way down to the little coffee place not too far away. It was quiet, secluded and the manager knew him well enough to know he didn't want any attention.

Oliver would hate to feel the wrong side of Katie's fist in his ribs. That woman packed a mean punch.

* * *

It was close to six p.m. when Oliver got home. He was both mentally and physically exhausted. He loved Katie, but she was hard work. They'd met on the set of one of his porn shoots; she'd been writing an article for a well-known lifestyle magazine on the relative difficulties of sustaining a true relationship given what the men involved did for a living. It had been a tasteful, sensitive article, highlighting the conflicts between separating the day job from the emotional and physical needs of having a lover, and had focused on the few monogamous relationships in the crew that Oliver had worked with.

Katie had been with him when he'd woken up, bleeding and broken in the hospital, in the aftermath of his coke-and-drink-fuelled orgy. She'd been his rock and his tormentor through the weeks and months that followed, refusing to give up on him.

Oliver poured himself a drink and sat down in the armchair overlooking the tatty garden. He got comfortable and draped his legs over the chair arm as he sat back at an angle, sipping his gin and tonic.

His iPad sat on the side table and he picked it up and idly flicked through his social networking sites. He used the name Justin Brown on most of them, Justin being his middle name, but kept his private details hidden and interacted only as much as he needed. It kept him in touch with the outside world to some small extent.

Oliver frowned when he saw a particular email in an inbox he monitored but had no reason to use any longer. It was on his old website, *www.nickystarr.co.uk*. The site was still active but he hadn't refreshed it in years. He still received a mountain of emails, mostly from men asking him if he was around either to fuck or be fucked. He ignored them all, but this one piqued his interest when he saw it was a Jacqui Lawson e-card sent by one Leslie Scott. Surely, it couldn't be the same man, could it? Curious, he opened it.

The card was called 'Monkey Business' and as Oliver watched, his lips curved in a smile. *This man is seriously goofy*. He was also cute as a button, plus stunningly beautiful. Oliver couldn't deny the warm feeling in his chest at the fact Leslie had actually taken the trouble to send him the card in the hope it would find him. When the little sketch with the organ grinder and the monkey had finished, the card read,

I hope you get this. Your website is one of my most browsed. Sorry I was such an idiot. I really didn't mean to offend you so I hope you can forgive me if I said anything. Sometimes my mouth runs away with me.

Oliver snorted with laughter, feeling cheerier than he had in a while. He didn't doubt the truth of *that* statement.

I'd appreciate the chance to make it up to you. I'm giving you my mobile number and perhaps you'll call me and we can have coffee sometime. I'm not a stalker, promise.

Your # 1 Fan, Leslie Scott.

PS I pinkie swear that I only told my two BFFs about you. They won't talk. They know better. I honestly couldn't NOT tell them

Another statement Oliver didn't doubt, even though it made him a little twitchy.

PPS I hope you get a chance to wear the suit. I think you'd look awesome in it.

A mobile number was listed at the end.

Glowing warmly inside, Oliver thought that maybe he might have made another friend. Someone who'd seen him at his worst and still wanted to be with him. He might just take Leslie up on his offer of coffee soon.

His old porn slogan, 'Get it On' flitted across his mind. Perhaps he'd do exactly that. The thought made him fall asleep with a soppy grin on his face.

Chapter 5

"Leslie. There you are." Laverne's strident tones echoed in Leslie's ears. He stopped what he was doing, which was unpacking a recently arrived bale of silk into the storage cupboard, and smiled. He always welcomed an opportunity to speak with his boss.

"Morning, boss. And may I say you look stunning today? Very professional."

Dressed in a smart grey suit of her own design, with a ruffled white blouse and heels Leslie would kill for, Laverne grinned back with pale pink lips. "Well, thanks for noticing," she chirruped as she came to a halt before him. "I have a meeting with the bank today so I thought I'd better tone it down a bit." Laverne smiled wickedly. "I don't want to overshadow them with my more fabulous self when I'm asking them to give me money."

She grimaced as Leslie quickly finished arranging the bale *just so* on the shelf and closed the door. "I hate the bastards, watching their eyes glaze over when they see me then having to kow-tow to their officious arses. I suppose that's just the way of it."

Leslie nodded sagely. "My bank manager always insists on calling me Mr. Scott, which makes me feel like my dad and then proceeds to tell me yet again what an overdraft is made for." He sniffed. "Apparently it's not supposed to go over the limit all the time, and he gets quite agitated when I try to explain that that's what I thought it was *for*. Hence the word, *over*. I've no idea what the 'draft' thingie comes from though. That doesn't make any sense at all. I mean, that's something a writer does, like, with his first story, or when a cold wind blows through your door." Leslie shrugged.

Laverne chuckled, a deep, amused sound that made her broad shoulders shake. "Oh, I'd love to be a fly on the wall when you speak to your bank manager. You are too damn adorable."

Leslie grinned. "Maybe next time he phones me up with that apprehensive quiver in his voice, I should take you with me as my financial advisor. Now *that* would be a fun meeting."

Laverne rolled her eyes and snorted. "Leslie Scott, you are a demon incarnate. I wouldn't wish the two of us on any unsuspecting bank manager. Now, sweetie, I need a BIG favour from you." Her eyes glinted with mischief.

Leslie's gut roiled just a little.

"What do you need?" he asked cautiously, casting a furtive eye at the door in case someone was looking for him and he could be called away.

"Well, Dasher can't make it to the fashion show tomorrow night, some family emergency, so I need you to fill in for him." Laverne showed white teeth as she smiled.

Leslie's arse clenched in fear. "Oh hell, no. No way. Nuh-huh. Not me."

Dasher Godfrey was an icon in the fashion team, a man with nerves of steel and an unrelenting demeanour of tough, no-holds-barred attitude, who rousted all the models for the fashion shows and ensured they got on the catwalk on time and appropriately attired. It was a job he relished and everyone else dreaded. For him not to make it to an event, the family emergency had to be dire.

The models, male and female alike, with a few exceptions, it had to be said, were known in the company as *the spawn from hell*, and Leslie had no desire to be their next meal.

Laverne tut-tutted. "Now, Leslie, I know you can do it. Dasher isn't there but Bruce is, so all you'll really be doing is helping him herd the troops, do little jobs, stuff like that. Nothing too onerous."

The news that Bruce Mitchell, Dasher's part-time and very put-upon assistant, would be there was definitely a more palatable idea, but still Leslie demurred. "Laverne, you simply *cannot* ask that of me. I know nothing about getting the demons ready for the show, and hell, Dasher has an ulcer, is that what you want to do to me as well—"

A large, warm finger shut his flapping lips.

"Leslie, you can do it. And think of this as another thing to add to your CV. If you want to work in this industry, honey, you need to man up and grow a pair and face the terror that is the dressing room. It will be a wonderful experience for you." The finger was removed and Leslie opened his mouth to argue but Laverne waggled that finger in front of his face.

"No, no, no. It's a done deal. Tomorrow night, six p.m., at Mystique. I'll tell Brucie you're more than happy to help." With an airy wave and a waggle of her taut, muscled bottom, Laverne left the storeroom, no doubt prowling down the corridor to find another victim for a life-or-death favour.

Leslie scowled. “Crap and fuck,” he muttered to himself as he picked up another bale of silk ready to pack away. “That’s all I need.” His face brightened as an idea came to him. “Maybe I can convince Taylor to come out tomorrow night with me and help. Eddie’s had his turn to keep me company so I have a feeling Tay may be next to be subjected to the puppy-dog-eyed look. I did share my secret with him, after all.”

Having met the infamous Nicky Starr, Leslie had been catapulted to almost superstardom in Eddie and Taylor’s eyes. They enjoyed his films as much as Leslie and were keen to encourage him to pursue *Oliver Brown,* as it meant they might get to meet him, too. He’d made them pinkie swear not to tell anyone, including Gideon and Draven, even though he knew that was a lost cause. Eddie couldn’t keep a secret. His freckled face was too expressive. But Leslie knew he could trust all four men to keep Oliver’s situation under wraps.

Buoyed with his idea of having moral support and having backup for the event from hell tomorrow night, he finished packing the material and then went in search of sustenance in the form of Red Bull and a chicken Caesar salad.

* * *

“Kill me. Kill me now.” Leslie’s muttered growl was aimed at his rather limp BLT sandwich as he took the last savage bite out of it and threw away the empty wrapper. He glowered as he surveyed the maelstrom of activity that was the models’ changing room. Beautiful men and women in various stages of undress assailed his weary eyes. His fingers were pricked bloody through various efforts to pin up fabric and tuck away bits that both the models and Laverne deemed unsuitable. He was bone tired, ratty and ready to go home.

He’d known he wasn’t cut out for the constant pandering and sycophancy that went with keeping a fleet of highly paid divas in control, but this evening had been more than he could bear.

And that traitor Taylor, whom he’d thought would be sympathetic to his woes, was chatting up the naked man-hottie, a model called Reuben, on the other side of the room, and he was smiling and laughing as if he was born to be in a room with dicks, crotches, bums, tits and other unmentionables that Leslie wasn’t prepared to name. Leslie wondered spitefully if his fiancé, Draven, knew about his lover’s proclivity to flirt like a man-slut.

“Saying the forbidden name Voldemort has nothing on this,” he muttered darkly. “There are lady bits everywhere…I can’t even…” He shuddered. One of the models, Sasha, aimed a gimlet eye in his direction, and he closed his eyes, wishfully thinking if he couldn’t see her, she wouldn’t see him. It was a fruitless exercise. When he opened them, she stood in front of him, dressed only in a blue, sequinned thong which he might have fancied himself, her pert breasts only two inches from his face.

Leslie swallowed at having so much female flesh in close proximity. One of her manicured hands held out a stick of what looked like chalk.

“Rouge me,” Sasha demanded and he stared at her blankly. From the corner of his eye he noticed Taylor glancing his way and moving toward him.

“Err, what?” Leslie said blankly.

Sasha clucked in impatience and stepped back a little. “Rub this,” she held up the chalk, “On these.” With her other hand, she indicated her breasts.

Leslie’s jaw dropped wide open. Of all the things he’d had to do tonight, this had to be the worst.

“Why?” he said feebly. “I mean, you’re going to be wearing something over them. A suit, aren’t you? No one will see them…” His voice tailed off at the narrowed and angry eyes of the model.

“*I* will know,” she imperiously. “It is a custom for me, and I want you to do it. Now. Put it on my nipples.”

She forced the chalk into Leslie’s hands and his gut churned. If Laverne hadn’t been watching him with hawk eyes from the other side of the room, he’d have turned tail and run.

“I’d suggest you get to it, Leslie.” Taylor’s barely contained chuckle at his side caused Leslie to glower darkly at his friend. “I mean, you don’t want to mess with Sasha’s traditions, do you? That’s bad luck.” He snorted loudly.

“Fuck you,” Leslie mouthed at him. Taylor bent over in laughter.

“*Da*.” Sasha nodded fiercely, her eyes conveying her approval of Taylor’s words. “Bad luck not to do it.” She thrust her chest and dusky nipples out toward Leslie. He gave a heart-wrenching sigh of resignation and with shaking hands, raised the reddish chalk towards the pinnacles of female perfection. Wincing, he circled one with the chalk, once, twice then did the same to the other. The nipples now stood out darkly against Sasha's tanned skin and she stared at them critically. Then she bestowed a dazzling smile on Leslie and leaned forward to kiss him on the forehead.

"*Spaseeba*," she squealed, turned and disappeared with a flourish of tanned, very firm arse. Leslie levelled his fiery gaze at Taylor who was struggling to keep his composure.

"You are such a prick," he said evenly as Taylor gasped in amusement.

"I have one of those, yes," Taylor spluttered. "Oh God, Leslie, your face. It was too damn precious. You looked as if someone had asked you to eat a baby."

"That might have been preferable," Leslie muttered. "Honestly, what else are these people going to expect me to do tonight?"

His question was answered sooner than he'd anticipated. Another of the models, Bernsen Jenner, sauntered over, all one hundred and fifty pounds of him, stark naked, with a dick that looked as if it could be used as a third leg to kick start a jumbo jet.

Bernsen waved toward his crotch. Leslie stared and he noticed Taylor was having a good look, too.

"Leslie, my dumpling," he crooned. "I need you to trim some stray hairs for me. My B is looking a little untidy."

Leslie shook his head in disbelief at the vision that was Bernsen's crotch. His groin was artfully shaved with the initials B and J either side of the meaty appendage that swung between his legs. This was still better than dealing with lady parts, and Leslie was quick to nod his head. After all, dicks and balls were more his speciality.

"Sure," he burbled, "Glad to." He reached over to a nearby dressing table and grabbed a pair of clippers.

"More your thing, then," whispered Taylor in his ear as he continued staring at Bernsen's dick. "I'm really glad you invited me tonight. This has been an awesome evening."

"Uh huh," Leslie said as he knelt down before Bernsen, feeling uncomfortably as if he was about to give a blow job. "Wait until I tell Draven how much you enjoyed yourself."

He revelled in the sight of Taylor's discomfort at that veiled threat as he worked. Bernsen gave a mournful sigh as he watched Leslie busy himself tidying up the man's bush, pushing his dick away gently to one side.

"You pay two hundred pounds for a manscape and this is what you get," the model fretted. "There is no sense of service anymore. Everyone is just out for a fast buck."

Leslie nodded. "Well, I manscape, too. Sometimes I do it myself and sometimes I go to the salon. And it looks nothing like *this*." He narrowed his eyes as he snipped stray hairs. "Is this one of your pre-show customs then, Bernsen?"

The model gave him a sly look from under perfectly manicured eyebrows. "Custom? No, my plum, I just think you are too adorable and I like your hands on my body."

Leslie blushed pink in pleasure. He finished up and stood back to admire his handiwork. In truth, he thought that there was little difference, but he'd tried to make Bernsen happy.

The model looked down and inspected his groin. "Looks better. Thank you, my sweetheart." He patted Leslie's head and turned and disappeared into the throng that milled around.

Leslie chuckled. "I love the whole BJ thing. I wonder if he gets much action with that design. Do you think he just drops his pants and pushes his crotch out at someone and he gets an instant blow job?"

Taylor flapped a hand. "I'm still in shock finding out how much he paid for the damn shave. I'd have done it for him at half the price. The shave, not the BJ. Although…" He leered and Leslie pursed his lips.

"You, my friend, are a complete tart." He grinned. "That makes two of us. I still wouldn't have paid that much though for a treatment."

Just then, Camilla, one of the models currently standing around, waiting to be dressed, gave a loud unladylike snort. She put her thumbs in her barely there, canary yellow thong and pulled them down. "Huh. What do you think *this* is?' She indicated her crotch and stared at him.

Leslie wasn't really sure what she was asking or pointing to. There was so much bronzed and pink-lipped flesh on display he felt a little nauseous.

"Uhmm, a vagina?" he proffered weakly.

The model gave him a withering glance. "Darling, you are definitely *so* gay if you think a woman's vagina is on the outside of her body."

Leslie's face heated up at the sniggers around him—Taylor's the loudest. "I know where a woman's vagina is," he said haughtily. "But honestly, I wasn't sure what you were pointing to." He swallowed. "It was rather open to interpretation, really."

Taylor's chuckles grew louder and Leslie turned to glare at his amused friend. Bruce had joined them and was watching the proceedings with laughter on his face.

Camilla's hand waved at her crotch. "This, my clueless friend, is a *three* hundred-pound wax job. We all pay a lot to look as good as we do. So I don't think your Bic razor job comes close." She sniffed and stalked off as Leslie watched her, open-mouthed.

"Bitch," he sniffed. "I don't use a Bic."

Taylor exploded in laughter, his face pink. Despite himself, a smile tugged at Leslie's lips. "Bastards," he said affably at Taylor. "If you were forced to stare at women's bits, I'd bet you'd sing a different tune." He cast a glance at Bruce. "Except you, old man, because everyone knows you *love* the ladies…"

Bruce guffawed. "Working around this lot of divas is enough to put you off 'em for life," he snorted. "But I do admit this job has its perks."

* * *

An hour later Leslie was sitting in a small storage cupboard, surrounded by various old props, clothing, towels and smelly laundry. He'd had enough of everyone, so he'd slunk away to check his emails and texts for the first time that day. His overriding hope was that Oliver had responded to his cute monkey card. Leslie had known it was a long shot but he lived forever in hope. He made himself comfortable on a pile of old towels, stretched his legs out before him and heaved a sigh of relief as he pulled out his smartphone. No one would think to look for him in here.

He wrinkled his nose in distaste at the reek in the room. "Smells freaky," he grumbled to himself. "But at least it's private and I can think."

He flicked quickly through his messages and his heart skipped a beat when he got to his texts. In fact, Leslie was sure he squealed like a *Supernatural* fan meeting Dean up close and personal. "He texted me!"

Hands trembling with excitement, he opened the message.

Hi Leslie. Got yr card. Tks, it was rly cool. Hope u r well. Coffee sounds gd. Oliver.

Leslie sat back against the wall and took a deep breath. "Oh hell. He wants to go for coffee." He texted back quickly.

OMG, gd to hear from u. Glad u lkd card. When do u wnt to meet up?

His eyes watched the small screen, willing a reply. After about ten minutes had elapsed, he sighed.

He's probably not got his phone on him.

Leslie kept telling himself that even after the day from hell ended. Taylor had been philosophical about the fact Oliver had texted him, but not called back yet.

"Give him some time," he'd advised, a twinkle in his eye. "He might have lost signal or something. Maybe give it a day or so, see if he gets back to you."

* * *

Now Leslie was home in his small, minimally decorated apartment, curled up on the couch with his favourite fuzzy socks on and a warm tracksuit. He wouldn't been seen dead in what he called his *sloth clothes* in public, but at home, on his own, he rather enjoyed the freedom to be a slob. It was hard work looking as good he did all the time.

He fed his fish, added an extra castle he'd bought to the fish tank so Glenda, a small clown fish, could try something new—the fish seemed to have a thing for hiding behind castles—then made himself a cup of hot chocolate.

He watched the news on television with eyes that barely took it in and kept darting to his phone every five minutes. When the phone finally rung and he was dozing on the large red throw pillow, he sat up with a start. The strident tones of Lady Gaga's 'Born This Way' echoed in the stillness of his lounge and he scrambled dozily for his mobile. It was an unknown caller and for a moment, Leslie was tempted not to answer. He'd been the subject of harassment before from a guy he'd given his number to and now he was a little wary. The thought in his head though that this could be Oliver calling made him waive his natural tendency to ignore the insistent ringing and he answered.

"This is Leslie." He mentally crossed his fingers hoping psycho stalker Brian hadn't managed to track him down.

"Leslie?" The hesitant voice on the other side made Leslie want to squee in delight.

It was him.

"Oliver?"

"Uhmm, yes. You recognise my voice then?" He sounded amused and Leslie's heart beat faster.

"Of course. It's only been a couple of weeks since I saw you. My memory isn't that bad."

"Yeah, I'm sorry it took so long to reply to you. I was…busy." There was a short silence. "I thought we could meet up somewhere on Thursday evening. You know, just for a chat and a cup of coffee." His voice was hesitant but firm.

Leslie pursed his lips.

Ah, setting the expectations. He sounds a little skittish. I can be his friend if that's all he wants. I don't want to scare him off. I know I can be a bit…intense.

"I'd like that; coffee sounds good. If you text me the address where you want to meet, I can meet you there after work on Thursday."

"Uh, sure. It's a little place called Fidalgo's, not far from my house. I'll text you the details. The owner knows me, so just mention my name when you get there and he'll show you through."

Leslie nodded happily. "That sounds good. I look forward to it."

Oliver sounded more relaxed when next he spoke. "Yeah, me, too. It'll be good to chat to you. I'll see you then."

The phone went silent and Leslie did a little jig around the lounge. He saw Mrs. Camberwell from across the courtyard in the opposite block of flats watching him from her window.

He pranced over to the large picture window and waved. "Hi, Mrs C. I've got a coffee date with a porn star—well, ex porn star." He knew she couldn't hear him but she waved back and disappeared.

Ever since he'd danced naked in front of the window one evening and she'd seen him, she'd been very friendly. He'd been rather drunk at the time, he had to admit. Luckily she hadn't seen the sexual calisthenics that had occurred after Leslie's date had pulled him back from his exhibition of Michael Flatley's *Riverdance* routine and pushed him onto his knees on the carpet. The guy—Darren, Darryl?—had had the presence of mind to close the curtains before fucking him senseless.

That image brought back some fond memories. After sending a message to both Taylor and Eddie with the joyful news Oliver had called him back, Leslie used that memory to jack off later to the face of Nicky Starr in his heyday, blissfully content that on Thursday, he'd get to meet the real man behind the mystery.

Chapter 6

Oliver sat at his usual table at Fidalgo's, his fingers nervously tapping the red-chequered tabletop. His stomach was in knots and he'd barely slept last night. He'd even thought of crying off today and telling Leslie that something had come up and he wouldn't make it. However, the thought of Katie—who'd highly approved of the coffee plan—bitching at him for *not* going was worse than the alternative.

And he really did want to see Leslie again. He'd thought of nothing more from their last phone call. It would be good to talk someone who was so bright and bubbly and, he admitted to himself, sex on a stick. Although that wasn't what he wanted from this, he reminded himself. He needed a friend, not a lover. And besides, he doubted Leslie would be interested in him that way. He probably had a string of undamaged goods at his beck and call.

For God's sake, stop analysing everything and get on with it.

Despite that thought, his cock throbbed in his black jeans when he saw Leslie enter the coffee shop. The man looked like he had just stepped out of a fashion magazine. Dressed in tight black chinos, finished with high-heeled black boots, with a white collared shirt and a leather jacket, wearing the biggest pair of sunglasses Oliver had ever seen, Leslie looked mouth-wateringly tempting. His jet black hair was styled artfully over his face, one strand of hair falling down, making Oliver want to brush it away. He took Oliver's breath away.

Down boy, he cautioned himself. *Keep it simple. Just friends, remember?*

Alberto, the owner, approached Leslie and gestured, then his coffee date looked over to where Oliver sat and the most beautiful smile flooded his face.

Oh dear God, Oliver thought desperately. *I am in so much fucking trouble.*

He didn't dare stand up for fear the hard-on he sported would spring free in celebration of Leslie's presence. Instead he remained seated, uncomfortably so, and as Leslie approached the table, he waved at the chair opposite, willing his erection to go down with thoughts of copulating old men with hairy bodies and limp dicks.

"Leslie. Glad you could make it."

Leslie seated himself at the table and flashed another grin. "I like this place. Very trendy. And that guy on the front desk is yummy." His blue eyes cast a mischievous glance toward Enrico, one of Alberto's sons who'd just arrived at the reception stand. Enrico looked down at the desk, a smile on his face. A sudden rush of jealousy assailed Oliver.

Where the hell did that come from?

He quashed the unreasonable emotion and waved toward one of the passing waiters. "What kind of coffee would you like?"

"Oh, just a plain latte for me. I'm not one of those 'caramel macchiato, venti, skim, extra shot, sugar free, no foam, extra hot' crazy people."

Oliver blinked. "That's a drink?"

Leslie huffed. "Oh my God, yes. Before I got this job at Debussy, I worked at Starbucks. You cannot believe the fussiness of some people out there with their coffee orders. I needed a dictionary sometimes to look up some of the words they used."

Drinks ordered, they settled into chat about the recent week. Leslie's hilarious account of his evening at the fashion event, including the side-splitting nipple-rouging, made Oliver laugh as he hadn't in years. Leslie's dry, sarcastic account of his escapades was delivered in a voice that Oliver thought could melt hearts, and his facial expressions and hand gestures were classic. His sides were aching when Leslie finished his story and threw him another dazzling smile.

"So that's my week. What have you been doing with yourself then?" His eyes slid appraisingly down Oliver's body. Oliver's dick took notice.

"I have to say, that colour green really suits you." Leslie murmured. "That shirt brings out the colour of your eyes and the cut is really flattering. But then what would you expect from a Ralph Lauren?" He shrugged slim shoulders as he removed his sunglasses and tucked them into his man bag.

Oliver had spent close to two hours debating what to wear and the fact he'd chosen well made his body glow. "It's an old favourite. Team it with comfortable jeans and it's a no-brainer for a coffee date."

Leslie's eyes met his and Oliver's hand moved unconsciously to his hair as he made sure it covered his scar.

"You look perfect," Leslie said softly. "Honestly, stop worrying about it."

"It's a habit," Oliver muttered. "Especially when I'm out in public." His hand strayed to his hair again and he took a deep breath when Leslie reached across and stayed his nervous movement. Leslie's touch ignited something in his heart and his groin.

"I'm not the public." Leslie said softly. "I'm just someone hoping to be your friend."

Oliver nodded then moved his hands away from his hair and picked up his coffee. Leslie unnerved him like no one in a long, long time. "I think that can be arranged." He grinned and the awkward moment passed.

An hour later there was a lull in the conversation as Enrico bought them another cup of coffee. Oliver frowned. Enrico didn't normally do table duty. In fact, he hated being a waiter, considering it beneath him as the owner's son. Oliver scowled as Leslie flirted and their waiter's normally monosyllabic responses got chattier. Oliver's ire grew even worse when he pressed a business card into Leslie's hand with the whisper to 'call me.'

"That guy is a prick," Oliver growled when Enrico was out of earshot. "I don't want to interfere in your love life, but you should know that."

Leslie's eyes widened innocently. "But he's so darned cute." He laughed as Oliver growled again and drained his coffee cup. "I tell you what, let's forget about the hot Italian stud over there and tell me more about yourself. I'm dying to know what you've been doing the last couple of years, being out of the industry. What do you do for a living? Do you have a job?"

Oliver nodded. “I do web design. Mostly, I get referrals and build customised sites for people. It’s a good living and I’m lucky—I have rather a captive clientele.” He cleared his throat. “I build a lot of adult sites, sex aid sites, some BDSM ones, that sort of thing.”

Leslie’s eyes got bigger. “Oh my God, really? How cool. Give me some examples; let’s see if I know any of them.”

Oliver leaned back in his chair. “Well, I built Leo’s new site, Leo Loving, but that wasn’t porn. It was his new film studio site. Then there was Donny Dickson, Jerry Jarvis and that new guy, Luke Lecher.” He grimaced at Leslie’s snort. “I know, terrible name. What’s with these guys and all the alliteration? But the guy threw a lot of money at me to create his website so I tried to give him what he wanted. ”

Oliver was enjoying himself. He didn’t really get to talk about his current work much. He warmed to his subject. “There’s something about sitting in front of a computer and listening to what a client wants, then trying to put it all together. It’s pretty creative, actually, to try and be different, when everyone thinks a porn site is all about hot bods and fucking. Of course that’s the main thing, but there’s also the merchandising aspect, the advertising revenues, the ability to let your fans interact with you too, and share their fantasies. It’s about creating something special where people can lose themselves. I created the Nicky Starr site myself and let me tell you, it’s damned hard work.” He stopped at the look of merriment on Leslie’s face. “What?”

“God, you are such a geek. It’s adorable.” Leslie’s blue eyes twinkled with mirth.

Oliver flushed. He *had* been rambling a bit. “Sorry, I get carried away sometimes.”

“I love it,” Leslie purred. “It’s a bit like me when I talk fashion and fabrics. Then all anyone wants to do is stuff something in my mouth to make me shut up.”

And didn’t *that* thought make Oliver harder than a stick of dynamite. His expression must have communicated his thoughts because Leslie’s pale face pinked up.

“Oh, wait, I didn’t mean it *that* way…”

Oliver couldn’t help himself. He burst out laughing and soon Leslie had joined in and they were both chortling like school kids.

Enrico cast them a dirty glance—Oliver thought it might have been directed at him.

When the dirty thoughts stopped circling his brain at just how much he'd like to shut Leslie up, Oliver wiped his eyes.

"Hell. That just tickled me." For one brief moment, he forgot his scar and tucked the hair that hung down his face behind his right ear. No sooner had he realised what he'd done, than he flicked it back again in panic, covering it up.

Leslie leant forward and ran a warm finger down his jawline, taking care not to touch the jagged scar. Oliver hadn't had anyone touch that side of his face in years. His heart and body thrummed with need and yearning.

"Maybe one day you'll tell me exactly how you got that." Leslie moved his hand away as Oliver swallowed and then looked down at the table. A long moment later, he looked up into Leslie's cerulean eyes. They were warm and there was no pity in them.

I can do this.

He took a deep breath. "I was twenty-three and I thought I was immortal. Untouchable. It was the height of my career and I had everything a man could want. A career, more money than I knew what to do with and a radical motorbike." His lips twisted in a smile. "His name was Hulk and he was huge and green just like Bruce Banner when he turned. I'd been to a party and got shit-faced on coke." He stopped, his throat dry. "I was pretty addicted to the stuff. It helped me cope with the demands of performing and the pressure to be *someone* constantly." He didn't want to get into the reason for him being at that party that night and getting out of control. That was a story for another time.

Leslie's calm face watched him without judgement. The only trace of emotion in his face was the slight tic in his jaw.

"That night all the guys wanted to check out the porn star, see how good he was. I ended up screwing about three or four of them. I needed some encouragement so I was as high as a bloody kite. Coke and booze. Then I got on Hulk to race one of them. It was a macho display that everyone knew wouldn't end well. But I didn't listen." He closed his eyes as the memories flooded back. "I hit a bend, slid and then hit the side of the road. It was pretty rocky and I went flying, straight over a barbed wire fence and into a field. The thing was, there was a load of scrap metal in a pile in the middle of the grass and it ripped my face and my right arm wide open, as well as the side of my body."

Leslie made a small sound of horror and reached over to take Oliver's hand in his. Oliver curled his large fingers around Leslie's fine-boned ones. The touch of the other man grounded him and he carried on.

"I broke some ribs, my left arm and a couple of my fingers. I had a ruptured spleen and as well as the side of my face being damaged, it affected my eye. Tore the muscle which is why it droops slightly. My right arm was virtually ripped open from wrist to shoulder and I have bad scarring along it, along with a bit of muscle loss. But physical therapy helped me get it back to almost normal. It just aches sometimes and I can't pick up anything too heavy."

"Oh my God." Leslie's face was white and Oliver saw his eyes glistening. "I'm so glad you made it out alive. I mean, it could have been much worse."

Oliver sighed tiredly. "I was very lucky to avoid blood poisoning afterward. The emergency services were quick to get me to hospital, and I had the best medical care money could buy. My film studio, Vanguard, went all out on that one." He tightened his fingers around Leslie's.

"I spent a long time in hospital, having plastic surgery and skin grafts for it all." His memories of the pain and frustration he'd suffered through too many surgical procedures made his stomach lurch. "And this…" he motioned toward his face, "was the end result." He gave a twisted smile. "As well as some other nice scars."

Rounded off by having my lover of a year walk out because he couldn't stand the sight of me. And getting over a cocaine addiction.

"Where was your family?" Leslie asked. "Didn't your parents help you though this?"

Oliver shook his head ruefully. "My folks live in Australia. Dad works a low-paid job and Mum is a housewife. They still don't know about my time in the porn industry. I didn't want them ever knowing either, so I didn't tell them about the accident until after it was all over and I was much better. They had no money to come out here. It would have bankrupted them and they may have found out what their son was doing." He gave a tired laugh. "I just told them I'd had a fall off the bike but never told them how bad it was. I haven't seen them face-to-face in years. We Skype now and then and I make sure they can't see my face properly."

"God, that's so sad, having to lie to your folks like that. My folks live in Scotland with my older brother, Nathan. I see them now and then." Leslie managed a wistful smile. "I think you look a lot like Jon Bon Jovi with that shaggy-hair look. He's damn hot; well, he was when he had that hair style. And I rather like the metrosexual bearded look."

"Thank you," Oliver said softly. "I don't get too many compliments anymore on how I look."

Leslie's eyes narrowed and he leaned forward, pursing soft lips that Oliver really wanted to kiss. "That, my friend, is because you don't get out much. It's your own damn fault for hiding away in that house with only a wardrobe of suits to keep you company." He grinned and Oliver's insides melted. "I know about your love of them, of course. I've seen your website. Plus I looked back at your purchases. You, my friend, have a problem. You must have bought about twenty suits from Debussy's over the past couple of years." He made a moue. "Not that it's a problem. Keeps me in a job buying that fabric you love so Laverne can make your suits. She loves you, by the way. You're her best customer."

Oliver chuckled. "No doubt she does. Her designs just have this appeal for me; they're so classic and sexy. I can't help myself."

Leslie cluck clucked. "Then we need to get you out and about in them more. Show you off."

Oliver shook his head, his heart heavy. "Not going to happen, Leslie. I go out only when I have to. Otherwise I'm fine by myself. I've managed so far."

Leslie's eyes softened. "I didn't mean get you out in the middle of a film premiere with 101 cameras sighted on you, doofus. I meant perhaps going to a great dinner in an intimate restaurant where I know the owner will protect your privacy and chase away anyone that bothers you. Gideon can be pretty scary when he wants to be."

Oliver had to say the idea tempted him, both getting into a new suit to go out and spending more time with Leslie. He nodded hesitantly. "Maybe we can do that." His heart beat a little faster. "Are you asking me out on a date, Leslie?"

Leslie looked taken aback then shook his head. "No, as one friend to another. Now that my two housemates have both moved in with the men of their dreams, I'm no longer part of a threesome. I miss having someone to hang out with."

Oliver raised an eyebrow. He couldn't deny he was a little disappointed at Leslie's response this wasn't a date. "A threesome? Are you into ménage then?" It was something he'd been involved in many times in his porn career and perhaps a few times after he retired. He was taken aback by his coffee partner's vehement response.

"Hell, no. I'm not into that sort of thing." Leslie's beautiful face contorted in a frown. "I know you are, but to tell you the truth, they weren't my favourite scenes of you. I prefer my actions man-on-man, not men-on-men."

"Oh." Oliver was nonplussed. "There's a lot of that in the industry. Sometimes I had to do the scenes, and they were fun, but not a personal preference." He shrugged.

"I want a relationship, not a fuck-fest," Leslie muttered. "Some of the guys I went out with in the past, all they wanted me for was to be the meat in the middle of a man sandwich and sometimes I had to think quickly to get out of being the hole in a full on gang bang."

Oliver gaped as the rising fury in his chest surfaced. "Did they try and force you? Did anyone hurt you? I swear I'll fuck them up—"

Leslie's face lit up and he laughed as he placed a warm hand on Oliver's. "Oh God, that is so damn sweet. My protector. No, sometimes it got a bit hairy balls and I had to make a swift exit, but I was always careful." His face fell. "Well, apart from this one time I already mentioned, when a friend saved me from a fate worse than death because he can see things. He knew I was in trouble and came to find me." He smiled wryly, holding up his thumb and index finger only slightly apart. "I was this close to being mauled by a couple of guys who I still think slipped me something in my drink, but my friend Taylor found me. He's a psychic."

That offhand comment left Oliver curious. "Really? A real one?" He'd never met someone with that particular talent before.

Leslie nodded, eyes sparkling. "Oh, yeah. He saved Eddie's cousin Luke when he tried to kill himself, and he helped solve a suicide, and he even helped Draven's little brother move onto the other side when he managed to contact him somewhere." He flapped a vague hand. "Somewhere in between here and heaven I suppose, and Draven turned off Jude's life support and we all hope he's gone somewhere really cool to be with his parents. They're dead, too."

Oliver was reeling from all the names and information thrown at him in this rather surreal conversation.

"Taylor is amazing," Leslie sighed, a faraway look in his eyes. "My bestest friend, really. I love Eddie, but Taylor and I, we just click together. He's awesome."

Oliver was beginning to take a distinct dislike to the paragon of virtue who was Taylor. "Are you and he, you know, partners?"

Leslie broke into peals of laughter. "Oh no, we'd kill each other. We've jerked each other off now and then and shared a bed a few times, but that's about it. God, Draven would kill me if I touched Taylor. " He winked at a slightly mollified Oliver. "And you don't want to get on Draven's bad side. He can be a real grouch and he has wicked self-defence skills and boy, can that man drive a car."

Oliver began to wonder if he was man enough for all these super hero he-men characters that Leslie seemed to know.

"So what does Eddie do then?" he asked snarkily. "Toss dwarves, fight rabid wolves, maybe slay a dragon or two?"

Leslie collapsed into snorts of laughter then raised a hand to his mouth. "Sorry, you got me snorting again. You're the only man who can do that, I swear." Oliver was gratified that there was something he could do that the Marvellous Avengers couldn't. "Nope, Eddie is a chef. An award-winning one. He just won the London Chef of the Year award a couple of weeks ago. "

Oliver wanted to roll his eyes, but that would have been rude. Now he had to contend with super chefs as well. He couldn't help feeling a little put out. "Oh, well, that's cool I suppose. I—"

Leslie nodded eagerly as he butted in. "He's one of the chefs at the restaurant I want to take you to. Eddie's boyfriend, Gideon, he owns Galileo's in Soho. He's a chef, too, only he's just starting to cook again because he got burned in a fire and lost a couple of his senses. Now that he's starting to get his smell and taste buds back, he's returned to the kitchen again. You'll enjoy meeting them, and Galileo's is like, the best place ever." He stopped to take a breath and Oliver saw his chance to actually participate in the conversation.

"Okay, that sounds like a plan. I can meet these two friends of yours and try out one of my suits and get a good meal, too. Win-win situation, I'd say. Any idea when you want to do this da—this dinner?"

Leslie pulled out his really fancy phone and flicked through it, muttering to himself. Oliver sighed. He should have known a guy like Leslie had a heavy social calendar and probably had to book his events weeks or months in advance. He was about to tell Leslie that it was fine and to forget dinner if he was that busy when Leslie waved his phone at him and beamed brightly.

"How about next Friday, the thirtieth? That's only eight days away." His face fell. "I'd like it to be sooner, but this weekend I'm working at a fashion show, helping them out with the setup and organising, and Laverne will have my balls if I cancel. Plus, I could use the overtime money she's paying me."

It seemed a bit far away, but Oliver tamped down his disappointment at having to wait over a week to see Leslie again.

"Sure," he agreed nonchalantly. "It's not like I have many other plans. Except, maybe drinks with my friend Katie. You'll have to meet her. I think the two of you will get along really well. She's crazy, too." He flashed a grin at Leslie who grinned back.

"I'd love to meet her, just as long as she isn't one of those women who insist on telling me all about her girly bits. I get enough of that at work, thank you very much."

"I think I can safely say that's not something you have to worry about."

Oliver was truly gutted when the afternoon came to an end. He stood up as Leslie collected his belongings, which had been strewn across the table like debris from a rock fall and stuffed everything into his fancy man-bag. For a moment, the two men looked at each other awkwardly. Finally Leslie stepped up and placed a soft kiss on Oliver's undamaged cheek and hugged him tightly.

"Thanks for this afternoon. I really enjoyed it. I'll text you the details of where to find Galileo's, unless you'd like me to pick you up? I can always borrow the work car."

Oliver shook his head. "No, it's fine, I'll tube it. I quite like the trains. All anonymous and no one really cares who you are."

Leslie nodded. "Okay. Well, I look forward to next Friday then. Enjoy your weekend. Tell your friend Katie I say hi." He slung his bag across his shoulder and with one last wave, he turned and walked away.

Oliver watched him go with mixed feelings. One part of him wanted to grab the man and take him home and pound the hell out of him. The other, a warm fuzzy feeling, told him he'd just made a friend and not to fuck it up.

He sighed as he put on his jacket. Oh well, he had Friday next week to look forward to. In the meantime, he'd use the image of Leslie's pert arse as his masturbation material for the coming week. He might even give Maxwell a call, see if his friend was in town. Maybe getting laid would rid him of this ache he had inside, the dread that coiled persistently in his stomach. It had been with him as long as he could remember.

Sex would help him forget, let him enter the zone where he could switch off and just enjoy the physical exertion. Yes, he'd definitely be giving Max a call.

Chapter 7

In bed that night, Leslie lay on top of the covers, clad in his favourite pair of red satin boxers and a pair of matching Christian Louboutin heels. His hand was inside his underwear and wrapped firmly around his dick. He loved the feeling of silk on his hands as he jerked off. It also made clean up less messy, although the laundry bill took a beating.

The room was warm and cosy, with just the dim bedside light highlighting the activity on the TV screen. Leslie watched from beneath half-closed eyes as Nicky Starr disrobed slowly, stripping off the suit he wore bit by bit until only his shirt and tie remained, the tie loose and strung around his neck like that of a naughty schoolboy flouting authority. Nicky's hard and rather pleasing cock jutted upward and Leslie imagined taking it in his mouth, licking it from root to tip, then swallowing it whole. The thought raised goose pimples on his skin, and he could almost taste the man in his mouth, the rich scent that Nicky would exude on his tongue, and smell the man's cologne in his nostrils. Oliver had been wearing Hugo Boss and the smell of it still lingered in Leslie's imagination.

“Oh God, yes,” he whispered huskily as he stroked his lubed cock, and his body embraced the rising pleasure that was unfolding. He opened his legs wider, planting his stiletto heels deeper into the bed cover. “God, Leo is so damn lucky.” He watched Nicky move onto the bed like a panther, still half dressed as he loomed over the waiting man on the bed. This film, a nautical-themed dalliance called *Scent of Semen* was one of Leslie’s all-time favourite Nicky Starr and Leo Loving performances. The two men had on-screen chemistry and Leo’s slim, lithe frame currently writhed in pleasure on the bed as Nicky lowered his head and took him deep into his mouth. Leslie imagined those lips around his own cock, sucking and licking and teasing and he twisted on the bed as his hands grew firmer on his dick. The action on screen got intense as Leo turned over and got on his hands and knees then sank down to the bed on his elbows and looked back at Nicky with a cheeky grin.

“Go on,” he murmured, “Eat me out. I know you want to. Want to feel your tongue in my hole, stretching me, then your beautiful cock inside me, making me scream. Fuck me, Captain.”

Nicky growled, a sound that struck the nerve endings in Leslie’s body, and he panted slowly as he watched Nicky lower his mouth to Leo’s arse. What followed nearly made him cream himself but he wanted to hold out just that little longer, feel himself come as Nicky’s tongue pushed his way fiercely into Leo, imagine that was *him* on the bed and Oliver behind him. The image he had on his screen might have been Nicky Starr, porn star, but it was Oliver, beautiful damaged Oliver, who Leslie had in his mind right now. Oliver, who he wanted to do that to him, Oliver who would finally push inside him and make Leslie cry out in pleasure as he came.

The noises on screen got louder as Nicky finally lubed Leo up enough to grab his hips and ram inside him. The sight of that perfect cock disappearing inside Leo and Leo’s strangled cry of pleasure was enough to make Leslie frantically jack himself off harder, all the while imagining that cock inside *him*, until he came, hard, with a shuddering of limbs, a heaving of breath and a spurt of semen that looked as if it was trying out for the National Semen Javelin Championships. Unfortunately that powerful orgasm hadn’t contained itself to his satin boxers. His belly was sticky and his treasure trail matted with come.

"Oh my fucking God," Leslie panted as his body shivered and jerked on the bed, his semi-hard dick still clutched in his hands. "That was awesome." The pleasure suffusing his post-orgasmic body was buoyed by the knowledge he'd actually had coffee with the man on screen today and that in just over a week's time, he'd be seeing him again. And yes, Leslie knew he was trying to be friends with Oliver first but he was also honest enough to admit that he wanted the man to fuck him just like Leo had been. He wanted Oliver here, in his bed, to cuddle and wake up to, wanted the warmth of that hard body next to his, smiling sleepily at him in the morning.

And one way or another, Leslie Tiberius Scott was going to get that wish.

* * *

Oliver was horny. Fed up that Maxwell had been out of the country—again—and he was left to his own devices, he'd already jerked off in the shower soon after leaving Leslie today. The relief had been short lived. He'd finished washing, wrapped a towel around his waist and as he'd gone to put his shirt into the laundry, he'd caught a whiff of Leslie's scent. It was some warm, spicy fragrance that had him sniffing deeply at the sweaty shirt, and getting hard again as he imagined those soft lips on his cheek and the taut litheness of Leslie's body against his as he'd hugged him goodbye.

Now, with a groan, he shoved the shirt into his wicker laundry basket and put the towel back on the rail. He padded naked over to his DVD collection and opened the door to one of the cupboards. Eyes quickly perused the contents; he soon found what he was looking for. It was one of his own performances, one he'd done with a cute guy called Adam, who bore a remarkable resemblance to Leslie. Oliver remembered him fondly. Adam had been all black hair and soft chuckles, with a body that had been sublime and the way he used it even better. Oliver had never been ridden like that before in his life, and truth be told, Adam had the knack of making a man feel like a prime stallion. Especially when he'd worn his heels, something Oliver was partial to in a man.

With a sense of anticipation, he put the DVD into his player and got comfortable on the couch. For these sessions, he tended to put down a towel first to keep the couch clean from sticky fluids. Even though he didn't get many visitors, Oliver was house proud. Dried semen on the seats tended to be off-putting to guests.

The film, titled *The War Whore*, started and Oliver wondered if he was a narcissist watching his own movie. However, he wanted to see Adam in action, imagine it was Leslie above him, see those cobalt blue eyes staring into his as he fucked him. His cock rose and Oliver sighed in satisfaction as his hands got busy. There was something to be said about living alone and having the privacy to jack off in your own living room using the lube that was scattered around the place.

Through lazy eyes, he watched himself lying on a medieval divan, dressed in an opened leather waistcoat, chest hair showing. He remembered that those pants had been the most uncomfortable leather ones he'd ever worn. They were opened to show his cock upright and purpled, already glistening and definitely ready for the slave who stood in front of him. Adam smiled invitingly on screen and dropped his tunic to reveal an impressive dick and a slim, muscled body. He also had a backside that you could bounce coins off. The man's arse had been bite-worthy, and Oliver's mouth filled with saliva as he imagined what Leslie's would be like. From what he'd seen today, the man had a tight, bubble arse and Oliver really wanted in.

Languid strokes to his cock made his pulse race; his mouth opened and his heavy breaths echoed in the room. He watched the events playing out on screen, as Adam straddled him and then rammed down on his cock with a fierce battle cry and began to bounce up and down like a yo-yo. Oliver closed his eyes and imagined that scene, but with Leslie in the slave role. Black bangs over blue eyes framed a face that was pale and delicate, yet with the strength of a man's jaw and square cheekbones that made no mistake about the gender of the person currently riding Oliver's cock.

He opened his eyes as his hands tightened around his dick, and the lube and his own fluids slicked him and sent waves of pleasure down to his feet, his arse and pooled in his groin.

"Oh, God, Leslie," he gasped, as he watched Adam rise and fall against Nicky's thrusting hips and heard the sounds of pleasure as Nicky Starr pushed deep inside the slave. "I want you so damn badly…" His voice caught as the pressure in his groin grew relentless and he cried out as he climaxed, come jettisoning across his stomach in white streams, the sheer volume leaving Oliver feeling empty and drained. He hadn't realised how tense he'd been and he slumped back against the couch arm, waves of lethargy washing over him as he relaxed.

Thank God for the towel, he thought drowsily as he closed his eyes, pulled a blanket he kept close over him and imagined Leslie lying next to him, curled up against his side like a sleepy kitten. He'd love to have the warmth of a man's body next to him, hear the slight exhalations as he slept, wake up to the sight of blue eyes staring into his.

What the hell is happening to me? was his last coherent thought before he drifted off into sleep. That man is going to be *so* much trouble…

Chapter 8

Leslie stood at the bar, drumming his fingers on the top. It was more of a habit than the fact he was impatient. As he waited for the rather hunky bartender to put his drinks order together, Leslie watched his friends with a fond smile. It was one of those rare nights when all of them could get together and they were gathered at a favourite cocktail bar on the outskirts of Chelsea.

He watched as Eddie mischievously teased his boyfriend Gideon's dark blond, wavy hair into a faux Mohawk. Leslie was sure that no one had ever done that before, firstly because Gideon's hair was longer than it used to be and secondly, because Gideon would probably have bitten their fingers off. Eddie, however, managed to smooth the hair into a short, upstanding facsimile of something similar to Elijah Wood's version and topped it off by placing the umbrella from his cocktail drink in the centre. It certainly looked ridiculous but Gideon was grinning and gazing at Eddie with so much affection Leslie felt a lick of envy. He wished someone would look at him like that.

Next to Gideon sat Taylor, his dark hair waving around his face as he chuckled at Gideon's new look, and his hand reached up idly to tuck his own irreverent curls behind his ear. Taylor's fiancé, Draven, leaned over and smoothed the hair away from Taylor's cheek and then the two men leaned in to each other for a kiss hot enough to melt metal. Leslie's dick twitched at the sight of the two men so obviously enjoying themselves.

"And here I am, the bloody fifth wheel on the bus. It sucks."

There was a chuckle from behind the bar and Leslie turned to see the bartender smiling at him.

"Did you say it sucks or you suck?" The barman enquired with a cheeky wink. "'Cos if it's the latter, I wouldn't mind testing it out."

Leslie returned the grin. He liked being hit on. It gave him confidence that the universe was in balance.

"Oh, I don't know about that," he said airily as he picked up the tray and turned to join his friends. "Maybe I'll catch up with you later." He blew a kiss at the barman and sashayed his way across the floor with his drinks tray. He deposited the tray on the table and sat down beside Eddie.

"I'll get the next round as well," he said with a wink. "The bartender is pretty cute." He picked up his lime daiquiri and took a long slurp.

Eddie chortled. "Go for it, Leslie. He is hot." He eyed the bartender closely. "Really hot. He has arms that could—" He squeaked as Gideon took hold of his ear and twisted it. "Hey, don't be like that. I'm allowed to look, aren't I?" He cast an injured glance at his lover.

Gideon released his ear. "Look, not drool. I'll need to give you a damn bib if you inspect him any closer."

Draven let out a bark of laughter. "He does look as if he works out a lot. Nice chest." He leered at Taylor. "But you're much hotter than him."

Leslie blew a loud raspberry. "Look at you trying to get some." He affected an American accent which he thought wasn't half bad. "Butter me up, baby, 'cause I am *so* gonna to get laid tonight…"

Taylor chuckled. "You mean he doesn't already *every* night?" He rolled his eyes and nodded at Draven. "The man's insatiable. I only have to bend down and he's like, oh Taylor, shall we indulge in a little bit of hanky panky…"

Draven smirked. “That’s because you’re hot, like I said. Don’t go putting all the blame on me either. You’re the one who hides handcuffs all over the house ‘just in case.’”

Taylor’s face turned darker, which meant he was blushing under his caramel skin. “Fuck, Draven, don’t tell everyone about that. Honestly. You have no damn filter.”

Leslie listened to the banter, the sense of loneliness at times like this intensifying. He was really happy for Eddie and Taylor having found the men of their dreams, but he wished he could do the same. That thought made him think of Oliver and he had a sudden yearning to call him. He put down his drink and stood up quickly.

“I need to make a phone call, guys. I’ll be back in a moment.”

He ignored his friends’ cat calls and dirty comments about phone sex and made his way to the quieter front lobby of the restaurant. He looked at his watch. Ten p.m. Surely it wasn’t too late to call Oliver? He squashed down his misgivings and dialled the number which he already knew by heart. They’d been texting each other and even had spoken a few times. He knew there were only two more days to go before their dinner ‘date’ but he really needed to hear Oliver’s voice again. The phone rang a few times and just as Leslie was about to disconnect the call, it was picked up.

“Hello?” Oliver’s voice was thick, sounding sleepy and Leslie mentally kicked himself. It sounded like he’d woken him up.

“Hi, it’s Leslie.” He knew the phone would show an unknown caller as Leslie always suppressed his number after his stalking incident.

“Leslie? Is everything all right?”

“Yes, everything’s fine. I just wanted to call and say hello.” He shook his head in shame at that lame response. Normally he was pretty eloquent but Oliver made him a little stupid. “I hope I didn’t wake you up.”

“I was watching a film. I might have dozed off a little so I’m glad you woke me. Are you calling to cancel our dinner thing on Friday?”

Leslie was horrified. “No, not at all. God no. Why, do you want to cancel it?” His stomach had butterflies at that thought.

Oliver gave a low, sexy chuckle. Leslie remembered hearing that exact noise on a Nicky Starr movie he’d watched (they were fast becoming an addiction) in the last week and his cock grew hard.

Down, you poxy thing. I can't go back to the table with a hard-on. Those guys notice everything.

"No, Leslie, I don't want to cancel. I'm looking forward to it. A little nervous about going out in public to somewhere that isn't one of my safe places, but I'm willing to take the chance."

A wave of relief swept through Leslie. "Oh, good. Me, too. You'll be awesome. I mean, the date will be awesome, although you will, too, of course." He closed his mouth, wondering why it was that this man turned him into a babbling idiot.

"What are up you tonight then that you called me?"

"I'm just out with some friends at the moment, having a drink or two. I feel a bit out of things actually because everyone has their significant other with them." He sighed. "Although the bartender has hit on me, so I suppose that's a good sign I still have my mojo."

"The bartender hit on you? You might get lucky tonight then."

Leslie didn't think he imagined the tinge of jealousy in Oliver's voice and he hugged that thought close as he smiled crazily into the phone. "I s'pose. Anyway, that wasn't why I called. I just wanted to say hi."

"I'm glad you did," Oliver said quietly.

There was a comfortable silence then Leslie sighed. "Well, I guess I should be social and get back to the crazy bastards currently trying to build a pyramid on the table with their drinks. I'll see you Friday then?"

"Yes, I'll be there. I won't let you down."

"Friday it is then. Night, Oliver."

"Night, Leslie. Thanks for the call." The phone went dead and Leslie knew he had a stupid grin on his face a mile wide. He sashayed back to the table.

Taylor looked at him knowingly. "You called Oliver, didn't you?"

Leslie's jaw dropped open. "Get out of here, how did you know that, did you see something in that head of yours?" He narrowed his eyes. "And you do know he's a secret, right?" He huffed. "You were supposed to keep it to yourselves, guys. Not tell the boyfriends."

Gideon snorted. "Good luck with telling Eddie something and expecting him to keep it a secret. He let it slip that you'd met Nicky Starr and all I had to do was tickle it out of him. As well as another thing I did to get him to talk." He smirked. Eddie flushed and went a deep pink.

The whole table erupted into laughter.

"No, you daft bugger, I didn't 'see' anything." Taylor grinned. "It's just that whenever you say his name, you get this goofy look on your face. You had the same look when you went to make your phone call. And don't worry; none of us would ever spill the beans about him. You know that."

"You've got it bad for this guy, Leslie," murmured Eddie with a smile. "Are you falling for him?"

Leslie tossed his head haughtily. "We're just friends."

There were more hoots around the table. "Yeah, we believe that one," Taylor scoffed. "Like we believe you didn't send that blow-up dinosaur to Gideon for his birthday."

Leslie fluttered his eyelashes and affected a southern accent. "Well, I do declah, sir, you have me all wrong. I swear on my pinkie finger that I did not send that big, green, six-foot dinosaur to this man, and I will swear that 'til my dying day."

Gideon snorted. "You bloody little liar. You might have gotten someone else to post it but I know it was you who sent me that damned monstrosity." He shivered in remembrance. "All green and fuck, it glowed, too."

Eddie snorted drink out of his nose and for a moment everyone was distracted as they cleaned up the beer that had sprayed over the table. Leslie grinned. Laverne had had the time of her life posting the horrible thing to Gideon. The post office worker had blushed as they'd stood there filling in the recorded mail slip that said what was contained in the box. They'd been fairly vocal about their 'package,' which had led to more lewd jokes. Leslie was still surprised they hadn't been kicked out of the premises.

He looked around at the people closest to him, his heart warmed by the sight. He was very lucky to have such good friends and was really looking forward to introducing them to Oliver one by one. He intended to try and bring the man back into the world again and hoped that in the process, something would happen between them that wasn't just friendship.

A man could hope couldn't he?

Chapter 9

Oliver leaned back in his chair and burped loudly.

Leslie burst into a fit of giggles. "Oh God, excuse my pig. He's a friend," he said to the man sitting at the next table. The man smiled benevolently and continued eating what looked like grilled salmon.

Oliver grinned, his face alight with mischief. "Sorry about that. The food is just so damn good, I was showing my appreciation."

Leslie smiled back at him. At first, Oliver had been nervous upon arrival at the restaurant, hanging behind Leslie as he walked into Galileo's. After meeting Gideon, who had been at his most charming and who'd personally escorted them to their intimate table in the corner behind a wooden screen filled with fragrant red flowers, Oliver had finally begun to relax.

He was dressed in a pair of black chinos, coupled with a white, open-necked, long-sleeved shirt which hugged his muscled frame like a wetsuit, with a black-and-white-striped waistcoat, closed, but for the top two buttons. Leslie was definitely a fan of the look. Oliver's wavy blond hair was artfully styled and held in place with gel, and the scar Leslie knew was there was hidden behind thick strands that framed his handsome face.

"I told you he was a great chef. Your prime rib looked really tasty. I have to say my calamari was delicious." He sipped his third glass of wine. He was feeling rather mellow. The man across the table looked incredibly sexy and Leslie was really beginning to get impatient. Yes, he knew the whole 'let's be friends' thing was a start, but honestly? His dick was raring to go and get Oliver into bed. He didn't think his libido would hold out much longer. It had been on high alert ever since seeing Oliver standing outside the restaurant, looking slightly overwhelmed. The sheer vulnerability of the man had struck a chord in Leslie's tender heart.

He didn't think he was mistaking the looks that Oliver was throwing his way either. They were hot, wanton glances of need that Leslie felt were probably reflected in his own eyes. He knew Nicky Starr's preferences in men, having read his interviews and watched the movies, and Leslie definitely fell into the 'right type' category. That was his ace in the hole, he decided while he observed Oliver over the rim of his wine glass, chatting animatedly about a new website design he was doing for some mega new porn star.

Leslie was exactly what Oliver Brown was looking for. The man just didn't know it yet. Or rather, he knew it but wasn't ready to act. It was going to be up to Leslie to get things moving along and he decided the time had come to try his luck.

His foot gently brushed against Oliver's under the table, and he was gratified when he started, seeing his dinner partner's eyes heat up as he took a sip from his whisky glass. Leslie took it one step further and ran his booted foot (he hadn't worn heels tonight, preferring to ease Oliver into that side of him a little more gradually) teasingly along Oliver's calf.

His lips curved in a smile that said Leslie was courting trouble. The sight of those rich, pink lips around the rim of the glass, and the amusement in his eyes that said Oliver knew full well what was going on, made Leslie as hard as adamantine. He saw the Nicky Starr persona behind Oliver's casual lick of his lips; his narrowed eyes were almost alive with hunger.

"Bit of a twitchy foot, there Leslie?" Oliver said softly, his tone dangerously seductive. "You might need some medication for that condition."

"Oh, sorry, did I touch you? My bad. I was just getting…a little uncomfortable. I needed to stretch."

Oliver nodded slowly. Leslie felt the slow stroke of a shoe against his left leg, a gentle sweep that made him want to rip off his clothes and beg Oliver to take him right there. Manfully, he controlled that impulse. Gideon would be as pissed as hell if he didn't.

The two men stared at each other over the remains of their dinner, each silently acknowledging that things were changing between them.

"So," Oliver drawled as his foot crept slowly up Leslie's thigh. "Do you think perhaps we should get the bill and get out of here? Back to my place, perhaps?"

Leslie swallowed, finding it hard to speak as that wandering foot nudged his groin. Said groin was on fire.

"What about the friends thing?" he squeaked, all the while wanting push his crotch into the foot causing him such turmoil.

Oliver's mouth curved in a wide, sexy grin. "I kind of think that's a little passé now, Leslie. I am so damn horny if I don't have you soon, I'm going to come right here at this table. You have no idea how bloody sexy you look," he murmured huskily.

Leslie knew he'd dressed to kill in his tight black jeans with a huge dragon buckle, a tight wine-red tee shirt, teamed with a black suit jacket with fine red stripes. But the lust and desire in Oliver's eyes made him quail a little. This was a man who had lapped at other men's arses for a living and then fucked the daylights out of them. As much as Leslie had his fantasies, he was a little overwhelmed at that thought.

"You look spooked." Oliver sat back, the moment gone, his eyes wary. "I'm sorry. Did I come on too strong?"

Leslie leaned forward in panic. "Oh God, no, everything's fine. Sorry, I just had a brain fart moment, thinking about us, together. It sort of overloaded my circuits."

Oliver laughed softly, the tension in his body easing. "I thought you were having second thoughts."

"Oh, hell no. I want to go home with you. I haven't been able to think of anything else. I'll ask the waiter for the bill then we can get a taxi back to your place?"

That course of action duly agreed, soon Leslie and Oliver were in a taxi heading back toward his house. Despite the intimacy of the under-the-table shenanigans, Oliver was subdued as they sat in the back of the taxi. Leslie really wanted to get close to him, press his own lips against those only inches from his, but something warned him to not to push it. Oliver was in full defensive mode, folding his arms across his broad chest and gazing out of the window.

It was only when they were inside Oliver's home and the door had closed behind them that Leslie got his wish to see and feel the man the way he wanted. He had only taken two steps inside when he found himself being yanked into Oliver's strong arms, and a hot, wet, greedy mouth found his in a frenzy of want. There were no lights on in the hallway other than a soft glow emanating from a room nearby.

"God, you drive me crazy," Oliver growled as he propelled Leslie toward the open door and shoved him through. Leslie nodded eagerly, his mouth too busy kissing any part of Oliver he could find.

Somehow he ended up on his back on the large, soft couch with the strong, firm body of Oliver on top of him, rutting against him.

Frantic hands scrambled at his jeans and Oliver cursed as he realised the barrier between them.

"Button-down jeans? No easy peel zipper?"

Leslie stared at him aggrievedly despite the fact he was as eager to get out of his pants as Oliver was to remove them. "I love my five-O-ones. Much more fashionable. They, oh fuck." His serenade of the benefits of the button fly was interrupted as Oliver managed to get some of the buttons undone and reached inside and took him in hand. His mouth lunged at Leslie's who could do nothing but lie there in the soft lamplight and be ravaged.

Strong fingers tangled in his hair as he kissed the crap out of Oliver, and Leslie floated in a sense of bliss. The scent of the man on top of him, his hardness digging into Leslie's groin, the feel of lustful lips on his and the roughness of stubble on Leslie's skin were all conspiring to send him out of his mind. He reached down and unzipped Oliver, desperate to feel that hardness in his hands. Oliver gave a heartfelt groan as Leslie's fingers gripped his dick tightly, and his mouth grew even more ravenous. When they finally came up for air, Leslie's lips were swollen and his brain completely scrambled by his lover's greedy tongue and the rough strokes on his dick. He'd never felt so taken and assaulted and wanted in his life, and he loved it.

"You haven't had any for a while, huh?" Leslie managed to get out between hungry, sloppy kisses and Oliver's hand roaming all over his body, yanking up shirts, and rubbing his passion-hot skin.

"Christ, it *has* been too damn long," Oliver panted as they stroked and mauled each other. "I'm sorry I'm not going to last enough to fuck you right now, Leslie, but we have all night. I want so badly to be inside you, but I need to take the edge off first."

And that thought sent a thrill through Leslie's groin and his dick exploded with creamy spurts of come that flooded his designer jeans and his groin, and he gave a strangled cry, pressed his mouth hard against Oliver's neck, and bit down in the throes of his orgasm.

Yup, I'm a biter. Hope you can deal with it, Oliver.

Oliver yelped as Leslie's teeth nipped skin and then he threw back his head and roared. Warm fluid coated Leslie's hand, the scent of sex in the air overpowering. Oliver collapsed against him, both of them sticky and replete. Leslie closed his eyes to savour the fact he'd just jerked off Nicky Starr, his personal wet dream. Satisfaction radiated through his limbs and he smiled against Oliver's sweaty shoulder.

"Wow," Oliver murmured. "Sorry that didn't quite go as I had planned, but I…you know, needed that. Needed you."

"Needed you, too," Leslie sighed. "That was pretty awesome anyway. I can't wait to see what else you have to offer." He shifted uncomfortably. "Not that I don't like you on top of me, but you're pretty heavy. Do you think…?"

Oliver pushed himself upward with one powerful move of his left arm and hovered above Leslie. He leaned in and gave him a gentle kiss. "Your wish is my command." He rolled off and lay beside Leslie, on his back. Leslie unthinkingly reached out a hand to caress his face and move damp strands away from his eyes.

Oliver pulled back with a grunt. "Don't do that please."

Leslie dropped his hand and gave a deep sigh. "Oliver, I don't care about the scar."

"I do." Oliver's tone was uncompromising. "It's the only thing off limits. Don't touch my face."

Leslie's heart ached at the vulnerability behind those words. "So you can stick your tongue in the back of my throat, but I can't touch you there? Oliver, you are one incredibly sexy package and the scar is part of it. Part of who you are."

Oliver's eyes darkened in the dim light. "You don't know me well enough yet to know who I am, Leslie. You might not like the man when you truly get to see him in all his damaged glory."

Leslie sat up and looked at Oliver, his brows lifting. "Really? We've just had hot, mad monkey sex of a sort and you start getting all maudlin on me? I think I must have lost my touch. Normally guys tend to be a little more upbeat after sex with me." He hoped his attempt at levity might lighten Oliver's mood. His lover snorted and Leslie thought it was with amusement and not anger at his forthrightness.

"I think that's probably very true." Oliver's fingers lazily trailed down Leslie's semen-sticky stomach. "You're the sexiest man I've ever seen. And my good intentions at just being friends went out the window when you started playing footsie with me under the table."

It was Leslie's turn to snort now. "Oh, I think we both know that whole friends things wasn't going to last too long."

There was a comfortable silence then Oliver raised himself on one elbow and brushed warm lips over his forehead. "Maybe we should clean up then get into bed. It's a damn sight more comfortable than this couch."

Leslie pursed his lips. "I don't know. I'll have fond memories of this couch. Being manhandled by a sexy porn star has always been a fantasy of mine."

Oliver stiffened and Leslie wondered what he'd said. Oliver's next words cleared it up.

"So you're only here with me because I was a porn star?" He sat up and catapulted off the couch angrily. "It's Nicky Starr you want then?" he spat as he stood above a wide-eyed Leslie who wondered what the hell had gone so suddenly, horribly wrong. "Well, I'm sorry, but I'm all out of porn star. The only thing that's left is a damaged Oliver Brown." He zipped his chinos up with trembling fingers.

Leslie knew this was a make or break moment and he swung his legs around and stood up.

God, this man is so broken.

Oliver watched him with both fire and uncertainty in his eyes. Leslie reached him and enveloped him in his arms, tightening his grip when Oliver tried to pull away.

"I didn't say that," Leslie whispered into Oliver's ear. "I said Nicky was the fantasy. You're the real deal and I know who I'd rather have. Oliver Brown. The man in my arms, the one whose heart I can feel beating—that's the man I want. Stop being so damn prickly. I know I say the wrong thing sometimes—I wouldn't be me if I didn't—but you're going to have to learn to live with it if you want to be with me." He nibbled on Oliver's ear. "I'm a package deal. You get the kooky with the sexy."

He took a chance and leaned away, then framed Oliver's face with his hands, hoping he wouldn't be pushed away. "You're pretty special just as you are. And I think you should take me to bed now and fuck the daylights out of me. I have a hankering to meet Mr. Brown up close and personal."

Oliver sighed deeply and rested his forehead against Leslie's. Leslie did a mental fist pump that he'd gotten to touch Oliver's face without incident. That had to be good sign.

"I'm sorry," Oliver muttered. "I'm not used to this sort of stuff anymore. I…"

Leslie didn't let him finish, just stuck his tongue in Oliver's mouth and proceeded to mine it. His lover responded with a moan, gripping Leslie's hips and grinding against him.

Good God, the man is already hard. How the hell does he do that? I guess in his past profession he got it trained like a performing monkey.

The thought made Leslie giggle and Oliver pulled away in confusion. Leslie didn't have the heart to tell him that he'd just compared Oliver's prick to a monkey, so instead he went back to mining. His own cock was starting to come to life again, and the thought of a bed and perhaps even getting to stay over for the night and wake up to him was a real turn-on.

"We need to get to bed," Leslie panted as he pulled away from Oliver's seeking mouth. "I need skin, flesh and your cock in my arse. What do you say?"

Oliver seemed not to need encouragement. He took Leslie's hand and dragged him up the winding stairs to the top landing. Leslie was unceremoniously pushed into a bedroom, a lavishly decorated royal blue and burgundy concoction of satins, cottons and plush armchairs; thick, heavy curtains and a chandelier in the middle of ceiling that took his breath away.

He stared at it in awe. "Oh my God, you are *such* a porn star." Immediately, he clapped his hands to his lips and turned to Oliver. "Oh crap, I'm sorry, my mouth ran away again."

Oliver put his hand across Leslie's mouth, his eyes dark with hunger. "Strip," he commanded. "I want you naked on my bed, right now."

Leslie was faint with the thought of being shagged and hastily he disrobed, feeling a slight prickle of discomfort at leaving his already crusty clothes in a heap on the floor. When he turned around, now stark naked, Oliver's smile turned wolfish as he took in Leslie's hard-on and naked body.

"I think I said get on the bed," he murmured gently, eye-fucking Leslie from top to bottom. "I'll get the stuff we need."

Leslie nodded and climbed onto the bed, lying face down, rubbing his cock shamelessly against the silk of the duvet. He didn't care that he was staining Oliver's cover. All he knew was that the fabric felt good against his swollen and heated skin and he moaned a little as he writhed in pleasure. There was a choked gasp behind him and he looked back over his shoulder to see Oliver watching him, lube and condoms in hand, his face twisted in lust. His hair was mussed, but still it covered the scar. Leslie had a plan for that later, to get Oliver to be less self-conscious about it. He also saw for the first time the twisted skin that ran down the outside of Oliver's right arm, and the thin scars that bisected the same side of his torso. None of that mattered to him.

"Fuck, you look so hot," Oliver said as he leapt onto the bed and straddled Leslie's calves. "You have the perfect arse, you know that? Tight and just waiting for me."

Leslie shivered, those words causing goose bumps to form on his over sensitive skin. "It could be the heel-wearing," he mused. "I like to exercise my butt muscles when I wear them and dance. They say it's a good way to tone up." A hot body covered his and he closed his eyes in bliss.

"You wear heels?" Oliver's tongue licked at his ear. "That is fucking sexy. I love that image." His voice was husky, full of desire. "Will you wear them for me one day? Let me fuck you in them?"

Leslie's heart filled with joy. He had a picture of himself on his phone in a corset, hat and heels. He'd have to show it to Oliver one day and get his engine even more revved up.

"Oh, God yes," he exclaimed as Oliver's tongue trailed down his shoulder blades and back. He gripped the bed sheets tighter at the sensation. "I have this pair of red ones you'll like, and…oh, hell yes…" His voice tailed off in pure pleasure as Oliver parted his arse cheeks and lapped at his hole. Then the bliss of having fingers inside him, opening him wide, rendered him speechless. He gyrated and made little mewling kitten noises as Oliver proceeded to probe his hole, pushing his tongue inside him with wet, sloppy sounds that made Leslie's cock throb.

He lost himself in the feeling of being explored, dominated and well and truly prepped. When he felt the cool dribble of lube at his hole and between his cheeks he sighed in relief and pushed his backside toward the man currently taking him to such pleasurable heights. When his hips were pulled up and Oliver's cock nudged his entrance, Leslie pushed back and groaned as it sank deep inside him.

"Are you okay, Leslie?" Oliver's husky voice was strained. "Tell me if I hurt you."

Leslie huffed loudly. "Just bloody get going, will you? I'm chafing my cock rubbing against this silky stuff, but it feels so damn good. And you inside me…God, it's heaven..."

There was a warm chuckle behind him and Leslie arched his back as Oliver began pounding into him in earnest. The smooth slide and slap of flesh was a welcome sound in the room, as the two men moved together, finding each other's rhythm. The unsteady movements caused them to grunt and swear in equal measure.

Leslie was lost in the moment and when Oliver reached around, his breath hot against Leslie's ear, and took his cock in his strong hand and jerked him with smooth, practiced ease, Leslie gave a cry of delight and came all over Oliver's satin cover. His body trembled, his skin prickling with heat and his balls contracting as he spewed forth what seemed like a never-ending stream.

Behind him, Oliver continued pounding Leslie's tender hole then tensed and gave a strangled gasp as he bucked against Leslie's arse, clutching his hips with fingers that Leslie was sure would make him bruise. His lover collapsed against Leslie's back, sinking him down into the wet, sticky pool beneath his stomach.

The strong, erratic beat of a heart against the skin of his back made Leslie smile as he closed his eyes and let the lethargy of their lovemaking take over. Oliver was heavy and he couldn't really breathe, but he felt so good plastered across Leslie like a second skin. It was only when he realised that actually, he *couldn't* breathe, that he began to panic a bit and gasp.

"Do you mind getting off me so I don't expire in the wet spot?"

Oliver grumbled as he unpeeled himself. "I was comfortable there. Why do you have to make me move?" he whined as he thudded down next to Leslie, staring up at the ceiling.

Leslie turned onto his side to stare at the man beside him. "I don't fancy being carted out of here covered in come even with a big smile on my face," he teased. In the intimacy of the moment, he took a deep breath and reached out to Oliver's face. Oliver watched him, eyes vigilant. "Plus I wanted to do this, please let me," he whispered as he moved the hair back from Oliver's face and shifted up so he could kiss the scar that showed. Surprisingly, gratifyingly, his lover flinched but didn't recoil or push him away. Leslie trailed his lips down the damaged flesh, a gentle kiss that ended at Oliver's mouth.

"There," he said softly. "See, you're not the monster you make yourself out to be. You're stunning, honestly." He touched his lips to the scar on Oliver's arm, kissing from wrist to shoulder.

Oliver swallowed and stared at Leslie with eyes that shone wet in the dim light. "Gregori said I was."

"He said you were what?" Leslie stopped his tour of Oliver's arm and snuggled into his side.

"Said I was a monster, because of the way I looked after the accident." He shrugged one shoulder. "But he was pretty mad with me at the time."

Leslie wanted to kill Gregori Golovin. "How could he say that to you? And especially when you were hurt?"

"He was an arsehole. A complete and utter bastard. I just didn't realise it until it was too late." Oliver stared up at the ceiling and Leslie reached over and wrapped an arm across his chest. His lover's skin was still sweaty from their lovemaking and his heart beat erratically beneath Leslie's outstretched arm.

"About three weeks before the bike accident, I found Greg dealing E to some kids." Oliver's voice was quiet, but anguished. "And when I mean kids, I mean twelve, thirteen-year-olds."

Leslie's insides churned. "Hell," he whispered. "I suppose as an adult it's a choice you make to take drugs. I don't agree with it but...kids? That's just disgusting."

Oliver nodded in the dim light. "That's what I thought. It's one thing me going off half-cocked and killing myself slowly with coke, but to deal to children? That was a new low, even for Greg." He shifted in bed and Leslie stroked his matted chest and waited for the story to unfold.

"I threatened to tell the film studio about it, get him kicked out. I was a bigger star than he was so they would have done what I asked." He snorted drily. "It was another thing that pissed him off about me. That I was more popular."

"Why the hell did you stay with a man like that?" Leslie reached up and caressed Oliver's cheek. "You deserved better than him." He snuggled closer into Oliver.

There was silence for a minute. "I loved him." Oliver stroked the top of Leslie's head softly as Leslie's heart beat faster at those words. He'd known Oliver had feelings for Gregori, but hearing him actually voice them hurt a little. "He was everything to me at the time and I guess I was willing to look past the cruelty and the bad times. We did have some good times. Just not that many."

He sighed heavily. "Anyway, he told me he wouldn't do it anymore. I believed him. My first mistake. Then Leo found him with an eleven-year-old kid who hung around the studio, selling him baggies of all sorts of stuff. Leo told me. He didn't like Gregori at all and he'd have done anything to get him kicked off the set." Leslie heard the smile in Oliver's voice. "He said the same thing as you. That I was better than Greg and deserved more."

"Leo was a clever man," Leslie murmured as he moved across Oliver and his lips kissed a soft path down his chest.

His lover chuckled. "Like you, you mean? Little brat." He hitched a breath as Leslie moved lower down his body. "You're not helping. How am I supposed to tell you this story if you keep doing that?"

Leslie waved an airy hand. "Oh, you'll cope." He blew a raspberry on Oliver's stomach and grinned at his lover's surprised exclamation. "I'm doing my bit to ground you here, so lie back and enjoy it."

"I'm not so sure about grounding me," Oliver murmured. "I look ready to take off."

Leslie sniggered as he palmed Oliver's rising cock, causing him to gasp. "I'll climb aboard in a little while, Captain. Go on, tell me the rest."

He looked up to see Oliver watching him with an expression that took Leslie's breath away. It was a look of longing, of need so intense Leslie wanted to board the aeroplane right that minute. Instead, he held himself back and sat up, crossing his legs, sitting Buddha-like at the bottom of the bed.

"There. No more distractions. Carry on. Tell me the rest."

Oliver snorted softly. "*You* are one big distraction." He reached over to the side table and took a sip of water. When he put it down, his face was once again serious.

"I had to tell the studio about it. I didn't want to, I knew Greg wouldn't react well and it would fuck up our relationship. But I didn't have a choice. I wasn't about to let him get away with ruining kids' lives. Reggie, the owner, didn't take it well. He'd lost a brother to drugs so he had a bit of a bug up his arse about it. He hated us using drugs but he knew he couldn't stop it. But when I told him about Greg dealing he went ballistic and gave him notice. He was kicked off the set and told not to come back."

Oliver fell quiet.

After a while Leslie spoke. "Is that when you two broke up?"

Oliver nodded. "It was the beginning of the end. I kicked him out of the flat we shared, and he and the twins, he had these two sycophants that used to hang around him, moved in together." His tone was guarded and Leslie wondered what Oliver wasn't telling him. "I didn't want to stay there anymore so I went to stay with Leo for a few weeks until I found another place." He waved a hand around him. "This house. I wanted something outside of the city centre and this fit the bill." He gave a twisted smile. "My principles broke us up, I suppose. And the house certainly came in useful after the accident. No one really knew about it, so I had the privacy I wanted."

Leslie scooted up over him fiercely, straddling his hips as he looked down. "Your humanity broke you up, Oliver. And his selfishness and arseholiness."

Oliver gave a soft snort of amusement. "Is arseholiness even a word?"

Leslie nodded emphatically. "Oh, definitely. It's *my* word." He laid himself flat on top of Oliver and took his mouth in a deep kiss. Beneath him, Oliver's cock moved and Leslie grinned into the kiss. When he sat up, he ran his hands down Oliver's stomach.

"Permission to come aboard, Captain? I have a feeling this is going to be a short flight."

Oliver's husky tone sent a shiver down Leslie's spine. "Permission granted."

Chapter 10

In his persona as Nicky Starr, Oliver had revelled in the chance to go out on the town, wear the suits he adored and flirt with anything that moved, male or female. Of course, he'd never have taken the offers from women wanting to 'convert him to the dark side' seriously. He was far too into guys for that. However, flirting was a natural tendency with him, no matter what gender. And you never knew where it might get you. It had defused a few difficult and sensitive situations. However, looking across at the darkened face of Katie, sitting opposite him, he didn't think flirting with her would work to reduce the ire she currently sported.

"You are so full of shit," she snapped. "I don't know why the hell you talk such crap about yourself." Katie picked up her wine glass and took a gulp. "That man adores you, anyone can see it. It's just you who are too bloody minded to let him in and accept that someone can actually like you." She slammed the wine glass down on the restaurant table, slopping the contents messily onto the tablecloth. It was a quiet lunchtime at Fidalgo's and the place was not too busy.

Oliver scowled. "It's my opinion. I'm allowed to have one, aren't I?" He started when she snorted and threw her napkin at him. It hit his chest then dropped onto his lap. He picked it up and chucked it onto the table. "Wow, that's mature. Next we'll be having a food fight."

"Don't bloody tempt me. I still have some bourguignon left in my bowl."

They glared at each other and it was Oliver who dropped his eyes first. "I just said he can do better," he muttered softly.

He'd been seeing Leslie for the entire month since their dinner. They'd spent time together having satisfyingly mind-blowing sex, and Oliver had even managed to go to a couple of movies with Leslie, since they sneaked into the darkened theatre when the lights were off and generally sat in the back and made out.

Leslie told him he didn't mind the scar, or the fact Oliver's damaged eye tended to twitch a little when he got tired. He'd cut Oliver's hair to what he called 'a more flattering style' and Oliver agreed that while it still covered the damage, it did look better. He'd tentatively offered to wear concealer over the scar when they went out. Leslie had just kissed him and told him that if Oliver wanted to do that for himself, it was fine, but he didn't have to do it for him.

"I know what you said, you idiot. And you know I don't agree. And neither does he from the way he looks at you." Katie and Leslie had met each other recently when they'd all met for coffee. The two had hit it off straight away.

Katie's tone was a little less hostile now and she reached out and placed one plump, bejewelled hand on his. "Listen. I know better than anyone what that twat Gruesome Gregori did to you. I know how much he hurt you. But he was wrong. You deserve the very best, you know that. And Leslie has been good for you. He's a keeper."

Oliver toyed with his fork and didn't look up. "Exactly. He's cute, sexy, gorgeous, on his way up in the fashion world…did you know he was actually head-hunted from Debussy's by one of the huge Burberry stores but he refused to leave? He's intelligent, funny and lights up a room when he walks in. That's why I say he needs someone without the baggage, someone he can have on his arm that goes to all these fashion shows with him and isn't afraid to be seen in public."

"And he makes you happy," Katie said softly. "I've not seen you like this in two years, Ollie. Not since that bastard of an ex-boyfriend did such a number on you."

The use of the diminutive for his name—something Oliver wasn't partial to, but tolerated from Katie—warned him he was about to get the *talk*. The same one Katie had been giving him since he left the hospital, broken in both body and spirit, by a man he'd thought had once loved him.

"Don't start," he warned Katie. "I'm not in the mood for the whole rah-rah speech today."

"Fine. I won't say how much I hate that bastard for what he did to you in hospital. Or how I'd love to string him up by the balls and wallop his fat arse with a cat-o'-nine-tails. Or tell you that you are definitely a great catch and he missed out on the chance to be with a great guy…" She waggled her eyebrows and Oliver couldn't help chuckling at the expression on her face.

"You just have to have the last word, don't you?"

She nodded, eyes sparkling. "I'm a woman, dahlink. Of course I do." Her face grew more serious. "Have you told Leslie anything about your ex yet?"

Oliver's chest tightened. "He knows about the drug bust thing, and Greg getting chucked off the film site. I haven't told him much more."

No, he hadn't told his current lover about the fight he and Greg had after Oliver told the studio bosses about the drug dealing. Or the fact that his boyfriend had beaten him so badly that night he'd needed a week to recover. Or that the night he'd had the accident, he'd come home to his London apartment to find his ex-boyfriend (he hadn't gotten his key back yet) impaled by Pierce—one of the twins—as the other twin, Payton, fucked Greg's mouth. There had been a ménage of note going on in Oliver's own bed.

He'd escaped their taunts and insults, their laughing derision and drug-fuelled aggression and found a party where he could drink and forget and then…the accident had happened. And Gregori's cruelty hadn't stopped after that either.

"Hey, you okay, honey? You're looking terribly pensive all of a sudden. I'm sorry if I'm going on. I just love you, and I want you to be happy."

Oliver managed to twist his face into a smile. "Yeah, I'm fine. Can we stop with the memories now and think about something else?" He smirked and reached for his phone. "Leslie showed me this new Salad Fingers video, maybe you'd like to see it?"

Katie shrieked in horror. "Oh God, please don't. You know that damn thing scares to me death. It's so creepy. That guy has to be completely psycho to make such twisted stuff."

Leslie had introduced Oliver to the character and he'd become hooked.

He laughed loudly. "It's just a drawing, Katie. I find them kind of funny myself."

"You two are just weirdoes. You deserve each other." She grinned at him and finished her wine, motioning for the waiter to come over for another order.

Oliver chuckled. "I have something else that will make you laugh. Remember we went to Galileo's for dinner on Valentine's Day?"

Katie nodded, a wistful look on her face. "You have to take me there, Oliver. I'm dying to see this place."

Oliver reached over and took her hand. "I'll make a plan, I promise. Maybe for your birthday we can get a group together. Anyway, Leslie has this friend called Eddie, Gideon's boyfriend. He's this amazing chef and honestly, his pistachio ice cream is amazing."

He took a sip of his drink, smiling as he recalled the events of that evening. "He's also got a bit of a reputation for being a klutz. Really nice guy, sexy, too, for a redhead, but a bit like a gangly Dalmatian who's been let loose." Oliver sniggered. "He came over to say hello, talking and waving his arms all over the place and managed to knock some poor guy's toupee off his head." He laughed out loud at the memory of the restaurant patron's red face and Eddie's stammered apologies.

Katie let out a peal of laughter as she snorted wine all over the table and Oliver. "Oh my God, that must have been so damn funny." She wiped her mouth with her napkin.

Oliver grinned as he dabbed white wine off his shirt. "Yep. Gideon was like a master of urbanity, like, 'So sorry, sir, accidents do happen, and please have the meal on the house,' while glaring at Eddie and Eddie looking like a puppy who had peed on the carpet. It was hilarious. And Leslie was too damn adorable, with that snorting thing he does. I love it when he laughs like that."

Katie reached over and squeezed his hand. "You realise when you talk about Leslie, you get this look on your face and your voice changes? Oliver, that's all the proof I need that you two are so absolutely right for each other."

Those words still rang in Oliver's ears when he got home that night. He wasn't so sure Katie's words were true.

* * *

The loud cry of distress behind him caused Leslie to drop the bale of cloth he was busy stacking, and jump about a foot into the air. He clasped a hand to his chest as he saw his boss's face staring at him in horror.

"*Oh. My. God.* Laverne, what the hell is wrong with you? You made me pee my pants a little."

Laverne strode over to him, appearing to be hyperventilating—badly. "Is that my Dormeuil *ikonic* fabric lying on the floor with the dust and the mouse droppings? Oh please tell me it isn't."

Leslie glanced down at the floor where the bale of exorbitantly expensive grey suit fabric lay. "I can't tell you that," he said guiltily. "Because it is."

Laverne shrieked and Leslie winced. For a man, Laverne could pierce the eardrums.

"Leslie, you need to pick it up right now." Leslie was sure his boss even stamped her foot a little like a diva-esque My Little Pony.

Leslie gently kicked the bale he'd dropped to the side and walked over to the errant cloth. He leaned over and hoisted it up, holding it in his arms then laid it out on a nearby cutting table. As Laverne opened her mouth to say something, Leslie placed a finger to his lips telling her to *shh*. Laverne's eyes narrowed and as she moved toward him rather threateningly, he took up a soft cloth and began dusting the fabric gently. Out of the corner of his eye, he kept a cautious look out for his boss in case he got hit around the head with a handbag or perhaps just Laverne's large hand.

"Sorry, poor baby," he murmured to the material as he caressed it gently. "I'm sorry I left you all alone down there, among all the muck. I mean"—he raised his voice slightly—"I know there are no rats or mice in here, so there's no poo on you, but you deserved better. Let's get you cleaned up and on the shelf where you belong."

Laverne looked slightly mollified as she bore down on Leslie like the Titanic. "This carelessness just isn't like you. You've been a bit distracted lately. Is everything all right?" At the thought of just how all right everything was with Oliver, Leslie grinned to himself. His arse was still sore from last night's activity, and their Valentine's Day celebrations.

"I knew it, you're getting laid," Laverne chortled. She tapped the side of her nose. "A little bird told me you were seeing a certain customer of ours with the initials OB. Is that true?"

Leslie gaped at her. "What? Who told you that? How…" His voice tailed off at Laverne's deep chuckle.

"Oh, sweetheart, Laverne gets to know everything. You mentioned his name once in passing then went all gooey eyed. I had to find people in the know and get the full story." She waggled a finger at him. "I told myself then he was something special to you, not just a delivery." She grinned wickedly. "Although he may be that, too. I was waiting for you to tell me about him yourself, but I saw I'd just have to pry it out of you."

Leslie flushed and tried to keep his air of insouciance. "God, you are one big gossip bitch, girlfriend."

Laverne's eyes softened. "Oliver is someone special, isn't he?

Leslie didn't kid himself. "Yes, he is," he admitted. "I really like him."

I even think he could be the one.

Leslie knew he was falling hard for the blond-haired, moody and insatiable Oliver Brown. They'd spent a lot of time together, but he just wasn't sure whether Oliver felt the same. The man had a way of hiding his thoughts and emotions and sometimes Leslie felt there were two distinct people inside him. The Oliver who was warm, tender and laughed at Leslie's jokes, and loved it when he wore his heels to bed, and the other, darker Oliver, who was morose and sullen and looked at Leslie as if he didn't quite understand what he was doing there. Leslie didn't like that side of his Oliver at all.

He looked at Laverne, a niggling feeling of worry in his stomach. "Is it okay to see Oliver?" he asked haltingly. "Because I don't want it to become a problem at work."

"Oh, honey, it's fine. Do I look like an ogre? As long as you don't sell my suits to him for nothing to sweeten him up to play with that cute arse of yours, it's fine."

"Oh." Leslie heaved a sigh of relief. "Thank you."

"Well, I'll tell you a secret." Laverne leaned in, her pink lips curved in a slow smile. "I've been seeing a guy, too, this really sexy, gorgeous guy, and we've hit it off a few times if you know what I mean."

Leslie's ears pricked up. "Oh, you have? Anyone I know?"

Laverne shook her head. "I doubt it." Her eyes took on a starry look. Beneath the female persona, Leslie knew the man, Lenny James, was something of an incurable romantic. Lenny was one of those people who simply believed the best of everyone and everything.

"We've had dinner a couple of times and then, you know." Laverne grinned.

"So, he's met you as Lenny then? Does he know about Laverne?" Leslie asked the question innocently, but wasn't prepared for the shadow that crossed Laverne's eyes.

"No, he only knows me as Lenny James. I haven't introduced my other self to him yet. It's still early days, you know? I want to ease into it."

Laverne sounded suddenly shy and Leslie reached over and hugged her tightly. "Well, you're both awesome people so he can't help but love you both."

"I hope so," Laverne mused, her face a little worried. "He's quite an old-fashioned guy, a little set in his ways. Brook has this charm about him…" She stopped, suddenly conscious that she'd let slip his name.

Leslie laughed. "Don't worry. Your secret is safe with me. I won't tell anyone about Brook." He broke into song. "Laverne and Brook, sitting in a tree, K-I-S-S-I-N-G." He leapt nimbly out of the way of Laverne's raised hand coming down to thwack him across the head and scuttled over to the other side of the cutting table. Unfortunately he slipped on a wayward swatch of silk on the floor and went barrelling down onto his arse, frantically trying to stay his fall by clutching at the table. Alas, that didn't go too well, as all he got was a handful of suit fabric, which came flooding down like a wave and covered him like a swaddling blanket. He lay on his back on the floor, winded and unable to see much through the dark material. He did hear Laverne's hearty, unmistakeably male, guffaws of laughter.

"Oh God, that was too precious. I wish I'd had my video camera on that. I would have made myself £250 easy with *You've Been Framed*. Leslie, honey, you just made my day. Are you okay under there?"

More wails of laughter rent the air as Leslie tried to extricate himself from the cloth, which was threatening to suffocate him. He finally stood up, trying to retain as much dignity as he could, despite having hair that stood on end and a face that felt as red as a beetroot. It wasn't his most auspicious moment.

"I'm fine, thank you." He swept his hair back from his forehead haughtily. "My hair needs a Valium after that escapade, but the man who is Leslie Tiberius Scott is ready to go. Now if you'll excuse me, I really need to pee."

With that, he swept past a still-chuckling Laverne and escaped to the bathroom to repair both his hair and his decorum.

On his way home that night, he heard a loud whistle and his name being shouted from the construction site next door. He looked up to see Frankie's cheeky face beaming at him from a ledge about twenty feet up.

"Hey, sexy man. How are you today? Loving the outfit, by the way."

Leslie preened at the compliment. He had to say his dark blue pinstriped suit and pale blue shirt did make him look rather natty.

"Hi, Frankie," he called.

The labourer grinned. "When are you going to join me for a drink at the pub?" he called out. "Just as friends. I know you're spoken for."

Leslie smiled up at him. The man had been trying to get him go for a *friendly* drink for weeks. Frankie was a big, affable man, a few years older than Leslie, with muscles and a wide smile, a cute, boy-next-door face and a swathe of dark brown hair that fell over his forehead. It had become a bit of a tradition for them to meet up when Frankie had his smoke on the pavement below as Leslie left work. Leslie smirked. He rather thought Frankie waited for him and then dashed down to see him right on time. Leslie might have Oliver, but the attention of another guy was always welcome. Even if he was a smoker. Leslie didn't like smoking.

"I heard you and some of the guys were invited to the fashion show on the fifteenth March? Laverne said she'd given you some tickets. Maybe we can catch up then?"

Leslie was working hard on getting both the show and the event organised with his boss and he didn't think Oliver would come, as much as he'd like that.

Frankie went on. "Yeah, me and my mate Stewart are coming. Not really our thing but we get to dress up in pretty clothes and have a few free drinks and eat some good food, so we're in. Plus you're there." He flashed a wicked smile down at Leslie. "That makes it even better."

Leslie flushed. "Okay, then, I'll see you there. It should be a really good event." He waved as he continued walking by him. "See you tomorrow."

"See you, gorgeous. It's the one highlight of my day. I wouldn't miss it for anything," Frankie teased.

Leslie grinned at that and sashayed down the pavement with an extra sway in his hips. It was always nice being appreciated.

Chapter 11

Oliver stared moodily into his soup as he drew the spoon around in circles, sloshing the liquid over the side of the bowl. He'd been having major problems with a website that he was building and he'd needed a break. The tin of tomato soup for a later dinner had seemed like a good idea, coupled with crusty day-old bread, but now he just thought he should curl up in a dark corner and sleep. He knew it was all down to his bad mood and the sheer capriciousness of the current internet connection he had, as he vaguely remembered that he'd seen a notice somewhere that his service provider was working on upgrading the lines in the area. He hadn't paid much attention to it at the time.

He was also suffering from withdrawal symptoms at not having seen Leslie for the past few days. His lover had been busy at work, organising some future fashion show or other, and had been working nights and weekends to get it sorted.

So when the doorbell rang, he didn't scramble to answer it. Perversely, he ignored it. He wasn't expecting anyone and it was probably some door-to-door salesman. He did peer out into the garden, but it was dark and he could see nothing. The doorbell rang again, more insistently as if someone had their finger pressed on it. Oliver growled loudly.

"Fuck off, will you? Can't you tell I'm not here?"

His mobile rang. He scrambled to pick it up and his heart leapt when he saw it was Leslie. *This* summons, he answered.

"Leslie, hi. I thought you were working tonight."

Leslie sounded rather exasperated when he replied. "I managed to get the rest of the night off. Instead, I thought, you know what, I'll go and pay a surprise visit to my boyfriend. So I doll myself up and rush post haste to his house only to find he's not answering his bloody doorbell!"

Oliver shot up from his chair and dashed to his front door, phone melded to his ear. He was surprised in a number of ways. First, that Leslie was here. Secondly that he'd called him his 'boyfriend.' They hadn't got to that discussion in their six-week relationship yet, and he was both a little scared and exhilarated at the term being used.

"I'm on my way," he blabbered. "Sorry, I thought it was a salesman or something. Hold on."

He reached the door, turned the lock then yanked the door open. His jaw dropped, the phone left his shoulder and clattered to the floor.

"Holy shit," was all he could manage. His cock managed much more than that, going from droopy to sledgehammer in about two seconds flat.

Leslie smirked from beneath eyes rimmed with guy-liner, his full lips pink and pouty with clear lip gloss. He wore a black coat, open in the front, under which he slayed, killed and worked a dark grey corset, which clung to his slender figure as if painted on. Teamed with sheer black stockings and red stiletto heels, Oliver had never seen a more erotic sight in all his life. And, given his former line of work, he'd seen quite a few.

"Can I come in then?" Leslie's husky voice made Oliver's dick jump and he nodded speechlessly.

"You came across town looking like that?" Oliver gaped. "Leslie, that's a bit dangerous, isn't it?"

Not to mention he didn't want anyone seeing his lover dressed like *that.* This was for his eyes only.

"Oh keep your pants on," Leslie drawled as he sashayed into the house. Then a wicked grin flashed across his beautiful face. "Or not…and don't worry. I didn't wear these shoes across town." He waved his man bag at Oliver. "I had jeans on and a pair of flats. I changed just before getting here."

"Changed where?" Oliver said dazedly.

"There's a coffee shop about four houses down. I popped in there and did the deed. So, are you happy to see me?" He licked his lips lasciviously as he cast a glance at Oliver's crotch. "I'd say that's a big, fat yes."

Oliver closed the door and tried to control the urge to rip Leslie's clothes off and drag him caveman-like into the bedroom. "Of course I'm happy to see you. I missed you these last few days."

Leslie's face softened and he drew Oliver into a fragranced hug. "I missed you, too, sweetie." His lips found Oliver's in a tender kiss, gentle and loving and Oliver succumbed to the sublime creature in his arms and sighed happily into his mouth. When they drew apart, Leslie grinned at him.

"That's more like it." An expression of uncertainty flitted across his face. "Oh and hey, I just realised I called you my boyfriend back there. It just sort of slipped out. I quite understand if you don't want me to call you that…"

Oliver reached out a finger and held Leslie's lips closed. "It's fine. That's what we are, isn't it?"

Leslie's—his *boyfriend's*—eyes shone and the smile on his face would have lit the whole of London on a dark and dreary night. "I'd hoped so."

They looked at each other and Oliver realised that at that moment, something had changed. He was terrified by the realisation that someone had come to mean more to him than he'd ever wanted—which meant he could be broken again. He quashed the squirming fear inside and waved toward the lounge.

"Shall we have a drink, you can tell me about your day and then perhaps I can peel those stockings off your legs. And that corset… fuck, you look incredible."

Leslie waved airily, a pink flush suffusing his cheeks. "A drink sounds like a good idea. For now." He smirked and walked past Oliver with a waft of fresh-smelling eau-de-cologne.

When they were settled with drinks and light chill-out music playing in the background, Leslie settled back into Oliver's arms with a happy sigh, his legs stretched out sexily in front of him.

"This is the life," he declared. "I had such a rough day at work, but you make it all okay."

Oliver loved hearing about Leslie's days at the fashion house. There was always something going on, some quirky tale to tell. He was having a tough time not pouncing on his boyfriend, though.

"Tell me all about it. Did any more material try to attack you?" he murmured, as he drank in the scent of Leslie's shampoo and watched his elegant legs fidget around getting comfortable. He'd enjoyed his lover's last dramatic account of the fabric that had 'tried to eat him.'

Leslie huffed. "No, that was a one-off, thank God. But Laverne has been on this mission with this latest fashion show to really make her mark. As part of the show, she had me practicing draping fabric over all these naked statues on the catwalk. That way she can see what look she wants on 'the night.'" He warmed to his subject. "I mean, I seem to have become her *go-to* toy boy. I thought I was the fabric buyer, not the set designer and general factotum." He scowled adorably and Oliver hid a grin. He knew Leslie *loved* being included in anything to do with the fashion house, but sometimes he felt he simply had to make a fuss.

"What kind of statues?" he asked idly as he ran his fingers through Leslie's hair.

His boyfriend's eyes lit up. "Naked ones, like David, you know? All these mock guys in all their glory. I have to drape the material strategically over them. Later, part of the show will be when the models release the fabric and reveal what's underneath. Some sort of Grecian fantasy Laverne is putting together. It looks really cool. I wish you could see it."

Oliver's heart skipped a beat. His earlier bad mood had disappeared seeing Leslie at the door in that sexy getup. Perhaps he could take their excursions a step further. Give himself a little bit of shock therapy and see how he fared.

"Do you mean that?" he said quietly. "If I decided to come down and watch the show, would that be something you'd want?"

Leslie swung around and stared at him. "I'd want? Oliver, you know I'd love to see you get out to a function like this, show everyone you're around." He gave a slow smile. "That you're mine."

Oliver's dick liked the idea of being Leslie's. His heart did, too. "No promises," he warned. "But I do think I owe it to you to try and be a little bit more public. Get over this whole recluse thing." His insides quailed at what he was proposing. "Just get out and about a bit, let people see I'm around. I mean, it's not like they think I'm dead or anything, and people still see me when they go the shops and shit, but at a fashion show a lot of people I knew once will recognise me."

"You don't owe me anything," Leslie said quietly. "I understand you're scared at what you think people will say. But honestly, you really don't look that much different. It's only in your head that you see the change, think it's worse than it is. That's what I've been trying to tell you." His hand reached out and caressed Oliver's cheek. "If you want to come with me, it would be awesome. I'd love it."

Leslie grew more animated. "I could get Laverne to put a little table at the back for you, and you could sit there like the mysterious stranger and let people wonder who you are. Maybe even wear a masquerade mask over your eyes, like the ones in V for Vendetta. Ooh, I could even get Draven to be your official bodyguard. He can stand there beside you with that glower he has making sure people can't bother you. Taylor would love that, seeing his man all dangerous and tough. I bet it would mean Draven would get a lot of nookie when he got home."

Oliver was laughing at the flow of words from Leslie's beautiful mouth so he shut him up the best way he knew how. He kissed him. Kissed him with all the feeling he had for this whimsical and quirky man-child, this man who made his heart beat faster and his soul soar. He knew it hadn't been that long, but he knew he was falling fast for the irrepressible Leslie Scott.

Leslie sighed and kissed Oliver back with fervour, soft lips nibbling at his, hands reaching in and touching skin. The soft whisper of Leslie's stockinged legs against Oliver's own made Oliver crazy with want.

"Please," he whispered. "Undress for me so I can see all of you. Naked is your best outfit, Leslie."

Leslie smiled wickedly and stood up. He wandered over to the DVD player and fiddled about with it. The soft, sensual music of Beyoncé's 'Dance for You' began to play. Then he bent down, arse to Oliver and removed one of his high-heeled shoes, slowly, tantalisingly, in time to the music. The corset tugged up and his tight, round cheeks made Oliver's mouth water. He watched the sexy, lithe and limber form of his lover perform a strip show of note as Beyoncé wafted through the speakers. Leslie's eyes closed as he removed his shoes, waving them teasingly at Oliver as he lay feet up on the couch. So turned on, Oliver was afraid to move in case the simple friction of his cock against his underwear and pants made him come. He wanted to savour the gorgeous man gyrating languidly in front of him, appreciate every moment and then make love to him, taking his time, breathing in Leslie's moans, which would become music to his ears.

Leslie mouthed the words to the song as he danced, then reached behind him and began undoing the clips to his corset. Oliver was so hard he was like the proverbial diamond in an ice storm. Slowly, teasingly, the vision in front of him taunted and teased, eyes half closed, as Leslie removed the garment. The corset was carelessly whipped to one side and Oliver lost his breath. His lover wore a tiny black thong underneath, the fabric already stretched and wet with arousal by Leslie's own hard-on.

"Liking what you see?" Leslie asked huskily, his eyes never leaving Oliver's. "See how I dress for you? Only for you, I promise." His face promised Oliver delights and Oliver so wanted to take advantage of them. He reached down and pushed his jeans and underwear off, throwing them to one end of the couch. Hastily, he pulled his shirt above his head until he was naked. He held the base of his cock tightly as Leslie undulated in front of him, rolling his stockings sexily down his legs. Oliver didn't want this to be over too soon. But, the lustful look in his lover's eyes as his hips and shaved crotch moved closer toward the couch was clear. Oliver's mouth wanted to take Leslie's beautifully upright cock in and show him just what he thought of his strip tease.

Slowly, Leslie stepped out of his not-really-there thong, and stood swaying to the finishing bars of the music as Beyoncé's voice tailed away. The sight of the man naked was one Oliver would take to his grave. Coltish, long limbs, an elegant yet strong build, a face that could sink ships with its open-eyed beauty and legs that looked as if they should be wrapped around Oliver right now.

"Put those heels back on and come over here," he growled. "I need you. So damn much."

The soft smile Leslie gave him was like the sun coming out on a grey day. Teasingly, he slipped his shoes back on, tantalisingly waving his beautiful ankles at Oliver as he did so. Then he moved over to Oliver and straddled his hips, his cock only inches from Oliver's yearning mouth. Slowly, Leslie eased forward until the tip touched Oliver's lips and he took him in, revelling in the musky taste, the smooth and heated flesh who was his lover. Leslie gasped and pushed deeper into Oliver's mouth. He loved it when Leslie fucked his mouth, loved the sounds he made, needy and desperate as those blue eyes watched his own cock moving in and out as Oliver's tongue and lips paid homage to the beauty that was Leslie Tiberius Scott.

The music continued to play in the background and Oliver closed his eyes and surrendered to the feelings building in his chest. This was something sublime, something to be savoured.

He got into his teasing torture, and not too soon after, Leslie's hands gripped his shoulders tightly, hips rocking as his panting grew louder. Oliver smiled around the cock in his mouth. He knew Leslie's breaking point, the point at which he could no longer hold back. He decided it was time to end it, as his own cock wanted inside Leslie so badly he didn't think he could last much longer. His tongue dipped into the slit, and his mouth tightened, and sucked and Leslie gave a cry of bliss and came hard. Wet, sweet-tasting come flooded Oliver's mouth and dribbled down the side. He relished every drop as Leslie slumped forward, holding Oliver's head tightly against his sweating belly.

"Oh God, every time you do that, I swear it's the best ever," he groaned as Oliver kissed the skin over his mouth. "You are just so good at it."

Oliver shrugged as he moved his head away so he could breathe and not be smothered by toned abs. "Plenty of practice," he said cheekily and Leslie laughed as he shifted position.

"Oh yes, Mr. Porn Star, that's definitely one of your best talents."

"I have other talents," Oliver murmured. He frowned. "You taste sweet. How come?"

Leslie chuckled. "I read this article that says incorporating fruit into your diet makes a difference. I tried eating pineapple and berries this week. Obviously, it worked." He waggled his eyebrows as he positioned himself above Oliver and stared down in amusement. "Maybe we should try different flavours, see if it's true? I could eat curry all week, then seafood and maybe you'll be able to taste the difference."

Oliver grimaced. "I'll skip the seafood and curry thanks. I rather like fruity Leslie."

Leslie laughed loudly. "Oh, I'm fruity all right. Don't you know that yet?"

"Fruity and the sexiest man I know," Oliver said huskily. "Now do you think we can get back to what we were doing? This hard-on isn't going away by itself."

"Your wish is my command," Leslie whispered as he picked up the tube of lube on the nearby table. There was always lube somewhere in Oliver's house. He figured it was an occupational hazard.

One of the things Leslie liked to do, and Oliver loved to watch, was to use his fingers inside himself as he readied himself for Oliver's cock. He made these strange grunts and sighs, and his face scrunched in pleasure.

"One of these days, I'm going to do this to you," Leslie murmured as he squirmed above Oliver. "I know you're not much of a bottom, but I really want to be in your arse at least once or twice."

Oliver nodded, his eyes feasting on the sight in front of him. "I've bottomed before. You know that, just not recently. But there is nothing I'd like better than you inside me. I'm ready when you are…"

Leslie used Oliver's sweats to wipe his sticky hands, tossing the pants on the floor once he'd finished. Grabbing a condom, Leslie unwrapped it with a quick, wicked grin and slid it onto Oliver's ready dick, sheathing him, making sure to flick his leaking tip as he did. Oliver heaved a shuddering, needy sigh at the contact. When Leslie finally straddled Oliver, teasingly lowering his body onto his cock, they both gasped, and Oliver gave a groan of satisfaction. He held back the impulse to push upward, and instead watched as he disappeared inside Leslie's eager hole. Wet heat engulfed his sensitive flesh as Leslie's fingers rested on his chest. Leslie rode Oliver gracefully, in balletic movements that were fluid and focused, his sexy heels adding to the sheer eroticism of his movements.

"My God, you do that so well, " Oliver gasped as his hips began thrusting impatiently upward as he strived to bury himself as deep inside Leslie as he could. "You are wicked, you know that?"

Leslie's reply was to bounce even harder on Oliver's dick, twisting his nipples and gripping skin until Oliver succumbed to the sight and sensation as he and Leslie became one. It seemed to Oliver that all those moments spent as Nicky Starr, all those sessions with men he'd knew as friends, colleagues or didn't know at all, were nothing compared to the moments of completeness he felt when he was with Leslie, making love.

The feeling of belonging was amplified as his groin exploded, his skin prickled and the orgasm that thundered through his body rocked his world. He clutched at Leslie's slim hips and bellowed out his satisfaction.

Leslie leaned back, resting his hands on Oliver's thighs and moaned. "I have two words. Fucking. Awesome. I love to make you flip like that. God, you look so damn sexy when you do."

Oliver's heaving chest needed air so he took in some deep breaths. "You are going to bloody kill me."

Leslie's soft laugh made his dick twitch—just a little. "Not the intention. Dead body sex is so gross. I need you alive and horny." He lifted himself up, expertly removed the condom, tied it…then flung it on the side table. He slipped off his shoes and laid them gently on the floor.

Leslie winced as he settled next to Oliver on the couch, feet tucked up beneath him. "Why do we always seem to end up on the couch when we do this? I don't think we've made it to the bedroom more than about three times since we met." He nestled into Oliver's side, gently tracing the scars on his body with warm fingers.

Oliver chuckled tiredly as he wrapped an arm around his lover. "Because you do things to me that no one has ever done before. Drive me to distraction."

Leslie moved up onto one elbow and stared down at him, brow furrowed. "Really?" He sounded uncertain. "I'd have imagined you'd have had another man in your life that might have made you feel that way. Gregori Golovin didn't do that?" He bit his lip. "Sorry. Bad form talking about an ex-lover to your present one especially after mind-blowing sex."

Oliver's stomach had lurched at the mention of his ex. "Greg never made me feel like you do." He stopped, not really wanting to tell this story now, but feeling it was due. "Greg was controlling, very charismatic. I was only twenty-one when we met. I was flattered that a man like him would be interested in someone like me. He was dominant, strong and I enjoyed that aspect. I was crazy about him."

Leslie's soft breath brushed his ear but he said nothing. His hands simply stroked Oliver's belly and torso, grounding him.

"We had some good times. But when I got him chucked out the studio for the whole drug thing, he turned really nasty. He'd always had a violent streak in him." He took a deep breath. "He beat the shit out of me that night. I needed a week to get over it. He'd hit me a few times before then, and apologised. I always took him back. Like an idiot."

"That bastard," Leslie growled. Even in this emotional state Oliver thought it was as sexy as hell. "Honey, you thought you loved him. That plays havoc with your common sense. I can't believe he beat you that badly, the prick. I'm never watching his films again." The determination and disgust in Leslie's voice made Oliver laugh.

"He may look like a blond god with those green eyes and platinum hair but he could be very cruel. I found out just how much the night I went back to my apartment, after we broke up and found him there with two other guys, the twins, remember I mentioned them before?" Leslie nodded against his shoulder. "I'd forgotten to get my key back." He fell silent as he remembered. "Greg was there being spit-roasted by these two guys. He didn't even care that I was there, seeing it. They just carried on. I screamed and ranted and they laughed at me."

Leslie's hand tightened on his shoulder. "Fucking bastards," he murmured. "I hope you stuffed them up."

Oliver's chest tightened. "I should have done, I suppose. I didn't." His voice was hollow in the quiet of the room. "Instead I rushed out, found my own party, got doped and boozed up and went on a motorbike ride."

Leslie sat up swiftly. "That was the night you had the accident? Oh, Oliver."

The grief in his voice made Oliver pull his boyfriend down closer into his arms as he kissed his fragranced hair. "I was a fucking idiot. I shouldn't have done it. I can only blame myself."

"Maybe, but you weren't thinking straight. God, I wish I could kick that motherfucker in the balls with my heels." Leslie growled again.

Oliver smiled at the feral sound. "I love it when you do that," he chuckled. "It's pretty hot."

Leslie smiled against his skin. "I'll have to do it more often then." He kissed Oliver's chest softly. "What happened after the accident? Did Gregori at least come to see you in hospital, say he was sorry?"

Oliver laughed harshly. "Oh, he came to visit me all right. I was in and out of consciousness, all doped up on all kinds of shit. I woke up to find him there, sitting by the bed." He paused, remembering the gladdening of his heart that perhaps everything was okay again, that Greg had come to ask forgiveness and wanted him back. "I told him I still loved him, needed him. He just smiled and leaned down and said that now I looked like a monster, there was no way anyone would ever want or need me again."

Leslie's horrified gasp echoed in his ear.

Oliver's chest ached with pain. "He told me that I was a pathetic, useless fuck-up and that I was finished in the porn industry because the only way they'd be able to pay anyone to fuck me was with a paper bag over my face." He smiled twistedly. "Then he left."

The room was silent. Against his chest, Oliver heard a muffled sound and he reached down in surprise to lift Leslie's face to his. His lover's eyes were wet with tears and he was vainly trying to hold back a sniffle. "Leslie, honey, please don't cry. It's all over now, and I have you, remember?" Tenderly he smoothed locks of Leslie's damp hair off his wet cheeks.

I have you for now, at least.

"I can't believe someone would say something like to you when you're all busted up in hospital," Leslie sniffed. "He's such a tosser. I am definitely burning all my films with him in. Then I'm going to pack them in a box and send him a letter telling him what I think of him. It will include the words *fuck you* and *twat.*"

Oliver laughed. "You do that, you devil, you." He was warmed at the reaction to his story, that Leslie cared about him that much. Warmed and scared at the same time. He was back at his old *I'm getting too close to this man* scenario, the one that meant he could end up getting hurt again and hurting Leslie in the process. That was his biggest fear.

I'm not the right guy for a bright, shining star like Leslie to have a future with. What if I can't be what he wants, what he needs? Maybe my own damn insecurities are going to drag him down, and he doesn't deserve that. He's too special to have anything but the best in his life.

They lay together, quiet, each busy with their own thoughts. And when Leslie reached up again with wet, salty lips and claimed his in a fierce, possessive kiss, Oliver closed his eyes and let all the bad memories of the past fade away for a fleeting, wonderful moment.

Chapter 12

Oliver loved lazy Sunday mornings. Especially when he woke up with Leslie curled beside him. There was something about having his lover's pert, warm arse snuggled against Oliver's already aroused body that really made it worthwhile sleeping in. He smiled and kissed the back of Leslie's neck, making him chuckle softly and wriggle against his already hardening dick.

"Someone's ready to go again," Leslie murmured sleepily as Oliver ran a hand though his messy bed hair. "Wasn't last night enough for you? You made me come so hard I saw stars."

Oliver trailed his lips across the bare skin of Leslie's shoulder. "I could never get enough of you," he murmured as his lips trailed down the soft skin of his boyfriend's back. "You're this irresistible force of nature who I have to contend with."

Oliver loved the way the body in his bed arched back, and Leslie's languid arm reached back and pulled Oliver's mouth to his for a hot, slightly stale-breath-smelling kiss. Morning breath really didn't matter when it was Leslie's.

For a moment they lost themselves in the shift of skin on skin, the press of a cock between firm, willing cheeks and the promise of something in passionate kisses and questing tongues. The moment was lost when the doorbell rang.

Oliver lifted his lips from Leslie's and frowned. "Who the hell can that be? It's eleven a.m., for God's sake." They waited with indrawn breath and the doorbell rang again.

"Well, whoever it is, they aren't going away," Leslie murmured as he settled back down on his pillow, with no intention that Oliver could see of getting up to answer the door. Since it was his house after all, he wasn't surprised when Leslie said, "I s'pose you'd better go see who it is." He snuggled back under the covers and closed his eyes.

Oliver muttered as he got out of bed and pulled on his sweatpants. "Bloody rude of them coming at this time of the morning."

There was a snort from under the covers and Oliver leaned over and swatted Leslie's arse hard. The squeal that followed made him smile. He wandered out of the bedroom, down the hallway to the front door. He yawned and scratched his belly.

This had better be something damned important.

He definitely wasn't expecting what he found on his doorstep. Packaged in a slender five-foot-seven frame with styled dark hair, twinkling dark brown eyes, a cheeky grin and bearing a McDonald's bag, Maxwell Lewis was not someone Oliver thought to see.

"Hi Ollie, long time no see. I come bearing gifts. Can I come in? I only just got in from the flight from Mexico and oh my God, worst ever. I had some woman trying to grope my balls all the way back. And let me tell you, spending thirteen or so hours in the air with some crazy chick feeling you up, that is *so* not cool. Can I come in? Did I ask that already?"

The complete diarrhoea that flowed from his friend and sometimes-bed-partner's mouth, coupled with the hated diminutive of his name had Oliver reeling. Maxwell beamed at him and pushed him out of the way to come inside and make his way to the kitchen.

"You're looking good, Ollie. Love the whole sweaty bare top, sweatpants thing you've got going on there. Very Brad Pitt. Très sexy. So who is he?"

Maxwell planted the McDonald's bag on the kitchen top, and turned to give Oliver a sly wink. "Can I meet him? Or is that taboo—one fuck-buddy meeting another one?"

Oliver finally found his voice and the welcome gap in Maxwell's verbiage to actually talk. "Max, wow. I didn't know you were in town." He glanced anxiously down the hallway wondering if Leslie could hear. "I have to say I wasn't expecting you."

"Oh, you know me." Maxwell waved a hand airily. "I like to keep people on their toes, surprise them." His eyes narrowed. "And you, my friend, have the freshly screwed look, plus there's dried come all over your chest. Is he here? Can I say hi to him?" He made a move toward the hallway and Oliver knew that Maxwell would have no hesitation in marching into Oliver's bedroom and introducing himself. He barred Maxwell's way.

"Hold on a minute, Max. Dial down the Duracell bunny a notch. You're making my head spin."

Max grinned at him. Truth be told, Oliver was really pleased to see him. He'd missed his quirky friend and part-time lover. Maxwell was one of those people who took every day in his stride, faced it head-on like a relentless juggernaut and didn't do commitments. Apparently, he kept a spreadsheet detailing the name of each of his conquests, with their height, age, weight, telephone number, orientation (top, bottom or side), fuck ranking from 1-5 (5 being the best) and dick size. That way, he'd told Oliver smugly, he could use his pivot table to narrow down whether he'd a) seen the guy before and b) wanted to see him again. The latter occasion was rare. Maxwell had never told Oliver what his ranking was, but he kept coming back for more so he supposed he must be a 4 or 5.

"I'm on an unexpected layover. I picked up some guy in a bar in Mexico City. It turned out he was the married-to-a-woman son of some bigwig who like, almost owns the airline I fly for, if you can believe that, and he's 'in the *closet*.'" He sighed. "The powers-that-be have put me on a four-day leave while they assure the guy I won't be putting the pictures I have of him fucking me onto the net, or the video on YouTube. I am hoping I still have my job though. It'd be a bummer to lose it because of some dickwad who can't admit he likes men." Maxwell gave Oliver a ferocious grin. "I told them if they get rid of me, those pictures and the video will definitely be getting airtime. So I think they saw my reasoning." He stroked his neatly trimmed goatee with a wicked glint in his eyes, looking for all the world to Oliver like an old-time villain in a black-and-white film.

Oliver blinked. It was too early for the likes of Maxwell. The man was a dynamo in bed and out. "Huh. Great story. Well, yeah, I do have someone here, so now isn't the best time for a catch-up. Maybe we can meet at Fidalgo's later…?"

"Oliver, is everything okay?" Leslie's voice echoed behind him and Oliver turned. Leslie stood there, eyes sleepy, sheet wrapped around his waist. His hair was tousled, and Oliver's heart leapt at the sight. He looked so damn beautiful standing there.

"Hi," Maxwell bounded like a puppy over to Leslie and held out a hand. "I'm Maxwell, occasional lover of this guy and others, and full-time slut." He grasped one of Leslie's hands and his boyfriend made a panicked grab at the sheet that threatened to drop. "I just popped in to say hi, and wow, you are really gorgeous. Are those eyes real or are they contacts?"

Maxwell leaned in to peer into Leslie's eyes in admiration. "I think they're real. Oliver, what do you think?" He turned back to Oliver with an expression of hope on his face. "Is he, like, into threesomes? 'Cause I would so like to…"

Leslie's eyes widened in sheer confusion and Oliver jumped in to rescue him, cutting Maxwell's words off with a hand on his mouth.

"Maxwell, A, they are real, B, no, you can't have us both, and C, you really need to tone it down a bit. You're scaring my boyfriend."

Now it was time for Maxwell's eyes to bug out. "Boyfriend? *He's a stayer*? Oh my God, Ollie, that's awesome. You found someone. I love it. It's about time." He reached over and hugged Leslie tightly, who clutched his sheet for dear life. Then Maxwell reached out and did the same to Oliver, who tried to give Leslie a reassuring look. His lover's lips twitched in amusement.

Leslie seemed to have found his composure after being mauled and inspected like a slab of meat. "So you're Maxwell, huh?" He shuffled forward taking care not to catch his feet in the sheet trailing behind him. "I'm Leslie. So nice to meet you. Oliver's told me…some stories about you. I have to say, it's great to meet the legend."

Maxwell flushed in pleasure. "Legend? Oh how kind." He blew on his fingernails. "If somewhat true." He glanced slyly at Oliver. "I suppose this means that you and me are no longer doing the *hide the sausage* thing? Unless, as I said, maybe we could all…"

Oliver moved forward to stand next to Leslie. "No. Just no, Max. Leslie isn't into that sort of thing and we're exclusive." He placed a possessive arm around Leslie's shoulders. "Leslie is mine. And I'm his. So no sausages are getting hidden other than ours." He grinned at Leslie who grinned back.

Oliver saw Maxwell's face shadow, his eyes darkening. It was only a fleeting expression, but he looked almost sad, a little whimsical. Oliver wasn't used to seeing anything close to that expression on Maxwell before.

"Well, that's put me in my place. I understand. You make a stunning couple, by the way. Ollie, I love what you've done with your hair. Suits you. Glad to see you getting over that whole scar thing. You always looked just gorgeous to me. And I heard you're even getting out and about a bit more? I guess that's due to this lovely man next to you? Well done, is all I can say." He made a moue at Leslie. "I could never get him to go out with me."

"That's because you wanted to drag me to every gay club in town," Oliver remarked dryly. "And every party and social event in the London calendar, all in one night. I don't think I could have borne the excitement." He kissed the top of Leslie's head. "And I'm actually attending my first event in a few days' time. A fashion show. I'm a bit nervous but with this one by my side, I'll be fine."

He kissed Leslie's forehead. Leslie smiled softly and presented his face for a proper kiss.

When Oliver finished his boyfriendly duty and looked back at a rather quiet Maxwell, he was surprised to see a look of longing on his face. It was quickly replaced by the mischievous grin he knew well, but he knew he hadn't imagined the other expression.

Was Maxwell growing up? Did he want a little bit of stability in his life instead of just a string of lovers? Someone to come home to instead of simply bang the daylights out of? Oliver wasn't sure, but he resolved to speak to him about it.

"So…" He gestured to the bag on the counter. "Are those for us then? I hope you bought enough of them because I am damn hungry. And you know I love their breakfast muffins."

Maxwell nodded. "I bought six of each. Bacon and sausage." He rattled about in the bag and laid the muffins out on the counter. "Put the kettle on, Ollie. I need black coffee. I'll have mine then get out of your hair. I'm sure you've got better things to do rather than entertain me." He smirked at them.

"Ollie?" Leslie murmured with a quizzical glance at his boyfriend. "I thought you didn't like that name?"

Oliver scowled. "I don't. But he"—he waved his muffin at Maxwell who was happily chasing a random bit of sausage falling out of his breakfast bun—"insists on it. It drives me crazy."

Maxwell pulled a tongue at him then went back to devouring his muffin. Oliver shook his head as he headed over to make coffee.

Two of my favourite men in one room. This is a turn-up for the books. I never thought I'd see the day. My now ex-lover with my current one.

He watched as Leslie and Maxwell chatted, enjoying the sight of the two together.

I could get used to this domesticity. It scares the crap out of me, but I want it so badly.

Oliver just hoped his insecurities and demons stayed away long enough to make that happen.

Chapter 13

The night before the fashion show, Leslie was taking a well-earned night off. He had a myriad of things to do—wash his hair, manscape and make sure his outfit was ready for tomorrow night. He was feeding his fish when his mobile rang. Hoping it was Oliver, he rushed to answer and he grinned when he confirmed it was indeed his boyfriend. Sprinkling a few more flakes of Golden Delicious Fish Food on the top of his tank, and hoping that his fish wouldn't explode from eating too much, he answered.

"Hiya, sexy. It's late, nearly midnight. What are you doing up?"

"Now *there's* a leading question," Oliver purred, his voice sending shivers down Leslie's spine and inflating his cock. His voice was husky and slightly slurred. "I was enjoying some wine, and thinking of you. Thinking of you led to a hard-on and I decided I really needed a hand with it." The sound of rustling clothing filtered down the phone.

Leslie's dick liked that idea. He chuckled and put the now-sealed fish food container back on the table. "Is this like, a phone sex call, or something?"

"Or something," Oliver said silkily and Leslie swallowed at the incredibly seductive tone. He made his way over to the bed. If he was having sex now, he wanted to be comfortable.

"What are you wearing?" Oliver growled.

Leslie looked down at his dark blue Andrew Christians and comfy white tee-shirt. "My blue high-heeled pumps and a thong."

He was damned if he was going to tell Oliver the truth and be *bleh.*

His boyfriend's indrawn breath and moan of desire went straight to Leslie's groin.

"You're wearing that around the house? Jesus. You are one sexy fucker." Now Leslie heard the sound of flesh against flesh and he swallowed, his cock inflating.

"Have you got Skype?" Oliver murmured.

Leslie's groin flamed as if he'd suddenly rubbed Deep Heat into his nether regions. "Yes," he squeaked. "I use it to speak to my folks. Oliver, are you beating off?"

His lover laughed softly and Leslie could see how this man had become a world-famous porn star. It was the Nicky Starr sound Leslie had heard so often in his films, a sound so dirty, so tantalising, so damned lust-inducing that Leslie thought he might self-combust.

"Oh honey, you do *not* want your folks in on this show," Oliver murmured. "The things I want you to do for me…"

Leslie looked around for a paper bag, sure he was hyperventilating from the feeling of breathlessness in his chest. His dick was already wetting the front of his underwear, pushing out like the Queen Mary about to set sail. "You want Skype sex? Oh fuck, Oliver. That is so hot. I haven't done that before."

"Good. Your first time can be with me. I can say I popped your c2c cherry."

"c2c?" Leslie fiddled with his laptop as he clicked on the Skype programme to open it. The familiar opening sound made him realise he was definitely doing this. He was going to have sex on camera. The penny dropped. "Oh. You mean camera to camera. I'm just getting it open now. Skype I mean. Hold on a minute."

"Send me an invite. StarrSex69. Hurry up. I'm all set up and ready to go…" There was a low groan and a sudden intake of breath from the other side of the phone.

"Yes, give me a minute. The connection isn't very good. I'll be with you in a sec. I'm going to put the phone off now. Buh-bye. Speak in a sec." Leslie terminated the call and sent the invite and within seconds, it was accepted. He put the call on hold and got to work. He'd never stripped and re-dressed as quick before in his life.

He rooted through his underwear drawer for his blue silk thong, slipped it on and then slid his feet into his heels.

He gave a quick look at himself in the mirror, satisfied himself he had nothing stuck in his teeth and he looked good enough for Skype. Then he got back onto the bed and pulled his laptop onto his lap. He hastily clicked the video icon to reveal himself then finally focused on Oliver's profile. When he saw his boyfriend, he definitely needed that paper bag.

Oliver sat in the armchair in his bedroom. His tanned legs were stretched out in front of him, sprawled open and he was naked. One large hand was wrapped around his jutting, pink cock and he grinned sloppily as he saw Leslie. "Hi, sexy. What took you so long? I was thinking about you."

"I love what you've done with that thing." Leslie motioned toward Oliver's cock as he peered closer at the screen. "You're a little drunk, aren't you?"

Oliver nodded vigorously. "Yep, and horny as fuck."

"I can see that." Leslie laughed as he scooted back up to rest against his satin pillows then arranged the laptop strategically just beyond his heeled feet so he could be seen at his best advantage. Luckily it was a nineteen-inch laptop screen—HD to boot—and the picture was excellent.

In the small frame at the corner of the screen he saw himself laid out languidly, his dick bulging in the skimpy thong. Unconsciously, he let his legs fall apart, revealing his arse cheeks. His face flamed with the wantonness of it. He was a slut putting himself on offer and he loved it. He especially loved Oliver's lick of the lips and the hungry expression in his eyes.

"Hell, you look beautiful. That arse…" The longing in his lover's voice made Leslie's skin prickle. Goose bumps formed on his skin.

"Thank you. I aim to please." He palmed his dick and closed his eyes at the feel of the fabric on his swollen, heated skin. "So, you want me to jack off for you to see?"

He squinted his eyes at the screen, thankful his eyesight was 20/20. He saw Oliver stroking himself. The sight spurred him on to wriggle on the bed and touch himself a little faster.

Oliver's throaty growl had him harder in seconds. "Yes. First I want to see you take that thong down, slowly. Then I want to see you get off. I want to see that gorgeous hole, too. Spread your legs more. Imagine me with my tongue in there, licking you, getting you wet, ready for my cock." The commands were softly spoken but there was no doubt who was in charge. Nicky Starr was in the house.

Leslie's whole body was aflame and, as he lifted his legs, he heard a stuttered moan from the other side of the screen. He peeled the thong from his backside, making sure he opened his legs wide, stretching his cheeks apart for his voyeur then lay back again. He was wet, but not enough. He reached over and took out the lube from under the pillow, squeezing some into his hand. Then he slid his fingers up and down his cock, uttering little sighs of pleasure, his eyelashes fluttering as he succumbed to the sensation.

"This feels so good, wish you were here with me. Want to feel your mouth, taste your cock, feel you inside me, filling me…" He opened his eyes and blew a kiss at his lover.

At the foot of the bed, Oliver's breathing quickened, his eyes never leaving Leslie's hand. "God, you look so damned gorgeous doing that. That pucker of yours….I want to be buried so deep inside that you taste me. Want to fuck you so hard you feel me forever. Make you mine and leave my mark."

The dirty words and the soft slapping of Oliver's hand on his cock drove Leslie crazy. He had no doubt Oliver was hearing the same thing on his side. He couldn't stop the grunts and moans that rose and fell from his mouth as he pleasured himself. For a while, he was lost in the feeling of his aching and heated groin and the knowledge Oliver was there with him.

When he opened his eyes, the expression of bliss on his boyfriend's face sent Leslie into a tailspin. He loved to see those half-closed eyes; that look of concentration as Oliver worked himself, and the white teeth that bit into lips he wished he could kiss. The faint sheen of sweat on Oliver's body triggered memories in Leslie's mind of his man, that strong, unique scent that remained embedded in his brain. He breathed in deeply, trying to *will* the smell stronger.

"God, Oliver, I'm ready. Try and come with me."

His arse clenched and his heels dug into the covers as he gasped loudly, and the prickling that started in his toes and ended in his groin and ultimately his dick, intensified. He shouted Oliver's name as he climaxed, his spunk streaming forth, covering his hand, his thighs and his belly. His trembling legs spasmed as his body did the same and from haze-filled eyes, he saw Oliver fisting his cock and spraying his semen in jets that seemed to never end. Oliver's panting and loud expletives made Leslie smile. In true porn style, Oliver was always vocal when he came. Leslie couldn't help chuckling when he saw a blob of spooge sliding slowly down the screen.

"You have some reach, there, cowboy," he gasped out, in between laughing. "Like a damn jet stream."

Oliver's lazy and satisfied smile made his heart beat faster. "Imagine if we ever did it without condoms," he murmured. "You really would taste me. It'd be better than a protein shake." His half-hard cock lay against his thigh as he leaned back in the chair and closed his eyes.

Leslie looked around for something close to hand to clean himself up. Seeing nothing, he huffed and went to the kitchen to pick up a roll of Kleenex and take it back to the bed. Oliver looked as if he were sleeping, slumped in the armchair with a beatific smile on his face.

Leslie watched him, feeling a warmth inside that he knew was far more than simply sex. "Don't you go to sleep on me," he warned. "You know we always talk after sex."

He began to wipe the sticky fluid off his belly and legs.

Oliver opened his eyes and his beautiful amber stare filled with affection nearly made Leslie blurt out the words he really wanted to say. He refrained, not wanting to scare his boyfriend away.

"Not just sex. Making love. Even when we Skype and say dirty, sexy things to each other, we're making love," Oliver rasped.

Leslie bit his tongue. Now wasn't the time for a declaration of love. Not right after *making* love. He didn't think it had the same impact. "I like making love with you. Now you look tired and I have to be up early for the show prep," he said softly. "Go and get some sleep, Oliver. I'll see you tomorrow night."

Oliver nodded sleepily. "Okay. I really enjoyed this little session. We should do it again soon."

"'Kay. Good night. Be sure and wear that suit I picked out for you tomorrow. You look damned fabulous in it."

"I will. Night, love." The screen went black.

Leslie put his laptop back in its customary place on top of his dressing table and got into bed. He snuggled into his pillow with thoughts of Oliver, his warm body and the opportunity to show him to the world tomorrow night.

* *.*

Leslie hummed as he straightened the fabric around a rather well endowed Greek statue and couldn't resist the urge to run his fingers up the stone cock.

"You like that, hmmm?" he murmured as he did it again. "You're as hard as rock; you must do." He sniggered. "I have no idea where Laverne got all of you, but I want one for home. Then when Oliver's not around, I can play with you instead."

"Oh you are one dirty, dirty, boy." Laverne's laugh echoed through the hall. "I might have known you'd be here fondling the men."

Leslie turned and bowed low. "I live to serve. Even statues need a little Leslie-love."

He turned and looked around at the display hall. "It's looking amazeballs, boss. This event is going to be a smash hit."

Laverne scratched her cheek. Leslie grinned at the move. She only did that when she was nervous. "Thanks to you and everyone who got it ready."

The hall did indeed look superb. The models' catwalk made up the centre of the room, and around it were scattered tables and chairs, ready for people to sit down for dinner. One section of the room was cordoned off for press, and the Grecian theme had been lavishly applied wherever possible. Grapes and vines hung from the roof; the statues stood, richly decorated with colourful fabrics from the store room. Huge, mock white pillars stood firm against the walls, and elsewhere, Grecian art and sculptures framed the room on trestles covered with white chiffon. It looked elegant and very posh, indeed.

The best thing about the space, though, was the small two-person table set back from the rest, almost in the eaves of the room. That was for Oliver when he arrived in about an hour. The lights would have been dimmed and although his boyfriend was psyched up to come—he'd talked about nothing else this week—Leslie wanted him to feel comfortable. He knew this was a huge step forward, appearing in public where probably he would be recognised.

"He's going to be fine, Leslie," Laverne murmured when she saw his glance towards the table. "Oliver is really trying so hard to be here for you. He's a brave soul. He must care about you very much."

Leslie couldn't stop the smile that formed. He and Oliver hadn't ever said anything concrete about how they felt, but he knew there was something there, something deep and, he hoped, lasting. "I think he likes me a bit," he said carelessly. "But then, you know, I'm a likeable character, me. Who wouldn't like this sexy package?"

He gestured down toward his Debussy suit, a slim-fitting, pastel blue worn with a matching waistcoat, a blue-and–white-striped formal shirt and a deep blue tie with white polka dots. He even had his favourite tiepin on, a small silver panther Oliver had given him. Apparently it had been his and he thought it suited Leslie as he was *lithe, mean and sexy.* Leslie wasn't sure how a panther could be sexy, but he loved it anyway.

"You look very handsome, but then it's one of my suits, so I'd expect that," Laverne acknowledged as her eyes dated around, checking the room. "Have you seen Dasher or Bruce? I thought they might be here. I couldn't find them in the dressing room."

Leslie's heart sank. "They are here, though, aren't they? You're not going to make me go down there again and help, because, you know, the trauma last time was enough for me to claim workman's compensation." He knew he was laying it on a bit thick but he had no desire to be at the beck and call of ladies who wanted unmentionable things done again.

Laverne guffawed. "No, Leslie, I won't send you there tonight. Yes, they're both around somewhere. I need to go find them. Camilla was pitching a hissy fit earlier about some fitting not being quite right." She moved away, her mind already occupied with other things from the look of her expression. "Later, Leslie."

Leslie gave a sigh of relief that he wasn't being summoned to the bowels of hell and glanced at his watch. Oliver should be arriving any time, as well as all of his friends. They'd all bought tickets tonight in support of the fashion show to support the Franklin Moore Trust for Homeless LGBTQ Youth, a charity Laverne patronized. He took one last look around the room and nodded in satisfaction. Everything looked superb and he was ready to rock and roll.

"Bring it on," he muttered. "Let's show my boyfriend how we do things in the fashion industry."

* * *

Oliver sat in his chair at the back of the room and watched the crowd around him swell and surge as people greeted each other. It was loud and busy, and he was totally out of his comfort zone. He took another large drink of his red wine and glanced around anxiously. Leslie had promised him he'd be back in fifteen minutes and now it was more like forty-five. The show had been a huge success, the runway models perfection personified and Oliver had to say, he could see a few more suits being purchased based on what he'd seen tonight. He grinned at the thought of what Katie would say about that. She'd been supposed to be here tonight, too, but she'd gotten stuck in Bristol when her plane was delayed and been spitting mad that she wouldn't be there to support him.

He had to admit that putting a suit to go on the town for the first time in a long while had given him a newfound confidence. Leslie had picked it out, fussing through his 'dressing room' (which was simply his spare room kitted with wall–to-wall closing cupboards) and exclaiming in delight every time he found a Debussy. He'd also been delighted when Oliver had pushed him into one of the large cupboards, pulled the door closed and given him a blow job right there.

The deep dove grey suit with the blue-and-white-striped shirt and electric blue silk tie was one of Oliver's favourites and wearing it with a paisley scarf in the top pocket tonight, it looked very dashing, indeed. Leslie had certainly liked it from the smouldering look in his eyes when he'd seen Oliver all dressed up and given him a murmured promise to peel it off him later.

Leslie's friends were über cool. They were all out in force tonight and seemed to be taking turns to check upon him. Gideon and Eddie had wandered over earlier and chatted, and he'd waved at Taylor and Draven as they walked past. It looked like all Leslie's housemates were dutifully love-birded up with only the one stray member of the flock to find his mate. Oliver wished he could say he was Leslie's forever, but his old insecurities were kicking in. Public gatherings like this one certainly triggered his vulnerabilities. However, so far everyone had practically ignored him, apart from a careless glance or quick hello, and he was grateful for that. Perhaps his career as an ex- model and porn star wasn't quite as widely known as it used to be.

He smiled as Taylor sauntered over to him. The man was definitely gorgeous, and Oliver felt a twinge of jealousy that he and Leslie were such good friends.

"Hey, Oliver, how goes it?" Taylor pulled out a chair with a grin and sat down. "I thought I'd come see how you were doing, see where that friend of mine is. He owes me a drink."

"He was supposed to be back a while ago. He's been delayed. Probably Laverne got hold of him."

Taylor chuckled. "Leslie can be a will o' the wisp. He's a real social darling. Everyone wants a piece of him."

Oliver scowled.

Taylor flapped a hand as he laughed. "Come on, you know the guy. He loves to talk." He grew more serious and leaned forward. "I've never seen him this way about anyone before, though. You and he are really getting along, huh?" Dark brown eyes gazed quizzically at Oliver.

"I guess. He's definitely unique."

"Oh that he is. Leslie is one of those who fall for someone, heart and soul." Taylor's eyes met his. "I hope you realise what a special guy he is. I'm pretty protective over him. I wouldn't want him getting hurt."

Oliver nodded. His hand went to his hair in an automatic gesture as he checked it covered his scar for about the tenth time that night.

Have I just been warned?

"Yes," he muttered quietly. "He is. Special I mean."

A shadow loomed over Taylor and a large hand clasped his shoulder. Draven Samuels stood behind his fiancé, a wide grin on his face.

"I heard that, Tay. Are you playing best friend 'don't hurt my buddy or I'll hurt you?' Way to make Oliver feel better." He sat down next to Taylor and covered his hand with his.

Taylor smirked. "Was it working? Was I badass enough without overdoing it?" He winked at Oliver who couldn't help smiling at the adoring look the two men gave each other.

Draven cocked his head to one side. "I have to say there's a much better badass side to you, one that we can try out when we get home. I prefer that bad boy." His hand reached out and caressed Taylor's cheek.

Taylor leaned into his hand. "I look forward to that later then." His eyes sparkled as he looked back at Oliver who was feeling both a little uncomfortable and turned on at the wanton expression of want in both their eyes. "I think we're making Oliver a bit nervous. Maybe…"

A slim hand reached out and twisted Taylor's ear. He yowled as he looked up at a glaring Leslie. A surge of relief flooded Oliver's chest as he observed his lover.

"Tay, are you teasing Oliver? I have two words for you. Dressing. Room." His blue eyes flashed a warning and Taylor blanched. Draven looked curious.

"Oh yeah, so not teasing." Taylor stammered, casting a quick look at Draven. "Just getting to know the guy. Look, we'll leave you two lovebirds alone. Draven and I have a dance he promised me. See you later." He pulled Draven away, who looked confused and was mouthing the words, "Dressing room?"

Oliver broke out into laughter as Leslie sat down beside him, looking smug.

"I can't believe you threatened your best friend with that one. I mean any guy in a dressing room is going to flirt with the models, right? Especially when they look like Reuben Tanner." Leslie had told Oliver about Taylor's recent flirtations when Leslie had dressing room duty from hell.

"He had it coming." Leslie smirked. "I knew I could play that card sometime. And it worked."

Oliver leaned forward and kissed Leslie gently. "You're awesome. And, have I told you yet how bloody beautiful you are tonight? The most incredible man here." His kiss grew deeper and he pressed his tongue against Leslie's mouth, loving the sound his lover made when he kissed back. For a moment, the din, hustle and bustle of the room went away and there were only soft lips, hot mouths and seeking tongues. When they pulled apart, Oliver was gratified to see Leslie looked a little dazed.

"God, you kissed me, right here in front of everyone."

Oliver shrugged, feeling like he'd just run a mile and won a medal. "I did. I wanted to show everyone you belong to me. That I'm yours."

"Oh." Leslie's happy whisper went straight to Oliver's groin, which was already hot and bothered. "That's…so…" Oliver hadn't seen a Leslie lost for words before. Apparently a PDA did that to him.

"Anyway, where did you get to? I missed you."

Leslie's brow furrowed and his eyes darkened. "I met someone I know and we got talking, and then time slipped away from me." He reached over and lightly ran his fingers down Oliver's shirted arm. "And now I need to go and make sure all the prizes are ready to be awarded for the raffle. Laverne's a bit nervous about going up on the catwalk to announce the winners; she doesn't really like going in public like that. So I said I'd check they were all ready, so she doesn't make a fool of herself up there."

"Oh. Okay. But hurry back." Oliver reached over and framed Leslie's face with his hands. "When this evening is all over I'm taking you home and I am going to make love to you until you forget your name. I'm so glad you invited me here tonight. I've enjoyed it."

He kissed him again and then looked into Leslie's wide blue eyes. The emotions he saw there both scared and elated him.

"You'd better get off before your boss comes looking for you."

Leslie nodded and stood up. His face shone with mischief. "Now I have a boner, you dickhead. You'd better make sure this gets put to good use when we get home. Maybe this time I'll be the one on top."

With a grin and a wave, he disappeared into the throng. Oliver watched him go, his body warm and content. Tonight he'd give Leslie whatever he wanted.

"Well, look at you getting it on in public. I thought it was you." The sneering voice catapulted Oliver back into a dark place. He blinked as he looked up into the smarmy face of Gregori Golovin. He was flanked by the twins, Pierce and Payton, who, as usual, were simpering behind him.

"Greg. And acolytes." There had been a time when Greg's long platinum hair and brilliant green eyes, his lithe, limber body and tanned skin had been Oliver's everything. Now, his mind conjured only dark blue eyes and black hair when he thought of someone he cared about. "I can't say it's a pleasure to see any of you. Now could you just turn around and leave?"

Gregori snorted and hooked a chair over with his foot, then sat down next to Oliver. "Go fetch me a drink," he commanded to Pierce. "Payton, can you grab me some food before that greedy bunch of vultures eat it all? I want to talk to my boy Nicky on my own." The twins nodded and melted into the crowd behind them.

"I'm not Nicky anymore, Greg," Oliver said quietly. "I'm just plain Oliver."

"Oh, I know that," Gregori replied with a smirk. "You were washed up the minute you trashed your face. Booze and drugs will do that to you." He leaned closer and peered at Oliver's face. "Wow, they did a really bad job of patching you up. I can still those scars." He reached out a hand to move Oliver's hair from his face and Oliver grabbed it tightly.

"You don't get to touch me," he snarled, his fingers gripping Gregori's wrist. "You don't have that right anymore."

"Oh but twinky boy does?" Gregori grinned nastily. "You seem to be slumming it now, Nicky. I guess that's all you're good for with a face like that."

Heat rushed through Oliver and he wanted to punch the smug face in front of him for those comments. He held back. This was a public place and the last thing he wanted was a lot of attention. Gregori no doubt knew that from the glint in his eyes that told him to bring it on.

"Fuck off," Oliver growled. "I'm over you, so piss off. Go find your toy boys to drill you a new one."

Gregori pulled out his phone. "I was watching you from the minute you walked in and I recognised you," he said dangerously. "So I had my boys follow that twink around and guess what they found? He doesn't just belong to you, Nicky. He has someone else on the side." He held up his phone and waggled it in front of Oliver, whose hands trembled under the table and breath seemed to be getting shorter. He didn't believe Gregori; it was all just a plot to rile him. So when Gregori laid his phone down on the table and there, in full HD colour, was the picture of Leslie kissing another man, a well built, hunky fellow, Oliver felt faint. The date stamp was clearly marked tonight, at ten-thirty pm when Leslie had been gone.

Gregori was watching him closely. "I wasn't lying, was I? He's a bit of a slag, leaving you here like that and then getting off with another guy."

Oliver leaned forward and poked Gregori hard in the chest. "Don't you call him that, you bastard. Leslie is no slag."

He had no doubt there had to be a reason for that picture. Perhaps it had been something innocent, something misconstrued. He'd have to ask him. Leslie wasn't the sort to do that to a man. That much Oliver knew.

Gregori shrugged his broad shoulders. "Well, pardon me. I suppose denial comes easy in your situation. Denial that you don't look like a monster. Denial that your *man*"—he spat the words out—"isn't off fucking someone else. Denial that you aren't a has-been porn star and drug addict who needed coke to get it up on set and make it through the day."

Oliver tried not to let the words get to him but he was shaking. He remembered the pain of the accident, the surgery, the skin grafts, the pain he'd faced with only Katie by his side. He remembered too well Gregori's sneering rejection. The withdrawal process had been painful and difficult. Although he hadn't been on the coke for too long, his addiction was bad enough that he'd suffered plenty through giving it up.

"So," Gregori drawled. "I just wanted to share that with you and tell you that honestly, you need to let it go. This guy isn't going to want you, *Nicky Starr*. He already has someone else anyway, someone who probably hasn't had half of London up his arse. You fucked up our relationship with your high morals and you'll do the same to this one sooner or later. You always do." He stood up. Oliver saw Pierce and Payton approaching the table with drink and food and Gregori waved them over.

"Guys, leave that here with our friend Nicky. He looks like he could use a drink. Probably the first time he's been out in public since his face was torn off. Disgusting, subjecting everyone else to it, too."

The twins laughed.

Even though Oliver knew no one could see the jagged scar, his hand still instinctively went to his face.

"Yeah, we saw 'his' guy over at the bar. He's luscious." One of the twins winked suggestively. Oliver had no idea which one it was; he'd never been able to tell them apart. "I wouldn't mind putting this between that tight arse and giving him one." The man grabbed his crotch and rocked his hips crudely.

Gregori laughed harshly. "I'd fuck him myself. Love to get inside that hot hole."

Oliver stood up, fists clenched. “I’m going to fucking kill you, Greg.” He moved toward him and the men formed a flank together like a wall of Armani suits and gold jewellery. He didn’t care if they beat him up. No one insulted Leslie like that.

“I wouldn’t if I were you,” Gregori said dangerously. “I’ve got someone at the bar keeping an eye on your little bit of fluff. You start something, he’ll get hurt.”

Oliver stared at the three men helplessly and unclenched his fists.

Gregori gave an unpleasant smile. “That’s better.” He flicked an imaginary piece of something off Oliver’s collar, “I’d suggest you quit while you still can. Go back to your miserable, solitary life and be the man you were born to be. Nothing.”

Oliver’s despair flooded him but he tried not to let it show. He didn’t think he was succeeding from the victorious grin on Gregori’s face. Old insecurities and fears invaded his body and his mind like soldier ants on their way to a tasty feast. Gregori looked as if he’d just won the lottery, the smirk on his face growing wider with every beat of Oliver’s bruised heart.

“So, why not sit down and wait for your boyfriend? Maybe you can ask him about the other guy when he comes back. The two of you can have a cosy little tête-à- tête and he can find out exactly how bloody pathetic you really are. Come on, you two.”

Gregori moved off, his two shadows close behind him. Oliver stood there for a while, swaying on his feet, wanting to be sick. He had no idea how much time had passed until he felt a warm hand on his arm as an anxious familiar voice murmured in his ear.

“Are you all right, Oliver? You look as if you’re going to faint.” Leslie’s strong hands helped him back to the table and he sat down, closing his eyes, wishing he was anywhere else but here. Leslie fussed around him as he handed him a glass of water.

“It’s probably nerves,” Leslie soothed. “All this activity and people after being a hermit is bound to give anyone a bit of anxiety. Here, drink this.”

Oliver obediently drank the water, waiting for his racing heart to calm down. Leslie’s blue eyes looked at him with concern.

“Feeling better? Sorry, I tried to get as back as soon as I could…”

The words left Oliver's mouth like vomit. "Someone said they saw you kissing another guy. Is this true?"

Leslie's face paled. "Oh my God, is that what got you all aflutter? It was just Frankie—he was drunk. I gave him a good slap, told him I was out of bounds. He apologised but not before he tried to kiss me. God, Oliver, I'm so sorry. It really didn't mean anything. Like I said, he'd had too much to drink and was a feeling a bit amorous." He sat down beside Oliver, placing a tentative hand on his.

Oliver passed a trembling hand over his forehead. "Who's Frankie?"

"He works at the building site next door to work. He's been trying to get me to go out with him for ages but I've been telling him no. Because I have you." His voice quailed. "I do have you, don't I?"

Oliver tried to process all the thoughts spiralling in his head. He rubbed his eyes tiredly. "I don't know. I can't think."

Leslie reached for his hand. "Frankie is just a friend. He's the son of the guy who owns the construction company. We see each other now and then when he goes out for a smoke, or pops in to say hi at work."

The kiss, Gregori's words, the knowledge of who Oliver had been and who he now was, the fact someone else wanted Leslie, someone who could probably offer him so much more…they all flooded his brain with images and sensations and he felt the familiar darkness creeping up.

"Look, Leslie, I don't feel so well. I'm going to call a taxi and go home and get some sleep. I need to be alone for a while, you know? This is all a bit much and I need to shut off for a bit." He stood up, hating the stricken look on his boyfriend's face, the pain in his eyes.

"Uhm, yes, okay. If that's what you need to do. Of course. Let me call you a cab…"

"No." Oliver's voice came out sterner than he'd meant it to and Leslie's eyes flickered. "I can do this myself. You get back to your party and celebrations and I'll call you tomorrow." He walked away, tears stinging his eyes, not wanting to see whatever devastation he was leaving behind. He needed to do this—leave and not look back before he lost it completely.

* * *

Leslie slumped down on a chair, his hands trembling, the numb feeling in his chest threatening to take over. What the fuck had happened tonight? One minute everything was going fantastically and they were well on their way to Oliver's house for a night of loving, and the next, his lover was walking away, alone, with a look on his face that left Leslie cold inside. Over a kiss? He wondered who'd told Oliver about it.

"Fuck you, Frankie," he muttered softly. "Why did you have to do that?"

In truth, he couldn't blame Frankie for this one. The look in Oliver's eyes, the despair on his face—that hadn't simply been from the kiss incident. Something else was going on, he was sure of it. Perhaps he had pushed Oliver too hard. Perhaps seeing all these beautiful people around him had pushed him over the edge.

"He looked so lost," Leslie whispered. "Like he has nothing. But he has me."

He knew he had fallen head over heels for Oliver Brown. The desire to shout out the words 'I love you' had taunted Leslie more than once, but he'd resisted. It was too soon, surely, he'd told himself, even when he knew it was the truth. He'd never felt about anyone the way he felt about Oliver.

And now it seemed his world had changed and all he could hope was that he'd get the chance to tell Oliver the words he'd been holding back. And the night had only just begun. In the distance, he saw Taylor frown and start walking toward him. The man's sixth sense was uncanny. Leslie could only watch with dread in his heart as his friend approached with a worried look as Leslie tried to hold the tears at bay.

Chapter 14

Oliver paced up and down the lounge as he watched the street. He was on tenterhooks waiting for Leslie to get here. After he'd got home last night, he'd stripped off his clothes and fallen straight into bed. His sleep had been uneasy, troubled with thoughts and emotions that he didn't want to name. Finally he'd fallen asleep, after making the decision that was currently making his stomach grumble and cramp in anxiety.

The text he'd sent to Leslie this morning had been simple enough.

Morning. Can you maybe come over later? I really need to see you.

Leslie's reply text had come over within a minute of him sending his.

Of course. Hope you're feeling better. I'll be there around midday. Got something to tell you too. xxoo

He saw Leslie walking up the path, hugging his arms around his body. Oliver moved away from the window and waited for the doorbell. It sounded and he walked over and opened the door. Leslie stood there, impeccable as always in tight dark jeans, high-heeled boots and a deep blue turtleneck. He had a bright rainbow-coloured scarf draped around his neck. He looked a little uncertain.

"Hi. Come in." Oliver stood back, his heart hammering with apprehension and grief. He wanted to vomit the cereal he'd eaten this morning into the nearest receptacle. Instead he watched Leslie brush past him, a worried smile on his face.

"I was so pleased to get your text to come over. You worried me last night. The guys were worried, too. I said you'd had a bit of a panic attack and needed to go home." His look of concern made Oliver want to run and never come back. He didn't think he could bear to see the hurt on Leslie's face when he told him the news.

It's the right thing to do, he told himself. *Leslie deserves more than this. He's too damned good for the likes of someone like me. I'll just hold him back.*

"Sit down, Leslie. Please." He waved toward the sofa and Leslie looked at him curiously.

"Are you okay? You sound a bit strange." Leslie came toward Oliver, his intention to steal a hello kiss obvious. Oliver moved away and stood behind the couch. If Leslie kissed him, held him, he'd cave in and not do this. He needed to be strong for Leslie's sake.

His lover's face shadowed, and Oliver saw the realisation on it that whatever news he was about to be told, it wasn't good. Leslie's eyes widened, his face paled and he stared at Oliver like someone had just stolen his favourite teddy bear. His voice, when he spoke, was husky, uncertain.

"Oliver? What's going on?" His shoulders hunching over, Leslie gripped the top of the couch.

Oliver took a deep breath and broke his own heart. "I've been doing some thinking and this isn't working anymore for me."

Leslie's blue eyes darkened. "What isn't working for you, Oliver? Us? Is it because of that damn kiss from Frankie?" His fingers gripped the couch, his knuckles whitening. He swallowed and gazed at Oliver steadily.

Oliver nodded and wanted to crawl into a dark pit at the flash of pain that crossed Leslie's face. "No, I believe you on the kiss. I just don't think I'm ready for all this yet. I thought I was and I know this is coming as a bit of a surprise to you, but I don't want to lead you on anymore."

Leslie's tongue came out and wet his lips as he nodded. "I see. What happened between last night and today? Your text said you really needed to see me. I thought it was all okay…"

"Nothing happened. I just figured out what I wanted, that's all."

"And it isn't me." Leslie straightened up, and Oliver saw his hands were trembling. His eyes glistened. "What did I do? Did I do something wrong? I know I can come on too strong, but I can tone it down, I promise…"

Oliver's heart shattered into a million tiny shards that threatened to drive deep into his flesh and bleed him dry. Leslie's persona was exactly what made him love him so much. This man should never have to change who he was.

Oh God, give me strength to do this.

"No Leslie, it's not you at all. It's just this all went too far, too quickly, and I need space. And I don't want the pressure of being in a relationship while I figure out what I want to do."

You need to find somebody who will worship you like I do, but without all the baggage. Not a washed up ex-drug addict porn star with a scarred face and a trunk full of insecurities. You deserve to shine, like the star you are.

"Oh." Leslie's eyes shimmered and he swallowed again. "So that's it then? It's over?" His shoulders hunched, and his eyes sparkled with tears. Oliver watched as one trickled down and he ached to wipe it off his porcelain cheek.

"I'm sorry, Leslie. I didn't set out in this meaning to hurt you, but you know my background. You know what I've been doing the past two years and I need that solitude back. It's better that way."

Leslie shook his head. "What if I don't accept that? I don't want to break up, Oliver. I love you. That's what I wanted to tell you. I don't want to leave." His voice grew stronger as he stood up straight and glared at Oliver. One hand came up to fiercely brush the tear off his cheek. "When do I get a say in this? I'll give you time if that's what you need, plenty of it. Just please don't send me away. Please don't do this."

Oliver tried to keep the quake from his voice at the words *I love you*. They struck his heart with the ferocity of an arrow and left him mortally wounded. "I'm sorry. I've thought a lot about this and it's what I want. There's nothing you can say that will change my mind."

You don't really love me, Leslie. You just think you do. Now, you have to leave, now.

The tension in the air was palpable and when Leslie spoke again, his voice was tight and controlled. "Suit yourself, Oliver. I can see you've convinced yourself that this is what you want to do, so I guess I can't argue. I don't know what the hell is going on with you, but I don't think this is what you really want. "

He knows me too well. He sees right inside me.

Leslie moved toward the door, his slender frame taut and angry. "I'll leave then. When you come to your senses, call me. I'll be there, waiting. And if you don't call…" he shrugged. "Then I guess I'll know I was wrong about you and about everything I thought we had." He laughed harshly. "It wouldn't be the first time and it probably won't be the last. I guess I'm too damn trusting."

He reached the door and put his hand on the door handle. Oliver waited, ready to bolt to the bathroom and be ill the minute Leslie left.

His lover turned around and the despair on his face was more than Oliver could bear.

He stood firm. "Thanks for understanding, Leslie. I hope you find the right man to love you one day."

Leslie stared at him, his face flooded with pain. "I thought I already had," he said quietly. Then he opened the door and walked out of Oliver's house—out of his life.

Oliver had never felt so dark and despairing, even when he'd been in the hospital. His legs threatened to collapse and as Leslie shut the door behind him, Oliver sank to the floor and wept tears of blood and grief as his broken heart exploded.

Chapter 15

Leslie burrowed down deeper into the covers and tried to ignore the persistent throb in his head from the alcohol he'd drunk the night before. He opened bleary eyes and peered at the clock. His heart pounded when he realised it was already eight-thirty am He was supposed to be at work.

"Shit. Fuck." He pushed back the covers, and sat up, wincing as his brain felt like it was smashed against the inside of his skull.

"I am never drinking tequila again," he vowed as he made his unsteady way to the shower. He thought he might still be a little bit drunk. "And I am definitely not doing karaoke with Eddie ever again. Who knew the man could sing like that?"

Last night his friends, worried at his depression over Oliver splitting up with him, and fed up of him wallowing in his flat for the past week and a half, had taken him to a karaoke bar in Soho, not far from Galileo's. They'd all four come by, threatened to knock the door down and then, when he opened it, made him shower, dress and come out with them.

He scowled as he got into the scalding shower. Getting on stage with Eddie, and hearing him belt out 'Mustang Sally' like a pro, complete with the gravelly voice, had left Leslie as envious as hell. He'd always wanted to be able to sing, but didn't really have the voice. Gideon's pride at his boyfriend's achievement had definitely promised dividends later and the gooey-eyed looks they thrown at each other had made Leslie sick with despair because he had lost Oliver and had no one anymore.

Well, except Frankie. Sort of. If Leslie chose to go down that road.

He and Frankie had been on a couple of non-dates *as friends*, as Leslie had told him firmly. They'd been to the movies, eaten pizza and had a few drinks together. As much as he enjoyed the ebullient Frankie's company, Leslie really wasn't ready for any sort of relationship now. The last one had taken it all out of him.

Last night Draven had been showing Taylor magic tricks and making him all *wow, look at you, you stud,* which again promised some late-night activity, and Leslie had got fed up with being the fifth wheel. He knew they didn't mean to be insensitive about his single status, but they just couldn't help themselves.

He'd finally left his friends singing 'Dancing Queen' on the stage and gone home to a bottle of his own tequila. *That* decision he was really regretting.

He smirked. At least he'd got something out of the evening. He'd videotaped the guys singing ABBA and already uploaded it to his YouTube account. Now *that* was a decision *they* might regret.

He got into work around nine-thirty, prepared to face his boss's ire. Surprisingly enough no one said anything to him and he thought he might have gotten away with it.

When he was summoned to Laverne's office around ten, he sighed. He knew it had been too good to be true. He knocked on his boss's door and heard her loud 'Enter.' When he went in, Laverne waved a hand toward the chair.

"Have a seat, sweetie."

Leslie's eyebrows lifted. Maybe the endearment meant he wasn't in trouble.

Laverne looked at him from beneath strong brows. "How are you doing?"

"In what way?" Leslie was puzzled.

Laverne sighed. "Leslie, since Oliver broke up with you, you've been a little distracted. Nothing affecting your work," she forestalled Leslie's panicked denial, "but I've noticed you're not your usual bubbly self. I know this is normal, of course, all things considered."

She frowned as noise from the building site next door threatened to drown her out. "Those boys need to keep it down a bit. They've been really noisy today for some reason."

She leaned forward. "I've been concerned about you and just wanted to check in."

Leslie looked down at his shoes. "I'm okay," he muttered. "Getting over it."

In fact, nothing could be further from the truth. His heart was still raw from Oliver's rejection. Leslie had hoped that he would hear from him, and he hadn't been proud enough to keep from sending a few texts asking Oliver if they could talk. He'd gotten one terse text back.

It's over. Please stop contacting me.

After that, he'd fallen apart and realised that it really was over and Oliver didn't want him anymore. Taylor had been there to pick up the pieces, wipe up the tears that fell copiously from Leslie's eyes and tell him fiercely that he was going to go over to Oliver's and kick his arse. Leslie had managed to convince Taylor that Oliver wasn't to be touched, but he wasn't so sure about convincing Draven.

Taylor's man had got this gimlet-eyed look as if was about to take out a hit on someone. He'd gruffly patted Leslie's head like a puppy and told him that Oliver was a complete arsehole letting someone like Leslie get away, and that in his future there might be some *payback.*

Leslie had shivered at the way he'd said that and hastily asked Taylor to please tell Draven not to interfere. The last thing he wanted to read in the news that an ex-porn star recluse had been found beaten or tortured in his house.

"No you're not." Laverne stood up, focused Leslie back to the present, and came over to him, pulling him to his feet. "Come here. You need a hug."

Leslie was enveloped in strong arms and it was all he could do not to cry at such concern. Instead he closed his eyes, breathed in Laverne's perfume and revelled in the firmly muscled chest under which a strong heart beat. Laverne might be woman on the outside but underneath that person was all man.

Finally Laverne released him and watched with kind eyes. "You're a tough little bugger, Leslie. You'll get over this." She grinned. "Maybe it's time to take that sexy Frankie up on his offer. God knows if I was a bit younger, I'd want to tap that."

Leslie sniffed. "Maybe I will. He called me yesterday actually, asking me to go with him to a rock concert. As a date, not a friend. I might…"

There was a mighty roar outside and the building shuddered. Leslie yelled in panic and grasped Laverne's arm. "My God, what was that?"

Outside, there was the sound of people screaming and crying and both of them dashed over to the window. Leslie's throat clenched as he observed the carnage outside. The scaffolding from the renovations next door had crumbled to the ground, lying in the street in a tumble of concrete, wood and metal. People ran around, trying to get to the injured obviously trapped under the debris. In the distance already there was the sound of sirens.

"Oh, Christ." Laverne's face was white. "Leslie. Get all the staff rounded up to help." She moved away from the window. "Anybody who can render assistance should come downstairs and give us a hand to get those people out from under that wreckage. And if anyone mentions they can't because of bloody health and safety, tell them they're fired."

Leslie nodded frantically. He didn't really think you could fire people for observing the safety laws, but Laverne was a law unto herself. He followed her as she rushed from the room.

What about Frankie? he wondered helplessly. He might be buried under there, hurt, even dead. Leslie swallowed as he darted around the office mustering the Debussy troops.

"Please be okay, Frankie," he whispered to himself. "I need you to be safe."

* * *

Oliver sat flicking the channels on his remote control. He didn't really see what he was looking at. His mind was still too crowded with blue eyes filled with devastation and a face that had etched itself into his painful memories. The words *I love you* still circled in his brain like hungry sharks, slashing at his thoughts, drawing blood.

If it was the right thing to do, why do I feel like shit?

For the thousandth time, he wondered what Leslie was doing now. Was he with Frankie, with a man who could laugh and take him places without falling apart? Had he moved on already, or was he too like Oliver, pitiable, useless, reduced to takeout food and alcohol to take the pain away? Oliver hoped not. That hadn't been his intention. One pathetic arsehole was enough.

He threw the remote down next to him on the couch, and pressed himself tighter into the corner of the cushions.

Why? he asked himself, second-guessing his decision to cut Leslie free. *Did you make the right decision? Or were you just overreacting to that bastard Gregori and his damning words about being a nothing, just a hole to fill? Did you just send away the best thing to ever happen to you?*

He stared at the television, seeing the pictures flash across it of some building or other that had collapsed but not really caring. It was only when he heard the words *London* and *Debussy's* that he started to pay attention. He frowned and picked up the remote to turn up the volume.

"To repeat, earlier this morning, building scaffolding collapsed in Diamond Street, Hackney." The presenter's voice was subdued. "At this moment it is not known how many people are injured, but we do know that there have been two fatalities." The camera focused on a scene far away and then zoomed in. "It has affected local businesses in the area, notably the fashion house, Debussy's, and well-known auctioneer Raymond Powell's. The local cafe below was also a popular gathering place for workers in the area. At this time it is not known whether any of these staff were involved in the accident."

Bile rushed up Oliver's throat. He could make out a hand covered by a tarpaulin. From underneath, he saw only the top of a head, a head covered in black hair just like Leslie's. He stood up, shaking, the blood rushing from his head, pooling in his stomach; his skin rose in goose bumps and he had to take deep breaths to centre himself.

"Oh my God, Leslie," he whispered, his heart clenching. The sick feeling in his stomach increased. His mind blanked out and for a moment, he couldn't breathe.

"The emergency services were on the scene quickly and the injured are still being moved to the local hospital. Rescue teams are attempting to locate people who may still be buried under the rubble." The presenter turned and waved at the scene behind her. "As you can see, they have help from many of the local businesses that have come out to assist the rescue team in moving the debris. At present, there is no explanation for the collapse but some of the construction crew have said it appeared to be a faulty building pillar that was weakened by recent drilling activity. I understand the reason for the tragedy still remains to be investigated and we will bring you more news as we have it."

The television reverted to the in-studio team on the news and Oliver stood, swaying slightly. A feeling of dread coursed through his body and he knew he had to get down there. Find out whether Leslie was safe. With trembling fingers, he dialled Leslie's mobile.

"Please answer," he prayed fervently. "Please, Leslie, answer."

The ringing tone in his ears mocked his distress and he cut the call off as it went to voicemail. He wasted no more time. He rushed to the bedroom, threw on jeans and a sweatshirt and ran out of the house. Flagging down a taxi and clambering in with instructions to take him to Diamond Street, he tried calling Leslie again. There was still no reply.

"You do know that place is a mess, right?" the taxi driver told him, catching his eye in the rear view mirror. "A bloody building collapsed. I might not be able to get you too close."

"That's fine," Oliver said distractedly as he called Leslie again. "Just get as close as you can. I have a friend there who might be hurt."

Or worse.

"A'right mate. I'll get you there. Hold on. This could be a bumpy ride." The vehicle swung out into the busy traffic and Oliver sat back, palms sweating, hands trembling, hoping to all the gods and fates in the universe that there was still time to make things right with the man he loved.

It took almost ninety minutes to even get close to the accident site. The distance was only about six miles but the traffic was horrendous. The driver, Emmett, kept up a running commentary about the vagaries of the London roads and transport system and more than once, Oliver thought he would get out and run the rest of the way. Emmett was always optimistic, saying they'd be there soon, but by the time they hit gridlock again not far away, Oliver was beside himself. There was still no reply from Leslie. The business phone was busy, and he hadn't anybody else's personal contact numbers.

When the taxi stopped once more behind a stream of exhaust-spewing, stationary traffic, Oliver could bear it no longer. He fumbled in his wallet for the money he owed and tucked it between the windows of the front of the cab.

"I have to get there," he said desperately as Emmett's eyes widened. "Thanks for the ride."

He checked; there were no bikes or motorcycles coming past, opened the door and leapt out into the street. His feet hit the pavement and he began running. A steady jog, nothing fast, but he knew that every step he took brought him closer to Leslie. Luckily Oliver was fit; his own little home gym was paying dividends. His hair bounced and bobbed around his face as he ran but the state of his face and that fucking scar meant nothing, absolutely nothing compared to what might have happened. The only thing on his mind was saying sorry to a man with hair as black as coal and begging him to give him a second chance.

If he wasn't too late.

Finally, Oliver saw the crowd in the distance, and he sped up. The area looked as if it was still being cordoned off, and Oliver hoped he wouldn't be stopped by the rescue services or police. He thought grimly that there was no way in hell they were stopping him finding Leslie. He'd fight to the death if he had to.

Panting, he stopped on the outskirts of the carnage and stared around in horror. The quaint building of Debussy's appeared intact but the site next to it was a wreck. It was a low building, probably three storeys high and while most of it was still standing, the left-hand side was ripped open. Plaster and beams hung down, metal poles dangled thirty feet off the ground, and long wooden struts lay smashed to splinters on the pavement.

Men and women in high-visibility jackets, police and paramedics, surrounded the scene in well-organised chaos. Everywhere Oliver looked, there were people moving planks, struts and pieces of concrete. Several cars were dented and squashed and the glass front of the little coffee shop where Leslie often bought his coffee was smashed to shards.

Oliver ran over to the front entrance of Debussy's, chest heaving. The door was locked and he had no idea whether anyone still remained inside. He hoped that it was the case.

A woman standing smoking saw him pulling at the door. She shook her head. "Everyone's out helping," she told him. "The guys locked the door so they didn't get looted while they cleaned up. You know what some people are like." Her eyes conveyed disgust as such a scenario.

Oliver stared at her blankly. "Were there any casualties from this place, do you know?" he waved at Debussy's. "Anyone get hurt?"

She shrugged and took another drag of her cigarette. "Don't know."

He turned and moved forward as if in a dream, eyes anxiously searching for the form of his boyfriend. The area was taped off and people milled behind the barriers, watching the events unfold. No one stopped him as he slipped through the bollards across the street and pavements. They all seemed to be occupied in the area outside the coffee shop. He'd been lucky.

Oliver moved through the frenetic activity. "Leslie," he shouted. "Leslie Scott!" His shouts brought him no response other than agonised glances as people spattered with blood and dust moved around the site. Once or twice he thought he saw the slim form of his lover and his heart raced in anticipation, but when he got there, he was disappointed.

He got closer to the coffee shop and saw a pile of planks and metal beams with half a dozen people standing around the heap. Desperately he grasped the nearest person, a broad-shouldered man coated in dust.

"Have you seen a man called Leslie? Slim, black hair, blue eyes? I really need to find him."

"Mate." The man's voice was quiet. "He's over there." He motioned to the rubble and Oliver's whole being went cold. The man realised his mistake and his eyes widened.

"No, *he's* okay. It's his friend…" The man's voice tailed off. "He won't leave him. We're waiting for the paramedics; they should be here anytime soon."

Oliver nodded a wordless *thank you*, his eyes brimming with tears of relief at the realisation that Leslie was all right. He moved around the waist-high pile and lost his breath when he saw him.

Leslie sat cradling a man in his arms, a man whose face was waxen-white, eyes closed and so full of blood Oliver thought he couldn't possibly be alive. Leslie was hunched over the still form, stroking the man's face, murmuring something. His lover looked like a dark phoenix about to rise from the ashes. His white dress shirt was ripped and bloody, his hands scraped and bleeding. Leslie's dark hair was covered with dust and pieces of plaster. He looked up and spoke to the man beside Oliver, not even seeming to recognise he was there.

"Dasher, where are those paramedics? Frankie's really cold."

The big man Oliver had spoken to moved forward. "They're on their way over, Leslie. I can see them. Just a couple of minutes, little 'un."

"But he doesn't have minutes," Leslie's agonised whisper tore at Oliver's heart. "He's dying, Dash. And we haven't even had that first date yet."

Oliver quelled the fear those words caused. There were more important things to think about right now. He needed to be there for Leslie.

"Leslie, sweetheart? It's Oliver."

Leslie's eyes flickered, looking dazed. "Oliver?"

"Yes, love. I'm here." He clambered over the boards and knelt down beside both men. "I heard about the accident and I rushed over. God, I was so worried about you."

The blank stare he got back in return scared him.

"He won't wake up," Leslie whispered, looking down at the man in his arms. "I've been talking to him but he won't open his eyes." His voice cut off as he choked up.

Oliver reached over and laid his fingers against the Frankie's throat, trying to track down a pulse. He smiled in relief as his fingers found what he was looking for.

"He's alive. Faint, but it's there." He looked up as two people, the paramedics, pushed their way through with a stretcher and crouched down beside them. The man and woman looked tired and drawn but the woman smiled softly at Leslie as they got to work.

"Hi, there. We're going to try and help your friend, okay? Do you think you could move a bit so I can get in, see what needs doing?"

Leslie stared at them unseeingly and Oliver wrapped his arms around him and tried to move him away. "Let's let them see to Frankie, shall we? If we move over here, they'll have room to work. Come on."

He helped Leslie up with a little resistance, and they stood and watched as the paramedics worked on the unconscious man. Leslie was trembling and cold and Oliver thought he might be in shock. He enfolded Leslie into his chest with a feeling that this was exactly where he should be. He was never letting go of him again, if Leslie took him back. From the sound of it, he might already be too late to make amends.

"I was so bloody scared, Leslie," he murmured into his ear. "I saw someone covered up in a bag and he looked like you. I died inside."

Leslie said nothing, but his heart beat steadily against Oliver's chest, his cheek against Oliver's shoulder, as he watched the paramedics with Frankie. The man Leslie had called Dasher was looking at him with a challenging look and he moved over to them.

"You're the git who broke up with him?" he said quietly.

Oliver couldn't deny it. "Yes, I'm that git."

Dasher nodded. "Broke his heart, you did. I'm glad to see that you're here for him now, but don't ever fucking do that again." His tone was threatening, but conversational. Leslie shifted in Oliver's arms.

Oliver nodded. "I won't." He kissed the top of Leslie's head. "But now's not the time to talk about it."

Dasher's eyes narrowed. "You got that right. This is a fucking disaster." He squinted and looked around. "I'm going to go see if I can help some more. You look after him, you hear? Or I'll be coming after you." He started to move away but was stopped as the paramedics moved across his path bearing the stretcher with Frankie on it.

Leslie pulled away from Oliver and walked toward them. "I want to go with him," he murmured softly. "I need to be there with him when he wakes up."

The paramedic looked a bit uncertain. "Are you his boyfriend or family perhaps?" she asked as she bit her lip worriedly.

"I'm his friend. And I've been sitting with him there talking to him and making sure he stays alive until you got here." Leslie's voice was pure steel. "And I *am* going in that ambulance."

Dasher snorted. "*There's* my boy." He turned to the paramedics. "I'd really suggest you let him go with you unless you want a strop.

And he's right. He's the one who kept that young 'un alive, and was there for him. He deserves to be with him."

The male paramedic nodded curtly. "Come on, then. We need to get him in the ambulance." They walked away and Leslie moved to follow them. Oliver touched his arm and Leslie looked at him.

"I'll see you at the hospital," Oliver said. "Is that okay?"

Leslie's blue eyes regarded him evenly. "I'd rather you didn't. Frankie needs me right now and I don't have time for anything else. I'll call you." He walked after the paramedics and Oliver watched him go with a sense of helplessness and dread.

Dasher gave him a sympathetic glance. "Best leave him be at the moment," he advised gently. "He's got enough to think about without wondering what the ex is doing here when he wanted nothing more to do with him."

Those blunt words stabbed Oliver in the heart and he nodded as he swallowed the lump in his throat. "I know. It's just hard seeing him so upset, you know? I just want to be there for him." His voice trembled. "And I fucked up so badly and I don't know if I can get him back now."

"That's a tale for later, my boy." Dasher looked around. "Right now, we could use your help cleaning up. You in?"

Oliver nodded. "Of course. Just tell me what you want me to do."

Later that night when he lay in bed, his muscles stiff and sore, chest aching and wondering how Leslie was doing, Oliver closed his eyes and sent into the ether of the universe both heartfelt thanks that Leslie was safe and a desperate plea that he still had a chance to win Leslie back. This event had opened his eyes once again to the fact life was fleeting and you had to make the most of every minute while you could, and stop feeling sorry for yourself.

I promise I'll do better this time. I'll be the best boyfriend ever. Just love me still, Leslie. That's all I'm asking.

Chapter 16

Eddie Tripp nudged Leslie on the shoulder and smiled at him from beneath untidy red locks of hair that spilled over his forehead. “Come on, Leslie,” he shouted over the clamour of the stage and the fans surrounding it. “At least look as if you’re having fun. You’re at a Killers concert, for God’s sake.” He waved his hands over his head and sang along to the lyrics blaring out of the speakers all over the park.

Leslie sighed heavily and looked around the crowded venue. It was filled with happy people for the most part, a few drunks, stoners, and in the corner one man was stark naked and being escorted away by security staff. Even that sight did nothing to lift Leslie’s darkened spirits.

In the two weeks since the construction accident, he’d seen Frankie through his surgery to repair multiple broken bones and lacerations, hugged him close when he had a bad day. Frankie was now back home in Suffolk with his parents, who were taking care of him until he was fully recovered. Leslie had also tried to forget the memory of Oliver’s stark white face at the accident site. The sight of him standing there shocked and scared had made Leslie’s heart beat faster despite his own panic at seeing Frankie injured. In the middle of calamity, being in Oliver’s strong, warm arms had been heaven.

But he couldn’t forget that Oliver had pushed him away. That Leslie had had his tender heart well and truly stomped on and then ground into the dirt. He’d said *I love you* to Oliver and it had counted for nothing. He didn’t think he could go through that pain again.

In the days following his trip to the hospital with his friend, Oliver had texted him simply asking if they could talk. Leslie had texted back, telling him thanks for being there, but asked him to give him some more time.

Oliver had texted back one simple sentence.

I’ll wait. Call me when you’re ready.

Leslie’s eyes had misted up reading that, but his resolve to take things slowly was at the forefront of his mind. He wanted Oliver back so badly it was all he thought about, but he wasn’t sure he was ready to face him yet. He sighed again and decided his bladder definitely needed respite.

He tapped Eddie on the shoulder. "I'm going to the loo, Edster. At least," he looked doubtfully at the Portaloo about a hundred people away, "I'm going to try get there. Send out the Mounties if I don't come back in a while, will you?"

Eddie nodded and danced around to the music. Leslie rolled his eyes. His friend had a real thing for the band, and Brandon Flowers in particular. Although, who wouldn't have a thing for him, Leslie mused. The man was drop-dead sexy. He battled his way through screaming women, men and kids; his bladder about to shed its load and he fervently hoped he got there in time.

When he eventually arrived at the rather foul-smelling Portaloo, he almost decided not to go through with it. He looked around furtively. Maybe there was a spot he could just whip it out and no one would see. One grey-haired granny woman (really, at a Killers Concert? It just went to show that appearances could be deceiving—or perhaps it was Brandon Flowers' granny) gave him the evil eye as if she knew he was about to try to pee in public and he scowled at her.

"I hope you're not going to do what I think you are," she shouted at him across half a dozen dancing, waving, screaming people.

"Wouldn't dream of it," he called back and with a hidden snarl he made his way into the loo. It was as bad as he thought it would be and as he took out his aching dick and pissed into the grey, black-smeared urinal, (he didn't want to even imagine what that stuff was) he closed his eyes and pretended he was in the Ritz Hotel, aiming his pecker at a beautiful, porcelain vault, ready and waiting to catch the stream of his golden pee as it flowed effortlessly into its waiting mouth. When he opened his eyes and shook his dick, using some scrunched-up toilet paper to dry himself off, reality hit him and he shuddered.

"Ughh. This is just *so* not cool," he muttered as he tucked himself away and zipped up his Calvin Kleins. "Why do I let Eddie drag me to these bloody concerts? He knows I hate this public toilet stuff."

He knew the answer. His friends were once again trying to take his mind off Oliver. He wished his mind could take *itself* off his ex-lover.

As he left the Portaloo and stepped gingerly down the rickety stairs, drying his hands on his pants, someone gripped his shoulder. He turned, half defensively because who knew what tossers hung around public toilets at rock concerts, and his jaw dropped when he saw the shining blond hair of a person he now considered his archenemy. Gregori Golovin stood before him, a smirk on his face and eyes so dilated and black Leslie knew he was on something.

"I was right the first time," Leslie muttered to himself. "It *is* a tosser."

Gregori stared at him blearily and Leslie looked at the hand still on his shoulder.

"Do you want to remove that?" he said as loudly as he could. "It doesn't belong there." He looked around. "And where's your entourage? I though you always travelled with a pair of twats." He felt brave enough to chance being bold seeing the condition of the man standing before him. Leslie knew some moves. He'd watched Bruce Lee.

"I thought it was you," slurred Gregori. "Pretty boy, with the nice, tight arse. I told Nicky I wouldn't mind fucking it."

Leslie frowned.

When had Oliver seen Gregori? While they'd been apart? And they'd talked about fucking his arse?

His stomach lurched uncomfortably at the thought Oliver might have gone back to Gregori since they'd split up. The next words put his mind at ease a little but gave him something else to think about.

"You know, at that fancy fashion party you were both at, the one with all the naked guys," drawled Gregori. "I had a little chat with him. Told him a few home truths, showed him the picture of you getting off with your muscle man." He belched and Leslie stepped back, fearing he might be vomited on from the state of the other man's foul breath.

His heart was beating faster with every word spewing out of Gregori's mouth.

All this had happened the night before he broke up with me.

“What did you say to him?” Leslie demanded fiercely. Hope flared in his chest that perhaps now he might understand what made Oliver send him away.

Gregor grinned and swayed. “Told him he was an ugly loser, and that you were off kissing other guys anyway, so he wasn’t going to keep you.”

A light bulb went on in Leslie’s head. “What else did you tell him?” His temper sparked at the look of greedy satisfaction in Gregori’s eyes.

“Just the usual truths. That he’s a worthless prat that didn’t deserve to have anything good in his life.” He squinted at Leslie. “You do know he got me kicked out of the best gig I ever had, yeah? Just for giving some kids what they needed.” His face twisted into a snarl. “He turned the whole crew against me. They thought I was shit. I’ll never forgive him for that. Fucking Nicky Starr, always more popular than me and I could never figure out why.”

He took a step toward Leslie, reaching out a hand. “He looked so fucking happy with you. I had to teach him a lesson. Told him no one would want an ex-drug addict porn star who’d screwed half of London. You should have seen the look on that fucked-up face of his. It was priceless.”

Leslie’s blood was boiling. He wanted to punch this useless, interfering piece of shit in the face. This cruel, foul arsehole who took pleasure in beating Oliver down.

Finally, Leslie understood why Oliver had broken up with him. While part of him was furious at Oliver’s lack of self-esteem and for letting Gregori prey on his insecurities to the point they got the better of him, the other part rejoiced because it all made perfect sense. Oliver did want him. He just didn’t think he deserved him.

Well, Leslie was going to show Oliver just how wrong he was. After dealing with the prick in front of him who’d ruined Oliver’s life.

He looked around, seeing a clear plastic cup of what looked like white wine perched on the bottom rung of the Portaloo next door. He pushed a startled Gregori out of the way, picked up the glass and flung the contents into Gregori’s face. Leslie grinned in satisfaction at seeing the man howl and step back, falling over the stairs and landing flat on his arse.

"You little bitch. You just threw piss at me," Gregori screamed, spittle and what Leslie now knew to be urine bubbling on his lips.

"Oh, was that what it was? Sorry. My bad." Leslie was enjoying this. "You deserved to be pissed on, arsehole. If I hadn't already gone and drained the lizard, I'd piss on you myself. I have a message for you, you nasty piece of shit. Stay away from my boyfriend and stay away from me. Because I know a man who would enjoy killing you quietly and they'd never find your body. Right. I bet he'd just love to take you on."

Leslie wasn't sure Taylor would appreciate him pimping Draven out as a hired killer, but hey, that's what friends were for.

Gregori's eyes widened and he looked a little scared. Leslie smirked. The man was a bully and when you stood up to bullies, they tended to back off. He sniffed and turned away, hearing Gregori's curses and threats to ram something up his arse that wasn't his boyfriend's dick.

Leslie felt quite pleased with the turn of events. He looked at his watch. Ten p.m. Still time to leave the concert and get to Oliver's to confront the arsehole. He debated sending Eddie a text to tell him he was leaving then sighed. Eddie wouldn't hear it above the noise and he was probably belting out the 'Human' lyrics, the song now playing on stage. It was his favourite tune by the band.

Leslie made his way through the crowd, a little worried that he might not find his friend in the throng of people dancing about. Finally, after what seemed a trek through an Amazon jungle filled with dangerous dancing beasts and arms waving like tree trunks out to get him, he saw Eddie's red hair above the crowd. He heaved a thankful breath and latched onto Eddie.

Eddie turned, his eyes shining. "Isn't this great?" he yelled. "They are so radical, I love these guys."

"Yeah, they are," Leslie agreed. "Listen Eddie, I'm going to make a move. I need to see Oliver."

Eddie's mouth dropped. "Really? You need to do this now?" He cast a yearning glance back at the stage. "Can we just wait until the song finishes? I…"

Leslie laid a finger on his lips. He was warmed at the thought that without question Eddie would come with him. "No, Eddie, this is for me to do alone. You stay here and enjoy the rest of the show. I'm a big boy. I can make it on my own."

Eddie looked uncertain. “Are you sure, I can come with you if you need me...” He threw another pensive glance back at the stage.

Leslie leaned in and kissed his cheek. “I’m sure. Stay. Enjoy.”

Eddie nodded. “Okay. Text me later, let me know you get there okay. I’ll keep checking my phone.” His eyes softened. “Did Oliver call you, or you him, is that what this is all about?”

Leslie shook his head. “No, let’s just say I met someone who helped me put things in perspective. And now I really need to talk to Oliver.”

“Okay. Remember to text me.”

“I will. Enjoy the rest of the gig.” Leslie kissed Eddie’s cheek again softly then turned and made his way for the third time back through the throng, fighting to break through to the entrance, which seemed miles away.

His mind raced as he pummelled and pushed people out of his way. He knew the minute Oliver opened his door, and he saw his beloved face, that all the carefully planned words he’d rehearsed would disappear from his head like dissipating fog. But it gave him focus and quelled the feeling of apprehension in his belly that perhaps he was wrong after all.

* * *

Leslie reached Oliver’s house an hour and a half later. It had taken him ages to get out of the frenetic stadium then catch a tube to Oliver’s. Now he stood on the doorstep, seeing no lights on and wondered whether he was doing the right thing. What if Oliver was sleeping? What if—and his heart lurched—God forbid, he had someone there? Maxwell perhaps, back from a flight and making a quick pit stop?

“You’ll only find out one way, Leslie,” he muttered and gritted his teeth as he rang the bell. The chime rang inside and he waited. The chill of the late-night air made him shiver and he wrapped his twill bomber jacket tightly around his body. An owl hooted somewhere and he started.

“Come on, Oliver, one way or another, you have to be here.” He rang the bell again and after the final chime had dwindled, he heard someone at the door. He stared into the peephole, hoping his fierce stare conveyed to whoever might be behind the door that he meant business.

When the door swung open, he heaved a sigh of relief. Oliver stood there, clad in black joggers hanging low on his hips, hair tousled, face pale and drawn, eyes hooded in sleep. Leslie's cock stirred just at the sight of him.

Thank God. I thought it was broken.

"Leslie? Is everything all right? What are you doing here?"

Leslie pushed past him and let himself in. "I was in the neighbourhood and thought I'd stop by."

Oliver's face was the picture of confusion. "You were in the neighbourhood? What for?"

Leslie's insides jellied and his hands shook but he jutted his chin out and stared at Oliver in defiance as his ex-boyfriend (*soon to be not ex*, he hoped) shut the door. The words that came out definitely hadn't been the ones he'd rehearsed.

"There was this guy I know who decided to do something really fucking stupid because he felt he didn't deserve the best thing that ever happened to him because some ex- boyfriend plonker fed him a load of shit about himself. So I thought I'd come run that past him, see how he felt about it all?"

Oliver's eyes grew wide as Leslie unzipped his jacket, threw it carelessly on the hall table then sauntered though to the lounge, hoping he gave an air of aplomb that he certainly didn't feel. He heard something muttered behind him as he sat down on the couch, swung his legs up to settle comfortably and regarded Oliver.

"I'm sorry it's so late, but I was out at a rock concert. I met a friend of yours there who told me a few things, so I wanted to talk to you about them."

"What friend?" Oliver moved over to the couch and sat down gingerly on the arm. He drew his arms across his chest defensively.

"Gregori Golovin."

Oliver leapt up, his face twisting into a snarl. "That bastard. Did he hurt you? Because if he so much as touched you, or even breathed on you, I am going to break him apart bone by bone."

Leslie's attempt to be a bad boy wore off at the look of fear and hatred in Oliver's eyes. And the fact Oliver still cared enough to kill somebody for him.

"No, he didn't hurt me. It was the other way around, actually. I threw pee at him and he wasn't very pleased about it."

"He…you what?" Oliver passed a hand over his eyes. "Hell, Leslie, it's late, you woke me up, I'm really not sure why you're here so could you please tell me what's going on?"

Leslie wasn't feeling as confident as he'd been. "Okay. Here's the short version. Did you break up with me because you didn't think you deserved me and you thought I could do better?" Oliver's hitch in breath told him he'd hit the mark. "I mean… I know Gregori said some cruel stuff to you. He told me what he said. What I want to know, is anything you said to me the night we broke up true? About not wanting me anymore? Or was it just you being all noble and letting me go so I could find someone you thought was better?"

Oliver's shoulders slumped and his hands moved to his hair and ran through it absently. Leslie stood up and moved over to him, standing in front and looking into his hazel eyes. He ached to touch him, but he wasn't sure yet if he should.

"I know you care about me or you wouldn't have come down to the accident site, or sent me that text telling me you'd wait. But I have to know." He swallowed. "Do you still want me around?"

"Oh, baby." Oliver's voice was just a whisper, his voice broken. "I never stopped wanting you. I love you so damn much. Every quirky, beautiful, loving, warm, incredible bit of you."

Leslie hadn't realised he'd been holding his breath and he exhaled in a rush of warm air. Oliver's eyes closed and he seemed to breathe it in.

Oliver loved him.

"Then why…?" His fingers reached out and stroked Oliver's jawline, relishing the feel of the man's skin on his fingertips. Oliver's eyes held his and for a minute neither of them seemed able to breathe.

With a soft cry, Oliver pulled Leslie into him, his arms tightening, and when their lips found each other's, Leslie sighed and surrendered to the warm, male scent of sweat, shower gel and a desperate mouth seeking his. He'd missed Oliver's unique taste and fragrance and this was heaven.

When Oliver's hungry mouth pulled away, Leslie groaned and pulled it back.

Oliver chuckled. "Steady on. My dick's already thinking it's Christmas and I don't want to rush this. I need to apologise to you first."

"Don't care," Leslie moaned. "Just take me to bed, please. I missed you."

Oliver shook his head and plucked Leslie's hands out of the inside of his joggers. Leslie growled at the loss of the warm, velvety skin he'd been about to grasp.

"Oliver, I swear, I am going to self-combust if you don't do something to me. I've been a damn monk since you left and I'm really horny."

Oliver laid his forehead against Leslie's and stilled his eager hands.

"You've not been with anyone?" His voice was wondrous.

Leslie scowled. "Well, no. Duh. I was too busy getting over you, and I didn't want anyone else. I had my chances, I can tell you. There was Frankie, before he got all busted up, bless him. And I did have an offer from one of the guys at the karaoke evening we went to, but he was a bit skanky. He kept showing me all of his Grindr profile and it was just PPP… prick after prick pic." He warmed to his subject. "Oh, and there was a guy Tay introduced me to who was pretty cute looking, but he lived with his aunt and all he could talk about was these damn birds she bred. Honestly, I think I know everything there is to know about Belgian canaries. I didn't even know canaries came from other countries, I thought they were just canaries..."

He stopped as Oliver's body was shaking and he was making a strange noise. He peered at him anxiously. "Are you okay?"

Oliver looked up and Leslie's heart warmed to see the smile on his face, that soft twist of lips he'd missed seeing, and the eyes that shone with tears as he laughed silently.

"Oh, God," Oliver spluttered. "How the hell could I have gone so long without that crazy mouth of yours? You are unique, Leslie Tiberius Scott. The most incredibly beautiful and amazing person in the whole world."

Leslie stilled. "Then why did you send me away?"

Oliver framed his face in warm hands and nudged his nose gently. "Because I was an idiot. Because Gregori told me I didn't deserve anything good in my life and I believed him. I listened to my own insecurities instead of my heart."

He led Leslie over to the couch, sat down and pulled him into his lap. Leslie settled against him with a happy sigh and wriggled his arse against Oliver's hardened dick.

I don't think it will be too long now and we'll be doing the horizontal mamba. Or maybe the vertical. I'm sure I saw a cowboy hat in Oliver's bedroom sometime...yee-haw.

"I wanted you to do better for yourself." Oliver moved underneath him, trying to get comfortable and Leslie smirked. "Not be stuck with some guy who was still busy trying to make a life, get back into the world outside. You shine so brightly. I didn't want to be that guy dragging you down."

Leslie kissed his chin. "Well, you were an idiot. Just saying." He nibbled at Oliver's earlobe. "I like shining with you."

Oliver's face shadowed. "God, when I thought I might have lost you that day, nothing else mattered than making sure you weren't hurt. I realised nothing else mattered other than telling you I loved you."

"Message received and understood. I love you, too. Are we going to put this behind us now though? I really don't want anyone else." He laughed softly. "It just means training someone all over again."

Oliver nodded. "If it's okay, I'd like to start over."

Leslie slid his hands across Oliver's bare chest, seeing him shiver and his eyes darken. "Good. Now can we go to bed and fuck each other please? Tonight, though I'm going to drive. Want to be inside you."

He could tell Oliver really liked that idea by the way his cock jumped under Leslie's backside. In their previous sex life, Leslie preferred being the passenger, as he called it, but tonight—tonight he just need to make Oliver his. Then, he hoped everything would be all right and he'd have his boyfriend back.

* * *

Seeing Leslie's hopeful face, Oliver knew he was a lucky man—lucky enough to have him back and to have been given this second chance. He desperately didn't want to mess it up.

"This time we are doing this in the bedroom," Leslie muttered as he propelled him toward his room. "I want a soft bed, mood lighting and ambience for this session."

Oliver snorted in laughter as Leslie pushed him inside and onto the bed. "I'm okay with that. My couch and that damn kitchen counter have never seen so much action."

He thought he and Leslie had probably christened every surface in the house, including the dining room table and the gym bench he used. That had been quite a notable event, including handcuffs and a lot of body contortions.

Leslie crawled on top of him and straddled his hips. He ground his backside against Oliver's groin as he smiled down at him and ran his fingers across his chest. His nipples hardened in response and his butt cheeks clenched as he anticipated Leslie between them.

Oliver groaned softly. "You're asking for trouble doing that," he whispered huskily. "I might fuck you before you get a chance to do me. So be careful what you wish for."

Leslie wiggled and puffed a soft breath on Oliver's face, making his nose twitch. "Just do as you're told," he warned, with a mock glower. Oliver thought his lover had never looked more bewitching and sexy than perched above him, blue eyes staring at him with avarice and need.

Immersed in a rush of love, Oliver felt warmth flush his veins and flesh with the knowledge this man was still his. He lost his breath and the room tilted in a strange kaleidoscope of colour. Reaching up, he pulled Leslie fiercely down on top of him, arms closing around his slim body in a loving vise.

"I'm glad you're here," he managed in a choked voice. "You mean the world to me, and I'm sorry I hurt you. I love you so much."

Leslie's mouth tickled his neck as he lay supine. "I know," he whispered. His tongue licked a sweet trail down the skin of Oliver's throat. "Now let me take care of you."

He sat up and pulled his shirt over his head and his smooth, lithe body was revealed, a sublime being, all planes, grooves and beauty. The front of his jeans jutted out with the rigid cock hidden inside and he smiled slyly as he began to unbutton his jeans teasingly.

"You want me inside you, Oliver? Deep inside, touching you, coming in you?" He licked his lips lasciviously and Oliver's groin burned with the fire of a thousand flames. Leslie stood up in one fluid movement and took off his jeans. Oliver gasped in awe at the sight of him in an emerald green thong, cock bulging against the silky material. Leslie turned around and presented his tight backside to Oliver. Two beautifully rounded and flawless cheeks bisected by a string that led to where Oliver wanted to be right now. Leslie waggled his arse at him.

"My turn with yours first. Then you can have this one."

Oliver couldn't speak. He watched as his lover slid the thong off his arse, down his legs then turned and knelt back down across him.

"Now to get rid of these," he murmured as he motioned for Oliver to lift his bottom and pulled the joggers off. Oliver's cock sprung up, wet, hot and aching, and Leslie's eyes dilated at the sight.

"God, I missed that," he whispered, then proceeded to wrap his mouth around the soft, velvety, swollen skin of it so tightly Oliver's hips left the bed and he cried out with the pleasure of it.

Leslie's hot, wet mouth circled, licked, sucked and teased, his hands resting on Oliver's thighs as he took him to a place in his head and body he'd not thought he'd find again. His hands clenched at the bed sheets, his legs shivered with the sensations running through his body and his vision ebbed and flowed as his lover gave him the blow job to surpass all others. He heard his own panting, his entreaties to Leslie to keep going, his garbled expletives and sobs as he spurred his boyfriend on.

Somewhere in the deep recesses of his brain, Oliver acknowledged this lust was caused by his celibacy since Leslie had been gone, having only his right hand and a vibrator to release the pent-up frustration he'd felt. The other sensation, one of being where he was supposed to be, in Leslie's mouth, his arms, his life, was the one trumping the horniness. It just felt so right.

He shuddered as he climaxed, his loud cry of satisfaction echoing in the bedroom as he shot his load into Leslie's waiting and greedy mouth, the rush seeming never to end. He was drained, sated, and as Leslie crept up his body to find his lips and kiss him with a hunger that promised even more, Oliver tasted himself, and the residue of his own fluids in Leslie's mouth.

"Lift your legs up, honey," Leslie murmured. "I need in you so badly."

He did as he was told and gasped when fingers breached him, already sticky with lube—*and when had Leslie done that?* Probably when he'd been passed out with the force of his orgasm. Oliver pushed his hole up to those questing fingers, desperate to impale himself deeper.

Leslie chuckled. “Easy, you greedy bugger. Let me do this properly.”

Oliver closed his eyes and relished the fullness in his arse. Then he heard the rip of a foil packet.

“Leslie,” he groaned, “Do we need a condom? I want to feel you inside me just as you are. You know my test results already. And I haven’t been with anyone else since you left.”

He and Leslie had already shared their results with each other before the breakup. They’d been debating whether to lose the condoms at that stage.

Leslie stilled. “I haven’t either, but are you sure?”

Oliver traced Leslie’s cheek tenderly. “Yes, love. I’m sure. I want this.”

Leslie’s smile lit up Oliver’s world and as he pushed inside, their eyes met and Oliver was lost. The heat of Leslie’s cock in his arse, the feeling of being taken, possessed so completely by him threatened to undo him.

Leslie’s sighs and whispered endearments as he made love to Oliver and owned his body were the perfect soundtrack to what Oliver was feeling. It was their own personal romance film, the culmination of years of loneliness, insecurity and pain being transformed by the love of one man, a man who truly wanted him. Oliver smiled up at Leslie as the movie played out to its picture-perfect ending. There may still be a few trials ahead, but with Leslie by his side, he’d face them. The alternative wasn’t an option.

When he felt the warmth of Leslie’s semen inside him, the multiple ‘*Love yous,*’ he sighed as he climaxed, and with the feel of skin against his as his lover collapsed on top of him, Oliver finally felt at peace.

They lay together afterward, half dozing, Leslie curled into Oliver’s arms, head on his shoulder.

“So…” Oliver had been dying to ask but hadn’t wanted to disturb their post-coital bliss until then. “How the hell did you manage to throw piss at Greg?”

Leslie giggled and Oliver was enchanted. “I didn’t know it was pee,” he retorted. “I thought it was wine someone had left on the step.” He shrugged. “Turned out I was wrong.”

Oliver spluttered with laughter. “God, he must have been mad.” He stroked his lover’s arm idly. “Still, things could have gotten nasty.

That night of the fashion show, he threatened to hurt you if I hit him. I had to back off because that *so* wasn't happening."

"He was pretty drunk and drugged up, so not much of a threat." Leslie threw his leg over Oliver's as he got comfy. "And I know some karate, too. I'm not just a pretty face." He huffed indignantly and Oliver wanted to kiss him senseless for being so damned cute.

Leslie carried on. "Plus he was spilling the beans about what he'd said to you that night and I just had this feeling, I knew why you did what you did…."

Oliver kissed his dark head. "Thank God you had that feeling. Or we might not be here now." He hesitated. "I was going to call you again, I was going out of my mind, but I wanted to give you space."

"I suppose you could say Gregori Golovin did us a favour then," Leslie said sleepily, His eyes were half shut, lashes dark against his pale cheeks.

Oliver grinned happily in the darkness. "Yes, I think we can safely say for once in his miserable life, he did something right. I'm going to make sure I keep you by my side, Leslie Tiberius Scott. Right where you belong."

Soft lips brushed his side. "I like the sound of that. Now can we go to sleep please?" his boyfriend grumbled, giving him the stink eye. "I'm tuckered out and I need my beauty sleep." He frowned. "Although I have this feeling I should have done something and I haven't…"

"You couldn't be more beautiful," Oliver murmured softly as Leslie smiled at those words and closed his eyes again. "And whatever it is, it'll come to you. It couldn't have been that important. Sweet dreams."

Sleep wasn't long in claiming Oliver, and as he sank into the welcoming darkness, he wrapped the man in his arms in a protective embrace and gave thanks to the universe for bringing him back.

* * *

In the middle of the night, rousing when Oliver's arm knocked him in the nose as he turned over, Leslie awoke with a start and the little thing that had been in the back of his mind niggling him as he'd fallen asleep came to the surface. "Shit. I forgot to text Eddie and tell him I got here safely. Hell, he's going to be pissed off."

He looked over at his sleeping lover, taking care not to wake him as he reached over to the bedside table and picked up his phone which lay charging. It read 3.12 am. He groaned softly.

"Four missed calls and half a dozen texts. Crap." He scrolled down, angling the phone away so the light didn't disturb Oliver and read the texts. It looked like Taylor and Eddie had worked in tandem in giving him hell.

Eddie: 11.30 pm. ***You didn't text. Did you get to Oliver's okay?***

Eddie: 00.30 am. ***You little shit. Where are you?***

Taylor: 00.34 am. ***Eddie called. Are you okay? Text me.***

Taylor: 00.45 am. ***Not talking to me? Call, me for God's sake. I'm worried.***

Eddie: 01.00 am. ***You are in so much trouble, mister.***

Leslie winced when he read that one.

Taylor: 01.20 am. ***Eddie's mad. Me too. Just hope you're okay. Text me ASAP!***

Eddie had called twice; Taylor, too. He didn't listen to the voicemail messages. He knew they'd simply be cursing at him for scaring them.

Leslie sighed and texted back, including them both in his message.

I'm fine, so sorry, my bad. I'm at Oliver's. Please don't be too mad with me. I forgot 'cos I was BBDIMBF xxoo

He sniggered as he hit Send. Let them figure that one out. He laid his phone down and pulled the duvet back up. He was only just starting to get comfortable when his phone vibrated crazily. He reached over and picked it up. The Taylor/Eddie conversation was highlighted.

Taylor: ***Glad you're okay. You're still in trouble though. All cool with you and Oliver?***

Eddie: ***Little bastard. Glad you two made up. About time he got his bloody head on straight.***

Leslie laughed softly. He knew his two friends would still have plenty to say to Oliver when they saw him next about what a prat he'd been for hurting Leslie. He might have to play mediator and make sure his lover wasn't tarred and feathered.

Taylor: *So you were buried balls-deep in the boyfriend, huh? High-five.* There was a picture of a hotdog in a bun attached to the message, which Leslie giggled at. He did scowl though. Trust Taylor to have figured that one out.

Eddie: *LOL like that one. I'll have to use it on Gideon*

Taylor: *btw the video you put on YouTube of us singing ABBA songs? You are so dead.*

Leslie laughed loudly then glanced guiltily over at Oliver. He started when he saw that his boyfriend's eyes were open and Oliver was watching him with a lazy smile.

"Sorry I woke you up," Leslie murmured. "It's the guys, they were worried about me. I forgot to text them."

"Do you mind if I see? I'd like to tell them something if I may?" Oliver held out his hand and Leslie passed him the phone. Oliver read through the messages and chuckled when he'd finished.

"They are good guys, aren't they?"

"The best," Leslie agreed.

He watched, a little confused as Oliver texted something, something quite long- winded, then hit Send, gave him back his phone and lay back with a grin.

Leslie read the last outgoing message.

Thanks for looking out for him, guys. You can beat me up when you see me. I'm ready for you. I'm glad he has friends like you. The Three Houseketeers are now all formally spoken for He's mine now and I promise I'll take care of his heart. I love him. Now if you don't mind, I'm about to be BBDIMBF. Oh and I loved the drunken Dancing Queens. Night chaps

Leslie's chest beat faster as Oliver reached for him, definite intent on his face and he allowed himself to be drawn down into his boyfriend's loving and passionate embrace. The phone vibrated again but this time, Leslie didn't even bother. He had more important things on his mind.

FEAT OF CLAY

Chapter 1

Cold. Dark. Silent.

The naked man lying shivering on the cold concrete floor had no idea of the time or day. All he knew was he hurt in every unimaginable place possible. Curled up into a foetal ball, he dug his fingers into cold arms as he tried to hug himself warm. Pain from ragged nails pierced his clammy skin, reminding him he was still alive, albeit in hell. His mouth was so dry from lack of water, he couldn't even cry out anymore. Agony riddled a stomach clenched and knotted from lack of food; he didn't remember the last time he'd eaten.

The only thing keeping him sane was the silence. As long as that remained, he knew he was safe. It was when his captor returned to the room that the air was broken with cries of pain and agonised breaths amidst the whispered gloats from his torturer of just how much his keeper could make him suffer. So when the man on the floor heard the click of the door lock opening, his stomach heaved in fear and pain. He retched strings of bile, knowing that what was coming was far worse than lying broken and beaten half to death on a cold floor.

"Ready for me?" The hated voice was mocking. "Let us begin again."

****

"You bastard, leave me alone. Fucking leave me alone, will you? I won't tell you anything. Fuck off."

Clay Mortimer woke to these words being spat into his ear as an arm beside him thrashed wildly in the throes of a nightmare. It was nothing new; he'd faced this scenario many times. His chest tightened with agonising pain at the utterance of words borne of an experience no man should have endured.

Awake instantly, thanks to his past training in the SAS, Clay reached out and gripped the wrist of the man floundering next to him in their bed. His other hand reached out and pressed itself into his lover's scalp with its thick covering of russet fuzz. Clay's gentle fingers pushed the fevered brow back onto the pillow, trying to stay the man's agitation.

"Tate? Love, it's Clay. Wake up. Come on, wake up. That's it."

As Tate Williams's cloudy hazel eyes opened, panic rife in their depths, Clay stroked his lover's forehead and murmured soothing words of comfort. "Easy, it's just a nightmare. It's over. Look at me." His words grew in urgency as Tate stared at him, no recognition on his face. Clay's stomach tightened and he lost his breath, the familiar anguish with which he lived rising in his chest.

"Look at me, Tate." His voice rose, commanding. "It's Clay. I'm here."

Tate's eyes slowly cleared. "Clay?" He blinked, his gaze focusing as his trembling hand came up and held onto Clay's arm tightly, making him wince. He was used to bruises as Tate came out of his fugues. Clay's partner needed to make sure the man beside him was real, solid.

"I was dreaming…" Tate whispered as he passed his hand across his eyes. "Armerian was there."

Clay swallowed, the mention of the other man's name making his gorge rise, and his blood boil in hate and anger. "Armerian is dead, Tate. He can't hurt you anymore." It was the same litany he repeated every time he drew the man he loved back from the hell he'd been in. Kidnapped, tortured and emotionally abused by a madman just over a year ago, the physical scars on Tate's body may have healed, but his mind was another thing. He was tough and proving steadfast in his attempt to get through each day, but to get his head to its current state had taken a lot of time, tears, frustration and grief. Clay had no doubt there was more of it in store.

Tate nodded slowly and sat up, the covers slipping down his muscled, lightly furred chest, to pool on his hips. "I know. I remember." His upper body was soaked in sweat, the dark curls on his torso damp and matted. Faint silver scars transacted his belly and ribs like a grid. Two deeper, rounder and thicker indents marked his upper left shoulder and pectoral muscle. Another one splayed across the left side of his ribs.

Clay sighed. He rose naked from their bed and walked over to the chair. A damp towel still sat there from their recent shower-sex marathon. He picked it up, went back to Tate, sat down beside him and dabbed the soft fabric across his face then across the pools of moisture on his body. Tate watched him do it, and Clay was glad to see his lips curve in a small smile.

"You're always looking after me. My very own defender—my knight in shining armour."

Clay snorted loudly. "Well, aren't we being literary. I just like to make sure you're okay, that's all." He finished what he was doing and threw the towel to the floor. He stood up to move around to his side of the bed and Tate reached out with both hands to grip Clay's hips.

Despite the fact his partner had just woken from a nightmare, Clay's cock stirred at the feel of Tate's warm hand on his skin and the desire in his eyes. Sex had become something of a sleeping aid to Tate, as he used it to dispel the nightmares he held. For the most part, Clay was fine with that. Sometimes, though, he felt as if he was simply a distraction, a living, breathing placebo for Tate to find his inner solace. He supposed wryly that there were worse ways for his partner to deal with his issues than using Clay as a human dildo.

"Stay there," Tate murmured as Clay's dick began its slow rise upward. "I want to taste you. Then you can fuck me."

As Tate's lips closed over his cock, Clay closed his eyes and gave in to the pleasure.

****

After Tate was sated and once more resting uneasily, Clay lay watching the restless form of his lover. The covers had fallen off and Tate lay on his side, back to Clay. Tate's honey-toned skin and the firm curve of his backside were a welcome sight. Clay reached out gently and traced the tattoo on Tate's right arse cheek. It was a dragon, teeth bared, wings spread, in shades of grey and black. It covered the whole taut muscle and while it looked stunning, Clay knew it hid something much more sinister.

Beneath the powerful beast roaring on Tate's flesh lay the word *Reino,* carved out with a scalpel in Tate's skin by the man who sixteen months ago had kept Clay's lover prisoner for four days, tortured him, then shot him three times and left him for dead in a city street. A snarling twist of deception had left Tate the victim after his undercover drug sting went bad. The dragon covered up what Tate thought was a shameful scar, but Clay, who'd chosen the image for him, had always thought it reflected his lover's inner strength and resilience.

Tate stirred and murmured sleepily and Clay hastily moved his fingers away so he didn't wake Tate completely. He settled back in the bed and pulled the duvet up over them both.

I hope he manages to sleep, was Clay's last conscious thought as he sank into darkness. *I don't know how long he can go on like this.*

Chapter 2

Tate sighed heavily as he fielded his way through the three computer screens set up in his home office. As a researcher and strategist for Clay's business, Mortimer Investigations, Tate spent a lot of time checking out information, inspecting facts and fiction supplied by snitches and leads and finding the real truth behind the stories. He'd always been a geek, loving gadgets and anything digital.

"I suppose it's just as well I had this kind of interest now that I'm 'retired' out of field work," he muttered to himself as he logged into yet another government agency site to collate information for his boss and partner. "I'd rather be out shooting someone though."

That thought made him scowl. He'd been trying to convince Clay he could go back to field work as one of his investigators, but Clay was adamant; Tate wasn't ready for that yet. Clay had a rod of steel when it came to his business, putting personal feelings aside, doing what was best for his company and his other operatives. He felt Tate would compromise the others' safety. No amount of cajoling or seduction techniques would work. Tate had tried them all.

He yawned and stood up to stretch his legs. His side ached where the second bullet had cut through like butter, the right arse cheek with its sensitive scar always appreciating an opportunity not to be sat on. Tate caught sight of his reflection in the mirrored glass of the sliding door leading out to the garden. He assessed himself critically.

He saw a clean shaven, well-built man of thirty-three, his body toned and muscled, with buzz-cut hair and hazel eyes. There were dark bags under his eyes and he reached up and touched them with a frown. His old but comfortable tee shirt rode up as he lifted his arms to stretch, and he got a sense of satisfaction as seeing his stomach was still tight, thanks to the regime of crunches and sit-ups he did every day in his well-kitted out home gym in the spare room. A dark treasure trail led down to his groin, to the waistband of his joggers, which sat low on his hips.

Tate grinned as he remembered this morning—Clay tracing that trail with his mouth, those warm, tantalising lips teasing and sucking until reaching Tate's needy dick. He loved Clay's mouth, the one that could look so stern and forbidding sometimes then melted into an expression of love and desire at seeing Tate. He also loved the fact that Clay could suck cock with those lips like no one else could.

He took a deep breath as the pleasurable memory gave way to one not so pleasant. Yet another nightmare last night had taken a lot out of him. They *had* been getting better though, going from virtually every night to two or three times a week. They left him debilitated and on edge. Since the shooting it had been rough for them both, no matter how much work-designated therapy Tate attended.

He scowled at his reflection. "Still no matter how much 'meditation' I do before bed, I'm still a fucking wimp, waking up and having to have my man wiping my damn face like I'm a kid. I was an undercover drug cop, for Christ's sake. I should have more discipline and self-control." He knew, deep down, the feelings of guilt, shame and self-recrimination lurking deep in his soul had as much to do with the nightmares as what had been done to him.

He kicked out moodily at a wastepaper basket sitting innocently at the side of his desk. It fell, rolled over and dispersed copious amounts of wadded-up paper onto the carpet. Tate's temper flared, something that happened all too often, and his foot lunged out, scattering the paper to the four corners of the room.

"Fuck you," he growled as he stomped and beat one unfortunate ball of paper into a flattened mess. "Damn you all to fucking hell." He didn't really know who he was swearing at, but the violent action felt good. When he finally stopped, his breathing faster and a slight ringing in his ears from the pressure in his head, there was a loud clapping noise from the door.

Adrenaline rushing through his veins, he swung around to see the tall, wide shouldered figure of his lover behind him.

"Tate Williams: one, Paper Ball: nil." Clay stepped into the room. "Do you feel better now? If you needed to release any energy, we could always have sparred for a while in the gym." He flashed a quick smile. "Or we could have done something else just as energetic and far more…pleasurable."

Tate waved a hand at him, fear rising in his throat. "It just shows you how bloody useless I am. I didn't even hear you come in. What if you had been someone else?"

Clay's eyes darkened. "I have keys, remember? For all three locks on the front door. No one's getting into Fort Tate, love."

It was their joke. After he'd been tortured by a maniac, Tate had equipped his flat in Kentish Town with alarms, sensors, extra steel locks and other paraphernalia to make sure that in Fort Tate, as Clay had coined it, Tate felt safe. It was probably not needed—after all, the man who'd hurt him was dead—but his paranoia ran deep. There had been a time when he'd left his doors open and hadn't had panic buttons on the wall. To be fair, a lot of the protective measures had been Clay's urging. The man had been a wreck after seeing Tate in the hospital, and Tate's safety and protection had become Clay's number-one priority. Sometimes it felt like a warm blanket; other times it felt like suffocating smog. As no one knew the extent of their relationship as lovers, the two men still kept separate homes. Clay had a huge Victorian house in Twickenham, which Tate loved unreservedly, while Tate had his ground floor flat. It was an ongoing thorn in Tate's side, keeping their secret.

Clay wasn't convinced it was the right thing to be open about them yet. "Tate, the job I do involves making enemies," he'd said quietly one night after a bout of passion. "If they know we're together in this way, it gives them an edge. They can use you to get to me, hurt you again. And I will never let that happen. You need more time to get over what happened to you. Let's wait a bit longer."

Tate didn't really appreciate being treated as if he were made of glass. In any case, he thought anyone watching them would probably make an assumption anyway about their relationship, but he hadn't been able to budge Clay on his decision. The man was as stubborn as hell.

Tate snorted as he moved over to kiss his partner. "Yeah, well, still."

He reached up to frame Clay's stubbled cheeks with his hands as his lover brought his face down to kiss him. Large hands came out and spanned Tate's waist, drawing him closer. Clay smelt of Fahrenheit, and shampoo and man. He was strong, muscled and wiry, and taller than Tate at six foot four.

Tate liked slotting into Clay's arm like a piece of a well-fitting jigsaw. One lock of jet-black hair swept over Clay's forehead and he raised a hand to absently brush it away. Long, dark eyelashes—like a giraffe's, Tate always thought—framed piercing green eyes that currently gazed at him with affection. Tate's man was indeed damned handsome and Tate never tired of looking at him.

Tate nudged Clay's hip. "What are you doing here anyway? I thought you had some fancy schmancy meeting with Draven?"

Clay shrugged. "I did. We got through the briefing quicker than I'd expected. He's on his way to Spain tomorrow night for a couple of days on the Medina Pharmaceutical case you did the research for. He'll get that sorted in no time, no doubt. So I thought I'd surprise you." He grinned. "I didn't think I'd find you kickboxing with a piece of paper when I got here."

Tate nodded. "He's going to track down Rupert Medina then?" He might not be in the field but Clay was always willing to talk about his cases with Tate and kept him in the loop.

Medina was the owner of a profitable and well-known pharmaceutical company that'd been selling illegal and ineffective versions of drugs for various life-threatening illnesses. From his involvement in the case, Tate knew at least ten patients had died using the company's ineffective and low-quality products. It had become a nationwide hunt to bring the man to justice and Clay had happened to find him first. Things had gotten nasty; one law enforcement officer had already died in trying to bring Medina to justice and Tate hoped both Clay and Draven would be careful.

Clay's face darkened, his face grim. "Medina looks as if he's fled to Spain, hence Draven going over there to find him and bring him back. That murderer is fucking lucky it's not me. I'd have no hesitation shooting the bastard and leaving him in the bay for the fishes to feed on."

Tate had no doubt of that. One of the things that turned him on about Clay was his tough, no-holds-barred attitude in his work. Seeing Clay in full macho and interrogator mode got Tate harder than he'd ever thought possible.

"And the toxic waste case?" Tate enquired. "What's the latest on that one?"

Clay's eyes narrowed and his nostrils flared. "We think we've found a connection to someone who might know what's going on. We're trying to find him so I can ask him some questions." He smiled wolfishly. "The man won't know what's fucking hit him when I finally get hold of him." His emerald eyes glinted in devilish anticipation. It was damned sexy and Tate had no doubt the unfortunate individual would experience the indomitable force of Clay. It was as sexy as hell.

"How are Draven and Taylor's wedding plans coming along?" Tate asked as he traced the five o'clock shadow on Clay's face, charcoal black laced with silver, like his thick head of hair. Clay had only just turned thirty-six but Tate was forever teasing him about those errant silver strands.

Clay chuckled. "Still on the go. Both of them are in no hurry; they're fine with a long engagement, and it's only been six months. Neither of them wants a big wedding. Knowing them both, we'll probably just get an invite one day to something low-key but intimate." He snorted with laughter. "Probably up in the wilds of Scotland or something. Taylor apparently has this thing for the Highlands. I think it's more he enjoys the men in kilts myself."
Tate's nodded. "Wow, that's...cool." He flicked a guilty glance at his partner as he moved away from Clay's embrace.

Clay's face was noncommittal but no doubt he was remembering, as was Tate, the night nearly eight months ago when he had asked Tate whether marriage, even kids, might be on the cards for them at a future date. Tate had been surprised, given Clay's stance on not making their relationship public. Clay had said quietly had said that he liked to think there would be a time when they could shout it from the rooftops.

Tate had said no to marriage and kids. He'd been rather more aggressive than he'd meant to be in his refusal. He'd still been so fucked up at the time, and hadn't felt he could make that kind of decision then. He'd gotten over it, as had Clay—the man had a knack for putting things behind him and moving on—but Tate knew he'd hurt his lover. And he hated himself for it.

"Don't worry," Clay said softly. "I'm not going to mention it again." He smiled but Tate saw the wariness behind it.

His stomach lurched and his heart ached at the look in Clay's expressive jade-green eyes. "I didn't think that. Stop putting words in my mouth. And we both know I wasn't ready for that conversation yet."

Clay regarded him evenly. "I get it; don't worry. Like I said, I won't bring it up again."

Tate swallowed. He'd known Clay since he was six years old, and Clay had been nine. They'd grown up together in Guildford in Surrey, gone to the same schools, albeit Clay ahead of him. They'd discovered they liked guys together and bonded as unlikely best friends.

Tate decided to let it go. "Lucy called. She said Rick got that promotion he wanted. I'm pretty proud of him." Lucy was Tate's older sister. Rick was his nephew and following in his uncle's footsteps in the police force. He was the only other person who knew the true nature of Clay and Tate's relationship. There'd been an unfortunate incident at Tate's home once when Rick had popped around and found them in flagrante delicto. It had been a few months after the shooting and they'd both been careless. Rick had muttered darkly that he needed to bleach his eyes now he'd seen Clay buried balls deep in his uncle.

Clay smiled warmly. He had a soft spot for Rick. "He did? That's great news. He's a great policeman; he deserves it."

Tate nodded. "Lucy's lucky to have such a level-headed kid. He'll go far."

The note of longing he heard in his voice for his old job didn't appear to escape Clay, as his lover's face darkened. The man knew him too well, knew that Rick had something Tate could no longer have. His career as an undercover cop was over, as his cover had been blown, and no amount of persuasion could make the powers that be reinstate him. When Clay had offered him the research position, Tate had decided it would fill in until he could get back into the saddle one hundred percent.

Tate found himself pulled into a fierce kiss, one that made him forget for a while, as Clay's mouth bruised his in an act of possession. Clay's mouth tasted of sweet sauce and burger, mixed with the sweet taint of Coke. When they finally drew apart, Tate still breathless, he wiped a finger across Clay's shining lips.

"You've been eating those damn Big Mac things again. How the hell do you not put on a stone and look like a house? Do you know what that garbage is doing to your cholesterol levels?" Tate tended to eat a lot healthier than his lover. He was quite a fan of salads, lean meats and low-fat foods.

Clay chuckled. "Like I tell Draven, tequila, hot sex and the gym keeps that weight away." He patted his toned stomach. "The hot sex part being my favourite bit of that."

Tate's dick plumped up in his jeans, happy with that scenario too. He pulled Clay's mouth down for another heated kiss. Maybe he could persuade Clay to get his clothes off and fuck him.

Judging from Clay's groan of satisfaction and the hardness pressed against Tate's stomach as Tate explored his mouth with his tongue, Clay would need little persuasion.

They were interrupted when Clay's mobile rang.

He unglued his lips from Tate's and scowled fiercely as he reached into his trouser pocket to answer it. "This had better be an emergency or someone's arse is getting kicked. I said no fucking calls." His eyes smouldered. "I had plans for you this afternoon."

Tate's insides danced with pleasure at the promise of those words. Clay winked then turned and Tate watched as he went outside onto the small balcony overlooking the green.

He bent down and picked up the crumpled piece of paper lying under the desk, dropping it into the waste bin. As he did, a series of loud, stuttering bangs from outside rent the air, rapid-fire sounds that caused Tate to freeze. His heartbeat sped up, his throat dried out and he reached out to grab the edge of his desk as dizziness assailed him. Flickers of light blurred his vision as the noises outside rose in crescendo and the shrill sound of a siren could be heard in the distance. Flashes of memory sped through his mind like the fast-forwarding of a DVD film. Immersed in the roar in his ears, he heard the faint echoes of his own voice crying out as bullets smacked into his body. Remembered pain and humiliation soaked Tate like a drenching acid rain from hell, burning and scalding him with his own shame and guilt.

"Bloody kids; they shouldn't be allowed to sell firecrackers until Guy Fawkes—Tate, are you okay?" Clay's worry and concern settled over Tate like a stifling fire blanket, dulling his senses, causing his limbs to become heavy as he struggled to get his racing heart under control. Vomit welled in his throat, rancid, foul-tasting bile that reached his mouth, causing him to gag and retch onto the floor. Clay's hand steadied his arm and Tate lashed out in anger and self-hatred as he pushed him away.

"Leave me alone, Clay," he snarled as he wiped his mouth. The darkness in his soul claimed him; sneering caustic jibes about just how pathetic he was buzzed in his ears. "I'm not a child and I don't need you picking up the pieces every time I have a meltdown."

The words were meant to hurt and yet for the life of him, he regretted hurling them at the man he loved. A chance children's prank and yet another realisation of his frailty had ignited a self-hating flame that couldn't be extinguished.

"I wasn't 'picking up the pieces'," Clay said evenly. "You were having a panic attack. I wanted to make sure…"

"You wanted to make sure that I was all right, that the sound of fucking bangs hadn't driven me crazy and that poor, damaged Tate could still function." Tate spat the words and Clay's eyes darkened as his lips thinned. "Well, you know what? You're fighting a losing battle. Because Tate *isn't* okay. He's a useless piece of shit who'll always be like this, so you'd be better off moving on and finding someone who can cope with hearing kids letting off firecrackers in the middle of the fucking street and who doesn't wake you up in the middle of the night with fucking bad dreams."

Tate was on a roll and he had no way to stop himself. That was how it worked. The freight train that was his tormented psyche gained momentum and rolled forward, crushing everything in its path.

"Christ, I love you, Clay, you know that, but I can't take this anymore. I need some space. I need to be alone and figure this out."

Clay moved forward, the bulk of his body both commanding and familiar. Tate wanted to enfold himself in those arms, feel the beat of Clay's strong heart against his chest, the warmth of his man's body against his, but he couldn't let that happen. He needed to get his head right, be someone Clay could respect again, not this broken, haunted man in front of him—a weakling.

"We tried that," Clay said softly, the pain in his eyes stabbing into Tate's heart with every blink of his eyelashes. "Remember? I came and fetched you and brought you home."

Tate stared at him. "You broke into the hotel I was staying at, tied me up and brought me back to that safe house, where you continued to lock me up while you talked the shit out of me. Some people call that kidnapping."

Clay took a shuddering breath. "I call it love. And it worked, didn't it? Those slashes on your wrist healed and you told me you wouldn't do it again. You even started going to therapy again."

Instinctively, Tate stared down at the scars on his wrists, reminders of that time ten months ago when he'd decided he'd had enough. He'd booked a cheap room in a hotel, drank himself stupid then attempted to slash his wrists. He was a cop; he knew how to do it properly, and yet he'd slashed across instead of down. Something had held him back. He had no doubt had he done it the right way, he'd be dead now.

Clay had tracked him down. How, he never knew, but his lover had his ways. He'd been forcibly bundled him into a van and a doctor had come to the house to patch him up. Then Clay had kept him under luxurious house arrest for a week in a radical one-man intervention. Tate had sworn at him, cursed him, but in his heart of hearts he'd been glad Clay hadn't let him die that night. His suicidal tendencies had abated over these long months and he was trying to put that whole sorry episode in the past.

"Yeah, well, maybe if we'd had someone else to talk to, had friends around that we could share stuff with, it would have been better for us both. Instead we creep around like a dirty secret because you're scared for me." He slammed his fist down on the table. "God knows I've tried to get you to make our relationship public but you insist on molly coddling me, hiding me for my *own good.* It's been over a year that we've been living like this, Clay." He spat the words then paused, his chest heaving.

Clay folded his arms across his broad chest and observed with tired and shadowed eyes. This conversation was familiar to both of them.

"You know why I feel that's the right thing to do, Tate. We've discussed it."

"That doesn't mean I've agreed." Tate passed a hand over tired, sore eyes. "Look, I need to be alone for a bit. I think you should go, and I'll call you when I'm ready. Leave your house keys."

Clay's eyes filled with pain so deep Tate wanted to vomit again. "Tate, love, please don't do this. Don't push me away."

Tate swallowed bile. "Go, Clay. Like I said, I don't want you around right now. I need to get my head round all this again."

His lover shook his head. "No."

He stood firm and Tate knew he had to do something to get Clay to go, so he could wallow in his own self-pity and come to grips with the disease that was his damaged self. Maybe that way he could become more of the man Clay needed.

"I *will* fucking hit you," he warned as he strode toward his partner and held out his hands for the keys. "Make no mistake. Give me the keys."

Clay's hands clenched but he made no move. "No."

"I swear I'll take them from you." Tate became desperate. The darkness inside him swelled to a crescendo and sent grasping, greedy ice-cold feelers out to clasp his twisted guts.

"Then try." There was steel in Clay's expression, a *don't fuck with me* attitude that Tate had seen fell bigger and stronger men than him. But he had one thing on his side. Clay *loved* him. And sometimes love was blind.

Tate made as if to lower his arm, and knowing Clay as well as he did, seeing the imperceptible lowering of his defences for someone he loved, he struck at a time when the man wasn't expecting it. His fist shot out, catching Clay on his jaw. Clay gave a shout of pain and surprise as he stumbled back, hands instinctively coming up to block himself. Tate moved in for another strike and was stopped by the look of despair that crossed Clay's face.

Clay held up his hands in surrender. "I'm not going to fight you, baby," he whispered, his face bleak. "I get it. I'll go." His hands trembled as he reached down and took the house keys from his pocket and threw them on the floor. "There. Satisfied? You got what you wanted."

No I didn't. I only got what I need. What you need right now.

The sour taste in Tate's mouth intensified. "Thank you."

Clay nodded curtly, but his eyes were haunted. "Just promise me you aren't going to do anything stupid, Tate. That's all I'm asking. And keep seeing Doctor Jakes for your therapy." His voice shook. "I'm sorry you think I'm so possessive. I want to let go, I promise, it's just that…" he shrugged helplessly. "I don't want you getting hurt again."

"I'm not going to try and off myself, Clay," Tate said quietly. "I promise. I just need some time. A few days. Maybe a week. Then I'll call you."

"I'll be waiting." Clay made as if to touch Tate then reconsidered and dropped his hand. "Call me soon. Remember I love you. Never doubt that. Never forget it."

Clay turned and left without a backward glance, leaving Tate standing there, sick to his stomach and cursing a dead sadist with all the vitriol in his soul. He stared at the closed door for a few minutes, trapped in his memories and filled with self-loathing.

Why the fuck did I just chase away the best thing that ever happened to me?

Deep down inside Tate knew why, but it was a secret only he and his therapist shared. And *that* had only come about because Dr. Natalie Jakes was a master at getting to a person's core—of digging deep and finding the vulnerabilities inside. Tate knew he was lucky to have her; he also knew he *needed* her. Needed her help in coming to grips with what had happened to him and what he'd done, but that didn't make it any easier in the telling of his tale. His shameful secret was something he regretted every day and not yet something he was prepared to tell Clay about. God knew how Clay would react.

The operation with Sonny Armerian had taken more from Tate than his dignity and self-confidence; it had taken his soul.

Tate turned and slumped down on the couch, covering his eyes with trembling hands.

"I'm going to have to tell him soon," he whispered to himself. "This can't go on like this, making us both miserable. I just need the right time to do it…"

He lay back on the couch and huddled into a ball, hugging himself tight. The devil on his shoulder gloated that if he did, he could lose the man he loved. The angel on the other told him softly that Clay loved him regardless and Tate should take the chance.

I guess I'll have to decide which camp I'm in. Heaven or hell.

Tate closed his eyes and let the darkness of sleep claim him.

Chapter 3

Clay peered blearily at his watch, trying to see the time through blurred eyes. He tried to focus on the swimming digits and raised his wrist closer to his eyes. Around him, the chatter and noise of the bar buzzed in his ears.

"It's nearly midnight, boss. Time to be heading home, I think," the amused voice of Draven Samuels murmured into Clay's left ear.

Clay grinned at him. "Dray, how the hell are you?" He squinted at his employee and friend. "What are you doing here? Is Taylor with you? How did you find me?"

Draven shook his head with a grin as he sat down on the barstool next to Clay. He waved at the bartender.

"Can I have some strong black coffee for this man, please? Just keep them coming."

The bartender nodded and turned to the back of the bar to prepare the drinks.

Draven's dark eyes regarded Clay with some curiosity. "No, Taylor is home in bed. The same place you need to be I think. And you always come here when you're upset. This is your go-to place." He narrowed his eyes. "You, my friend, are as pissed as a newt. Considering you don't normally drink like this, I'm thinking Taylor's sixth sense was right. Something is wrong."

"Taylor had a premoniti—" Clay's voice faltered. "A vision of me?" Taylor Abelard was a psychic—a damned good one that Clay and his police colleagues sometimes used for a case. He was also Draven's fiancé.

Clay's stomach roiled and he swallowed bile. He'd had this acidic taste in his mouth ever since Tate had kicked him out of his apartment.

"He woke me up in a panic saying something was wrong with you." Draven's tone was dry. "And we all know I don't ignore my man when he has one of his touchy-feely things going on." He reached over and touched Clay's chin gently. "From the looks of it, he was right. Who hit you?"

The fierce protectiveness in Draven's voice gave Clay a warm, mushy feeling. Draven was right; Clay didn't often drink to excess and certainly not here on his own, in his favourite bar. Being told to leave and seeing the pain in Tate's eyes when he'd left had made forgetting the image through alcohol a more palatable option. His head swam and he passed a trembling hand over his eyes, trying to clear them.

"Tate hit me. He was scared. I didn't want to fight him though. So I left."

"Who's Tate, Clay? The man you've been seeing?" Clay had never made his relationship with Tate public at work, not even to Draven. He had his reasons. Draven knew though that he had someone special. Maybe now was the time to share the news with a man he respected and liked more than anyone else in his life—other than Tate.

Clay snorted. "Yep, my secret lover, the man I've wanted for what seems like forever. He kicked me out of his home tonight."

He heard the anguish in his own voice and swallowed. The bartender placed a steaming cup of coffee down in front of him and he stared at it as his eyes prickled.

"Drink the coffee, boss man," Draven muttered quietly. "Then I'll take you home."

Clay picked up the cup and took a large gulp from it. The liquid burnt his lips and he swore. "Fuck. That hurt."

Draven's lips curved in a small smile. "You *are* in a state. So why did Tate kick you out… or hit you?" The swift change of subject was a Draven special, designed to put people off guard and take them unawares. Clay should know; he'd taught him his interrogation techniques. As a senior operative of Mortimer Investigations, and probably the best, Draven was a man not to underestimate. Clay really needed to share and he could think of no better man to trust.

Clay shrugged. "He needed time on his own. He's fucked up. I've tried to hold it together but tonight…" his voice trailed off.

"Tonight he really flipped out again. He has panic attacks after the shooting incident. He gets aggressive. He thinks he's weak, but he's not. He's the strongest man I know."

Draven's eyes widened. "Your friend Tate—is this Tate Williams that we're talking about? Taylor's friend Rick's uncle?"

Tate's shooting had made the papers, so it was public knowledge.

Clay waggled a finger at him. He was feeling sicker by the minute and the black coffee wasn't really helping. "Now you know my secret. I shouldn't have told you; it might put Tate in danger. You can't tell anyone else. Except maybe Taylor, 'cos I know he won't talk. But God, Draven, I'm so tired. He didn't deserve what happened to him and I can't make it right for him." His heart ached and he wanted nothing more than to go home to Tate's house, gather his man in his arms and kiss the shit out of him.

Draven's watchful eyes regarded him. "He got shot, Clay. That's bound to fuck anyone up."

Clay snorted sadly. "That's not all that happened to him, Dray. Armerian got his hands on him long before the shooting. Did things to him that you can't imagine, including some stuff Tate's never told me about but I suspect it was worse than he's told me." His suspicion that Tate had suffered more than physical torture—that he'd suffered some form of sexual abuse at Sonny Armerian's hand—lived deep in his gut and made him crazy with hate for a man who was already dead.

Draven stiffened. "Tate was *tortured* by Sonny Armerian? *That* never made the papers." Of course it made sense that Draven would know exactly who he meant when he said the name 'Armerian.' The man was an astute investigator and thrived on all things law enforcement.

Clay waved a hand. His own hand movements made him dizzy. "No, it was all hushed up. That motherfucker held him for four days, trying to get him to spill the beans about the whole drug sting operation. The bastard did unspeakable things to him, and he shot him. *Three fucking times.* Armerian thought he was dead so he pushed him out of a moving car in front of the gym where they'd met. Thank God Tate is made of tough stuff." He finished his coffee and like magic another one appeared.

His friend let out a long sigh. “I always knew there was more to that story than was made public. Tate was working undercover in the drug squad then?”

Clay nodded. “Yes. He’d been in deep cover for close to three months. They were trying to find the head honcho that Armerian reported into, someone really high up in the organisation…” He closed his eyes, remembering the drawn features and pale face of his lover. “I don’t even know the full story about his time undercover; he never talks about it. But Tate was a mess, living on a knife edge.”

It had been a difficult time for them both, in their then-relationship as “just friends.” Staying apart and only making contact with each other when the need arose. They’d had to be ultra-careful, but both men were trained in techniques to keep themselves safe and stay off the grid.

“Armerian was killed by a car bomb about two weeks after Tate was shot,” Draven observed, his eyes searching Clay’s. “Was that your doing?”

There was no accusation in Draven’s tone, simply curiosity. Men like him knew the value of revenge.

Clay shook his head tiredly. “I went looking for him while Tate was in protective custody at the hospital. I was going to kill that bastard for what he did to him. But the Renaldo cartel got to him first. He pissed them off and they took him out.” He sipped his coffee. “I was following Armerian. I watched as he got into his Maserati and the thing blew sky high. That’s how I knew he was finally dead. It was such a fucking relief. At least I knew they wouldn’t come back to finish Tate off. The other cartel members all defected to Renaldo and thankfully they didn’t care about a half-dead man.”

“And you never trusted me to tell me all this? You dealt with this on your own?” Draven’s voice was pained. “I thought we were friends, Clay. You know I’d keep any secrets you shared with me. You did the same for me with Jude.” Clay remembered the heartache when Jude, Draven’s little brother who was injured in a car accident and left comatose, was at the point of never getting better. Draven had made an agonising decision to turn off his life support, something which haunted him to this day.

Clay reached out and gripped Draven’s muscled arm tightly. “I couldn’t. Tate was so bloody damaged and I couldn’t risk anything else happening to him. You and I have enemies, Draven. It's the nature of the work we do. Tate has always been my Achilles' heel. No matter what our relationship, I couldn't have anyone finding out how much he means to me and using him against me. If they'd known exactly what he was to me, it would have made it worse."

Draven stared at him and then nodded slightly. "That makes sense. People could get to you through me then to Tate. I'd do the same if it was Taylor who'd been hurt like that."

Clay's head was clearing a little now. "I know I'm a bit paranoid, and Tate's told me the same thing. It's just hard, you know?" He stared down. "I've known him since we were kids. We lived on the same street; our parents were friends." He got lost in the half-full coffee cup. God it felt good telling someone about this.

"He was three years younger than me. We went through school together, came out together and we were best friends. But I'd always known he was more than that to me, even when we were so young." He drew a deep breath. "I needed to stop any temptation before I did something illegal to Tate, so I went straight into the RAF at eighteen. Tate was only fifteen then. He stayed behind to finish secondary school and then college. I was travelling around so much, never in one place, and it was tough to see each other, apart from an occasional meet-up when both of us were in town together. We kept in touch with Skype, messages, emails…God, the emails. I think I must have a damn novel on my computer."

His voice trailed off. "Tate found his way into the police force and worked his way up to detective in the drug squad. I'd joined the SAS and was never around." He snorted softly. "Six years ago we each found time to meet up face to face again at a family function. It was like physically being apart had never happened. We took up as mates again but I definitely wanted more. Tate'd had a couple of old relationships and wasn't ready to start anything with anyone, least of all me. I just didn't think he thought of me that way."

Draven shifted on the barstool and shot a glance at the bartender, who was obviously waiting for them to leave so he could close up. Draven ignored him. "So you became close again?"

Clay nodded. "Yes. Then all the shit happened. Somehow Armerian found out about him. We still don't know how. The investigation is ongoing, but it's unlikely we'll ever see any further developments." He stared unseeingly at the bar counter. "From the time Tate woke up in hospital, I was there for him. Things changed between us after that. I guess a near-death experience makes you reconsider your priorities." He grinned wryly. "A couple of months after his shooting, we had sex for the first time. It blew my mind. What was equally mind-blowing was when he confessed he'd always had a thing for me but had never acted on it. He didn't think I felt the same way about him and neither of us wanted to blow the friendship we'd had since childhood."

"No. Just blow each other maybe," Draven observed drily. "Christ, you two were stubborn arseholes not admitting your feelings for one another." He snorted. "I can relate to that." He scowled. "I always knew you had someone special, friend or lover. You were always so damn secretive about the man in your life."

Clay nodded and then wished he hadn't as his head exploded. "I've always loved him; I just didn't tell him. It was fucking torture."

The bartender cleared his throat. "Gents, I need to close up the bar. Sorry about that but…" he rolled his eyes. "It's way past closing time."

Draven stood up. "Come on. Let's make sure you get into a taxi home. The tube won't be running now."

Clay drained the dregs from his coffee cup and got to his feet. He stumbled and Draven's strong arm gripped his elbow.

"Easy, champ. Good thing I'm here." The two men made their way outside and Clay's head swam as the cold air hit him. The empty feeling in his chest amplified at the fact that he was going home to his empty house. True, he and Tate had their own places, but more often than not, when he got home, Tate would be found curled up on Clay's old, comfortable sofa, in sweats and a cut-off tee shirt. The bad days were something they faced together; the good days were heaven. Only now Tate had decided his past was his cross alone to bear.

"I don't want to lose him, Dray," Clay muttered as Draven opened the taxi door and motioned him in, giving the driver his address.

"I know," his friend said softly. "But you've had your drink binge and gotten it out of your system; now work on getting him back. You're Clay Mortimer, for God's sake. You can figure this out. Just keep being there for him and give him the space he needs." His eyes darkened. "One word of advice. Tate is a grown man, Clay.

You have to let go sometime, let him be his own man, take his own risks. Or you're going to stifle him. Especially given what he was. The man's used to taking care of himself, taking risks."

Clay blinked at him. "Since when you did you get to be so damn wise?" he murmured. "Is that Taylor's doing? That man has been good for you, you know that?"

"I'm very lucky to have him," Draven agreed. "And you'll get your man back too. Just go home, sleep it off and I'll see you tomorrow. You know where I am if you need me. Make sure you call me if you do. Don't be fucking Captain Lonerguy and try and do it on your own."

He stepped back onto the pavement and rapped his knuckles on the roof of the taxi. As it pulled away, Clay leaned back into the vinyl-smelling seat and closed his eyes. Draven's words about letting Tate go echoed in his ears. They stayed with him long after he finally got home and stumbled into bed for a restless, uneasy sleep.

Chapter 4

Watching a film containing multiple car chases and picking up all the continuity errors in the story wasn't really the way Tate wanted to spend his evening, but after a day of nonstop web browsing and compiling reports for work, he needed something mindless to distract himself.

He lolled on his two-seater couch, clad in old joggers and a soft sweatshirt, a bowl of Kung Pao chicken on his chest as he watched one of the *Fast and Furious* movies. He picked at his food as he watched Vin Diesel getting it on with some busty blonde. Not that *he* wouldn't have minded getting it on with Vin, of course. He'd bet on the fact that if Vin was gay, he'd be one hell of a power bottom. Everybody else thought he'd be a top but Tate thought differently. Tate rather fancied that idea of having a naked, buff Vin Diesel bent down on the bed, muscular, delectable arse in the air.

Thinking of sexy arses made him think of Clay. It had been four days since he'd last seen him. Clay had texted and Tate had replied, and the conversation had been fairly non- committal. Clay asked how he was and Tate told him he was fine. Both of them knew he was lying. Tate's soul burned with the shame of pushing Clay away. He ached with his need for the man who'd turned his world upside down and he languished in despair once again at how he managed to keep fucking up anything good that they had.

Tate had been to his usual session at his therapist. She'd subjected him to some gruelling interrogation and once again given him a lot of perceptive insights. He always felt better after seeing her. Dr Natalie Jakes was a master manipulator and an excellent psychologist, plus she didn't take Tate's bullshit. She'd been really miffed to hear he'd kicked Clay out. Her small, elfin face had creased in a scowl behind her spectacles and she'd chastised him in that gentle, completely *I'm going to kick your arse* way she had.

"I appreciate you feeling that way, Tate," she'd said gently. "But Clay is the one person who can help you in this struggle you have. Take your time off, but don't take too long. Don't fuck it up for yourself. I know you're frustrated because he protects you too much and that *does* need to change for both of you to be comfortable. He can't wrap you in cotton wool too much longer. But give him a little more time."

Her words had struck fear into Tate's heart that Clay may get tired and give up on him, or that they'd be forever hidden from each other's outside lives. As he sat now, picking the chicken out of his dinner and feeling as lonely as a ball bobbing on an ocean, he decided enough was enough. He'd wallowed and stared into his soul enough this week and it was time to stop. He knew in his heart that he couldn't guarantee it wouldn't happen again but he'd have to live with that fear.

Tate picked up his mobile and took a deep breath as he called Clay's number. It was answered almost immediately.

"Hey." Clay's gentle voice was like a soothing balm on a stinging cut. "Are you okay?"

"Yeah, fine. Sitting here thinking I want to plough Vin Diesel's arse and wondering if he'd let me."

The husky chuckle from the other side of the phone perked Tate and his cock right up.

"You always have this thing for him. I'm not sure of the attraction myself." There was a garbled muttering in the background, laughter and the sound of soft music.

Tate frowned. "Am I interrupting? You sound as if you're in the middle of something." Part of him felt a little peeved that Clay was having fun without him. It was completely illogical. He'd been the one who'd kicked him to the kerb.

"I'm having dinner with Draven and Taylor at Galileo's. They knew I was down so they bought me one of Eddie's famous 'Chocolate Orgasm' desserts to get me through it." Clay's voice was matter of fact, not at all judgmental about Tate being a bit of an arsehole and pushing him away. Tate closed his eyes as a wave of guilt swept through him.

"I miss you," he murmured softly.

There was silence then, "I miss you too."

"I'd love to see you. Do you think—" Tate hesitated. "Do you want to come over later after you finish stuffing your face with pudding?" He took a deep breath and waited for Clay's response.

There was a sudden quiet and a whispered conversation in the background then it sounded like the phone was grabbed as someone came onto the line with all the subtlety of a Force Twelve hurricane.

"Tate, is that you?" Taylor's voice was slurred, and Tate sighed.

"Yes, Taylor, it's me." They'd met on various occasions and Tate really liked the wild, unconventional being that was Taylor Abelard.

"You need to stop being such a fucking prat and giving Clay gray hairs. He's a really nice guy and he's been bloody miserable and I for one—wait, Clay, what the fuck are you doing? Ouch, stop that, you bully. Draven, what the hell are you doing with that fork—fuck, that hurt, you bastard. You are *so* not getting any tonight—"

Taylor's indignant tone was cut off as he squealed loudly and there was muffled laughter on the other side, deep and amused. Tate knew it to be Draven. He'd heard that laugh often enough before at the office. Tate was also curious about Taylor's words. It sounded as if the man knew the real nature of his and Clay's relationship.

What has Clay been telling them? Has he finally confided in someone?

With a small flicker of hope in his soul, he grinned into the phone as he imagined the scenario being played out in the restaurant.

Finally there was a loud scuffling noise and the next he knew, Clay was on the phone again. He sounded out of breath and rather apologetic.

"Love, are you still there? Sorry about that. I swear I haven't been bad mouthing you. Taylor came to the whole prat conclusion all by himself. He's had one B-fifty-twos too many and he's a menace to society when he gets tipsy. His mouth knows no bounds. Dray's not much better off either."

"Don't worry about it. I can see you have your hands full with those two." Tate snorted with laughter.

There was a sudden flurry of words, a loud guffaw and then Clay groaned.

"Yeah, Taylor, tell the restaurant *exactly* what your mouth does with Draven. God, Dray, shut him up will you? I don't care how. Oh, shit. I didn't think you'd actually *do* that whole 'stick your tongue down his throat' in public to keep him quiet..."

Clay sounded flustered and Tate felt better with each minute with the events being enacted on the other end of the phone. His one regret was that he wasn't there to see it himself. He broke into quiet chuckles at Clay's next mortified words.

"Oh hell, Gideon, I'm so sorry. I understand you don't need a porn show in your dining area. I promise to get these two drunken sods out of here. Just let me say goodbye to my boyfriend. Love, I'll come over once I've off loaded these two, okay? See you later. Love you."

The line went dead and Tate stared at the phone with a sense of longing. He wanted that camaraderie too. He wanted to be with Clay, in public, instead of hiding who they were to each other. He wanted to sit in a restaurant and fool around with friends. It did sound as if Clay had perhaps opened up a little about their relationship. Maybe Tate's last words about being molly coddled, spoken the night he told Clay to leave, had finally struck a chord.

It was close to ten-thirty when Clay finally arrived. There was a tentative knock at the door, almost as if he was expecting him not to answer. Tate took a deep breath. He'd had a shower, shaved and put on a clean pair of jeans and polo shirt and he was ready. The bedroom was well stocked with lube. The toys, an electro wand and torpedo plug they'd bought together at a sex fair in Manchester, had fresh batteries. He didn't think that sort of play was on the cards tonight; no, tonight he just wanted to be close to Clay—but who knew?

He opened the door and his heart beat faster at the simple fact that his lover stood there. Clay looked tired and a little frazzled, but the scent of him and the hesitant smile on his face made Tate's world a little brighter.

He reached out and pulled Clay inside, not even stopping to say anything. His mouth found Clay's, his tongue pushed inside a warm, chocolate and whisky-scented mouth and from that point on, the clock stopped. Clay's answering moan into his mouth, the way he pulled Tate's hips against his groin, the already-hardened cock Tate found pressed into his crotch; those actions spoke louder than any words.

They grappled with each other, both ravenous, each of them trying to say something in the pressure of lips on lips, the thrust of tongues, each seeking dominance, releasing soft groans as hands found skin. For Tate, it was 'Welcome Home,' 'I'm sorry' and 'I love you' all at once.

Clay pushed Tate back against the wall and pinned his arms to his sides, his mouth sucking on Tate's bottom lip. Tate heaved a shuddering sigh and gave into his lover, his body becoming pliable and surrendering to whatever Clay wanted to do with it.

"You smell like sandalwood," Clay finally murmured when his lips stopped assaulting Tate's. "Did you shower?" His pupils were dilated and there was only a thin green line around them. It was sexy as hell and Tate loved that he was the cause of it.

"Yes," he whispered. "And I fingered myself too, tried to get ready before you got here." He noted Clay's flared nostrils with a deep sense of satisfaction. The man was so turned on.

"God, Tate, I missed you so much." Clay's lips trailed a heated track down Tate's throat. "I thought you'd never call, but I didn't want to be a needy bastard and call you."

Tate's hands were finally released and they wandered down to the hardness at Clay's groin. His lover hissed as eager fingers rubbed his cock. "I missed you too. I'm sorry I'm such a prat like Taylor says; I just get so damn frustrated sometimes—" He hitched a breath as Clay bit his shoulder, pushing the shirt aside to get at the skin.

"Let's not play the blame game right now." Clay's hands were under Tate's shirt, his touch searing Tate's skin. "Let's just go to bed so I can fuck some loving into you. I was going to suggest double-Dutching but I really want to be inside you myself."

Tate's balls contracted and his cock swelled at those words. They tended to be pretty versatile in bed, giving and getting on an equal basis. What they called double-Dutching was always a firm favourite. Pushing something into Clay at the same time Tate was being filled, the fact they fucked each other with their own personal favourite toy; that was a huge turn-on for both of them. There were nights when Clay would drive him insane with it all and the constant assault on his body and his senses. And then there were nights like tonight when he just wanted to be as close to Clay as possible and feel him inside him.

He tugged Clay toward the bedroom, already set with candles flickering in the darkness and the smell of incense permeating the air. The covers were already folded back neatly to the bottom of the bed.

Clay's eyes smouldered as he looked around the room. "You had this all planned out then? Are you trying to seduce me, Mister Williams?"

Tate laughed huskily. "I did and I am. Now get your clothes off and into bed. I need to feel skin, cock and your mouth everywhere. As for the candles—you can put them to good use later. Round two, maybe."

The shiver that ran through both his own and Clay's body at those words was anticipation. Tate enjoyed having hot wax on his skin and Clay enjoyed putting it there. There were a few other things they'd experimented with: ice against Tate's prick and balls, then rubbed on his arsehole until it froze so that Clay's warm tongue could warm him up. Another favourite was using the pulsing wand on Tate's cock, taint and balls until Tate was ready to scream with the tension before begging Clay to finish it.

Both men disrobed hastily and Tate's skin prickled in pleasurable response to the sight of Clay's heavy balls, and the erect cock curving against the muscles of his groin and stomach. A dark line of black hair ran into a neatly clipped bush above his cock and as Tate watched, his breath deepening, Clay's stomach muscles contracted as he palmed himself and looked at Tate with a wicked grin.

"Ready for this? I'm too damned horny and I can't promise this is going to be slow or easy. In fact, I think I can pretty much guarantee I'm going to pound the life out of you." His voice deepened. "Get on the bed, Tate, onto your back."

Sometimes not making love, but taking it rough and hard, was necessary. This was one of those times. Tate hastened to do as he was told. He scooted onto the mattress, lying back on the continental pillows against the wrought-iron headboard. Endorphins raced through his blood as his anticipation built, and his prickling skin screamed for Clay to touch him and anoint him with his own sweat and come. To claim him. To make things right, at least for a little while.

Clay watched with hooded eyes and slightly parted lips as Tate deliberately spread his legs, dropping them to the side so he was exposed, then gently ran his hand over the flat planes of his stomach and down toward his prick, which jutted up, proud and ready. Keeping his eyes on Clay's face, Tate stroked himself, making sure his hand swept over the head of his cock. He gasped as his calloused palm hit a particularly sensitive spot and was gratified to see Clay's cock swelling, the purple head glistening.

"You look so damn sexy like that." Clay's voice was thick with desire. "I've been dreaming about you like this. Lying there, open for me, ready to take you, be inside you."

Tate smiled lazily. "Yeah? Then you'd better get over here before I finish myself off, because it won't take long." He twisted his hand around his cock again and drew in a deep breath at the sensation.

The bed dipped as Clay got on and before Tate could even make another stroke, his wrist was gripped and pinned above his head.

"You will come when I do," Clay growled. "Just from me fucking you, you hear me?" His body covered Tate's, the feel of hot, slick skin against his frying his brain and making his insides churn.

He nodded wordlessly, loving the dominance that Clay brought to the bedroom. In Tate's career as a policeman, he'd always had to be in control. With Clay, he could lose that part of him and succumb to someone else. Tate thanked God each time he submitted like this that his enforced incarceration with Sonny Armerian hadn't taken this part away from him. He might have been bound then and had no choice about what was done to him, but with Clay, he knew there was always an out.

"I hear you," he murmured breathily. "Just fuck me already, for God's sake."

Clay's mouth covered his and his forceful kiss would have made Tate's knees buckle had he been standing up. He moaned, and his groin pushed up to rub against Clay's. God, he needed release so badly. His cock ached, his balls were tight and his arsehole waited in anticipation for Clay's breach.

From under the pillow, Clay brought out the lube. He moved back, straddling Tate's hips as he opened the cap and rubbed it onto his fingers.

"Bring your knees up," Clay murmured and Tate obliged, lifting his knees almost to his ears. Clay's face flushed in the dim light, and the look on it at seeing his lover open like that was almost Tate's undoing. The look was reverent and worshipping but also filled with pure lust. Then cool, vanilla-scented liquid was pushed into him together with Clay's fingers—two of them from the feel of it. Tate arched his back and whimpered at the feeling of being filled.

They had no need of condoms; they'd been together exclusively for long enough for each of them to commit to that. And while it was messier and they needed to change their bed sheets far more often, Tate wouldn't have given that up for anything. The heady feeling of Clay's naked cock in his arse, with its smooth heat and slickness, and the feel of Clay's semen leaking out of him afterward was manna from heaven.

He groaned as he was breached more deeply, Clay's fingers pushing in, finding that place inside him that made him see spots, that caused his body to tremble as waves of pleasure coursed through him. "Just there…feels so good. Need you in me."

Clay kissed his cheek softly as his fingers withdrew, and then his warm, hard body pressed against Tate's as he slid inside him.

Tate cried out as Clay stretched him, silken flesh pressing against his inner walls. He pushed his hips toward the welcome intrusion. Clay gasped as he sank deeper and leaned down and bit the side of Tate's neck gently, no doubt marking him.

"I missed you," Clay whispered as they moved together, lost in the sensation of each other's bodies and murmurs of need. "Thought about you every damn minute…"

His thrusts grew frenzied and Tate gripped his backside and urged him deeper still. He caught sight of Clay's face above him, sweat gleaming on his cheeks and forehead, eyes half closed as he bit his lip. His look of concentration was intense and Tate reached up and gripped his face, bringing him down for a kiss, claiming the man inside him with the possessive need borne of love.

Tate's cock was near to bursting, and he wrapped a hand around it then moaned when Clay pushed his hand away.

"No, you come just from *this*," Clay growled, "Me inside you. You've done it before; now let me see it. Think about my cock deep inside you, marking you, giving you my seed..." He leaned in to Tate's ear. "Me *fucking* you like this. Making you mine." He pushed Tate's legs back, gripping him tighter and drove even harder, to the point of near pain.

Those words and the aggressive passion with which he was being well and truly screwed drove Tate to the edge. As Clay reared back and rammed into him again, Tate managed one sly twist of his cock with his hand and climaxed. Shuddering as his body rode out his orgasm, dimly he heard Clay's shout and the warmth flooding his arse as he came too. Breath heaving with the force of his release, Tate lowered his aching legs and lay beneath Clay's heavy body. His heart pounded madly, his arse was sore and the room bore the scent of sex, sweat and Clay's unique fragrance. His lover toppled off him onto the bed and lay there beside him.

"You cheated," Clay finally muttered as he raised himself on one elbow and observed him with a smile. "Think I didn't see that little move you did when you palmed your cock?"

"Yeah, yeah; you don't miss a thing do you?" Tate wiped a strand of sticky semen off Clay's stomach, raising it to his mouth and sucking on it. Clay's eyes darkened. "Mister Hawk Eyes, that's you."

Clay chuckled. "Next time I'm going to tie your hands to the headboard so you can't touch yourself."

Tate's cock jumped a little. "*That's* no punishment," he said softly as he trailed his tongue along Clay's jawline.

Clay grinned tiredly. "Oh, yeah. What the hell was I thinking…? You love that stuff." He rolled his eyes as he settled back onto the pillow on his side, facing Tate and pulling the duvet over them both. "Time to sleep. Are you okay to talk in the morning about things?" His tone was hesitant.

Tate took a deep breath. "I guess. I know we should." He frowned. "Did you tell Draven about us? I know Taylor knows and Draven is the only common connection I can think of."

Clay was quiet for a minute before replying. "Yes. I had a rough night the night you kicked me out. I got drunk, spat my mouth off." He shrugged. "Either Taylor read his mind or Dray spilled the beans. He can't resist that man of his. But I know both of them will keep it quiet."

I don't want it kept quiet. But I'm not going there right now. Clay will be surprised enough at the next therapy session when it comes to that sensitive topic.

Under the cover, he ran a hand across Clay's stomach then turned himself into the little spoon. Clay's strong arm swung across him as he pulled him closer, his half-soft cock pressed against Tate's cheeks.

"'Kay." Soft lips brushed against the back of his head. "I hope you manage to sleep well, love. I'm glad I'm back."

Tate nodded as he closed his eyes. "Uh huh, me too." He was already drowsy and feeling safe with Clay's arms around him. Maybe the nightmares would stay away tonight.

Chapter 5

In his time in the RAF and then the SAS, Clay had faced many dangers. He'd been thrown out of an aeroplane by a manic instructor, kicked in the head by a rogue donkey in Afghanistan, been submerged in below-freezing waters, been shot at, stabbed and beaten more times than he cared to remember. He'd encountered crazies intent on his destruction, drunk more alcohol than was healthy for him and killed many men and a woman. The latter had been a lady (and he admitted he used that term loosely) hell bent on slitting his throat during a deep cover operation in Prague. Nothing, however, had ever prepared Clay for the relationship skills and patience that he needed to manage the volatile being that was Tate Williams.

Dr. Jakes smiled at him. "Something on your mind, Clay? Want to share?"

Clay smirked. "Your last question reminded me about our school years together." He waggled a finger in Tate's face. "Even as a teen, he was a damn handful. When he was thirteen, he was the first one of us to come out." He chuckled and saw Tate grin at the memory. "He made this huge, six-foot-long, two-foot-high banner at the mock junior prom and hung it across the dessert table. It said, 'Yeah, I'm a fucking fruit. Get over it.'"

Both men sniggered loudly. This was their third session as a couple and Clay really believed that it was helping them both manage Tate's behaviour and moods. He'd been giving a lot of thought to Draven's words too. He knew he needed to tackle it sooner rather than later, despite his fear for his lover's safety.

Dr. Jakes raised her eyebrows at Tate. "Confrontational much?" she said with a warm smile.

Tate laughed. "That's what happens when you call me fag and queer. I had to hit back somehow."

Clay prodded Tate's arm. "You hit back in more than that way. You beat the crap out of those two jocks who called you that because they saw you kissing that boy in the schoolyard. Then you decorated the town and got caught, leading to more damn trouble."

Clay had been unhappy with that for two reasons. Firstly, that the boy Tate had deep- Frenched wasn't Clay. It had been some geeky straight schoolmate who had dared Tate to kiss him and everyone knew you didn't dare him because…well, it was just downright stupid. He was Tate, for God's sake.

Secondly, he'd been concerned for Tate for fighting back and injuring the two other boys. Tate had been suspended while the school board investigated the incident. Luckily, one of the teachers sympathetic to Tate had seen the event unfold and confirmed that Tate hadn't started it.

Tate scowled. "So I went on a bit of a binge to celebrate my newly declared homo status. Some of those shop owners had no sense of humour." He grinned. "All I had to do was clean it up. I got off with a caution."

Graffiti was an art talent that Tate still possessed. He'd go off by himself occasionally when he needed solace, and Clay had no doubt that somewhere in the neighbourhood there'd be a new piece of art on the city streets.

Clay glanced at the doctor, who appeared highly amused by the stories. "Less than a year ago, we went to Croydon and Tate felt the need to spray the police station with his genius. We were rather drunk, and it was three in the morning. It seemed like a good idea at the time. I was shitting bricks that we'd get caught."

Tate laughed loudly. "Yeah, one of the senior detectives at the station was an ex-lover of mine and he was a complete prat and a cheating arsehole. It was payback time."

Both of them grinned at each other, and Clay guessed they were both remembering the two-foot-high rendition of a backside and an arsehole painted on the station wall. It had been painted over quickly after discovery but they still chuckled when they drove past the wall.

Natalie Jakes nodded and leaned forward, her eyes observing Tate carefully. "You guys sound like a right pair. Well matched, I'd say," she remarked drily.

Then she got back to business. "So, Tate. The halfway house."

Clay knew Tate had a temper. He'd been on the receiving end himself more than once. Now, as he watched his man scowling fiercely across the table at his therapist, he hoped Dr. Natalie Jakes had bigger balls than his lover. She was going to need them.

"Yeah, I heard you on that. You want me to spend time at a kid's halfway house. Why?"

Clay tried to hide his smile at Tate's ferocious snarl. His partner actually loved kids, and in his career as a policeman, he'd always been the first to volunteer for the school talks and Career Day opportunities. Tate just simply had to challenge everything. It was the nature of the beast.

Clay sat back and waited in anticipation for Dr. Jakes's reply.

The psychologist mock-frowned at Tate who frowned back. "It's a great halfway house, for abused and troubled teens. The owner, Randall Pierce, is a friend of mine. He thinks the young people would benefit from an older role model, someone who knows what they've been through and can identify with them. You wouldn't need to tell them your whole story. Just talk to them, make them understand you know where they're coming from. Tell them some stories about when you were a policeman."

"How? I wasn't a troubled teen," Tate said mulishly. "And I wasn't… abused. I was tortured by a psycho in the course of my job." His voice lowered and he glanced across at Clay quickly then back to the doctor.

Clay had heard the slight hesitation in Tate's voice when he said he hadn't been abused, and from the look on her face, so had his therapist. Her eyes darkened and she threw a wary glance at Clay, whose stomach clenched at what he suspected Tate wasn't telling anyone.

Dr. Jakes leaned forward, a sympathetic glint in her eye. "These kids suffer from PTSD, Tate, and that, my friend, you definitely have in common with them."

Clay hitched a breath. His boyfriend wouldn't like that statement.

Dr. Jakes forestalled Tate's next words as Clay had no doubt he'd try and refute that statement. "And we've had this conversation before. You might not acknowledge it, but it's a fact."

Tate muttered under his breath and leaned back in his chair, long jeans-clad legs stretched out in front of him. He turned and glared at Clay, who wisely kept quiet.

She warmed to the subject. "I think it would be good for you to see these kids, interact with them. We aren't talking sexual abuse only, we're talking actual physical and mental harm, and some of these children are as young as eight years old. I think you have the empathy to help them. At the same time, it would be good for you to see what they've been through. It might give you all some perspective." She smiled at Clay. "Clay tells me you're good with kids. They respond to you. So one day a month isn't going to kill you, is it? I'm sure the boss will give you the time off."

Clay nodded, trying to keep the grin from his face. "Oh, I think I can safely say the boss will be happy to give Tate some leave."

He heard a snort and what sounded suspiciously like 'Fucking Jezebel' from Tate. But it looked like he wasn't going to argue anymore and was resigned to the suggestion. Her next words threw him.

“And Clay—it’s time you and Tate started being open about your relationship, with other people and in public.” Her tone was even but Clay heard the steel in it.

Clay’s eyes widened as he stared at her. “Where the hell did that come from?” He felt a stir of resentment. Even though he’d reached the same conclusion himself, and had been meaning to discuss it with Tate, he was irked at being blindsided. He suspected ruefully that this was the real reason for his last attendance at the three sessions he’d been to.

Tate shifted in his chair and then raised troubled eyes to Clay’s. The two men stared at each other. Clay waited for Tate to go first.

“I need you to let go a bit, Clay,” Tate said quietly. “We’ve talked about this, so it’s no real surprise. I don’t want to be protected or kept secret. I need to feel—” his voice caught. “I need to believe you still see me as strong enough to look after myself despite what I went through. You need to have confidence in me that I know what’s best for me.”

Dr. Jakes watched their exchange with narrowed eyes. She twirled her pen around in her fingers as she observed them.

Clay reached over and took his hand. “God, baby, I know that. You’re the strongest man I know. You are without doubt my damn hero.”

Tate’s eyes softened. “Then trust me to be that hero, Clay. Stop worrying that the bad guys out there are going to get me again, and be the man I love. *That* I can live with. But being sheltered, having you see me as half a man—that I can’t do anymore.” He swallowed and his fingers tightened in Clay’s grasp.

Clay’s jaw dropped. “Half a man? I have *never* thought that of you.” His heart beat faster. “You’re my world, Tate, my everything. I can’t bear the thought of someone hurting you again; that’s why I keep us a secret.”

“And therein lies the problem, Clay.” Dr. Jakes’s soft voice echoed in Clay’s eardrums. “This isn’t about you. It’s about Tate. He needs to feel you still see him as the man he was before Armerian got hold of him. Not someone to be wrapped up in cotton wool. It’s hindering his healing process.”

“I realise that,” Clay said gruffly. “It’s all I’ve been thinking about for the last damn week myself.”

Tate stared down at their clasped hands then raised anxious eyes to Clay's. "I understand your fear, I do. But I can look after myself. I was an undercover agent for Christ's sake. I failed at that once. But I won't fail again." His jaw jutted in determination. "Have you ever thought that I feel the same way about you? That you go off to work, might get involved in dangerous situations and you might not come home one night?" His voice cracked. "I would fall apart if anything happened to you. But I don't expect you to do anything different because of who you are and what you do. Well, this is who I am, Clay. You need to deal with it." He swallowed. "We spend so much time together, sleep at each other's houses. Anyone who really wanted to hurt me through you would put two and two together anyway. What you're doing means jack shit in keeping me safe. They'd know how much you mean to me and me to you just by looking at us. That's why I get mad, because you don't see it that way."

Clay was dazed. He didn't want to admit it right now but he knew exactly what Tate was talking about. He *had* been hiding his head in the sand, pretending no one would figure it out if they kept the semblance of not being in a relationship.

As for danger to him—Clay *had* been getting some threatening phone calls recently telling him something nasty was going to happen to him if he didn't back off a certain missing-person investigation his team was working on.

His agency and the police were now involved because it looked like there was a tie-in to a case they were working on, involving toxic waste being dumped illegally in an abandoned quarry in Oxfordshire. The scenario had the potential to be similar to the Monsanto scandal in Wales a while ago. Clay had been down at the police station with Tate's nephew Rick at the time, who'd convinced Clay to file a report on the threats, 'just in case.' Clay had done so to placate Rick but he didn't really think anything would come of it, or anything would happen to him. He got threatened all the time.

Tate didn't know about the threats and now wasn't the time to tell him.

Clay nodded jerkily. "I get it. I'm sorry—"

Tate leaned forward and placed a warm finger on his lips. "Don't ever be sorry for trying to keep me safe. Just turn it down a notch. Let *us* breathe."

Clay reached up and kissed the hand at his mouth. He nodded. "I'll try. Do you want me take out an ad in the newspaper saying 'Tate Williams and Clay Mortimer are in a relationship, having mind-blowing sex and will continue to do so for the foreseeable future'?" The thought definitely gave him a buzz. He wanted nothing more than to tell the world Tate was his, but his fear had held him back. But now was the time to make it right.

The wide smile on Tate's face at his attempt at humour made the world a brighter place. "I think we can give the banners a miss," he grinned as he leaned back in his chair. "But we can go out and do it with graffiti if you like. That would be cool. I miss doing that now I'm supposed to be 'respectable.'"

His body was more relaxed and Clay wondered if that capitulation on his part was all it had needed to achieve that. If so, he felt a real prat for not listening to Tate sooner.

Dr. Jakes grinned at him. "There. That wasn't too bad, was it?" she said jokingly. "And as for that graffiti thing you do, Tate…" She pressed her hands over her ears. "I heard nothing."

Both men smiled sheepishly. She leaned forward and slid a piece of paper across her desk. "This is the address of the home. It's called Castaways and it's in Camden. Randy is expecting you, so just call him and set up when you fancy going in." Her face grew serious. "I really think this could help as part of your therapy, so be very aware that this course of treatment is mandatory. If I get a call from Randy asking me why you haven't called yet, I shall be displeased." She grinned wolfishly. "And you won't want that, trust me."

Clay had no doubt that statement was true. Natalie Jakes's reputation was legendary. She might only be a slim, five-foot-five, bespectacled, red-haired woman, but she had determination and grit. She'd been recommended by a former colleague of Clay's in the SAS. She'd had him sobbing like a baby in his own session.

She looked at her watch. "Time's up, gents. Go home, fuck each other's brains out and let off some steam."

Both Tate's and Clay's mouths dropped open.

The therapist smiled wickedly. "What? I watch gay porn. It's hot. I read gay romance books too. So shoot me." She shrugged. "Are you going to report me for unprofessional behaviour? You know I'm not all that conventional at the best of times."

Clay guffawed at that understatement. Tate grinned but there was an element of wide-eyed surprise in them at her words.

"Doctor's orders, love," Clay said with a leer. "I think she has something there, with fucking as therapy."

Tate's tanned cheeks pinked up. Clay shook his head. Tate could shoot the wings off a gnat at a hundred paces, talk dirty with the best of them and had some kinks Clay wouldn't ever reveal to anyone, but discussing his sex life with his doctor got him all embarrassed.

"Thanks, Doctor." Tate held out a hand and shook hers. "So, same time next week? And I'll give Randy a call. I promise."

They left the office, and on the drive home as Clay manoeuvred his Audi through the city traffic, little was said. Tate had reached over and laid a hand on his thigh as Clay drove. The solid contact had warmed Clay. He felt that somehow today they'd turned a corner—one that he had probably been guilty of delaying with his paranoia. This thought rankled all afternoon and night, even when he climbed into bed that night at his home where Tate was staying over.

His partner was reading a Norman Mailer book called *The Faith of Graffiti*. It was a well-worn copy that he browsed through every time he wanted to read something familiar. Seeing it, Clay instinctively looked at the far wall of his bedroom where a painting hung. It was a large, square, silver-framed picture of Tate's tag signature. It was a simple *TW* in some funky script, in bright red, because that was Tate's favourite colour.

Tate had never understood Clay's reasoning for having the print done and framing it. Yet in Clay's head, this was a unique portrait of everything Tate Williams stood for. Unconventional. Brave. Quirky. Headstrong. Fearless. Not to mention his whole 'stick it to the man' philosophy, which was contradictory to him being a detective. And *so* Tate.

Tate looked up at him and laid the book down on his side table. His chest was bare, the covers pooled at his waist. "Work stuff finished for the night? And it's not even midnight," he said teasingly.

Clay took a deep breath as he slid into bed, clad in his sleep boxers. "I finished work stuff a while ago. I was busy with personal stuff."

Tate nodded. "Bills and things? Hope you paid the electricity bill. I put that load of fresh fish from the market we went to earlier in the freezer. You don't want that going off." His nose wrinkled.

Clay turned to face him and reached out a hand to idly stroke the bullet-hole scar on Tate's chest. "No. I called home actually. Spoke to Mum and Dad."

Percy and Angela Mortimer still lived in the neighbourhood where he and Tate had grown up. They'd been neighbours to Tate's parents, Sam and Rachael. Tate's folks were now deceased; his dad had a heart attack when Tate was in his twenties, and his mother died four years later from a brain aneurysm. Clay had been devastated when he'd learnt that. Tate didn't talk about them much, but Clay knew his own folks had been there for Tate when Clay had been off roaming the world. They were exceptionally fond of Tate and his big sister Lucy.

"Oh?" Tate's eyebrow lifted. "How are they? Still looking to win Garden of the Month?" he snorted. As youngsters, he and Clay had spent a lot of time toiling in the garden trying to win the coveted village trophy.

"They're fine. I, ermm, I told them about you. About us being together."

Tate stilled. "As in *together*-together?"

Clay nodded. He lay back on his pillows and crossed his hands under his head as he stared at the ceiling. "It was a bit of a let-down actually. They said they knew. Something about how I looked at you whenever you walked into a room." He rolled his eyes. "I didn't know I was that transparent. But they didn't want to bring it up until I did."

There was silence. He risked a look at Tate, whose face was glowing, his eyes shining.

"You really mean to keep your promise, don't you?" he whispered. His hand came out and brushed a strand of hair of Clay's forehead. "I know this isn't going to solve everything, Clay. I'm still going to struggle; there's no quick fix. But it means a lot to me that you listened today."

"I just wish I'd done it sooner," Clay said sadly. "I feel like a dick for making you feel less than you are. That was never my intention. I'm a man. I should have understood how you felt being treated like a kid. I just wanted to keep you safe."

Tate shifted over to run his fingers down Clay's chest and push the covers down past his hips, revealing his already semi-erect cock.

"Oh, yes, indeed," Tate murmured as his lips traced down from Clay's hardening nipple and trailed down his skin. "You are definitely a man." He gave Clay a wicked smile, his eyes heated under long lashes. His fingers curled around the base of Clay's aching hard–on. Clay gasped as Tate licked the tip and then licked a long, wet path down the underside. "And I need to test out the doctor's advice about fucking being therapy. So hold on to your balls, honey, because you are about to get the ride of your life."

Clay choked down a laugh even as his body thronged with sensation at what Tate was doing to his dick. "I'd rather *you* held onto my balls, actually. Oh, God, yes. Just like that…"

Clay closed his eyes and braced himself.

Chapter 6

Tate stood in front of a large house in the leafy suburb of Camden and gazed at the building perched at the top of the stone steps. It looked innocent enough—an old Victorian house, similar to Clay's, built of red brick with a white door. The sign bolted to the left of the ornate iron gate read simply 'Castaways.' He grunted moodily as he walked up the steps to the front door then pressed the bell.

The house was on a busy street, the hustle and bustle of traffic behind him drowning out the sound of any bell that may have rung inside. He waited. It had been a week since he'd promised to make it down here, and although he'd kept his promise to Dr. Jakes, he wasn't really in the mood.

After a minute, the door swung open. A harassed-looking woman in around her mid-forties or so stood there, dishcloth in hand and a weary smile on her face.

"Yes? Can I help you?" She glanced quickly out into the street then her gaze swung back to his face.

He forced a smile. "I'm Tate Williams. I'm here to see Randall Pierce?"

Her face cleared. "Oh, yes. I'd heard someone was coming. I hadn't expected you so soon. I thought you were coming later in the afternoon."

Tate cleared his throat. "If it's inconvenient, I can always come back later."

Yep. Like much later.

He was grumpy; he hadn't slept well, had been restless and the remnants of his bad dream from last night still haunted him. Clay cutting the strings on the overprotectiveness a little had changed something. Tate felt more at ease and the nightmares had lessened somewhat, but they could still invade his sleep like an unwelcome guest. The other day a car had backfired and while Tate had started and his gorge had risen in fear, it hadn't caused an extreme reaction similar to the firecracker incident. He'd been able to control it.

She waved at him with the dishcloth. "Oh no, it's fine. Please come on in. Randall is around somewhere. I'll get him for you."

Tate stepped into the hallway and his ears rang as the woman bellowed out loudly. "Randy. Your guest is here."

A harried voice called out from somewhere in the distance. "I'll be there in a moment, Jen. Please show him to the lounge. Tell the kids not to bother him if they're in there. No need to scare him off before we even get started."

Tate shook his head at the fact that this Randall guy thought a few kids could scare Tate. He'd faced far greater perils.

Jen laid a hand on his arm. "If you follow me, I'll show where to wait." She motioned him over to a room on the side. "Would you like a cup of tea, or coffee?"

Tate shook his head as he followed her into the room. "No, thank you. I—" His voice cut off as he encountered a few pairs of eyes staring fixedly at him. It *was* as unnerving as hell, like something out of *Children of the Corn*. The kids, ranging in age from about seven to twelve years old observed him with the fixation of a cat about to devour a bird. Tate could now see what Randy had been warning Jen about.

"Uhm, hi," he proffered as he waved a hand in their direction and cursed Natalie Jakes for putting him in this situation. The youngest looking kid in the group was a podgy, dark-skinned boy with black, shining eyes, and cornrow hair. He barked at Tate.

Tate blinked in confusion at the shrill 'Woof' emanating from that stocky little frame.

Jen tut-tutted. "Now, Damian, stop that nonsense. You know you're not a dog, sweetheart." Her eyes narrowed fiercely at the others. "No matter what this lot tells you."

The room broke into sniggers as the kids all looked around at each other with sly grins. Damian smiled too, and sidled over to Tate with what looked a half-eaten string of red liquorice. He held it out solemnly to Tate who reached for it with some trepidation.

He held it uncertainly and caught Jen's eyes. She shrugged apologetically.

"I think he wants you to eat it. You don't have to, though. I mean, I don't know where it's been."

Tate nodded, and swallowed. Then he took a deep breath and shoved the liquorice into his mouth. He chewed on it—it did taste a little gritty—then gave a thumbs-up to Damian.

"Very nice," he managed to say after he swallowed what tasted to him like something out of the garbage. Tate hated liquorice.

Damian's face lit up and he nodded. He woofed again and went back to the group, who now had dropped their degree of intense observation and looked a lot more relaxed. Tate started when someone spoke behind him. It was a warm voice traced with laughter.

"Guys, stop messing with Mister Williams. He's here to see Randy, not eat your leftover yucky sweets."

Tate turned and hoped he managed to hold back the shock at seeing the face of the young man behind him.

"There you are." Jen sounded relieved. "I'm going to let young Jackson here be your host, Mister Williams. I'm sure that Randall will be with you in a moment. It was lovely meeting you." She waved her cloth at him once again and disappeared out of the room.

Tate was left facing a young man with the visage of a stricken angel. His skin was creamy porcelain, with a shock of thick, unruly blond hair curling above it. His face was pitted with small, silver scars and a few deeper pockmarks. Both of the young man's eyes were milky blue orbs floating in a picture of flawed beauty. Jackson held himself straight, his slim frame proud as he stared at Tate with a smile that radiated warmth and light.

He stepped forward without hesitation and held out a hand to Tate. “Hi. Call me Jax—with an x.” He grinned, revealing straight, white teeth. “I help Randy out with stuff here.”

Tate noticed Jax’s chin tilted up when he spoke, and his eyes looked down, as if he was trying to see out from under his eyelids. It was a little disconcerting.

Tate shook the hand, which gripped his firmly. “Call me Tate. Pleased to meet you, Jax. It must be a pretty full-time job that, especially taking care of these ones,” he waved at the now chattering group, “I imagine they’re quite a handful.” He stopped, wondering whether Jax could actually see the hand gesture through those damaged eyes. The teen had come into the room without any white cane or support so Tate assumed he had *some* vision.

Jax smiled. “I’m not totally blind,” he confided. “I don’t see well, but I can make things out, especially when I’m about to hit a wall, or a dumpster or something. I just need the right angle to get a little vision.” He snorted softly. “I’ve done the dumpster-bashing thing before, so now I’m a bit more careful.”

There was no self-pity in his tone, simply a wry awareness of his shortcomings. Tate’s heart ached for such maturity and self-deprecation in one so young. He also wanted to maim whoever had done this to Jax. He’d no doubt this had been no accident but a deliberate, wilful act of violence.

Jax moved forward slowly until he stood in front of the other kids. He tilted his face upwards, his chin rising. “Right, you lot, bugger off and get outside. It’s lovely out, so go and play and I’ll call you when it’s time for lunch.”

Damian stepped forward and hugged Jax around the legs. “‘Kay, Jax. I hope it’s spag bol, ’cause I love that stuff.”

Jax ruffled the top of his head. “It’s macaroni cheese, not spaghetti Bolognese. Maybe Vicky will make that for you tomorrow. Now scarper, you lot. Mr Williams needs to speak to Randy.”

The group ran out of the room, calling to each other. One child remained behind. She

came forward and touched Jax’s arm. She was thin and pale with sunken brown eyes, and was no more than about ten years old.

Jax turned his head to look down at her. Tate noticed he was very careful with every move he made, his actions deliberate and slow. "You okay, Lucy?" His voice was soft. "Do you want to go outside or would you prefer to sit here and read?"

Lucy shook her head. When she spoke, Tate's stomach clenched. Her voice was strangled, hoarse, as if her throat didn't work properly.

"No. I'll go play with the others. Krispin hid my book. Can you ask him to give it back, please?"

Jax nodded. "I'll speak to him. He's just having fun. You know that, right? He's teasing you."

Lucy's lips tightened. "I want my book back. It's the one you gave me."

Jax's expression softened. "I promise to get it back for you." He ran a hand over the girl's lacklustre hair. "Maybe later you can wash your hair? Jen will help you look all pretty."

Lucy's eyes widened. "With apple shampoo? I like that smell." She smiled slightly and left the room.

Jax sighed, a deep, heartfelt sigh that seemed to come from the very depths of him. Due to the damage to his eyes, Tate couldn't see much expression in them but Jax's sad face spoke volumes. Tate didn't want to pry just yet; he was starting to think he'd rather *not* hear the stories behind each of these seemingly tragic individuals.

Just then there was a loud noise behind them and Tate turned to see a short, portly, bearded man bustle into the room bearing a tray of tea and biscuits. He smiled at Tate as he set the tray down on the small oak table in the middle of the room.

"Mr Williams? I'm Randy. It's lovely to meet you. Natalie's told me all about you." Tate's startled glance must have unnerved him because he continued hastily. "Oh, nothing confidential, of course, she'd never breach patient/doctor confidentiality. She shared just enough to make me curious." His wide grin would have put the Cheshire Cat to shame. "Please, have a seat, and I'll play mother. Jax, are you joining us?"

Jax shook his head. "Thanks, but I've got some studying to do." His mouth twisted. "I have an exam soon." His pale blue eyes turned towards Tate. "Nice meeting you, Tate. Hope to catch up with you soon."

Randy reached over and grasped Jax's shoulder. "Thanks, lad. Don't overdo the studying. Remember to break often, and give your eyes a rest."

Jax made a moue. “Thanks, *Dad*.” He chuckled. “I promise I’ll be careful.”

He gave one last affectionate look at Randy and left.

“That young man is an inspiration,” Randy murmured. “He’s one of the bravest people I know.” He glanced at Tate. “I’m sure you’re dying to know everyone’s story and find out why you’re here, and I have to confess, I’m anxious to find out yours too.” He began to pour strong tea into large mugs. “Natalie told me she thought you could help these youngsters and vice versa.”

Tate blew air out. “I’m not sure how I’m supposed to help them, but I’m all ears.” He poured milk into his tea. “Natalie thought this would help me.” He shrugged. “I’m not sure what she hoped me to get out of it.”

“That woman works in mysterious ways,” Randy chuckled. “I’ve given up trying to understand women, and I’ve been married to Jen for almost twenty years.”

Tate nodded his agreement and sat back. “So what’s Jax’s story?” The man had sparked a fierce protectiveness in him and he wanted to find out more.

Randy nibbled on a biscuit as he sat back, mug in hand. “Jax has been with us for just over two years. He was fifteen when he arrived. He was part of a loving family, with a very privileged background and a father with an obscene amount of money. Sounds idyllic, doesn’t it?” His face darkened. “Except Jax had an older step-brother called Terrence who wasn’t right in the head. Terry was mean, cruel and made Jax’s life a misery.” He bit down savagely on his biscuit. Tate blinked at the act of aggression towards an innocent cookie.

“Jax’s birth mother died when he was twelve and his father remarried a year later. Without going into detail, Jax lived in a state of hell, being picked on, harassed and beaten. His father refused to see what was going on. He travelled a lot. One night it went too far. Terry came into the house while everyone was out. He was high on something. He found Jax in his bedroom—Jax says he’d been asked to put some laundry in there by his step-mum and he’d forgotten to do it earlier—and he beat Jax almost senseless for being in his room.”

He put his mug down on the table as Tate listened in horror. “Jax’s dad is some megastar photographer and had his own photographic lab out the back, in the garage. Terry went out there, picked up a container of some fluid Jax's dad was using for the photo development and took it back inside." His tone was grim. "The fluid contained some sort of acid. He threw it into Jax's face while he lay there bleeding on the floor with broken ribs, internal bleeding and a bad concussion. Then he left." Randy heaved a deep sigh.

Tate gasped in horror. He might have been tortured and beaten himself but the thought of someone that young being subjected to the same pain and misery he'd experienced was horrific.

"Christ. What happened then?"

"Luckily, two things helped him keep some of his sight and negate the damage. His eyes were closed at the time because he'd been beaten half unconscious. But unfortunately it's a natural reaction to open your eyes when something splashes in your face and it didn't save his sight altogether. Secondly, the housekeeper had come back to check on the oven; she was one of those OCD individuals who thought she'd left it on.

She heard his screams and had the presence of mind to flush his eyes out with soda water or milk or something, and called nine-nine-nine. It took Jax months to recover and he's also had a lot of plastic and eye surgery. What you see today is worlds apart from what he looked like straight after the attack." He sighed. "He sees better when he tilts his head up apparently. If he looks at you straight on, it's all black and he can't see shit. It's a bit of a quirky mannerism but it works for him."

Tate was speechless. "Where's his family now? Why is he here instead of with them?"

Randy's face saddened. "Terry was arrested and because he was over eighteen—just—he got a prison sentence for grievous bodily harm. I don't know whether he's still inside or not. Jax's dad passed away about three months after the incident—a heart attack. Jax was still in the rest home at the time, having all the recuperative surgery. His step-mother sold the house, packed up and left. No one knows where she went. Jax was an only child so he had no one else. He did have a trust fund though, a good one that paid for everything and became his when his father died. It's administered through his father's lawyers and Jax becomes complete custodian of it when he's twenty-one."

Tate still wasn't clear. "If he has all that money… no offence, but why is he here, in a halfway house? Shouldn't he have his own home with a guardian and doctor at his beck and call?"

Randy's eyes lit up. "You'd think that, wouldn't you? We met at the hospital he was in. Jen and I were visiting another child, we got talking to Jax and over the months we became friends. When he heard what we did for a living, Jax asked if he could come and stay here and help us. The doctors said it would be good for his recovery, to feel useful, and if that's what he wanted, then let him."

He picked up another biscuit. "He's just never left. He's part of the extended family really. He's a stubborn little blighter, extremely independent and intelligent indeed." He popped the whole biscuit in his mouth and Tate watched, fascinated, as his muzzled jaw moved up and down.

He finally drew his gaze away. "What's he studying?" Tate asked curiously.

"He missed some school because of the attack, but he caught up and now he's doing his A-Levels in psychology via distance learning with a local college. He has special software—non-visual desktop access or NVDA—set up on his PC which he can use when he doesn't want to strain his eyes too much. The last thing we need is the last remaining vestige of sight he has disappearing altogether, so we're quite strict in trying to enforce his eye rest sessions. The college has been good about bending over backward for him, even given him some textbooks in Braille, which he can read. Plus he attends a couple of workshop sessions every month so it gets him out of the house."

Randy's eyes shadowed. "He used to be a promising young artist, but he hasn't picked up a paintbrush since. He was also involved in music and played piano; he has a real creative streak. Now he doesn't go out much and has no real friends his own age. It does worry me. He insists he's fine, but I wonder. Sometimes he gets this look…" His voice tailed off and Tate waited to see what *look* this might be. When Randy didn't continue he simply nodded.

"It's a damn tragic tale for one so young. Makes mine seem paltry in comparison…" Tate hesitated at the wicked glint in Randy's eyes and the sudden knowledge that he'd had been played. That was *exactly* the reaction he knew that Dr. Natalie Jakes had been looking for.

He raised his cup of tea to Randy. “Touché,” he acknowledged. “Therapists are manipulative bastards, aren’t they?”

The other man chuckled loudly. “Tell me your story then.”

And Tate did. Not all of it, admittedly. There were aspects of his torture at Armerian’s hands that he’d never revealed, to either his therapist or Clay. It was too intimate, too shaming and he’d probably go to his grave with his secret. When’d he finally finished his story, and Randy had eaten half of the packet of biscuits and drunk most of the pot of tea, Tate felt…purged. It had felt good sharing it with someone who wasn’t close to him like Clay or someone who was trying to heal him. Randy simply listened.

“Shit, that’s some pretty heavy stuff,” Randy said, drawing a breath between his teeth. “Thanks for telling me. I’m sorry you went through that.” He leaned back in his chair and gave a soft burp, then smiled apologetically. “You can certainly empathise with some of our kids here, even though your story is vastly different. Damian—he was sexually abused by his uncle for years. Lucy—,” his voice grew quiet. “She was kept in a basement for close to three years by her folks. They thought she was evil because she burnt her backside on an open electric fire and they said the burn looked like the mark of the devil. Her father tried to strangle her and damaged her vocal chords. They were religious nutters. Luckily for her, one of the kids of the new next-door neighbours was a little thief. He climbed into the basement window, came out pretty quickly and told his folks about the ‘weird kid’ living in the basement. They told the authorities.”

Tate shook his head in disbelief at the stupidity and ignorance of the human race. “What the hell is wrong with people?”

Randy shrugged. “Human beings can be the worst sort of cruel. Krispin was physically abused by his father from an early age; Cathy is six and was abandoned when she was three when her folks found out she was deaf…they wanted a perfect child and she didn’t fit the bill. So they left her with a sister who was a drug addict and who didn’t treat her well.” He cleared his throat. “The only good thing is that they all found their way here, and are relatively stable and happy. Jax contributes to that. They love him.”

“I’ve only just met him and even I can see how special he is.” Tate agreed. “He has this calming effect, this light about him.”

"That's our Jax." Randy said proudly. "I know one day he'll have to leave us and that will be a sad day when he does, but until then we're fortunate to have him." He grimaced. "Don't get me wrong, he has his bad days. Then he hides in his room and won't talk to anyone. Not even the kids can get him out of his funk. But those episodes are few."

Tate spent another half an hour talking to Randy. When he finally left that afternoon, he called Clay. He planned to let him know he was on his way to his house and he'd pick up dinner and wait for him there.

Clay answered. He sounded a little preoccupied. "Mortimer."

"Wow, that's a bit brusque, isn't it? What if I'd been a client?" Tate said in amusement.

Clay chuckled. "Sorry, I've been working from home this afternoon and was in the zone. It didn't even occur to me check who was calling. How did your visit go?"

Tate was pleased he'd get to see Clay sooner. "I can tell you I have much more of an appreciation for the work that the halfway house does."

Tate crossed the street to his car, an aging VW Golf, and clicked the key fob to open the door. "I think this whole visit was orchestrated to show me that there are others worse off than me. Randy even got me to agree to go back and give a talk to the youngsters on being a policeman." He grinned as he got into the driver seat. "I think that damn doctor was trying to give me a new perspective on things. She's one sneaky lady. She might even be in your league, my maestro of manipulation."

Clay's husky laugh went straight to Tate's dick. "Yeah? I'll show you manipulation when you get here. Your legs over my shoulders."

Tate's dick grew harder and he groaned. "Don't do that. I'm about to drive home and a hard-on will just get in the way." He started the car and put his mobile into the Bluetooth cradle.

"You could always pull over and we can have car phone sex," his lover purred seductively. As much as Tate fancied that idea, the biscuits he'd had earlier hadn't filled him up and his stomach was growling. He intended stopping to pick up Chinese food on his way home and eat *then* go to bed with Clay.

"It's an attractive offer, but I'm ravenous, and not for cock." Clay's splutter of laughter warmed Tate's heart and he laughed. "I'll pick up some Chinese and see you in a while." He shifted gears and sped up. "Oh and I met this really incredible young man called Jax. There's just something about him that makes me want to get to know him a little bit more."

Clay's voice was a little edgy when he next spoke. "Really? Does he know you're spoken for?"

Tate's stomach tingled pleasurably at the tone of possessiveness in Clay's voice. If his man had one particular fault, it was that he was jealous as hell. Not to the point of being unreasonable, but the green-eyed monster never lurked far from his cool surface.

"No, you jealous bastard, he's only seventeen. Kiddie-bait. He's been through such a lot but he just radiates this positive energy. Remarkable kid from what I've heard. I'll tell you all about him when I get home."

"Ahh." Clay didn't sound convinced. "Okay. Could you pick me up some of that crispy chilli beef please? I could really go for that."

"Roger," Tate said as he steered his way through the traffic. "I'll see you soon."

Chapter 7

Clay put down his mobile and rubbed his chin thoughtfully. Tate had sounded upbeat, more so than Clay had expected. They'd had a couple of altercations about that particular part of his therapy. Tate hadn't been looking forward to the visit to Castaways, which had led to heated, expletive-filled arguments. One had led to hot make-up sex. The other had Clay storming off to visit Draven.

Now Clay frowned, wondering who this Jax was that had Tate all warm and fuzzy. His mobile rang again. He smiled, thinking it was Tate, and didn't even bother to check the caller ID.

“Hi love, haven’t they got any chilli beef then? I’ll settle for something sweet and sour, you choose.”

A loud snort of laughter blasted his eardrums. “Much as I like you, Clay, I have no intention of giving you anything sweet or sour. I’ll leave that to Tate.”

Clay chuckled at the sound of Rick’s voice. “You cheeky little blighter. To what do I owe the pleasure of this call?”

Rick sighed heavily. “Sometimes I wish I’d never got that promotion to Sergeant. Now I have to do all sorts of stuff I didn’t have to do as a constable. Which includes attending some sort of black-tie event and I don’t have a tuxedo. I happen to know Tate hoards all his old ones in one of your cupboards. I wondered if I could borrow one; I’m sure I’ll find one to fit. I haven’t been able to get hold of him, and I’m in the area, so I wondered if I could pop in and rummage.”

Clay snorted. “Sure, if you think you can navigate the horror that is Tate’s closet. It’s all cut-off jeans and sleeveless, tatty tee shirts that he can’t bear to part with because they’re ‘comfortable.’” Tate’s flat didn’t have much space and Clay’s home had four bedrooms—plenty of spare capacity, which meant he’d inherited a lot of Tate’s *junk.*

Clay frowned as he focused on Rick’s other comment. “You can’t get hold of him? I spoke to him just a minute ago.”

Rick’s voice was wry. “Clay, don’t go worrying. He’s probably engrossed in conversation with Mister Yung at the takeaway. You know how they love to yack.” There was the sound of scrabbling and a muttered curse then Rick came back on the line, sounding a little breathless. “Sorry about that. Some kid ran past and knocked me. I nearly dropped the phone. Okay, I’ll see you in a while then.”

Clay’s mobile went silent and he laid it back on the table.

He wondered whether to call Tate again and find out if everything was okay. Part of him wanted to do it right now, the other, the bit that had promised his partner he’d stop being so protective, said a firm *leave it alone.*

So Clay chose to make some more business calls, mess around with some paperwork and ignore the tight feeling in his stomach that meant he was worried. When Tate walked in half an hour later, bearing fragranced bags of food, Clay was relieved.

"Got your beef," Tate announced as he threw his jacket over the chair back and disappeared into the kitchen. There was the sound of packets rustling and plates being pulled from the cupboard. Clay followed his lover into his kitchen and stood watching as Tate busied himself arranging food on plates.

"Smells good. By the way, Rick's popping over. Something about wanting to borrow one of your tuxes for some fancy do." He frowned. "I'd expected him here already." He glanced at his watch.

"Rick's coming over? Okay…" Tate's voice tailed off and he looked a little shamefaced. "Did he say anything about anything?" His tone was hesitant.

Clay looked at him. "Define *anything*." He quirked an eyebrow, curiosity spiking. Tate seemed ill at ease as he took a deep breath. "I haven't told my sister about us yet and he's been pushing me to. It's just—I know you told your folks and some of the people at work, but Lucy hasn't been around much, and every time I think I'll do it, I get distracted and Rick has been nagging me."

He rifled through the food bags with jerky movements and laid more food out on the counter. He didn't meet Clay's eyes.

Clay walked over to Tate and stayed his fiddling, his large hands grasping Tate's tightly. "Tate, it's fine. You've had a lot on your plate to deal with." He caressed Tate's cheek gently. "This isn't a race to see which one of us can tell as many people as possible."

Privately he thought the slower the news dribbled out the better. But Lucy was a bit of a firecracker and to find out she'd been one of the last to know could cause Tate a few big-sister problems. Like a slap to the side of the head.

His partner looked at him with darkened eyes filled with self-recrimination. "I made a big deal about you telling people about us but when it comes to my own sister, I just haven't gotten around to it," he muttered. "That makes me a bad person."

Clay snorted. "And when she finds out you waited so long, her wrath will be punishment enough." He grinned at the panicked look in Tate's eyes. "To be honest, I think she probably knows."

Tate's eyes widened. "Why would you say that?"

Clay leaned forward and bit Tate's earlobe, causing not only a slight yowl from him, but a shiver to run through his body.

"Because everyone tells me I look at you as if you're the whole world to me. I can't help it. It's true." He reached over and framed

Tate's face, then leaned in and took his lover's mouth in a bruising kiss. The moan Tate breathed into his mouth had him hard in seconds. He never failed to love the way Tate responded to him, the feeling of his mouth on his, the eagerness with which he shoved his tongue into Clay's mouth with a fierce possessiveness.

When they pulled apart, Tate's mouth was swollen, his eyes heavy lidded. His hands had burrowed themselves inside Clay's shirt, his warm fingers on Clay's skin.

"I don't think we should do this now," Clay growled huskily. "If Rick finds us getting busy again, he'll need therapy."

His lover snorted with laughter. "Hell, yes. Last time the poor guy couldn't sleep for a week, he said." He grinned wickedly. "I still think it's because he harbours this secret fantasy about older guys and the sight of you and I going at it like rabbits turned him on."

"I heard that, you freak." The indignant voice behind them made them both swivel round. Clay saw the faint panic in Tate's eyes at the sudden interruption but it disappeared quickly when he saw his nephew smiling behind them. Rick was obviously off duty as he wore jeans and a blue tee shirt. He was carrying a cardboard carrier loaded with coffee.

Tall, broad shouldered with light blond hair and an easy grin, Rick had been *involved* with Taylor Abelard for a short time; as far as Clay knew it had been as friends with benefits, but all that had changed when Rick had met Lauren. Rick was bisexual, in his own words 'an equal opportunity employer of my dick,' but Lauren had taken hold of his heart and his senses and her red-headed beauty had captured him body and soul. They'd been together for a while now and Clay had heard marriage rumours floating about. Privately he thought that at twenty-five, they were too both young, but Rick could be stubborn like his uncle.

Tate waved a hand at his nephew. "You come bearing gifts. Good lad." He reached over and plucked a coffee out of the tray. "I understand you're scrounging for a suit?" he narrowed his eyes. "What makes you think one of mine will fit you? Better still, you really think you'll look as good in it as I do?"

He dodged Rick's slap at his head and darted out of the way.

Clay chuckled as he picked up a coffee. "He does look good in a tux." He smirked. "He looks even better out of it…"

Rick scowled. “No images, please. The sight of two guys doing the dirty isn’t a problem, but when it’s my uncle and his main squeeze…” he shuddered. “Not going there.”

“Main squeeze?” Tate chortled. “Clay, you just got downgraded from hot-shot lover to something that comes out of a toothpaste tube.”

Rick grinned and slurped his coffee. Then he flicked his eyes up to gaze at Tate.

“Have you told Mum about you and Clay yet?” His words were mild but Clay saw the effect they had on Tate.

His partner flushed. “No. I thought I’d pop over, see her tonight.”

Rick nodded. “Okay. I know you’ve had stuff on your mind. I think she knows but she’ll be as mad as hell if she doesn’t hear it from you. And you know what Mum’s like. *She’ll* have your balls, let alone Clay having them.” He sniggered then stared at Clay, a more serious look on his face. “Have you had any more death threats?”

Tate started and his expression darkened. Rick’s tone faltered as he darted a guilty glance at Clay then at Tate. Clay’s heart sunk and from the look on his face, Rick seemed to know he’d make a faux pas. Clay *had* told Rick that he’d let Tate know about the threats, and Clay hadn’t, so Rick wasn’t to blame.

Busted.

“No,” he said quietly. “Nothing since the last ones.”

Tate’s jaw tensed. “What threats are these?” he said tightly. His mood had changed in the blink of an eye with the rapidity of a tornado changing course. PTSD was a bitch.

“It’s that toxic waste case. The one you helped me with. It seems to have another element now, a missing person. About ten days ago I had a couple of threats, just the usual stuff, warning me off. The kind of threats I get because of the type of business I run.”

“And you didn’t tell me…why?” Tate said caustically, his eyes flashing.

Rick looked uncertainly at them both then flapped a hand. “I’m gonna go look for that tux,” he stammered, and scarpered.

Clay wished he could have done the same. Tate looked thunderous.

"I didn't tell you because it was being handled. I gave a report to the cops because Rick insisted, and since then, there have been no more calls. It's gone quiet. I don't think our missing person wants to be found. If he is, he'll go to jail, maybe worse, so…" He shrugged. "It's no big deal."

Tate went ballistic. "*This* is your fucking way of not molly coddling me?" he spat at Clay. "By not telling me someone wanted to fucking kill you? And Rick bloody knows before me?"

"Rick knew because he was there when I got the call," Clay said evenly. "Not because I chose to tell him over you. Tate, you're overreacting to this." Clay's heart thudded in his chest, and a sick feeling of dread washed over him, soaking him, suffocating him.

Tate's jaw clenched as he leaned into Clay's face. "Fuck. You." He hissed and spittle hit Clay's cheek. "I thought we'd taken one step forward, Clay, but it looks like nothing has changed. You still think I can't cope with the seedy side of your life. Of *our* lives."

Clay's temper was rising now. "That's not it at all," he exclaimed. "I didn't think it mattered because they've stopped and nothing has happened to me. For Christ's sake, stop being such a bloody drama queen and listen to what I'm saying. Not everything is always about you."

No sooner were the words out than he regretted them. Tate's eyes flickered and his Adam's apple bobbed and then in one quick movement, he grabbed his leather jacket from the back of the chair where it had been resting, and strode away. The door opened and slammed on an image of Tate racing down the front steps toward the street.

Clay belatedly dashed to the front door but Tate had already crossed the street and vanished at the intersection. Clay slammed the door shut and turned and swept the flowers from the vase on the entrance table with a violent shove of his hand.

"Fuck, fuck, fuck." The petals from the fallen tulips drifted to the ground and coated the terracotta tiles with leaves of colour.

"God, I'm sorry." Rick's quiet voice invaded Clay's raging psyche. "I had no idea you hadn't told him, and I shot my mouth off. I'm so fucking sorry, Clay." Rick looked as miserable as Clay felt.

Clay shook his head tiredly. "It's not your fault. He's got a trigger temper at the best of times and this just set him off. He'll come home when he's calmed down."

“He seemed to be doing much better.” Rick’s tone was hopeful. “I really thought…” his voice tailed off.

“He *is* doing better,” Clay said softly. “Part of the PTSD. Hair-trigger reactions. Sometimes, he gets these ideas and there’s no stopping him. He hates to feel like a burden or that he’s being protected.” He gave a wry smile. “I thought I was doing better too at not being such a damn control freak, but I guess we both have a ways to go.” He smiled at Rick, trying to reassure him, although Clay’s heart wasn’t in it.

His heart bled and raced through his bloodstream like acid. This whole emotional crap wasn’t like him either. Tate brought out the nurturer in him, made him more vulnerable. Clay had never had these highs and lows in any other relationship before, but then he guessed you didn’t often fall in love with a man who’d been kidnapped and tortured before, or who you’d worshipped since you were ten years old.

He nodded at the suit draped loosely over Rick’s arms. “You found a tux then?”

Rick nodded miserably. “Yeah.”

The two men were silent then Clay heaved a deep sigh. “Best get off,” he murmured. “I’m sure you’d rather be with Lauren than waiting here.”

Rick stared at him, his face worried. “Are you sure? ’Cos I’ll wait here with you.”

“No, you get off. I’ll try and call him in a little while, see if he’s calmed down.”

Rick moved toward the door, the suit clutched in his hands. “Okay. Text me when you hear from him, though. Let me know he’s okay. I’m on call tonight so I’ll keep an eye on my phone.”

He squeezed Clay’s arm and then was gone. Clay closed the door behind him and leaned against it, closing his eyes.

Tate, you had better take care. Stupid moody bastard, just look after yourself. Come home to me.

Chapter 8

Wall to wall paint cans. Tate wandered down the aisle of his local hardware store and stared idly at the spray cans layered on the shelves. He had an itch to spray a wall somewhere, to thumb his nose at the norms of society and leave a lasting impression of his current turmoil and anger.

It had been two days since he'd raced out of Clay's house. He knew he'd overreacted. It was the nature of the beast inside him, the one that tore its teeth into his belly and lashed its stinging tail into his heart. But hearing Clay being so blasé about a threat to his own life had brought back memories of his own incarceration and near death, being imprisoned in a warehouse, chained like an animal and forced to endure indignities and pain to his body and mind that, at the time, he thought he'd never get over. Armerian had been a master at torture, both physical and psychological. Tate shuddered as he plucked cans of paint off the shelves and went to the till. He never wanted that to happen to Clay.

Clay's last words had cut him to the core.

Not everything is always about you.

Hearing them from his lover's lips had made them all the more real. He didn't want anything to be all about him; he wanted to be a whole man again and be Clay's equal. He was trying so hard, but then the whole fucking house of cards had come tumbling down around him. The thought of anyone harming Clay made him breathless with fear. Once again they'd kept in touch with text messages, and Clay's last message had been simple.

Come home.

The till assistant smiled at him and wished him a nice day as Tate handed over his cash for the paint. Tate nodded his head and tried a weak smile back.

Ten minutes later, he found himself in an old, dilapidated part of town that housed a derelict swimming pool and leisure complex. It was a haven for graffiti artists and there were normally some spraying away at the dull concrete canvases at any one time. Tate knew a couple of them; he nodded to them as he passed and made his way toward a fairly clean part of wall. Numerous pockmarked buildings dotted the quadrant of the area, all decorated with slogans and messages.

Luckily Tate looked the part to be one of the masses down here. He still had on his old sweats and a tee shirt with his leather jacket, and he always carried a beanie in his jacket pocket. It had become his method of dress when he'd been trying to infiltrate the Armerian drug operation. He'd not shaved or washed his hair and had been known to snort the occasional coke and take E, among other things. Realism was the name of the undercover game and it could save your life.

He uncapped his cans and got to work. When he painted, he got *in the zone*, ignored everything and everyone around him as he concentrated on painting his images.

By the time he'd finished, dusk had set in. He was sweaty, his hands ached and he felt a sense of achievement. He put the finishing touch to his tag and grinned as he stood back. The three-foot mural of a cartoon man hunched over in a green tee shirt, with a clockwork key sticking out of his back epitomised how he felt. Wound up, winding down, out of control, manipulated and only alive when someone turned the key. Well, that might be a little over the top but it was how he saw himself in his head.

"Meh. Not bad," said a voice from behind him. Tate swung around. A young girl of about thirteen stood there, dressed in a sloppy sweatshirt, jeans that looked too big for her and a knitted mauve cap on her head. She was scrawny, her eyes sunk deep into her face.

He scowled at her as he packed his cans back into the plastic bag. "What, you're some sort of expert?" He laid the bag on the ground.

In his days undercover on the street, he'd met plenty of these young people, the unwashed and unloved of the city with sordid histories, chips on their shoulders and dreams that had been trampled on and ground into the dirt. They expected no kindness and were as cynical as hell. He'd found the best way to deal with them was on an equal basis. Not as children. These teens had seen more pain and heartbreak than most adults.

The girl waved a hand. “I said it’s not bad.” She scrunched her face up and peered at the image. “Although he does look a little constipated.” She giggled and Tate grinned at the sound.

“He does a bit. Like he has something stuck up his arse.”

She giggled louder and then coughed, the amusement turning to hacking, chesty sounds as she turned away and hunched over. Tate watched in concern. He didn’t want to invade her space or touch her. Unless she passed out or anything—then all bets about personal space were off.

Finally she stopped, but when she turned to him her eyes looked even darker, her face more pinched. “Fuck. That hurt.” She wiped her sleeve over her nose. “Sorry ’bout that. Had this cough for a while. Can’t seem to shake it.”

Tate knew better than to ask her if she’d been to a clinic or doctor. These kids stayed away from places like those. Perhaps he could take her somewhere later, once they’d chatted. It might be worth the ask.

Instead he pulled a pack of chewing gum from his inside jacket pocket and offered her a stick. “Fancy a bit of peppermint? It might help.”

She stared at him in suspicion. “How do I know you haven’t drugged it or something? Guys do that all the time.”

Tate’s stomach clenched at the thought someone so young might be vulnerable to predators. “I’ll eat one and you’ll see. I promise you they’re fine. I bought them earlier. See, it’s a new pack.” He split it open then unwrapped a piece and popped it into his mouth. The girl moved forward, watching him then silently stretched out a hand. Tate placed a stick on her palm.

A few seconds later both of them were chewing gum like cows with a cud and observing Tate’s art.

“I’ve seen you here before,” she said softly. “You did that one over there.” She pointed to one of a big blue dragon surrounded by flames. “You should have made the dragon pink, it’s my favourite colour. But I like him in blue, and he looks over me when I sleep. This is my favourite spot.” She gestured around her. “It makes me feel at home. Plus it’s a bit more sheltered from the wind.”

Tate nodded even as he cringed at a cold spot in a deserted building being called home. “Yeah, I did that one. About six months ago.” It had been his protest to the one tattooed on his backside. He glanced at her. "What's your name—the one you *want* to give me?" He noticed an oval pendant around her neck with the initials AK carved on them. It looked cheap but worn.

She observed him evenly for a while, her blue eyes cautious. "You can call me Lily."

Tate held out a hand. "Hi, Lily. I'm Tate. Pleased to meet you."

Her hand in his felt frail and hot. Her cheeks were pink and he thought she might have a fever from the brightness of her eyes.

"So, Tate. What's your story?" Lily sat down cross-legged on the ground. Tate followed, his legs stretched before him.

He shrugged. "Needed to let off some steam. This helps."

She grimaced. "I know how you feel. I don't have an arty bone in my body but I like to watch the artists getting busy."

"So what do you do to let off steam then?" Tate watched as a bunch of youths on the other side of the open area began pulling out spray cans and adorning the wall with bright green strokes.

Lily sniffed. "I don't. My mum used to tell me I tend to bottle stuff up inside."

"Where are your folks now then?" Tate asked nonchalantly.

She snorted. "Nice try, buster. I don't have any parents anymore."

They were quiet, both of them watching the antics of the kids, laughing and shouting as they started the picture of what looked like a giant marijuana plant.

Lily coughed again, wiping her mouth with her sleeve. She tried to move her arm quickly to her side but Tate's heart thudded when he saw bright red streaks adorning her tatty sweatshirt.

"That doesn't sound good," he said quietly. "Have you had that cough checked out at the local homeless clinic? There's one not too far away from here. If you like, I'll come with you."

I can't leave her like this.

Lily shifted as she glared at Tate with fierce eyes. "Don't need a clinic. It'll go away on its own. It won't matter much soon anyway. For either of us."

Tate tried to push. Her last words worried him. "I saw the blood, Lily. That's never a good sign. I think you should it get checked out."

Lily sprang up angrily. "Who the fuck are you? My father? I told you, I don't need any help."

She cast a scornful glance his way as he rose to his feet. “You’re just like all the others, trying to get me alone so I can give you a blowjob or something or screw me. You guys are all the same.” Her voice was tight but Tate heard the fear and loneliness in it. He knew those sounds well.

“Lily, I’m not wanting anything from you. I’m not into women, let alone kids.”

She gave a harsh laugh. “You telling me you’re a homo? You don’t look like a fag.”

Tate drew a deep breath. “Well, sorry to burst your bubble of what a fag looks like but yes, I’m gay. I have a boyfriend.” He raised his hands palm side up. “In fact, that’s the reason I’m here. We had a bit of an argument a couple of days ago.” He waved around him. “This helps me focus, get over stuff. That’s why I come here.”

She peered at him suspiciously. “Yeah? So are you going home to him now?”

Tate shook his head. “No, I’m at my own place at the moment.”

Tate would maybe call Clay in the morning. Perhaps it would lead to more frantic make-up sex. He supposed there was an upside to being a prima donna.

Lily stared at him from eyes that said she still wasn’t sure about him. Tate chewed his gum, slid back down to sit on his arse and watched the kids across the quadrant and waited. Finally she sniffed and sat down beside him.

“When I first saw you painting here, I thought you were a copper. You had that air, you know? You can always tell a man in blue.” She sniffed and then coughed again, her face twisting in pain. “I wondered what a man in the force would be doing down here, painting with a bunch of rebel kids. Didn’t seem the sort of thing a policeman would do. Now I’ve met you, I *still* think you’re one of them. Am I right?”

Tate glanced at her. “I was a policeman, yes. Then something happened to me and I wasn’t. Short story.”

Lily gave a hoarse laugh. “Did you do the dirty on someone, take a bribe? Maybe shot the wrong person in a beat down?”

Tate frowned. “You’ve been watching too much telly, you have. Those phrases are straight off U S television shows.”

Lily flushed. “So what if they are? I sometimes sit outside the pub and watch the shows through the window if they’re open. I like *Law and Order*.”

Tate grinned. He rather liked this young lady.

She cocked her head. “So what happened to you that you left the force then?”

Tate stared across at the youths on the other side. “I got… hurt,” he murmured. “So I was forced to leave.”

“You get shot or something?” Lily asked curiously.

Tate nodded. “Yes.” He wasn’t rehashing his whole sorry story to someone as young as Lily.

She scowled. “You don’t like talking about it, I gather. Okay, I know how that is. I don’t like talking about me either.” Her voice faltered. “Not much to say, really.” She sounded sad and Tate looked at her.

“Why are you here, on the streets?” Tate asked quietly. “Haven’t you got somewhere else you can go? Can I call someone to come and fetch you?”

Her eyes shadowed and her lips tightened. “No. I don’t have anyone. I like it on the streets.” Her voice was brave but the expression on her face was anything but.

Tate tried again. “I know this halfway house that takes on kids like you.” He had no idea whether Castaways could take on a teenage runaway but if not, he knew other people he could contact. “I could see whether they could offer you somewhere to stay.” A stray thought of Jax with his blue eyes and angelic visage flashed into his head. Despite the fact Tate didn’t know Jax that well, he’d no doubt the young man would extend his compassion and help to someone like Lily.

“I said I’m fine. I don’t need anyone. Will you stop fucking meddling?” Lily spat as she leapt to her feet. She looked ready to run and Tate didn’t want that.

“Okay, I’m sorry. I’ll stop fucking meddling. I just wanted to help.” Tate raised his hands in a gesture of surrender. His heart ached for the teenager, and her stubbornness at insisting she needed no one when she so clearly did.

She scrutinised him with a sneer. “If you really want to help me, you can buy me something to eat. I like hamburgers. There’s a place down the road that does good ones. Maybe bring me a Coke or something too."

Tate narrowed his eyes. It sounded like she wanted to get rid of him. His instincts told him something was wrong. He didn't remember seeing a burger place anywhere close by. It was all warehouses and old factories. He said as much and Lily rolled her eyes.

"There's a mobile burger van that gets here around this time every night, just down the street. I've seen it."

Tate was unconvinced. "Why not come with me?" he suggested. "You can see what you want."

She shook her head vehemently. "I'm not going anywhere. You want to help me, you bring me food."

Tate sighed. He still had misgivings but he couldn't hound the kid. "Fine, I'll go get you something and bring it back." He looked around. "It's getting dark. Are you going to stay here or is there somewhere else you want me to bring your dinner back to—somewhere warmer?" And safer, he thought.

Lily snorted. "Here's just fine. This is *my* place. I'll be waiting here."

Tate supposed that if he could help her with food, at least that was something. He thrust his hands into his jacket pockets and started walking away. "I'll get you some food. Be back in a bit."

"'Kay. Don't be long. I'm really hungry." Lily's vice faltered and Tate looked back at her.

She stood there, shooting him a defiant look. "What? Go already."

It took Tate over an hour to find a burger place much further down the road, order some food and then get back to the abandoned baths. Contrary to what he'd been told, there was no mobile takeaway in the area. Or perhaps there had been one but it had already left for the evening.

It was dark when he got back, the area where he'd been painting deserted. The kids painting the huge plant on the wall were nowhere to be seen. Neither was Lily.

Tate called out. "Lily? It's Tate. I have your food. Where are you?"

There was no reply, only the faint whistle of the wind as it blew across the deserted quadrant. He took out his mobile phone and used its flashlight app as a torch. There were no signs of life. Icicles trailed down his spine as his misgivings deepened. Something was wrong. As he approached a secluded area near to where he and Lily had sat, Tate smelt it. *Blood.* He was familiar with its pungent scent, both his own and that of other people. As he rounded a corner of one of the buildings in search of the young girl, his nostrils flared. The rich tang of the substance flooded his senses as aimed his phone at a motionless bundle lying in a heap of blankets against a wall.

"Lily?" he said quietly as he approached. As he got closer, he saw it *was* her—pale face, slack mouth, half-closed eyes, and he knew without any doubt that she was dead. He'd seen that look before, that dull, vacant expression that heralded death.

He tried to quell the panic in his belly, the rising sickness in his throat. Putting the now cold food on the ground and crouching down, he pulled back the red sodden blanket and gagged. Tate thought he was hardened to death, having seen junkies and gang members dead when he was undercover, but he'd never seen a young girl drenched in her own fluids, blood spread around like a fallen can of red paint. Her sweatpants had been removed and were folded neatly by her feet, only her grey and grubby daisy-printed panties covering her modestly.

His police training allowed him to dispassionately observe what looked like a fisherman's filleting knife lying next to her outstretched hand, covered in blood. From what he could see, she'd cut her femoral artery, a ragged wound marking her left thigh. Tate's first thought was that death would have been quick for Lily, although the action of cutting herself must have hurt like sin, not to mention the psychological trauma of performing such a determined act on oneself. In her other hand she clutched her pendant tightly. A tattered piece of paper peeped out from underneath the sweatpants.

Tate reached out a hand and unfolded it. The writing was scrawled, untidy and as he read it, his eyes prickled and his throat closed up.

Hey there Graffiti Man

I didn't think you'd come back. They normally don't. But if you do see this, then I'm sorry if you're the one to find me. You said you were a policeman in a past life so I guess this kind of thing is something you're used to. I like it in this spot so I needed you gone so I could do what I had to do. It's just the way it is. Don't feel sorry for us. I think we're going someplace better, some place safer.

Keep painting, you're actually pretty good.

Lily

"Oh, Lily," he whispered brokenly into the silent darkness. "Why didn't you wait for me?"

Tenderly he leaned over and brushed a strand of greasy hair from her forehead before standing up and pulling out his mobile phone. With instructions given to the emergency services, who assured him they'd be there in ten minutes, Tate sat down next to Lily's cold body and let hot tears fall.

Chapter 9

Clay was half asleep when the call came in. Groggily, he reached for his phone and became more alert when he saw who the caller was. His blood froze. Three in the morning was never a good time for a phone call.

"Tate? Is everything okay?" He sat up and swung his legs out of the bed. He was ready to move at a moment's notice. There was a silence. "Tate? You're scaring the shit out of me. Where are you?"

Finally there was a soft whisper. "I'm at the police station in Kentish Town. I'm okay. It's not me."

Clay was out of bed already, grabbing clothes and pinning the phone under his ear as he tried to get dressed. "Who is it? Is it Rick?"

Tate's voice echoed down the phone. "No, he's fine. It's—" His voice broke. "She was just a kid, Clay. And she's dead. I should never have left her. I knew something was off." A sob caused Clay's stomach to tighten and his throat to close in fear. Tate never cried. Perhaps when he was in the throes of one of his nightmares, but he'd never shed a tear during his waking hours since Armerian had gotten hold of him.

Clay cursed as he hopped around trying to get his pants on and finally succeeded. He shrugged his arms into an open shirt and slid his feet into loafers. "I'm coming down to fetch you. Hold on there, love. I'll be there soon."

There was another silence then Clay heard a soft shuddering exhaled sigh. That sound scared him more than anything. It sounded as if Tate was simply letting go. It was the sound of defeat, and that was something Clay wasn't going to let happen to the man he loved.

"Tate, I'm out the door now." He left the house and moved swiftly to his parked car. "I'll be there soon. Hold on for me, okay?"

When Tate spoke again, his plea broke Clay's heart. He'd never tried to start his car so fast in all his life. His man sounded so damned lost.

"I need you. Please hurry." The line went dead.

Clay thought he'd broken the land speed record by the time he reached the police station and struggled to find somewhere to plant his car. Growling at the lack of parking, he eventually parked on a yellow line and decided any traffic warden giving him a ticket would get a long fuck-you letter if they ticketed him.

He tore into the police station as if all the demons in *Supernatural* were on his tail. The duty officer behind the desk stared at him in surprise as Clay leaned over the desk and barked out, "My partner is here. Tate Williams. Where is he?"

The duty officer blinked. "Sir, I have no idea where he might be I've just got on shift. What was he admitted for?"

"I haven't got a fucking clue," Clay said, panic overriding good manners. "He just called me and told me to come down here. It was something about a young girl dying?"

The officer's face still looked puzzled. "Let me find out for you. Hold on."

He reappeared about five minutes later as Clay tapped his fingers impatiently on the counter. "He's in one of the interrogation rooms, sir, with Sergeant Fisher. He's being questioned."

"Questioned? What the hell for? Has he got a lawyer?" Clay snarled. If it was the same Fisher he knew of, the man had been one of Tate's partners in the past. He was a big, burly, bearded man with a good heart.

The duty officer rolled his eyes. "Tate doesn't need a lawyer. As far as I know he's not accused of anything. He was simply the witness who found the body."

A sliver of cold ran down Clay's spine. "He found a kid's body?" Inside he raged at the unfairness of it all.

Christ, how much more does he have to go through? Wasn't having him tortured and shot and his mind fucked up enough for you, God? Now you have to throw a dead kid at him too? Well, fuck you.

"Please take me to him." Clay demanded.

"He's being moved to the waiting room and you can see him there." The duty officer smiled sympathetically at Clay. "We all know Tate here. He's been through hell in the past and we didn't want to cause him any more trouble. He's in a bit of a mess at the moment though. I think he'll be glad to see a friendly face."

Feeling rather a heel at his high-brow attitude, Clay tried to smile. "Thank you. I'm sorry if I seem a little agitated, but you know…" He shrugged and took a deep breath. "He's special to me." He had no idea whether his and Tate's relationship was common knowledge yet, so he thought it best to play it quiet. Tate had enough on his plate.

The policeman grinned. "No need to be circumspect, Mister Mortimer. We know you two are *together* together. Tate's nephew Rick is a frequent visitor here."

"Ah. I see." Clay wasn't sure he liked the fact that Rick had been the Gay Town Crier about his and Tate's relationship but the damage was done. "Thanks." He looked around. "Can I see him now then?"

The other man nodded. "Sure. Follow me."

His portly frame led the way to a colourless, soulless room in which slumped a man who had definitely seen better days. Tate's face was drawn and pale, his eyes dark circles in his face. He was wearing unfamiliar clothing—an old Iron Maiden tee shirt and what looked like a ratty pair of long grey joggers. He sat looking down at his hands twisting around and around in some frenzied parody of hand washing. Clay's heart ached to see him looking so vulnerable and beaten.

"Tate?" he murmured quietly. Tate looked up, eyes widening, and then stood up, only to launch himself into Clay's open arms. Clay pulled him close, feeling Tate's body shivering as he wrapped his warm arms around him with the fierce determination never to let him go again.

"Christ, it's good to see you." Tate's muffled words against his sweatshirt had Clay swallowing down his emotions.

"I'll leave you two alone then," said the duty officer, who turned and left the waiting room.

Clay held Tate to him, feeling his heartbeat through the fabric of his clothing.

"Not sure I like your fashion choice," he murmured, breathing in Tate's smell. "You look like the remnant of someone out of a drug dive search."

Tate's hands tightened on Clay's hips. "I had to give them my other clothes. They were covered in blood."

Clay shuddered. "God, love, what the hell happened?"

Tate told him. Everything.

Five minutes later, his heart cracking open with pain and empathy, Clay sat as he watched his lover fall apart. All he could do was stand there and hug the man crying silently against his chest in his arms and promise him things would be okay.

***

Three days after the incident, Clay sat and watched Tate sitting on the couch, freshly showered, in his own comfortable clothes and staring unseeingly at the television. Lately he'd eaten listlessly, but tonight Clay had managed to get some pasta down him. Tate had a glass of neat whisky next to him, which had been hardly touched.

The inroads they'd made on Tate's nightmares had been dented by this latest tragedy but Tate was still coping better than Clay though he would. His lover did sometimes wake up with a start with all the monsters in his head and all Clay could do was hold him or sometimes make love to him, until Tate settled back into an uneasy and restless sleep.

The one thing he wasn't prepared to let Tate do was feel guilty for the situation he'd been forced into once again. Guilt was something Tate had in abundance in his over-packed suitcase of emotions, along with self-recrimination and shame. Any more shoved in there and the suitcase would burst open, showering them all with the acrid aftermath of the explosion.

Clay sat down beside Tate and pulled him against Clay's side. With a soft sigh, his boyfriend leaned against him, and his hand ran across Clay's stomach, seeking the warmth and solace of his skin under the open shirt he wore. Clay's hand moved up to gently stroke the bristles of Tate's hair, bristles that were longer than normal and which Clay thought suited him.

"I'm going to say something to you and I don't want you to go off pop," he murmured against Tate's hair.

Tate huffed. "*That's* a helluva positive conversation starter," he muttered and closed his eyes as Clay massaged his scalp with strong fingers. A faint, pleased growl of satisfaction from Tate made Clay smile. The big, bad, tough undercover cop had a secret weakness when it came to this particular action. He turned into a great big puppy.

Clay tried to find the right words. "It's been a few days now so I think I can say them. Whatever you'd have done differently the other night—don't let it take you over. Don't second guess yourself and think *if only*. That's not going to help anyone. This whole thing wasn't your fault. I know you will, but I don't want it to consume you. You've suffered enough, love. You still suffer."

He kept massaging Tate's scalp as he waited for the reply. Finally it came. It was a soft murmur of assent that made Clay's heart beat faster.

"I know, and you're right. I did some thinking of my own." He gave a strained chuckle. "And at the station the other day Clem laid into me too about how narcissistic I was being if I thought I could cure the world's ills or stop people killing themselves." He sighed. "I guess the old adage about 'there's always someone out there worse off than you' is true after all."

Tate valued his ex-partner and Clay was glad the man had spoken to him. Tate's sister, Lucy, who was now aware of their relationship and happy about it, had also come by to talk sense into her brother.

"I'm glad you listened to him and Lucy." Clay pressed a soft kiss to Tate's head.

Tate sighed. "Yet you tell me the same thing and to quote your words, 'I go off pop.' Why does it always make more sense when you hear stuff from other people?"

Clay snorted. "It's like kids. You tell your child to get off the furniture and they don't listen. But let someone else tells them and the chances are that they'll listen."

Tate sat up and stared at him with narrowed eyes. "You're calling me a child?" He reached over and palmed Clay's groin suggestively. "Would a child do that to you?"

Clay grinned, pleased to see his old Tate coming back. "I'd fucking hope not. That would be wrong. But a sexy man with eyes like yours and a mouth that looks like it needs shutting up with mine—that I wouldn't mind."

He was growing harder at Tate's slow brushes against his cock, and from the look in his eyes that was exactly what his lover wanted. In his head Clay chuckled.

Tate using sex as comfort. I'll never complain about that. As long as it makes him forget things for a while.

He grinned as his pants were unzipped and Tate's tongue came out to wet his very kissable lips. At that sight, Clay's cock instantly plumped up. The sly caress of Tate's thumb across the head of his dick made it even perkier. Clay settled comfortably back against the couch, stretching his arms across the back, hitching a breath as Tate's mouth swallowed him down. The image of Tate's mouth on him, dark head bobbing up and down with his little moans of pleasure teasing his cock, never failed to arouse Clay. Tate was exceptionally good at sucking cock and enjoyed it immensely. His hot, wet tongue flicking against Clay's tip, those long, steady licks against his shaft as Tate glanced up at Clay, holding him mesmerised. The fact this was *his* Tate was a turn-on itself.

"Your mouth is too good at this," Clay hissed, eyes closing in bliss as Tate took him deep, throat massaging his sensitive dick. "I know I say that every time." His voice caught as Tate's tongue did something to him that sent all the nerve endings in his body aflame. "Christ that felt good. Do it again."

Tate's gave a wicked chuckle as his dirty mouth drove Clay crazy. When he pulled off, Clay moaned pitifully.

"Don't bloody stop," he groaned huskily. "Finish me off, please, in your mouth."

Tate shook his head. "No. You need to get those jeans off," he growled. "I'm going to fuck you this time. Make you come when I'm inside you."

Clay needed no prompting. He shifted his hips, lifted his arse and had his jeans and briefs off in record time. He left his shirt on. Tate liked it when he was half dressed. His lover wasted no time unbuttoning his own jeans, and as he pushed his black briefs down, his cock sprung out. Clay's backside throbbed in anticipation of having it inside him.

"You want to move this to the bedroom?" he murmured as he watched Tate run a hand up and down his erection, eyes dark and needy.

"Nope. Going to do it right here, on the couch. Get on your knees and hold on. I'm coming in for landing."

Clay laughed softly as he switched around to kneel on the couch, arse stuck out in the air, hands gripping the arm. "Don't forget the oil, Maverick," he breathed as Tate's fingers slid over the curve of his backside. "It's been a little while."

Tate sniggered as he reached under one of the throw cushions and found the lube. There was always a tube handy in the Mortimer household. Clay thought he might have been a Boy Scout in a previous life.

"Don't worry. I'll make sure you're all oiled up before I fly you."

Clay gave a snort of laughter. "Where the hell are all these aviation references coming from anyway? Have you been reading those bloody Dale Brown books again…? Oh hell, Tate. Yes…"

Tate had crawled on the couch behind him and the cold slickness of lube with its minty fragrance being rubbed against his hole made Clay lose his train of thought. His cheeks were spread open, and insistent fingers circled his opening and then slipped inside, opening him up. Talented fingers pushed their way in to stroke Clay's prostate and the zings of pleasure made his skin prickle and his arse clench tightly around Tate's welcome intrusion.

Soft kisses peppered his back, as Tate leaned over him and trailed his tongue down the skin that was already goose bumped with needy sensations. His lover's warm skin pressed against Clay's own heated flesh and a quick bite to his shoulder made Clay's cock jerk. He moaned softly and heard Tate's quiet laugh.

"You taste so damn good. Ready for take-off, Captain?" His cock nudged Clay's hole and Clay nodded, as he took a deep breath.

"God, yes, I need you inside me, to feel you. Stop the damned flight deck talk and just fuck me, please."

Tate sputtered with laughter as he pushed inside Clay. "I like talking dirty flight talk. Oh God, yes…" He gave a hiss of satisfaction as he slid deep inside, filling Clay with his heat and hardness. Clay pushed back against Tate's groin.

"You can do better than that," he gasped as he closed his eyes and concentrated on the heady feeling of Tate inside him. "Come on, where's my big, bad hard arse of a cop? I want him. I need him to show me just what a bastard he can be."

Tate gave a low, dangerous snarl and began pounding Clay in earnest, the denim of his half-mast jeans rubbing against Clay's skin. When Tate had been in the force, one of the things they'd done had been role play. In the early days, fucking each other while Tate had his old police uniform on had been something they'd both enjoyed. The handcuffs still came into play and were enjoyable, but Tate in his uniform, shirt unbuttoned, pants open and that cock of his rising from the depth of the formal trousers had been a sight for sore eyes.

Clay closed his eyes and surrendered to the power and passion of the man behind him, the grunts and heavy breaths and occasional expletives music to his ears. He revelled in Tate's scent, his presence and his sweating skin and heated flesh. Clay's own rising emotions and awareness of just how much he loved the man inside him filled his heart, just as Tate filled him.

He grunted when Tate's hand came around and fastened around his cock, jerking him off in rhythm with his thrusts, inflaming Clay's senses and bringing him to the brink.

"Just like that," he panted, "Don't stop. Make me come."

Tate's nip of Clay's ear nearly drove him over the edge. "Oh I intend to," Tate hissed. "I love to feel you come around my cock. Love it when you tighten on me, pulse like a fucking strobe light. I can lose myself when you come like that, Clay."

His thrusts grew deeper, fiercer and his teeth closed on the tender flesh on the side of Clay's shoulder.

This fucking hurts but I love it...

With a strained cry, Clay felt his balls contract, felt his groin tighten and the familiar wash of sexual gratification as it soaked his body and ushered in his climax. Arcs of his release jetted across the couch, flooding Tate's hand and Clay's belly with sticky fluid. His body tensed and then slackened, and his arms threatened to give way on the arms of the couch with the intensity of his orgasm. It was made worse as Tate rammed harder into Clay, causing him to almost fall over the chair arm. With a soft snort, Clay braced himself for his lover's last final pushes into his now tender hole.

When Tate topped, Clay always knew when he came. He made a hoarse, throaty grunt and gripped Clay tightly, fingers digging into his flesh and leaving marks. He was a biter too, as evidenced by the teeth marks on Clay's body and the nips to his ears. Tate's groin was all but melded to Clay's backside, as if he was trying to fuse with him, as his cock throbbed while he shot copious amounts of come inside Clay. Clay loved the feel of it inside him, marking him.

Tate lay across Clay's back, breath warm in his ear. "That was fucking awesome," he panted. "It's been some time since I had you like that."

Clay made a face. His arms were tired from supporting himself and his partner's weight. Thank God he worked out. "Yeah, except you nearly made me fall arse over face on the bloody floor," he laughed softly. "I thought you were trying to launch a rocket up there. Lose yourself in me."

Tate moved out of him and off him, leaving Clay to push himself up and try not to get the come from his arse all over the couch as well as everything else.

"I always lose myself when I'm with you," Tate murmured, his lips curving in a warm smile. "It's where I belong." He hitched his jeans and stained underwear up. "I'm going to shower. You can join me if you like, and I'll wash you down."

Clay stood up and bent down to pick up his trousers off the floor. "I'll be there in a minute. Get it hot for me." He snorted at Tate's cheeky grin. "Not that, you fool, although if you think you can get it up again…" He shrugged as Tate cackled.

"I'm the younger one in this relationship," Tate teased. "I should be saying that to you." He evaded Clay's fist aimed at his arm and escaped into the hallway.

Clay shook his head as he used his underwear to clean up the mess they'd left on his expensive fabric couch. Thank God for Scotchgard, he thought with a wry grin. It was probably time to get the cleaners in again though and have another dose of it applied. Couch- fucking looked as if it could become a regular occurrence.

Chapter 10

The smell woke Tate. It pervaded his nostrils with its stink and left a sour metallic taste in his mouth. He opened his eyes in disgust and panic, hands fumbling in front of his face as if trying to push someone away. He took a deep breath, imagining the lingering essence of blood on his tongue. In the darkness of the room Clay slept on, and Tate was glad he hadn't shouted out this time and woken up his lover. He shivered in the aftermath of his nightmare and sighed tiredly.

I am so damn tired of this shit.

Tate had once again been dreaming about Lily—and Armerian. In the dream, he'd seen the young girl lying there still and cold, the blood pooling about her body. Tate lay next to her, drenched in blood, cold, shivering and hurting. In the shadows, a man lurked, invisible but Tate knew it was his dead tormentor. Deep in the pools of his mind, the deep, dark lakes of his psyche, Sonny Armerian always lurked, like a silent, grinning predator ready to eat his flesh.

At times like this Tate wished he smoked so he could light up a cigarette and sit by the window, staring out in the darkness beyond it, blowing plumes of smoke and focusing on it as it swirled in the still air. It always looked so cool in the movies.

He shivered, remembering the weariness in Lily's young voice and the look of defeat on her face. The fact he'd not pushed her into accepting his help would always rankle with him. But he'd acknowledged, despite what everyone might have thought about him trying to blame himself, he was *not* to blame. He'd been spending more time at Castaways, trying to make sure he made a difference to kids who needed him. Trying to show them that people could be trusted and not everyone was an abuser. Jax was especially a delight for Tate. The young man was funny, occasionally moody, intelligent and one of the warmest and empathic people that Tate knew. He was like a little brother and that was something Tate could get on board with.

He sat up, leaning over to pick up his mobile on the nightstand. He flicked through the picture gallery and came to the picture he'd always carry around.

The photo of the note Lily had left him.

The police had taken the original but Tate had taken a picture of it with his mobile before it had disappeared. He wanted something to remember her by other than the dreams he had.

"Can't you sleep?" Clay's husky tones caused Tate to turn and look at him. His partner's eyes were sleepy, and his face furrowed with sleep lines.

Tate smiled softly at him. "I had a bit of a bad dream. I'm fine. Go back to sleep."

Clay yawned and stretched, the covers slipping down until Tate could see the firm planes of his stomach and the treasure trail of dark hair that led down to his sleep shorts. It was a sight he'd never grow tired of.

"I'm awake now, and it's"—Clay squinted at the wrist watch he never removed—"five a.m. anyway. So, the middle of the morning, really."

Tate snorted. "For a soldier like you, maybe, Mister SAS. For those others of us a little more refined, it's fuck o'clock."

Clay's face lit up. "Really? Is that an actual time then? Because I like the sound of that time of day." He chuckled as Tate huffed in exasperation. "You walked right into that one, babe." His face grew serious. "So what woke you?"

Tate sighed and leaned against the headboard, hands clasped behind his head. He hated that Clay had to ask that question. "Just memories."

Clay shifted in the bed, getting comfortable. "I wish I could take it all away for you. It pisses me off I can't reach inside that head of yours and pluck it all out."

Tate sighed heavily. "Me too." He managed a wry grin. "We'd be millionaires if we could." His hand moved up idly to touch the scar on his chest. "This was bad enough but then the thing with Lily…it's just not fair, you know? She was so damn young."

Clay nodded. "When kids die, there's something about it..." his voice trailed off and Tate knew he was remembering something from his past. Clay's jaw clenched; the tic in his cheek became more prominent when he was emotional.

“Tell me about it, please,” Tate murmured, moving to his side and propping himself up on his elbow. He fixed his eyes on Clay’s face. “How do you get over it?”

Clay’s eyes shadowed. “You don’t. It’s always there with you. But the memory gets less painful as time goes on. That’s what I’ve found and what I keep trying to tell *you.*” He smiled to take the sting out of his words. He looked as if he was considering his words carefully. “I was with a group in Israel about eight years ago. We went over to do recon on some Palestinian activity, some rebels who were operating in a camp out in the desert. It was all ultra-secret, of course, one of those field ops where plausible deniability was the buzz word.” He snorted in derision. “Bastards who sit behind a desk, and who’ve never seen blood close up in all their damn lives, telling us that if we fuck up no one’s coming to fetch us. We were on our own.”

Tate nodded in fascination. He’d heard many tales of Clay’s past, but only the ones that could be told. Clay had a lot of stories that Tate suspected remained hidden away in the recesses of his sharp, agile mind, never to be shared—never to be forgotten.

“There were a number of young boys among the rebel camp. Three of them, aged between about ten and twelve. They carried guns, looked too young to be there in such a damn inhospitable terrain. It was blistering hot; the sand flies bit any open flesh they could find and even found their way up your butt crack.” He smiled slightly as Tate made a noise of disgust. “I found smearing Vaseline around my hole and between my cheeks at least protected me from the bites and made sure they didn’t crawl up my arse.”

Tate’s backside clenched in sympathy. “That sounds like a fate worse than death,” he murmured, running his hands over Clay’s furred chest.

Clay nodded. “Not pleasant.” He turned and plumped up his pillows, punching them to make them fluffier then sat back with a satisfied sigh. “We staked out the place for a while, checking what was going on, taking photos and relaying information back to base. It was rumoured that there was an Israeli reporter who’d been captured and was being held. Our brief was if he was there, to extract him and get out. It turned out to be a crock of shit. There was no damn reporter. We were told to get out of there, as they were planning an air attack and hadn’t wanted the reporter getting blown to smithereens if they could help it. He apparently had some big wig political father back in Jerusalem." He huffed. "It would have been bad form having his son smeared all over the damn desert."

His eyes grew distant. "As we were sneaking out, one of the kids found us. My point guy hadn't seen him leave the encampment and we came face to face with him with his dick out, taking a piss." Clay's body stilled. "We had decision to make. We couldn't afford him crying out to warn the others, which is what he would have done. It would have jeopardised the air strike."

Clay's face darkened and Tate swallowed. He hoped this wasn't headed where he thought. "What did you do?" he asked quietly.

Clay exhaled loudly. "None of the group wanted to kill a kid. In an ideal situation, with a man or woman, we would have done it there and then. I'm both ashamed and relieved to say we all hesitated. Not good when you've been trained for that eventuality." There was a poignant silence. "Then one of the older rebels came across us and screamed at the kid to shoot us. The look in that kid's eyes…" Clay's voice trailed off. "He couldn't do it. So the guy raised his weapon at the kid and shot him point blank in the head. It was like a fucking melon exploding. The bastard was entertained by it all, and it probably saved our lives."

Tate groaned in horror.

"We had to get out of there pronto before the rest of them came running. I was nearest. While the sick SOB was gloating, I jumped in, snapped the bastard's neck, watched him fall to the ground and yelled to my men to get the hell out of there. Our transport wasn't far so we made it." His voice was matter of fact but Tate heard the pain in it.

"Jesus," Tate had a sick feeling in his stomach at what Clay must have felt. He sat up straight. "You've never told me that story before."

Clay shrugged. "Not one of the highlights of my career, seeing a kid killed like that," he said quietly. "Plus we ignored our training. We could have all gotten killed and stuffed the mission up by getting caught because we couldn't shoot a kid pointing a weapon at us."

Tate swallowed. "That's admirable to me, not something to be ashamed of. You make me feel so damn stupid, like a coward," he whispered.

His lover frowned as he sat up, covers pooling at his waist. "Why would you say that? You're no damn coward." His fierce tone warmed Tate's heart but still he felt a sense of failure.

"Because you have things in your past that could drive you crazy," Tate explained. "You've killed people, been shot at, been in war zones and seen horrible things but you don't have nightmares like I do. You've seen things I probably couldn't even imagine, but you're so damn strong, you can put them to rest. Me?" He sneered. "I fall apart at firecrackers, have bad dreams about kids who've killed themselves, agonise over what happened to me with Armerian when you've probably seen much worse. How do you stay so strong?" He heard the agitation in his voice. "Am I just a fucking wuss that I'm like I am? All damaged?" He threw himself back against the bed, breathing heavily and throwing his arm over his eyes. The sense of emasculation, the feeling he was a weakling tasted like acid in his mouth. He huffed loudly, opening his eyes as a strong, warm weight landed on top of him and his arms were yanked off his shamed face and held above his head.

Clay was aflame with passion, his eyes bright green glints in a tanned face. He looked like a man about to take on the world. "Don't *ever* talk about yourself that way again," he snarled, as his body held Tate's still. Tate gulped at the vehemence in his lover's voice. "You are one of the strongest men I know. What was done to you by that fucking bastard was something you wouldn't have done to an animal. I saw you afterwards, love." His voice cracked with pain. "I saw you shot three times and left to die like a dog on the sidewalk. I saw what he'd done to you. The horrors he'd inflicted."

Tate wanted to close his eyes and not remember but his eyes were hypnotised by Clay's. They stared into him and Tate swore he could see into Clay's soul. He'd never stopped to consider what Clay might have gone through when Tate had been hurt.

"The knife cuts, all the broken bones, the burns. The damage to your balls and cock where he'd kicked you. The brand he carved into your backside as if you were some sort of animal that he fucking owned. The coke up your nose." Clay's voice quietened. "The bites and teeth marks everywhere and the bruising and finger marks around your backside."

Now Tate struggled, the memories of what he'd called 'that which will never be spoken of' rising to the fore like some giant, monstrous leviathan. His shame and his guilt at what he'd done for 'the mission.'

"No, fuck you," he snarled. "We don't talk about that, you bastard." He flailed his arms and Clay pinned him tightly.

"That's the problem," he murmured softly. "You hide it away from me, and deep down, you need to let it out. I think we've both waited long enough." His hands gripped Tate's wrists like a vise. His body shifted on top of Tate's, its warmth and strength both comforting and scary.

"Let me go, Clay." Tate's vision blurred as tears threatened to fall. "I won't talk about that to you." Dr Jakes knew about Tate's deception with Sonny Armerian and his rape at his hands but he'd never told her everything about the sexual savagery that Sonny had inflicted upon him during his torture ordeal. He knew she suspected there was more than he'd told her.

"It's time." Clay's gentle voice was closer now, his lips brushing Tate's cheek.

Tate shook his head stubbornly. "No," he spat at him, still trying futilely to get free. But fighting against someone like Clay, single minded, tough, protective and physically strong, wasn't an option. The man was a fierce warrior, a man used to getting his own way.

"If you love me, Tate, and want us to get through this, you need to tell me." Clay's commanding voice overrode Tate's, which was telling him to hide, keep a secret. He cried out in anger and distress, the tears seeping from his eyes now, bringing back the memories of what Armerian had done to him in those four days. He hadn't only taken his freedom away but his self-respect too. How could any man raped by another not feel that way?

Clay gripped his face and stared into Tate's face with haunted eyes. "What he did to you was not your fault. You were tied up, chained, with no say in what happened. And when you admit that, maybe, just maybe, the nightmares might go away."

Tate was tired. He stopped struggling and simply listened to Clay's voice, hearing the love and grief in it for him.

Maybe it is *time to tell him everything. I'm so tired of keeping it a dirty secret. No one else knows what my relationship with Sonny actually was and the guilt is tearing me apart. Clay deserves to know too.*

"I was with you when they brought you into the hospital, virtually dead." The dead tone of Clay's voice reached out to Tate. "You flat-lined once, and when they brought you back, I cried like a fucking baby." His voice choked. "We were just friends then but I knew, just knew, that if you got through it I was going to make you mine. No more of this best friend shit. I was going to have you, body and soul. I love you so damn much. I've loved you forever."

"You don't know what I did, Clay." Tate heard his voice but it didn't sound like him. It sounded like a man with everything to lose. "What I did for that damn case. How hard I fell to get what I wanted—to put him away."

What he did to me.

Clay's voice was steady. "Then tell me. Right here, right now. Tell me what you did. What causes you to wake up at night."

He loosened his grip on Tate's wrists and his weight lifted as he rolled to the side. Clay didn't let go of him though; he kept his arm across Tate's chest as he cradled his back.

"I can't," Tate whispered in agony. "You'd see me differently and I never want that to happen."

"Listen to me." Clay's voice was steely. "Nothing you can ever say to me will make me love or respect you less. You are it for me, baby. Everything I want is here." He stroked his fingers down Tate's flanks and his touch grounded Tate. "You need to tell me what went down or you will never fucking heal."

The only sound was both of them breathing and the clamour of Tate's rapidly thudding heart in his aching chest. He was surprised Clay couldn't hear it.

Maybe it's time to admit what I did. What I really was. A whore.

Tate's cheeks were wet. He took a deep breath, then started speaking, his emotions suppressed. "I was told to meet Sonny, get friendly with him."

He heard Clay's indrawn breath at the mention of the man's first name. They'd always called him Armerian in the past, as if there was no personal connection. "We met at the gym he dumped me at when he threw me out the car that night. I took one look and figured it wasn't a hardship trying to get to know him. He was sexy as fuck. Tall, dark-skinned, swarthy, built like a damn powerhouse."

There was another hiss of breath from Clay and his fingers tightened on Tate's hips momentarily before once again stroking his skin. Tate had a sinking feeling Clay knew where this was going. "Yeah, he was a major drug dealer, but hey, that's what it made fun. Knowing what I was there to do, that I was going to bring him down." Tate took a deep breath. This was the hard part. "So I got to know him very well indeed." He stopped and so did the Clay's hand.

"You two were fucking *before* all the shit went down?" The incredulity in Clay's tone made Tate feel dirty and unclean and he wanted to lie. But he'd come this far. He couldn't back out now.

"Yes," he said quietly. "Of course, no one knew. It was bad street cred to have a bisexual head honcho as the kingpin of a drug cartel like Reino. And I never told anyone on the force or in the team we'd become lovers. They just believed I was acting as one of the gang."

Clay released him and sat up, his eyes wide and blew air out of puffed up cheeks. His face was pale. "I knew he was bisexual. It came out in my investigation. He was married to a woman after all. But the two of you together? That's news to me."

Clay stared at Tate with eyes that looked as if he didn't know him at all. It cut Tate to the core. Tate took a deep breath and laid a hand on Clay's arm. Clay stiffened and Tate's throat closed up.

God, he hates me.

"Just, leave me a minute, will you?" Clay's voice was choked. "I need a moment to deal with this."

Despair wrenched at Tate's heart and dealt it a heavy blow. He knew Clay well enough to know that his admission was hurting him. The fact Tate had been fucking a man while he and Clay had been friends and trying to deny whatever was between them for the sake of that friendship *had* to wound Clay deeply. He needed to explain more, see if he could fix this.

Tate sat up, taking a sip from his water glass. "It was for the job," he said softly. "It was the best way to keep him close, get him to trust me." He fiddled with the sheet over his groin, pulling it into folds nervously. He cleared his throat. "I had to do coke now and then just to make sure he trusted me. Other stuff as well, but never anything heavy. I'd seen guys get into the like of H and that shit and there was no way I'd do that, not even for the job." He gave a short bark. "Prostituting myself—I guessed that was okay."

Clay's brows furrowed and he glanced away to look at the wall, eyes distant.

Tate felt the old shame leaking back into his mind. "There was no emotional connection though, at least on my side. It was just sex. Or so I thought." There'd been other things they'd done together—bondage games and other kinky shit—but Tate would never tell Clay about that part of his relationship with Sonny Armerian. That he definitely *would* take to his grave.

Tate stared at Clay, trying to will him to look at him. Perhaps if he could see Clay's face, he'd know what was coming next. Tate didn't like surprises.

"He obviously kept it discreet and made it known if I ever outed him I'd be a dead man. I don't think I was the first, and while I was undercover, I learnt a bit about other guys he'd had before me who had 'disappeared.' Some of them must have tried blackmail, or maybe he simply he got bored of them and couldn't take any chances." Tate shrugged. "Not many people in his crew knew about his other sexual preferences and those who did were fiercely loyal. I managed to keep his interest until the day he got the phone call in his office telling him about me. We still don't know who leaked it or how it happened." He shrugged. "I doubt we ever will." He cleared his throat. The memories of Sonny's flat eyes looking at him over the top of his John Lennon glasses, the ones he'd worn when he needed to read, still chilled Tate to his core.

"I could see what was going down. I knew I needed to get out of there fast or I'd end up dead. The problem was the door was locked because just minutes before, he'd fucked me on the desk."

Clay finally looked at Tate. His jaw was tight, the tic in his cheek throbbing. Tate knew he had to finish this story. It was as if the dam had burst and the floodtide of self-recrimination and guilt had come rushing out like oily, tainted sludge and was soaking them both with its stench.

"He took his gun out of his desk drawer halfway through the conversation and laid it on the desk. I knew something was wrong then. My gun was still in my holster, on the floor with my pants. I couldn't get to it. He pistol-whipped me across the head before I could even do anything, and then kicked me senseless. When I woke up, I was in a garage, just me and a whole bunch of fancy cars. I knew then it would be a miracle if I got out alive."

Tate's voice was hoarse from talking. He took another gulp of water. His hands were shaking.

What the hell does he think of me? Should I have kept quiet? No, he'd never let it go. This is Clay. He'd have dragged it out of me sometime, might as well be now.

Clay finally spoke, his voice tight. He still didn't look at Tate but kept his gaze centred on the sheets at his waist. "Did you not have any backup to support you? Someone who'd know where you were, and that you hadn't called in? Isn't that standard operating procedure for an undercover op like yours?"

Tate nodded. "There was backup, of course. I couldn't wear a wire of any sort. Too dangerous and in any case, he'd have found it."

Especially with the regularity I had my clothes off.

From the look on Clay's face, he'd had the same thought. Tate wanted to crawl into a dark tunnel and hide.

"So I had a throwaway phone stash, a number to call and told to check in twice a day, using code words—all that shit." He shifted uncomfortably. "But the house we were in was one of his safe houses, and it was a new one. When I finally realised where we were, and that my team didn't know about it, I needed to get away and tell them." His face burned. "Sonny was feeling rather amorous and he jumped me before I could do that. So I thought I'd have time to do it afterwards. Then the call came in and everything went tits up."

"Christ, it sounds like a damn cluster fuck." Clay sounded as if he was trying to hold some emotion back and Tate just hoped it wasn't disgust. He couldn't bear if Clay lost respect for him after this. Their relationship was worth shit without it. He kept quiet, heart aching, the fluttering in his stomach making him nauseous.

"And that's when he decided to torture you?" Clay's tone was soft but dangerous. Tate had no doubt it would strike fear into someone else; shit, he was already scared at the possibility he was going to lose him.

"Yes. He made it a 'project' to do whatever he could to get me to spill the beans about the operation, whether there was anyone else undercover. I kept telling him I was the only one, that there was no one else. I told him I'd never tell him anything about the operation so he might as well kill me now." Tate's eyes burned, and they were gritty with fatigue. "He said he believed me. And that he knew I'd never tell him anything of value no matter what he did. He knew I'd die before that happened."

Clay's nostrils flared. "He believed you, but he carried on. To pay you back for what you'd done to him as opposed to needing information?" He looked up at Tate now, his eyes burning with a violent darkness that Tate had never seen before.

Tate exhaled. "Yes. And yes. The rough sex, rape, whatever you'd call it happened and the rest—" He broke off. There was no way he was telling Clay about what had been done to him with bottles and other household implements during his incarceration. "—that was to punish me too. For leading him on, making him feel something for me. He told me he'd been starting to fall in love with me."

Clay's face was white. "The word rape is the right one." His face was pained as he reached up to touch Tate's jaw softly. Tate wanted to rejoice at the fact his lover was touching him. "And an animal like him didn't know the meaning of the word love. He was a man who thought he could own people. Use them." He frowned. "What did you mean 'the rest'?"

Tate ignored that question. "I was pretty drugged up and in pain. I couldn't do much to fight him off. That first day, after he'd smacked me unconscious, I woke up to him beating me with a golf club. One of his fancy ones he was fond of. He broke my ribs, my arm, and cracked my tibia. He kicked the fuck out of me and then pushed coke up my nose until I was so high I couldn't think." He shuddered and Clay reached out again, laying a hand on Tate's arm, stroking his skin gently.

Tate's eyes prickled with tears at that gesture. "He'd release me, untie me, but I was pretty broken. I wasn't given food or water regularly so I didn't have the strength to fight him off. I tried; believe me. But he broke my nose and collarbone and beat the shit out of me and still took what he wanted anyway. He said it was his right. That I was his."

His voice cracked. He was exhausted and wanted to shut down, curl up in a ball and hibernate. His soul was bruised black and at that moment, he wanted to howl with pain and grief. Memories of the worst time of his life welled up like acid waste. All he wanted to do was hold onto the man who stared at him with eyes that saw into his soul and never let him go.

"God, Clay," Tate whispered brokenly. "Please tell me you still love me. That I haven't fucked this up for good by what I did. By what happened." It was then that his tears fell, hot, burning rivers of shame and guilt. He crumpled the bed sheets in trembling hands, unable to look up at his lover.

Clay gave a shuddering sigh. He sat up, pulling Tate into his arms to lie against his chest, stroking his hair with one hand while the other wiped tears off Tate's cheek.

"Jesus, Tate. You went through hell. Of course I still love you, you stupid bastard. I'll *never* stop loving you."

Clay's arms tightened possessively around Tate as his hands stroked Tate's back. His chest ached with relief at simply being there, at still being loved, and he couldn't stop more sobs escaping from him.

"God." Clay sounded choked up. "I can't believe you've kept all this inside you. Why the *fuck* have you never spoken about this to me or anyone?"

Tate wiped tears from his eyes and tried to take control of his crying jag. "Because I pimped myself out. I was sleeping with a man to get information from him. I'd never done that before, but with Sonny…I *wanted* to. I was crazy about you, but didn't think you felt the same way. I didn't want to spoil our friendship. So I thought, fuck it, I'll find someone who does want me. And he was around. And I was ashamed at what he did to me, the fact I couldn't stop him. I felt dirty, used."

Tate cleared his throat, taking deep, shuddering breaths. His nose was stuffy and he needed to blow it. "Then afterwards—we happened—*we* became *us* and I didn't want to sully our relationship with the fact I'd whored myself out for the job and got fucked up for it. It just didn't feel right telling anyone about that part of the deal. And you can be possessive and I thought perhaps you might feel…cheated." He stared wildly around the room, looking for a tissue.

Clay gave a soft growl, his arm tightening around Tate. "I'm a fucking possessive bastard, yes, but no one should hurt you like that. God, you should have told me this sooner. What's done is done, Tate. And you shouldn't be ashamed of anything that happened to you." He stroked Tate's cheek tenderly then leaned over and reached inside his bedside drawer. He passed a packet of tissues spotted with Minions over to Tate, who gave a watery chuckle at the sight of the bright yellow characters.

"Really? *Despicable Me* tissues? What's next—Pooh Bear pyjamas?"

Clay laughed softly and Tate opened the packet and blew his nose loudly then wiped the wetness from his cheeks and eyes.

He relished Clay's arms around him and leaned against his lover's chest, feeling his beating heart as he closed his eyes. The comforting, rhythmic sound soothed him, eased his aching soul and he never wanted to lose that feeling of belonging. Now he knew Clay didn't resent him or what he'd done, he felt lighter than he had in months. The storytelling *had* been cathartic.

"I didn't want you to see me as weak, Clay." Tate whispered. "Or as some sort of slut. It was the only time I ever did that because I believed the end justified the means. And—" he swallowed, "I never thought I could have *you*."

Clay's answer to that was to drink in Tate's lips like a parched man needing water. Tate surrendered gladly to that possession, heart gladdening that he was still wanted. His lips devoured Clay's with a possession of his own. Finally they came up for air. Both men's lips were swollen and wet.

Clay rubbed a finger over Tate's lip and Tate sucked it in, delighting in seeing Clay's eyes blacken as his pupils expanded.

"I'm not going to push you for more, but don't think I didn't notice you evaded my question about 'the rest.' You'll tell me in your own time, and if not, I can live with that," Clay murmured as he watched Tate's mouth suck his finger, his eyes passionate. Tate's cock hardened at that look. "You went through hell and kept this all locked inside you. I don't see you as weak. I'm not happy about what you did. Another man having you that way? It hurts. I won't lie to you. But I can't be jealous of a sadistic, manipulating bastard who hurt you in unimaginable ways. You did what you thought you had to do and I know that feeling well. Following orders, making the mission successful."

He gripped Tate's jaw tightly, forcing him to look at him. "You ask me how I cope with everything. I was trained by one of the best fighting forces in the world. They teach you how to deal, how to compartmentalise and rationalise what you do. I don't say it's easy, just that it's easier to believe in it when you're doing it for a cause. For your country and for the benefit of other people who will live because of what you did." He kissed Tate again fiercely and Tate moaned at Clay staking his claim. He wanted so badly to be taken, possessed by this man.

"We had a choice to perform that service or not. You didn't. You had that taken away from you with Armerian when he tortured you. That doesn't make you weak. You didn't deserve what you got just because you were sleeping with the guy. In battle we often do things we never thought we would."

Clay's eyes smouldered as he brushed a hand over Tate's hardened cock. "I need to show you how I feel. Make love to you again until you come so hard you explode. Show you that sex with someone you love is better than with someone you merely lust over. And make no mistake; you are mine now and no one else's. I'd fight somebody to the death for you."

He didn't wait for Tate's reply, just slid under the covers and sucked the skin of Tate's stomach into his mouth. Tate's back arched as Clay ran a hand over Tate's thigh, then stroked between his legs, finding that sensitive part of him. When Clay's mouth finally found Tate's cock, and that hot, wicked mouth licked and sucked with abandon, Tate had no choice but to forget and surrender.

He cried out loudly as he came into Clay's hot, greedy mouth; and when Clay pinned him down, Tate's body rejoiced in being loved, being cherished by Clay's loving thrusts inside him. Tate's hands never left Clay's skin; his need to hold his man close and absorb him was so desperate he thought he might stop breathing. His arse ached from Clay's passion, his mouth was bruised from Clay's possession and his mind was so in tune with his lover's that they were one.

Make me yours. Possess me.

"You are mine," Clay growled as he jerked inside Tate with the force of his orgasm. "I will always be here for you no matter what."

Tate felt the warmth of Clay's seed inside him, marking him, owning him, and he pressed his face into Clay's neck, finally acknowledging that the truth may just have set him free.

Chapter 11

Two weeks after his emotional confession, on a warm early July afternoon, Tate went back to Castaways. He was feeling positive about it being a great day to give a group of kids a talk on what he'd done as a policeman all those years ago. When he got to Castaways and saw Randy and Jen's harassed faces greeting him at the door, he stepped inside with a frown.

"What's wrong? Are the kids all okay?"

Randy flapped a hand at him, as he shook his head. "Oh no, they're fine. Well, all except one." He pursed his lips. "Our Mister Jackson Grady—Jax—has been pitching a hissy fit. He's locked his bedroom door and refuses to let anyone in."

Tate's heart sank. "What happened? Do you think he'll talk to me?" He'd storm up the stairs if need be and insist Jax talk to him.

Randy's face brightened. "Would you mind? He's quite fond of you. I know the two of you have been in touch. I can't get anything out of him other than the command to fuck off and leave him alone. Jax doesn't swear often so we know it's bad when he does. He's not usually so disrespectful."

Jen touched Tate's arm. "I'll go pop the kettle on," she said softly and left the hallway.

Tate nodded his thanks as he hung his windbreaker on a hook on the wall alongside various coloured cardigans and jerseys belonging to the kids. He grinned when he saw a baseball cap there with the words 'Diesel Rules' emblazoned across the top and a picture of a scowling Vin Diesel on the front. He conjured his own fantasies about the man and tried not to blush. "Who's the Vin fan then? He has good taste."

Jen glanced at the cap and smiled. "Oh that belongs to Krispin. He adores the man. His bedroom is plastered with pictures of him." She shrugged. "He's eleven and Vin is his hero and Krispin thinks Vin would protect the little blighter from his dad." Her tone was sad.

"His dad's been in prison for child abuse for quite a few years now so he won't be calling anytime soon, but still Krispin worries."

Tate's throat ached at the story of a child who could need a hero like Krispin did. "I've seen people do bad things, but abusing a kid has to be the worst of the worst." A loud bang from above made them both look up the stairs.

Randy sighed heavily. "That'll be Jax. He tends to throw stuff when he gets upset." His face twisted in a wry grin. "Thank heavens it's not often. That young man has a temper on him."

Tate smiled. "I know the feeling. Let me see if he'll talk to me." He made his way up the stairs to the sight of two wide-eyed kids sitting on the landing, half-eaten sandwiches in hand, staring at a door that Tate presumed was Jax's. It was the little kid who'd made Tate eat liquorice—Damon, no, Damien—with an older child Tate hadn't seen before. They gazed at him curiously.

He lifted his chin in greeting and gestured to the door. "Is that Jax's room?"

Both kids nodded solemnly.

"He's not feeling so good, huh?" Tate crouched down beside the two children and smiled sympathetically. "Anyone know what put the bug up his arse?"

Both kids shook their heads. Damien giggled a bit at Tate's words.

"He just got grumpy and said he was going to his room," the unknown child muttered. "He got a text and it made him mad."

Tate filed that away for future reference. "Do you know who it was on the phone?"

Again there was the shake of two small heads. Damien spoke softly. "Krispin said we should maybe go downstairs and ask Jen if we can bake him a cake to make him feel better. Jax likes chocolate cake and maybe it will make him smile again." His lower lip quivered. "I don't like it when Jax is sad. It makes me sad 'cos he's always so happy."

Tate's heart ached. "That sounds like a really good idea to me," he agreed, looking at the kid he supposed must be Krispin, lover of all things Vin Diesel. "Why don't you go down and ask her and I'll see if I can talk to Jax and find out what's wrong with him?"

Both boys looked doubtfully at each other.

"You can try," said Krispin quietly. "Normally we just leave him alone and he comes down to dinner sometimes." He stood up and took little Damian's hand. "Come on, squirt. Let's go downstairs and see if Jen will let us bake."

He nodded his head at Tate and the two boys made their way down the stairs. Tate took a deep breath and knocked on the door.

"I told you all to fuck off!" An expected reply said vehemently.

Tate sighed. "Yeah, well I've just arrived and I have no intention of leaving just yet. Stop being such a damn drama queen and open the door and let's talk."

There was a silence. Then, "Who the hell are you?"

Tate rolled his eyes. "We've spoken enough on the phone, Jax. You know who it is. It's Tate."

"Just go away. I don't want to talk to anyone." There was a soft muttering from behind the door and Tate grinned. No doubt Jax was asking himself why nobody wanted to listen, to leave him alone. Tate had done it often enough himself.

He sat down on the landing outside Jax's door. "I'm not going anywhere, so I'll just wait here until you open the door. I have a cup of tea on the way and maybe a piece of chocolate cake too. I'm in no hurry." He got comfortable sitting against the wall next to Jax's door and took out his mobile and texted Clay.

Guess what I'm doing? Trying to talk a sulky teenager out of his room.

He closed his eyes as he leaned back and smiled. Clay had done this often enough to him, wheedling, cajoling and finally threatening Tate out of a locked room. Tate knew how this all worked. The key word was patience. His mobile buzzed. He sniggered when he read Clay's message.

Talk about payback. See what it feels like on the other side of the door. Good luck

Jen arrived then with his cup of tea. She snorted and placed it next to him.

"You might have a long wait," she advised. "He's a stubborn little cuss." Her voice rose loudly at the last words, no doubt hoping Jax heard them.

Tate shrugged. "I have time. I'm busy mulling over my speech I was going to give the kids, which has now been delayed." He deliberately spoke louder too. Jen gave him a soft smile and disappeared into one of the bedrooms. Tate shifted, getting comfortable.

There was a scuffling on the other side of the door. "Why are you being such a dick?" the voice asked sulkily.

"It's in my nature." Tate said airily. "My partner accuses me of it all the time, especially when I lock myself in my room and refuse to talk to anyone. Normally his use of the word dick is preceded by another bad word which I won't repeat, because there are small ears around."

There was a soft snort from the other side of the door and Tate's heart lifted. "That's not all he calls me either. His favourite is usually preceded by the bad word and has arsehole after it. So I guess he's an equal opportunity insulter, insulting both my front and my back side."

There was a louder snort now. Tate waited. Then there was the click of a lock turning and Tate stood up, his scarred arse cheek stinging from sitting on it. He tried the door. It swung open and he walked into a darkened room, leaving the door part open behind him.

A huddled shape lay on the bed, duvet cover over his legs and hips, facing away. A dim bedside light was on. The curtains were closed and under the sweet smell of incense, which burned on a side table, the room stank of stale sweat and old deodorant.

Tate's nose twitched. "Quite the aroma café you have going on here. Do you mind if I open a window?"

"Yes."

Tate sighed heavily. "Fine. I'll just asphyxiate with teenage odours."

"I didn't ask you to come in. You bullied your way in here. So put up with the *aromas*."

Tate once again rolled his eyes.

Heaven save me from teenage angst. I think maybe I should have stuck to psychotic drug dealers.

He walked around to the chair by the window, one in front of where Jax lay. He sat down and observed the face of the young man on the bed, lying in what looked like a sweatshirt and jeans. Even in the dim light, he could see the swollen red eyes, the pink nose and the duvet tightly fisted in one pale hand. Jax had been crying and Tate wanted to find out why. He had an overwhelming need to be of solace to this boy curled up in his bed. He was uplifted by the fact that Jax had let him in; it meant he wasn't as averse to being helped as he pretended.

Everybody needs somebody to talk to—even you.

Clay's words echoed in his head and Tate scowled. He wasn't sure he liked being on the other side of the equation. It meant Clay was right.

"Why are you scowling like that?" Jax's voice was thick with crying and from a blocked nose. "You look like you want to punch someone. Is it your partner—your work partner?" His tone was indifferent but Tate heard the underlying curiosity about his use of the word.

"Yes and no. I work for him but he's also my life partner. Clay is my boyfriend."

Jax stilled. The hand clutching the duvet unfurled and Tate heard a slight gasp. He leaned back in the chair and stretched his legs in front of him, and waited.

Finally the bundle of clothes and duvet moved and Jax sat up. His eyes stared at Tate and while Tate couldn't see the expression, his tone indicated surprise—wonder even.

"You're gay?"

"Uh-huh. All my life. Born this way, as Gaga says. Is that a problem?"

"Er, no." Jax stammered. "Of course not. Do I look like a fucking homophobe?" he hissed angrily.

Tate smiled inwardly. Finally, some real emotion.

"Nope. Just wanted to make sure that you weren't one of those 'bad-word' dick arseholes."

There was silence. "Shouldn't it be one of those dicks 'bad-word' arseholes instead?" Jax asked acerbically. He swung his legs over the side of the bed and, head tilted, stared challengingly at Tate who ran the words through his head and grinned when he realised what Jax meant.

"Clever. Not that I'm getting into my sex life with you or anything, but you are a quick one, aren't you?"

Jax's next murmured words would normally have been out of earshot, but Tate's hearing was damned good. He wondered if this was what was bothering Jax.

"Yes, well, that's not anything I'm ever likely to *get into* anyway." Jax crossed his arms over his chest.

Tate leaned forward. “Jax, the kids said you got a text that upset you,” he said softly. “Anything you want to talk about? I’m a damn good listener.” He felt a pang of guilt suddenly because he hadn’t managed to help Lily even though he’d listened to her too. He shoved that thought from his head. He’d been doing okay keeping those emotions at bay and he wanted it stay that way.

Jax’s eyes shifted to his mobile on the bedside table. His hands fidgeted in his lap. “Nothing I want to get into.”

“Fair enough. So is that the reason you’ve been a real diva and locked yourself in here? Everyone was worried about you.”

Jax shot up so quickly he almost hit Tate on the nose with his flailing arm. He stood and stared down at Tate.

“God, I have one bad period from trying to be so damn happy all the time and everyone gets all bent out of shape about it. Aren’t I allowed to be selfish every now and then? To wallow a bit?” His voice shook. “I’m fucking human too, you know, even though people don’t think so. They think I’m a freak.” He swallowed and Tate saw the sheen of tears in those ruined eyes. His heart ached at the pain etched on Jax’s marred face.

“You’re not a damn freak,” Tate said firmly. “Who the hell’s been telling you that nonsense?”

Jax moved over to the window, hugging himself. “Maybe you should go. I’m really not good company right now.” His voice broke and what little self-composure he’d been holding onto disappeared as his body shuddered with silent sobs. Tate certainly wasn’t going to leave him in this emotional state. He stood up and pulled Jax to him, wrapping him in his arms and patting his back. Jax resisted at first but then heaved a shuddering sigh and leaned into him.

Tate hadn’t thought too far ahead on this one. He did think briefly how this would look if anyone walked in and he was found holding Jax this way, but Tate wasn’t prepared to let this young man do everything on his own.

“It’s fine,” he murmured soothingly. “You don’t have to tell me everything but I’m here if you want to talk.”

Jax sniffed and moved away from Tate, wiping his eyes on the sleeve of his sweatshirt. “Sorry. I didn’t mean to do that. I think I got snot on your top.”

Tate chuckled. “Don’t worry. It won’t be the first time. Normally it’s my own though.”

Jax gave a watery laugh. "Thanks for the image." He walked to his dressing table and fumbled with a tissue box then blew his nose loudly. When he turned around he was more composed.

"You're not a freak." Tate waved a hand. "You're a bright, incredible young man who has his own fan base in this house and who, despite everything he's been through, is strong and independent. And yes, sometimes I think we're all at fault for expecting someone to always be upbeat and not have down days. Of *course* you get to have hippo days."

Jax frowned. "Hippo days?"

Tate grinned. "When you wallow. Like a hippo in mud."

Jax snorted, the corners of his mouth lifting slightly. "Another great image." His face shadowed. "I'm just tired, you know? Of always trying to be Happy Jax. Sometimes I want to scream, tear things up and just feel sorry for myself. The kids…" his voice trailed off. "I love them, and I want to be positive for them but sometimes…" His voice hardened. "Then I get a text from some fucking twat who has no idea who I really am other than what they see outside and it just pisses me off."

Tate didn't *want* to push but he remembered the last time he *hadn't* and how that ended. He wasn't doing it again. "What twat was that?"

For a minute he thought Jax wouldn't answer but then the young man shrugged. "Someone I met whom I thought might be a friend. Or more."

"More? Like a girlfriend?"

Jax hesitated and a shadow flitted across his face. "We met at the library and I really thought maybe I'd found someone who saw past my face to the real me. I was obviously wrong." He gestured to his phone. "I asked the person to coffee and I got a text back saying, sorry, but no thanks. 'Going out of town' was the excuse, without an idea of when they'd be back." He grunted. "I know a brush off when I see one. It's why I don't get friendly with people."

Tate remembered Randy saying Jax had few friends. "So what? Maybe she *is* going out of town. Maybe she'll get hold of you when she gets back."

"And maybe they won't." Jax's tone was bitter. "All I want is someone to be with me, even kiss. Do you know I've never kissed anyone properly? Like with tongue?"

Tate cleared his throat uncomfortably. He was a bit out of his depth in this conversation about French kissing.

Jax gestured to his face. "I kissed someone once before this but it was nothing special. I want a real kiss, maybe more. A *lot* more."

Tate didn't know what to say. Giving sex advice to a teenager was a little out of his comfort zone.

"Maybe you should wait until the right person comes along," he proffered weakly. "They will, Jax. You're no freak, honestly. Someone will see the real you."

Jax shook his head in frustration. "Yeah, right. My face isn't exactly a beacon for hope in that regard and the fact that I'm half blind? I'm a real catch." His voice was scornful. "How do you think it feels to be a seventeen, nearly eighteen-year-old virgin? My hand has never seen so much action."

Tate winced. It wasn't that he was a prude, far from it with his kinks, but this was *so* not a discussion he wanted to have with a seventeen-year-old. "It'll happen, in time. Maybe you need to get out a bit more. I've been told you don't do that much. The odds are more in your favour if you do."

Jax's pale blue eyes stared at him fiercely. "I've resigned myself to the fact that I'll probably die a virgin," he spat. "No one wants damaged goods." He threw himself down onto the bed and wrapped his arms around himself. Tate sat down next to him.

"You're wrong," he said softly. "*I'm* damaged goods, Jax. I went through a really bad time a couple of years ago and nearly died. It left me with a lot of issues." He hitched a breath as he rolled up his sleeves and Jax's eyes widened at the scars on his wrist.

Tate pulled up his shirt, revealing his scarred torso. "Someone did a number on me with a razor blade and a scalpel. He was having fun trying to create a chess board. Then he decided he'd had enough and shot me. But I survived."

Jax's eyes widened in horror as he tilted his head to better see Tate's chest.

Tate shrugged. "I'm still getting over it. Some people aren't so lucky. A couple of weeks ago I was down at the old swimming baths and met this homeless girl called Lily. Thirteen years old. I went away to buy her some food, and when I came back, she was dead. She'd killed herself."

Jax gave another gasp of horror, his hand raised to his mouth.

Tate carried on. "It made me realise something. It made me remember that I *do* have someone, unlike Lily. I have Clay, who loves me, cares enough about me to try and help me fix myself. It took us a long time—over twenty years in fact—to realise we wanted and needed each other and now I'll be damned if I ever let him go. He's my rock." He leaned forward and touched Jax's shoulder gently. "And one day you'll find yours."

Jax stared at him speechlessly. Then his lips twisted in a wry smile. "Wow, this is a real Hallmark moment, isn't it?" His tone wasn't derogatory, more self-deprecating. "I'm sorry, I don't mean to be facetious, Tate. I'm just processing everything you've told me. First you're gay, and then that you've been some through shit yourself. One day maybe you'll tell me all of it. Like why you got those." He waved at the scars.

"One day maybe," Tate agreed. He knew he'd never share all of it but if he could make Jax feel better for the moment, then so be it.

They sat in companionable silence for a few minutes then Jax sighed. "I guess I should shower, clean up my room and get rid of the stench of teenager." He punched Tate lightly on his arm. "Then maybe I'll join you for some of that chocolate cake the kids are baking for me." He gave a wicked smile as he stood up.

Tate chuckled and got up too. "You are too much, young Jax. Clay's going to love you when he meets you."

Jax stared at him uncertainly as he nibbled his bottom lip. "Can I ask you something, and please don't take offence. What's it like being in a relationship with a man?"

Tate's warning bells rang at that question. "Like any other relationship. Two people getting through the day and doing stuff together. Other than the physical sex bit, there's no difference." His tone grew wry. "Or at least there shouldn't be."

Jax's tongue protruded as he considered his next question. "How did you know?"

"Know what?"

"That you were gay?"

Tate considered. "I think jacking off to *Sports Illustrated* and sucking Billy Grant's dick back in school when I was thirteen was a pretty big indicator." Jax's amused snort warmed his heart. "I'd been eying Billy out for a while and when I got the chance in the showers to try him out, I did." Tate shrugged. "It all made perfect sense. I'd never been interested in girl parts like boobs and stuff." He'd never told Clay about *that* little cock-sucking episode either. Knowing Clay's jealous streak, the least he knew about Tate's foray into gay man life back in school when they'd been friends the better. "And that, my friend, is between you and me. Clay isn't to know."

Jax sniggered as he picked up clothes from the floor and went to draw the curtains and open a window. "Right, pinkie-swear." He waved at the door. "Now get out and let me get my shit together."

Tate nodded. "On my way." He moved toward the door.

"Tate, wait."

He turned to look at Jax.

"Thanks, for everything." Jax said quietly. "Sometimes a person needs a little perspective, you know?"

Tate grinned. "Better than anyone." He left Jax behind, his body buzzing with energy and a warm glow. He might be a bit of a fuck-up himself, but he seemed to have done someone some good today. His therapy session next week? He was *so* going to impress Dr. Natalie Jakes.

Chapter 12

"So you think you're some sort of psychotherapist now, do you?" Clay teased as he negotiated a bend in the road with expertise. "Like I said before, I bet talking about sex with a seventeen-year-old really made your day." He laughed loudly as Tate gave him the finger.

"I didn't say that," Tate growled, as Clay's car swung into the tight country lanes both with ease and speed. "I simply said I'm glad I got through to him the other week." He smiled smugly. "And Dr. Jakes said the same thing yesterday. She was quite impressed at my teenage handling skills."

He swore as Clay avoided a dead badger in the road and narrowly missed the hedge on the opposite side. "Fuck, Clay, I can see why Taylor moans about Draven's driving. What the heck are you trying to do, kill us?"

"I went on another defensive driving course a couple of weeks ago." Out of the corner of his eyes, Clay sniggered as Tate's jaw tightened when the SUV bypassed a slow-moving tractor with only an inch to spare. "It's fun testing out my driving skills. And besides, this car is made for this sort of driving."

Testing out some newfound skills wasn't all Clay was doing. He'd also noticed a car that appeared to be following them, a dark grey BMW. His suspicions had been aroused as they'd gotten onto the motorway and the car had seemed to keep pace with them. Moving into the country lanes had been a great way to shake off a potential pursuer. He hadn't noticed the vehicle since he'd done that though so he was beginning to doubt his earlier suspicion. Perhaps he was simply being paranoid. It had been a long week.

He was also proud of himself for telling Tate about the BMW as well. There was no way Clay wanted a repeat of the last time he'd kept things from his lover.

"No car is made for your sort of driving," Tate muttered as his fingers tightened on the seat. "Christ, I thought going undercover was dangerous. It's nothing compared to this daredevil shit you're doing. Fuck, Clay, can you watch where you're going? Can we get back on the motorway?" He glanced behind them. "I don't see anyone following us now. Maybe the guy was just out for a drive in his fancy car."

Clay chuckled as he slid the Audi between a slow-moving white van and a dip in the road, which would have meant a broken axle or worse had they gone in. "Stop being such a damn baby. I know what I'm doing. I'm a trained professional."

"Smug bastard," Tate groaned, looking a little green.

Clay grinned. "Well, you wanted to come with…" he pointed out slyly.

There had been a break in the case that Clay was working on with the police regarding the toxic waste dumping. A call had come in to his office, been verified by his team and now he and Tate were on their way to Oxford to meet with some local government councillor. The man said he'd gotten the evidence that toxic chemicals *were* being illegally dumped in the old quarry and had the names of those involved.

Clay's missing person hadn't made an appearance yet and Clay hoped that this lead would check out and point him in the right direction to the missing Glen Walkerman, who Clay believed was the kingpin behind the multi-million-pound illegal activities. He also believed Walkerman was a killer.

Tate glared at him. "You offered me an overnight stay in a quaint little bed and breakfast in the heart of Chipping Norton in the Cotswolds afterwards. I fancied the idea of having an intimate rendezvous with you, away from home. Bite me."

"Maybe later…" Clay drawled and laughed as Tate muttered something intelligible. He did have a faint smile on his face and Clay went warm thinking about what might be in store for him later. He could definitely use Tate's talented mouth around his dick…and on his lips.

The warm July air rushed through his window. The scent of warm grass and Tate's aftershave gave Clay a good feeling—until he saw the familiar headlights and number plate in his rearview mirror. The car was closing fast and didn't look as if it was about to slow down. "Fuck," he swore, casting a quick glance at Tate to make sure he had his seatbelt on. "That BMW is behind us again. I knew I wasn't imagining it."

Tate's eyes widened and he turned to stare behind at the rapidly approaching car.

"It's the same one," he said quietly, nodding. "Can you outrun him? Looks like he intends ramming us."

Not for the first time Clay blessed having a fellow law enforcement officer as a partner who was quick to catch on and didn't ask unnecessary questions or freak out.

He grinned. "This guy doesn't know who he's messing with. If he wants to fuck with me, he'd better be prepared to get fucked in return." He sped up and widened the distance between the cars. The lanes were narrow and winding and Clay hoped to God there wasn't much traffic ahead. The last thing he wanted was to get innocent people hurt.

"I'll try find somewhere to pull over rather than take this on the roads." His eyes flicked back to the mirror. The BMW was gaining on them again. "We might have to shoot our way out of this one."

Tate nodded as he opened the glove compartment and took out Clay's Colt .38 revolver. It was a Detective Special, a piece Clay swore by.

"I'm ready," Tate said grimly. "You drive, I'll shoot. Maybe we can get this fucker before too much damage happens." His jaw clenched as he checked the weapon.

Danger and the resulting adrenaline were always a turn-on for Clay. His cock jumped in his chinos at Tate's tight jaw and the fierce look in his hazel eyes. "I love the way you think."

God, the man looks sexy with that gun in his hand .Definitely going to do me some role play soon. Excellent time to be thinking with your little head, Clay. Focus.

"You're thinking about sex, aren't you?" Tate murmured, his eyes drawn to Clay's groin. "I can't believe you just sprang a boner. You like seeing me with a gun." He smirked and then it changed to quiet determination as he glanced behind them. "He's pretty close, Clay. We need to get off this damn road in case someone innocent gets hurt."

"I know." Clay gritted his teeth and floored the accelerator. The Audi shot ahead but the BMW must have been souped up; it kept pace with Clay's vehicle no matter what he did. Ahead, the road twisted to a blind bend. Then the BMW rammed into them.

Both of them swore loudly. Tate gripped the dashboard and the gun as he glanced behind. Clay tightened his grip on the wheel and tried to keep control as the BMW rammed them again. His eyes assessed the situation ahead in an instant.

So far no traffic. Trees either side, embankments a few feet high, no room to pull off. Just got to keep going and hope we don't encounter any other cars.

Tate twisted around in his seat. "I need to shoot this arsehole. Give him something to think about. Slow him down." He looked down at the seatbelt restricting his movement.

Clay shook his head vehemently. "Don't you fucking dare take that off," he commanded as he strove to drive faster. "If we crash, I don't need you flying through the damn windshield."

"It's not giving me much of a damn shot, Clay." Tate snarled. He managed to get the seatbelt slack enough to turn on his seat and kneel, looking behind him. He positioned himself between the seats and aimed as the vehicle careened around another bend. Clay heard

Tate swear, heard the fire of the gun and the shattering of the Audi's rear windscreen. Tate fired another shot, then another. Clay had no way of knowing whether any of the shots were hitting their target. He hoped one of them would blow the pursuer's head off.

"Got him," The triumphant satisfaction in Tate's voice was hard to miss. "At least it went through his damn windscreen. I think he's intact, more's the pity."

The BMW rammed them again, at a different angle and the Audi went sideways, wheels spinning in the dirt of the foliage-covered embankment.

"Christ, Tate, hold on." Clay shouted as he battled with the steering. Thankfully the car remained on all four wheels and righted itself. The road opened a little wider and Clay saw his chance. He geared down and braked suddenly, the loss of momentum causing Tate to cry out in surprise. The BMW hadn't seen that coming either and drew almost level with the Audi. Clay thrummed the engine and rammed the other car side on, driving it against the embankment. He pulled away and did it again. The screeching of tyres from the BMW as the driver struggled to control it was music to Clay's ears.

"Let's see how you like that, you bastard," he snarled. "Fuck with me and mine and I *will* hurt you."

The BMW looked as if it was having trouble staying on the road and Clay rammed it again for good measure. The road opened into fields lined with huge trees and as Clay went back in for the kill, Tate fired off another shot from his position. There was a loud pop and one of the BMW's tyres burst. It lost traction and as Tate and Clay watched, the car slid off the road and plowed head-on into the trunk of a tree. Both men growled in victory at the grinding noise and resultant smash, but they had more important things to focus on than satisfaction. Clay's own vehicle was all over the road and as he geared down, trying to right the Audi and slow it down, he heard Tate's panicked roar.

"Jesus, Clay, watch out for that damned cyclist. You're heading straight for him!"

Clay glanced to the side and was confronted with the vision of a red helmet and someone on the side of the road on a bike. He swung the steering wheel urgently, trying to move away from the cyclist. The manoeuvre caused the car to slip wildly across the road, hit a ditch, bounce in the air then flip sideways.

We're going to fucking roll.

Clay shouted a warning to Tate. He instinctively reached out, letting go of the steering wheel with his left hand, using that arm across the front of Tate's chest as a brace. Clay knew that that was a worthless gesture given the circumstances, but like a mother with her child, his first thought was to protect his boyfriend. Then the vehicle went arse over bonnet into green fields covered in purple flowers, and Clay's head hit the doorframe as everything went dark.

***

Throbbing head. Eyes glued together with something sticky, a pain in his shoulder that made his eyes water and an overwhelming silence.

Clay groaned and moved his hand toward the passenger seat. Immediately a stab of pain shot through his left shoulder. He gritted his teeth and reached out again, ignoring the agony. "Tate? Are you okay?" Nausea rose in Clay's throat and he coughed, trying to get rid of the taste of blood. "Tate?" There was no response and Clay fumbled around as best he could with his right arm, trying to unhook his seat belt. His body throbbed with pain, his head more so, but he persevered.

I have to get to Tate. God, please let him be all right.

Finally there was the welcome sound of a click and the seatbelt drew back. Clay struggled upright from the position he was in. The car had landed upside down, and his boyfriend lay motionless beside him, blood trickling from his mouth, eyes closed. Panic set in as Clay pushed at his door with his feet, biting back a cry of pain as something in his leg protested.

"Hold on, the ambulance is on its way." A woman's voice floated in through the pain and as Clay finally kicked the door open, a hand reached down and gripped his. "Let me help you. Then we can get your friend out."

Clay nodded and between them, they managed to extricate him from the wreck of his car. The woman, still in her cyclist helmet, stared at him with concerned blue eyes. "Is everything okay? I was trying to get the door open myself but it was stuck and I couldn't manage it."

Clay heaved a shuddering sigh as he checked himself for damage. "Yes, I think I'm fine. Bruised and I have a helluva headache, but I'll live." He moved around to the Tate's side of the car. "I need to check on my boyfriend. He doesn't look too good."

Heart racing, he pulled at the door. It was jammed and Clay lost it. "Bloody fucking hell," he snarled as he pulled and kicked it. "Tate, love, please talk to me. I'm trying to get you out—just hold on."

There was a low groan from inside the car. "Shit, this is a cluster fuck of note." Tate sounded really pissed off.

Clay laughed with relief. "Just hold on. I'm going to get you out of there."

He pulled at the door as the cyclist took hold of it with him and together they managed to wrench it open. In the distance Clay heard sirens.

"Sounds like the cavalry is here, so hold on. Let me get that damn seatbelt off then we can get you out."

"Better hurry. I can smell fuel and I don't fancy being a crispy critter." Tate's voice was husky and he coughed. Clay saw the wince of pain cross Tate's face as Clay tried to free his lover.

Clay's fingers worked the seatbelt loose and then, between he and the woman, they managed to get Tate out of the car and well away from it lest it explode. Clay didn't think it was a possibility despite the smell of fuel, but better safe than sorry.

Tate looked battered and bruised, had a split lip and a rather nasty rip to the flesh at his collarbone. From the looks of him and the way he moved, Clay thought he might have damaged ribs as well.

"I'm fine," Tate said tiredly as Clay checked him out again. "How are you? That head wound of yours looks nasty."

The woman shook her head. "It's just a flesh wound. I checked your boyfriend out already. I'm a nurse. My name's Anne." She smiled at them both. "Thanks for not riding me down, by the way. I'm sorry you had to crash to avoid me. What happened? Did you serve to miss something?"

Clay snorted. "No. Some arsehole tried to ram us off the road. He crashed a little ways back." He looked at Tate. "Speaking of which, I want to go see what happened to him. I'll be back in a minute."

Anne's startled gasp of horror made Tate smile tiredly and he waved at Clay. "Go. I'll tell Anne here all about it." The sirens grew closer. "Sounds like they're nearly here." He cast a dire look in Clay's direction. "Not that I'm going anywhere with them."

Clay rolled his eyes. “You could do with checking out.”

“I’ll go if you go,” Tate said mutinously. “Otherwise forget it. I hate fucking hospitals.”

“Fine,” Clay muttered in exasperation as he turned and walked down toward the smashed car in the distance. “Bloody stubborn git.”

His leg ached, his back ached, and the little people in his head were trying to tunnel out of his skull to the surface using pickaxes, but Clay was grateful neither he nor Tate was badly injured. He couldn’t say the same about the man in the BMW once he reached the vehicle. Clay knew he wasn’t supposed to be scrabbling around in a dead man’s pockets trying to find out who he was, but the guy wasn’t going to be going anywhere. His neck was broken, his skull crushed and Clay’s sense of justice was mollified.

“Try to kill me and my man, and you’ll end up second best,” he murmured to the body as he rifled his pockets, anxious to do it before the police and ambulances arrived. He gave a hiss of satisfaction when he found the man’s wallet and driving licence.

“Well, Mr Glen Walkerman, I guess I found you. Pity the cops won’t be able to put you away in prison but I guess dead fits just as well. Bastard.” Clay knew he sounded callous, but the man lying with open eyes in the car before him had killed two people and just tried to kill two more. Clay was in no mood to be sympathetic.

He trudged back to the scene of his accident, having wiped down the wallet—just in case—and removed all traces of himself from the BMW. Tate raised an eyebrow at him as he sat on the ground.

“Our guy is no longer missing, or alive,” Clay said grimly. “I’m guessing he thought ramming us off the road, maiming us would slow us down or kill us so he could get to the guy we were going to see.” He waved his mobile. “I already called the team and asked them to make sure the council guy is kept safe. Bring him in for questioning. He obviously has something worth telling.”

Tate shrugged. “One less villain in the world to worry about if Walkerman’s dead.”

Both of them watched as the ambulance and two police cars pulled up. Anne was closer and she approached them, gesticulating wildly, obviously explaining what had happened.

"She's a nice woman," Tate said softly. He grinned. "Very happy we didn't pulverise her into a hedge like bramble jelly. Her words, not mine."

Clay laughed as he stretched, trying to ease the kinks out of his body. "I guess we have a lot of explaining to do," he sighed. "This is going to be fun." He cast a jaundiced eye at his SUV. "And that's a fucking write-off. I s'pose I have an excuse to buy a new one now. A faster one."

Tate groaned, no doubt hearing the relish in Clay's tone. "Really? Like this"—he waved at the mess in the road—"wasn't enough for Mr Adrenaline Junkie?" He winced and held his ribs. Clay sat down beside him and draped an aching arm over his shoulders.

"I'm just glad we made it out of that wreck," he said quietly. "I'm glad we can sit here together and laugh about it. I don't know what I would do if anything happened to you."

Tate smiled at him, his agreement obvious beneath the pain. "Ditto." His eyes narrowed as a paramedic walked toward them. "Heads up. Looks like we're going on a ride."

Clay turned to look at the paramedic and sighed. "Yep. I guess we're both going to get checked out at the hospital if that's the only way I can get you to go. No doubt the cops will be there too, wanting an explanation. Especially with the dead guy down the road and the bullet holes." He leaned over and kissed Tate gently on the lips. "Sorry we won't get that romantic night away. Looks like we're going to be busy for a while."

Chapter 13

Tate lay in bed at Clay's house, the warmth of the duvet on his naked body a welcome solace to his aching bones and limbs. They'd both been patched up at the hospital; Tate had bruised ribs, a couple of stitches in the torn flesh of his shoulder and a swollen lip. Clay had a nasty gash in his head, which had required cleaning and taping and not much else. Both men knew they'd been past lucky.

Tate settled down with a sigh into Clay's king-sized bed. It had been the afternoon from hell what with the accident and then the myriad questions at the hospital and police station. The dead man had definitely been a complication. Thanks to some eyewitness testimony from a young couple who'd been parked in the woods making out, heard the noise and seen the BMW's blowout, it looked like he and Clay were off the hook as far as actually causing his death. The bullet holes and shattered front windscreen had of course taken some explaining, but Tate had managed to impart that it had been purely in self-defence. There was probably still a little fallout to come, but both Tate and Clay were confident that they'd weather that storm, given the connection to the Met case and Rick's intervention.

The car had been towed off but was probably a write off. It looked like Clay would definitely be getting a shiny new toy.

Tate was still edgy. They could have lost each other today and for Tate that was a scenario that he couldn't accept. Life without Clay in it meant nothing.

His skin prickled as if being teased with tiny surges of electricity that ebbed and flowed as he moved. His legs couldn't keep still, moving restlessly beneath the covers. His dick ached, hard and needy. He tried taking a few deep breaths to calm the raging soul inside him, but it didn't appear to be helping. And when Clay came into the room, dressed in boxers, the dark hair on both his head and chest matted with moisture from the shower, Tate's cock immediately took notice. He growled softly and Clay's eyes narrowed, his lips curving in a soft grin as he observed the rapidly tenting cover under which Tate lay.

"Feeling agitated? Danger does that to a man," Clay murmured as he slipped his thumbs into his boxers and slid them off. He threw them onto the rattan chair in the corner as he regarded Tate with heated eyes.

Tate's cock hardened further at the sight of Clay's own hard-on, and the fine line of hair leading down to his dark-haired groin. Clay's toned stomach contracted and tensed as he moved, flat planes of skin and golden muscles that Tate wanted to bite and ravage with his mouth and teeth.

Clay chuckled softly. "No need to ask what you're thinking about." He lifted the cover and got in beside Tate, pulling the duvet down over their waists. His warm legs pressed against Tate's, the touch of heated skin and flesh against flesh making a seductive sound. "Are you up to this now? I know you bruised your ribs, and that cut on your shoulder doesn't need to start bleeding again." Clay grimaced. "My head is feeling better, but it still aches like shit."

At this stage, Tate really didn't care about his injuries. He'd taken his painkillers. Right now, all he wanted was Clay. If truth be told, he was having a little trouble breathing, his need and desire to fuck so strong he wasn't sure he'd be able to control himself from literally riding Clay's dick there and then, lube and aches and pains be damned. He was as horny as Hellboy, no doubt from the adrenaline residue in his blood and the knowledge that they both could have been killed today.

He shook his head as he pulled the duvet off their bodies and swung his legs over to straddle Clay's hips. His balls made contact with the tight skin of Clay's lower stomach and he hissed in pleasure at the sensation.

"No time for thinking, only fucking," he moaned as he leant down and violently took Clay's mouth in a kiss that made them both gasp in pleasure. Tate tasted blood from his split lip and probably from where one of his teeth had nipped Clay's lips. Emboldened by the taste of blood and the pain, he thrust his tongue into Clay's mouth roughly, tasting his man, feeling the wetness of his mouth against his.

The noise Clay made, part growl, part groan made Tate harder than he thought he'd ever felt in his life.

“Christ, I am going to come just like this,” he groaned, as his wet, swollen cock pushed against the bare skin of Clay’s stomach. “I’m just so damn turned on, I can’t think—”

He gave a moan of frustration as Clay’s mouth left his but his disappointment was soon overshadowed when strong hands gripped his hips, fingers digging deep, hurting, and no doubt bruising his flesh.

“Up on your hands and knees, over me,” Clay growled hoarsely. “I need to feel my fingers inside you, opening you so you can ride my cock. Want to split you open.” He reached under the pillow for the tube of lube. Tate’s heart stuttered as Clay opened it and squeezed fluid onto his fingers. His balls contracted and he nodded desperately, the sight of Clay’s pupils, black and dilated, the snarl of ferocity on his face nearly undoing him.

“Yes,” Tate panted as he did what he’d been commanded. He leaned forward, placing his hands on either side of Clay’s waist and leaned over so Clay had easier access to the eager hole. “Need to feel you in me. First your fingers then that big, beautiful cock of yours. Want to ride you ’til I can’t think.”

Clay snarled and thrust his fingers deeply into Tate, pushing and twisting Tate’s hole until he cried out. As he loomed above Clay, half lying, half sitting over his body, the feeling of those rough fingers inside him was exactly what he needed. As Clay opened Tate up, his other hand gripped Tate’s jaw and pulled his mouth down to his. Lips and teeth ground together and both men moaned in pain and pleasure. Tate’s cock was squashed against Clay’s flesh, every move causing friction and he cried out as the slick wetness of his pre-come coated Clay’s stomach and left trails of white across Clay’s belly.

“Don’t come yet,” Clay commanded him, his lips glistening and swollen, eyes darkened with passion. He made another fierce twist inside Tate’s arse. “You wait for me to be inside you before you do that.”

Tate hitched a deep breath. “God, you bastard, then I suggest you fuck me sooner rather than later. Because I am going to come so damn hard in a minute.”

Clay’s face flushed and his teeth bit down none too gently on Tate’s jaw, causing him to yip in pain. “Then do it. Now.”

Tate needed no further urging. He lifted himself up, trying to ignore the pain in his battered body, and stared down at the man who half sat, half lay beneath him. Clay's face was twisted in lust and want, and his cock jutted proudly from the thatch of dark curls at his groin. Tate bit his lip and then lowered himself down onto the hot, slick and eager dick waiting for him. Clay's deep gasp of satisfaction made his hole throb, as did the burn of Clay in his arse. Tate spread his legs to take Clay deeper then began to slowly move above him, his hips undulating and his inner muscles tightening around Clay's cock.

The feeling of power he got from watching his lover slowly lose it was like nothing else. That Tate could take such control of this man he loved, that he could watch his self-control unravel like a skein of wool—that was something for a man to be proud of.

As Tate rose and fell, his hands resting behind him on Clay's strong thighs, Clay's cock sliding in and out of him, he revelled in the primal urge to be impaled and fucked to destruction. He was flying so high, the bruised ribs and plastered-up shoulder were of no consequence.

Huh. Sexual endorphins make for great painkillers.

Tate's inflamed cock had no chance when Clay's hand wrapped around it. It took barely three pulls before he was crying out, shooting ribbons of come over Clay's belly and chest, his muscles tensing around Clay's cock as he climaxed. The feeling of Clay's own orgasm, the hot, sudden heat filling Tate's tender passage and Clay's hoarse grunts as his hips thrust upward—it appeared nirvana was here and now.

Tate had found his paradise in the scent of sweat and semen, and the soft exhalations of his lover as he spent himself inside him. He leaned down, still feeling Clay inside him. Tate pressed fevered, dry lips to Clay's, wanting to breathe him in, taste him—own him.

Fuck, I want to consume him.

For a while, the only sound in the room was the soft fleshy smack of lips, mewls of pleasure as both men strove to absorb the other. Finally, needing to breathe himself, Tate released Clay's mouth and smiled as he stared down at the thoroughly debauched sight before him.

"You look like you've been well and truly fucked," he muttered softly. Clay's lips were red and bitten and there was a small smear of come on his jaw. Tate leaned down and licked it off. "I'm sure I look the same. My arse is damn sore."

He knelt up and uncoupled himself from Clay's sticky groin. Between his cheeks and down his legs, Tate felt and smelt Clay's come and he smiled to himself. He reached down and wiped a bit of Clay's spunk off his thighs then slowly, teasingly, he painted Clay's lips with it. Clay's eyes grew blacker and he made a noise that sounded like a snarl. Tate was ready for a second round there and then with that sexy noise.

"Love it when you claim me like that," he whispered as Clay's hand reached out and he pulled Tate's fingers into his mouth, sucking them, his eyes never leaving Tate's.

"You are mine, Tate. Never forget that." Clay flipped Tate onto his back and held Tate's hands above his head with one hand as the other found its way down to Tate's arsehole. Tate lost his breath at the expression of possession in Clay's eyes. His prick ached as he grew hard again.

Clay's fingers pushed gently into Tate's sensitive hole and he held his breath as Clay scooped up his own come from Tate's arse. He opened his mouth instinctively then Clay's fingers pushed into his mouth, smelling of musk and his own sex. Tate swallowed down what he was being given, the taste and scent of Clay arousing his senses and his cock again.

"This is my spunk inside you, and in your mouth," Clay whispered, "*proving* you're mine." Clay bit down on Tate's ear as he watched Tate sucking his fingers. His hardness pressed against Tate's stomach again. "We took long enough to get here, to this point, you here with me. I don't ever intend losing you. I could have lost you today and that scares the shit out of me. I don't ever want a life where you aren't in it."

"I know," Tate whispered as he licked the final bit of Clay off the fingers in his mouth. He pulled his hands free from Clay's grip, desperate to touch the man in his arms. "I feel the same way. I need you. You're mine as much as I'm yours. Remember that too."

Clay nodded, green eyes staring at Tate with tenderness. "I'll never forget that. Count on it."

Tate felt those eyes on him as he padded naked to the bathroom to get a bunch of industrial-strength wet wipes. When he got back to the bed, he handed some to Clay and they cleaned themselves up.

Tate took the used ones and wadded them into the rubbish bin. Then he got back into bed and snuggled himself into Clay's arms, head on his lover's shoulder.

"How are your ribs?" Clay stroked a hand over his hair, fingers caressing his forehead.

Tate waggled a languid hand. "Sore. I'll live." He chuckled softly. "How's the headache, dear? Do you need an aspirin?"

Clay snorted tiredly. "Shut up. Like you, I'll live. Sleep will do me the world of good." His voice already sounded sleepy. He yawned widely.

Tate couldn't help but yawn too. He closed his eyes and trailed his fingers gently over Clay's lavender wipe-fragranced stomach. "I'm glad we got out of that mess okay today. It could have been nasty."

Clay nodded drowsily. "You were awesome with that gun though. So damn badass. It fucking turned me on, danger or not."

"Yeah? You liked that? Maybe we need to role play. Cop and villain. You can bend me over the interrogation table and fuck me when I don't tell you the truth."

"Jesus, Tate, don't say things like that just when we're both so exhausted. I don't need another boner when I'm trying to get to sleep."

The smile in his lover's voice warmed Tate. He grinned against Clay's skin. "I see me with my trousers down round my ankles, arse in the air just begging for it, you wearing my old uniform trousers, unzipped, your big, thick cock pushing out, and then you push me facedown onto the table and ram into me—"

His words were broken off as Clay's hand clamped down over his mouth.

"Enough, you bastard. Go to sleep. Hell, I'm sporting wood now." Clay's voice was aggrieved. "How am I supposed to sleep like this? Arsehole…oh hell, that feels good."

Tate grinned as he wrapped his hand around Clay's semi-hardened dick and took his mouth in a dirty, open mouthed kiss. His man's recovery time was admirable and a hand job before bed was a definite sleeping tablet in his book.

***

Clay emptied the coffee refill into the jar as he waited for the kettle to boil. He moved the two coffee cups around the kitchen top as if playing a game of cups and balls. The feeling of nervousness that had plagued him since he'd made up his mind two days ago to do what he was about to do was still there. He could make life-or-death decisions in an instant but something like asking Tate to move in with him permanently was freaking him out.

He shook his head ruefully then grimaced at the pain. Hangovers were not conducive to rapid head movements. Luckily he and Tate were recovered from their car accident, and the last two weeks had been fairly normal as their lives went. Clay's part in the toxic dumping affair was over. He'd found the man *he* was looking for and now it was up to the police to see what they could do with the remnants of the case. Their informant had been taken into protective custody and the whole toxic waste dump affair was unfolding like a concertina.

He stared out at the wild garden of his backyard. He hadn't had much time lately to maintain it and it was looking overgrown—beautifully tangled and wild, but still overrun with thistles and weeds.

He turned as Tate came into the kitchen, dressed in tight green briefs and an open white shirt. His hair was growing and what had once been a close buzz cut was now more a spiky auburn mess, a mess Clay really liked. It made Tate look younger, more vulnerable and less like the hard-arsed undercover agent he'd once been. Hazel eyes crinkled in welcome as Tate saw Clay standing there.

"I could die for coffee," Tate said, throat still husky no doubt from the deep throating he'd done last night. He and Clay had come home last night from a visit to Rick and his girlfriend, where they enjoyed a dinner worthy of Gordon Ramsay, but without the foul language. They'd also drunk far too much, and had stumbled into Clay's place in a veritable fit of giggles at something they'd seen or heard on the way home that had seemed hilarious at the time but in the stark light of day, probably hadn't been. In fact, Clay couldn't even remember now what had been so damned funny.

Whatever it was, Tate had been determined that he could 'buck the trend' and decided to swallow Clay's cock the minute he'd gotten home—with gusto. Tate was particularly skilled at blowjobs, having an impressive ability to take Clay deep—a favour Clay wasn't able to quite return although he didn't do too badly, thank you very much.

"You sound a bit rough," Clay smirked as he made Tate his coffee, strong and black.

Tate snorted. "Yeah, well, what the hell was I bloody thinking last night? I definitely had one too many tequila shots."

Clay nodded. "I think we both did. And what the hell did we think was so funny you had to prove you could stick my dick down your throat until it reached your stomach?"

The two men stared at each other in bemusement for a while, trying to recall the memory then burst out laughing. Clay lost his breath both with his own laughter and his sheer relief at the sound of Tate's. It had been a long time since he'd heard his lover make that incredibly infectious noise, a mix of belly laughter and snorting at the same time. Finally, the hilarity ceased and they both wiped their eyes and picked up their coffee cups.

"I guess we'll never know," Tate chuckled with a teasing glance at Clay's crotch. "I guess as long as you, me and Clayzilla down there enjoyed it, there's no harm done." He took a sip of his drink.

"Oh, it was definitely enjoyable," Clay murmured. "And honestly—*Clayzilla*?" Tate's snigger of amusement was cut off by Clay leaning in and taking his lover's mouth in a deep, tastes-like-coffee, good morning kiss. Tate's breath and his low moan into Clay's mouth clearly made Clayzilla happy too.

They were interrupted in their tongue calisthenics by the ringing of Tate's mobile phone.

They unglued their mouths and Tate swore. "Christ, it's only nine on a Saturday morning." Tate reached over and picked up his phone. "It's Rick," he answered. "Rick, you just interrupted morning sex with my man. You'd better have a damn good reason for calling me this early." He winked at Clay who chuckled. There was a loud squawking on the other side of the phone.

Tate rolled his eyes. "What do you mean, TMI? You've never had morning sex? You don't know what you're missing. It's the best time to make use of morning wood."

Clay shook his head in amusement as the squawking grew louder. "Stop baiting him," he whispered with a snigger. "The man's going to have serious issues."

He frowned as Tate's face darkened and his mouth slid into a tight line at whatever Rick was now saying.

Something was wrong.

Clay took another gulp of his sweet, strong coffee and watched the rest of the conversation play out. Emotions rippled across his boyfriend's face—sadness, anger and resignation all appearing. Some minutes later, Tate sighed and passed a hand over his eyes.

"Yeah, thanks for telling me. I 'preciate it. Tell that sister of mine I say hi and it's time we got together for that roast dinner she promised me."

Rick rang off; Tate put his phone down and turned to face Clay. His face was set, a trace of sadness on it.

"What is it?" Clay asked softly.

"They found out who Lily really was," Tate said quietly. "And it's not a pretty story." He picked up his coffee cup, made a face and then put it down. "Her real name was Amy Knight. She was fourteen years old and had been on the streets for about a year."

Clay reached over and placed his hand on Tate's. "That's shitty, being on your own like that. What else did Rick say?"

Tate huffed, his eyes distant. "It's a bit stereotypical really. She had an argument with her parents about her not being able to see some boy, got the hump in and ran away from home. They never saw her again. They'd been trying to find her but it wasn't until her picture appeared in a local newspaper up north that they recognised her. They contacted Rick yesterday and drove down from Manchester to identify her body. How she managed to get to London is anyone's guess. Her mother told Rick she had an online friend down this way—perhaps she was trying to find her. We'll never know."

Tate stared at Clay with troubled eyes. "Apparently she was quite a regular at the clinic down the road, not far from where I met her." His face tightened and the welling emotion was evident in his face. "She was treated for various STDs and pneumonia. She was coughing blood when I saw her." He went silent and Clay saw the pain in his eyes when he looked up. "When she died, she was also six weeks pregnant."

Clay's stomach lurched. "Christ, that poor kid, and the baby. Stupid question I know, but do they have any idea who the father might have been?"

Tate shrugged. His body language made Clay want to pull him close and never let go. He wasn't sure that was what Tate wanted right now so he held off.

"They have no idea. I doubt they'll try and find out either." Tate's hands clenched. "She stood no fucking chance. She was young and vulnerable and chose to kill herself because she was in trouble, with nowhere to go." His voice thickened with rage. "If I ever find out who made her pregnant, I'll bloody well kill them."

"You think she knew that she was pregnant?" Clay asked softly as he ran a finger down the side of Tate's fisted hand.

Tate nodded. "She said something about it being too late for either of them. At the time I didn't understand." He stopped then blurted out, his expression anguished, "I should have nagged her more. I should have made her go to that damned hospital."

And now it was time for Clay to pull his tormented lover into his arms and murmur words of comfort in his ear. "Baby, you did what you could. There's only so much you can do for someone. You're spending time at Castaways trying to help kids who need it, that's something. Those kids love you like a big brother from what Dr Jakes told us in our sessions. So please don't let this one thing fester inside of you. You need to let it go."

Inside Clay raged that each step forward that Tate took, there always seemed to be a step backward attached to it. Some sort of piss-poor karma delivered by a fate that loved playing sick jokes on people who were already hurting.

Clay held Tate close for a while as they both stared out into the unruly garden and watched the next-door cat try and catch an unsuspecting sparrow. The sparrow realised its vulnerability at the last minute and eluded the cat with an indignant chirp.

"It's looking like damn Borneo out there," Tate muttered as he pulled away from Clay. "We need to get a gardener in here and get it seen to before the tigers breed and eat us in our beds."

Clay chuckled softly. "I don't believe there are any tigers in Borneo. Some civets maybe and definitely orang-utans." He was glad Tate appeared to have taken his advice on board. Time, however, would tell how far *that* went. His man was a stubborn as hell. It was what had kept him alive in the past.

Tate gave him a look of disdain. "Listen to you, David Attenborough. Mr bloody know it all." But his soft grin took the sting out of his words.

Clay cleared his throat. “Speaking of the garden. I’m glad you said ‘we.’ There’s something I’ve been meaning to speak to you about.”

Tate’s face flushed. “Sorry, when I said ‘we’ I obviously meant you. I mean it’s your house.”

Clay ran a hand down Tate’s cheek. “Unless you want it to be *our* house. I’m up for that if you are.”

Tate’s eyes widened. “What are you saying?”

Clay scratched his head. How come this was so damned awkward?

“I mean maybe you want to move in here. You’re here most of the time anyway, and half your clobber is in my spare room. So now we’re out and proud, and everyone knows about our relationship, and I’ve stopped being such a protective Daddy Bear, then I thought perhaps…” his voice tailed off. Tate’s face was a picture in…something…and Clay wasn’t sure whether it was good or bad. His boyfriend hid his eyes behind his arm and his body shook. Clay was a little peeved. It looked like Tate was laughing and Clay didn’t think the request was that funny.

“What the hell is so damn amusing?” he growled, his pride a little hurt.

Tate snorted as he moved his arm away and his eyes shone with mirth. “Protective *Daddy Bear*? Oh my God.” He collapsed in a fit of giggling. “And yes, you crazy bastard. I’ll move in with you.” His eyes softened. “I thought you’d never ask.”

Clay grinned his heart filling with both relief and joy. Tate never giggled. This was pretty new and he liked it.

“Yes,” Clay purred, moving toward Tate and gripping his hips, pulling him against his body. “All the better to eat you with, or however that damn fairy tale goes. Or was that something else? I’m not very good with fairy tales.”

Tate was still chuckling when Clay hefted him onto his shoulder and took him into the bedroom where he proceeded to show the man writhing eagerly beneath him exactly how a Daddy Bear ate someone.

Chapter 14

Galileo's buzzed with activity as Clay walked back from the bar with a round of drinks. His friends were all seated in a corner booth, chatting animatedly. He grinned at Tate who already looked a little under the weather as he tried to convince Eddie of the benefits of briefs versus boxers. Eddie gave Clay a 'please help me' puppy dog look which Clay ignored. He knew exactly what happened when Tate got onto that subject, Clay being a boxer man himself, and he didn't want to get involved. He smothered a laugh as he sat down and heard the words 'dangling junk' seeing Eddie's panicked look around the restaurant to check if anyone else had heard Tate's rather loud ode to the delights of wearing briefs to keep his junk "contained."

Taylor waved his beer bottle in Clay's direction. "More booze. Just what we needed." He slugged down the remains of his current drink and picked up another one.

His fiancé, Draven, sighed. "Tay, remember what happened the last time you got drunk? You gave Tate hell, and then it ended up with Gideon politely kicking you and me out of the restaurant with poor Clay as the babysitter."

Clay laughed loudly. "I remember that night well. I thought poor Gideon was going to pitch a fit."

"Poor Gideon *did* pitch a fit," was the dry rejoinder from behind and Clay turned to see the man in question standing there. He was immaculately clad as always in a grey suit, as befitted the owner of Galileo's. He sat down in the empty chair beside Eddie and leaned over to kiss his cheek.

Gideon grinned. "If I recall, it was a bit like the Nicky Starr porn site in here that night." He frowned. "Talking about Oliver and Leslie, weren't they supposed to be here?"

Taylor nodded. "Yep. Something happened to one of Leslie's fish—again—so poor Oliver had to go around and console him. They'll be a bit late."

Eddie laughed loudly. "If by *console*, you mean that Oliver had to go round and flush the little fishy tyke down the toilet because Leslie was in hysterics and couldn't do it, you hit it on the head." He grimaced. "I don't know what it is with that man and his pets. He has this nasty habit of losing them."

Draven shook his head in amusement. "I bet that's not all that's getting *consoled*," he said slyly.

The table burst into raucous laughter. Clay chuckled at the merriment and thought not for the first time what a great bunch of people he had the pleasure of knowing. His relationship with Tate and Draven had brought him into contact with men he was really proud to call friends. The fact Tate had also agreed to move in with him made it even better. There was quite a bit to organise in terms of the move, but the fact that *his man* was going to be living with him definitely made the evening better.

Tate raised his drink at him and the warmth in those hazel eyes made Clay smile. His lover looked more relaxed than he'd seen him in a long while. That was partially down to the therapy he still underwent and Tate's unburdening of himself to Clay. He was so proud of Tate in coming to terms with his demons, he could burst.

Draven leaned over and touched his arm. "Tate is looking great," he murmured softly. "I'm so pleased for you both. I know you both went through a lot and to see him like this—it's pretty admirable. He's one tough bastard, isn't he?"

"That he is," Clay remarked fondly, watching and listening as Tate told some dirty joke about a penguin and a dwarf nun. He winced at the punchline. "God, that was a bit sexist even for him."

"That's what comes of working with misogynistic bastards like Sonny Armerian," Draven mused. "So big on proving they don't suck dick, they treat women like objects." He chuckled. "I guess in Tate's case, you can take the man out of the undercover cop—"

"But you can't take the undercover cop out of the man," they finished together and laughed.

Clay leaned in toward Draven. "I wanted to ask you how Taylor was," he murmured quietly as he watched the antics around the table. "You said he had a bit of a turn when we were in that accident—is everything okay now?"

Draven nodded, eyes on his fiancé. "Yeah, he was a bit under the weather for a while. Did the whole passing-out thing and shit."

His lips twisted in a wry grin. "I guess it's all part of the fun of being involved with a psychic."

"But you wouldn't have it any other way," Clay said, nudging his friend's shoulder. "I know the feeling. Can't live with 'em; can't live without 'em." He glanced at Draven with a smirk. "I never thought I'd see the day Draven Samuels was in love. And yet here we are."

"Back atcha." Draven shot back. "And you, with Tate Williams? I never saw that one coming."

"Yeah, well." Clay shrugged. "We've known each other forever. We still take it day by day, but yeah. He'll be fine. Especially now he's moving in with me. I can keep an eye on him."

Both men shared a look that said they knew what it meant to take care of someone, even if the other person didn't really think they needed it. In their profession, protective instincts were a must.

A tornado in the form of Leslie Tiberius Scott chose that moment to make his entrance. Leslie was adept at making an entrance and Clay couldn't help but feel a surge of affection for the young man who'd manage to tame a former porn star and bring him out of hiding.

Oliver Brown, aka Nicky Starr in porn circles (and someone all of them had watched at some time or another) smirked at Taylor and Eddie as he sat down. "Sorry we're late," he announced, his hand reaching up and smoothing his hair over the scar Clay knew was there on his face. "Glenda died and we had to have the funeral there and then." He rolled his eyes and glanced fondly at his boyfriend.

Leslie pouted, brushing a stray lock of black hair away behind his ear. Clay thought Leslie was adorable.

"I wasn't going to let her sit around and be eaten by a cat or something," Leslie sputtered indignantly. "That damn tabby next door slipped into my flat the other day and ate all the salami I'd left out for my sandwich and I had to make do with boring ham. God knows what it would have done if it found Glenda lying in state. She'd have been gobbled up like that." He clicked his fingers and sat down.

Taylor and Eddie burst into loud fits of laughter.

"Leslie, did you just say a cat ate your salami? Oh my God, there has to be a joke in there somewhere." Taylor howled. He could always be counted on for a laugh, and Eddie wasn't much better.

They nudged each other in mirth. Draven rolled his eyes and Gideon just shook his head. The two men shared a sympathetic glance at their respective partners' schoolboy humour.

Leslie glared at them, blue eyes flashing dangerously. "Ha-ha. You two are like dirty little kids, you know that?" He gave a smug grin. "Besides, my *salami's* too big to be eaten by a cat."

Eddie laughed louder. "Oh, please don't start on the whole eight-inches thing again."

Oliver leaned over the table with a grin. "Lads, my boyfriend's dick size is classed as need-to-know information. And you don't need to know." He smiled fondly at Leslie who batted his eyelashes back as he imperiously ordered his drink from the waitress.

The juvenile banter caused Clay a slight sense of insecurity. At the ripe age of thirty-six he was almost the daddy of the group. The thought irritated him and he scowled.

Tate leaned over and ran a hand down his jawline, warm eyes assessing him shrewdly. "Everything okay?" he murmured as his other hand caressed Clay's thigh under the table.

Clay sighed. "Just feeling like old Father Time," he admitted softly. "Look at this lot. I have about ten years on them all."

Tate snorted. "So do I when it comes to some of them. We're a right pair." His hand travelled further up Clay's leg and palmed his groin suggestively. "You are definitely sexy for an old bloke though." He squeezed hard and Clay tried not to make a noise as his dick hardened. He reached down and pushed Tate's hand off his crotch.

"Stop it," he hissed. "You start something and Gideon will throw us out." He cast a quick glance at the man in question but he was too busy kissing Eddie to hear them.

Tate chuckled and removed his hand. "Easy now, old-timer," he said, putting on a twang. "Don't go getting your panties in a bunch."

Clay snarled softly and reached across to grip Tate's jaw, loving the spark of lust and desire that flared there. "I'll show you who's not so damn old." He took Tate's mouth in a bruising kiss, owning him and forgetting for a moment just where they were. When they finally came up for air, both men realised the lack of conversation at the table.

"Oh. My. God," Leslie said, fanning himself with a menu. "That was so fucking hot!"

"Er, yeah, just a bit." Eddie's face was pink and he threw a heated glance at Gideon. "Pretty much a scorcher."

Both Gideon and Draven nodded in agreement. Taylor was too busy sitting with his mouth open to say anything, but from the dangerous look he flashed Draven, he had *something* on his mind.

Clay's face flamed. He'd never expected to be the centre of attention like this although it seemed they might just have contributed to everybody else's getting lucky later. For an *old-timer*, he was quite proud of that.

"Yeah, sorry," he said sheepishly as Tate snickered again and his hand crept up Clay's leg to the dick that was trying to punch its way out of his trousers. Clay gripped that wandering hand tightly.

God, my man is being such a prick tease tonight. I need to keep him away from alcohol when we're out. It does something to him, especially here at Galileo's.

Oliver grinned wolfishly. "If you guys fancy the idea, my old studio Vanguard is always looking for guys to perform for the more mature audience. I can give them a call if you like?"

The gleam in his eyes and the wicked twitch on his lips forestalled Clay's 'fuck you,' at that comment. Since meeting Leslie, Oliver had definitely come out of his hermit's shell. He'd proven to have a wicked sense of humour, a really dirty mind and knew every porn star in the business and their secrets, which kept them all entertained.

He was also clearly besotted with Leslie, but Clay didn't see how anyone could resist the blue-eyed minx. Everyone around the table had a great affection for him. He was the warm and fuzzy team mascot that got under your skin and you couldn't get him out.

Leslie gave a shriek of horror. "Babe, you can't say things like that to Clay and Tate." He smacked Oliver across the head with a menu. "Sorry, guys, Oliver sometimes has a big mouth."

The howl of laughter and Leslie's rapidly reddening cheeks at the dirty comments that followed, once again about the size of Leslie's cock, took the heat off Clay and Tate for a while.

When they finally left the restaurant, with the promise to all to arrange another 'Dirty Dinner' night, as Eddie had dubbed it, it was close to midnight. Clay definitely wanted to put the heat back into the bedroom. Tate had been a tease all night and now it was time for payback. And from the dangerous look in Tate's eyes, his lover was ready to pay the price.

***

Moving was a bitch but the results were worth it. Tate stared around the bedroom he now shared with Clay with a sense of accomplishment. He gave a nod of satisfaction and made his way to the patio. The French doors were open and a light, warm breeze blew in, caressing his face with tendrils of its warm breath. He stared out at the tangled garden with its overgrown foliage and unclipped greenery. It had been a hot and heavy weekend moving all his stuff out of his flat in Kentish Town into Clay's place, and putting some things into storage.

The past three weeks had been hectic to say the least. Organising removals, ensuring the utilities were stopped, changing his address, fobbing off his sister Lucy's offer of casseroles and stews (something Tate hated but Clay loved) and cleaning out the flat; it had taken a considerable amount of time.

Now he was firmly ensconced in a house he'd always considered home anyway. He loved Clay's huge Victorian house with its vineyard and peaceful garden. It bore so much of his partner—the classic wooden and leather study, with wall-to-wall books. The comfortable, old-style Quaker kitchen with its pale wood and centre island just perfect for eating around in the evenings. The ornate wrought-iron table and chairs on the private cobbled patio were perfect for warm summer evenings. It all spoke of warmth, safety and Clay.

Warm arms encircled him, pulling him against a strong, familiar body. Tate closed his eyes and breathed in Clay's beloved scent. Now, he *really* felt he was home.

"I'm wondering why the hell it took so long for us to get to this point," Clay whispered in his ear. "What the hell was I thinking—we could have done this a long time ago." He kissed the back of Tate's neck. "It was my fault, I know that. Me being all Daddy Bear and not wanting to risk you being hurt."

Tate reached back and pulled Clay's mouth down for a kiss. "You still make me laugh when you say that. Not to mention when I read 'Goldilocks' now I shall have really dirty thoughts." He turned and wrapped his arms around Clay's neck, laying his forehead against his. "Thank you for believing in me and staying with me after all the shit I've put you through." He pressed a finger to Clay's lips as he tried to speak. "Nope, be quiet. This is my turn to say important stuff." He smoothed a stray strand of Clay's hair from his cheek. "You inviting me into your home like this—it means everything to me. You once told me I was your world, your everything. Well, I need you to know I feel the same way. I love you, Clay Mortimer. To quote Mr Darren Hayes, 'Truly, Madly, Deeply.'" He grinned and saw Clay's eyes soften. "And the mind-blowing sex is good too."

Clay's chest rumbled as he laughed. "Good to know," he murmured as his hands slid around Tate's waist and found the warm skin under his polo shirt. "I'm really glad you're here too. Waking up every day with you—that's all I need."

"That, and a good gardener," Tate remarked drily. "I'm pretty sure I saw an orang-utan earlier in that tree." He pointed to a giant tree in the garden laden with some sort of pink bloom. Clay chuckled and kissed the smirk off Tate's face with his usual thoroughness. His hands gripped the back of Tate's head as he pressed his lips against Tate's. Clay's tongue made slow, sensual swirls in his mouth, on his lips, teeth clicking together. Tate had the sense of being emotionally branded and owned and he fucking loved it. Loved that someone like Clay would make him his over and over again.

Clay's hard body pressed against his in a wanton display of possession. His cock pressed against Tate's groin, which was already aflame, and Tate moaned as Clay bit his bottom lip then sucked it into his mouth.

"I need to be inside you," Clay said huskily. "Want to christen the fact you're living here with me by making love to you until you forget who you are. 'Til I forget who I am." He chuckled. "I can feel you're up to it, so maybe we should take this inside?"

Tate finally remembered to breathe. "The study," he gasped as his hands fumbled with Clay's zipper. "I've always had this fantasy about being bent down over that desk and taken and it's the one place we haven't done it yet."

The look in Clay's eyes said he thought that was a great idea. Clay took hold of his arm, propelling him forward as they stumbled to the inner sanctum of Clay's—and now Tate's—home.

Tate's arsehole clenched in anticipation of being bent over that huge leather-topped desk. His dick pushed against the front of his stained and dusty sweats and the minute they reached the room, he tugged off his pants together with his briefs. He breathed a sigh of relief at being free. Pulling his polo shirt over his head, he flung it into the far corner and turned to see Clay pushing his jeans down to his ankles. He made to remove his open-necked button shirt and Tate stopped him.

"Leave the shirt on, just open it." he growled. "I love it when you fuck me that way."

Clay hitched a breath, his green eyes deepening to slits of emerald. "God, you drive me insane when you say things like that." He did as he was told though and his eyes roamed around the room. "I don't think we have lube in here," he muttered. "I think this is the one place—"

He stopped as Tate triumphantly reached under a pile of papers and unearthed a tube.

"You planned this?" Clay's mouth quirked in a grin; a hot, slutty, needy grin that took Tate's breath away.

"Hell yes. I knew we'd need it sometime. Now come here."

Tate drew Clay to him roughly, taking his mouth and groaning as their cocks pressed together, wet and slick, and he knew his was about ready to blow. "God, I want you," he grunted as they rutted together. "There's something about this whole move thing that has made me as randy as fuck."

Clay picked up the lube and opened it, then slid a warm hand down Tate's flank, reaching around to grip the tight globe of his arse. "Bend over," he instructed, his breath deepening as Tate did what he'd been told. He lay flat on the table, arse in the air. He gripped across and over the table, unable to get his hands around the two sides as it was too wide. "I love your arse."

Clay leaned down and kissed Tate's ruined cheek, tracing the dragon scar with his tongue. "I love this." His mouth gently bit at the flesh on his hip. "I love this." His finger slid inside Tate, now coated with cold coffee-scented lube. Tate clenched and unclenched and as another of Clay's fingers pushed inside, he let out a slow growl of satisfaction. He surrendered to the sensation of being filled, and when Clay's cock nudged his hole and slid deep, he gripped the table tighter and pushed back.

They were adept at this slow serenade of lovemaking, of meeting each other's needs and the teasing, needy seduction of skin against skin while mouths grasped greedily at each other's as the chance arose.

Clay's deep sighs as he pushed deep inside Tate were a serenade. Tate made noises of his own when his lover sunk in and touched his prostate, causing his body to spark with fierce, unbridled pleasure. The murmured endearments as Clay made love to Tate made him feel cherished and adored and banished any memories he might have of another time, another place, a tormentor. For Tate, there was only the here and now, as the gentle breeze blew in through an open window and the fragrance of honeysuckle touched his nostrils.

"Going to make you come now," Clay gasped as his hand encircled Tate's cock and he began to stroke it fiercely.

Tate grunted as his swollen prick responded to the movements of Clay's hand. His arse pushed back frantically against Clay as Tate's balls contracted and he covered Clay's hand and desk with warm strings of come that also painted pearly pictures on the floor. The warmth of Clay's own orgasm inside his channel caused Tate to smile fiercely, and he clenched his muscles, milking Clay dry and leaving him a sobbing, gasping mess splayed across Tate's back. Sweat, semen and honeysuckle all combined to make a recipe for a perfume Tate thought he'd definitely buy. It was intoxicating, primal, erotic and all *them*.

Splayed out on the desk like a flattened starfish Tate knew he should have felt uncomfortable but he wasn't. Instead, he twisted so he could embrace that sweaty man of his as he lay heaving above him.

"Hell." Clay's raspy laugh tickled Tate's ear. "There will definitely be more of that. That was fucking hot. *You're* hot." He gripped Tate's face, turning it to face him then seductively licked Tate's mouth. "And you taste like more."

"I'm not sure I can manage that right now," Tate gasped. "But later you can count on me being there."

Tate's skin tingled at Clay's dirty laugh as he slid out of him and moved away.

Tate groaned as he unglued himself from the desk. "I got spunk everywhere," he moaned as he stood up and stretched. "Do we have a housekeeper?"

Clay snorted. "No housekeeper. Just good old wet wipes and Kleenex." He rummaged in a small wooden cabinet and Tate raised an eyebrow when he produced said goods.

"You've done this sort of thing before then, to have *that* in there?" Tate gestured to the items Clay was using to clean up, feeling a prickle of jealousy that perhaps maybe he hadn't been the first one to be had on Clay's table that way. He tore a piece of tissue off and wiped up the random spooge that glistened on the side of the desk.

"No," Clay said softly. "I've never fucked anyone in here. Only you. It's just I have a habit of coffee spills and ink stains. And you don't want to see what my hands look like when I change the printer cartridges."

"Oh." Tate felt better at that. "Not that it matters, of course." He gave a careless shrug. "I mean you had a life before me."

Clay reached over and caressed Tate's cheek, his green eyes warm with satisfaction at the jealousy in Tate's tone. "Liar," he said softly. "I *had* no life before I had you in it like this."

Tate's throat closed at that statement and he was horrified to feel a prickle of tears behind his eyes. He coughed to cover it up.

Since when did I become so damn needy?

"Sex makes you all emotional," he murmured. "You want to watch that. It could be catching."

He didn't miss Clay's smile as he finished cleaning up and tossed the dirty wipes and tissue into the waste bin. His boyfriend looked decadent standing there in only an open shirt, his cock hanging heavy between his legs and trails of dried come on his stomach.

Tate looked down at himself and grinned when he realised he looked even more debauched. He was naked, with dried come everywhere. His arsehole hurt too. "Maybe we should get in the shower and clean this off. I think I need a little TLC; my backside feels as if it's had a tree trunk rammed in it."

He sauntered out of the door into the hallway, and along to the winding stairs. The best shower in the house was upstairs in the master bedroom. Tate had a hankering to see what it felt like being in there as master of the house and not an overnighter. Judging from the footsteps following him up the stairs, and the hand resting lightly on his back, Tate had a feeling he wouldn't be in there alone.

Chapter 15

Liquorice had never been one of Clay's favourite things to eat, especially when it was covered with lint and speckles of dust. He and Tate had the same dislike of the stuff.

His boyfriend had left him in the small reception room at Castaways while he went to find the famous, or infamous, Jax that Tate talked about incessantly. He had promised to take Jax to Tate's usual hangout to do some graffiti painting. He'd wanted Clay to come along to meet his new young 'apprentice.'

Clay prayed that Tate going back to where Lily had died wouldn't affect him and push him back to that dark place he'd lived in for so long. Christ, he was moving forward now and Clay didn't want that to change. Tate hadn't been back to the abandoned baths since Lily's suicide. While he had quietly assured his lover he was fine with it, Clay had to decide whether to trust Tate's judgment or hover, which, Clay admitted, hadn't gone down well in the past. He worried over it, but at the end of the day, he wasn't going to undo all the progress they had made by letting his insecurities for Tate's well-being colour the outing.

The problem now? Clay hadn't been left alone. He'd been quickly introduced and now two small faces watched him eagerly as their proffered gift of a string of apple-scented green liquorice had been pressed into his hand. Before he'd sped up the stairs, Tate had chuckled and said he thought it was some baptism of fire all newbies went through. Clay hadn't quite understood it at the time.

The two children, introduced as Damien and Krispin, stared at him expectantly. They didn't seem to say much at all. There had been some shy smiles, some giggling and a few whispers between them and that had been it.

Clay cleared his throat. He was obviously expected to eat the item he'd been given. Or perhaps he could be the bigger person and say he was saving it for Tate. That thought made him hopeful. He was about to declare his noble intention when someone tweaked the skin on his ribs and he uttered a soft curse as he turned to face his pincher.

Tate stood there, a young, blond man beside him, and Clay was stunned. When'd he expected to see Jackson Grady, he hadn't expected to meet a flawed angel. The man was simply breathtakingly beautiful, even with the scars on his face and the blue eyes that regarded him evenly from underneath a tilted chin.

"Aren't you going to eat that?" Tate gestured to the item in his hand with a smirk.

Clay stared at the liquorice. "I, er, I thought I'd save it for you," he muttered, knowing Tate would see through that but giving it a shot anyway.

Tate shook his head vehemently. "Oh no, I insist you have it. I've already had a bit."

Jax chuckled softly and placed a hand on Tate's arm. Clay narrowed his eyes, knowing it was childish to be jealous of a seventeen-year-old.

"It's a thing with Damien," Jax said, his voice deep and rich. "Think of it like a university hazing ritual."

Clay glanced at the kids watching him and decided *fuck it.* He'd been in the SAS, and a sweet and two kids weren't going to get the better of him. He popped the green string in his mouth and chewed it. It was really sour and his eyes began to water.

"Fuck," he sucked his lips together as the sourness intensified. Tate laughed loudly and placed big hands over the little kids' ears.

Clay's face burned with guilt. "Sorry about the swearword, but, wow. That's a little tart." He managed to swallow it at last.

The two children were giggling and smirking, no doubt at Clay's language. Jax grinned and went over to the boys. He leaned down and whispered something in their ear and their faces lit up.

"Really?" Damien's face lit up and Krispin seemed to look at Clay with a new respect. "Will he do it for us?"

"Maybe one day," Jax promised and Clay wondered what the hell he was in for now. "But right now, you guys need to disappear into the garden and go find Jen. She has a picnic outside for you."

With whoops of glee, the two boys ran out of the room.

Clay narrowed his eyes in suspicion at an innocent-looking Jax. Tate was grinning from ear to ear and Clay wondered what they'd been cooking up.

“What have you promised I’d show them?”

“Don’t blame Jax. It was my idea.” Tate grinned. “The kids have an outing coming up and they all wanted to go the airfield to see the planes take off and have a barbeque. I might have suggested to young Jax here that you could parachute out of a plane while we were there.”

Clay’s jaw dropped. “Honestly?” He could do that with his eyes closed but he wasn’t sure he wanted to be a fair-side attraction.

Tate snorted. “Yes, Mister SAS man. It would mean a lot to the kids to see someone they knew doing that. And you have to keep up your jumping hours so I thought it might make a nice trip out for us. I mean we’re talking you, jumping out of a plane.” He grinned wolfishly. “That’s something I’d like to see myself. Hell, maybe I’d join you.”

Clay didn’t miss the look of yearning that crossed Jax’s face at Tate’s words.

“You ever thought of doing something like that, Jax?” Clay asked softly.

Jax started, nibbling on his lips. “I’d love to do that. Jump out of a plane. Feel the wind racing through my hair, the rush…” His voice tailed off.

Tate reached over and chucked Jax on the chin with a mock fist. “I’m sure we could organise a tandem jump…?” His eyes searched Clay’s.

Clay nodded. “Of course, that shouldn’t be a problem. Jax could jump with me when we do this whole day out.”

He warmed at seeing the expression of gratitude in Tate’s eyes. His man really had a bond with the young man.

Jax’s face brightened. “I could do that? I’d need to check with the doctors though that they don’t have any objections. My eyes might need some special covering or something so they don’t get damaged, but hell, I’d love to do it if I can.”

“Then it’s settled.” Tate gave Clay a quick smile. “I’ll talk to Randy and he can find out what we need to do to get this medically approved. The last thing we want is anything happening to what’s left of your sight.”

Jax gave a wide beam and Clay’s heart melted. Between Jax and Leslie Scott, Clay’s whole tough-guy act was going out the window. He’d have loved to have had a child; a son would have been nice. He sighed. It wasn't really something they talked about too seriously other than in passing, but he knew Tate had been averse to the idea before. Now? Perhaps. He wanted to pursue the marriage idea with Tate once again; talk to him about it and see how he felt because, really, who knew? Anything was possible in this ever-changing relationship they had; even the prospect of having a child one day.

Clay was interrupted from his musings by Tate's heavy thump to his arm. "Hey," he glared at his boyfriend. "What the hell?"

Tate mock boxed around him, throwing fake punches. "You looked in a brown study there. We need to get going. I've got an art lesson to give to my protégé here…"

He picked up his rucksack, which Clay knew was loaded with paint tins, and slung it across his shoulder. Tate helped Jax get his own satchel on board then turned to Clay with a raised eyebrow.

"Right, we're ready. Let's go. We've got trains to catch and it's a bit of a trip. I need coffee; we need to stop at Starbucks. And maybe a Danish or something. I'm starving."

Clay rolled his eyes and laughed when he saw Jax doing the same thing. This was going to be an interesting afternoon.

***

When they got to the derelict swimming bath with its concrete canvases, Tate got quieter as they walked toward a wall emblazoned with a green-clad clockwork man. Clay recognised Tate's tag on the side of the mural.

"You okay, baby?" Clay murmured softly. He'd noticed Tate's stillness and the stiffer body language as they approached the wall.

Tate nodded. "Yeah." He grinned softly. "I'm the big, tough cop, remember?"

Clay reached out and squeezed his hand. "I remember."

Tate smiled softly. "Besides, this isn't for me. It's for Jax. He needs a boost. I think he'll get a kick out of it."

Clay chuckled. "I never thought I'd see the day my 'big, tough cop' got all soft over a teenager." He reached up and brushed Tate's cheek softly. "I'm so damn proud of you. You've been great with him and he really likes you. Trusts you. It's a big thing inspiring someone like that."

Tate looked over at Jax. "He's a great kid. It's like having a kid brother. I like it."

Jax gave them a both a faint smile as he walked beside them.

On the train, the teenager had been quiet, gazing down at the floor of the tube behind dark sunglasses and gripping his satchel tightly. Tate had spoken quietly to him and Jax had nodded and then stuck his earbuds in his ears and listened to music on his mobile phone. On the walk to the complex, Jax had insisted he could walk on his own.

Tate and Clay had made sure to be either side of him, as he walked *über* carefully, chin held high. When he'd stumbled once or twice, misjudging a step or the kerb, both of them had swiftly steadied him. Clay wasn't sure how much was politically correct and what could be construed as patronising. He was following Tate's lead, as he seemed to have Jax's measure.

As they drew closer to the wall, Clay nudged Tate and gestured to the picture. "I like it. Very expressive. Feeling a bit manipulated at the time, were you?" He knew Tate's murals depicted his moods and he was pretty adept at picking up on his lover's emotions.

Tate stared at the man with faraway eyes. "Yeah. Something like that."

Beside him, Jax murmured softly.

Clay wasn't sure what he'd said, and whether it had been at his words or the picture itself. He stood, unsure what to do next. So he sat down against the wall, crossed his legs in front of him and leant back. Then he waited for his two damaged souls to take the lead. He closed his eyes, enjoying the afternoon sunshine. In the far corner of the quadrant, older youths swore and joshed with each other and he heard the rattling of paint cans.

"So what are we doing then?" asked Jax uncertainly. "I haven't painted anything in a while. I'm not sure I remember how to."

Clay opened his eyes to see Tate's empathic glance at his young friend.

"You paint from the heart, Jax," Tate murmured softly, pressing a primed paint can into Jax's hand. "You aim the nozzle and in your mind, you see what you want to say. I've seen your paintings. You're good and your instincts will take over. Pick a spot and just let yourself go." He reached out and ruffled Jax's blond curls affectionately. "Do anything you want."

Jax nodded and shuffled over to a blank bit of wall. He considered it for a while, in a birdlike fashion with his delicate chin raised. Clay saw the fingers of his free hand clenching and unclenching. Then he lifted his paint can and began spraying.

Clay didn't have a creative painting bone in his body. He could write a bit and had published a few articles on violence, life in the military and such for various publications. But drawing anything meaningful other than a stick figure—*that* he couldn't do. He admired people who could translate their emotions into painting and/or graffiti like this.

He watched Tate as he studied the wall, rubbing his chin, raising his arms and sketching something in the air. Tate nodded once or twice, deep in thought, then aimed his spray tin and painted a white swatch on the wall. The rebel that dwelt inside him was taking over, flaunting convention and leaving his lasting mark.

Clay loved seeing him like that—immersed in his task, so focused on what he was doing that everything else disappeared. Including Clay, he realised ruefully.

He closed his eyes and enjoyed the warmth of the sun, its soft touch making him drowsy. Around him, he heard the hiss of cans, the murmurings as Tate or Jax pondered their mural, soft huffs from Tate as he worked and in the distance, faint shouts and laughter from no doubt other graffiti artists, who were busy making their mark. It was peaceful, and the sun was warm and Clay relaxed.

"Wow. He looks so peaceful, seems a shame to wake him up." Jax's voice with its hint of laughter roused Clay and he opened his eyes to see Tate and Jax peering down at him. He swallowed; his throat dry, his eyes slightly gritty. He hoped like hell he hadn't been drooling.

I must have fallen asleep.

His boyfriend observed him with a sly glint in his eye. "Afternoon, old-timer. You were having a nice snooze but it's getting late so we thought we'd better wake you up."

Clay scowled. "Fuck off. Enough of the 'old,' thanks."

He squinted up at the two men sniggering above him. "Are you two done creating the new Picassos?"

He clambered to his feet and looked over at the walls, which had once been plain and grey and now abounded with colour. The pictures leapt off the wall and assaulted his eyes with a visual feast that was both bold and vibrant. They took his breath away. His Picasso comment hadn't been far off the mark.

“What do you think?” Tate asked, and Clay heard the hesitation in his voice.

He shook his head in wonder. “Baby, it looks—wow. Just damn wow. And Jax—I hope I’m not being PC here, but hell, you paint better with bad sight than I could ever hope to manage fully sighted and with a modicum of talent. It’s stunning, truly.”

Jax’s face flushed in pleasure and he shifted on his feet. “Thanks,” he said awkwardly. “I just did like Tate told me to. Let my instinct guide me. And Tate’s mural is radical. He is really talented.” He threw Tate a look of hero worship and Clay bit back a smile. That look on Jax’s face was the way he felt every minute of the day.

Tate’s mural was about five feet high, the same wide and was rainbow coloured; a giant pink dragon graced the wall, orange fire blowing from its nostrils. In the belly of the dragon, the initials AK were written in bright, vivid green. The dragon held a small green and white flower in its outstretched claws. Tate’s signature tag of his initials formed the prong of the dragon’s tail. Clay’s heart ached at what his rebellious lover had done and he had to push down the emotion that swelled inside.

“It’s a mural for Lily,” he said softly, looking at Tate, who was observing his creation with critical eyes. “You said she wanted a pink dragon and you gave her one.”

Tate nodded. “I wanted her to know she hadn’t been forgotten, that she was real, hence the AK. It was who she was, even if she called herself Lily when I met her.” He scowled. “I’m not good with flowers, so hopefully that looks like a lily. Maybe I should try and get it a little more defined—”

Jax reached over and gripped Tate’s arm. “It looks perfect to me,” he said gently. “Leave it. If it’s a little flawed in your eyes, that just makes it all the more real.”

Tate frowned at his protégé. “Since when you did you get so damn smart? That sounds like something Clay would have said.” But he smiled, his face softening. “Love, what do you think of Jax’s music score? Isn’t it sheer genius?” He beamed with pride and Clay’s heart once again swelled with emotion.

God, this man will be the death of me. How did I get so damn lucky to have a man like Tate?

"It's phenomenal," he agreed, looking at the three-foot mural of a music sheet with notes, clefs, staffs and various other symbols imprinted upon it. It was classic black and white, and had a white space in the middle in which a figure, roughly drawn in black, sat gazing up around him at the detail of the sheet. It lacked the detail of Tate's creations, and there were places where paint had run and overlapped. But it was beautifully expressed and instantly recognisable. For a young man who was half blind and hadn't touched paint in years, it was an incredible feat of perseverance. Something Clay understood all too well in his struggle to rescue Tate from his demons.

"I'm speechless, actually, Jax. Is that you in the middle? Is music something you enjoy?"

Jax nodded, and a shy smile crossed his face. "I love music. I was taking piano lessons when I got hurt and I had to give it up." His face shadowed. "I wanted to do it again but I just couldn't. I kept thinking it would be too damn hard and I couldn't see the sheet music or the keys and it would just be too damn awkward, plus who's got patience to teach a half-blind guy the piano?" The words rushed out like a verbal assault. "I enjoyed the music side more than the painting. I even wrote some songs."

Clay reached him before Tate did and laid a finger on Jax's lips. "Stevie Wonder plays the piano and he's been completely blind from birth. You can do it, Jax. You're a remarkable young man. You'll find a way to bring the music back. I have no doubt. And if we can help at all, you let us know."

Tate nodded and reached out and pummelled Jax on the arm. "What he said. He's pretty wise for an old, sleepy geezer." He threw a blinding smile at Clay and then bent down to start shoving empty paint cans into his bag. "Come on. We need to get this cleaned up—"

Just then, two youths that had been loitering on the periphery sidled up to them. Clay tensed but Tate nodded at them.

"Freddy. Mitch. How's it hanging, guys?"

The tall, skinny, ebony-skinned teen of about sixteen bobbed his head and reached out to fist pump Tate's outstretched knuckles. The other teen, a pale kid around the same age with untidy ginger hair, stood shuffling next to him.

"Coo, dude, cool. Me and my homey Mitch here are liking that dragon. The music one's not bad either." The boys' eyes flittered to Clay and he tried not to look threatening as he smiled at them.

Jax stood quietly, hands clutching his satchel. His chin lifted as he watched the other two young men.

"So." Freddy nodded then turned to look at Tate. "Is that for Lily? You're the guy who found her, right?" His jaw tightened.

Tate nodded. "Yeah. It's for Lily. She deserved it."

Freddy's head bobbed up and down fiercely. "That she did, man. She was legend. Such a damn little trooper. Me and Mitch here, we tried to get her to hospital to see about that cough, but she was having none of it. Bit our heads off if we even mentioned it." His face darkened. "Damn shame she did what she did. Sorry you had to find her that way, bro. Musta been a shock."

"Yeah." Tate's Adam's apple bobbed as he swallowed. "But it's done. And now she has a dragon to watch over her, so," he shrugged. "It is what it is."

"Word," Mitch finally said solemnly, darting a curious glance at Jax. "You did some damn fine art there, with the music shit. Looks good."

"Thanks," Jax murmured. "It's my first time."

Mitch stared at him. "Cool." He stood staring at Jax, and Clay saw the teen's face begin to flush.

Mitch gave Jax a huge grin. "You're really fucking beautiful, you know that?"

Jax's face went bright pink and he fumbled with the straps of his rucksack. Clay was pretty sure that speechless was a rare occasion for him. He swallowed a snort of laughter and Tate seemed to be doing the same.

"Er, thanks," Jax stammered.

Freddy smacked his friend on the back of his head, causing Mitch to yowl in pain. "You got no manners, you know that? Don't go telling guys that sort of thing unless you really know they swing your way, you fucking idiot. How many times do I have to tell ya?"

He cast an apologetic glance at them all. "Please don't beat us up, I'm really fucking sorry. Mitch here is a *homosekshual*," he drawled the word teasingly, "and his mouth runs away with him sometimes."

Clay wanted to burst into laughter. It sounded like the two things weren't mutually exclusive and it amused him no end.

"No problem," he said, seeing the glisten of tears in Tate's eyes as he tried to hold back his own mirth. "No offence taken." He glanced at Jax, whose face was less red now and whose lips curved in a slight smile.

"Well, we need to get off." Freddy announced with a dark glare at his friend, "Before my friend here decides to hump yours and then we'll really be in trouble. Later, dudes."

He yanked Mitch's arm and the two men walked away, Mitch casting a cheeky grin over his shoulder at Jax, whose smile grew wider. Clay was still struggling to hold back breaking into great guffaws of pure amusement.

Tate reached out and bumped Jax's shoulder with his. "See? I told you people would find you cute," he teased. "Mitch thinks you're beautiful, Jax. It's those blond curls."

"Fuck off," Jax said with a smirk. Tate chuckled and finished picking up the cans and stuffing them in his bag. Clay knew Jax hadn't definitely come out and said he was gay to Tate, but it was something Tate suspected. Based on his reaction today, Clay thought it was probably the case. Jax hadn't appeared uncomfortable at all with Mitch's admiration; he had in fact welcomed it.

Clay watched as Tate bent down and his arse strained the seams of the tight black jeans he wore, jeans that were stained with pink paint. Clay decided that later he'd definitely be peeling them off his lover and perhaps even putting the study desk to good use again. He stood back and took one last look at the murals that had sprung from nothing into statements of affection, remembrance and compassion. Tate looked at Clay and the love in his eyes spoke volumes. Clay grinned back at him and hoped his eyes conveyed the same look.

Oh yes, there was definitely going to be crazy, passionate sex when they got home. Then pizza. With anchovies, whether Tate liked it or not. Clay thought that might be the perfect ending to a perfect day.

Chapter 16

Seven p.m. on a Friday night and Tate was on his way back from a retirement party being held for a fellow policeman. The local pub near the police station where he'd worked was warm, friendly and had cheap drinks. Tate was driving so he hadn't imbibed too much. On a whim, knowing Clay was working late tonight (having texted him only ten minutes before) he decided to pay his boyfriend a late-night visit at the office.

Maybe we can catch a quick drink together before going home.

Happy with his plan, Tate swiped his own office key card to gain access to the building and took the lift up to Clay's office. He knocked briefly on the door and entered. He didn't bother waiting to be allowed in.

As he stepped inside Clay's office, his partner waved a hand at him, motioning to him to sit down. The scowl Clay had on his face disappeared momentarily at the sight of Tate to be replaced by a warm, albeit distracted grin. The scowl was soon back in all its ferocity. His mobile was glued to his ear and Tate bit back a grin at the poor unfortunate soul on the other side of the phone who was earning Clay's ire. Tate made himself comfortable in the plush visitor's chair in front of Clay's desk and sat back to enjoy the show.

He admired the sight of his man standing in full aggression mode. Tate drank in the sexy lines of Clay's broad shoulders in his rumpled white shirt, top button open, tie loosely slung around his neck. The tight curve of Clay's arse in his dark blue trousers and the shirtsleeves rolled up to his elbows was another tantalising image. Tate's cock began to swell, his fantasies taking reign. In his mind, he slowly undressed Clay, unzipping his trousers, pushing them down around his ankles and then slowly, teasingly, undoing the buttons on his shirt one by one…

"Fuck you, you miserable piece of shit." Clay's infuriated roar jolted Tate out of his dirty daydream. He sat up upright, watching Clay as he stormed around the room, phone gripped tightly in clenched fingers. "Don't you fucking tell me I can't fucking get my guy out of that damn place. Find me a way to get Graham out of that fucking hellhole. I don't care what it costs. The man has family waiting for him back here, and the last thing I want is him rotting in an Estonian prison cell. You're the negotiator. Fucking negotiate!"

There was a loud quacking sound from the other side of the phone and Tate raised an eyebrow as Clay looked over at him and shrugged apologetically.

Tate shook his head and gave Clay a slow smile. "Don't stop on my account," he murmured softly. "I think it's hot, you getting so mad. All that testosterone makes me horny." He ran a hand suggestively over the front of his jeans where the outline of his hard-on was already evident. Clay's face flushed and his eyes darkened. Tate licked his lips and chuckled when Clay turned away from him, obviously intent on ignoring his seduction. He continued his conversation with the negotiator on the phone.

"That sounds like a better idea; now you're talking my language. Like I said, no problem with expenses. Just get the man back home. Phone me later. Let me know when I can tell Janey she'll have her husband back. And Wally, don't fucking let me down. Or I will come over there, hunt you down and kill you myself."

The threat in his voice was unmistakeable. Tate was now so turned on it was all he could do not to bend Clay over his desk, rip his trousers off and take him right there. He gave a satisfied chuckle at that thought and tried to look innocent as Clay slammed his phone down on his desk and glared at him.

"What?" Tate said indignantly. "I'm not allowed to have fantasies?"

"Fantasies?" Clay growled. "You looked like you were about to blow right there. You had that look on your face."

Tate stood up and sauntered over to Clay, who leaned back against the desk, arms folded across his chest. His green eyes were watchful, but there was the hint of a grin on his lips. From the looks of the bulge in his crotch, he was beginning to get turned on too.

"What look?" Tate asked as he reached out a hand and slid Clay's tie through his fingers. "The one that says I find you so damn sexy I can't keep my hands off you?" He twirled the tie around in his fingers. "The one that says I want to rip your clothes off and fuck you right now?"

Clay's breathing was shallow, his pupils dark as he watched Tate's mouth. Tate was having a bit of trouble of breathing too. "Or the one that says that I want to taste you in my mouth, right here, right now?" He leaned in and swiped his tongue over Clay's lips, loving Clay's throaty moan. He pushed against Clay, rubbing their groins together as Clay gripped the side of his desk, knuckles white.

"We can't do this in here," he groaned softly. Tate brushed his hand against Clay's cock, which pushed forward instinctively. "There are cameras everywhere."

"I like the idea of putting on a show," Tate whispered in Clay's ear, as his tongue delved into its depths. A delicious shiver ran through Clay's body. Tate loved it. Loved that he could do this to a man who with one phone call could probably start a small war in some distant country. He loved hearing Clay's breaths deepen and his eyes become black as his pupils dilated with pleasure. He loved the control he currently had over this man who meant the world to him.

"We can't…" Clay groaned again. "I'm the damn boss, the last thing I need is them seeing me with my arse in the air with you inside me."

Tate's dick grew harder. "You want me to take you?" He licked a trail from Clay's jaw up to his mouth. Clay's lips parted and Tate slid his tongue against Clay's eager one then pulled away. "Push inside you until you scream, ram my hard prick into you and call your name when I come?"

Clay's breathing was ragged. His hands had slid inside Tate's shirt, finding warm skin, and Tate was in need of more of Clay's naked skin himself. "Christ, Tate. We need to go somewhere else to finish this, baby. It's gone too far already." He pulled away from Tate, slipping to the side and zipping himself up. He took Tate's hand and motioned to the door. "Come with me. I know where we can continue this seduction you have going."

Tate gave a sultry laugh as he was dragged out of Clay's office. "Seduction? Is that what I'm doing?"

Clay nodded as he tugged Tate along the darkened corridor. "Oh yes. That's exactly what you have going. And may I say I like it, so don't stop." He halted at a closed door and looked back at Tate, his eyes quirking devilishly. "This room has no cameras. You've been here so you know it's pretty comfy. Come on." He opened the door and pulled Tate inside.

The office common room, known fondly as the Chill Room by the employees, had a couple of couches, a luxurious shaggy pile rug and even a fireplace. In winter, the fireplace burned cosily and the room became a haven to escape the pressures and often ugly aspects of the work Clay's team did. As they entered the room, Tate found himself propelled backward to the floor, landing on the thick rug with an 'oomph' as Clay towered above him, fingers already unzipping his jeans.

"Oh no, you don't," Tate muttered and with one limber move, he shot up, unseated Clay from his hips and had him pinned beneath him. Clay shouted out in surprise but didn't struggle. Instead, he relaxed and grinned as he lay back, stretching his arms above his head with an air of nonchalance.

"I see which way this is going," he said, lips curving into a soft smile. "I hope you brought lube with you because I sure as hell don't have any in here."

Tate smirked. "I do, actually." Tate reached around to his back pocket and drew out his wallet. "It's only a sachet but I think it'll do."

"You *think*?" Clay's eyes widened in apprehension. "Hell, you'd better make sure it's mega-size for that huge cock of yours to fit in me. Economy just won't do."

Tate chuckled again and drew out the sachet. "I'll get you ready," he said slyly. Tate straddled Clay and once again unzipped him. "Up," he commanded and Clay obeyed, lifting his hips so Tate could draw the trousers and his boxers off his lean hips. "Turn over," he instructed, kneeling over Clay.

Clay did as he was told and was soon face-down on the rug, on his knees with legs apart. Tate could have spent hours staring at that sexy sight—Clay clad only in his shirt and tie, his tight, rounded backside, the dusky puckered hole, the balls that hung low with the jutting cock as Clay moaned and rutted down against the rug.

"Christ, hurry up and do something will you? I need you."

Tate stroked Clay's cheeks and ran his hands loving down his lover's hips. "Patience, you randy bastard. Who's running this show?"

"You," Clay whispered as his hips thrust against the rug. "Always you."

Those husky words spurred Tate, their timbre and passion inciting the flame in his groin and in his heart. He stood up and dropped his jeans and briefs to the floor, leaving his shirt on. Then he knelt down behind the prone and groaning man on the floor and ripped open the lube. Tate's own dick was so hard he thought he might have been able to drive nails into the wall with it. He was already leaking and wet and ready to be buried inside Clay. He dripped the lube onto Clay's hole, hearing Clay's hiss of pleasure, then slowly, deliberately, he pulled Clay's cheeks apart, thumbs sliding inside his man, widening him, delving deeper and deeper as Clay moaned in ecstasy.

"Oh, God, Tate, your fingers. It feels so good, love. Want your cock inside me, need to feel you. Love to feel you split me open, own me. Please, make love to me. Now."

Seeing Clay come apart in this way thrilled Tate in a way nothing else could. His tough man, his protector…the tables were turned and now it was Tate's turn to make sure Clay got what he needed.

"I'll make love to you," he whispered as he pushed inside that warm, tight place. "Not fucking tonight. Want to make you feel good."

Clay's groans below him as he rocked back against Tate's cock, impaling himself deeper, turned Tate's insides to mush. Clay's moans and whispered entreaties to go deeper was what Tate needed. He loved to see Clay give up, be taken and controlled. He wanted to be the one giving solace to him, loving him.

As they moved together as one, slow strokes and muffled cries, the fusion of their bodies performed a dance of both adoration and possession of each other, and to Tate, the world seemed to stop. His dick was aching for release and as he moved toward the welcome sensation of spilling his seed inside the man he loved, he whispered Clay's name.

That single utterance pushed Clay toward his orgasm. Clay shuddered beneath Tate as he came, muscles tightening around Tate's cock, causing him to lose him breath. As Clay emptied himself onto the rug, Tate cried out softly and gave one last thrust, then pulsed inside his lover, filling him and spending everything he had in payment of his debt of love. Boneless and content, Tate kissed Clay's shoulder, dropped soft kisses across his back, before moving out and off him to lie beside on the rug. The air had grown chilled and both of them shivered as they lay there half naked.

"I'm cold but I can't get up," Clay murmured as he raised a hand to stroke Tate's cheek tenderly.

Tate closed his eyes at that gesture. "Uh-huh. Me too." He snorted. "This rug of yours is going to need cleaning. There's spunk everywhere."

Clay waved a hand tiredly. "I'm sure it's seen worse. I'm not too sure what goes on in here after hours. I'll get it cleaned up."

He leaned up on one elbow and gazed down into Tate's eyes. "Thank you," he whispered softly and traced Tate's lips with a finger.

"For what?"

"For being here. For making love to me like you did tonight. For moving in with me. For just being you. Tate Williams. The man I love."

Tate's throat closed up with emotion at those heartfelt words. "I love you too, Clay Mortimer. I doubt I'd be here if it wasn't for you. I know I'm a pain in the arse sometimes, but you keep forgiving me, taking me back."

Clay chuckled. "Pain in the arse is right. There could have been a tad more lube." His face softened. "And forgiving is all part of loving someone." He shivered. "I don't want to break up the romance but I'm fucking freezing. What say we get dressed and get home, get into bed and we can do a little more lovemaking? Where it's nice and warm." He shivered again, goose bumps breaking out on his skin.

Tate nodded and struggled to his feet. "I say a big fat yes to that proposal." He hunted around for his pants and put them on, watching Clay do the same. "Can we go home in your car, and I'll pick mine up tomorrow? I don't think I've enough energy to drive."

Clay rolled his eyes. "I guess. I'll need to pick up my keys from my office. Let me go get them." He gave Tate a lingering kiss from cold lips then disappeared into the hallway. Tate followed, limbs tired, body satisfied and heart warmed.

When he got to Clay's office, Tate saw him standing there, holding a small white card in his hand. Clay turned, almost guiltily, as he came in. He seemed a little uncertain of himself,

"What you got there? Are you ordering Chinese? Is it from Wongs or that other place?" Tate reached out to take the card and Clay held it away.

"No, it's not bloody Chinese. It's something I was going to give you tomorrow, but I think maybe I should give it to you now." Clay shrugged. "I think the time is right."

Tate's curiosity was piqued. "What is it?"

Clay handed him the card silently and cocked his head to one side, waiting.

Tate stared down at the card and his eyes prickled uncomfortably. He looked down at the card, then up at Clay. "Is this for real?"

The business card read:

Tate Williams. Lead Investigator, Mortimer Investigations.

Clay nodded. "Of course it is. You deserve to come on board more than anyone I know. It's time you went back out into the field. You're ready and I want you to know I have faith in you." He shuffled uncomfortably. "I also want to talk to you about becoming a partner in the business, a shareholder, with equal rights. I want us to manage this business together. But I guess that's a conversation for—oomph."

He didn't finish his sentence because Tate's mouth was on his, kissing him with every fibre of his being. Tate wrapped his arms around Clay's neck and held on as passion and love spent itself in every flick of a tongue, every press of lips against lips and every soft murmur of breath into each other's mouths.

Finally Tate let Clay go and rested his forehead against his lover's. "Thanks," he said huskily. "For believing in me."

"That's no hardship, love," Clay said softly as he nudged Tate's nose with his. "It's a privilege."

He grinned and moved to pick up his keys from his desk.

Tate's heart was full and he had no more words. They'd both come a long way since those early days of pain and grief. It had taken endurance and patience on both their sides to get to where they were now. It had taken a feat of Clay.

Tate knew he would still have some way to go to be completely healed and that perhaps he might never put his ordeal totally behind him. But he had Clay. And friends. People who cared about him. Some people didn't have the half of what he had.

Clay was his rock, his soul mate. And Tate knew without a shadow of doubt that he was Clay's. And that simple fact meant that whatever life might throw at them in the future, whatever dangers or sadness they may encounter, they would do it together.

CROSS TO BARE

Chapter 1

Fashion faux pas were something designer Laverne Debussy-Smith could handle. Clothing that was an assault on the eyes was regularly relegated to the rubbish bin. Laverne had been known to strip the garments off some unwitting soul at her company and replace it with something a little more appropriate. She also had a knack for consoling pouting, excitable, needy models of both genders.

But a wild-eyed, naked man standing in the reception of the company premises fell well outside of her comfort zone.

Lenny James, gay, transvestite, and aka leading London designer Laverne Debussy-Smith, stared at the sweating, unkempt man currently presenting his bare backside to the receptionist, whose eyes were as wide as a cheap polyester tie.

"Mr Morgan says he needs a new suit, and he needs you to make him one," the receptionist, Lauren, stammered as she averted her eyes from the spectacle in front of her. "He took off all his clothes and threw them at me then asked to see you." She gestured to the sad pile of garments on the floor behind her.

Lenny nodded as he stepped forward and eyed the nude man out with a practiced eye. "I see. Am I to assume this is my ten o'clock appointment then—Mr Nathaniel Morgan?"

Mr Morgan swallowed and nodded. "Yes, that would be me." His modulated tone was at odds with his salt–and-peppered hairy chest, his slight paunch, and from what Lenny could see, a rather well-endowed set of genitals huddled in a messy bush of grey hair. "I couldn't wear that dreadful suit any longer, and I insist you fit me for a new one."

The man clearly had a screw loose but a fine sense of fashion, Lenny thought as he circled the naked Mr Morgan. "I'm flattered you feel the need to be so enthusiastic, but perhaps you could come into the fitting room so I can see what I can do for you? May I offer you a towel or something to wrap around your—"

"No. I'm not wearing anything other than one of your suits." The man's voice was firm, and Lenny sighed. He really wasn't in the mood to force a grown man to get dressed here in an open-plan office.

"Very well." He cast an eye around at his open-mouthed, astonished staff and beckoned to one of them. "Lance, could you make sure fitting room one is clear please, so I can ask Mr Morgan to step in?" He knew there'd been some other customer due for a fitting in there and didn't want to shock them with an unsolicited porn moment. It was also the nearest fitting room, and Lenny really didn't want to escort Nathaniel Morgan down the corridor to the other one at the end of the building. "If it's occupied, move them into number two."

Lance nodded, a faint grin on his face, and hurried away to do his boss's bidding. Lenny smoothed down his navy blue wool business dress with its geometric collar and tried to look as if having a naked man in his reception area was indeed an everyday occurrence.

"Have you come far today for this appointment, Mr Morgan?" Lenny enquired. Perhaps if he could find out from where the man had come, he could be returned there.

"Only from home. I slipped out when Mallory wasn't looking."

"And Mallory would be?" Lenny raised an eyebrow at his would-be customer.

Mr Morgan sniffed. "My partner and carer. He never lets me go anywhere unless he comes along. But I wanted a new suit and he didn't listen to me. I knew he wouldn't let me come here alone so I started a fire in the microwave and then slipped away." He smiled proudly. "I'm not totally useless, you know. I can do some things for myself. I walked here on my own."

Lenny's heart broke at that brave statement. The man obviously had dementia or something similar and this was his way of making sure he asserted himself.

"That is brave, my lovely," Lenny murmured gently. "But I'm sure Mallory will be worried about you. I think we need to get in touch with him and let him know you're safe."

Mr Morgan's eyes narrowed. "I don't remember the number," he muttered slyly.

Lauren motioned at Lenny from behind the desk. She gestured for him to come over. Lenny sidled over, smiling at Mr Morgan as he did so. No point in spooking the man.

"I saw some cards with his name on them in his jacket pocket," Lauren whispered. "When he flung his suit at me, they fell out. I thought they were business cards, but on second thought, they looked more like identification cards, the sort you give people when they forget who they are. I'll have a look at them too see if we have a number for this Mallory guy. Or a home number."

Lenny nodded as Lance came back into the room. "You do that. Otherwise, chicken, Google is a marvellous place. Check those cards, and see if we can find out more about Mr Morgan. I'll keep him occupied in the meantime."

"Fitting room one is now free, Laverne," Lance said with a wicked smile. The boy was enjoying this far too much, Lenny thought in irritation. Thank God his employee Leslie Scott was on holiday or who knew how this would play out. Lenny knew Leslie would be heartbroken he'd missed all the fun.

"Well, let's get you into that fitting room and have you measured up for that suit, Mr Morgan. Would you like to follow me?"

Lenny gestured to the nude man to follow, and like a shepherd with an errant sheep, Lenny led the way into the fitting room, hearing the squeals of laughter and pent-up amusement giving way behind him. He grinned. He could safely say that at this office there was never a dull moment.

An hour later, having taken measurements and listened to Nathaniel Morgan's random comments about grooming cats, how to avoid bad theatre makeup, the vagaries of the National Health Service, and numerous curses about how mobile phones were the devil's work, there was a knock on the door. Lauren came in with a burly, worried middle-aged man who sagged in relief at seeing Nathaniel Morgan currently clad in grey suit fabric wrapped around his hips.

"Nate. For God's sake, what on earth were you thinking? I was so worried about you. And it took me ages to sort out that microwave emergency you created."

"Laverne, this is Mallory Crane. He's Mr Morgan's life partner and carer." Lauren smiled softly and left the room.

Lenny stood, grimacing as his knees creaked and his back protested from kneeling down taking inner seam measurements. If Mallory was taken aback at the sight of a man in a dress and a blonde wig, he didn't show it.

"Mr Crane. I'm glad we managed to get hold of you. I'm almost done here and then perhaps you can get your partner home."

Nathaniel's face creased in a frown. "I had to get out, Mall. I was going crazy and you just didn't understand I really needed this suit. I have a premiere to attend later this month and a Debussy will really make everyone sit up and take notice."

Lenny didn't miss the look of sadness that crossed Mallory's face. "I know, darling. You're going to look absolutely fabulous. But you know you should have brought me with you. I didn't say no to the suit, just that we needed to wait so I could go with you. I had no idea you'd made an appointment already. That was very enterprising of you." His voice was teasing but Lenny heard the despair in it, and his heart ached.

Mallory held up a black carrier bag. "I brought you your old Debussy suit to wear back home. I'm sure when your new one is ready, Ms Debussy-Smith will make sure you get it for the event. Isn't that right, ma'am?" His eyes flicked hopefully at Lenny.

Lenny nodded. "Of course. I'll make sure it's personally delivered. Now if you'd like to change over there behind the screens, I'll finish up the measurements."

Mallory smiled at Lenny gratefully and, taking Nathaniel's elbow, he escorted his partner over to the dressing area. "You get dressed then I'll take you home. I think we both need some refreshment; maybe a good whisky will go down well."

Mallory left Nathaniel to get dressed and walked back to Lenny. "Thank you so much," Mallory said with a sad huff. "Nate is in the mid stages of dementia and it's a full-time job making sure he's comfortable and that he sees some quality of life."

Lenny heaved a deep sigh. "I'm so sorry. It must be a dreadful thing seeing someone you love go through that."

Mallory nodded. "We've been together over thirty years. Nate used to be on the stage and he's been in a few big films. He still lives in the entertainment world, and to be honest, I let him. Why not. It makes him happy." He cast a loving glance at his partner who was shrugging his arms into his suit jacket. "I love him as much as I did then and it's hard to see him this way." Tears glistened in Mallory's eyes. "But you made him happy, and for that I thank you. It can be hard for others to deal with these sorts of situations."

Lenny had a lump in his throat. "I can't even imagine."

"He doesn't really have a premiere next month. But at least he'll have his new suit. As you might have gathered, he's a big fan of your work."

"I'll make sure he gets his suit," Lenny promised. "It's the least I can do for a fan."

"Just let me know what I owe you for the garment and I'll settle it up."

Lenny shook his head. "There'll be no charge, sweetheart," he said. "If it makes your man happy, that's enough for me. He deserves some pleasure out of his life given what it's thrown at him, and you."

Mallory's eyes welled with tears and he couldn't help a sniffle. "Oh God, that is so sweet of you, dear lady. You cannot even know how much I appreciate that. Money's always tight of course, and a new suit was a bit of an extravagance. But it makes him happy, so how could I have refused?"

Later, watching Mallory escort his partner out of the building with a winsome smile and a cheery wave goodbye, Lenny felt a sense of bitter sweetness sweep through him. One day he hoped to have what they had: an overwhelming love and devotion to another man that transcended anything the world may throw at them.

The story of Nathaniel and Mallory was tragic. But it also showed there was always hope in finding that special someone who's accepted life's challenges, and that acceptance was something to aspire to even if it had eluded Lenny all his life.

Chapter 2

Sweat, musky-scented skin and five o'clock shadow stubble. Skin slapped against skin, amidst grunts and sighs of passion, as Lenny lay on his back in bed, knees pulled up, and watched the man inside him lose it. Lenny gripped his hands tighter around his lover's hips, forcing him deeper. The burn in his arse intensified as the thrusts grew frenzied.

"I'm feeling it," Ryan Bishop panted. Sweat beaded his forehead. "You know how to use that arse of yours. No matter how many times we do this, it feels like the first time."

Lenny reached up and brushed a hand across the sweaty auburn curls of Ryan's head, eyes drinking in the flushed face of a man who had been his occasional lover for more than three years.

"Yeah," he gasped as he surrendered to the sensation of his cock slapping against the other man's stomach. "I'm feeling it too, almost there, honey. Keep going."

Hungry lips claimed Lenny's in a frantic kiss that made him harder. He pumped himself to climax then groaned as his balls contracted, and his dick ached as he shot. Ryan shuddered then collapsed in a boneless heap on top of him.

After a minute of heavy breathing into his ear, Lenny chuckled. "Hey, I'm not a continental cushion. Get off me. You're damn heavy even though you're a little fella."

Ryan wasn't one of those tightly toned muscle jockeys Lenny was used to, but slim, curvy and wiry with a winning smile. His bed partner laughed and rolled off. He slid off the condom, tied it and threw it on the bedside table. "Are you saying I'm fat *and* short, Len?" He pouted. "I'll have you know I'm going to the damn gym three times a week." He patted his flat tummy. "I have to work hard to keep it like this." He gave Lenny an envious look. "I'm not like you with those natural fucking sculpted abs and tight arse. You put me to shame you do, you gorgeous bastard."

He reached over to the bedside table and lit up a cigarette, inhaling then blowing perfect circles, which floated across the room. Lenny settled back in the bed and pulled the duvet up across his waist. He was sated, tired and didn't give a fuck about the sticky mess on his belly and sheets.

"It's been too long since I got laid," Lenny said.

Ryan lay on his side. His blue eyes were soft, his hair curling around ears that were pointy and elf like. Lenny loved them—loved biting them and tugging on them until Ryan could take it no more, cursing him as he came.

Ryan pouted. "Yeah, I'm sorry about that. I've been travelling so much with the theatre company lately with the new production that I'm nowhere near around as much as I used to be. These booty calls with you have become quite infrequent." Ryan was also Delilah Delish, a renowned drag queen and one of the stars of the current hit musical 'Come to Bed Baby', which had swept the West End and other counties alike.

Ryan's body stretched out, catlike, as he settled back on the bed, arms resting on the pillow. He observed Lenny affectionately. Neither of them had ever felt the chemistry for each other to make their relationship anything other than fuck buddies. Ryan had another lover he saw regularly, a man who Lenny thought Ryan cared about more than he'd admit. But Mango Munroe was commitment-phobic and not prepared to be in a monogamous relationship. Lenny liked Mango, and it broke Lenny's heart seeing Ryan pine after a man he couldn't have the way he wanted.

Lenny reached out to caress his lover's dimpled chin. "I know that, honey. I enjoy you when I can get you. In the meantime there's my left hand and the occasional blowjob or fuck at the club. You know me. Not exactly the most eligible bachelor in town."

His tone was dry but the truth behind his words hurt. Lenny's penchant for dressing up as a woman during the day and becoming Laverne Debussy-Smith didn't help his love life either. He and Laverne were a package deal. He hadn't yet found a man who could or would take them both on. One who wouldn't try and convince him to give one persona up for the other, or mollycoddle him, thinking he was weaker than he was.

He'd had two relationships in his life that ended badly, not counting his most recent experience. One in his twenties with a much older man who at first had accepted the quirkiness and unique nature of Lenny a.k.a. Laverne. However, six months in, Vincent had met some young, Latin lover boy and decided that in fact, Lenny's dual personality had become somewhat tiresome and Lorenzo, 'such a sweet young man' (emphasis on 'man') had promised him so much more. He'd left to go to Sicily and as far as Lenny knew, he'd never come back.

The other, a man eight years his junior, had been a DJ with a local dance club. It had been a passionate, fun and sex-fuelled affair that had fizzled out when Dorian got tired of Lenny's rising success as Laverne. The younger man had been happy as long as Lenny had been a nobody and could do things like attend rock concerts and festivals at will, without what Dorian called 'boring, plebeian commitments.' However, as soon as Lenny's fashion career began to take off, Dorian had begrudged the time Lenny had spent building both the career and Laverne. Dorian said he was a young man and deserved more. They'd agreed to call it a day.

Recently, Brook, Lenny's sexy lover with skin the colour of polished mahogany, had gotten under Lenny's skin. Lenny didn't want to think about Brook too much. He'd really liked the man and thinking of how the relationship had ended made him feel both regretful and a little pissed off.

Ryan frowned as he took another drag of his cigarette. "You're a fine catch for any guy. Don't bring yourself down. I've tried to set you up with dates and you always say no. How are you going to find someone if you don't go out there and socialise?"

Lenny snorted as he sat up and picked up his wine glass from the bedside table. He tossed the dregs back and then waved the glass at his friend. "I will never, ever, go out on any blind date you set up ever again. Remember you tried to pair me up last year with a casino player from L.A. who wanted to take me back to Vegas with him and had insisted on me being Laverne twenty-four-seven for the rest of my life? Then there was that real cutie, the tennis player on his way to being a star who thought I might like to be his 'daddy.' I might be thirty-five, but I am *not* old enough to be anybody's daddy. Not like he wanted me to be anyway."

Lenny winced when he remembered the abortive end of his date with the sexy twenty-six–year-old athlete Mitchell Cross. Mitchell's kink had involved a request for a golden shower. He'd then asked if Lenny would tie him up while he was covered in pee and spank him. And it hadn't stopped there. Mitchell had asked Lenny to fuck him with the biggest, nastiest dildo Lenny had ever seen. The whole scenario had made his cock shrivel, his balls retract and his guts churn. He liked a bit of a kink, but Mitchell took things too far. Lenny's answer had been a resounding 'No' to it all.

"Then you introduced me to Cock Robin." Lenny shuddered. "I mean, first, that was his real name, which should have been a red flag, and second, who knew the guy liked taxidermy and had a house full of stuffed animals?"

Ryan giggled and slapped Lenny's arm. "Oh, I'd forgotten that one. He seemed like such a nice guy. A real stunner."

Cock Robin had indeed been a stunner, with huge green eyes and wavy black hair like a man from a Renaissance painting. The blowjob Cock had promised had been okay to start with as Lenny had closed his eyes and tried to ignore the recriminating stares of animals shot for pleasure then mounted on walls and tables. It was when Cock had conversed with a stuffed owl about his progress that Lenny's spine had tingled and his skin prickled in horror.

Hearing 'See, I told you he'd like it' and 'Watch his face, see how good I make him feel?' being spoken to a large barn owl perched on a side table as Cock's blowjob progressed had been the last straw. Lenny had muttered something about remembering he was supposed to meet an out-of-town friend, pushed a surprised Cock off his dick and zipped up his pants. He'd never been so glad to get out of a house in all his life.

Ryan blew another plume of smoke into the air. "I admit my track record hasn't been good." He laughed at Lenny's disgusted harrumph.

"Good?" Lenny grumbled as he settled down to try and get some sleep. It was after midnight after all and he had work in the morning. "It's atrocious. I'll find my own partners, thank you very much. Now hurry up and finish that damn smoke so we can get some shut eye."

Lenny snuggled into his pillow. He heard Ryan take one last drag then grind the cigarette out in the ashtray next to the bed. The bed shifted and a strong, slim arm wrapped around his waist from behind.

"Night," Ryan whispered as he spooned Lenny, his legs pressing into his.

“Night, honey,” Lenny murmured. “If you fancy waking me in the morning to give me head, feel free. I know you hate wasting morning wood.”

A pinch to the skin on his stomach and a soft mock growl in his ear made him yowl but smile. Lenny closed his eyes and surrendered to the pull of the sandman.

Chapter 3

There was a certain satisfaction in sitting across a table in front of a pair of tight-arsed, stuffy business brokers while fluttering one's mascaraed eyelashes at them. Lenny didn't usually camp up his persona as Laverne, but he already knew that the two men across the table from him had no intention of giving him the loan he needed. One of them had made it clear with his smirk and loaded questions. The other looked as if he was still on the fence. Resigned to that fact, Lenny thought he'd have a little bit of fun.

He shifted in his chair then leaned forward, making sure that his mock boobs swelled and heaved like the rising bough of the Titanic. One man's eyes were drawn inexorably to Lenny's rather tight but padded tits and he choked back a chuckle. The guy had been casting veiled disgusted looks at him during the appointment and it was time for some payback.

"Well," Lenny drawled. "It appears we're at a bit of an impasse, gentlemen. You want me to sign over my life blood to you and I'm declining to do so because I think you're greedy. I have no problem sharing, but twenty-five percent of my business as a shareholding to grant me a small initial loan of thirty thousand pounds is rather over the top. I can offer you ten percent as a stake, and that's as much as I'm prepared to give."

He tucked a piece of blonde wig back behind his ear. Damn business angels. Lenny had a lot of time for them because they were fair and a necessary evil, but to ask for a quarter of his hard-won business as an investment against future borrowing was damn cheeky. He knew he'd have the ten percent paid back as soon as possible and regain control of his business, but he'd have one helluva long time doing that at twenty-five percent. The fashion industry incurred a high price in operating as he did and while Debussy's was a well-known brand and highly profitable, it wasn't Ralph Lauren.

Lenny raised one brow at the group and waited.

"Ms Debussy-Smith, we believe it to be a fair percentage given the risk you're asking us to take." The man who'd been giving him the stink eye, Keith, looked like a rotund seal, all grey skin and flabby jowls. “Your business is doing well, your reputation is sterling, but let’s face it, you are a little over-extended. And, of course, you’re known to be a little, well, eccentric in your business dealings. I mean, you give away large amounts of your profit, which should be being ploughed back into the business. How do we know we’ll get our money back when you’re giving it away like that?” He looked around at his colleague, whom Lenny had dubbed Grey Hair because he couldn’t remember his name, who stared at Keith with horror. It was obvious he didn’t like the way this was going and for a minute, Lenny felt sorry for him. Then he steeled himself. Either of them could stop the drivel if they had the balls.

Lenny wanted to punch Keith. He imagined ‘eccentric’ to the sneering Keith also meant the unstated ‘*You dress up like a woman. Oh, and you’re a poofter.*’ Reining in his urge to plant his fist in Keith’s nose, Lenny leaned forward and placed a well-manicured hand on the table, tapping the surface gently. He didn’t wear false nails, but kept his own neatly trimmed and varnished with clear nail polish. The ominous thudding sound made the man across from him gaze at Lenny’s moving fingers as if hypnotised.

“I see,” Lenny mused. “You mean those charities I support? The Albert Kennedy Trust for homeless LGBT youth? Galop? Pace? And of course, let’s not forget Stonewall.” He bared his teeth in a snarl. “Gentlemen, giving to these charities is my way of giving something back to my community. I know what it’s like to be a gay kid on the streets, so to me this is a non-negotiable aspect of my business. I put money into these charities so I can sleep at night. My business profits may suffer a little but all it means is that its takes longer to get where I want to be.”

“Well, perhaps if you didn’t give your money away, you wouldn’t be asking us to borrow more money now,” Keith said, a smug expression on his face. “Perhaps you could put your money back into your business and leave the donations to these minority groups to other people,” he said disdainfully. “I’m sure there are other more deserving charities out there that might not need so much money. I mean, these *homeless* people run riot all over the city and everyone panders to them like damn sycophants.” He flapped a careless hand to illustrate whatever point he thought he was making. His condescending tone echoed in the room like the knell of doom.

There was a deathly silence as Lenny digested Keith's words with a sense of disbelief. Grey Hair had a panicked look on his face and he half raised himself from his chair.

"Now, Keith, that's not really the spirit we came in," he stammered, casting a panicked glance at Lenny, whose face was probably twisting into something resembling Quasimodo—he was that furious. "I assure you, Ms Debussy-Smith, we don't all hold that same opinion—"

His voice trailed off as Lenny rose up from his seat like a leviathan and pointed a finger at the puzzled-looking Keith. Lenny was glad he'd worn his highest heels today; he towered over the others, a change from his average five foot nine.

The man doesn't have a fucking clue how insensitive and rude he's just been. I want to fucking deck him one.

"Minority groups? More deserving charities?" Lenny blasted. "Are you insinuating that I shouldn't give to these charities because they support LGBT causes and that's a 'minority' in your eyes? People dying on the street, being beaten to death for being different, having nowhere to stay because their families don't want them anymore, like a damn dog bought for Christmas and then abandoned. We're minorities to you?"

I don't want to do business with people like you anyway, arseholes.

His voice got louder with every sentence and both men were now on their feet, clutching briefcases and looking very uncomfortable.

"Ms Debussy-Smith, I can assure you that's not our judgement to give. Keith was totally out of line saying what he did." Grey Hair glared at his colleague who looked back, seemingly stupefied that his crass comment had caused such ire.

"You bet your fucking life he was," Lenny spat. His bosom heaved inside his ruched tailored blouse and for a split second he wondered if his falsies would hold firm. "I'd suggest you both get the fuck out of my office right now before I rip your damn heads off and shove them up your arses."

The men's eyes widened as they clutched satchels and made a beeline for the door. Keith opened it and turned back, mouth open as if to speak. Grey Hair muttered something to the effect of, 'The boss is going to crucify us, and he won't be happy with this turn of events.' Lenny hoped with all his heart that was true.

He strode forward and waggled his fingers menacingly in front of Keith's face, as the man appeared about to speak. "Not another damned word from you, you little thundershit," he warned as he pushed them out into the corridor. He loved that swearword, stolen from a past mentor. "I might look like a lady but under this skirt, I'll damn well kick your arse anytime, you prick."

There was a hush in the open-plan environment as Lenny's employees watched the two men beetle quickly over to the lift. Lenny's PA, Naomi, was seated at her desk outside his office. She stared after the fleeing men with wide eyes. Lenny watched them go, smoothing down his Donna Karan jersey pencil skirt.

"So…good meeting then?" There was a gentle snigger at the end of the comment.

Lenny whipped around and glared at the black-haired, blue-eyed vision in front of him. Leslie Scott, one of Lenny's trainee buyers, and his favourite employee stood staring at him from the foot of Naomi's desk. His sapphire eyes sparkled and his face bore a cheeky grin.

"I don't have time for dickheads or homophobic wankers," Lenny growled angrily. "Shouldn't you be working and not listening to my business conversations?"

Leslie waved a slim hand. His face creased in merriment. "Well, one couldn't help but hear, Laverne, dear. You were so loud," he snorted. "Would you really have shoved their heads up their bums? 'Cause I have to say, I'd love to watch that…"

Naomi chortled then put a hand over her mouth as Lenny glared at her.

Sometimes he thought this young man needed a good spanking, although Leslie probably got that at home with his ex-porn star boyfriend Oliver. Lenny's eyes narrowed when he saw what Leslie was wearing. His anger at his abortive meeting disappeared and a familiar amusement took its place, sprinkled with a fond frustration.

"Leslie, is that my new waistcoat design you're wearing?"

Leslie flushed. "Yes, but it's not what you think," he gabbled. "Sophie was fitting it on me to see how it looked and when I heard the noise from your office, I came over. I'm not taking it home, Laverne."

His voice broke off wistfully as he ran loving fingers over the fabric of the silk waistcoat. Leslie loved good fashion and had a great eye for it, and for the fabrics needed to make the garments.

Sophie was one of Lenny's trainee designers working with him on a new style and loved using Leslie as a model. However, Lenny had no doubt that if Leslie could get away with it, the waistcoat would disappear and become a Sherlock Holmes mystery to solve.

"Make sure it doesn't," Lenny commanded. "That's earmarked for some music awards next year, for Jett Pepper from Windfall. He's commissioned it especially for the event."

Leslie's jaw dropped open and he stared down at the garment he wore with wonder. Lenny smirked. He knew Leslie had a thing for the sexy and burly lead singer of one of the most sought-after alternative bands in the country.

"Jett Pepper's going to be wearing this?" he breathed. "Oh—my—God. I'm wearing his waistcoat. That is radical, I can't even…"

His voice tailed off and Lenny grinned at the hero worship in his young protégé's eyes. Just seeing Leslie seemed to have restored his good mood. The younger man had that effect on people. Naomi smiled as she went back to her typing.

"Not that exact one, chicken," Lenny murmured. "That's a prototype."

"Oh. But still…" Leslie sighed deeply. "It's still special."

"Very special," Lenny agreed. "And I still want to see it in the Arbour at the end of the year, as a sample, and not in your closet. That's my one and only warning, Leslie, my sweet pea."

Leslie had a habit of acquiring soiled spec suits and garments for his own personal use. It wasn't often, and Lenny knew about each one of them in advance. Leslie worked on the 'May I borrow it and then never bring it back' principle of ownership. Lenny didn't begrudge him them as they were of no use to anyone once they were slightly soiled, and the younger man put in a lot of overtime and was always willing to help out. He was so in love with the items that Lenny was glad they went to someone who adored them as much as he did. Still, Lenny thought he needed to assert his 'boss' authority before half of Debussy's stock went missing.

Leslie stuck a small, pink tongue out at him. "Oliver's buying me my own suits," he said haughtily. "His are too big for me to wear, so now we have a special closet at his house for my stuff. So there." He smirked and Lenny wanted to spank that bubble butt.

He narrowed his eyes instead and drawled, "I know. I saw the order come through. One deep grey Debussy Fashionista in size…small." Now it was Lenny's turn to smirk.

Leslie's face flushed pink. "I am *so* not small all over," he sputtered. "In case that's what you're inferring, boss. Yes, I might be slim and not so tall but I'll have you know—"

Lenny interrupted him with a grin. "Yes, I've heard all about the monster in your pants." He rolled his eyes. "Oliver's a lucky man indeed, I imagine then?"

His PA gave a muffled sound and turned to scramble in her bag for something. A tissue to wipe her streaming eyes from an amusement overload, Lenny guessed.

"I am *so* not talking to you about *that*," Leslie sniffed. "You need to get your own sex fantasies." He smiled wickedly. "I remember you telling me about some guy, Brook, a while ago that you were seeing? You seemed quite keen on him last time you mentioned him. How's that whole thing going?" He waggled his hands like fluttering birds.

Lenny felt a squirm of unease. "I haven't seen him in a while," he muttered.

Make that I haven't returned any of his calls or made the effort to stay in touch in the past weeks.

The one man Lenny had thought he might have developed a relationship with had spoilt it all one night with one unthinking comment after watching *Ru Paul's Drag Race*. Lenny thought he'd probably overreacted to the casual comment, but it was too late now. The damage was done. Brook might have been 'the one,' but, in the end, he'd turned out to be like everyone else—conservative. And not in the political sense.

"Oh?" Leslie's look of concern was sweet. "I thought you guys had something special going on."

Lenny frowned. "It didn't pan out, Tinkerbell. Not everything can be a happy ever after, you know."

He thought his knee-jerk reaction to an off-the-cuff comment from Brook had been as good a reason as any to distance himself from someone that could be dangerous to his heart.

He regretted his terse words as a shadow fell across Leslie's lovely face. Lenny didn't begrudge Leslie his own HEA at all. Lenny reached out and chucked Leslie under the chin. The younger man's eyes stared at him uncertainly. "I'm sorry, sweetie. I shouldn't have said that. I'm being a bitch."

"You really liked him," Leslie said. "Did things get so bad that you couldn't fix it? Because everything can be fixed, you know." His tone grew earnest. "Maybe you should give him a call? Send him a Jacquie Lawson card like I did for Oliver?"

Lenny couldn't help a chuckle at that. "I'm not sure sending him a cheeky monkey card will help. But thanks for the thought." He sighed. "No, he said something I didn't think boded well for the future and—"

"What?" Leslie's eyes widened and he pursed his lips. "Hell, I say things all the time that people don't agree with or like but they still talk to me."

Laverne bit back a smile at that. Naomi made a choking sound as she tried to contain her laughter at Leslie's ingenuous comment. His predilection for putting his foot in his mouth was well known in the office.

Leslie put his hands on slim hips and scowled. "Perhaps you were being a tad over-sensitive?"

Lenny snorted. "A *tad*? Who are you, bloody Little Lord Fauntleroy?" He grinned to take the sting out of his words. Leslie pressed lips together, sapphire blue eyes staring at Lenny as he waited for his reply. A curl of black hair swept down onto his forehead and he brushed it away absently.

The regret in Lenny's voice was self-evident when he answered. "I appreciate the worry, love, but it doesn't matter. He'll have moved on by now, no doubt."

Brook had been a catch of note. He'd been tall and wide shouldered, with burnished bronze velvet skin and the most beautiful twinkling brown eyes. Coupled with a sense of humour and a deep, melodious voice, Brook had sent Lenny's insides and emotions into a spin.

"Humph," Leslie sniffed. "I hear nothing but an excuse there, boss."

Lenny scowled at his employee who gazed back at him, wide eyes innocent. "Yes, well, we're all entitled to our opinions, aren't we?" Lenny said.

Leslie rolled his eyes again and heaved a deep *I'm so put upon* sigh.

Laverne ignored it. "Anyway, I'm sure you have work to do, my young lad, so if you wouldn't mind getting back to it, I know that the boss would be *ever* so grateful."

Sarcasm was wasted on Leslie, Lenny knew, but it made *him* feel better.

Leslie shrugged. "Okay, your wish is my command." He turned and waggled his pert arse cheekily. "This is me, leaving to go back to work, before the big, bad, boss throws a hissy fit because she's so *wrong*." He sang the last word loudly, and Lenny reached out and picked up an eraser sitting on Naomi's desk and wound up to throw it at the back of Leslie's head.

Naomi sent Lenny an exasperated look. "Honestly, you know he'll evade it. The man is like a greased piglet with eyes in the back of his head."

Lenny threw it as hard as he could, and true to form, Leslie dodged the missile and gave a cackle as he wriggled his backside again and disappeared into another office.

Naomi gave a soft chuckle. "See?"

Lenny gave her a mock frosty look. "That's enough from you, missy. Now do you think you could run along and get me a latte from downstairs? I have a hankering for one."

Naomi stood and picked up her bag. "No problem. I'll have a quick smoke break while I wait for that new yummy barista to get your coffee." She winked at him.

Lenny's eyes widened. "There's a yummy barista? Hell, gurl. Sit your little ass down. I'll go myself." He waved his hand at her as she sat down with a pout. "But you can go for your smoke when I get back, I promise."

He left Naomi grumbling about the unfairness of it all as he sauntered across the office floor towards the lift. A sexy barista and a latte was what he needed to soothe his soul and brighten the day.

Chapter 4

Brook Hunter glowered at the file in front of him. His brow furrowed in a scowl worthy of a king about to behead his favourite courtier. The man in front of his desk sat still, eyes staring down at nervous fingers, his demeanour one of defiance no doubt coupled with a sick knowledge he'd gone too far.

Brook leaned back, steepling his fingers together. He didn't like Keith Turner at the best of times. Keith was an opinionated, insufferable, homophobic twat and if he hadn't been the son-in-law of the owner of the business, Brook would have fired him a long time ago. But this latest incident was not one he was prepared to let go. He ran this specialist broker finance unit and he'd hold people accountable for their actions.

"You insulted a customer, made judgemental comments about the way the woman ran her business, probably broke the law, and ended up getting both you and Derek thrown out of her office in front of a whole room of people. You asked for far more collateral to cover the risk than we needed, based on your own personal prejudices." Brook's voice was deceptively quiet. Inside, he raged. "I'm not sure that's how we choose to conduct business at Lively, Lewis and Hardcastle. Our reputation is everything and you've gone and tarnished it."

Keith muttered something and Brook leaned forward in his chair, eyebrows raised.

"Sorry, Keith, I didn't quite catch that."

"That person was a bloody weirdo." Keith snarled, looking him in the eyes. "It's a bloke dressed as woman. I mean who does that? Can't they decide if they're a man or a bloody woman?" His lips twitched in disgust and Brook had to physically restrain himself from launching across the desk to smack the man.

While it might not be *his* personal choice to wear women's clothes, he knew he couldn't judge those who did, even if he thought it was a bit—well, strange. Brook was a conservative man, and he'd been raised by two diplomats with old-fashioned, traditional family values.

Thinking of men in women's clothing brought back memories of Lenny and him laughing at "Ru Paul's Drag Race" as they cuddled up on the couch. Lenny had loved the show although it had taken Brook a little time to warm up to it. It wasn't something he'd have chosen to watch on his own, but he'd enjoyed the fact Lenny had chuckled at it so much. The sweet memory of being together caused a pang of regret in his chest. He'd no idea what he'd done to make Lenny incommunicado and not return his calls, but he wished he could find out. Brook's texts and phone calls had gone unanswered, a terse, '*Thanks, it's been good but I think it's best we not see each other again*' the only indication he'd had that something was wrong. Those three weeks and the sweet, delicious nights they'd spent together made Brook wish for more.

Shorter than his six foot one, with shaggy, light blond hair, unusual aqua eyes and a tanned and toned body that screamed gym and good genes, Lenny had been Brook's wet dreams come true. He'd been funny, warm and one of the most compassionate people Brook had ever met, doing a lot of charity work within the LGBT community. It was how they'd met, at a pride rally.

Brook came back to earth when he realised Keith was still whining. "I mean, come on. We're men. Shouldn't men dress like men and not wear damn pantyhose and a wig? And she-he-whatever it was - was giving away all their hard-earned money to charities that pick up bums and runaways off the street. I mean, what the hell happened to a person finding a job instead of waiting to be given a hand-out from taxpayers like you and me?"

Keith seemed to be taking Brook's dumbfounded silence as agreement with his views, as he warmed to his subject. He probably thought being the boss's son-in-law gave him extra kudos to say whatever the hell he liked. "And let's face it. He must be really gay to dress like that. I mean, real men don't wear women's underwear and heels. That's damn perverted." His self-righteous tone echoed in Brook's brain.

He'd had enough. He stood up slowly, letting the fury in his soul temper itself out before he did bodily harm to this stupid wanker in front of him. He knew he made an imposing sight: tall, broad shouldered and, as one of the ladies in the office's admiringly said, 'Falcon like.'

He was used to being compared to the Marvel Avenger after he'd attended a Christmas party kitted out as the superhero and to be honest, there was a resemblance of sorts. He was quite proud of the nickname. To him, the Falcon stood for a lot of good things, but he ruefully acknowledged that he didn't quite have the muscles or the weapons his alter ego had. If he had, the man across from him would be a blistering scorch mark on the wall right now.

"You bloody idiot," Brook growled loudly. "I'd stop if I were you, before you say something else that will make me put my fist in your face. I cannot believe what I'm hearing. Firstly, you're damn lucky the lady didn't decide to sue the firm for that crass outburst of yours. And this woman is not an 'it,' you insufferable ass. She simply chooses to be something you don't. Secondly, you do know *I'm* gay, right?"

From the horrified look on Keith's face, he hadn't known until this moment. Brook prowled around the desk to loom over the other man who sat staring up at him, wide-eyed and pale. His fingers clenched the arms of his chair.

Brook sneered down at him. "It's not a secret I like men. I don't go blurting it out to everyone I meet, but I feel the need to tell you now in case you missed the office grapevine." He imagined Keith was so wrapped up in his own little world he'd missed that broadcast.

"Oh I didn't mean *you*," Keith stammered, eyes darting around wildly as if hoping another superhero may appear to rescue him. "I mean these other people…" His voice tailed off and he shifted in his chair as Brook shook his head angrily.

"Don't try and wriggle out of this one, Keith. I have no place anymore for someone like you on my team. I've given you enough slack. It's time to haul the rope back in. I'll clear it with Lawrence, but I don't want you here anymore. He can move you somewhere else, if they'll have you. If not, well…" He shrugged. "It's no great loss." He'd make sure his boss, Lawrence Lively, got all the facts about his daughter's screw-up of a husband. Hopefully he'd see Brook's side, if not—well, he'd tackle that when it happened. He doubted he was at risk.

Keith stood up, his face red with anger, jowls wobbling. Brook was glad it wasn't Christmas. The man might be mistaken for a turkey. That image made him chuckle and Keith glared at him.

"You don't have the fucking authority to kick me off this team, you young punk. Lawrence will never let that happen—"

"Lawrence put me in charge of this team for a reason," Brook said, steel in his voice. "Despite my '*young punk'* age, I'm the biggest grossing broker this team has." He was thirty, at least ten years younger than the man in front of him. "This firm's revenues have increased by forty-five percent since I came on board, plus most of the firm's top clients—who I've brought in—will move with me if I go. Compared to your track record, one I've been trying to improve since you got here, by the way without success, I think I know whose side Lawrence will be on."

Brook gestured impatiently at the door. "Get out, pack up your desk and go wherever it is you spend half your time, the pub across the road or wherever. Your days of lording it over as a member of the boss's family are over. It's time for you to move on from my team." He folded his arms across his chest and stared implacably at Keith. The man's face was flushed, his breathing erratic and Brook hoped like hell he wasn't about to have a heart attack. There was no way he wanted to perform CPR. The thought of his mouth on Keith's fleshly lips made him vaguely nauseous.

"You bla—bastard," Keith spat at him and Brook heard the slur at his Kenyan heritage remaining partially unspoken. "You think that will make Lawrence choose you over his own flesh and blood? You're mistaken in that assumption."

Brook ignored that outburst, simply gave a deep, bored sigh and rolled his eyes towards the ceiling. He wasn't feeling as confident as he hoped he looked. While everything he'd said to Keith was the truth, family was always a rather personal business. He had to hope Lawrence Lively could see past that. His boss had always been a fair man.

"I'll leave your office, but I'm not going anywhere until I've seen Laurie." Keith's smirk as he used his father-in-law's pet name irked Brook but he stood his ground. "And Pattie will never let her father do *anything* to me I don't want to do."

Privately Brook thought Patricia Lively would be glad to be rid of the husband who drank too much, was a complete prat and who, she'd once confided in Brook when she'd been off her face with booze, she wished she'd never married at all. The words, "push him under a bus" had been drunkenly uttered as a solution. The fact

Keith was also simply clueless as to her random affairs with various 'coaches' she supposedly had training her in a variety of sports was also a saddening indictment of the marriage. The man had blinkers on where Pattie was concerned. And it wasn't Brook's place to enlighten him on his cheating wife.

"I suppose we'll have to see," Brook drawled as he waved his hand again in dismissal. "Piss off, Keith. I have work to do."

Keith's eyes narrowed. He trundled his bulky frame towards the open door and half in, half out, he turned and threw Brook a smouldering look of dislike.

"Oh yes, we'll see," he spat. He turned and strode down the corridor, ignoring the curious glances of everyone else in the open-plan office.

Brook rolled his eyes and made sure to close the door after what he hoped was now an ex-team member. He slumped down in his high-backed executive chair and stared out the window, his fingers idly turning a stray paperclip into a straight line as he gazed at the folder on his desk and muttered to himself. "Ms Laverne Debussy-Smith, you must be some woman to kick two supposedly hard-assed financial brokers out of your office like that. I believe you're a force to be reckoned with. I think I might pay you a personal visit to see if I can redeem the company and perhaps try and do some business with you."

His gaze strayed to a pamphlet lying on his desk. With a twinge of nostalgia, he picked it up. It was a brochure to Ripley's Believe It Or Not! in the West End. He remembered going there with Lenny one night on a 'not-date' as they'd agreed, but as friends. Of course that hadn't lasted the evening as by ten o'clock that night they were fucking each other's brains out—but their intentions had been good.

"And then you wouldn't even return my calls," he mused, turning the brochure in his fingers. "What the hell did I do to piss you off? I wonder if I should make another call. If I knew where you lived, I'd send you a bottle of wine and some of those Belgian truffles you liked so much."

Brook scowled. He had no idea where Lenny lived, what he did as a job other than him telling him vaguely he was in the rag trade and had a 'little business.' For all Brook knew the man sold garments at Primark or had a market stall somewhere. Lenny had been fun but he'd not given much away about himself. Mind you,

Brook had only told Lenny that he was in finance in the city and that was about it. Between shagging each other senseless and watching re-runs of *Supernatural* on television to lust over the two lead men, they hadn't really gotten to know each other that well. Brook had hoped to learn more about the man he was seeing until it all went pear shaped.

He opened his desk drawer and threw the brochure inside, his mind made up. He'd try and call Lenny yet again and find out what the hell he'd done wrong. He'd also make an appointment with the feisty Ms Debussy-Smith and see where that went. From the research Brook had seen on the company, it was indeed a good business to be in bed with, and he quite fancied a small slice of the pie that was Debussy's. He was sure he could be charming enough to sway her opinion of the firm and bring in a new client. As for Lenny—he'd call him tomorrow and try to woo him back. He had a real yen to have the blond, sexy goodness that was that man back in his life and in his bed.

Brook's shitty day didn't stop there either. He sat in the crowded tube train on his way home, eyes closed, leaning back against the window, when someone nudged him. Brook opened his eyes to see a rheumy-eyed old woman smiling toothily. He reflected moodily she probably had less than half her birth allotment. Her breath was bad but her eyes were kind. She looked to be in her seventies.

"You dropped something, lad," she said loudly. "Looks like it might be important, like." Her voice hinted at a Welsh heritage.

Brook looked down to see his battered copy of his London tube map at his feet. He really didn't need it, and it certainly wasn't important, but he smiled his thanks and bent down to get it. "Thank you."

She waved a gnarled hand. "Oh, no problem, lad."

The youngster sitting across from Brook gave a loud cackle. "It's a fucking tube map, you old cow. Nothing important about it at all."

He didn't look like the proverbial hoodie teenager everyone was warned about. He was in his early teens, casually dressed in jeans and a FCUK sweatshirt. His sneakers were Skechers and his hair was styled with gel. He had what looked like an expensive haircut.

Brook scowled at him. “Mind your damn manners. There’s no need to be rude.”

People about him shifted uncomfortably, seeming to sense there might be trouble. He didn’t care. He could take care of himself. Being both black and gay had made it fairly necessary when he was younger.

The youth shot up to his feet, aggression oozing out of every pore. He clutched the roof bar as the train wobbled from side to side. “Shut it, you wanker. Nobody was talking to you. Don’t you have a bloody plantation to work on or something?” He grinned, obviously thinking he was being witty. The old lady gave a loud snort and started rummaging in her large, rather tatty handbag. People’s murmurs grew louder and around him, eyes looked down at the floor or the copy of the *Metro*, not wanting to get caught up in whatever might be coming.

Brook rolled his eyes. He should be so used to this by now. “No, you ignorant brat. Why don’t you sit the hell down and shut your mouth? People here are trying to get home. They don’t need your crap.”

The brat scowled and reached inside the pocket of his sweatshirt. Brook tensed and readied himself, wondering if a knife or something equally dangerous might come out. He wondered exasperatedly why this was happening now, in a closed space, with so many people. Maybe he should have kept his mouth shut. But his father had taught him better manners than that.

Brook didn’t get a chance to do anything after all. No sooner had the young man pulled nothing more innocuous than a mobile phone out of his pocket than all hell broke loose. The youth screamed as the smell of oranges flooded the air. His phone dropped to the floor of the carriage. The old lady cackled in glee as whatever she was spraying at him lodged in the youth’s eyes. The other passengers stared in horror, some getting up and moving along out of the area.

Some of the mist hit Brook, whose eyes immediately began watering. The young man must have been in a lot of discomfort as he’d taken the brunt of whatever it was.

“Teach you to bad-mouth your elders, laddie.” the woman screeched as she emptied whatever was in the can into the air. “My chemist friend gave me this for such a situation.” Brook was valiantly trying to remove the can from her grip but she held on for dear life and he didn't want to hurt her bony fingers.

"You crazy bitch," the youth screamed as he frantically rubbed at his face. "What the hell is that stuff? You're gonna make me go blind."

"Well, you should have minded your manners, then," she spat at him. Brook managed at last to wrestle it from her as the can ran out, fizzling to nothing more than a pathetic drizzle over his hand. The train slid into the station, stopped and the doors opened. No one got on other than a portly station security officer who stepped into the train, stared at the can in his hand, then at the youth then at the chuckling old lady.

Brook took a deep breath. He didn't want to get the old lady into trouble but he also didn't fancy being arrested for assault with a spray can. Luckily, the decision was made for him.

"Arrest that bitch," the young brat screamed, as he tried to wipe the crap out of his face and eyes. "She made me go fucking blind."

The security guard sighed heavily and leaned over to pluck the can out of Brook's fingers. "No, she didn't," the guard muttered. "It's only orange essence in a can. The effects will wear off but it stings like hell before then." He turned to the grinning woman. "Cally, you promised me you wouldn't do this again. Now I'm going to have to have you come to the office and speak to the boss again. He's going to be well angry with you."

Brook crouched down and picked up the youth's phone. The guard gestured them all off the train onto the platform. Brook didn't quite know what was expected of him so he followed them. The train doors closed and it left. Onlookers on the platform gazed at them curiously.

"He started it." Cally pointed at the youth and pouted, her pale face set. "He was being damn rude to this gentleman here. Racist, and plain nasty. He deserved it."

"Yep, maybe he did," the guard said agreeably as he rolled his eyes at Brook. "But the two of you are going to have to come with me." He pointed at Cally. "You, because you did it again, and you"—he pointed at the youth whose face was red and eyes streaming— "you need to have that looked at and your eyes flushed. Come on, the pair o' you. Follow me."

Brook stared at him. "Do you need me to come with too?" His eyes still stung and he decided instead of going back to the office, he'd go home, take a quick shower and knuckle down to some work. He had a deadline to meet on a future customer proposal and he was running out of time.

The guard shook his head. "Nah, I think you were the piggy in the middle in this whole thing." He flashed an angry glance at Cally, who glowered, her face defiant. "She rides these trains all day looking for an excuse to use her 'orange mace' as it's called. It was bad luck she happened to start it before the train pulled into my station. The minute those doors opened and I smelt that damn orange, I knew she'd been up to mischief." A faint smile crossed his face. "She's a real character, is our Cally."

"Will she be in trouble?" Brook asked worriedly. "Because, honestly, all she was doing was standing up for me, even though it wasn't necessary." He handed the phone he held over to the guard. "This is his phone." He jerked a finger at the moaning youth. "You might want to give it back to him when he stops whining."

The guard nodded. "Yeah, you look like you can take of yourself," he said appraisingly. "But no, she won't be in too much trouble. The boss will give her a dressing down and a warning and send her home." He became business like. "Thanks for the phone. Right, you two, let's get going so I can get back to work. You've both fucked up my schedule to catch train jumpers with your stupid stunt."

Brook leaned over and touched the old lady's arm. "Thanks, Cally," he murmured. "I hope his boss goes easy on you."

The woman's eyes twinkled. "Oh he will," she purred. "He's not likely to do anything too bad to his poor old grandma." She winked as she sashayed off after the guard, the youth protesting angrily behind her. Once again Brook's jaw dropped. He clutched his briefcase close to his chest and shook his head in weary amusement as he waited for the next train to arrive. Today couldn't end soon enough.

Chapter 5

Lenny slammed his phone down on the table. "For fuck's sake, stop texting me. You're driving me to distraction."

The latest text he'd received from the relentless onslaught that was Brook Hunter was really playing with his head. Lenny was slowly, grudgingly coming to the conclusion that for some reason, his ex-lover had resurfaced and wasn't giving up on him. Part of him rejoiced in that fact; the other felt the first tremors of apprehension. Lenny didn't know if he could resist much longer.

A knock at his office door made him look up. Leslie stood there, a frown on his face.

"Okay to come in, boss?" he asked, bobbing impatiently from foot to foot like a beach ball on the waves.

Lenny squinted at him in suspicion. "You're asking now? Darling, normally you barge in like the bloody Queen Mary."

"Oh, puh-lease," Leslie waved a hand airily as he came in and plonked himself in the chair in front of Lenny's desk. "I may be a queen but I do have *some* manners."

"Since when?" Lenny asked gruffly. "I could be on my knees giving a blowjob to someone, and you'd waltz in. What's happened to the old Leslie I knew?"

"Ooh, we *are* a grumpy girl," Leslie chittered. His keen eyes glanced at Lenny's phone. "Did you break a nail? Who's pissed on your battery anyway that you have a face like thunder?" He ignored Lenny's snort. "And F-Y-I, Oliver told me last time he was here visiting he noticed my lack of pre-announcement when I came in here and thought it might be nice if I tried knocking now and then. I thought I'd try it out." His pink lips pursed in a moue. "*That* doesn't look like it worked too well. I think I'll stick to barging in."

Lenny leaned back and smoothed the front of his magenta-coloured silk blouse. For some reason the fabric kept creasing and he made the decision not to buy from this particular vendor again. It looked like her silk wasn't up to scratch.

"So who's got your panties all ruffled?" Leslie asked. "Anything I can do to help?"

Lenny sighed. "No. Someone who won't take no for an answer."

Leslie's face became animated. "Oh, I know *that* situation. The other night Oliver and I were out at a club and he went to the loo. Some guy came over to chat me up and he was very insistent. He asked if I'd go with him to some private party for a shag fest with some of his friends."

Lenny grinned at the indignant look on Leslie's face. He knew his opinion on *that* subject having been subjected to a passionate discourse more than once.

"I mean, what the hell says '*I'm into multi-fucking'* with this?" Leslie waved an expressive hand down his face and body. "Do I have an invisible tattoo somewhere that says 'Ménage Boy' or something?" He huffed. "Anyways, Oliver came out and saw the guy and I thought he was going to smack him into next week." He gave a satisfied smile. "I love it when he gets all caveman on me. I mean, when we got home that night—"

Lenny raised a hand. "No more, sweet. I don't think I can take any stories of how you and your porn star boyfriend managed to make mad, passionate, kinky caveman love when poor Laverne is going through one of her dry spells." He made a sad face and motioned to his phone. "And having one very determined man trying to get me to go out with him again *should* make me happy that situation might be remedied but I don't know…"

Leslie's eyes brightened and he leaned forward. "Is it that Brook guy?" he said conspiratorially.

Lenny nodded.

Leslie frowned. "So what's the problem? Go out with the man, get laid and poof! No more problem."

Lenny shook his head. "It's not that simple. Brook is," his voice tailed off. "Well, he's a pretty conservative kind of guy and I'm still not sure how he'd feel if he found out the man he'd slept with wore women's clothes to work."

Leslie gasped and clasped a hand to his chest. "Oh, Laverne, he wouldn't be that shallow, would he? I mean Oliver loves my corsets and heels; what man wouldn't?"

Lenny cleared his throat. "Those that watch *Ru Paul's Drag Race* with you then say, 'I wouldn't particularly want my man dressing up like a woman and put on display like that, but damn, some of them look beautiful when they do. Not my cup of tea, but they'd definitely fool anyone who didn't know there was a man underneath all that eyeliner.'" Lenny shrugged. "Then when I asked him what it was that he didn't like, he laughed and said he fancied me as I was without any cosmetics."

Leslie's blue eyes shadowed as Lenny continued. "When I heard that, I thought it was best to go our separate ways and not get more invested." Lenny's heart ached. His whole world changed when Brook made that remark—admittedly not in derision or judgement, more in thoughtful conversation. They had both been rather drunk by that time, but it had still hurt. Lenny knew his habits were a bit much for some men to take.

There was silence as Leslie's brows furrowed in thought. "Ah, I see." He seemed to be pondering and Lenny waited to see what pearls of wisdom might fall from his lips. Leslie was discerning and had a lively and intelligent mind. Advice from him was usually worth listening to. Unless it was watching films that he recommended. Their viewing tastes were not the same and Lenny had no desire to watch any of the *Pitch Perfect* series, something Leslie adored and about which there had been some heated debate on both the dancing featured and the leading man.

Leslie nodded sagely. "But he didn't actually *say* he'd have a problem with it, did he? I mean, it might not be something he'd ever thought about, but with the right man, someone he cared about? And he did say 'I wouldn't *particularly* want it' meaning that perhaps there was a little room for manoeuvre in there, as if he wasn't really being *particular*, he might consider it? And he thought some of them were beautiful, which means he must be attracted to them, right?" The words flowed from Leslie's lovely mouth like a deluge of glitter, and Lenny could only watch in horrified wonder as his protégé gained momentum.

"Laverney, do you think you maybe overreacted and did one of those 'knee-jerk' thingies people do when they get all panicked? I mean, you were quite into this man and it seems such a pity if he's trying to get back in touch that you don't give him a chance to explain and maybe talk it over with him. Over a nice Rioja and a fancy dinner at Galileo's perhaps?"

Lenny had reeled at the name 'Laverney,' which was a new development, and not one he liked. The way Leslie's eyes sparkled, Lenny had a feeling it had been spurted out simply to make him take notice. He was also dizzy from watching Leslie's slim hands wave around in front of his face like semaphores trying to direct an errant plane in to land.

Lenny stood up, pulling his dove-grey suit trousers from his arse crack, and smoothing them down. He fastened a stray mother of pearl button on his blouse, which had somehow come undone, exposing his boobs. Leslie stopped talking and watched in approval.

"Nice outfit. I haven't seen those trousers before; are they new? The colour goes beautifully with your blouse."

"Yes, they're part of the new Fashionista range."

Leslie huffed. "There's something I meant to ask you. I see that Tracy Trey is getting into *your* area of expertise? He's started doing men's suits. I hope he doesn't stop making his corsets and underwear. Oliver wouldn't be happy."

"I doubt he'll stop designing the things that bring him the most revenue, Leslie. I think you and Oliver are safe." Lenny nodded. "And, yes, I knew. I saw Tracy the other day at a lunch and he told me all about it. He gloated he was going to become a major competitor. The man's a prick."

Leslie's eyes narrowed. "Isn't that a bit dangerous?"

Lenny shrugged. "In my opinion, this market is big enough for us both. Tracy and I are not friends, but we work in the same industry. I can't begrudge him expanding his *plaid* empire to make items like these." He glanced down at them. "And let's face it, mine will always trump his." He grinned. "I made the Debussy suit famous by doing things differently and better."

Leslie frowned. "Still. I saw one of his jackets on the catwalk. I thought it bore a resemblance to something you were working on a few months ago…? That retro design you decided not to go with because it didn't look right."

Now it was Lenny's turn to frown. "Really? I didn't see that. It must be a coincidence. I decided the design wasn't good enough, so I binned it."

"Do you shred your old drawings, boss?" His employee's tone was all business. "We have that huge shredder out there, and the secure waste disposal service. You should be putting your stuff in there. Anyone could walk out of here with your thrown-away pieces of draft paper."

Lenny laughed. “I trust my staff, chicken. We’re a small team of fifteen people, and I doubt any one of them would steal things from my waste bin.”

Leslie didn’t look convinced. “I’d still feel better if you disposed of them securely.”

Lenny loved it when Leslie got all serious. He was adorably efficient at his job despite his flirty, ‘I’m-a-drama-queen’ demeanour. It was why Lenny had hired him.

“Fine. If it makes my young man happy, I’ll shove them in the shredder or pop them in the secure waste bag. Happy?”

Leslie rolled his eyes. “I’m only looking out for you. I don’t want your hard work to go elsewhere.”

Lenny walked over to him and hugged him. “I know,” he murmured against soft, black hair. “And I appreciate you for it. You are my favourite chicken.”

He released a rosy-cheeked Leslie. Lenny wasn’t sure if Leslie’s colouring was because he’d pressed him into his bosom or whether he was blushing because of the praise. It was possibly a bit of both. He remembered something else he’d been meaning to talk to Leslie about.

“Oh, by the way, I think it’s time to up the ante a bit on your continuing education here at Debussy’s and bring you into the fold of the actual business side of things. The boring nitty-gritty of finance and revenue. I want you in the next loan meeting.”

Leslie’s eyes glazed over. “Finance and revenue?” he murmured uncomfortably. “Really? You’re asking a guy who barely understands an overdraft into a financial meeting?”

Lenny nodded. “Yes. It’s about time you saw a bit of the behind-the-scenes work in action.”

Leslie’s face fell. “Laverne,” he whined. “The last time you made me go behind the scenes I had to put chalk on a woman’s nipples. I got into conversation about a va-jay-jay.” He shivered. “It was horrible.”

Lenny laughed loudly at the disgusted expression on Leslie’s face. “Yes, my pumpkin, I want you there. You remember those idiots I chucked out a couple of weeks ago? Well, I’ve had their manager on the line to Naomi, charming her into giving him another appointment so he can personally apologise to me for the dickhead’s behaviour. He wants to see whether he can help me with finance.”

He walked around the desk and stood at Leslie's side, picking stray pieces of what looked like silver thread out of his black hair. The man had probably been scrounging for bits of material in the recycle bin again. "I thought that if he's got the balls to come and personally apologise, then the least I could do was see him. Apparently he also fired the homophobic wanker that was out of line." He leaned over and peered at his diary. "So, a Mr Simon Hunter will be here on Thursday at two p.m. Put it in your diary—if you have one."

Leslie heaved a theatrical sigh. "If I must." He rolled his eyes. "Don't expect too much of me. I know I'm not daft but finance is one thing that really gets me confused. Someone tried to sell me an issy the other day and I didn't understand a word she was saying."

Lenny was puzzled. "An issy?"

Leslie nodded. "Some tax savings account thingamabob."

Lenny chuckled loudly. "Oh you mean an ISA, Leslie. Honey, you make me laugh."

"Whatever." Leslie pouted then gave a wicked grin. "I don't need a savings account. I have Oliver." He chortled in delight at Lenny's widened eyes. "I'm joking. I'm not with him because of his huge bank account. I'm with him because of his huge prick." He wiggled his brows. "And because I love him to bits."

Lenny laughed loudly. "Sweetheart, the things you say. I really feel sorry for that boyfriend of yours."

Leslie stuck his tongue out at him. "Don't. He gives as good as he gets, believe me." Realising what he'd said, both men collapsed in peals of laughter only to be interrupted in their mirth by Naomi putting her head around the door with a raised eyebrow.

"Sorry to interrupt, but your ten o'clock meeting is here, Laverne. Richard Grace, the fabric guy? He's in the waiting room having green tea. Shall I bring him in?"

Lenny wiped his eyes. "Yes, Naomi, please do. Give me a minute to freshen up and I'll be right with him. Leslie, remember Thursday, two o'clock. Please don't forget, or have some pet fish emergency."

The regularity with which Leslie's treasured fish died deserved its own CSI programme. There was definitely something *fishy* about it. At that silly thought, Lenny chuckled, ignoring Leslie's questioning look and Naomi's deep sigh.

"Private joke," Lenny managed. "Give me a minute then take Richard to the conference room. He's doing a presentation for me. It's all set up for him."

Leslie turned to leave then swung around. His blue eyes were warm, concerned. "Laverne, call your man back. Go and explain things to him. It might not be that bad. You deserve to tell him the truth at least and let him make his own decision. Not do it for him. He must really like you if he's been calling nonstop." He flashed a quick smile and disappeared out of the office, Naomi right behind him.

Lenny finished wiping his eyes, making sure he had nothing in his teeth, then sprayed some more antiperspirant under his arms. Silk tended to make him sweat. Then he picked up his tailored jacket from the hanger on the coatrack in his office. Shrugging into it, he considered Leslie's words. Perhaps he had a point. Maybe it was time to clear the air and tell Brook about Laverne. He guessed he had nothing to lose. He adjusted his wig, making sure it covered his own hair properly and picked up his folder from his desk.

Time to get to work. Then, perhaps later, he might have a glass of wine for Dutch courage and make that damn call.

***

"Hey, freak. My lady and I have a bet on. I say you're a freak of nature and she thinks you're a fag dressed like a woman. Can you put us out of your misery and tell us who's right?"

Lenny sighed, rolled his eyes, catching the sympathetic glance of the woman standing next to him.

I am so not in the mood for this. The train is delayed again and it's as hot as Hades down here. Perhaps if I ignore these arseholes they'll go away.

"Hey, dickhead. I'm talking to you."

Lenny groaned softly. The tube station was packed due to the late rush hour and the delay. He really didn't need the aggravation. Also his head itched from his wig but he daren't take it off because underneath he'd be a sweaty, mussed-hair mess. Lenny hated bad hair days, especially when it was his own.

Not going to go away then? You prick.

Occasionally, when he travelled home in his Laverne persona, it caused some raised eyebrows and invited more than a couple of derogatory comments and snide remarks. Normally Lenny changed back into his 'man' clothes after work but tonight, he couldn't have been arsed. He was eager to get home; it had been late and the thought of changing and removing everything had been too much bother. It was only three tube stops to home, so a short ride, but still. Usually no one seemed to notice him, everyone too busy staring into iPads or mobile phones, or simply gazing hopefully down the track as they awaited their ride.

Once or twice as Laverne he'd had to kick a guy in the balls because the men had gotten a little too aggressive and insulting. That must have been a sight to see for onlookers—a broad-shouldered woman in a skirt and low-heeled boots whirling her way through a series of Taekwondo moves—because Lenny could take care of himself. He'd studied martial arts and boxing in his twenties for close to five years, but he really didn't want to resort to violence on a crowded station platform if he could help it.

He turned to face the man passing comment. The man was well dressed, in his late forties, early fifties, with the red nose and blotchy face of a heavy drinker. His companion was a skinny, bottle-blonde woman of around the same age, and Lenny's discerning eyes noticed her tacky knockoff suit. She certainly didn't look like the type to afford the real thing. Lenny sniffed. Classy was not a word he'd have used for the pair.

Why the fuck do arseholes have to cause trouble?

He tried a polite smile. His lips were dry and devoid of lipstick because, after work he couldn't be bothered to apply more.

"I'm trying to get home, same as you. Why don't you mind your own business?"

He saw them start at his deep voice and the woman had the grace to look uncomfortable. She looked away, pretending to peer down the track for an approaching train. The man, however, didn't give up so easily.

"I mean, what the hell? You're a man in women's clothing. What's all that about?"

Lenny's temper flared. "Leave me the hell alone," he growled. "It's my business how I dress. Leave your fat, ugly nose out of it."

The heat in the tube station was causing rivulets of sweat to run down his forehead and into his eyes. And it was only mid-June. Heaven knows what it would be like in the height of the July and August summer months. He wiped the sweat away irritably. He smelt his own sweat beneath the antiperspirant he wore. Under his suit pants his barely-there silk briefs clung to him. The inside of his thighs were chafed.

Where the fuck is that damn train?

There was a flurry of activity on the platform and Lenny looked up to see his heckler standing right beside him. He tensed, hoping things weren't about to get ugly. Everyone around them looked at uneasily.

"You don't get to speak to me like that," Red Nose said angrily. "I was only asking you a question."

"A question you have no right to have the answer to," Lenny shot back. "Like I said, it's my business. Now fuck off." The time for niceties was definitely over.

Red Nose growled and his arm came up, as if to slap or punch him. Instinctively Lenny blocked it, and in one fluid moment, he had the guy in a headlock, the man pressed close to his own body as he growled softly into his ear. "I said leave me alone. You don't get to touch me. Now are you going to resist so I can knee you in the knackers and you can amuse your lady with your high voice or are you going to back—the—fuck—off?"

The panic on Red Nose's face was almost funny but Lenny was in no mood to be amused.

"I'll back off," Red Nose squeaked. "Let me go."

Lenny released him and the man scurried back, his bravado returning as he got further away, back to his stunned, open-mouthed partner.

"Wanker," Red Nose spat as he nursed what was probably now a bruised arm. "That's assault, that is. I should sue you." He looked around wildly, probably for a security guard.

Lenny closed his eyes and took a deep breath. He had probably overreacted, but the guy was a douche bag. He hoped he wasn't going to be harassed by the station authorities.

A quiet voice piped up from among the platform dwellers. "I think we can all safely attest to the fact you started this, you bully. This woman here was defending herself." The three women standing a few feet away smiled at Lenny. Behind them three big men, probably their partners, stood protectively. One of them nodded his head at him in support.

The woman continued. “You can call the authorities, but I think we’d all agree here that nothing really happened?” She waved a hand towards Red Nose. “Most of us here are all part of the same Sherlock Holmes tour, and I feel pretty sure we’ll all say you were the tosser and not this lady.” She looked around at the milling crowd. “Am I right?”

The crowd nodded in various stages of assent and there were murmurs of “Absolutely,” and “Sure. We all saw what really happened.”

Lenny felt a surge of warmth at the fact people were standing up for Laverne. A strong wind blew down the tunnel and he breathed a sigh of relief that the train had arrived. He mouthed a grateful ‘Thank you’ at the woman as they all clambered on board the train. She winked and then was lost in the melee of weary passengers struggling to get home. Red Nose and his lady friend were swallowed up in the same influx. He did catch a glimpse of the man glaring at him from among the other passengers and Lenny was childishly tempted to pull a tongue at him. But he resisted and instead held on tightly to the overhead rail as the train pulled out of the station.

When he got home he showered, changed clothes and poured himself a stiff drink. Then he sat down to watch the latest porn offering from Vanguard Studios, called *Boys of Bayshore*. He couldn’t concentrate on the onscreen action though, as one of the performers in the film, a very talented black actor called Griffin Damson, reminded him of Brook.

“Hell, Griffin is hot,” he murmured, as he reached inside his loose drawstring board shorts and fondled himself. “But nothing like Brook…”

Lenny closed his eyes, letting the warmth of the room wash over him, his arousal and slowly growing erection transporting him elsewhere, blocking out the street noise below. The noise and grunts of the men onscreen spurred him on as he smeared his own fluids into his palm and slowly, agonisingly, tugged himself to thoughts of Brook’s hands on his cock, the glistening smoothness of his ebony skin and the pink of his lips as he sucked him to distraction.

Lenny braced his bare heels against the couch seat, back arching as he thrust upwards into his hand. He remembered pushing inside Brook for the first time, and the first time he’d had his ex-lover’s sizeable cock up his own arse. Thoughts of that drove him on to jack himself harder. He'd not had sex for a while, what with Ryan being out of town and not being in the mood to have random stranger jerkoffs or blowjobs at the clubs he usually frequented.

With a stifled wail and a deep gasp of breath, Lenny came all over his own hands, saturating his clean shorts and the bottom half of his tee shirt in the bargain. He lay there with a hand on his semi-flaccid dick, satiated and knowing without any doubt he was definitely calling Brook back.

Chapter 6

Brook sat in Galileo's restaurant indulging in an orgasmically tasty chef's special, smoked swordfish with piquant blackcurrant jelly. Coupled with his glass of white Pinot Noir and the fact Lenny had eventually called him back, Brook was in a celebratory mood.

The conversation between him and Lenny a day ago had been brief. The usual "Hi how are you?" followed by "I think we should talk." (Lenny), and "I'm so glad you called." (Brook) then a mutual decision to meet for dinner at Galileo's next Saturday night.

Brook beamed at the waitress who delivered his second basket of crusty bread and butter. "Good news, sir?" asked the pretty blonde server with a smile.

Brook nodded. "Oh yes. It looks like I have a date here next Saturday night. One I never expected to have, so it's a rather nice surprise."

The waitress—Imogen, from her name badge—gave him a wink. "Wonderful, sir. I'll be here that night. Is there anything special you'd like me to do for you? Give you a specific table or make sure she has her favourite flowers on the table?"

Brook grinned. "My date's not really into flowers. Now if you'd mentioned Belgian chocolates, I think he'd do *anything* for you."

Imogen laughed softly. "Very well, sir. I'll try and organise that for you. I'm sure Mr Kent, the owner, won't mind splashing out for a few truffles. Is there anywhere specific you'd like to sit? I'll mention it to the duty manager if so."

He was touched. This young lady was delivering above and beyond the realms of good service in his book. "Well, if it's possible, I'd love the corner booth, the one over by the bronze telescope. It's quiet and out of the way."

So I can get up close and personal with my date. It's going to be tough to keep my hands off him.

Imogen nodded. "I'm sure I can get that sorted for you. I hope it all goes well on Saturday night, sir." She smiled and left the table with his first empty bread basket.

Brook took a sip of his wine and sat back in his chair. He enjoyed his occasional lunches here at the restaurant, only a few tube stops from work. Lenny had a good friend who knew the owner and his boyfriend, and the place had come highly recommended. He had to admit it was worth taking the time out to come here instead of one of those boring places around where he worked on Bank Street.

Galileo's was beautifully decorated in red and bronze, in a style worthy of the astronomer himself. The beautiful frieze of the world on the walls, the star-scape constellation painted on the ceiling and the medley of old brass and copper telescopes and other paraphernalia scattered lovingly around the room were both sophisticated and warm.

Brook finished his meal and was texting Lenny, saying he was happy he'd got back in touch and looking forward to their get together when he heard a polite cough at his elbow. He looked up into the eyes of a rather dishy, suited blond man.

"Afternoon, sir. My name is Gideon Kent. I'm the owner here." The man smiled at him. "My waitress told me you'd like something special next Saturday night for your date. She mentioned Belgian chocolates and the corner table. I'd like to reassure you we have everything in hand for your evening."

Brook was taken aback but delighted. "Wow, you really do take service to another level, don't you? Is this normal or have you mistaken me for a film star? I do get told I look a bit like Nathan Owens, the model."

Gideon Kent narrowed his eyes and appraised him thoughtfully. "I have no idea who Nathan Owens is, but if people tell you that, I'm sure it's true." He flashed a grin at Brook. "Actually Imogen said you looked like a bit like the guy from the *Avengers* films."

Brook grinned. "Well, I'm neither of them; simply plain old Brook Hunter. But tell her thanks for the compliment." He quirked an eyebrow at Gideon. "So is this simply a case of mistaken identity then, and now you're going to tell me I get to sit by the revolving doors outside the kitchen and if I want chocolates for the boyfriend, I have to bring them myself?"

Gideon chuckled, a low, husky sound that Brook really appreciated. Damn, the man was sexy. Brook's thing for blond men was definitely showing itself.

Gideon shook his head. "Not at all. You made an impression on Imogen so she mentioned you to me. It's all part of the service."

Brook raised an eyebrow. "So—I guess the question is how far do you take that service?"

The flirty words came out of his mouth before he had a chance to pull them back. His face heated up. He was meeting Lenny in a week's time and here he was propositioning the restaurant manager. "I'm sorry. I shouldn't have said that. I was out of line. I apologise."

The man standing at his side grinned. "No need to apologise. I'm flattered, but very spoken for. I appreciate the sentiment. Don't say anything like that in front of my chef."

"Your chef?" Brook queried.

"He's my partner. We live together upstairs." Gideon waved vaguely at the roof of the restaurant. He snorted in amusement. "I can assure you redheads *do* have the temper they're reputed to have. Eddie can be a little jealous."

"Well, tell him the food is incredible. He's truly inspirational. You're lucky to have him."

"Oh, don't I know it." For a moment, Brook thought he saw little hearts flying around Gideon's head as his expression softened. Then the man was all business again. "Well, I'll leave you in peace. Can I get you a coffee or anything?"

Brook duly ordered a latte and said goodbye to the hunky Gideon Kent. He watched Gideon stride off across the restaurant, stopping at patron's tables and briefly chatting.

The man has one fine arse in those tailored suit pants.

He glanced at his watch. He'd have his coffee then get back to the office. He still had to prepare for his meeting with the renowned Laverne Debussy-Smith tomorrow afternoon. He wanted to make sure he knew everything about her and her business before the meeting. The last thing he wanted was coming off second best, and being royally escorted from her office like his colleagues had been.

Brook gave a satisfied sigh as he sipped his steaming latte that had magically appeared on his table. He knew two things. One, he was definitely coming back to this restaurant again and again. Two, he was so going to convince Lenny to give them another chance. The man wouldn't be able to resist him.

***

Thursday afternoon Lenny sat down and had a stiff drink from the brandy bottle he kept in his desk drawer. He double-checked his lipstick—a pale pink, he hated bright colours on his lips—and applied a bit more mascara. These were the only two items of make-up he used, preferring the *au naturel* look. First impressions counted for everything in this business. Lenny was sure his dark grey pants suit, with his red chiffon blouse and pale grey and white silk scarf was a testament to power dressing. This Mr Hunter was going to end up giving him the damn loan he wanted and take the ten percent shareholding, or leave with a flea in his ear, Lenny reflected grimly as he swallowed his brandy.

It wasn't that Lenny was desperate for the money; he had a fairly substantial amount squirrelled away in various offshore and onshore accounts. It was simply he was loathe to dip into those reserves as he had plans to expand the business in the next two years and would need every penny. If he could get a small loan now for the new material he needed for his new designs at a good deal, then using someone else's money made sense. But he wasn't going to sell his soul to do it.

A loud, heavy *I mean you to hear me* sigh at the door made him turn. He already knew who he'd find standing there. Leslie's blue eyes regarded him soulfully, black bangs obscuring his forehead as he leaned against the door to Lenny's office.

"Laverne, do you still need me in your meeting at two?" His voice was hopeful and a little plaintive at the same time and Lenny wanted to chuckle at the woebegone expression on Leslie's lovely face.

"Yes, my sugarplum, I do." He shook his head. "I don't know what's so damn scary about this meeting, really I don't."

Leslie scowled. "They're so boring. And they make my head hurt. Honestly I'd rather watch *Top Gear* than be in here. And you know how I hate *Top Gear*. All those cars and macho testosterone. Oliver loves it," he said gloomily. "He makes me sit with him and watch those crazy guys doing all those stupid things. I try and distract him in…other ways." He grinned slyly. "But sometimes he resists me and I have to watch stupid cars zooming around a boring desert or something equally as bleh."

"Resist you?" Lenny said. "How the hell does he manage to do that? I doubt I could, my chicken. You are Leslie the Irresistible, after all."

"I know," Leslie remarked. "It should be a crime punishable by non-masturbation. Guys should have their hands tied behind their backs while I undress and dance in front of them, and they can do nothing about it. I'd be wearing my heels and my satin undies and really make them all hot and bothered." His eyes sparkled. "There's an idea. Maybe tonight I can get something to tie Oliver up—"

Lenny passed a hand over his forehead, the thought of that whole scenario making his own cock rise in his fairly tight suit pants. He wouldn't ever admit to the man in front of him that image turned him on or he'd suffer Leslie's glee and teasing for the rest of his life.

I am a red-blooded man, after all, and if that whole idea didn't give me a damn woody, I'd be a sorry specimen. But I don't want to have dirty thoughts here at the workplace about my employees and their porn star boyfriends. Hell, I need to get laid.

"Please don't bring your fantasies into my office." *Because they become mine.* "Could you go find Naomi and ask here whether Mr Hunter has called to confirm his appointment and see if she's got an update for me?"

Leslie checked the time on the wall clock. "He's only due in half an hour anyway. What's the rush?"

"Leslie," Lenny warned.

Leslie huffed and brushed his hair off his forehead. "Fine," he said. "I'll go." He shot what Lenny supposed was to be a fierce glance of pique, but in all honesty was nothing more than an adorably cute expression that made him want to eat Leslie all up. He really didn't know how Oliver could resist anything the man did.

Lenny busied himself looking over his projections and accounts, making sure he was ready. He lost track of time until a sharp knock at the door made him look up. His stomach plummeted to the floor and his heart beat erratically in his tightened chest.

What the hell was Brook doing here?

"Boss, Mr Hunter is here so I thought I'd bring him over personally. I've already introduced myself." Leslie graciously waved Brook to a seat right in front of the desk. "May I get you tea or coffee, or a soft drink perhaps?"

Brook smiled at Leslie. "No thanks, I'm fine." He stood, looking at Lenny, obviously waiting for him to stand up so he could shake hands. "It's lovely to meet you, Ms Debussy-Smith."

Lenny was stuck to his seat as if he'd grown roots.

What the fuckity-fuck do I do now? If he hears my voice, he might recognise me.

"Laverne?" Leslie's voice was uncertain. "Are you okay?"

Lenny swallowed and closed his eyes briefly. He'd never done a Mrs Doubtfire before but he was sure as hell going to give it a try now and hope Leslie didn't mess it up for him.

"Good afternoon, Mr Hunter," he said chirpily, as he stood up, raising his normal voice an octave—or two. From the dropping of Leslie's jaw and the widening eyes he thought he might have overdone it.

"Oh please, call me Brook. I like to be a little less formal than my other colleagues, if that's all right with you? I've been looking forward to meeting the legend that is Laverne Debussy-Smith. Your name is stellar in this industry from what I've heard." His voice was admiring, not sounding at all to Lenny as if he was trying to curry favour with compliments. They shook hands.

Lenny heard Leslie's squeak of panic at hearing Brook's first name and for a second, the two of them stared at each other as understanding for the reason for this new voice dawned in Leslie's eyes.

Lenny found his composure. "Please sit down. And yes, please call me Laverne. Have you been offered something to drink? Oh of course, you have. Sorry, I'm away with the fairies it looks like. It must be something in the water…" His voice tailed off.

Shut the fuck up. The man's looking at you as if you're a loon.

Brook sat down and laid his briefcase at the side of his chair. Lenny fiddled with the papers on his desk, trying not to make eye contact.

The man looks good. That suit looks fabulous on him. He's a walking Adonis and he's sitting here IN MY FUCKING OFFICE!

Leslie sat down nervously in the chair next to Brook and stared at him with bush baby eyes. "Er, I thought your business card said your name was Si—Simon?" he stammered.

That's exactly what I want to know about too. And when Brook said he was in finance, I had no idea it was this *sort.*

Brook chuckled, the sound stirring Lenny's groin and he was horrified at the slow swelling of his dick. He put a surreptitious hand under the table to press against it as he repeated all the mantras that had helped him out in situations like this before. He'd never had to think of them all at one time before though.

Fat old men with lady titties in steam rooms. Jabba the Hut—naked. Jar Jar Binks in my bed, in a cotton floral nightdress.

"Oh, I always have to explain this. Yes, my name is Simon Brook Hunter, but I don't like it. I got teased far too often at school with the whole 'Simon Says' thing. So I use my middle name. But someone forgot to tell my boss's secretary, and she went ahead and ordered reams of business cards which I have to use up before I can get any more." He flashed a charming, white-toothed grin at them. "It's easier really to explain in person than on the phone." He looked over at Lenny, who tried to avoid too much eye contact and focused on Brook's shoulder. A shoulder he'd bitten more than once in the height of his orgasms.

"Thank you so much for seeing me," Brook said. "I wanted to apologise personally to you for Keith's behaviour and assure you that the company certainly doesn't think the same way he does." He grinned wolfishly and at that sexy sight Lenny's heart gave another stutter. He'd seen that look before when Brook was fucking him.

Shit, shit, shit. Stop with the damn sex stuff.

"So," Brook leaned down and opened his briefcase, drawing out a file. "I took the liberty of drawing up an explanatory proposal based on your last meeting with my team. I made sure to reflect your offer of ten percent as well, although I'm not sure we need that much based on what I've seen of your business accounts so far. You run a very tight and profitable ship here. Perhaps we can see if this is more to your liking?"

He pushed the folder across the desk, sat back and waited.

Leslie stared at Lenny, his expression one of pure dread. His face mirrored what Lenny was feeling on the inside and hoped Leslie's expressive face didn't give rise to any curiosity on Brook's part.

How long can I keep up this bloody voice? And when he looks into my eyes, he's going to know. They aren't your usual shade and he's stared into them often enough.

Lenny got a lot of compliments on his eyes, especially when he highlighted them with mascara; a deep shade of aqua, they were a standout. Other than his dick and arse, Brook had been enamoured with them.

Leslie was fidgeting nervously, staring anywhere but at Brook. Lenny took a deep breath and levelled his eyes at Brook, pitching his voice higher then picking up the folder lying on his desk. He looked down at it, glad of the excuse to leave that chocolate-brown gaze behind.

"Thank you. I'm very appreciative you took the time to do this." He didn't want to say too much because his natural voice was low and husky. If he said any more, he had a feeling he'd fuck it up.

Brook's face creased in a frown and he stared at Lenny intently. Lenny ignored it, along with Leslie's sudden hiss of breath, and carried on pretending to read the proposal. In truth, Lenny couldn't see anything, only a blur of words. He tried to concentrate and made thoughtful nods now and then to show he was considering the document. He felt the curious gaze on him as he pseudo-read.

Then the silence was broken. "Excuse me for asking this, but do I know you from somewhere?" Brook leaned forward and his stare became more focused. "I have this feeling we've met before."

Lenny swallowed and waved a hand. "No, I don't think we've met before. I think I'd recognise you." He cleared his throat and stared fixedly down at the desk. His insides churned and he'd never felt so nauseous. Not even when he'd eaten some bad chicken in Honk Kong one business trip and coughed his lungs up.

"Huh. I guess so." Brook smiled and sat back. Both Lenny and Leslie breathed a sigh of relief. "So what do you think of the proposal? Do you think it might better meet your requirements?"

Lenny nodded desperately. It was an extremely generous offer and he'd be an idiot not to take it. He needed time to recover himself. "It gives me something to think about, certainly. Can you leave it with me and I'll get back to you?"

Brook looked a little nonplussed. "Well, of course I could do that. Don't you want to discuss it now then? Do you have any questions?"

Yes. How the fuck did I get myself into this situation?

Lenny made a humming noise, an inane sound that made him wince. "I'm really not feeling very well at the moment, sorry. Perhaps we can reschedule this meeting?"

Brook stood up, his face concerned. "You do seem a little out of sorts. Maybe some water might help?" He reached over and picked up the water jug on Lenny's desk, and poured a glass into a tumbler next to it.

With shaking hands, Lenny reached out for it, trying to smile as he did so but his face felt frozen, so who knew what it looked like—the Joker gone wrong perhaps.

“Thank you, that’s sweet of—oh, thundershit. Fuck it.”

The glass had slipped from his hands and spilled all over the desk, and all over Lenny, ice cold water flooding his crotch. It was Leslie’s soft shriek of horror that alerted him to what he’d done. In his flustered state, Lenny had completely forgotten to use the higher-pitched voice for those last few swear words. He’d also uttered his catchphrase swear word, and Brook no doubt would recognise it. He’d had said it often enough, even in bed when writhing beneath his magnificent, sweaty body. He looked straight up and met a startled gaze, one that was slowly turning to disbelief.

Resigned, his gaze locked on confused brown eyes as he knew with dread in his heart that he’d definitely been rumbled.

There’s no getting out of this one. The thundershit has hit the fan.

“Lenny?” Brook’s stunned face made him wince. Leslie was sitting stock-still, face pale, biting his bottom lip as he glanced between the other two men. Brook stood up, tension radiating from his wide shoulders.

“Leslie, would you mind leaving us alone for a minute?” Lenny’s throat was dry and his heart clamoured. Hell in a hand basket. At least he had his own voice back.

“Of course, boss.” Leslie stood up and shot him a sympathetic glance. He turned to Brook and fixed his vivid blue gaze on him.

“He’s still Lenny under there,” Leslie said softly. “Please remember that.”

With one last reassuring smile at Lenny, whose throat had tightened at the sincerity and caring in those words, Leslie left the room.

Once Leslie had left, gently shutting the door behind him, the two stared at each other. Lenny’s heart beat rapidly, his hands clammy. He had no idea why he was so nervous. After all, he was who he was and normally anyone who didn’t like it could fuck off. This was Brook though; it was different.

“Tell me.” Brook’s taut words broke the silence. “You want to tell me the hell why you tried to hide from me just now?”

Lenny closed his eyes briefly and opened them to see Brook's face tight with fury, his eyes fierce. "I didn't know how you'd feel about it. I wanted to tell you about Laverne at dinner on Saturday night when we met. Not have you find out this way."

"So instead you thought you'd treat me like an idiot, put on that stupid high voice and play me for a fool? You didn't trust me enough with the truth, no matter how I might have taken it?" Brook's jaw clenched, the angry tic in it evident.

Lenny raised his hands helplessly. "I never meant to make you feel foolish. I didn't think—"

Brook laughed harshly. "Oh, you got that right. You didn't bloody think at all. Your employee seems to think I'm some sort of arsehole who'll judge you badly for dressing up. Where the hell would he get that impression?"

Lenny swallowed. "I might have mentioned something to him you said a while back…" his voice trailed off at the incredulous look Brook gave him.

"What the hell did I say for you to think I'd be like that?" Brook levelled a stare at Lenny that, had it been a ball, would have thwacked him between the eyes and caused grievous bodily harm.

Lenny smoothed nervous hands down the front of his blouse, noticing how the other man's eyes followed them, and his eyes narrowed at the gesture. He looked…a little distracted at seeing the boobs across Lenny's chest.

"We were watching Ru Paul, remember? You said it wasn't your cup of tea, and you wouldn't want your man dressing up like a woman and put on display like that."

Brook looked a little taken aback at the reminder. Some of the tension left his body as he ran a hand over his short black hair. "Well, yeah, I might have said that. I'm a pretty old-fashioned guy and you threw me a bit. Doesn't mean I'd be a dick about someone who *did* like that sort of thing though. Each to his own and all that." He scowled. "Is that why you blew me off? Because you thought I'd get all funny about it?"

Lenny had nothing else to say other than the truth. "Yes."

The word hung in the air like a bad smell.

Brook nodded. "I'm disappointed in you. It might have been a bit of a shock to find out you were"—he waved a hand at Lenny—"Laverne, but it would have been my choice to figure things out. I'm not that much into the cross-dressing thing but—" His jaw clenched. "I really liked *you*."

Lenny's heart sank at the past tense. "I was going to tell you when we had dinner on Saturday night. I'd made up my mind already that whatever happened, I'd accept it. I really like you too." If Brook noticed Lenny's use of the present tense, he didn't acknowledge it. Instead he leant down to pick up his briefcase. He stood observing Lenny for a moment then inclined his head.

"I'll leave the proposal with you to have a look at," he said quietly. His face was sad. "I'm still interested in doing business with you as Laverne Debussy-Smith. I think it could be good for us both."

Lenny's throat burned. "But not interested in doing business with me in other ways," he managed to get out. "Because of this." He waved down his front and Brook shook his head.

"Not because of that. First because you broke up with me because you presumed you knew what I'd be like before you even gave us a chance. Then today, you lied to me about who you are. That doesn't bode well for 'resuming' anything, does it?"

He turned to walk out the door. Lenny took a deep breath.

Here goes all or nothing.

"Wait." Lenny moved around the desk to stand beside Brook. "When I saw you…I'm sorry I tried to pull the wool over your eyes. I panicked." He raised his hands in frustration. "I didn't want to tell you like this, here, in front of an employee. I thought if I could hide it for now, it would have been so much better telling you over a glass of wine and a good meal. Please let me still have that chance, with just the two of us. Then you can tell me how you feel about it, and I'll be fine with whatever you have to say."

Lenny held his breath as he waited for Brook's reply. He held it so long, he felt his chest tighten. When Brook remained stoically silent, Lenny exhaled then added. "And to be clear—at dinner I'll be Lenny, not Laverne. I don't wear this persona out of work." He hastened to qualify that statement with blabber. "Well, unless I'm at a fashion event where everyone expects her of course. Or out on the catwalk, talking to my prima donna models, or doing something else Laverney." He winced at using that word but it fit. "But weekends and out of work and in bed, of course, although you know that already, I'm all Lenny."

He saw the faint turn up of Brook's mouth at the corners at that last comment and Lenny took heart in that small sign of forgiveness.

Then Brook nodded and Lenny's heart gave a thump of relief. "Okay, let's still meet for dinner. But I'd rather make it dinner at my place than a restaurant. It's more private and we can talk. Can you come over for eight?"

Lenny nodded. "Of course. I'll see you there then."

Brook gave a curt nod then his lithe frame disappeared out the door. Once again, Lenny gave a sigh of relief. He'd barely had time to turn to go back to his desk to take another drink from his brandy stash when a fragrantly scented dervish came whirling into the room.

"Oh—my—God, that was epic—epically bad." Leslie's hands fluttered like flags in a gale. "How did it go? What did he say? Is he mad? He didn't look that mad; he even had a teensy weensy smile. Is everything okay?"

"Leslie, my love." Lenny's head hurt. "Please shut the fuck up. I need a damn drink." He plonked down into his chair, removed the brandy bottle from his drawer and took a swig from it.

Leslie regarded him with flashing eyes as he sat down in the visitor chair. "Tell me, damn it," he snapped. "You don't get to put me through that awful experience with that dreadful camp voice—I think I threw up in my mouth a bit, it was that bad—and then tell me to shut the fuck up."

"I do actually," Lenny said drily. "I'm your boss." He took another swig from the brandy bottle and then passed it to his protégé. He gave a silent snigger, expecting him to knock it back and choke, but instead, he was left gaping at the sight of Leslie swallowing it down like a champion. When the bottle was passed back to him with a smirk, it was far emptier than it had been.

"I'm good at drinking and swallowing," Leslie remarked slyly, no doubt seeing his look of disbelief. "And I happen to love brandy."

Lenny raised the bottle towards him. "Touché, little one. Touché." He drank deeply, and then put the bottle on the desk.

Leslie raised perfectly manicured eyebrows quizzically. "So?"

"We're still having dinner on Saturday night, at his place." Lenny murmured.

Leslie shrieked in glee.

Lenny winced. "It's early days yet."

Leslie shook his head vehemently. "He's seen you as both people and still wants to have dinner. That's a good sign."

Lenny sighed. "I hope so. I don't want to fuck this up any more than I have."

"You didn't fuck anything up." Leslie's tone was adamant. "To quote you, today was a major thundershit of a day which turned out better than expected." He grinned as a cheeky smile lit his face. "He is damn hot though. I can see why you fancy him."

"Yeah, he is." Lenny agreed. "Now, chicken, perhaps you should leave my office and let me finish this day in some semblance of peace. I'm sure you have some shelves to pack, or some orders to process."

Leslie stood up. "One word of advice. Please don't *ever* use that horrible voice again. You sounded like a chipmunk on crack." He gave a wicked smile and flounced out of the room, leaving Lenny wondering in bemusement what a chipmunk on crack might even sound like.

He contemplated the brandy bottle and then gave a sigh and tucked away the now half-empty bottle in his drawer. He had no desire to be pissed getting home on the tube tonight. The last time he'd done that, instead of getting home to his beautifully converted ground floor apartment in an old warehouse in Shoreditch, he'd ended up in Tower Hamlets, and that experience had been as scary as hell. He still didn't have any idea how he'd ended up in the slummier part of the city. Luckily he'd not encountered any trouble and gotten out of there fast. No, he'd be a good lad and finish the day off in style. Then he'd go home and probably jack off thinking of Brook and bask in the thought that in a couple of days' time, he'd be with him. Hopefully things would work out for the best. Or not. Lenny gave a mental shrug. One way or another he'd know whether he needed to move on.

Chapter 7

That special Saturday couldn't come around soon enough. Dressed in a pair of tight black chinos, a Ralph Lauren white button-down shirt with a black-and-white-striped tie, and his favourite rust-red, military-style jacket, open at the front, Lenny thought he'd power dressed well enough to get through the evening. He knocked on the door of Brook's flat in Camden, having been announced and let up to the third floor by the building concierge.

He heard footsteps and then the door opened. Brook stood there, all six foot plus of him, looking as handsome as Lenny remembered. A short-sleeved indigo blue polo shirt clung to his chest, highlighting every curve and toned muscle, and the jeans he wore hugged his groin and hips and emphasized the strong line of his legs. He was barefoot. Lenny's dick took notice of the whole sexy package. He was gratified to see those brown eyes sweeping across his body and there was no mistaking the appreciation in them.

"Come in," Brook's voice was husky as he beckoned him in. "You know the drill. Make yourself comfortable and I'll get you a drink. Would you like whisky or a beer?"

The fragrance of something spicy wafted from the open plan kitchen to the left. On the right, a tiled hallway led to where Lenny knew the bedrooms were. The whole apartment was spacious, open and minimally furnished, with a long red couch, a palatial beanbag and a small coffee table in the lounge. One wall was filled with TV and sound equipment. Brook loved gadgets.

"Whisky please." The scent of Brook's aftershave hardened Lenny's cock and he squirmed. They'd always had this crazy, physical attraction between them, hardly able to be alone in the same room together without jumping each other's bones. He was pleased to see it was still the same. For him, anyway. Hard to tell where the night would take them.

They'd spent a lot of nights here in the privacy of this flat, and one weekend they'd barely gotten out of bed except a couple of times to eat and then take a shower before Lenny left for home when they were satiated. It had been hot, dirty and as sexy as fuck. The mere thought of it made Lenny's groin ache.

He wandered over to the picture window that spanned the room, looking out onto the green two floors below. A memory of being roughly shoved against that cold glass while Brook fucked him made him shiver. Goosebumps blossomed on his skin and he hitched a breath. He traced a finger against the cold glass.

"I remember that time too." Brook's breath brushed his ear and Lenny closed his eyes, revelling in the sound of that deep voice. He took a deep breath and turned to face the man. Brook held out his drink and he took it, staring into smouldering eyes and wanting to claim the other man's kissable lips with every deep desire he possessed.

"It was…memorable." He took a sip of his whisky, enjoying the burn as it went down. Brook regarded Lenny steadily, focusing on his mouth. Lenny's skin prickled with want. His cock was hard and aching and he didn't think he'd be able to eat anything. His hunger was only for the man standing in front of him. He glanced down at Brook's crotch and was gratified to see he was feeling the same, the bulge against the front of his jeans certainly living up to his own memory of it.

Huh, I've only been here a few minutes and already we're getting busy. This chemistry thing is a miracle.

"I'm glad you came over." Brook brushed Lenny's shoulder absently with fingers that sent a thrill through him. "I had time to think about what you said and I think I understand why you did what you did. It was a bit of a shock to me though. I've never known anyone like you before." He grinned. "Sexy as a man and quite unforgettable as a businesswoman."

Lenny was mesmerised by the eyes staring into his. "It's not quite the norm; I get that. But I hope we can work it out."

Brook smiled. "The chemistry is still there, though. No doubt about that." His brows furrowed. "And if I remember from our last window encounter, you promised to return the favour," he murmured as he reached out and removed the glass from Lenny's hands. He put the whisky down on the table by the window then dipped his finger in the cool liquid. Brook's finger came up, and he slid it across Lenny's bottom lip, slowly. Lenny thought he was going to shoot in his pants with the eroticism of that gesture. The whisky flavour burned into his lips and he slid his tongue out and sucked the finger caressing his mouth. Brook's eyes widened in lust, the pupils expanding. His lips parted and Lenny wanted to thrust his tongue and his cock inside the hot, wet heat of that mouth.

"Let's get this over with, shall we, because obviously neither of us can wait," Brook whispered, as his tongue slid into Lenny's ear. His hands slid under the red jacket, tugging the shirt from his trousers, and then caressing the heated skin beneath. "Otherwise we'll not enjoy my wonderful chicken cacciatore that I slaved over all day. Let's fuck first, talk later."

Lenny agreed wholeheartedly. With a low moan, he mashed his mouth against Brook's and took possession of it. Familiar and wanton in return, Brook's questing tongue slid into Lenny's mouth. The slippery sensation of that deliciously heated organ, currently on a quest to drive him crazy, took him back to those passion-fuelled days when he and Brook had been together. The feel of strong fingers against Lenny's skin and the heat of that body pressed against his—it was if they'd never been apart. Lenny wasn't one for insta-love, but insta-lust he could definitely understand.

"I'd forgotten how damn good you taste and feel," Brook gasped as his hands fumbled with buttons, opening Lenny's trousers. He cried out as Brook's hand slid inside his silk boxers and slid fingers down his hardened and wet cock. "This—this is what I want, you inside me."

That phrase made Lenny thrust his cock harder into the tight confines of Brook's hand.

"You keep saying that and I won't have anything to fuck you with because you'll make me come," he managed to get out. "Turn around, face the glass." He didn't wait for Brook to obey, simply spun him round hard and slammed him against the cold, silken wall. "You'd better hope this *is* one-way glass, because otherwise your neighbours are going to see *you* being royally skewered this time." Lenny kicked off his trousers and underwear, giving a sigh of relief as his cock sprung free.

"I'm not *that* much of an exhibitionist. Of course it's one-way," Brook gasped, his hands splayed against the glass, his breathing erratic and wild. Lenny unceremoniously reached around and unzipped his lover's jeans, yanking them down his muscled thighs. He almost expired on the spot at the sight of that tight, rounded arse being pushed out at him. Brook wore no underwear.

“Jesus Christ,” Lenny managed to get out in between desperately wondering how he was ever going to be able to leave this man to get the lube and condoms he knew were in a drawer in the fancy wall unit. “Are you trying to kill me?”

Of their own volition, his hands gripped Brook’s cheeks and he squeezed them tightly, wanting to sink his teeth into those taut globes.

The low chuckle from in front of him made Lenny’s cock reach up and take more notice.

“No, that would be a waste.” Brook waggled his arse out, causing Lenny’s breathing to heighten and his chest to tighten. “Now hurry up and get the stuff. You always did talk too much during sex.” He ground his cock against the glass, giving a hiss of pleasure as he did so.

Lenny reluctantly moved away from the taut body holding him captive as he went to the nearest unit and rummaged in a drawer. He found what he was looking for and ripped open the packet, settling the latex cover on his aching cock. He opened the lube then pressed himself against Brook again, letting him feel his hardness in the crease of his arse. Brook gave a low cry and arched his back more, offering himself.

Brook groaned through gritted teeth. “Hurry up. I need that gorgeous cock of yours *right now*. I’m going crazy here.” He hissed loudly as Lenny’s fingers smoothed the lube around his hole then pressed inside him. “Don’t stand on ceremony, lover. Warm me up a bit.”

Lenny did exactly that. He fingered Brook until he groaned with need then Lenny yanked his hips back and pushed Brook down by his shoulders until he was bent over. Lenny slid into where he wanted to be with a strangled sigh, closing his eyes in beatification at being enveloped with sudden heat and tightness. There was no more talking, only the sound of grunts and groans, and the occasional squeak of sweaty fingers on glass as Brook’s hands lost traction with the force at which Lenny was pummelling his body. This was raw and primal, sex for sex’s sake, and he wasn’t too proud to admit it. There would be time for conversation and emotion later. For now, he simply wanted to take this man he so desired until neither of them could think or talk. Dirty words out of Brook’s mouth promising more delights of the flesh spurred Lenny on.

Lenny heard the hitch in Brook's breathing and his stuttered expletives as he pushed further back, his muscles tightening around Lenny. He knew his lover was close to coming. Hell, Lenny didn't know how he'd made it this far without shooting *his* load. It was taking all his self-control to hold out this long.

Lenny reached around and grasped hold of the dick that was currently ramrod hard as it smacked against the window every time he thrust in. Brook jerked and groaned at the gesture as spurts of spunk coated the windowpane and floor with thick, creamy ribbons of musky release. Lenny gave a thankful whoosh of breath as his orgasm hit and he slumped over his partner's sweaty, muscled back, breathing deeply and loving the pure animal smell of sex and sweat between them.

"I need to stand up," Brook gasped. "I feel like a damn rag doll bent down like this."

Lenny held the condom tight and moved away, pulling it off and tying it. Brook straightened up, rolling his shoulders with a wince. "That was hot as hell but I couldn't do it again too soon," he chuckled. He reached down and pulled his trousers up, leaving them open. His cock hung flaccid in front and all Lenny wanted to do was get it going again.

"Your window cleaner's going to get a surprise when he sees that." He smirked as he waved at the sticky goo on the glass pane.

Brook flashed him a smile. "Lucky I'm that guy then, isn't it?" He regarded the mess ruefully. "I'll clean it up later. Right now, it's time to freshen up and check my chicken."

"I thought I already did that," Lenny said slyly. "Your cock was fine, from what I saw."

Brook gave a deep, rumbling laugh. "Ouch. That was a terrible joke. In fact, dire is the word." He gestured towards the hallway. "If you want a shower or anything, feel free. I'll just go and wipe myself off. I'm hoping to get lucky again later." His eyes raked Lenny from head to toe.

Lenny swallowed. "Me too. I'm good for now, thanks." He retrieved his briefs and chinos from where he'd kicked them, used his underwear to clean most of the sticky spunk off himself then pulled on his trousers. The air was redolent with the musky scent of sex and cooking. And he was suddenly self- conscious. Here he was, stinking of sweat and semen and he still had to explain about Laverne. Lenny had never been this insecure about her before.

It was only when they were sitting down at the kitchen island, drinking wine and eating their meal that Brook broached the subject they'd been skirting around.

"So," he said quietly as he poked around his plate, probably looking for the chicken that was in there somewhere. "Now we've got that urge out of the way, tell me about Laverne."

Lenny took a deep breath and laid his knife and fork down. "I studied at the London College of Fashion when I was eighteen." He stared down at the table. "I knew then I wanted to design clothing people would wear and say, 'Hey, that's one of Lenny James's designs.'" He grinned softly as he looked over at Brook. "Trouble is, I'm a damn perfectionist. I was designing clothes for men *and* women, and to do that, I needed to know how it felt to wear fashion as both. I already knew how my designs fit as a man because I'd been doing it since I was fourteen—making my own clothes." He cleared his throat and took a sip of his wine. Brook's eyes were kind but cautious. "So I decided the best way to do that was dress like a woman, fake boobs and all, and see how fabric draped, how it rode up over the backside, how it fell from the hips, felt across the stomach. I spent days in costume, getting in and out of taxis, buses, toilets, anything that gave me an inkling of how some of my clothing would feel if I wore it as a woman." He took another sip of his drink and stared into Brook's eyes, almost challengingly. "And I liked it."

Brook raised his wine glass and took a drink. His face was noncommittal. "What did you like about it?" he asked quietly.

Lenny shrugged. "I liked the feel of the silk of the underwear and the softness of the fabrics. I liked the fact if I wore a corset underneath my clothes it held me in, made my posture better. I felt sexy. And wearing heels with it gave me this sense of power, of being bigger than everyone else. I felt more empowered somehow."

He saw Brook's Adam apple bob as he swallowed then Brook spoke. "I understand some of that, the need for someone creative like you to make sure that you get the research done for what you're creating, like authors do with their books. I don't understand quite how it became part of your everyday life. Not that there's anything wrong with it," he hastened to qualify his statement. "I'm trying to understand why you'd develop this whole other *you* as a result of that experiment."

"It wasn't any type of 'experiment,'" Lenny said gently. "I wasn't a confused gender queen trying to decide whether I was male or female, I—" He stopped, seeing the relief in Brook's eyes and hearing his soft exhalation of breath. "Fuck me. Is that what you thought? That I might one day run off and decide I wanted a damn lady cave?" He didn't know whether to be insulted or laugh. He thought he'd proven his masculinity and his love of being a man more than once when he'd pounded Brook's arse.

Brook looked ill at ease. "I didn't know, really. I don't know much about this whole cross-dressing thing. I mean, I Googled it, and it came up with words like transvestite and transgender…" His voice tailed off and he looked at Lenny with uncertain eyes.

Lenny drained his wine and pushed it over for Brook to refill. "Okay. Let me play it straight then." They both sniggered slightly at that phrase. "I *am* a transvestite. I wear women's clothing and have a whole different persona when I do. That doesn't mean I'm going to run out and get a va-jay-jay, or have boob implants. I love being a man and having a dick."

Lenny continued Brook's sadly lacking education. "I'm also not going to run off and join a drag show, although I have partaken in one or two in my lifetime. My best friend Ryan is a drag queen with his own club, and every now and again, I enjoy being flamboyant." He gave Brook a sly smile. "And I'm definitely not transgender because, as I said, I have no desire to be a woman physically. Hell, Brook, Google is your friend and Wikipedia does great things to explain all this stuff."

There was silence as Lenny took another gulp of his drink. He really needed something stronger than wine if he was going to continue this conversation. He took a deep breath.

"Look, I created Laverne Debussy-Smith back at university because it was fun to have a name to the woman I was when I cross-dressed. It entertained my friends, it made me feel good and somehow it stuck. I didn't always use her though, not until I got my fashion business. Then, I was so embedded in the fashion scene as both Lenny and Laverne; I decided it would be good to have the two sides of me. Laverne won the toss-up as the embodiment of the business, and looking back, I think it was the right decision."

"I'm not judging you, Lenny," Brook said softly. "I really enjoy your company. And if we're going to do this seeing each other thing, I need to understand you a bit more. And Laverne too, obviously." He smiled, but Lenny saw the hesitation in it. His stomach fell. He wasn't sure he was getting through to Brook, although his words gave Lenny some comfort Brook wasn't going to run screaming from the room.

Brook leaned forward as his fingers toyed with his wineglass. "Aren't you scared some people might take exception to you dressing as a woman and try and pick on you?" His voice was tentative. "Even hurt you somehow? I've seen that happen and it isn't something I could go through again."

Lenny snorted. "They can fucking try. I used to do martial arts and box. I can take care of myself."

Brook didn't look convinced, his face creasing in a frown. Lenny twirled his wine glass in his fingers and sighed sadly. "We have so many faces we have to wear each day as a man. Brother, son, partner, the bedrock of the family, the provider. That was how it was engrained in me when I was growing up. Men are men; that's what my father tried to teach me, over and over again." He heard the hate in his own voice. "Laverne allowed me to be someone else, someone where I could escape the pressures of being a man, be softer, be in control of who I am…" He stopped, aware he'd probably said more than he'd intended.

With a tender look, Brook leaned over and brushed fingers down Lenny's jawline. "You didn't like your dad." His matter-of-fact statement opened the floodgates in Lenny's soul. This was a story he didn't tell anyone. Only his dear friend and sometime fuck-buddy, Ryan, knew about this part of his life.

Lenny's tone was flat. "I never use the term 'dad' to apply to my father. *Dad* is someone you can respect, love." He rubbed his thumb over Brook's fingers. "My father was one of those who insisted his son be manly, be the strong one. He took me hunting, tried to make me kill things, wanted me to play rugby and be like him. I didn't live up to his expectations and he made sure I knew that. I was too soft, too girly in his eyes, because I didn't play much sport or go hunting. I preferred reading fashion magazines, tracing out patterns and creating my own clothes." His voice cracked slightly. He hated telling this story, hated pity of any kind when he explained what kind of man his father had been. But if it gave Brook more insight into the person that was Lenny, he was willing to do it.

Brook leaned over, concern on his face, and covered Lenny's hand with his warm one. "He sounds tough."

Lenny gave a harsh laugh. "I hated him. My father was a hard, unpitying man and all he wanted was his only son to one day run the family farm. My younger sisters, Jane and Patrice, were beneath that consideration, being female. My mother was a timid, frightened woman whose only mission in life was to please him."

Brook's hand tightened on his. "I'm sorry you had such an experience," he murmured, fingers stroking Lenny's.

Lenny nodded, his throat tight. "There was this one day when I was twelve. My father hit me when I refused to pull the trigger on a poor, petrified rabbit cowering by the side of the shed where we lived on the farm in Suffolk. He ignored everything I said to him about not wanting to and why, cocked the rifle and blew the poor creature to smithereens. Then he made me clean up the mess."

Brook gasped. "That's fucking wrong."

Lenny nodded tiredly. "I cried that night in bed. I was damned if I'd have done that in front of him. He would have smacked me around a bit more then locked me in the cellar for the night." He grinned twistedly. "I hated that fucking place. Dark, cold and noises no one could explain. I didn't want to end up down there again. I spent too much time in there as it was, locked in with no supper, until *he* decided to let me out."

Brook's look of horror caused Lenny to reach over and kiss him gently. "It's a long time ago," he murmured as his lips brushed over Brook's. "I try to forget that part of my life."

"Where is the rest of your family?" Brook's head tilted. "Your mum and your sisters?"

Lenny's heart clenched and he felt the familiar grief well inside. "They're dead," he said curtly. "They all died in a fire at the farm after I'd left."

He laughed again but there was no amusement in it. "Or rather after I was kicked out at fifteen when my father decided I wasn't the son he wanted. Some busybody told him I'd been seen in an alleyway doing disgusting things to another boy." His words were mocking. "It was only a damn blowjob. When I got home, he beat the shit out of me, pushed me out of the house and that was the last I ever saw of any of them. I wasn't allowed to go back. It would have been impossible to go home since my father told lies about me to my sisters, about what I'd done. I don't know exactly what he told them, but they didn't want to see me again. I got a letter from Jane a few months after I left telling me never to get in touch again. Mum went along with whatever Dad said. She wasn't a very strong woman." He smiled sadly. "The farm burnt down about three years later. I heard about their deaths from another relative. I wasn't even invited to the funerals."

Brook didn't even hesitate. He stood up swiftly, went over to a startled Lenny and pulled him up. Lenny found himself being enveloped in strong arms as soft kisses were pressed to his forehead. "He was an arsehole," Brook whispered fiercely. "He didn't deserve a son like you. I'm so lucky to have the parents I have. I can't imagine what you went through."

Lenny closed his eyes and inhaled Brook's scent. "It was an experience," he admitted as his lips trailed soft kisses down Brook's throat.

"Actually, I was lucky," Lenny continued. "When I was kicked out I found a place I could call home for a while. It was in an old dojo on the outskirts of town. The guy who owned it, Patrick, took me in and I did odd jobs around there until I was old enough to stand on my own two feet." His voice quietened as he remembered the gruff, taciturn man who'd changed his life. "He was a godsend for me. He was kind, rough and not interested in my body. He taught me how to defend myself, put a roof over my head, and when he died," Lenny's voice softened at the memory of watching someone he'd cared deeply about die slowly of cancer, "I learned he was very wealthy, and he left me everything. I was able to put myself through fashion college, buy a small place of my own and eventually, I started Debussy's." He placed a soft kiss on Brook's lips. "And I found you. Then I pushed you away, because I didn't want to get hurt." He made a moue. "I was an idiot."

Brook's eyes searched Lenny's face. "You are something else," he whispered and Lenny closed his eyes as hard, demanding lips covered his and Brook's tongue snaked in and took possession. Their bodies ground together and hardening cocks pressed against each other. Lenny moaned into Brook's mouth.

"Oh, what you do to me. You're like this incubus I can't resist."

Brook nibbled at Lenny's ear. "Incubus? Hmmm. I like that description of me as a wanton, sex-mad demon." He pulled away with a wicked grin, leaving Lenny aching and horny. "Come on, it's time for dessert. I made a New York cheesecake."

Lenny stared at him incredulously. "You give me a boner then expect me to eat cheesecake?"

"Stop pouting like that," Brook murmured. "It's pretty cute and makes me want to rip your clothes off." He chuckled as Lenny's eyes widened both in indignation and anticipation.

"I am not cute," Lenny spluttered. "I have staff who are cute but that's not me."

Brook regarded him in amusement. "Uh-huh. Definitely cute." He danced off towards the kitchen. "Cake first, and then we can get busy again. And we still have some more talking to do," he warned. "I'm sure there's a lot more you can tell me about yourself."

Lenny rolled his eyes. "I can see this is going to be one of *those* relationships," he griped. "You feed me until I'm fat and can't fit in my clothes anymore then talk me to death after wild monkey sex."

Brook turned slowly and Lenny's stomach fell.

Shit, had he used the R word? It was a bit soon for that, wasn't it? He didn't even know if, after all this talking, Brook was going to still see him.

Brook didn't look perturbed about it. Hope flamed in Lenny's chest that perhaps this might all turn out for the best.

Brook looked at him, his gaze heated. "Are you going to stand there and flap those gorgeous lips, or are you going to get over here, eat cake, and then let me fuck you?" His satisfied yet ultra-sexy smirk at seeing Lenny race over to the kitchen counter ignited another spark of desire in his groin. That damn cake had better go down smoothly and quickly because he couldn't wait much longer to have that promise fulfilled.

Chapter 8

The next few weeks were both a pleasure and a torture. Despite the great sex and the welcome company, Brook was aware there was an elephant in the room regarding his and Lenny's relationship.

Her name was Laverne.

Lenny and Brook had talked about the alter ego, and while Brook accepted she existed, he was struggling to accept it wholeheartedly. Laverne was the reason they didn't stay over at each other's places when they got together. Lenny would need a whole suitcase to drag to Brook's place to get ready in the morning. Instead, he preferred to go home in the early hours so he could get some sleep before work. For that reason, Brook tended to spend most nights at Lenny's place. It was still a little disquieting seeing his lover dress up as a woman before going to work.

Brook still worried about Lenny in public when he went out dressed like that. He was working on his insecurities with the situation, but given a past bad experience, it was taking time.

He'd decided he needed to better get to know the woman that was Laverne Debussy-Smith. And what better way to do this than at her workplace, during a fashion show tonight? Brook was looking forward to it but was a little nervous about seeing the woman in action. He chuckled to himself. He had a business excuse to be there. The loan Lenny had agreed to accept from his company had come through and Brook thought he'd check out his investment.

He picked up his keys and jacket, stepped into the corridor and was busy locking the door when he heard a noise behind him. He turned to see his neighbour stepping out. Brook had often had people knock on his door mistaking his flat 22A for 22B. The weirdly named occupant, Mango Munroe, of said 22B was a bit of an enigma and had the nocturnal habits worthy of a badger.

"Evening, neighbour." A soft, Somerset drawl echoed in the hallway. Mango was a little intimidating. In his mid-thirties, he was about six foot two, broad and well-built with knotted muscles in his forearms, and an untidy mess of golden brown hair that fell forward over his forehead. Brook had always thought he had a rather dangerous air about him. It lurked in his eyes; they were watchful, almost black and seemed to take a man's measure in one narrow-eyed glance.

Rumours from some of the other inhabitants of the building told the story of how, in his younger days, Mango had been at some fox hunting protest. When challenged with force and told to leave the area, he'd managed to take out a contingent of three police officers using only the cricket bat he held and an antique knuckle duster. The urban legend also said he'd spent a year in prison for some or other escapade, the details of which were unknown. The building tenants held him in some sort of worshipful regard.

"You off to the fashion show? You look pretty spruced up." Mango grinned. Brook frowned, wondering how Mango knew about it.

"Yes. Are you going too?" He didn't think so. Mango was dressed more for a casual night out on the town with his blue jeans and polo shirt.

"Nah." Mango shrugged. "Not my cup of tea, more the…" He hesitated. "The boyfriend's. He's into that stuff. We have a mutual acquaintance—your man Lenny."

Brook stared at him. "You know him then?"

Mango is gay?

Mango grinned. "I know Lenny well. He's a great guy."

Brook was taken aback. "Small world," he murmured. It explained how he knew about Brook and the fashion show. He must have seen them together.

"Well, enjoy yourself. Give Laverne a big kiss from me. I love that woman." Mango grinned and waved goodbye as he disappeared down the corridor towards the lifts.

Brook nodded. "Sure, I'll do that."

He huffed out a breath as he left the building to get to the tube station. Time to get to the show and see exactly what he'd let himself in for in getting involved with Lenny.

***

An hour later he stared around the room with wide-eyed yet horrified fascination. Coming here had been a brave decision and one he was beginning to regret.

Chaos. Complete, unmitigated chaos.

Around him he watched squabbling fashion models in various eye-popping stages of undress; tits, dicks and bits wobbling everywhere he looked. Shrill jibes, soft exclamations and resigned entreaties flavoured the air in a symphony of discordant music.

The bottom floor of the Debussy offices was a hub of beautiful, mostly naked flesh, frazzled employees, screaming queens, screeching divas and every now and then the voice of reason from a large, calm individual whom Brook only knew as Dasher. There was also the slim, rather hyperactive figure of the man Brook had met in Laverne's office the day of Brook's abortive visit.

Leslie Scott looked like a fashion model himself with those deep blue eyes and elegant frame, all draped in a classic, grey suit with a bright red tie. The man standing next to him looking like he'd stepped out of *GQ* magazine was watching him with laughing eyes and a swathe of blond hair that fell over his handsome face. Brook imagined that was Oliver, Leslie's boyfriend and the infamous adult entertainer, Nicky Starr. Lenny had mentioned them both fondly in conversation.

Oliver's eyes narrowed when a man approached Leslie with a cheeky grin and enveloped him in a hug fit enough to smother the smaller man while copping a feel of Leslie's admittedly pert arse. The man was dark-haired with a goatee, sparkling brown eyes and well-built with an easy smile. Leslie had called him Maxwell. Oliver watched the easy interchange of the pair, but Brook thought in amusement if Maxwell had got much *more* familiar with the laughing, admittedly sexy Leslie, he might be missing a few teeth by the end of the night.

He sighed heavily. Fashion shows weren't something he went to regularly, but for Lenny and of course, Laverne, he'd made the effort so he could see his lover in action. It was about time he observed Laverne Debussy-Smith in her native environment. He couldn't put it off much longer if he wanted to be with Lenny. And he *did* want to be with Lenny.

He smiled as Leslie bustled over to him, dragging his boyfriend behind him, followed by Maxwell. Oliver wore both a look of resignation and amusement at his hyperactive partner's antics.

"Brook," Leslie exclaimed as he came in for a hug, nearly knocking Brook off his feet. The man certainly didn't have any PDA issues. "How wonderful you're here. Laverne will be so pleased." His eyes twinkled, but behind them Brook sensed a warning not to fuck things up tonight for her in any way. "This is my boyfriend,

Oliver." He bounced excitedly and cast an adoring look at his partner. "And this is Oliver's friend, Maxwell. He's flown in from New York and he's on a stay over. Max is a flight attendant. He flies all over the world, the lucky bitch."

Brook grinned and hugged Leslie. "Of course, I wouldn't miss it. It'll give me a chance to see the lady herself in action." He extricated himself to shake hands with Oliver.

"Brook." Oliver nodded. "Good to meet you at last. He's told me a bit about you but it's good to meet the man behind the gossip." He grinned widely and cast an affectionate look at Leslie.

Leslie sniffed regally. "Uh-uh, I am not a gossipmonger, baby. I love a bit of idle chat."

Brook laughed as he shook Maxwell's hand, noticing the sly, slow brush of Maxwell's thumb over his palm and the swift glance at his crotch.

Hmm, this man is a definite player. He's cute, but he's not Lenny.

"Nice to meet you too, Maxwell." Brook released the hand that was holding his a little too long and grinned. "It must be an interesting job, flying all over the world?"

Maxwell shrugged. For the first time Brook noticed dark shadows under Maxwell's eyes. "It's a lot of fun. You get to meet people and see the world and fuck a guy in every port, so I guess people would think it was a cool job."

His smile didn't reach his eyes and Brook thought his words, probably meant to shock, had sounded a little contrived. From the quick, concerned glance Oliver threw his friend, he seemed to think so too.

"Maxwell is staying with me for a few days," Oliver said softly. "He's been a little unwell. He picked up some bug in one of those ports although he's over it now. Someone needed to make sure he eats properly and rests a bit more." He reached out an arm and gently punched his friend in the solar plexus in a mock boxing move.

"Yeah, I wasn't really in the mood to come tonight, but Leslie insisted." Maxwell threw a fond yet exasperated look at Leslie who stuck his pointy tongue out at him. "And we all know Leslie gets what he wants."

Brook chuckled. "I'm beginning to get that impression, yes. Lenny says much the same thing."

Leslie smiled wickedly then his eyes narrowed. “You look a little overwhelmed, Brook.” He chucked Brook softly on his shoulder. “Laverne is an absolute darling. We all love her so much. She rocks this place.” He cast a jaundiced eye around the heaving room. “Although I’m not sure having this event here was such a good idea. Transforming the lobby into a dressing room and having a catwalk event in Brilliantine’s boardroom might not have been the best idea anyone’s ever had.” He made a pout of dissatisfaction.

Brook was heartened by the fact that everyone seemed so at ease referring to his lover as a woman. “Brilliantine is the business on the first floor, the fake fur traders? The company with that huge, fancy boardroom that takes up a whole floor and the fake waterfall in the corner?” He’d heard all about it from Lenny when he was excitedly planning the event. It was a small but well attended private event, and one where the audience was carefully selected for best effect by the canny CEO of Brilliantine.

“Yep. Ostentatious much?” Leslie frowned. “This is a charity event for sick kids from Great Ormond Street and apparently one of the Brilliantine directors is on the board or something. She really wanted to use the boardroom for the event and show it off.” He rolled his eyes. “But this lot,” he waved at the frantic activity all around them, “are really *so* not appreciative of that. All I’ve heard is, ‘This place sucks,’ ‘Where’s my latte, I ordered it, like, minus ten seconds ago,’ and ‘Darling, you need to really clip that bush of yours, it looks like a hen’s nest.’” He shuddered. “I’m not good with the whole lady-bits part.”

Oliver chuckled loudly beside him. “You’re good with the man bits, love, and that’s all that matters.” He cast an enquiring look in Brook’s direction. “So, you’re seeing Laverne here for the first time since that meeting, then? I guess that could be a bit daunting if you’re not used to it. But you’ll be fine, I’m sure. Think of it like anyone else who dresses up differently for the day job. A clown wears their outfit, a go-go boy wears his, and we retired porn stars take it all off and hang loose. It’s another side of you, but it doesn’t mean it’s who you are.”

Brook nodded. “I do understand. It’s a bit weird being with a man, then seeing him dress up as Laverne for work in the morning.” He grinned.

He was already worried about a future weekend they'd planned. Lenny had badgered him into going to his best friend Ryan's club in Soho. Brook had heard of it; Club Delish was one of the trendiest clubs in the city. Brook hadn't watched a live drag show before but Lenny had assured him with a wicked grin that he was in for a treat.

Oliver flashed a warm smile. "I'm sure you'll get it right. Lenny is really into you, and as long you both feel the same, you'll get there."

"Oliver's so wise," Leslie said adoringly. Maxwell snorted in amusement and rolled his eyes. Oliver smiled back at Leslie, and Brook wanted a man to look at *him* the way Oliver looked at his fiery boyfriend. He supposed he might have seen a fleeting glimpse of something like it on Lenny's face once or twice, but it had been gone in an instant. Almost as if he'd been fighting it back. Brook thought wryly that Lenny had probably seen him do the same thing. He wasn't sure what this thing was they had going on other than the fantastic sex, but one day soon he hoped to have it figured out.

He caught a glimpse of yearning on Maxwell's face but as quickly as it flashed up, it was gone, and Brook wondered if he'd mistaken it.

Maxwell stared at him evenly then grinned widely. "They're dreadful together, aren't they? So damn lovey-dovey." He made a wicked but disgusting gesture with his hand. "Ollie and I used to be fuck buddies but there's no room for me now he has this one." Maxwell waved at Leslie and sighed heavily. "He won't even let me do a threesome. That's how serious he is about being monogamous."

Leslie's eyes widened in uncertainty as he bit his lip and looked at his boyfriend.

Oliver scowled. "Max, that's enough. The whole fucking world doesn't need to know our personal business. Besides, I thought you *had* someone special?" He cocked his head as Maxwell's brow furrowed. "Is there some trouble in paradise then?"

Maxwell didn't reply but he looked uncomfortable. Oliver carried on. "Now behave or I'll have to send you to your room without supper." His tone was light but Brook and no doubt everyone else present couldn't mistake the tinge of a threat beneath it. Oliver took hold of Leslie's hand and ran his thumb across the top, smiling at him.

"Sorry, my bad." Maxwell affected an air of insouciance as he looked around the room, but Brook saw the swallow and a look of sadness in his eyes. He wondered what the man's story was. Maxwell was a man who looked as if he had one.

They were interrupted by a loud screech from the other side of the foyer and they all turned to see two people, one man, one woman, fighting over a hair piece. Brook stared wide-eyed as the unfortunate feathered tiara was tugged and pulled to and fro, small pieces of feather drifting to the floor in the scurry. From the outskirts of the room a large, placid-looking man moved through the crowd like an ice breaker, and beside Brook, Leslie giggled.

"I wouldn't want Dasher's job for all the money in the world. I don't how he does it. He says it's like having kids again, and he should know. He has five."

Brook blinked. "Five? Hell, that's a lot of mouths to feed."

Leslie shrugged. "Most of them are out of the house but he does have this one adorable twelve-year-old daughter who's absolutely precious. He brings her to work sometimes and we play dress-up when Laverne's not looking." He shot an *It's our secret* look at Brook. "Please don't tell her that. She'll have my arse paddled for using her stuff and taking time out when I'm supposed to be working."

Oliver snorted. "The only paddling that cute arse of yours will ever get be from me." He leered at Leslie whose face pinked up. Once again Maxwell rolled his eyes and threw a *See, what did I tell you?* glance at Brook.

Brook laughed. "I promise to keep mum about it, honest. Sounds like fun."

Leslie nodded with a happy smile. "Oh yeah, I love it. I get to wear all sorts of stuff. Even makeup."

Beside him, Oliver shook his head in amused frustration. "He's still a kid," he explained to Brook. "My man is Peter Pan, I swear."

There was a deep, familiar laugh at Brook's elbow. He turned to see the eyes of his lover observing him from long lashes lightly flecked with mascara. Brook was fascinated by the sight, but also a little uncomfortable. And there was no mistaking the uncertainty in those aqua eyes, as they searched his anxiously. His boyfriend was as nervous as he was at this encounter.

“That’s an apt description of this minx.” Laverne smiled, lips rimmed with pale pink lipstick. “Chickens, the show will be starting in about fifteen minutes, so if you want good seats, I’d suggest you get upstairs before the stampede.”

Brook cleared his throat and his eyes darted nervously down Laverne’s body.

Laverne wore a classically styled dress, bottle green and form fitting, with a tight bodice, nipped waistline and flowing Grecian pleats to the floor. She wore one-inch high peep-toe shoes of shimmering silver. Brook’s eyes were hypnotically drawn to the bulge of two breasts over her chest. He swallowed and lifted his eyes to meet hers.

“You look really lovely,” Brook said awkwardly. “That colour suits you.”

“Thanks,” she said softly. She glanced out across the crowd then her eyes narrowed. “Prick,” she said softly.

Brook turned to look in the direction she was and noticed a thin, brightly dressed man with a spume of red and yellow hair on the top of his head standing beside a rather portly matron dressed in what looked like a gaudy type of plaid frock.

Brook looked at Laverne. “Who’s a prick? The guy with the parrot crest?”

Laverne nodded. “Yes. His name is Tracy Trey. He’s been shooting his mouth off about his new suit designs, which are terrible by the way, and just generally giving the industry a bad name because he’s so full of himself.”

Leslie butted in. “Laverne, I remember now what I wanted to talk about today in the office when I forgot.”

Laverne smiled at him. “You spotted a new shirt design on my desk and its brilliance made you forget what you came to see me about. I remember.”

Leslie nodded. “I noticed you were still throwing your old drafts into your bin,” he scolded. “I thought we agreed you were to going to get rid of them securely?”

Laverne opened her mouth to reply but Leslie was on a roll. “And I saw a suit cuff the other day with something that looked remarkably like a copycat of that design you showed me the other day. The one you wanted to experiment with.” He whispered conspiratorially. “On one of Tracy Trey’s suit jackets.” There was a stunned silence. Brook wasn't sure what was expected so he waited. He didn't have long before Leslie was off again.

"It was at a closed showing of his. I managed to get into it because the organiser loves me. Duffy lets me sit in as long as I gave him fruit candies and promised him—" his voice tailed off as he became distracted at the sight of a famous drag queen walking past. She smiled at him.

"Oh—my—God—Kiki Kittens, I love her," he gushed, gazing after the woman in adoration.

"Promised him *what* exactly, Leslie?" Oliver's dangerous voice brought Leslie back to the real world. Brook stared in amusement at Leslie's boyfriend, wondering how the hell he coped with him. Max gave a long-suffering sigh then started biting his nails.

Leslie blinked. "Promised him I'd get him the uncensored version of *Clockwork Orange*. What did you think, baby?"

He pursed his lips fiercely at his boyfriend who looked shame faced. "Anyway, Duffy hides me at the back because if Tracy knew I was there he'd pitch a hissy fit because he'd think I was there to steal his poxy suit secrets. Like I'd want *his* suit designs when I have Laverne's." He sniffed.

Laverne was looking a little concerned. "Leslie, are you sure? If so, it means someone at the office has access to my designs and is passing them onto him. I don't even want to think about what that might mean."

She looked ill and Brook reached out and squeezed her shoulder. "Love, we'll talk about this, and see what we need to do. There's nothing you can do now and you have a show to put on."

His lover nodded. "I just don't want to believe someone I employed and trusted is ripping me off." She sighed. "You're right. I can't do much now except kick Tracy in the knackers when I see him."

Brook chuckled. "Let's get the evidence first before you do that. I don't want you arrested for knacker kicking."

Oliver nodded and grasped Leslie's hand. "I agree. Let me get Secret Agent Scott upstairs and get primo seats to observe the action." Leslie looked smug at being described thus. "Come on, Peter Pan. Let's fly upstairs. Max, come on. You're going to have a blast watching this show, I promise." He pulled his boyfriend towards the long, winding stairs at the end of the foyer. Maxwell nodded at Brook and followed them up the winding staircase.

Laverne smiled at him. "I suppose I should be off," she said. "Leave the excitement of fashion espionage behind and focus on tonight." She turned to leave then turned back again, a vulnerable look on her face. "Look, I know this is a bit difficult for you, and I don't expect you to be a hundred percent with it. I know it'll take time, but I wanted to say how much I appreciate you being here tonight. It means a lot to me."

Brook's heart ached at the look in those eyes.

This must be so damned difficult for her. For Lenny.

Affection flooded his chest as he reached out and cupped Laverne's chin. That familiar curve brought back the memory of kissing it that morning in bed. They'd been long, languorous kisses down Lenny's jawline, then down his eager body until Brook had taken him in his mouth and driven him crazy.

"Baby, it's all right," Brook whispered, something stirring inside that seemed like hope.

He could do this.

"You look fabulous, these people adore you and you're going to be your amazingly talented self and go out on that catwalk and show them who you are. Laverne Debussy-Smith, designer extraordinaire. And the sexy man who shares my bed. Go and greet your fawning fans. I'll be upstairs in a minute."

The warm and loving look in Laverne's eyes was one he'd remember for a long time. Brook wanted to see it again and again, and with a sense of wonder, he asked himself what the hell was happening here. In his wildest dreams he'd never have imagined having a lover like this one, let alone having the depth of feeling Brook currently felt. He cupped Laverne's face in his hands and kissed her, his lips tasting flavoured lipstick. It was unfamiliar and Brook licked his lips after he'd finished his kiss. "Go be you, love. They're waiting. You may have to refresh that lipstick though."

Laverne flashed a radiant smile at him and turned. Brook watched him go and then she turned and winked at him. "Tonight," she murmured softly, "I'm going to ride you like a stallion. Think of that when you're sitting upstairs watching *this*." With a sweep of her hand down her body, a wicked chuckle and a flounce of her wig, Laverne strode towards the stairs. Brook's dick had gone from slumbering flag at rest to an upright semaphore in one second flat at the thought of those teasing words. He forced the dirty thoughts he had out of his head. It was time to see Laverne in action. Tonight was all about her night in the spotlight. There was time for crazy sex later.

***

Half an hour later he was clutching his sides in laughter along with the other sixty-plus people in the huge room. He knew Lenny had a dry, sarcastic wit but up on the stage, as Laverne, the snark and cattiness was amplified. His lover might not be a drag queen but her delivery of sly innuendos, downright filth and observations of certain poor members of the audience was as electrifying and an entertaining one.

"And now, we get to the crux of the show," Laverne's husky voice, familiar but different, echoed over the crowded venue. The burbling of birds and occasional parrot squawks that emanated from the speakers set high on the wall ceased—something Brook was quite glad about.

In the corner, a waterfall bubbled gently, the ten-foot high water feature a startling backdrop to what was otherwise a lavishly decorated boardroom now decked out as a jungle. Twisting vines in hemp buckets were the centrepiece for every table and more vines and fronds hung above them from the beamed rafters. The servers, male and female alike, were all dressed as natives in super-short grass skirts, of various hues and designs. The men were bare-chested and the women wore soft suede bikini tops. Soft chiffon, pastel-coloured blue, green and lilac curtains floated down all the walls, from ceiling to floor, like flowing coloured water that shimmered and shivered lightly in the cool air-conditioned room.

"Ladies and gentleman and others of indiscriminate description, because if I had to go through the whole damn alphabet describing you all, I'd be here for fucking *ever*"—the room exploded in laughter and Brook marvelled at Laverne's ability to get away with that comment—"this collection has been a while in the making. It's been designed especially for Brilliantine, the sponsors of this event." Laverne waved to a woman sitting in the front, wearing a large hat set with various tropical fruits. She had a silly grin on her face. "This lady here is the CEO of the company, Lydia Romano-Ruiz. Give her a hand, everyone, for giving us this fabulous room to stage this exclusive pre-peek event in." Laverne gestured lavishly around her and the bracelets on her wrists sparkled in the glare of the lights. The room exploded in clapping and after a while Laverne raised fingers to her mouth and blew a piercing whistle. Brook chuckled. He'd been subject to that ear-splitting sound before, normally when Lenny was trying to catch the attention of a bartender.

"Thank you all for that warm applause. Now can we get on with the bloody show? My models are growing old back there and we all know how they feel about that..." Once again the audience roared with laughter. A wave of sheer pride washed over Brook at the way his lover worked the crowd with such ease.

"As I said, this collection was put together for Lydia, as Brilliantine wanted to branch out with its own custom-designed clothing range. Some of the items *do* have fur, ladies and gentlemen, I will warn you, but for all those wankers out there who want to throw paint and make a PETA statement, it's Brilliantine's own fake fur, my darlings. No animal was harmed in the making of this clothing. I support PETA myself and in fact we have a couple of their people in the audience. Not those rabid extremist types," Laverne made a moue, her pick lips shining, "but the ones who work tirelessly to try and make a difference."

She turned and waved towards the back of the stage where more long swathes of pale green and blue billowed, "I present the '*La Jungla'* range, which for those of you who are less educated means jungle in Spanish, the native language of our lovely Lydia." Laverne waved a camp hand. "I class myself as one of those as I didn't have a fucking clue what it was until Lydia told me."

Brook chortled along with the rest of them at Laverne's self-deprecating statement. The woman could certainly hold an audience's attention. The lights dimmed to spotlights on the long catwalk that ran from one end of the boardroom to the other.

Brook watched open-mouthed as a parade of mostly scantily clad and beautiful models glided, strutted and crawled down the catwalk. He knew from post-coital conversations at home that Lenny disapproved of having too-thin models showing clothes. Laverne insisted that they all have enough meat on their bones to set an example. Apparently when Lenny had been at university, one of his best lady friends had starved herself to death desperately trying to stay slim to keep her modelling job, and Lenny had never forgiven himself for not being able to help her.

The rounded curves of women and taut arses of men vamped down the catwalk, clad in fur-trimmed bikinis and skimpy men's swimsuits, tailored ladies' suits, elegant coats and gilets and one man's suit in particular, an eye-catching ensemble of grey fabric with a soft, sleek black fur waistcoat. There were men's and ladies' jerseys, fur-lined parkas in bright white with matching brightly coloured scarves and sparkly gym-wear with fur trim. While it wasn't to Brook's taste, it was an eclectic and captivating display of decadence, elegance and uniqueness. It blew his mind, and for the first time, he appreciated the magic that Lenny as Laverne Debussy-Smith unleashed upon the world.

His heart swelled as, after the show, he watched Laverne working the room, flirting with men and women alike, her deep laughter ringing in his ears, those aqua eyes always searching out Brook's and meeting his gaze across the crowded floor. The smile on Laverne's face was uncertain at times as she inclined her head at him and Brook smiled back, hoping that his face conveyed both his respect and his affection. Although affection was beginning to be a term Brook thought might be too tame. The feelings Lenny provoked ran deeper than that. Seeing him tonight, unrepentant, proud and regal, completely at home as Laverne and being respected and adored in turn, was an eye opener to Brook's growing feelings.

It was close to eleven-thirty that night before Lenny appeared, in his jeans and a sweatshirt, looking tired, a little pale, yet wearing a grin on his face when he saw his lover that warmed Brook's heart. What he didn't enjoy seeing though, was Ryan Bishop holding Lenny's elbow possessively as they chatted as they walked towards him. They looked *too* comfortable together. Ryan's auburn hair against Lenny's blond waves; his shorter, slimmer build against Lenny's broader frame—they looked as if they *fit.* Brook shifted uncomfortably. Ryan understood his man better than Brook did. Ryan understood Lenny's need to be someone else; they even went shopping for women's fashion together.

"Thanks for waiting for me." Lenny kissed Brook warmly on the lips. "Let me introduce you to Ryan. Or, as he's better known, the gorgeous Delilah Delish." He grinned quirkily, throwing a fond glance at his friend.

Brook shook hands with the one outstretched in greeting. "Nice to meet you," he said, feeling insincerity washing off him like radio waves. Ryan grinned and Brook thought uncomfortably that those bright blue eyes saw right through him.

"So you're the man who has my friend all aflutter," Ryan teased gently. "Lenny doesn't stop talking about you."

Lenny huffed beside Brook, his warm hand stealing in to take hold of his. "Don't be such an ass, Ryan. I don't." But he smiled at Brook, who felt the stirrings of something in his chest, something deep and warm.

Ryan huffed loudly. "Yes, you fucking do." He fluttered his eyelashes dramatically. "Oh, my God, he's so divine, he's like, this big hunka man I have to throw down on my bed and have my way with. Ryan, my heart beats so much faster when I see him…" His falsetto voice rang out in the now mostly empty room.

Lenny growled. "Listen, you big queen, you're embarrassing my boyfriend. Now give it a rest before I pop you one." He made a mock fist and raised it at Ryan who chuckled even louder.

Brook watched the exchange with amusement and a sense of satisfaction that Lenny talked about him. "Well, I can see why you two are friends," he said with a laugh.

Ryan leaned over and ran his soft hand down Brook's jaw. Brook's mouth dropped open a little at that gesture.

"That's right," Ryan murmured softly. "Just friends. Lenny has been there for me through some bad times, as I have I for him. The fact we used to fuck doesn't matter anymore. He has you now. So take him home and do whatever it is that you two get up to, and enjoy, my darlings. I for one have some fruit to eat, so I need to get going before he finds someone else to do the dirty deed. My Mango isn't a patient man." He gave a low, sultry laugh.

Brook started at that name. There couldn't be all that many people called Mango around. It had to be his neighbour. The 'mutual acquaintance' Mango had mentioned had to be Ryan.

Lenny shoved his friend towards the door. "Bugger off then. Go find your man so I can get mine home and have my way with him."

Ryan chortled. "I know when I'm not wanted. I'll give you a call, Lenny. We can be *ladies who lunch.* Cheers, Brook."

He turned and walked towards the exit.

Brook stared at him. “Are Ryan and my neighbour Mango Munroe having it off then?” he asked Lenny curiously.

Lenny laughed. “Love, they’ve been having it off forever, but Mango won’t commit to him. It’s a whole ‘open-relationship’ crap from Mango’s side and they’re miserable without each other. It’s about time they got their act together.” He grinned. “I couldn’t believe it when Ryan mentioned Mango lives in your building. That’s such a weird coincidence.” He took a deep breath. “Anyway, enough about *them.*” He licked his lips. “I need to get you home to my place so I can have a little taster of my own.”

At Lenny’s lascivious look, Brook’s cock plumped up. He knew he *needed* Lenny. *Wanted* Lenny so badly his trousers were tight with his desire and he couldn’t wait to get home so he could have his lover to himself. His distinctly male, musk-scented, cock and balls–bearing lover who, with one look, could turn Brook’s world upside down.

“I can live with that,” Brook murmured as he pulled Lenny towards him. “I think we’ll get a taxi though so we can make out in the back.”

Lenny’s pupils expanded, and he gave his lips willingly to Brook, taking his mouth in a wet, open-mouthed kiss that made Brook’s groin ache.

When he managed to focus enough to hail a taxi, Brook only hoped they’d make it home before he pushed his eager way inside Lenny. He really didn’t want to be arrested for indecent exposure.

Chapter 9

Lenny loved adventurous sex. He was open to new things, being daring in the bedroom and performing acts that in some vanilla circles might raise an eyebrow.

He admitted though that sex with Brook was enough to replace all the daring things he'd done before. Not that sex with Brook wasn't exciting—far from it. The emotions Lenny felt added extra *oomph* to the relationship. Simply the scent, taste and feel of the man were enough to send Lenny into orbit in a way he'd never imagined. Lenny knew the old adage about finding a soul mate. He thought he might have found his. It was too early to say anything so he kept it tucked inside him like a scented handkerchief from a beau.

So when Brook propelled him, needy, greedy and grasping into the dimly lit entrance of Lenny's home, his arousal pressed against Lenny's jeaned backside, Lenny was only too glad to go with the sexual flow.

"I am so horny," Brook gasped as he rutted against Lenny. "You were fantastic tonight and you do things for me no other man has." His hands came out and grasped Lenny's jaw.

Lenny gasped his reply in between frantic, rough kisses as his head was pulled back while voracious lips bruised his. "I have that effect on some people." He winced as teeth caught his lip. The heat in his groin needed to be assuaged and Brook was the only man that could do that.

Brook growled. "There's no 'some people' about this. You're mine."

His rough hands yanked at Lenny's expensive Calvin Klein shirt and Lenny gave an indignant squawk.

"Hey, go steady there, Hulk. This shirt cost me a hundred and fifty quid. If you rip it I'll have to make you pay." He didn't mean moneywise either. He had plenty of ideas as to how the bloke manhandling him could soothe the pain of Lenny having his clothing ripped to shreds.

"Oh yes," Brook's eyes smouldered and he licked his lips slowly. Lenny moaned softly. "And how are you going to make me pay, gorgeous? By letting me put my cock in your arse and make you come so hard you'll think your prick exploded?"

Lenny groaned again, his hands fumbling with the buttons on his trousers. Damn button-ups might look trendy but they really hindered moments like these when he needed to release the aching cock in his pants.

Between them, they shed their clothing in a frenzied mating dance and soon both stood, spotlighted in the warm glow of the wall sconces. Brook stood tall and strong, his satiny skin shining with sweat, lips swollen with lust and the evidence of his desire jutting up out of a groin that was neatly trimmed and shaven. Lenny stared at him. If he'd been a wolf he'd have been licking his chops and salivating. Instead, he settled for a sly tug of his cock and grinned in satisfaction when Brook's eyes were drawn to his gesture.

"You want a taste of this?" Lenny taunted softly, his belly clenching in pleasure at the hungry look on his lover's face. "Maybe tonight I get to take you again."

He and Brook did take turns but in truth, Lenny preferred being the taken and not the taker. The wanton sound that ripped from Brook's chest and into his delicious mouth made Lenny faint with sheer animal want.

"Not tonight." Brook's velvet tones were edged with huskiness. "I seem to recall a certain someone telling me he was going to ride me like a horse. Going to climb me like a tree, sit on my cock." He stroked himself languidly and Lenny's heart pounded faster. "And fuck me into oblivion."

Lenny swallowed. "I don't remember saying all that," he said in a strangled voice as Brook advanced with definite intent to do wonderful bodily harm. Lenny found himself being yanked into his bedroom by a man clearly intent on not much more foreplay. He thought faintly that he'd been lucky to make it this far without having Brook's dick up his arse, lube or no lube. In all truth, his arsehole was fairly well used whenever his boyfriend was around. If foreplay were on the menu, Brook's tongue would be a great idea. Lenny loved being rimmed.

That wet dream became reality as he was pushed onto the bed face first, Brook kneeling beside him and leaving no doubt as to his intention as he growled in Lenny's ear.

"Get up on your knees and hold the rail. I need to taste you. Need to get my tongue inside you. Then you can keep to your promise of that ride."

Lenny couldn't do as he'd been told quick enough. He scrambled up the plush satiny bedspread, got on his knees and grabbed hold of the metal headboard low at the base. He looked back at his lover from under outstretched arms and he moved his body slightly back and down, offering his backside for the pleasure he was hopefully about to receive. Tongue or cock, either one was first with him. He wriggled his arse as an incentive and was gratified by the loud hiss to his rear.

"You look fine like that, all splayed out for me. So damn sexy." The bed dipped as Brook changed position and strong, warm hands grasped his cheeks, pulling them apart. Lenny gave a soft sigh as hot breath ghosted his hole. He shivered, goose bumps rising on his skin. His groin was on fire, his cock wet and swollen, and he wasn't sure whether he could hold on long enough to enjoy all the sensations being inflicted upon his needy body.

Then he moaned in satisfaction as Brook's mouth licked a path along his crease from top to bottom, once, twice, softly biting the soft inner skin of his cheeks. Lenny knew he wasn't going to last with those loving caresses to his rear.

"Yes," he panted as his arse instinctively pushed back towards that eager mouth. "That is so good. Get deeper, honey. Want to feel your tongue in me." He waggled his arse again for good measure and was delighted to feel and hear the sharp smack to his left butt cheek. He gave a low groan as it happened again, harder this time.

"You like that, don't you, you sexy bastard." Brook's mouth bit down on the area he'd smacked and Lenny's cock jerked in appreciation.

"Touch me and tongue me at the same time," he managed to say in between pants and moans as Brook's tongue delved deep into his crack. "I want to come in your hands, need you to get me off."

The wet nub of a tongue in his hole made Lenny dizzy and he pushed back, face-fucking his lover with his arse. "Your hand on me! What does a guy have to—oh sweet Lord…"

His wish granted, fingers encircled his cock and stroked him hard as he was assaulted at the rear. He didn't know which sensation to focus on so he tried to do both and it drove him to the edge. There was a movement behind him and Brook pushed sweet-smelling lube into him. Lenny shouted in surprise at the fact that after the warmth of the tongue he'd had in there, the lube was cold and his lover's fingers were burrowed deep inside him, hooking and curling until they hit that spot that he called his nirvana.

He lost his breath as he climaxed, losing control and shooting thick spurts of come over his bed sheets and his stomach. He cried out and felt sheathed heat push inside him, opening him, touching his heart with its depth. His orgasm continued as Brook thrust inside him and gripped his hips, forcing Lenny so deeply back on him, he could almost taste Brook. He knew there were men who might be too sensitive after orgasm to be fucked but he wasn't one of them.

"Hell," he gasped in between pants. "You made me come my dick off, you bastard."

There was a low chuckle then Brook withdrew leaving him empty and wanting.

Brook lay back on the bed, pulled pillows against the headboard and sat up. "Ride me," he said simply as he rolled on a condom.

The lust in his voice made Lenny half-hard again. He straddled his lover, eyes never leaving that steady gaze and he planted his hands against the hard flesh of Brook's shoulders and sank down onto him. His lover's eyes closed in pleasure and Lenny impaled himself, sinking down until he could go no further. Brook's face was dazed, his lips parted and Lenny thrust his tongue almost into his throat, wanting to punish his mouth as he had done to him. As they kissed, he sank gracefully up and down on the pulsing cock inside him, loving the burn as he took him in and relishing the sight of his man coming totally undone. The slow ballet of sex and lust, the scent of the room, with its musky, sweaty fragrance and the heavy breathing of the two men as they pleasured each other—never before had Lenny had never felt so in tune with another man.

There were no barriers, no judgements, no differences, just the hedonistic pleasure of enjoying each other's bodies, each other's mouths and attaining that common goal of their orgasms. Lenny had a feeling that it might happen again and his cock swelled with each slow stroke of Brook's hand and the sensual glide of him in Lenny's channel. Lips were hungry, greedy and fed each other's passion and it was perfect.

Brook gave a soft exhalation and his body shuddered. He was always quiet when he came, but had a tell-tale sign: he bit his lips tightly as he climaxed and stared intently into Lenny's eyes as if committing the moment to memory. It was such an intimate thing, and something he missed when Brook was behind him. The look on his face, that loving, warm expression and the tightening of his hand on Lenny's cock spurred him on and he joined in the hands tugging him until he could hold it in no longer. He came for the second time, making sure he coated Brook's chest and stomach with white ropes of his come. He wanted to mark him, make him his. He collapsed against Brook's chest, hearing his husky laugh as he did so.

"Epic," Brook murmured. "You certainly know how to ride a man, Lenny. You damn near gave me a heart attack."

Lenny lifted his face from where it was buried in Brook's sweaty neck. "Well, you made me come so hard I had a brain freeze." He nibbled Brook's throat. He didn't want to move, didn't want the softening cock slipping out from him. He liked this connection they had. For a while they lay stuck together, drowsy and satisfied until a gentle snore from beneath him roused Lenny.

He sat up and stared at Brook indignantly. "Are you going to sleep under there? Am I that boring?"

Brook opened his eyes and chuckled tiredly. "Sorry. You smelt so good and were keeping me warm."

Somewhat mollified, Lenny harrumphed. "Okay." He lifted himself up—in truth he was a bit stiff himself and it wasn't his cock—and moved off his lover. He rolled off Brook's spent condom, stood up with shaky legs and tottered to the bathroom to take a pee. He took back a bunch of wet wipes; wasn't he the romantic one? Some guys gave you warm washcloths, but he wasn't one of them.

Brook was already curled up on his side, arm outstretched across Lenny's side and seemingly already in the Land of Nod. Lenny watched him for a minute then gave a sigh of resignation and crawled into his side, lifting Brook's' arm and laying it gently across his broad chest. Then he spooned up against his man, drew the covers over them both and closed his eyes.

***

Lenny awoke drowsily to the scent of bacon frying. It was one of his favourite all-time smells and he sniffed in appreciation. The bed space next to him was empty. Yawning, he shifted over and looked at the clock, eyes widening when he saw the time.

"I'm going to have to change this man for another one," he muttered sleepily. "Nine a.m.—really? That's still bloody sleep-in time."

Lenny's general wake-up time on weekends and when he wasn't working tended to be closer to midday. However, the bacon smell and the warm, toasty feeling inside that said his man was cooking for him drew him into the kitchen. He stood there in his boxers, admiring the view of Brook's backside in his tight, dove-grey briefs. He was leaning over the stove turning pieces of bacon and nimbly plucking pieces of bread out of the toaster.

Lenny sidled quietly up behind him and slid a sly finger into the waistband of his briefs, sliding it down into Brook's heated crack. He was most put out when Brook hardly flinched and chuckled softly.

"Morning, sleepyhead."

Lenny scowled but kept his hand where it was, against the firm globes of Brook's cheek as he squeezed it. "You used to having a man's hands down your pants when you're cooking?" he asked. He pressed himself against Brook's back, grinding his hips, determined to get some reaction out of him. His morning woody needed some attention.

Brook laughed as he turned a piece of bacon. "I saw you coming in there." He waved at the shiny reflective surface of the toaster. "But I appreciate the gesture." He laid the spatula down and turned to face Lenny, who was gratified to see that he had indeed gotten a reaction. The front of Brook's underwear tented pleasingly. He smiled into the kiss as Brook's mouth covered his, tasting faintly of bacon. Lenny closed his eyes as the kiss got deeper and hoped Brook didn't mind morning breath.

When he was released, they both looked down at their groins and smirked at each other.

"Are you going to do something about this?" Lenny waved at his hard-on. "Why don't you leave the breakfast plans for now and come back to bed? I think we could both use a little TLC."

Brook leaned his forehead against Lenny's and shook his head firmly. "Nuh-huh. I'm hungry. Last night all I had to eat was those dainty little canapés at the event and they do nothing to fill a man up." He turned to tend to his cooking, reaching for an egg and expertly cracking it to put in the pan.

Lenny grinned. "I'm not even going to make the obvious comment about me having something to fill you up." Brook groaned theatrically and Lenny reached out, picking up a piece of crunchy bacon, deftly evading the slap of the spatula as he danced away.

"Fine. If you're going to get me up so damn early in the morning, at least tell me you made coffee?" He stared around the kitchen then spotted his cafétiere on the kitchen counter dutifully filled with what looked like his best Colombian blend. He cackled in satisfaction and pulled two mugs from the cupboard.

"Good man. You may have some redeeming qualities after all."

He ignored Brook's exasperated eye roll and poured coffee, black for him, and with a splash of milk the way Brook liked it.

"I don't want to bring up bad news so early in the morning, but you're going to have to think about the whole 'who's stealing your designs' thing soon." Brook buttered toast as Lenny sat down at the kitchen island and scowled. He hadn't wanted reminding of that betrayal so soon.

"I know. I can't do anything about it now, so it'll have to wait till I get into the office. I'll check all the employee files, see what I can come up with." He sighed heavily. "I just hate the thought it's someone I know. I guess Leslie is right. I have been a bit lackadaisical with my drafts. I'll have to dispose of them more securely," he said gloomily.

Brook leaned over and kissed him. "Check your files first and then we'll see where we get to. I'm here to help, whatever you need."

Lenny felt better just for that comment. Doing this together was far better than alone. Minutes later they were sitting down with a plate of bacon and eggs, toast and fresh, heart-warming coffee. Lenny made his into a sandwich and raised his eyebrows at Brook's small frown.

"What? I'm making a toastie." He busied himself breaking the yolk, before he placed the last slice of bread on top, sighing in satisfaction as it bled yellow onto his plate. He picked up one half of his toastie and dipped it in the mess.

Brook pursed his lips with an adorable huff of breath. Lenny debated jumping his bones at the table there and then. The sandwich won out. He was hungry too. The asparagus tips and tiny biscuits did nothing last night to stave off the hunger he'd had, and which had escalated now he had the frying bacon smell in his nostrils.

His lover nodded at him. "I've noticed that you make everything into a sandwich. Give you steak and chips and it ends up between two slices of bread. Chicken? You make a sandwich, with mayonnaise. Even the ribs I did that one night, you picked clean and shoved in a bread roll. What is it with you and bread?"

Lenny munched his toastie happily. "Comfort food, I guess. It makes me feel good. What's with you using a knife and fork all the time? Waste of good cutlery."

He grinned at Brook's snort and indignant rejoinder. "My parents taught me to eat with them, you barbarian." His soft, indulgent smile was like an emotion-coated arrow that lodged straight in Lenny's chest.

Crap. This guy is really doing things to me.

Lenny tried to deflect those rising feelings of *whatever the fuck it was*. "Talking of parents, I've told you about my misguided childhood and lack of family members to complicate my life. No blood-sucking commercial events like birthdays and Father's Day to worry about. How about your folks? You haven't told me much about them." He popped the last morsel of sandwich in his mouth and started on the other one.

Brook frowned slightly. "Don't be so damn flippant about your family, babe."

Lenny's eyes widened and he stopped chewing and looked at Brook.

Did he really say that?

Brook carried on evenly. "You were given a raw deal by your family and I'm really sorry you had to go through it. But I know you still hurt. I see it every time you see the news on the telly about kids being thrown out of their homes, or being abused, and the money you give to all those charities, the fact you created Laverne to have some control over who you are, and fuck your father who tried to make you into something you weren't. Please don't ever feel you have to hide that from me. I care too much about you for that."

Lenny was still staring at him, gob-smacked, food still in his mouth in what he imagined was a very unattractive sight. His first instinct was to rise to the challenge and tell Brook it was *his* life, *his* story and he'd tell it any way he fucking pleased. Then he saw the nervous tic in Brook's jaw, the white-knuckled fingers, and his Adam's apple bobbing as he swallowed. He also repeated Brook's last words in his brain and that little arrow twitched yet again.

I care too much about you for that.

So instead Lenny swallowed his half-masticated food and took a slurp of coffee. He cleared his throat. "Point taken. So is this where I get to hear about your family then?"

The flash of relief that shot across Brook's face like that same arrow being slung from a bow was all he needed to know. Lenny imagined his boyfriend may have thought he'd overstepped the mark and upset him

"Unlike yours, my family are loving and supportive. Always have been and I guess they always will be." Brook toyed with his last piece of bacon, sweeping it round the plate abstractedly.

"And this is why you've never told me about them before," Lenny said softly. "Because you don't want to rub salt in my old wounds?"

Brook nodded uneasily. "I guess so. It didn't feel right telling you about my happy childhood when you had such a crappy one."

Lenny got up and walked over to Brook, motioning him to stand up. Once they were standing together facing each other, he reached out and framed Brook's face. "Love, you give me the happy times now," he whispered as he brushed a soft kiss to Brook's lips. "And I don't mean *those* types of happy times. Although those are good too, of course."

Brook's mouth curved in a slow, sexy smile. "Yeah? Want one of those right now?"

Lenny grinned as he reached down into Brook's briefs and took his semi-hard cock in his hand. "You know, I think I might."

Chapter 10

Later that morning, lying on his bed and idly tracing whorls in Brook's sweaty, matted chest hair, Lenny raised himself on one elbow and tried to ignore the discomfort in his recently pounded arse.

"So, you still owe me a story about your folks. Tell me."

Brook shifted on the pillows and tucked his hands behind his head. The crumpled sheet lay gathered around his waist. "Mum's a translator with the UN here in London. Dad—well, my dad is a diplomat here. He works at the Kenyan High Commission. He's a financial attaché actually." He sounded vaguely embarrassed.

Lenny sat up in awe. "Get out of here, really? I had no idea you had such a highbrow parentage."

Brook shrugged. "Dad's Kenyan born, Mum is Jamaican." He laughed. "Dad always says he's descended from the Masai tribe, a couple of times removed though. We're still not sure if that's true or what he wants to believe. He loves to think he's descended from a great warrior nation." He chuffed softly in amusement.

Lenny was fascinated. "How many brothers and sisters do you have?"

Brook was quiet for a while. Lenny kept himself busy caressing the curve of Brook's ribs and waiting for his answer.

"Four. Two sisters. Two brothers. They're scattered all over the world. I'm the middle son."

Lenny couldn't help the pang that leapt into his chest and stomach at those words. He remembered sunny days of laughter and fun with his little sisters at the farm. Jane had been eleven when Lenny had been thrown out, and Patrice only eight. He'd been their big brother, the one they'd looked up to and adored. Until his father had tainted their young minds with his lies. And then they'd died and there'd been no way to get any of it back when he was ready.

He cleared his throat. "That's one big family. Are you close to them all?"

Brook nodded and his hand came out and stroked Lenny's hair gently. "Yes. Me and my dad in particular. He jets all over the world but always has time to send me a text, or a picture from wherever he is. He calls me once a week without fail. Mum too. So yes, we're close."

Lenny sat up, pulling the covers around his waist as he nodded. "I'm glad you have that."

There was silence for a while then Brook spoke. "You were incredible last night. Laverne, I mean. I've never seen anything like it before. It was—different."

Lenny's bones chilled.

What the hell did 'different' mean?

"Well, yeah, I imagine you don't have that many boyfriends who dress up as a woman and parade themselves on a catwalk," he said jokingly, fingers poking nervously at the swirls in the duvet. "I mean what would the odds be?"

Deep brown eyes regarded him steadily and Lenny plucked at the covers more frantically than before. "Let's face it, Laverne and I are pretty awesome together, and I doubt there's another one out there like me." He laughed nervously.

What the hell is wrong with me? Why do I need this guy to accept me so badly?

Brook reached out and brushed a stray strand of hair from Lenny's face. "Stop it," he instructed. "By different I meant pretty fabulous. You rocked that show, had those people eating out of your hands, and they loved you. They loved Laverne. It was astonishing to see. And yes," he smiled cheekily. "I doubt there are too many people out there who can say their *boyfriend,"* Lenny noticed the stress on that word and was heartened, "dresses up like you do. It's not something I ever thought I'd hear myself say, but I guess it's something I need to get used to if we intend being together."

Lenny lost his breath at those last words. They were telling ones, words that indicated that perhaps being Laverne and Lenny might be okay after all.

"That's good to know," he murmured. "Maybe now we can actually stay over at each other's places instead of sneaking out in the middle of the night so you don't get to see me dressed up in the morning."

Brook's face shadowed. "Lenny," he began but Lenny leaned over and kissed him, shutting him up. It was a tender, soft kiss and when they pulled apart, both of them were smiling.

"I know it's all been a bit weird," Lenny said as his fingers traced Brook's lips. "I realise waking up to a man and seeing him go out as a woman can be a little disconcerting."

Brook frowned. "I still worry about you going out dressed like—that."

Lenny frowned. "Worried? Brook, we've talked about this." Exasperation flooded his body. "I'm used to that. I can take care of myself. The other night I managed to avoid a fracas at the station. The guy got off easy." He smirked. "I can't hide who I am when I go to work in the morning. Or come home at night. Mostly before I come home, I change before leaving the office. It's more comfortable travelling when you're not wearing heels and a wig after a long day."

He'd been rambling on and missed Brook's silence. He looked up at his lover whose face was tight with displeasure. "Brook? What's the matter?"

"Someone tried to attack you? When was this?" Brook's voice was tight.

Lenny shrugged. "Some homophobic tosser who had too much to drink tried to plant one on me. I defended myself and he went away. No big deal."

"So the fear I have was founded and not something in my imagination."

Lenny gaped at his lover's serious face. "Honey, I handled it. I'm not being dictated to by some bigot who doesn't know his arse from his elbow. No bloody way. I've worked too hard to get where I am to hide it." Lenny had the distinct feeling this conversation was heading down a train tunnel straight into the path of an oncoming train. "I told you, I can take care of myself." He warmed to his argument. "Besides, all I have to do is be too gay, too loud, too something else and it will give any idiot who fancies it a chance to try and cause shit. Me being dressed up as a woman is another thing to add to an arsehole's list."

"What if one day you didn't see it coming? And you got hurt?" Brook sounded a little desperate and Lenny shook his head in puzzlement.

"Brook, where is this coming from? What am I missing here?" A trickle of unease slid down his spine; Brook's expression of frustration was tinged with fear.

Brook took a deep breath. "When I was first started at my job, I had a colleague called Aaron who was very femme. We became really good friends."

Lenny waited. There was obviously more to this story from the look in Brook's eyes.

"He didn't dress in women's clothes but he was a real flamer. And proud of it too. He didn't back down for anybody. It got him into quite a bit of trouble because, to be honest, he was a bit of a scrapper." He smiled fondly. "I was his wingman on quite a few occasions then no one seemed to bother him much. Sure, they made comments, but never picked a fight."

"What happened to him, because I'm assuming something bad did?" Lenny's eyes were concerned but watchful.

"One day when I wasn't around, a group of guys got hold of him and beat him so badly he was in hospital for over two weeks. This cute, funny guy was laid up in hospital with broken bones, internal bleeding and lost an eye, it was damaged so badly." Brook swallowed, remembering the sight of Aaron lying bloodied and beaten like a wax doll in a hospital bed.

"I'm sorry, love." Lenny reached over and stroked his hand. "Is he all right now?"

Brook nodded. "Yes. He recovered well enough, after all the surgery, met this guy and Nico took him off to France to live. Nico had a vineyard down south and he said it was the right place for Aaron to start over. I still talk to them both, not as much as I used to, but we keep in touch."

"That's a fucking awful story, and regrettably, nothing new," Lenny murmured. "But it's not going to happen to me."

Brook snorted. "That's what Aaron said, and look what happened. I'm really not comfortable with you being out on the streets dressed as Laverne. There are arseholes out there, and I think you're asking for trouble."

Lenny stared at him. "That's not your call to make, love. I understand your concern, and I appreciate it now that I've heard about Aaron. I really do. But I've been looking after myself my whole damn life. I've taken the knocks, and I've gotten up from them. And I might dress as a woman when I need to be Laverne, but that does not make me one. I'm a man who doesn't need a knight on a white charger. I'm quite able to take care of myself. I'm not Aaron."

His heart ached with the knowledge that perhaps Brook had underestimated him—that perhaps he didn't quite understand after all.

Brook's lips firmed and he shook his head mutinously. "Still, Lenny, I'd really like it if you didn't wear women's clothing out of work. I mean, it means changing before you come home, so what's the big deal?"

Lenny didn't trust himself to speak. He sympathised with Brook, but his request went against everything Lenny believed in. Instead he got out of bed and pulled on sweatpants and a tee shirt with shaking hands. "So because this happened to your friend, you think I should stop what I've been doing for the last, oh I don't know, for fucking *ever*, and play it safe? Is that what you're asking me to do?"

"Lenny," Brook reached out a hand and Lenny pushed it away savagely. "I understand, I do," Brook said softly. "But that doesn't stop me worrying about you. I thought that perhaps…" His voice tailed off as Lenny glared at him. He knew he was making more of this than he should, but fuck, this conversation really hurt. He'd been through this too many times with former lovers, like a song on repeat. He'd thought Brook would be different.

"You thought perhaps I should tone it down, stop being who I am to put *your* mind at ease? *Fuck. You.* Not going to happen. So if that's your expectation of this relationship, you may as well leave now. Right now."

The air was thick with tension, as the two men stared at each other. Then Brook sighed sadly and climbed out of bed. He picked up the clothes from where they'd been thrown hastily onto the floor and dressed. Lenny watched, hands clenched, wanting to say something but not knowing quite what. This had all gotten out of hand too quickly.

Brook broke the silence. "I'm not leaving because I want to. I'm leaving so we can both have some space to think. I'm sorry if I offended you. That wasn't my intention. This is all new to me, Lenny. I'm learning as I go along. I'm going to make mistakes."

Lenny swallowed but kept silent. He knew he was being a stubborn jackass, but somehow the words wouldn't come out, the ones that would absolve both of them.

Brook finished dressing, slung his jacket over his shoulder and turned to look at Lenny, his eyes sombre. "We'll speak in a couple of days." His lips twisted. "I understand your point of view, but you need to see mine too. Let me know the results of your personnel file checks. I'll be around to help if you need me."

He turned and left the bedroom. Lenny waited, heard the front door close then closed his eyes as he swept a hand through his hair.

Fuck, fuck, fuck and thundershit. That had gathered momentum like the rolling shit ball of a dung beetle.

A lazy day spent flicking through the telly channels to find something to watch and enjoying Chinese takeout did nothing to soothe him. Neither did the two whiskies before bedtime. He was still tense about the whole abortive conversation when he got into bed around eleven. The guilt didn't help either. Brook had only been worried about him, and said as much. And, he was up front about still figuring stuff out. Lenny supposed he could have been a little less confrontational. He gave a deep sigh as he tossed and turned, willing sleep to come. Perhaps things would sort themselves out when Brook called. If Lenny didn't call him first.

Chapter 11

Brook sat in his office and sighed as he picked up his phone to check for messages. Nothing from Lenny. Brook's mood soured. He'd hoped that he might have called him back over the last two days, but it looked like that wasn't on the cards. Once again, Brook thought he'd be the one doing the running. It pissed him off royally. Half of him, the proud side, said to leave it until Lenny called him. The other side, the one that wanted the man, said, *Hell, no.*

He supposed ruefully that the plan they'd had to meet at Ryan's club next Friday night might be a no go. He'd actually been looking forward to it. Meeting Ryan in his own environment and seeing Lenny there too would have been another facet to Brook's continuing education on drag queens, cross dressers and the club scene associated with them. A pang of regret flooded his chest. Maybe they'd have made up by then.

It was almost nine p.m. when he got back to his apartment. He'd spent the best part of the early afternoon and evening going through a new account with a particularly troublesome client. Now he was short one team member, the work had to be done somehow and Brook had taken on the extra weight. He was pleased his boss had agreed with his decision and the homophobic Keith had duly been permanently reassigned elsewhere. Brook had taken himself to a bar for a couple of drinks while he pondered whether to call Lenny. He'd decided against it for tonight.

He'd made himself a stir-fry and sat down to eat it, together with a beer while he watched the news, when his phone rang. His heart skipped when he saw who it was. He answered speedily.

"Hi, Lenny."

"Evening, Brook." The sound of Lenny's voice got Brook's libido tuned to high. "I hope I didn't interrupt anything?"

"No. I was sitting down to eat something and catch up on the news. Is everything okay?"

Lenny sounded tired. "Yes, everything's fine. Well, apart from I miss you and I wanted to apologise for being a bit of a prat the other night. I think I overreacted a bit." The line went silent.

"I miss you too. And I'm sorry I pushed you. I shouldn't have." Brook put his plate down on the side table and stood up to wander around his flat. "I worry about you."

"I know." Lenny's voice held relief and a trace of amusement. "I get a bit sensitive about that subject. Can we agree to put this spat behind us and move on?" His voice held a warning tone. "I'm not going to stop doing what I do, so don't get excited. I will keep your concerns in mind though."

Brook sighed. He'd expected no less from his feisty lover and there didn't seem to be another way around it other than him trusting Lenny to be able to take care of himself. "Sounds like a plan."

The awkward quiet that followed needed filling, so Brook forged ahead. "Are you at home?"

"No, I'm still at the office. I had an overseas client I had to entertain and he left about half an hour ago. He's Japanese and a damn workaholic. I had a quick shower and I'm on my way home now."

"Come round to my place. I have a stir-fry I can warm up and maybe we can sit and watch more Sam and Dean episodes. We need to finish season seven so we can move on to the next. I've heard good things about it."

The sexy low laugh that echoed down the line made Brook wonder if once again they'd even get to eating dinner when Lenny got here.

He heard the grin in his lover's voice through the phone. "Really, we'll watch *Supernatural*? I'm pretty knackered so if you're thinking of jumping my bones as soon as I arrive I have to say I might disappoint you. I slipped on my bloody heels this morning as well and wrenched my back. So I'm a bit of a mess—"

"Lenny, get your arse over here. I promise to behave myself." Brook grinned. "I might be able to be persuaded to give you a massage though; one without the happy ending if that's what you prefer."

He heard the interest in Lenny's voice when he replied. "Yeah? Are you any good at massage?"

"I did massage therapy as one of my extracurricular courses at college. I think I remember the basics."

"I'm on my way." The line went dead.

Three quarters of an hour later, there was a knock on his door. Freshly spruced up, Brook answered to see Lenny standing there, blond hair wet and dishevelled, his aqua eyes tired but still as warm as Brook had come to enjoy. Poured-on black jeans, cut-off white tee shirt coupled with a black suit jacket made a sexy ensemble and everything to encourage Brook's dick swelling in his loose pants.

Brook pulled Lenny into the flat, pulling him close as he kicked the door shut and took his mouth in a kiss that should have set off a fire alarm. Lenny tasted of minty toothpaste, brandy and sin, his tongue searching and desperate as he pushed eagerly between Brook's lips. Hands reached around and clasped Brook's arse. The groans emanating from his lover's mouth were a turn-on in themselves, even if Brook hadn't got a hundred and seventy pounds of warm, willing man pressed against his front and a pair of hands kneading his arse cheeks.

Gently, Lenny pulled away, mouth swollen, eyes hazy. "Jesus, I thought you said you *weren't* going to jump my bones the minute I got here?" His voice filled with laughter and he gestured towards his crotch. "Now look what you've done."

Brook was definitely looking at the tight bulge in those oh–so-snug jeans. Lenny reached up and removed his hat, throwing it onto the side table. "I thought the plan was for you to feed me then give me a back massage?"

Brook nodded, trying to find his breath. His heart raced at a pace that surely meant it was going to win whatever race it had entered. "Sorry. You looked so damn edible standing there I had to taste you." He pressed his hand against the front of his dick, willing it to stay leashed. Lenny grinned and shouldered past him into the lounge. He unashamedly reached down and adjusted himself and Brook's throat went dry.

"So where's dinner?" Lenny cocked an eyebrow at him and the rush of thankfulness that things seemed to be back on track with no hard feelings—other than the ones in their pants—took Brook by surprise.

I am so invested in this man, it's scary.

"In the kitchen. It's stir-fry so I'll reheat it and put a new cheese bread in the oven. I ate the last one." Brook disappeared into his open-plan kitchen and set about getting dinner on the table. "Can I offer you a beer? They're in the—oh."

Lenny appeared with a Peroni in each hand. "I know where they are. I've been here before, remember?" He cast a swift grin at his lover and peered over his shoulder at what was cooking on the stove. "Smells good. Am I going to be able to make a sandwich out of that?"

Brook mock glared at him. "Don't you dare, you heathen. Now go and sit down and relax and I'll bring it out to the table."

Lenny snorted with laughter. "Pity. You know how I love a good sandwich…mmm."

Brook found the opener and Lenny smiled, taking the beers to the dining table. Brook heaved a sigh of relief. *This* was how it was supposed to be. The two of them having fun, sharing a meal and perhaps even having raunchy sex later, despite Lenny's protests. Brook had sly plans for the massage anyway. He'd do Lenny's back but he definitely wanted to do something else as well. Front and back.

The meal went well without any awkward silences or talk of what had sparked their disagreement. Brook learnt Lenny had been through his employee files but was still no closer to finding out who might be deceiving him. They agreed a next step might be getting an external consultant in to deal with it and Lenny agreed to contact a few people Brook knew.

They relaxed, enjoyed each other's company and watched the Winchester brothers kick ass. Sam's arse was a thing of beauty, and as the two of them differed over which one was hotter—Lenny preferring Dean—it usually ended with them tussling on the couch as they struggled to reclaim control of the remote to freeze-frame their preferred arse. That activity normally led to sex. Tonight, however, Lenny seemed content to let Brook freeze-frame Sam whenever he wanted and simply snuggled closer into his chest as they lay on the couch. It felt right somehow, as if it were meant to be.

Lenny kept shifting on the couch to get comfortable, his lips tightening in pain now and then. Brook waited till the end of the programme then switched off the TV. Light blue-green eyes gazed at him in exasperation from beneath a blond fringe.

This man of mine is beautiful. He simply has no idea how much.

"It was getting exciting," Lenny spluttered. "In the next episode Dean beats the shit out of that demon."

"Yeah, and it's time for me to give you your massage, fidget-arse." Brook pushed Lenny off him and stood up. "Go into the bedroom and get your kit off. Then I'll sort your back out."

And perhaps anything else that takes my fancy.

"As if I haven't heard that before," Lenny grumbled as he stood, wincing as he straightened up. "Lenny, darling, take your clothes off, lie down and I'll make it all better. The next thing I know I have a cock up my arse." He sniggered as Brook's mouth dropped open. "Joking, honey. Just a joke."

Lenny took hold of his shirt and pulled it over his head as he walked toward the bedroom. Brook admired the sleek line of his back, the broad shoulders, trim waistline and the play of his muscles as he tossed the shirt on a nearby chair then disappeared into the bedroom. Taking a deep breath, Brook went into the bathroom to retrieve his basket of goodies from the cupboard. He made sure everything he needed was there—although he'd checked it before—and went into his room. His breath caught when he saw Lenny stretched face-down on the comforter, arms stretched above his head, bare-arsed naked and skin glowing in the light of the flickering candles. Shadows cast on the wall wavered and ebbed as the flames burned. Brook was more interested in the shadows dancing on the supine body, the play of them across golden skin, and the secret places Brook loved to explore.

"I lit the candles, thought I'd get a head start," Lenny said sleepily, eyes closed. "Nice setup you've got going here. Now all we need is music."

"That can be arranged," Brook said huskily, his dick full mast and aching. "Give me a minute to get my phone in the dock." He reached into his sweatpants pocket and took out his iPhone, setting it in the dock and setting the mood. The soft strains of Coldplay wafted through the room.

Lenny opened his eyes and stared at him incredulously. "Coldplay? I expected some fancy arse New Age music for this session."

Brook grinned and took his shirt off, watching in satisfaction as Lenny's eyes followed his every move. "I like Coldplay when I work. Now shut up and let me get started."

Lenny huffed adorably and turned his head to the side. Brook thought he'd be tempting fate taking his sweats off so he left them on and got onto the bed, straddling his lover's legs. He placed his basket beside him and picked up the oils. As he opened it, a vanilla-scented fragrance infused the air. He poured it into his hands, warmed it then leaned over and began sweeping his hands upwards along the back of strong, muscled thighs. Lenny groaned in pleasure, the sound heating Brook's groin even more. He nobly ignored it and concentrated on working out the kinks in the leg muscles.

"So how in hell's name did you fall off your damn shoes?" he asked in amusement.

Lenny's voice was dampened as he pressed his face into the pillow. Brook's dick had a vision of him doing that to hide the scream he'd make when Brook slid inside him. He tried to focus on the job in hand, which, to be honest, wasn't the job he'd rather have in his hand.

"Leslie dared me to wear these damn new shoes he's bought. Six-inch stilettos. I couldn't resist the challenge. Trouble was, I got one of them caught in a piece of loose carpeting and went arse over face down the stairs. Leslie couldn't stop laughing until he realised I'd actually hurt myself. Then he broke out the chamomile tea. That stuff is vile. Never let Leslie know you're upset. He's like a pit bull on steroids when he tries to get you to drink the damn stuff. "

Brook chuckled. "I'll bear that in mind. He sounds like a pretty formidable character, this Leslie of yours."

"You have no idea," was Lenny's muffled reply.

"How badly did you fall? Is it your lower back that hurts…like here?" He moved up Lenny's back and gave a few strong strokes up his lower back muscles. He kneaded the flesh, trying to work out the knots there. His lover flailed like a salmon out of water and cried out, wriggling underneath him. It didn't help Brook's horny state of mind at all.

"Ow, that bloody hurts. Yes, there, you big bully. Right there, where you pushed my back into my stomach."

Brook ignored his lover's indignant complaint and continued his massage, pressing a little more gently, using his thumbs to ease the strain of the muscles. "You definitely did a right number when you fell," he murmured as he trailed his fingers idly down Lenny's tanned and shining skin. "That'll teach you to try competing to wear six-inch heels with these younger types who have more flexibility in their bodies."

Lenny's head slowly turned, and the laser glare directed at Brook was worthy of a *Star Wars* fight scene. "Fuck you, bitch."

Brook couldn't hold back his laughter at those words. "Well, you are over thirty now," he teased as he continued his stroking up Lenny's back and ribs. "It's time to break out the rocking chair and slippers."

Lenny swore filthily and squirmed underneath him again, trying to turn around. Brook lowered his weight across Lenny's back, relishing the feel of his hot skin against his lover's own oiled body. Lenny stilled.

Brook whispered in his ear. "Stop wriggling. It's making me damned horny and I'll never finish this massage. You need it. You're as tense as hell."

"That's not the only place I'm tense," Lenny muttered. "My dick is going to bore a hole through this mattress in a minute. I've changed my mind. Maybe it's time to stop the massage and do some other form of stroking."

Brook shook his head. As much as he liked that idea, Brook could tell Lenny needed this TLC from the tightness of his back, and Brook wanted to make him wait. It would be all the more worthwhile.

"Wait a little while longer," he murmured, sitting up and continuing his careful exploration of Lenny's body. "Patience. Just lie there and relax."

Lenny grumbled into his pillow and Brook watched his lover's eyes close as he settled in to enjoy Brook's ministrations. For a while Brook lost himself in the slow movement of his hands, the feel of warm, pliable skin under his fingers and the focus on giving his man what he needed to rid him of the strained muscles in his back.

With a soft sigh, he leaned back, hands aching, and gently swept the last remaining vestiges of oil over Lenny's backside and hips. "I think that should do it," he muttered, wiping his oily hands on his chest. "I got most of the knots out, and hopefully that'll feel better."

There was no reply. "Baby, are you still with me?"

A soft snore was the only response he got and Brook grinned. The fact Lenny seemed to have fallen asleep was definitely something he'd be teasing him about when he woke up. His boyfriend had a particular vulnerability about his age and now Brook had more ammunition.

"Old man fell asleep on me," he said to the empty room. "I'm not sure if that's a compliment or not." He gazed down at the sleeping man, whose eyelashes lay black against his cheeks, his mussed blond hair and pink lips slightly open. The rush of feeling Brook had for Lenny both scared and elated him. He knew he'd fallen hard—about that there was no doubt.

It wasn't a case of understanding what made the man work or what Lenny had to give anymore. It was a case of Brook accepting whatever he had to offer, accepting who he was and living with anything that was thrown at him. Brook didn't think he had a choice. Having none of Lenny was far worse than having all of him—having *both* of them. Brook leaned down and planted soft kisses down Lenny's oil-glossed spine. The dozing man murmured softly but didn't wake up, his lips curving in a smile. Brook gave one last kiss to that special spot where his man's back ended and his arse began and climbed off the warm body below him. He draped the duvet loosely over the still body, stood watching him for a minute then sighed.

Okay. So no booty call right now. That sucks.

Brook went and washed his hands then climbed into bed beside his snoring lover. There was a simple joy in curling up beside a warm, scented body, a feeling of deep-down comfort as he headed into sleep.

Chapter 12

Brook woke to a distinctively pleasurable feeling in his groin. Heat surrounded his morning wood and he murmured in pleasure, lifting the cover to see what the hell was going on.

Lenny's blond head didn't even look up as it bobbed like a cork on water. The noise of licking, sucking and a little slurping made Brook's backside raise itself from the mattress and push his dick upwards towards the talented, heated cavern of Lenny's mouth.

"I like this way you have of waking me up," he managed to groan in between deep breaths. "I think perhaps it should become a regular thing." He hissed as Lenny's tongue swiped a deep lick up the underside of his cock. His boyfriend lifted his head and his beautiful eyes regarded him with a definite twinkle.

"You massaged me last night; I wanted to repay the favour. With my tongue." He went back down again and Brook closed his eyes, his crotch flooding with heat, and tingling and prickles and, fuck, anything else that was classed as a good sensation in this world. Lenny gave the best blowjobs.

"Maybe you should switch around and get up here, so I can suck you too," Brook panted, in between trying not to lose control too soon.

The tongue that was currently burying itself between his balls stopped as its owner considered the potential benefits of the offered sixty-nine.

"That works for me," Lenny said, giving a last, deep tug of the cock in his mouth. He scrambled up Brook's body and got comfortable. Brook found himself with a warm, scented man kneeling above him and an enthusiastic hard-on being pushed between his lips. He gripped Lenny's hips, pulling him closer into his wanting mouth, gasping as his lover's lips found Brook's dick again and rough fingers fondled his balls.

Brook breathed in the scent of sweat, musk, soap and vanilla-scented oil. He enjoyed sucking, licking and returning the favours currently being bestowed upon him. For good measure, he reached for the lube that was always kept under his pillow, and opened it to dribble some on his fingers. Then he pushed on his cock as Lenny pushed back onto his hand.

Brook groaned at the loss of the welcome heat of Lenny's mouth around him when his man lifted his head and panted, "More fingers please. Suck me at the same time." Those words spurred him on to push more digits inside Lenny. He found that nirvana spot at the same time he deep-throated Lenny again. The moan that reverberated around his dick as Lenny manfully kept up the pressure on Brook's cock was an aphrodisiac itself in its need.

Both men grunted, slick with sweat, the room filled with the smell of sex. Brook's climax built and he gasped. "Lenny, babe, incoming."

Lenny's warm mouth left his cock and instead he kissed Brook's hip, nipping at the skin with sharp teeth. Brook's climax washed over him and he came, gasping loudly and giving a yell worthy of an Indian brave. As Brook's sensitive body twitched and spasmed in the aftermath of his orgasm, Lenny lifted his head and looked back, face twisted in desire and desperation.

"Make me come, please. Push your fingers inside me. Go harder…I need to feel you." Brook did what he was told, twisting and hitting the spot that drove a man crazy. He let Lenny's slick cock slide out of his mouth and watched Lenny's body shudder with the force of his orgasm as Brook was coated with come. Lenny rolled off and crawled up to kiss Brook, his mouth still tasting of Brook's essences.

"Some wakeup party. I could make a habit of this."

"You and me both." Lenny gave a contented sigh and snuggled into the protective circle of Brook's arms.

"You do realise we're both supposed to be at work?" Brook murmured as he dozed. "I know you're the boss so you can get away with not going in. Me, I've got a boss to answer to so I guess I'll call in and tell him I'm working from home this morning. I do have a meeting I need to get to this afternoon at the office though, so I can't spend all day in bed with you."

Lenny grunted and shifted closer to Brook, splaying his hands over his stomach and trailing them down his sides. "I'll text the Leslie minion in a moment, tell him I'll be in late. I have to go in today, for lunchtime, though. Mr Miyagi is coming back in for yet another meeting on silk fabrics manufacture."

Brook glanced down. "Isn't that the name of the guy in *The Karate Kid*? Is that really your customer's name?"

Lenny's lips curved in a smile. "No. His real name is Akito Yosuke Hanaka but we call him AK for short because it's such a mouthful. He's pretty cool, one of the New Age mod businessmen. He's only thirty-two years old and heir to both a shipping empire and a fabric manufacturing plant. He's also extremely sexy eye candy, let me tell you. The man looks like Shun Oguri. Quite delicious…"

Brook sat up. *This* was the guy his boyfriend had been at the office with until quite late? Some sexy young Japanese stud muffin? And was going back to be with again?

"Who?" he asked, feeling a little put out at Lenny's obvious admiration. "Never heard of him."

Lenny waved an airy hand. "Well, unless you have a taste for Japanese films, something I *might* do on occasion, I doubt you'd recognise him. He was in this awesome film called *Crows Zero*. Hot teenage students and violence." He shivered theatrically. "Gives me gooseflesh thinking about it." He grinned and picked up his mobile from the side of the bed. Brook watched his fingers fly furiously across the screen.

"Yeah?" Brook scowled. "Bully for him. So what does he think of Laverne then?"

Lenny chuckled loudly as he put his phone back on the table. "Oh, he's absolutely fascinated with her. It turns out he's a big fan of *kabuki* and has even been known to perform an *onnagata* role now and then with a local theatre company. When he was a lot younger, of course." He cocked a devilish eye at Brook and fluttered his eyelashes camply. "*Onnagata* is when men dress as women—"

"I know what it is," Brook growled. "Son of a foreign diplomat and a UN translator, remember? When I was a teenager, we were stationed in Tokyo for six months in between Mum's postings. She speaks Japanese."

Lenny's face lit up. "Really? I'd love to hear that sometime. I love the language. What other languages does she speak?" His mobile pinged; he picked it up then gave a loud delighted laugh. "That young man is incorrigible."

"What young man?" Brook was becoming decidedly pissed off with all these other young men being flaunted in his face. He wanted to throw Lenny back against the pillows and show him exactly who he belonged to. And didn't that thought make him all flustered and confused. He'd never thought of owning someone like that before.

"Leslie." Lenny gave him a sly grin. "He has this fascination with your dick. Little slut texted me back saying I obviously got some and he hoped it was as good as he imagined given that you're, you know…" He clamped his lips shut, looking uncomfortable.

"What?" Brook was interested. They talked about his dick between them? This was becoming a bit like a dirty porn film in the making.

Lenny rushed ahead. "He seems to think I'm a lucky man and you have this huge cock. While he's not mistaken—it *is* a good size—he thinks you're hung like King Kong." He broke off abruptly and flushed. Brook was fascinated at the way Lenny's face turned bright red. He'd never seen that shade of tomato before. He suppressed the rising laughter in his chest as he waited with interest to see what could possibly come next. Could his man get any more adorable?

"Oh shit," Lenny stammered, holding one hand to his heated cheek like a damsel in distress, "I didn't mean to call you a gorilla or anything racist, it was an unfortunate turn of phrase and now…fuck, I'm making a real mess of this, aren't I?"

Brook couldn't help it. Lenny's lips needed shutting up so he did that, pulled him against his chest and proceeded to kiss the ever-loving crap out of him. The kissing led to a more— a lot more. Before they had time to think about anything, they were once again lying side by side, panting with exertion, sweaty, fulfilled and definitely not wanting to leave the comfort of Brook's rumpled and distinctly ripe-smelling bed.

"I love having you in me," Lenny whispered drowsily as he lay with his head on Brook's chest, his hair matted and sticky. "My King Kong man…I certainly will never be telling that little whippersnapper at work how nicely you fill me up."

Brook didn't reply. He was too tired and worn out from satisfying an insatiable Lenny. The man had a streak in him of liking his sex rough and dirty. Brook wasn't complaining, but it did take a lot of effort to please his lover.

"I never did get to know what other languages your mum speaks," Lenny murmured.

Brook roused himself enough to reply. "She speaks French, German, Japanese and Spanish. Some Italian too. She's studying it at the moment. She has this thing for languages; never happy unless she's learning something new."

"Hmm. Cool." Lenny fidgeted beside him then gave a deep sigh. "I suppose I should get up, have a shower and get home. I need to dress before I go into the office."

"Why not wear the clothes you wore last night? You didn't exactly wear them all that long, so I doubt they're mucky." Brook snickered.

Blue green eyes regarded him appraisingly. "Hello. Laverne, remember? Unless you have a skirt and blouse and a pair of silk stockings in your wardrobe I can use, I need to go home first."

"Oh, I forgot." Brook said shamefacedly.

Maybe I need to stock up on some women's clothing in case this happens again. Or perhaps Lenny can leave some of his stuff here. I need to get over this whole him going out in public dressed as Laverne thing. Lenny isn't going to change his mind.

Lenny sat up, covers dropping to his waist, and damned if Brook didn't feel the heat again.

"You still okay with everything?" Lenny asked. The uncertain look on his boyfriend's face made Brook want to pull him close and not let go. "I mean, we haven't really talked about the other night much, and I know how you feel, but I need to know you understand my point of view."

"I'm trying." Brook said quietly. "I mean I'll still worry about you, don't get me wrong, but I'm hearing what you're saying about being able to look after yourself."

Lenny looked relieved. "Thanks, love. That means a lot. I give you my promise I won't put myself in bad situations where I can help it." He swung his legs out of bed, sat and stretched. "Right. Time to get back to normal I guess." He stood up and padded into the ensuite. Brook admired his arse and sighed for lost opportunities.

Lenny came out a minute later. "Are we still okay for next Friday to go to Delish? Ryan was asking me if we were still planning on it."

Brook nodded. "Sure, should be fun."

Lenny cleared his throat, seemingly totally unaware that his nakedness was causing Brook to squirm. "It might be a bit more than a bit of fun. Ryan wants me to do a bit of a thing with him on stage, just a short drag skit, and I wanted to make sure you knew that beforehand."

Brook frowned. "What kind of skit? Will there be any nakedness involved between you two?"

Lenny spluttered in laughter. "Oh no. We're not sluts on stage—well I'm not anyway. Ryan is a law to himself. It's a few minutes of drag and that's it. Delilah Delish and Laverne Debussy-Smith having a laugh together with some raunchiness directed at the poor unfortunates in the audience."

Brook didn't want to say the wrong thing and have Lenny go off in a huff again. "Oh. Yeah, of course it's fine with me, if it's what you want to do."

The blinding smile Lenny threw Brook's way before he disappeared back into the bathroom made his stomach squirm in a good way.

Minutes later Brook heard the shower going. Usually he'd get up and join Lenny for a long, leisurely, steamy bout under the water but today they were short of time. It was already past ten and both of them had places to be. He'd probably regret it later when he was sitting on the train, but right now? He had plenty of good memories to get him through the day. And all of them involved Lenny James.

Chapter 13

Friday. The visit to Ryan's club rolled round fairly quickly. Lenny sat in his office, squirming because his lacy pants were stuck to his arse with the heat of the early August summer. There was a heat wave at the moment—if it could be called a heat wave. Twenty-eight degrees in UK terms was designated as such when the whole country came to a standstill, trains couldn't run and people ran the risk of becoming lobsters in the overzealous sun-worshipping that ensued. Lenny wasn't fond of heat unless it was in the bedroom. He swore as he stood up and wrenched his underwear away from his backside, snarling under his breath.

"Stupid bloody lacy crap, I don't know why the fuck I wear this stuff." He was irritated, sweating and grumpy. He'd taken clothes to Brook's place last night to change into this morning—a real coup for both of them in terms of Brook's acceptance of Laverne—and he wished he'd taken different underwear.

"Is that any way for a lady to talk?" His boyfriend's amused tone jolted Lenny out of the gym session with his arse, and he looked up in surprise at the grinning figure of Brook in the doorway.

Naomi stood beside him with a smirk. "You have a visitor, boss," she said slyly. "I'll get you something cold to drink. You look as if you're going to self-combust." She gave an evil chuckle. "*This* is why we keep telling you we need to get air-conditioning in this building."

Lenny scowled. "My lovely, for the sake of a week every three-hundred and sixty-five days when the weather heats up enough to warrant it, this lady is not using her hard-earned cash to pander to the needs of the suffering masses—of which I am one, I might add." He tossed his head back in mock disdain, causing a curl of his wig to fall over his face. He blew it back huffily, seeing Brook's eyes widen and his lips curve in a smile. "I bought all my ungrateful minions fans for their desks and a new fridge to stock your copious bottles of water and energy drinks. I think I've done my employer-ly bit." He sniffed in satisfaction.

Naomi shook her head as she rolled her eyes. "Oh, you are indeed our gracious benefactor," she teased. She turned to leave and glanced over her shoulder, eyes twinkling. "I give thanks to the generous being that is my boss."

"Cheeky mare," Lenny spluttered. He looked at Brook in indignation as his PA disappeared. "You see how my employees treat me? Not a shred of respect, nary a one."

His grumbling was stopped by the press of Brook's warm lips to his. The kiss was soft, sweet and over far too soon for Lenny's liking. He blinked at Brook as his lover sat down in the visitor's chair and crossed his legs. He looked delectable, Lenny thought dreamily, like a *GQ* model, in his blue suit and white shirt, with a striped red and blue tie.

"I was in the area so I thought I'd stop by and see what time we're meeting at the club tonight. I managed to lose that arsehole Keith permanently to his new team in another office in the city, so it's cause for a celebration tonight. He's gone for good." Brook loosened his tie, and Lenny's eyes watched, hypnotised at that slow, sensuous action.

"I told you this morning at your place. Nine p.m. Is the heat affecting your memory?" Lenny asked. In truth his lacy panties now had another problem: the stiffy he was starting to sprout underneath his linen dress.

Ugh. Stay down, you horny little bastard.

"Oh, I must have forgotten. My bad," Brook drawled lazily as he undid the tie completely and then loosened the top three buttons of his shirt to reveal the gleaming, muscled start of his torso. The tie lay draped around his neck and Lenny wanted to rip it off, tie Brook's hands behind his back and have his way with him. Instead he sat down behind his desk to hide his rising excitement and raised an eyebrow at his boyfriend.

"You came down here to give a lady shit, didn't you? This damned outfit is hot enough without you adding to the heat. I love linen, but it was the wrong choice today." He frowned down at his slightly crumpled, pale green Ralph Lauren sleeveless, lace yoke dress. "And my tits are really irritating the hell out of me today. I think I might stop wearing them altogether." He mused in contemplation. "They used to be fun; now, not so much." He scowled again. "And don't get me started on this fucking wig. Maybe it's about time I rethink this whole thing. Maybe I can get away with growing my hair and wear it longer." A strange sound came out of Brook's mouth but Lenny was too preoccupied on thinking of himself with his own curls and bouncy waves to respond to it. "I like that idea too. In fact, I think that's exactly what I might do…" His voice trailed off as Brook exploded into a fit of laughter.

Lenny stared at him in pique. "What the hell? What's your problem?"

"Oh, babe," Brook spluttered through what sounded suspiciously to Lenny like girly giggles. "You really don't do heat well, do you? You are *not* a summer person. What would you do if I took you to Kenya on holiday or anywhere hotter than this…?"

Brook wanted to go on holiday with him? Well, well…

He glared at Brook and wiped a stray rivulet of sweat from his hairline. "You're mocking me? A woman on the edge? Do you know what happened to the last guy that did that?" He moved around to where Brook sat and plonked himself down in his boyfriend's lap. Brook's eyes widened at being subjected to a groin-full of man-woman. Lenny latched an arm around Brook's neck and brought his ear closer. "He fucked me then did it again. And it was *good…*" He rolled the last word out lasciviously, pleased at the response he felt under his arse.

Oh yes, that is exactly the reaction I was hoping for. Make fun of me, you bastard, and I shall make you pay…

He wriggled a little for good measure and was gratified at Brook's low, breathy groan. Then Lenny stood up, adjusted his own package best he could, given he was in a dress, and went back to his own seat. He sat back down with a snicker. The heat in the room had definitely been turned up a few notches.

Brook's eyes smouldered but he made no move to hide the hard ridge lying under his snug-fitting trousers. "Playing hardball, eh?" he murmured with a sensuous look at Lenny. Lenny grinned back at him but swallowed at the sexy menace in Brook's voice. "Fine with me. Two can play at that game…"

Lenny shrugged. "Bring it on, chicken. Bring it on…" He waggled his head in true diva style and Brook's nostrils flared. They stared at each other for what felt like minutes until an amused voice broke into their standoff.

"The testosterone in this room is stifling. I can feel the heat from here, and I don't mean the weather."

Lenny rolled his eyes at Leslie leaning against the door jamb, arms folded and a huge smile on his face. "What can I do for you, Leslie? My fella and I are a little busy at the moment."

"I'll say," his employee sniggered as he walked unceremoniously into the room and stood behind Brook. Leslie frowned. "Laverne, darling, you need to powder. Your face is all shiny. And your mascara is running."

Leslie sidled around to where Lenny sat. Lenny opened his mouth to ask him what the hell he was doing, then closed it in disbelief as Leslie stuck out a pink tongue, wet his thumb and proceeded to wipe the spit-laden digit under Lenny's eyes. The same strange sound he'd heard earlier emanating from Brook was once again apparent, only louder and mixed with what sounded suspiciously like snorts. Lenny was, quite simply, speechless at the bold gesture of personal space invasion.

Leslie stood back and squinted at Lenny's face. "Looks better," he said doubtfully. "But you really need to get rid of all that shininess. It doesn't become you at all, nuh-huh."

Lenny finally found his voice. "Sweet Jesus, what the hell? You spat on my face." The one good thing was his hard-on had subsided somewhat.

Leslie shook his head vehemently. "Oh no, I tidied up a mess *using* spit. There's a difference. If I'd spat on your face you'd know about it, honey. A bit like if I'd given you a golden shower. Unmistakeable."

Brook now had tears rolling down his face as he laughed without reservation. Lenny wondered faintly how anyone coped with Leslie Tiberius Scott full time. Oliver Brown had to be a saint. There was no other explanation.

Leslie trotted back over to where Brook sat. "Anyhoo, boss, I came in here to tell you there's a Mrs Landry waiting in reception for you, for your meeting with her and Pixie. Pixie's asked me to let you know, she's getting coffee." Leslie flapped a hand. "She's weird, that girl. I've been trying to get to know her for ages, and she just doesn't seem to warm to me. I can't imagine why."

Pixie Blenheim was a recent appointment at Debussy's. She'd been recruited from a competitor two months ago because of her programming knowledge of the software Lenny used to design his merchandise. She was quiet, kept to herself and would have been overwhelmed by the magnificence that was Leslie Tiberius Scott. Lenny could well imagine why she hadn't become firm friends with him. The girl was rather strange though. She never seemed able to look Lenny in the eye when he said hello to her, or sat with her about the new developments he wanted in his design package. She was also one of the few employees he didn't know well yet and her name was on the list of people to be investigated when the security consultant came to visit next week. Lenny hated thinking of her in that way, but under the current circumstances, he felt he had no choice.

"Thanks, chicken. Tell her I'll be there in a while. Rita is early, so she won't mind waiting while I finish up here. "

Leslie nodded and waved a slim hand at Lenny as he walked to the door. "Make sure you tidy up before you go. Don't want to scare the customers away with that glazed-donut look." He gave a moue of distaste and then his face brightened. "Oh, and I'm looking forward to tonight. Everyone's going to be there, Taylor's dragging Draven along and Eddie's convinced Gideon it's for a good cause so he's coming too. It's so going be a hoot!"

He disappeared out of the office.

Lenny and Brook looked at each other and then both of them burst out into side-splitting guffaws. Lenny knew he had a visitor waiting and he'd need to repair his face but he didn't care.

"How do you manage a man like that?" Brook somehow got out between heaving sobs. "He is absolutely precious, one of a kind." He wiped his eyes and reached over to Lenny's desk to take out a tissue from the box that always sat there. He wiped his eyes and then blew his nose.

"I know. He's a pretty unique character," Lenny agreed as he tried to compose himself.

"A golden shower…I mean, honestly?" Brook was off again.

Lenny grinned as he stood up, sides hurting from laughing. "Love, I have to get to this meeting. You'll have the pleasure of more of Leslie's company tonight at the club. He's dragged all his friends down there, more fool them. I hope they know what they've let themselves in for." He wiped sweat off his face and grimaced. "Yuck, I really need to clean up. I'll see you later at the club then? Around nine, in case you'd forgotten again."

Brook stood up. "No problem. I'll be there." His hands reached out and framed Lenny's face. "I know you're all shiny and that but…" he said softly and kissed him sweetly. Lenny melted against him. Brook finished driving him crazy and stepped away, a strange look in his eyes.

"It feels weird kissing you with your Laverne clothes and makeup on, but I'm actually getting used to it…and I think you growing your hair is a great idea. It'll give me more to hold onto."

"Oh," Lenny said, head spinning. "Good to know." That simple statement floored him. He'd known Brook was more accepting than when they'd first started, but it meant the world to him that Brook could actually kiss him in his Laverne guise. The strange thing was, random thoughts had been flitting through Lenny's head recently about Laverne. He'd actually wondered if he could give up that persona if it ever came to a choice about having her or Brook, and the conclusion he'd come had stunned him to his core.

He'd never, ever considered letting her go before, but for Brook…Lenny thought he'd do it. That had shaken him, and caused a strange fluttering in his stomach at that shocking realisation. It was a decision he hoped never to have to make, as it would be a world-changing one. It would also go against everything he believed in about accepting someone for who they are and fuck the rest of the world.

And what the fuck is all that about? That's not me. This man has scrambled my brain.

He became aware Brook was kissing him softly on the cheek as he chuckled. "You look in a brown study there. I'd better go. I'll see you later." Lenny made his way to the door. Brook reached out and caught his arm. "Lenny?"

"Yes?" Lenny looked at him quizzically.

Brook dropped his hand. "Nothing. Have a good meeting. I'll see you tonight." He looked as if he wanted to say more but Lenny didn't have time to wonder what. He needed to freshen up and get to his meeting and ponder the strange thoughts he'd had in the recent week.

"Laters, baby," he mouthed at his boyfriend, doubting Brook would get the *Fifty Shades* reference. "Wear something sexy for me." He smirked then Lenny left the office for his meeting with a little more spring in his step.

***

Later that evening, Lenny was in the arbour doing a stock check on his new show designs. What with everything going on, he wanted to make sure that each and every one of his treasured designs was accounted for before the show next week. Leslie had already checked them but Lenny felt a burning need to make sure for himself.

The building was quiet and he assumed all his employees had left for the night. He was due at the club for nine o'clock tonight and it was only a tube stop away. When he stretched, wincing as his back snapped and popped, he looked at his watch. It was eight p.m. already.

"Shit, I'd better start thinking about locking up," he muttered as he closed the doors to the built-in cupboards along the walls. He tidied up, left and locked the room behind him, making sure to arm the special alarm for the room.

As he approached his office, he heard a rustling from within.

"Crap, I hope I don't have fucking rats," he swore as he crept towards the half-open door. "That's all I need—a rodent infestation." The thought of rats or other little nocturnal creatures getting into his precious store of fabric made him hyperventilate. He took a deep breath as he gently swung the door open to see not a rat, but a pair of distinctly human feet clad in low-heeled, grey court shoes sticking out from the side of the desk. Someone was behind his desk, by his chair and currently rummaging in his waste bin from the papers strewn across the floor.

Lenny thought he'd found his human rat. He made his way as quietly as possible around the desk, wincing when his one shoe squeaked. The rustling stopped. He held his breath and watched as the figure looked up and he gazed into the startled green eyes of Pixie Blenheim.

"Pixie. Can I ask what the hell it is you think you're doing?" He stepped forward, his eyes focused on what she held in her hand. It was a draft of a waistcoat design he'd done earlier in the day, modelled after Johnny Depp's coat in *Pirates of the Caribbean*. It hadn't been a serious effort, simply a whimsical look at how it would look in a crushed black satin fabric, with gold braid.

"Just emptying the trash. Laverne. I thought you'd gone home," she stuttered, her eyes darting around the room as if seeking a magical escape route, one that Lenny didn't block. Pixie was about five foot five, petite, with bobbed dark brown hair and pale skin.

"Obviously. Is that a new duty you've been assigned, then?" he said silkily. "Funny. I don't remember signing off on anything for one of my employees to become an overnight cleaner. I hope I'm not paying you overtime."

His inner bitch was in top form.

He prowled towards her. "Just tell me the truth, chicken. You're the fox in my henhouse, the rat in my cellar, the mouse eating my cheese. You're Tracy's little snitch."

Her nostrils flared, her eyes panicked. "He told me it wasn't doing anything wrong. That if you threw them away they were okay to use."

Lenny tried to control his rising temper. "So he's paying you to steal from me. Anything you find in the confines of this building, of this office, is not yours to take. It belongs to me. The sign says Debussy's, not Tracy Trey. I have to say I'm bitterly disappointed in him for stooping this low."

He moved to his desk and picked up the phone. "I think we should call the police." He had no intention of taking it further with the law, because they really wouldn't give a fuck, but it didn't hurt to scare the shit out of her.

She moved closer to him in panic. "Please don't call the police, Laverne. I'm sorry. I'll tell Tracy I can't help him anymore."

Lenny snorted. "Honey, you are so right. You are going to go to your office, with me as your escort, clean out your desk, give me your key card and leave this building. You're fired. And you're going to go back and tell that worm Tracy Trey that Laverne Debussy-Smith is onto him and he'd best watch his damn balls because I'm going to fucking kick them into his stomach."

Pixie gasped but nodded, her eyes bright with tears. "I understand. I'm sorry…"

The bitter taste of bile crept into his mouth. "I like to be able to trust my employees. We're a family here." He gestured to her. "Follow me. I want you out of here as soon as possible."

The walk of shame led to her small cubicle where he watched her pack her things with trembling hands. He said not a word, just glared at her. When she was finished, and held the empty photo copier paper box containing her possessions, he marched her down to the security desk and watched her hand over her key card.

"She's not allowed in this building, under any circumstances," he instructed Colin, the guard he'd known for over ten years. "Stick her on your shit list, Col."

Colin nodded. "Sure, Laverne. She'll go up on the Wall of Shame." This was a list the security guys kept of people not permitted into the building. It included a few exes, a certain well-known actor one of Lenny's neighbours had a problem with, and a Conservative MP who'd pissed off a fellow Labour MP who owned half of the building.

Ten minutes later both he and Colin watched Pixie leave.

Colin reached into his desk drawer and took out a bottle of bourbon. "You look like you need one of these, my lovely." He winked as he filled two small tumbler glasses of drink and passed one to Laverne. "Drink up."

Laverne downed the drink and felt a little better. "Thanks, Colin. What a shitty evening. And I've got to get to the club now, before I'm late for my own show." He smiled wryly.

At least I've found the thief. Brook will be pleased. So will Leslie. Fucking Tracy Trey. Wait until I get my hands on him.

Chapter 14

"Do you have a VIP pass? You need one to get in this entrance." The very large, affable-looking man smiled toothily at Brook as he stood at one of the entrances to Club Delish. It was the smile of a shark about to devour him slowly, taking great pleasure in eating him bit by painful bit. The bouncer's teeth were shiny white beneath the glow of the lights blinking above, but his eyes were hard and uncompromising.

The door Brook stood at was one of three along the street of the club, which stretched almost a small city block. To his left, the crowd milled as they stood in line to get into the main entrance under the flashing rainbow sign denoting Club Delish in flouncy script. To his extreme right, at the end of the building, adjacent to a dimly lit alley, there was a door leading into what Brook had been told loftily was the 'tradesman's' entrance and which apparently led directly into the kitchen. Another bouncer stood guard there, looking as formidable in bulk as the one who now stood glowering at Brook, a suspicious expression forming on his chubby face.

"I thought my name would be on a list," Brook said quietly. "I wasn't given a pass." He glanced above the door at the gaudily painted purple and silver sign bearing the Club Delish logo of a violet high-heeled stiletto. The words on the sign "VIP Passage - Exclusive entry" blinked off and on above the tall brushed-steel door.

"No ticket, no admittance," the bouncer growled, softening his words with what was possibly a grin, but looked more to Brook like the man had wind. "We don't keep lists. Sorry. I suggest you get in line with the rest of 'em."

Brook glanced uncertainly over the long line of people currently queued up, ranging from go-go boys to shorts-clad twinks and surprisingly, more than a few bears with large tattooed arms hanging all them. Brook sighed loudly. He hated queues and this one looked as if it could go on a long time.

He nodded resignedly and pulled out his phone. He'd need to try and call Lenny and find out what the hell was happening. He was listening to Lenny's answer message and wondering whether his boyfriend would ever check it when he spotted Mango coming round the corner from the alley. Mango was deep in conversation, looking up at a slim woman, or possibly a man in drag, with long, deep red hair, a long silver dress with heels Brook knew he'd never be able to balance on, and tanned, bare arms. Mango had a rucksack on his back, dressed in blue chinos, a polo shirt that showed off strong arms.

He left his message telling Lenny to get the fuck out here and let him in when Mango spotted him. He gave a wave of acknowledgement and a shouted "Hi Brook, be with you in a sec," and Brook waved back. The bouncer's attitude changed considerably. His eyes widened and Brook swore where before there had been wary boredom in them, there was now a look of respect.

"You're a friend of Mr Munroe's?" the bouncer enquired, looking a lot friendlier.

Brook knew when to milk a situation. "Yes," he said airily as he watched Mango give what looked like a pretty filthy kiss to the redhead, who then disappeared into the other entrance. Mango swaggered towards Brook. "We're neighbours actually, and good friends too."

Brook crossed his fingers by his side at the white lie. One altercation in the hallway of their flat complex and occasional greetings didn't really constitute the description of good friends, but Brook desperately needed to pee and wanted inside the club as soon as possible. It would take him five minutes to get out of the damn leather pants he had on, so time was of the essence.

Mango reached him and waved a languid hand at the bouncer. He clapped Brook on the shoulder as he grinned at him. "Wow, you look delicious," he said admiringly. "Love those trousers. Great package too."

Hmm. That answers the question whether Mango likes men I guess. Unless he's bi. I'm still not sure who the redhead was.

Brook blinked. Hubris aside, he knew he looked good in his black leather pants, silky bronze long-sleeved, button-down dress shirt and his Armani loafers. His leather jacket was draped casually over his shoulder. The trousers showed off his assets to his best advantage—it was the reason he'd worn this ensemble. Lenny had said, dress sexy.

Mango nodded at the bouncer. "Damon," he acknowledged. "How's the baby doing? Is she over the colic period yet?"

Damon aimed a high-wattage smile in Mango's direction. "She's doing fine, thanks Mr Munroe. The wife has calmed down and stopped panicking. That tea remedy you gave me really worked. I owe you one."

Mango shrugged modestly. "It's one I learnt from an Indian shaman who was a damned genius at that sort of thing. He had to be with the regularity with which his wife popped the little buggers out." He playfully punched the big guy in the arm. "And I've told you to call me Mango, you prick. Mr makes me sound so old."

The bouncer nodded his head. "Yeah, I know, Mr Munroe." His grin caused Mango to shake his head sorrowfully.

"You guys slay me…" He glanced at Brook. "You waiting to go in?"

Brook nodded. "Apparently I need a pass and Lenny never gave me one. I've left a message for him."

Mango gave a cackle. "Oh fuck the pass. Damon, he's with me. Come on, handsome, let's go find the ladies." He grinned wickedly. "Or rather the queens who think they're ladies."

Damon gave a beatific smile and without further ado, opened the door to the rumbling beat of music. Mango stepped inside and beckoned Brook in, shouting a little over the noise.

"First time here?"

When Brook nodded, Mango gave another wicked grin. "It's a fabulous place. Ryan runs a tight ship here and he's a damn genius at getting people moving."

He fought his way through the dancing, waving crowd, on his way to the front when Brook reached out and stopped him. He shouted into Mango's ear. "Mango, sorry about this but I really need to take a piss. Know where the toilets are?"

Mango gestured vaguely to the left side of the heaving humanity on display. "There's one over there, mate. It's a *special* one." He grinned. "You might like to wait 'til we get to the front and go to the other bathroom. Less going on in that one."

Brook's bladder was bursting and he couldn't wait. "I'll use this one, thanks. Don't want to pee myself."

Mango gave a loud snicker. "Be careful. You want to watch yourself in that one." He flashed a wicked grin at Brook and disappeared into the mass. Brook felt a little uneasy at that comment.

He'd been to gay clubs before and knew what went down *and* up in them, but Mango had sounded as if there was more to it.

He figured it out once he got into the toilets. They were spacious, luxurious receptacles of glistening, lilac booths, probably about fifteen in all. A glitter bomb had obviously exploded inside because the doors and walls were covered with various shades of purple, lilac, pink and pale blue. As if that didn't astonish him enough as his eyeballs ached, the number of drag queens engaged in pastimes he normally did in the privacy of his bedroom was mind boggling. The room was a hive of activity, with wigs, false boobs, shimmering dresses, stilettos and body parts. Some of the booths were shut and the grunts and exclamations emanating from them left Brook in no doubt what was going in there.

As he moved through the bathroom trying to get to the single unoccupied booth he saw at the rear, he passed a number of blowjobs, a full one-on-one sex session, what looked like a rimming job—he couldn't be sure; the sequinned dress was plastered over the head and face of the man on his knees behind another, who clutched the porcelain sink in ecstasy—and a threesome of some sort which Brook really didn't want to dwell on. All he saw were dicks, dicks and more dicks. He couldn't even be sure how many people made up the thrusting, heaving mass in the corner.

He managed to get through the orgy, sidestepped a few hands entreating him to join in, winced at more than a few hard gropes to his backside and balls and fell into the cubicle. He locked it behind him and passed a hand over his face, then unzipped his trousers. His cock sprung free and he heaved a sigh of relief as he peed into the toilet.

Bloody hell. What kind of place was this anyway? He'd never seen anything like it.

He finished, zipped himself up and took a deep breath, ready to face whatever lay outside the safety of the cubicle door. Then with a mental shake, he opened it and stepped out. The first thing he saw was a black-haired man leaning against the wall in front of the stall, examining his nails. The man's air of nonchalance at the activity around him was impressive, Brook had to admit. He smiled at the guy as he tried to push past him. It was a bit of a trial as the other man was about six feet five, broad, muscled and bearded and looked as if he'd stepped out of *Bears R Us* magazine. He also didn't move aside to let Brook pass.

"Thanks matey." Big Guy had an Australian twang. "I'm dying for a piss. The other stalls seem busy." He grinned. "This is a bit of an eye opener, eh?" He waved a hand around.

"Yes, a bit. Do you mind moving so I can get through?" Brook tried polite.

Big Guy narrowed his eyes. "In a hurry are you? Not quite your scene? Pity. You don't fancy a blowjob in there then? I'd do you a good one, mate." He motioned to the cubicle.

Brook shook his head. "No thank you. Have a good night." The man stepped aside reluctantly to let him pass. Brook moved quickly towards the door, feeling the man's eyes on him. He made it through the still-busy bathroom and out into the safe confines of the club.

Where the hell is Lenny? This place is making me nervous.

He sidestepped the people gyrating on the dance floor, finding himself at the entrance to a large, plush bar kitted out with tables, sofas and chairs. It looked busy as well but there was still room at the bar to stand. Brook went over and stood there, trying to catch the harried bartender's eye.

I need a drink. Or two. Lenny, where the fuck are you? You said to meet you here.

He'd gotten his first drink of the night when he heard a loud hail from one of the low set banks of couches on the side of the bar.

"Brook. Over here!"

He glanced over to see Leslie waving at him. He was sitting on someone's lap, someone half obscured by Leslie's body, and Brook assumed it was Oliver. A group of other men sat around, staring at Brook with interest. One of them had unruly red hair and was busy kissing the man next to him rather thoroughly. Another man with long, curly black hair pulled back in a short ponytail was chatting quietly to another man who looked tough and dangerous, and yet had such a goofy grin for the man talking that it made Brook smile.

My friend, you have it bad. I dare say I look like that when I see Lenny.

He acknowledged Leslie's greeting and held his drink tightly as he negotiated through the mêlée of the bar. Once he got there, he sat down on the seat that Leslie patted. He smiled at the group around the table.

"Good to see you all. I was beginning to think I'd entered the Twilight Zone. I went to that purple bathroom to take a pee and…"

He was interrupted by Leslie's loud squeal as he clamped a hand to his mouth in horror. "Oh, shit, Brook. You went into *Deep Purple*? Didn't anyone warn you about that place? It's the humping ground for the club. Delilah created it so that the usual bathrooms could be kept clear for what they're supposed to be used for. People were complaining they were peeing themselves trying to get through the guys using it for BJs and stuff."

Oliver reached over Leslie's body with difficulty as the man clung to him like he was a treasured teddy bear. "Good to see you again."

The redheaded man who'd recently had his tongue down the other man's throat gave a wide grin and held out his hand. "You had a narrow escape if you went in there and survived. I'm Eddie by the way. This is my boyfriend, Gideon."

Brook nodded at Gideon, recognising him. "Yes, we've met before, at Galileo's." He gave the redhead a wary glance.

Sorry I hit on your boyfriend.

Gideon nodded a greeting at him and gave him a grin. "Brook, nice to see you again. Looks like the date worked out."

Brook chuckled. "Yes, very well actually, although not in the way I'd originally planned. Sorry I cancelled my dinner date at your restaurant. I'll need to make another reservation to bring Lenny in."

Gideon shrugged. "No problem. Give me a call and I'll set it up." His nostrils flared as Eddie moved closer to him and a look of complete satisfaction crossed his face. Brook blinked as he wondered at that strange gesture.

Eddie beamed. "I'm assuming you know Leslie and Oliver, his boyfriend?" He reached over and stroked Gideon's cheek idly.

Gideon's eyes closed in satisfaction. "God you smell good," he murmured.

Brook stared at them.

Eddie must have noticed his puzzled face. He grinned. "My boyfriend had a problem with his sense of smell for a while, and now it's coming back. He's like this weird hound dog that has to sniff me all the time."

Gideon scowled. "I hardly think that's an apt description, Eddie. Brook is going to think I'm crazy."

The ponytailed man laughed loudly. “Crazy is as crazy does, Giddy baby. We all know you have this thing now for sniffing stuff and telling us about the orgasmic tastes of everything you put in your mouth now you’ve started cooking again.” He smiled slyly. “Thank God you keep *some* tastes to yourself.” He snickered and Mr Tough Looking slapped his arm lightly.

“Behave, babe,” he admonished, but the smile on his face belied his warning.

Eddie’s face was pink. “Tay, enough already.” He cast an apologetic glance at Brook. “Gideon lost his sense of taste too in a fire but it’s come back. Now he’s making up for lost time.”

Brook nodded. “I’m glad to hear things are better. I can’t imagine what it would be like to lose two of my senses like that.”

Eddie gestured around the table. “So this joker here is Taylor and his fiancé Draven. Don’t let Draven’s tough-man look fool you. He’s a pussycat, really.”

Taylor was the man with the swept-back black hair and coffee-coloured skin. He inclined his head in greeting. Draven rolled his eyes at Eddie’s statement. Up close he looked even tougher. His eyes held a wary amusement.

“Yeah, big old pussycat, that’s me. Nice to meet you at last, Brook. I’ve heard about you from a number of sources.”

Brook frowned. He wasn’t sure he liked being talked about. *A number of sources*? That sounded very official. Draven had the air of a policeman, which was a little disconcerting.

“Oh yes? Who’s been talking about me then?”

Draven snorted. “Well, Leslie doesn’t stop with Laverne this and Brook that. And I understand you live across the hall from an old friend and colleague of mine—Mango Munro?”

Brook groaned. Hell, that man was everywhere. Did the whole damn city know him? “Yes. He’s the one who told me about Deep Purple but he didn’t really go into details.”

The table erupted in laughter. “Mango is a bit of a bastard,” Draven acknowledged with a fond smile. “It’s just like him to test your mettle sending you in there. Well, you got out intact—I hope?”

He raised a quizzical eyebrow and Brook flushed. “I might need bleach in my eyes to wash away some of it, but yes, I made it out.”

Taylor spoke for the first time. “Lenny was here earlier looking for you. He was a bit worried. He expected you sooner.” His voice was soft and melodious.

“I didn’t realise I needed a pass to get in the VIP door. Mango helped me in,” Brook explained. “I haven’t seen Lenny yet.”

Leslie made a moue. “Lenny was like an old woman worrying where you were. He wanted to see you before he got all dressed up. He had something important to tell us but he wanted to wait until you got here.” His face lit up like a sparkler. “He has this fabulous outfit; it’s pink with the most awesome pair of heels you can imagine to top it off. I want a pair of sparkly Blahniks like those.” His yearning was obvious, and Oliver chuckled loudly.

“Baby, don’t you think you have enough shoes? My place has become a shrine to every kid of bloody footwear you can imagine.”

Leslie pouted. “Oliver, you can’t ever have enough shoes. Have I taught you nothing?” He proceeded to pull Oliver’s face to his and indulge in deep-play tonsil hockey.

Brook took a sip of his drink and tried to relax in his chair as the hot display of wantonness went on before his eyes. It made his cock plump up and without Lenny there to alleviate the situation, it was no fun.

The other men around the table seemed used to their friends’ close PDA, and the conversation turned to one of sport, the show ahead and for some reason, the latest cop shows on television. Suddenly a warm pair of hands encircled Brook’s neck and the familiar scent of his boyfriend flooded Brook’s nostrils with spice and sandalwood.

“Evening, love. I hope the gang is taking care of you?”

Smiling eyes regarded him. Lenny looked pumped up, his eyes roving down Brook’s body in appreciation. Brook felt a frisson of desire race through him at the heat in his lover’s eyes. His boyfriend’s tight, forest-green chinos and pale-green, button-up shirt clung to his body, with the faint hint of sweat and musk.

He tilted his head back and looked up into Lenny’s warm eyes.

“All the better now you’re here,” Brook murmured softly, and all at once the group around him uttered an amused. “Aww.”

“Piss off, you lot.” Lenny narrowed his eyes in mock anger at the men grinning at them. “You’re jealous I get to have this hunk of manhood in my bed and you don’t.” He planted a swift kiss on

Brook's cheek. "I have something to tell you and Leslie. I found the mole."

Brook stared at him and Leslie squealed. "Oh God, you found him? How? Where?"

"*She* was Pixie Blenheim. I found her rifling through the rubbish in my office. She confessed she was spying for Trey and I fired her and banished her from the building."

Draven gave a low laugh. "I think my boss needs to employ you, Lenny. We could do with your sort on the investigative team at our agency."

Brook grabbed Lenny in a hug. "Great news. What did the police say?"

Lenny squirmed. "I didn't call the police."

At Brook's eye roll Lenny hastily continued. "There was no point. Fashion espionage isn't exactly the type of thing the police focus on, and it would have caused more trouble than it was worth." He smiled grimly. "Next time I see Tracy, I'll get my own back, I can assure you."

"Well, okay." Brook was uncertain, but he wasn't going to argue. Lenny looked too relaxed and happy for that. "As long as she's gone I guess there's not much more can be done."

Leslie reached out and pulled Lenny to him in a fierce embrace. "Now please let's not have the same issues we had before and you start looking after your stuff, boss. The shredder is your friend." His attempt at a tough glare made Brook smile. He noticed Oliver and the others holding back a grin too.

Eddie reached out and tousled Leslie's hair. "You are so damn cute when you try to be tough."

Leslie gave a cry of outrage and slapped his arm. "Do you have a death wish, bitch? It took me ages to get it right."

The crowd cracked up laughing at Leslie's indignant expression as he fixed his hair.

Lenny chuckled. "I've got a little while before I need to go on stage with Delilah. Why don't I show you around the club?"

Brook stood up. "You're not going to take me into Deep Purple, are you?" he said tentatively. "Because, I have to tell you, I've been in there and it's not my scene."

The guys sniggered and Lenny's eyes widened in horror. "What in the name of thundershit possessed you to go in there? I left a note and your club pass on the table before I left your place this morning. The note said, 'Here's your pass and please, whatever you do, stay away from Deep Purple. It's a den of iniquity and you'll hate it.'"

"Oh, I never saw it. Well, Mango did warn me but he didn't tell me how disturbing it was." Brook chuckled. "It's fine. I'm not a fainting maiden. It was a shock to the senses, that's all. Like a damn Greek orgy scene."

Lenny sighed and brushed a blond lock off his forehead. "Yeah, Ryan needed somewhere for the guys to go when they wanted to get their rocks off outside the main club. We had a few incidents with people messing themselves outside the bathrooms because they couldn't get in for cocks and false tits and who knows what else. So there's a strict rule. No hanky-panky in the normal toilets, use Deep Purple for that. Of course it still goes on in the usual loos but the bouncers manage it. People can at least take a piss when they want to instead of having to dodge multiple semen bullets and pushy bottoms." He snorted loudly in amusement at the groans around the table.

"Jesus, that's disgusting," muttered Gideon with a wince of distaste. "That image is now seared in my brain."

Lenny waved an airy hand. "Glad to be of service. Come on, love. Let me take you on a personal tour of the place. See you guys later."

Brook waved a fleeting goodbye before he was pulled out of the bar. Lenny seemed in a real hurry to be somewhere.

"Lenny, where's the fire?" he protested laughingly as he was pulled along like a kid's toy on wheels, trying to avoid the dancers on the floor. "Slow down."

Lenny stopped to regard Brook with smouldering eyes. "I am so bloody horny, I can't think straight. You look so sexy in that leather getup and I really want you to shag me. We need to find somewhere that's fairly private."

At first Brook thought Lenny was joking. Then Lenny moved in and took his mouth in a kiss that told him he wasn't. They were surrounded by people, and his lover was deftly palming his crotch, pressing himself against Brook's body, causing incredibly hot reactions. When Lenny released him to let him breathe, Brook reeled from the onslaught of his passion.

“Jesus,” he managed to get out in a strangled voice. “You are a randy bastard.”

“Uh-huh,” Lenny murmured huskily. “So let’s go somewhere that will let me relieve my tension—and yours.” He snickered as he glanced down as the cock now pressing uncomfortably against Brook’s trousers. “Because that animal needs letting loose. On me.”

Lenny pulled Brook through the crowds—a man who knew where he was going and wanted to get there as soon as he could. Brook had no choice but to follow. His boyfriend stopped in front of a door. Lenny looked at him with a glint in his eyes and pulled down the handle. The door opened and Brook was yanked unceremoniously into the room. The door was closed firmly behind them. It was a small sound studio, with low desks full of equipment and one armchair. The room had small windows covered with closed blinds looking out into the back alley of the club.

Lenny raised his eyebrows. “Ryan never comes in here. It’s used more for storage now. And look, we have an armchair.” He licked his lips, his eyes predatory.

Brook was growing even more turned on, and he groaned. “What if someone comes in? That’s all I need to be found with my backside in the air screwing my boyfriend.”

Lenny's answer was to drag a small side unit over to the door and wedge it under the handle. Brook watched him, open mouthed.

His lover grinned wickedly. “Then we make sure we don’t get caught. I watch TV. I’ve seen them do that in the movies. Now relax, we don’t have much time. I have to get dressed for the show.”

Lenny reached out and took off Brook’s jacket, throwing it on top of a mixing table then started to unbutton his shirt, and he was powerless to resist. He loved this side of Lenny, the part that took Brook’s fantasies and played them out for him. He was always expected to be in control, be the sensible one in his day job, but Lenny? The man did something to him inside that no other man could do.

Brook heard Lenny’s deep breaths as Brook slowly caressed his lover’s chest and gripped his hands in Lenny’s hair to take his mouth in another mind-blowing kiss. Brook groaned deep in the back of his throat, which only served to excite his lover more. His shirt was now on the floor and Lenny sucked Brook’s nipples. There were so many sensations in his body he didn’t know which one to appreciate first.

His prick was hard and the sense of need to release or bury himself inside Lenny's body was overwhelming.

Lenny's voice was husky. "You are so incredibly sexy, do you know that? I never get tired of your body or your mouth." He reached down and unzipped Brook, their eyes never leaving one another's. Lenny knelt down and slid Brook's trousers down his legs, using a little force to get them down, then flicked his tongue against the slick tip of Brook's cock.

"Look at you, going commando," he whispered reverently to Brook's crotch. "Beautiful."

Brook drew a deep, shuddering breath at the feel of that warm tongue and the quick pressure, feeling as if he would explode. Lenny's hot mouth wrapped around him and he groaned as he grabbed hold of the thick hair in his hands and dug his fingers against Lenny's scalp.

"Mmm, that feels so good…" Thoughts of anyone finding them *in flagrante delicto* were banished to the furthest recesses of his mind as the man on the floor drove him crazy with his mouth.

Lenny gave one last swirl of his tongue then stood up, observing Brook's naked body with greedy eyes. "My turn," he murmured as he unzipped his chinos and stepped out of them. His cock rose, glorious and majestic, and Brook's mouth salivated at the sight. Lenny lifted his shirt over his head and threw it down. "I want you to do me like this."

He reached into his jacket pocket and pulled out a small wrapper of lube and a condom, which he placed on a surface filled with DJ decks. Then he turned, swept everything off the armchair onto the floor and presented his arse to Brook, his hands splayed on the top of the chair like a decadent actor in a porn movie. His balls swayed and his proudly weeping ramrod of an erection jutted out from his groin. Even as Brook admired the view, he choked down a laugh at the sweeping action, and he moved in to caress tight arse cheeks. He didn't want to ruin the eroticism of this moment by giggling at that rather grand gesture.

"I suppose you saw that done in the movies too?" he whispered as he his fingers travelled down the crease of Lenny's backside. His boyfriend shivered and Brook grinned as he tore open the foil packets. "I think I need to stop you from watching so many of those porn movies you like so much."

Lenny swore. “I’m dying here. Get me lubed up and then I want you in me. Stop the damn teasing.”

“Yeah, yeah, I'm moving as fast as I can. You’re a pretty distracting sight. That whole bent over the chair thing is really doing it for me.” It was too. His sheathed cock was ready to launch at Lenny’s hole like a rocket jetting for the moon, the taut arse that was fuzzy with blond hair, balls dangling between his legs like ripe plums, purple and swollen.

“Yes, well I don’t see you doing *me*, which is the whole bloody point,” Lenny said edgily, wriggling his arse. Brook chuckled and slid his lubed-up fingers inside him.

He gave a squawk. “That's cold.”

Brook continued his slow, teasing stretching of the man waiting impatiently for him then moved in for the kill. “This might be one of the stupidest things we’ve ever done but it’s one of the hottest.”

He grunted as he positioned himself then pushed inside, heat wrapping itself around him like a warm hand. Lenny pushed back, eagerly impaling himself more. Then there was nothing but the sound of sex on the air, deep, drawn-out sighs and moans, curses uttered under breaths that stuttered and crescendoed as both of them got closer to the end.

“Don’t stop, that feels so good,” Lenny panted. Brook gripped his hips, making sure he drilled deep, the way they both liked it. The slick warmth of Lenny’s passage was a welcome combination that inflamed his groin and his passion. Time stood still and there was only the two of them. Brook wondered not for the first time how Lenny managed to have this effect on him every time they made love.

“I always want you so much,” he whispered. “I’m not going to last much longer.” He slid his hands over Lenny’s back lingeringly, caressing the skin of his hips and backside.

Lenny gasped. “Neither am I. I’m about to blow and I haven't even touched it yet.”

Those words speared Brook on and he choked back a cry as he came, burying his face against Lenny’s back, feeling the warm skin against his lips as he pumped what was contained in his swollen balls into the warm body he filled. Lenny’s body jerked beneath Brook, as Lenny gave a low growl then spurted streams of semen onto the seat of the chair. They stood cemented together with sweat, both panting and Brook chuckled, his head dizzy with release and orgasmic well-being.

Lenny snorted. “Something obviously is entertaining you.” The tone of his amusement evident in his voice

Brook chuckled. “We’re in the middle of Ryan’s club having raunchy man sex on a chair in who knows whose office. I’ve never done that before.”

Lenny laughed loudly as he pushed off the chair, dislodging Brook from his arse and turning to face him. “First time for everything. That was intense. We’ll have to do that again sometime, in someone’s office, maybe yours?”

Brook's face dropped. “Hell, no, we’re so not doing that anywhere near my place of work,” he stuttered. “My secretary might walk in, a client, an investor—” He pulled of the condom, tied it and looked around for somewhere to dispose of it.

Lenny grinned as he stood there glorious in his nakedness. “Yeah, but it makes it all the more fun.”

Brook scowled. “Forget about it and strike it off your bucket list, Mr James. Not going to happen.” He decided the dustbin was as good a place as any for the condom and chuckled to himself at thinking what the cleaner might make of it.

Lenny gave a sly smile as he used his boxers to clean himself up. Soon they were both dressed and ready to leave. The smell of sweat and sex permeated the air.

Lenny sighed. “I suppose we should get out there. I have a show to prepare for after all. Do you think everyone will know where we’ve been?”

“If they see us coming out of here, both of us with a big grin on our face, your hair all mussed up like that and smelling rampantly of sex, I’d say, yes, they probably will,” Brook said drily. “Oh crap. We need to clean that up. We can't leave it.” He motioned towards the puddle of semen on the floor and on the chair. “There has to be something here…” He looked around for something to clean up the mess with and managed to find a toilet roll in one of the drawers of the side cabinet still barricading them in. He raised his eyebrows at that, not expecting to find that particular item in a desk drawer.

Lenny chuckled. “Maybe they had a cold, or the sniffles. Give it to me.”

He managed to wipe off most of the signs of their activity and threw the used paper into the dustbin to join the condom. Brook looked at Lenny.

"May I leave the room now?" he enquired with growing amusement. "Are you finished with me?"

Lenny shook his head firmly. "Oh no, not finished yet, only for now." He grinned and moved the unit away from the door. "No one's going to notice that we've been missing"—he glanced at his watch—"over thirty minutes?"

Brook nodded. "It's so busy out there we can slip away unnoticed." He opened the door and peered into the club. "It's pretty dim and absolutely jam-packed. Come on."

They made their way out of the room and were quickly swallowed up by the crowds. Lenny reached over and gave Brook a chaste kiss. "I need to go shower then get into my glad rags," he murmured. "I'll catch up with you after the show—we can go back to my place?"

Brook nodded. "I'll be here. Enjoy yourself up there. Break a leg."

Lenny laid his forehead against Brook's and kissed him again, deeper, hungrier this time. "Glad you're here with me," he whispered. "It means a lot."

"Where else would I be?" Brook murmured back. They stared into each other's eyes for a second and Brook wanted to say something more profound at that point. He'd fallen for Lenny, he knew that; the L-word hadn't been mentioned yet, but he was pretty sure this was what it was for him.

His boyfriend gave him a dazzling smile and melded into the crowd behind him. Brook watched until Lenny was lost from view then made his way to the separate room at the front of the club where table and chairs were set up in front of a small stage. He'd get a drink, sit down and enjoy the show. After that—perhaps tonight he might get to tell Lenny how he really felt about him and see if it was returned.

***

Brook had never really been into the drag queen scene. Not from any sense of being opposed to it but simply because he'd never really considered or been close to the concept. However, watching Ryan and Lenny on stage in their relevant personas as Delilah Delish (the sexy redhead Mango had kissed outside had turned out to be Ryan after all) and Laverne Debussy-Smith, Brook was rapidly becoming entranced.

They were dirty, irreverent and so non-politically correct. Brook wondered if the non-PC police would come calling anytime soon. Their jokes and barbs were clever, witty and downright salacious in some cases. He'd never laughed so much in his life.

Since meeting Lenny he'd had his eyes opened to a lot of things. Seeing his man on stage in a pale pink ball gown, with a long slit up the side, and seeing those beautifully shaped and stockinged legs attached to a firm arse strutting across the stage as the pair entertained the audience, he couldn't help but feel proud that it was *his* Lenny up there wowing the crowds and looking supremely confident and—might he even acknowledge it—damn sexy. It made Brook hard thinking about what they'd done a little while ago in the office.

At the tables around him, the men he'd met earlier sat chuckling and guffawing at the antics of the two queens on stage. Leslie was in tears from laughing, Oliver much the same. Eddie had a huge grin on his face, while Gideon had a smirk and was probably busier watching more of Eddie than the performance. Taylor was chuckling away while leaning close to Draven, who was probably the most stone-faced of the group. However, Brook had seen the curl up of his mouth when he thought no one was looking. He was pleased Lenny had people like these to call friends.

He looked around when someone pulled up a chair next to him, and sat down. It was Big Guy, the man with the Aussie twang that he'd met in Deep Purple. He looked very drunk and leered at Brook.

"Wanna fuck?" Big Guy slurred, reaching out and gripping Brook's arm. "I rather fancy a piece of that ass of yours."

Brook pushed the man's hand off his arm. "Get lost," he muttered. "I said no before and it's no now."

"Oh come on, I promise you I'll give it to you the best you've ever had." Big Guy gestured obscenely to his crotch. "My fat cock was made for your arse."

Brook stood up, fists balling. "Get lost," he growled. "Before I plant you one."

"Oh you're one of those, are you?" Big Guy sneered as he teetered to his feet, his fingers reaching down to grope Brook's crotch. "A prissy boy who thinks he's above the rest? A snooty cocksucker who's better than me?"

The room had gone silent and when Brook looked around, everyone was looking at them. A few of Leslie's friends looked ready to get up and come to Brook's defence, something he'd really hoped wouldn't happen.

Then a voice hailed them from the stage, and Brook looked up in surprise at hearing a rather different Laverne Debussy-Smith than he was used to. Her voice had a distinct nasty edge to it.

"Looks like we have a showdown going on, ladies and gentlemen. I smell the testosterone in the air. The gorgeous man in those enticing leather pants is my sexy and beautiful boyfriend, by the way. Everybody, meet Brook. My very own tasty piece of heaven. And I mean heaven, if you know what I mean." The room exploded in laughter, the tension abating. "I'm pretty sure the other guy is what we commonly call a douche bag in certain circles, meaning someone who can't take a fucking hint and move on. Am I right, chicken?" Laverne sauntered over to the front of the stage. Beneath the blonde wig and the makeup, the aqua blue eyes were more grey granite and the look of disdain on Laverne's face was hard to miss. "Sometimes it takes an outsider to call the shots."

Big Guy's face twisted in a snarl and he stared daggers at Laverne, his face reddening. From across the room, Brook noticed Mango appear and stare fixedly at them from the side lines. As Mango started moving in their direction, Brook readied his fists to punch Big Guy's lights out before Mango got here. Brook could take care of himself and didn't need Mango's intervention. He thought with a wry flash of understanding about what Lenny had said about not backing down, and fighting back the bullies himself.

He needn't have worried. Laverne seemed to have everything under control.

She waved a sweeping hand down the front of her. "Darling, the man has all of *this* fabulousness at home. So he doesn't need anything you might have to offer. However, I can recommend a bathroom where you might be able to meet someone. It's called Deep Purple and it's at entrance to the club, my sweet. You've probably been in there tonight anyway, and got yourself blown. So can I suggest you fucking head back there? Then you can leave what's mine alone and get your sorry arse out of this club." Her voice hardened and Delilah moved up to the front of the stage to join her. Together the two queens did a classic diva wave, hands twisting and pulling as they chorused together, "Bye, Felicia," and the room exploded once again.

Big Guy looked back at Brook amidst the laughing patrons. His eyes darted towards the rapidly advancing Mango and he blanched at Mango's fierce expression. The two bouncers advancing rapidly towards them didn't look as if they would give any measure either.

Big Guy waved a hand as he tottered on his feet. "Hey, no need to get your panties in a wad, lady. I'm going. He's probably not worth the effort anyway."

The bouncers had reached them by now and took hold of the troublemaker's arms as they escorted him away to the sound of clapping and cat calls. Brook looked at the stage. Laverne looked back at him, eyes uncertain, and then recovered her composure. "And that, my loves, is my famous 'bully ball-breaking' routine, although of course I do have another one involving balls that's much more fun. But you have to be *very* special to see that one."

Despite the tension he felt, Brook smiled fondly at Laverne as he sat down. Her eyes lit up and she went back to stalking around the stage with Delilah as they closed their show. The guys nodded at him from the other table and Leslie blew him a flirty kiss. Brook grinned when he saw Oliver place a finger across Leslie's lips in restraint and Leslie sucked in it. It looked pretty hot from where he sat, and from the look on Oliver's face, he thought so too.

Mango appeared at his side. "Laverne drive the bastard off, then?" he said quietly. He glanced fondly at the stage. Delilah waved at him and blew him a kiss, one that Mango returned.

Brook nodded. "Yes, I think he thought better of making a scene. I need another damn drink after all that. Thanks for the concern, Mango. I really don't know why you worry about me, but thanks."

Mango shrugged. "Ryan and Lenny are best pals. You're Lenny's guy. Ryan's mine. Of course I'm going to look out for you." He flashed a quick grin. "Right, I need to get back to the party. I have a willing twink waiting for me. See you around."

He cast another glance at the stage, at the strutting form of Delilah Delish, and a fleeting expression of longing crossed his face. Then he was gone, back through the crowds.

Brook wondered faintly that if Ryan was his guy why the hell he needed anyone else. He'd love to know *that* story. He blew out a breath as he beckoned the waiter across to get another beer. Now he'd sit back, watch out the rest of the show and then later, he'd thank Lenny up close and personal, and completely embrace his boyfriend's *fabulousness*. He was looking forward to it.

Chapter 15

Talk about a shitty day.

Brook strode up the few stairs to Lenny's front door and let himself in. He'd been in two minds as to whether to come over tonight. His mood was tantamount to a wave of negative matter sweeping out from a science experiment gone wrong.

Brook's boss had recently found out that one of the other team members, John Cotswell, had been siphoning money from the company account into his personal offshore one. The team leaders had been summoned to an emergency meeting and told they were all under investigation to make sure the firm didn't have any other 'fucking thieving bastards' in the mix, to quote an irate and highly inflammable Lawrence Lively.

It had been a gruelling day; being questioned and inspected like a microbe under a microscope had been taxing, and having his ethics and honesty questioned had really ticked Brook off. He and his team had been exonerated of any shady shenanigans, but the bitter taste of being thoroughly investigated like a man at his prostate exam still rankled.

"Fingers so deep up my arse we should be fucking married," Brook muttered softly as he laid his briefcase on the floor in the entrance and made his way to Lenny's well-stocked home bar for a stiff drink. He flung his jacket carelessly over the large armchair as he entered.

His mood was not helped when he walked into the lounge and found Ryan Bishop in Lenny's arms.

"What the holy fuck?" he growled, and the two men jumped apart, startled.

Lenny was the first to recover. "Hell, Brook, you scared me to death," he said exasperatedly. "I didn't hear you come in."

"Obviously." Brook walked over to the gleaming counter of the four-foot bar along the wall. "Did I interrupt something?" He took down a whisky tumbler and poured a hefty measure of Lenny's best bourbon into it. Ryan's eyes watched him uncertainly then flicked back to Lenny.

"No, you didn't interrupt anything, you plonker." Lenny frowned. "Ryan was a bit upset. The man needed a hug."

Brook took a deep swallow of his drink, leaned against the bar and regarded the two men. "Well, don't let me stop you. Please, feel free to get back to what you were doing. Don't mind me." He took another gulp, knowing he was being a prat but unable to stop himself.

"Fuck, what the hell is wrong with you?" Lenny said angrily. "Ry is a guest in my home, so stop being such an arse." His eyes flashed dangerously, lips thinning, and in any other situation, Brook would have enjoyed the sight of a pissed-off Lenny. He was sexy and downright off the charts hot.

"It looked like more than a hug to me," Brook muttered.

Ryan moved forward, his pale face anxious. "Brook, sorry if we upset you," he said, his voice soft. "I needed to get something off my chest. I'll leave—"

"No you fucking won't." Lenny's voice was dangerously soft. "You aren't being chased out of *my* home by someone who's had a bad day at the office from the looks of it, and wants to take it out on someone. That's my job, not yours, Ry. We have a fashion trip to plan this weekend, so we still have things to talk about."

Brook put his drink down on top of the bar with slightly more force than he intended. The contents of the glass sloshed and droplets splashed onto the polished surface. "What trip is this? I hadn't heard about any trip."

"That's because I hadn't told you yet," his boyfriend said with an undertone of menace. "If you hadn't come in like some sort of Viking warrior about to haul me over his shoulder and thump his chest, I'd have gotten around to telling you about it."

Ryan looked from Brook to Lenny, face troubled. "I'll go and leave you two to sort this out then," he murmured. "I'll wait in your office, Lenny, and get the itinerary up so we can check…stuff." He darted one last glance towards Brook and then walked out of the room.

Brook and Lenny stared at each other.

"So, bad day at the office, dear?" Lenny asked caustically as he went to the bar and poured himself a gin and tonic. He carefully cut a lemon and added a slice to his drink as Brook watched him.

"It was shitty. Thanks for asking. So what's this about going away this weekend? I thought we planned to go to that cinema at Leicester Square and watch that film you wanted to see."

His lover sighed and took a sip of his drink. "That was the plan, yes. But Ryan broke it off with Mango today and needed some cheering up. So I suggested we take ourselves to Paris for the weekend to check out a fashion show he wanted to see, and perhaps do a bit of fabric buying."

"And I'm not invited?" Brook said, fingers tensing.

Fuck, I need to stop being so damn needy. Lenny has a right to plan time away with his friends as much I do. What the hell is wrong with me? I'm looking for a fight.

Blue-green eyes regarded him steadily. "No."

Brook took a deep breath, willing his bad mood away so that he didn't cock up anymore. "I see." He picked up his drink and took another gulp.

Lenny sighed and walked over to him. "What the hell happened today to get you in such a snit? This is so unlike you, being such a dickhead."

"Oh well, thanks for that astute assessment of my character," Brook spat, feeling quite put out.

Lenny raised an eyebrow. "If the shoe fits…"

Brook glared at him. "I was hauled through the fucking coals at work, had my integrity questioned and had to give an account of everything I've ever done so they could confirm for themselves I wasn't a criminal mastermind," he snarled. "Some twat ripped the company off so there was a damned witch hunt."

"Sounds tough but I can understand their rationale," Lenny observed, eyes narrowing. "Wouldn't you do the same if it were your company?"

Brook scowled. "Yes, but that's not the point."

Lenny shrugged. "I kind of think it is. Don't take it so damn personally. They probably had to treat you exactly the same way they did everyone else. They couldn't be seen to have a favourite."

His boyfriend's logic was beyond argument, and something Brook had told himself on the way home, but he was still angry. "It still made for a crappy day. And then I come home and find my boyfriend in the arms of his old fuck buddy, someone he's planning on going away with this weekend."

Lenny's shoulders stiffened and his face tightened. "Brook, I'm warning you. Don't go down that route. Maybe you should piss off and not come back until you're in a better mood. I've had enough today dealing with Ryan and his broken heart. I don't need your shit too."

Brook drained his drink. "Maybe I'll do that. Leave you two alone to plan your 'trip' to Paris together. Nothing like a French city for a little romance." He knew he was pushing things but the blackness in his soul demanded to be heard.

Fuck, I knew I shouldn't have come here in a mood like this.

Lenny's eyes flashed. "Fuck. You. Don't slam the door on your way out." He wheeled around, motioned to the door, and disappeared in the direction of his study, where, no doubt, Ryan waited.

Brook watched Lenny leave the room then unleashed a string of invective, directed mostly at himself, then snatched up his jacket. "Yeah, sure. I'll leave the two of you alone."

He made sure to slam the door as he left.

***

A few drinks later, Brook had mellowed out enough—well, okay he was as drunk as a monkey on marula berries—to realise he'd cocked up royally. He stared into his whisky glass and winced as he replayed his boorish and completely irrational behaviour.

"He didn't deserve that," he muttered to his glass as he looked up at the wall clock on the back of the bar wall. "Lenny's never given you any indication he's still into Ryan that way, you stupid tosser."

His huge sigh attracted the attention of the female bartender who gazed at him in sympathy. "Rough night?"

Brook waved his glass. "I pissed off my boyfriend, over nothing. I was a bit of a prick, said some things I shouldn't have."

The bartender shrugged as she wiped down the bar surface. "Then unsay them. Go and grovel, tell him you're sorry. Normally works for me. Of course, then the make-up sex can be pretty hot too."

She winked at him and went to serve a customer down the end of the counter. Brook pondered the advice and came to a conclusion. Make-up sex sounded like a welcome idea. So rather than wait for the morning, he'd go round, *right now,* and apologise to his lover.

"No time like the present," he slurred to himself as he left money and a good tip on the bar. He weaved his way out into the cool night air. Lenny's place was only a few blocks away and the air would do him good, sober him up a little before he got there.

When he reached Lenny's place, which in his state was further than he'd thought, he thumped on the door. "Lenny," he shouted. "Let me in."

There was no response. Brook banged again and yelled louder. "Lenny, let me in. I'm sorry I was such an arsehole."

The door swung open to reveal a royally irate Lenny, clad in short, black sleep pants. His hair was mussed up in an adorable state of bedhead.

Brook's heart stuttered at the sight. "You are gorgeous," he breathed. "So damn beautiful."

Lenny shook his head in exasperation. "Brook, it's nearly bloody midnight." He glanced around carefully. "I hope you haven't woken my neighbours up with your noise. What the hell are you playing at?"

"I needed to see you, to say I was sorry. I've been at the Whistle Blower having a drink and the bartender told me I should come straight over and apologise so we could have make-up sex."

His boyfriend's eyes widened comically. "What? She said—oh crap, come in before you fall down in my doorway."

With a muttered "stupid drunken git," Lenny dragged Brook inside and closed the door. He held Brook against the wall and glared at him.

"So, you've been drinking there since you left my place and the bartender said you should come over to your boyfriend's house so you could have make-up sex. Did I get that bit right?"

Brook nodded. He was feeling a little sick. "Kind of. Not in so many words, but that's what I took out of our conversation."

Lenny nodded, but he didn't look as pissed off as he had. His eyes held a glint of amusement. "Of course you did. It had the magic word in it. Sex."

Brook reached out and cupped Lenny's face. "I'm sorry I was a prick. I was out of line."

"Yes, you were," Lenny agreed, as he steered Brook towards his bedroom. "You made Ryan feel uncomfortable and me mad."

His head swimming, Brook perked up at realising where they were heading. "But you'll forgive me? I hate it when you're mad at me."

Lenny pushed him down onto his bed with a snort. "I'll think about it. First you need to get your drunken arse into bed and sleep it off." He set about removing Brook's shoes and socks and then pulling his trousers off. Brook was only too happy to oblige even as his head ached. When his shirt was off, and he was clad only in his boxers, he gave what he thought was a sexy smile at his lover, but from the grin on Lenny's face, it didn't quite make the sexy scale he was aiming for.

"Honestly," Lenny muttered as he draped covers over Brook and got into bed beside him. "Sexy leers are so not your thing when you're drunk."

Lenny got settled beside Brook and his soft chuckle against Brook's ear was a sound wave serenading Brook's groin, even though he didn't really think he'd manage much tonight. He really was feeling ill.

"In a way, it's quite a turn-on seeing you get all jealous," Lenny whispered as his lips brushed his boyfriend's ear. "My sexy, hot lover getting all alpha male on my arse—there are worse things to fight about I guess." His teeth nipped Brook's earlobe and he flinched.

"Stop the seduction technique because I don't think I can get it up," Brook muttered, going for a determined tone but instead sounding sinuously like, *Don't stop. Ever.*

"Sure?" Lenny's breath ghosted his cheek as he pulled away, eyes mischievous. "You should be damned lucky I'm being so accommodating seeing as how you were awfully rude to my best friend."

Brook was feeling much better now that his lover's hands were all over him and creeping stealthily down his flanks. "I'll apologise to Ryan tomorrow," he muttered, closing his eyes as Lenny's hands stroked the small of his back.

"Good," his lover whispered then moved away to his side of the bed, leaving Brook with a sense of loss. His eyes were heavy, the room spun and he closed them.

That soft whisper was the last thing he remembered.

Chapter 16

Staring at his pale face in the bathroom mirror, Lenny now knew how Brook had felt the other night when he'd vomited copious amounts of liquid and doner kebab into the white porcelain bowl of Lenny's toilet. Lenny wanted to throw up too. The nervousness that currently plagued him was causing his stomach to churn. He tried to calm himself, closing his eyes to focus on his breathing. *In, out. In, out.*

When he opened his eyes, nothing had changed. He hadn't been transported to Lenny Land, his happy place, to a world of buff, sexy, bare-chested men wearing nothing but tailored (but tight) suit pants and a world with trees and leaves made of Belgian truffles. He was still in front of the mirror, staring into panicked eyes in a pale, set face. His blond hair stuck up from where he'd run his hands through it, hands that were slightly sticky from the mousse he'd applied to keep it in place.

"Lenny? Babe, we need to go. Are you coming out of there?" Brook's impatient voice interrupted his musings, and Lenny started.

"Yeah, in a minute. I'm fixing my hair." With shaking hands, he reached for more mousse and squirted some into his hair, smoothing down the unruly strands and scowling at the cowlick that seemed to plague him. Perhaps this hair-growing business wasn't for him. It was at that stage when it was too long to keep it in check and too short to do anything else with it. It curled around his ears, fell over his forehead and was generally a damn nuisance.

Brook loved it. Loved winding his hands in it when Lenny blew him, loved stroking it back from Lenny's face. He especially loved it when those soft strands trailed over his hardened dick as he was sucked dry. Brook had gasped out once that the sight of Lenny's eyes looking up between the blond strands was one of sexiest things he'd ever seen, and then promptly blown his load into Lenny's mouth. It was a move guaranteed to make his boyfriend come with force.

"Lenny." Brook's voice held fond affection. "It's my parents you're going to meet. Not the King and Queen of England."

"I'd be less neurotic if it was fucking royalty," Lenny muttered to himself as he dragged more mousse through his hair and checked his face, turning it this way and that in the dim bathroom light to see no stray hairs peeked out of his orifices. "I've never met anyone's folks before. What the hell possessed me to say yes to this?"

He knew why he'd said yes of course. It has been the day after his argument with Brook. The following morning, Brook had been hung over, bleary-eyed and reeking a little of vomit after spending time in the toilet. Brook's mother had called him and left a message. His boyfriend had been on the phone apologising to Ryan at the time so had returned the call.

He'd managed to be *compos mentis* long enough to find out why his mother was calling—it was to invite them to lunch the following week. His lover's bumbling attempts to try and find out whether Lenny was prepared to meet them had been pathetic. Lenny had taken pity on him and simply said yes. It was a decision he'd regretted ever since. His weekend away with Ryan in Paris had been a bit of shambles as they had both got drunk and ended up hung over for most of the weekend. They had, however, managed to make some worthy fabric purchases.

It was apparently a rare treat to get both parents together in the Hunter household and they desperately wanted to see their son. They knew all about Lenny, as Brook spent time on phone calls and Skype and wasn't one to keep something like having a boyfriend from them. From what Lenny had seen, they were a close-knit family unit. They even knew about Laverne.

He checked himself one last time and then decided he couldn't delay any longer. He unlocked the bathroom door and stepped out into the hallway. Brook leaned against the wall, impeccably dressed in charcoal grey chinos, a pair of black, shiny loafers, and a charcoal button-down shirt that clung tightly to his body and made Lenny want to rip it off despite his anxiety. Brook raised one eyebrow when he saw Lenny appear.

"Are you quite finished primping?" he asked lazily, a quirk to his lips. "I mean, you look tasty enough for me to drag you through into there"—he gestured to his bedroom on the side—"and ravish that gorgeous body of yours, but that'll have to wait for later. We're already cutting it fine because of your hair." The knowing look on Brook's face unsettled Lenny. They both knew the delay had nothing to do with his hair. It was unnerving having someone know him so well.

Lenny scowled. “Bite me for wanting to look my best. You’re lucky I’m going at all.” No sooner had he said the words, he wanted to take them back. “Brook, sorry. I’m nervous-”

Brook sighed. “Honey, I really don’t know why. My parents are ordinary people who want to meet my sexy, incredibly talented fashion designer of a boyfriend and spend some time with us.”

Lenny huffed moodily. “Yeah, your cross-dressing transvestite of a lover, who’s older than you and spends his day as a woman. I mean, maybe you should go without me, I don’t really feel—”

His half-hearted ‘I really want to get out of it’ plea was effectively stopped by a pair of lips taking his, forcing his lips open so a warm tongue could gain entry and shut him the fuck up. Lenny had to say it worked. He moaned, feeling Brook’s mouth claiming his, owning him, and wrapped his arms around Brook’s neck, pulling him closer. Senses on override at Brook’s fragrance, his hard body pressed against his, all Lenny could do was duel his way into the kiss and keep the battle raging. He pulled away reluctantly so he could speak. It was his very own Custer’s Last Stand.

“Maybe we should stay here like this and bang each other’s brains out—” Again he was silenced, barely having time to take in air. When he was released, he took a huge gulp of life-giving breath.

“Stop it,” Brook murmured in his ear. “They’re going to love you as much as I do. They won’t be able to help themselves.” With a final fierce kiss, he moved away. Lenny’s eyes were drawn to his bulging crotch.

“But *that* is a damn waste,” Lenny whined as he gestured to Brook’s visibly hardened cock. “And what about this?” He palmed his dick and hissed when that made it worse.

Brook grinned wickedly. “I know. I need a few minutes now to calm down before we go out in public. I’d hate to be arrested for sporting a weapon of mass destruction.” He smirked as he made himself comfortable. “I’m going to get the bag with the wine and the presents. You sort yourself out and we’ll leave in a minute.” He walked down the hall toward his kitchen, and it was only then as Lenny pushed his dick around trying to get comfy in his tight briefs, that he realised what Brook had said to him.

They’re going to love you as much as I do.

Thank you, Brook. Now, instead of feeling sick with nerves, Lenny was hyperventilating.

"What the hell does that actually mean?" he whispered to himself. "Brook *loves* me? Or was it a figure of speech?"

They'd not used the L-word in their few months-plus of seeing each other. Lenny thought he might have fallen arse-over-heels in love with the man. However, his natural reticence stopped him from saying it first or even truly accepting it. People you loved didn't always love you back. And people you should love, like your father, didn't deserve it. In Lenny's jaded perception, love could be a never-ending quagmire of emotions that could turn around and stab you in the back then dance on your cooling corpse with pointy shoes.

"Ready?" Brook appeared, looking calm and collected with no idea of the raging turmoil of Lenny's emotions. "Good. Let's get off then."

Without waiting for any acknowledgement, he turned and virtually sprinted down the hallway towards the front door. Lenny rolled his eyes and followed.

Grant me strength to get through this. Don't have them look at me as if I'm freak. If his mother asks me for makeup advice and whether I'm considering gender assignment surgery, I might pitch a hissy fit. Fashion—that I can do, I mean, it's my raison d'être after all.

"Lenny, get your arse over here, babe. Come on." Brook's tone was both amused and bossy. In another situation Lenny might have really enjoyed that. Like the one he'd proposed and been turned down for in favour of meeting the parents.

Scowling, Lenny ambled down the hallway, not wanting to appear as if he was obeying that demanding summons from his hot boyfriend.

"Yeah, yeah, keep your pants on," he muttered as he picked up his man bag off the table in the entrance. "I'm coming. Not." He sniggered at that as he joined Brook at the doorway and pushed past him into the corridor.

"Let's get this show on the road," Lenny said airily as he walked towards the lift. "Spit spot now."

***

An hour later he was seated in the airy expanse of a house that was probably a country all on its own. When he and Brook had walked up to the huge dwelling in the middle of Fitzrovia in the West End, Lenny's jaw had dropped. He thought his spacious property was a decent size, but compared to this house, it was nothing more than a broom closet. Brook had shrugged apologetically when he'd rung the buzzer at the huge wrought-iron gates.

"Because my folks are diplomats and need security, protection and the like, the Consulate insists on putting them in high-end places like this. They don't own it, it's owned by the government. Honestly, my folks would rather have had a small brownstone somewhere. My dad's been trying to get them to relocate him and Mum forever."

Not only was the house a palace but the security to enter the abode was nerve wracking. Lenny was patted down by quite a cute young security guard with a winning smile but a deadly expression in his eyes that said he'd as soon as shoot Lenny if he put one finger wrong. Brook was searched too, despite being the son of the people living there. He'd shrugged philosophically.

"It's to keep my folks safe so I do it. The security team insist even though I've been coming here for years."

Now, as Lenny sat awkwardly nibbling at the unlikely combination of savoury pastries and whisky—he'd eschewed tea for something stronger to get him through the afternoon—he really, really wished he was any place other than here waiting for his boyfriend to bring his parents into the room. Lenny inspected the contents of the pastry he held. He wasn't a particularly fussy eater but he did like to know what he was putting in his mouth.

He didn't realise the room had fallen silent and when he looked up, he found three pairs of eyes regarding him curiously, one more amused than the others. Brook's eyes sparkled and Lenny cleared his throat awkwardly and stood up.

He held the pastry up apologetically and waved it. "Good afternoon. I was having a look to see what was going in my mouth. I mean, I know what it is but I wasn't sure what was in it and I'm not a fan of fishy stuff…" His voice tailed off as the beautiful woman in a multi-coloured kaftan walked towards him with a warm smile on her face. She was statuesque, round faced and dark skinned, with a wide smile. Brook was the spitting image of his father. The man stood about six foot seven, regally attired in a pair of chinos and a golf shirt and a pair of gold-rimmed spectacles, and was looking at Lenny with a questioning expression on his face.

Lenny found himself hauled into a substantial bosom—far more than his own when he was sporting breasts—and hugged within an inch of his life. He met Brook's eyes over the top of his mother's head and was sure his lover read the panic in Lenny's eyes because Brook winked at him. The bastard *actually* winked as if he found this whole smothering thing hilarious.

"Lovely to meet you at last, Lenny. I'm Dianne Hunter, Brook's mum, and this man over here is my husband, Harold. Harry we call him. We've been looking forward to meeting the man who has my son all in a tither." She released Lenny with a beaming smile. "And it's cream cheese, chives and bacon chips that you're putting in your mouth." She grinned and winked.

Lenny flushed. Despite his embarrassment, his ears pricked up. Brook was all in a *tither* over him? He stared over at Brook, his eyebrow raised, and his boyfriend fidgeted uncomfortably and ignored it. Harold 'Harry' Hunter moved gracefully over to Lenny, hand outstretched. He was no longer frowning.

"Lenny, it's wonderful to meet you at last. Call me Harry, please. I've heard quite a bit about you from Brook." His voice was low and melodious and Lenny wished he had it. He was sure he'd make people melt at the timbre of that deep, rich tone. Harry Hunter cast a glance over at a faintly scowling Brook. "My son is not looking too happy that we are letting out all his secrets. He no doubt wishes to appear aloof and reserved, but I'm afraid that his mother and I believe in calling a spade a spade." Harry chuckled as Brook glowered at him. "Brook, however, has always been a child who plays his cards close to his chest."

"Dad, please stop it." While Lenny couldn't see Brook blushing, he knew he was. He'd known the man long enough to know that delightful warmth would be flushing his cheeks and making him pink below the deeply bronzed tones of his skin. Lenny had felt it often enough when Brook came in his arms. He tried to suppress that thought manfully. Having a boner in front of his boyfriend's parents wasn't something he needed.

He shook Harry's hand. "I'm glad to meet you both, it's an honour. Brook has talked about you both often."

They sat down in the large comfortable couches dotted around the spacious living room and Brook sat down next to Lenny. He was grateful for that. He was still feeling a little frazzled, although both of Brook's parents seemed terribly accommodating and pleasant. The conversation revolved around Brook's work, his parent's activities and talk of Brook's brothers and sisters, and Lenny was thinking it was all going terribly well. Until Harry Hunter leaned back in his chair, steepled his fingers together and regarded Lenny thoughtfully.

"So, tell me, son, what is it with you dressing like a woman? I'm really curious about what that's all about. I mean, I know this happens and I have no objections—if my son's happy, I'm happy—but why do you do it? I'm truly interested in the motivations. I study psychology in my spare time and I confess I find it all very fascinating."

Lenny's eyes shot open and he stared at Brook in panicked consternation. Brook sat forward, laid his hand on Lenny's leg and turned to his father.

"Dad," he said through obviously gritted teeth, "we talked about this. I asked you not to make Lenny uncomfortable…"

His father waved a hand impatiently, cutting Brook off. "Son, I ask because I'm interested, not for any vicarious or ulterior purpose." He regarded Brook over the top of his glasses. "And I seem to recall you *telling* me not to make Lenny suffer discomfort, not asking me to spare him. We all know how I feel about being told what to do by my children."

Lenny could imagine. Harry Hunter seemed an affable man but you could see the inner steel and the determination in his demeanour. Something Brook had some of himself.

Brook looked helplessly over at Lenny. "Sorry," he mouthed and Lenny felt a little better.

Lenny stared evenly at Harry. "It's simply a part of who I am," he said. "It started out as something to do when I was at college, to see how women would feel in my clothes. It ended up being more than that when I realised I controlled it; I could better show the other side of me in female clothing, the side that didn't have to be all manly and macho, and could show something softer. I can't explain it—it just was. If you've talked to Brook about me and my dress habits, then he's probably told you I didn't have the best of childhoods, and a father who didn't like the fact I was gay, and wasn't the son he wanted—someone brutish and masculine. Laverne allows me to be someone else for a while. I suppose I hide in a way behind that persona, but as much as I hide, I also show other facets of myself." He shrugged. "By the time I'd realised what I was doing, she was too ingrained in my psyche to let her go."

Harry nodded wisely. "That sounds like a fairly logical coping mechanism that's grown into a part of you, something integral. You are the sum of the whole parts, Lenny, you and Laverne, I think." His kind smile touched something in Lenny and he felt his next words flow out without even realising it.

Lenny swallowed and looked over at Brook. "Yes, that's true. But the only time I've ever considered letting her go was a while ago when I realised I cared more about your son than I did about her. It was a pretty shocking realisation."

He heard Brook's gasp of breath and felt his hand clench on his leg.

"Baby, I would never ask you to do that," Brook said fiercely. For a minute they were the only two people in the room as they gazed at each other. "I could never ask you to give up someone you love, someone who's part of you. I know I didn't understand at first but now, seeing you as Laverne, seeing how those other people love and adore you both—I would never be so selfish to ask you to change that part of yourself. You'd be too miserable and after a while, you'd resent me." He cupped Lenny's jaw tenderly and that gentle touch did something to Lenny's heart. "It's the whole package deal I lo—like." He corrected himself quickly but Lenny saw Harry's quick glance at his wife and their shared, soft smile. His insides turned to jelly at that almost declaration of love. It was definitely time to share that sentiment. Tonight, when he got home, Lenny was going to make sure Brook knew exactly how much he cared about him.

A gentle cough brought them both back to the real world. Diane regarded them with gentle affection. "Shall we go in for lunch then? I believe it's ready and I think after that lovely declaration, you both deserve a drink." She stood up and bustled out of the room. Harry stood up too and did something quite unexpected. He reached out and enfolded Lenny in a strong hug.

"Thank you for sharing that with me," he murmured in Lenny's ear as Brook watched wide-eyed. "I can see my son is in good hands with you."

He released Lenny, who had a lump in his throat and a strange prickling in his eyes. No father figure had ever hugged him like that before. It was a novel experience and one he could grow to like. Harry left the room and now it was only the two of them.

Lenny took a deep breath. "Thanks for that," he said to Brook. "I didn't mean to share that right here and now, but your dad has this knack of pulling things out from inside…"

The fierce, possessive kiss Brook bestowed on him made his toes curl and other parts jump to attention. He was boneless when Brook let him go.

Brook's breathing was laboured, his eyes heavy lidded. "Come on," he said huskily as Lenny tried to catch his breath. "Before we do something really stupid in my parents' house." He propelled Lenny towards the open door that led to the dining room. "I need a drink."

Lenny was quite happy when he could sit down at the long dining table draped with a chintzy red tablecloth and hide the evidence of his arousal under both the cloth and the napkin. He had a feeling it was the safest place to be even if his boyfriend sat next to him staring at him innocently while his fingers tantalisingly brushed Lenny's leg or arm. Lenny sighed heavily while trying manfully to eat his artfully arranged veal and vegetables. It was going to be a long lunch.

***

"Your parents are really something. You're lucky to have them." Lenny sat comfortably in the armchair back at Brook's place, as he idly channel surfed, trying to find something to watch that wasn't the eight o'clock news. It was too depressing hearing what was going on in the real world.

Brook stood in the kitchen, apron wrapped around his waist as he pottered in there making them dinner. The lunch had gone well; there had been no more embarrassing questions, and when they'd gotten home, they both had been feeling peckish. Brook had decided to make eggs Benedict. Having been banished from the kitchen, Lenny was sitting with his second glass of wine and watching the TV images flicker by. He still felt a little overwhelmed about today. Meeting Brook's parents, having to explain how he felt about Laverne, admitting he'd given a thought to giving her up and hearing what in his mind had nearly amounted to a declaration of love from his boyfriend…he sighed. Not to mention that tonight somehow he was going to tell Brook exactly how he felt about him. Yes, it might be in bed after making love, but that was as good a place as any in his opinion.

Strong hands landed on his shoulders and Lenny curled into them as his aching shoulders were massaged. He felt the soft press of lips on his hair.

"Tired?" Brook's voice was husky. "Dinner won't be a minute, just heating the sauce. Then we can eat."

"Mmm, sounds good." Lenny closed his eyes as hands eased the stress in his muscles. He gave a whimper of disappointment when they were pulled away.

Brook chuckled. "I need to check the sauce. I heard your stomach rumble, you must be hungry."

"That meal at your folks' was good but there wasn't enough of it," Lenny murmured. "I mean all this haute cuisine stuff really does my head in. You get a few strategically placed bits of random food artfully arranged on a plate, dribbled with fancy coulis or whatever they call it, that wouldn't satisfy a rabbit."

His stomach was much happier later that evening after a full plate of tasty food, another glass of wine and a half a bar of chocolate as he and Brook lay snuggled together watching *True Detective* on Netflix. Lenny had a real thing for Matthew McConaughey and his sexy Texan accent, and even sexier arse and shoulders.

He was dozing while dreaming of the pliant Matthew spread face down in front of him, naked and willing—because a man can fantasize even if he's in a committed relationship—when Brook interrupted his fantasy.

"Babe?"

"Uh-huh?" Lenny said sleepily, only slightly peeved he hadn't gotten yet to the good part where he took Matthew roughly.

"Were you serious today when you said you'd been thinking of stopping being Laverne—for me?"

Lenny opened his eyes and struggled to sit up from where he'd obviously been drooling on Brook's shoulder. He reached out a hand and patted the wetness apologetically. "Sorry 'bout that."

Brook stared down and shrugged. "It's cute when you do that. Did you hear what I said?" His voice was hesitant, something Lenny wasn't used to, and he nodded.

"Yes, I heard you, and yes, I was serious about it. I'm not saying it would have been easy, but if it ever came to a choice between having you in my life and Laverne out of it…" He swallowed. "I figured it would be *hasta la vista* Laverne."

Brook stared at him and Lenny stared back. "What about the business, Debussy's?" Brook asked softly. "She's who Debussy is, after all. How could you think of doing that and keeping the business the way it is?"

Lenny sighed deeply. "*I'm* the business, Brook," he acknowledged. "Me, the *man* behind the wig and the fake boobs. It's *my* designs, *my* talent and *my* drive that's got me where I am. Laverne is the figurehead, sure, but I knew if she wasn't there, I'd still be, and I'd have to think about how best to manage that."

He had a sudden sinking feeling and wondered if he might be forced to make a choice after all, despite Brook's vehement declaration earlier he'd never ask him to. Despite his brave words, Lenny knew giving up Laverne would be extremely tough.

His fears were proved groundless a minute later when Brook reached out and drew him in for a kiss that engulfed him, absorbed him and heated his limbs and other parts like soft licks of flame. Brook's lips parted Lenny's, his tongue took over possession of his mouth and his hands slid under his tee shirt and grasped hold of the warm flesh tightly, so tightly Lenny moaned in pleasure and pain. He was pushed back against the couch, Brook's body on his, his lover's hardness grinding against his and Lenny simply gave in to being mauled and ravaged and loving every minute of it.

When Brook pulled his mouth away and stared down into his face, his lips were swollen, his eyes wondering. "Why?" he whispered. "Why would you do that for me?"

Lenny heaved a shuddering breath and gazed into Brook's brown eyes, eyes that searched Lenny's face, as if he was looking for an answer that he wanted but wasn't sure he was about to get.

Time to tell him the truth. I suppose one of us has to go first.

"It's what you do for someone you love," he murmured, tracing Brook's cheek with unsteady fingers. "You compromise, give something up, if it means keeping them."

Brook gazed at him, eyes wide, and Lenny felt the first tendril of fear.

Thundershit, please don't tell me I've got this all wrong. That he doesn't feel the same way. I don't think I could cope with that. Say something, baby. The right something. Please.

Brook stood up and held out his hand. Lenny stared at it in confusion, then up at Brook. "Are we going somewhere?" he asked uncertainly.

What about Lenny's damn declaration of love?

Brook nodded, his face tender. "I need to show you something. Come on."

Lenny took Brook's hand, and he pulled Lenny to his feet then led him through the flat to the back bedroom. The last time Lenny had seen the room it had been full of boxes, papers, various pieces of old gym equipment and basically a real mess. He hadn't been in there since.

When Brook threw open the door, and pushed Lenny inside, he gasped. It was now a spacious room, light and airy, with grey and burgundy curtains, a dressing table complete with mirror, a chair and a huge cupboard that stretched the whole length of one wall. On the other wall, there was a floor-to-ceiling mirror with strategic lights on either side that looked as if they could be turned on at will. It was like a starlet's dressing room.

Lenny gaped and turned to look at Brook. "Have you taken up modelling or something—is that what this is for? I mean, don't get me wrong I think you'd make a great model, but I want to get to see you in the outfits myself—"

His rambling was cut off by the firm press of warm fingers against his mouth.

"It's for you," Brook said softly. "Well, for Laverne. I thought you needed somewhere to get dressed in the mornings without having to hang stuff up everywhere, and steam the creases out of it, or go home first in the small hours of the morning. Like you said—it's what you do for someone you love. You learn to compromise and live with every bit of who they are, no matter what."

Lenny lost his breath. He turned and waved at the room. "This is for Laverne?"

Brook chuckled. "Yes. I meant every word I said this morning. I appreciate you thought about giving her up, but I don't for one minute believe you'd be happier doing it. I love that you were willing to make that sacrifice, but you don't have to. I love you both. Well, I love the Lenny person a lot more because that's the man I'm in love with, but you know what I mean."

Lenny swallowed, at a loss for words. When he found them, they weren't literature but they were heartfelt. "Wow. No one has ever done anything like this for me before."

"I love you," Brook said pulling him closer. "I've tried to say it before but it never seemed to be the right time."

"Me too," Lenny agreed happily, pressing himself against Brook's hard body. "I wanted to say it so many times but I wasn't sure you felt the same way…"

Brook's voice deepened. "Say it." He nudged Lenny's nose with his own. "Tell me the words."

Lenny flushed. He wasn't used to declaring his feelings quite as openly as Brook. Warm eyes regarded him with laughter, as one sexy eyebrow raised enquiringly. The look of love in them was unmistakeable and Lenny felt a wash of emotion unlike anything he'd ever felt before.

"I love you," he murmured gently, running his hand over Brook's stubbly head and drawing his lips down for a kiss. "I love you."

Lenny had no idea how he got onto Brook's bed, minus all his clothes, with a hundred and ninety pounds of warm, randy man on top of him, but he didn't really care. All he cared about was the hot, flushed skin pressed against his, the taste of lips, then cock in his mouth. When Brook rode him, his sweaty, shining, burnished body poised above him like a living statue, with hunger in his eyes and stark need on his face, Lenny simply revelled in it, and embraced the fact he was loved.

Chapter 17

Lenny sat back in his office chair and sighed tiredly. He glanced at his watch. Eight p.m. The office was quiet and empty, and somewhere out on the deserted floor, an overhead light flickered and then went out. The external office plunged into darkness and Lenny glanced anxiously at the lamp that burned on the desk, hoping it wasn't a citywide power cut. There had been a few of those lately. But Cleopatra's contemplative visage remained staring out at him from her reclining position on her bed, delicate features highlighted by the soft glow of the bulb behind the etched glass fan. The solid brass art deco lamp had been one of his indulgences and he'd fallen in love with the item on first sight.

When he worked late, he preferred the restrained light of the lamp rather than the harsh glare of the overhead one, which always made him feel as if he were one of Leslie's beloved fishes, spotlighted in a bowl for the entire city to see.

Lenny stood up, stretched, yawned until his jaw clicked then began stuffing his satchel with his papers, various oddities he carried with him, and his iPad and phone. He was due home at nine to meet Brook. He was glad his boyfriend had a key; it made working late so much easier than having to dash home and open up. Then they were going for drinks. Lenny still had to go home, shower and change. If truth be told, he would have preferred to crawl into bed and forget today had ever happened. He'd left Brook's place this morning with a spring in his step and his spring had gotten progressively less sprung as the day wore on.

"It's been the worst fucking day ever," he griped to himself as he packed.

It started when the heel to his favourite pair of black shoes, his beloved Giuseppe Zanottis, had snapped off when it got caught in a grate as he'd rushed to work. Lenny had fallen arse over heels, laddering his stockings and nastily bruising and scraping his hand and forearm when he'd tried to stop his fall. It hadn't helped that the man gallantly trying to help him up had uttered a disgusted curse when he'd seen Laverne was actually a man and had hurried back down the street, leaving Lenny sprawled on the cold, grey pavement.

Lenny had given him the finger as he'd struggled to his feet and limped to the entrance to the tube station sans a heel. His back hurt from the lopsided gait he'd effected as he'd made the rest of journey to work. The snapped heel was safely in his satchel, though, in case the shoe could be redeemed—something he very much doubted.

Once he'd reached work, he'd found that a larger delivery of suit material from one of his most trusted suppliers had been delayed. Some shit to do with industrial action in France and a holdup at the ports for the shipping. That had meant rearranging a whole week's work, and telling his customer that his order of ladies' suits wasn't going to be ready on time for his launch. Lenny had to eat humble pie on that one and make it up to the irate customer by yet again shaving the price.

"And as if it wasn't already as low as I could go," he muttered to himself as he packed his satchel with some fabric remnants he was taking home to assess. "Bastard sucked me dry, and not in a good way." He scowled fiercely as he looked around the office, checking he had everything.

The cherry on the top of the crapalicious sundae that was his life today had been hearing that Tracy Trey had apparently criticised Laverne and Debussy's Fashion in a recent television interview. He'd obviously been miffed at being found out by Laverne. Calling her a 'lady that knew her stuff but still had a long way to go, with designs that didn't hit the mainstream' and simpering on stage about the fact he, Tracy, had made the list of nominations for the *Whirl Magazine* Best Up-and-Coming Designers list where Laverne hadn't, had really pissed Lenny off, more so than stealing his designs. He knew personally Tracy had only got the nomination because he was fucking both the organiser and the patron of the magazine. The man was a slut of note. Laverne and Tracy hadn't yet had the occasion to square up to each other, but payback was coming and best served cold.

Lenny had spent the rest of the day snarling at his staff, throwing things around and being a complete bitch. Even Leslie had scurried wide-eyed out of the office after he'd been growled at for trying to make Laverne some chamomile tea. In fact, Lenny thought guiltily, he might have shouted at Leslie to shove the tea where the sun don't shine and bugger off. The memory of that made Lenny squirm and he wondered if he should call his friend to apologise.

Sighing, he pulled his phone out of his bag and dialled Leslie's mobile number. It went straight to voice mail and Lenny closed his eyes in weariness as he left a message.

"Hi, Leslie. It's me. I'm sorry about today, chicken. I was being a prima donna and I shouldn't have gone off at you like that. I know you were only trying to help. I hope you'll forgive me. I'll see you tomorrow and apologise in person."

He disconnected the call then made another one. Brook's voice mail picked up.

"Babe, I'm leaving the office now. I should be home in about twenty minutes. Love you."

Lenny hefted his satchel over his shoulder. He hadn't changed into his 'man clothes,' as Brook teasingly called them; he was too tired to do that now and the public could damn well take him as he came. He'd change when he got home. Lenny *had* changed his shoes to a pair of flats that didn't really set off his cream pantsuit to its best. He pushed fingers under his sweaty wig, gave his forehead a welcome scratch, and then re-fit it so it sat better. Not too long to go and he thought he could give the wig a miss. His hair was looking quite something, with it waves and curls.

"Fuck 'em," he said to himself as he locked his office. "For once, I don't care what the hell I look like." Lenny made his way across the quiet floor to the lift. He wasn't walking the four flights of stairs. His back was still sore from his walk in this morning, compensating for his missing heel. Not to mention the large bruise he'd found on his hip when he'd gone to the bathroom earlier and which now hurt like hell. He tapped his foot as he looked impatiently at his watch. There was no grating or grinding sound of the lift as expected, and he frowned and pushed the button again. The light went out. He pressed it again, vexed. The light went on and then rapidly went out. Still there was no sound from the lift shaft.

"You have *got* to be kidding me," he swore. "Don't tell me the damn lift isn't working now. This day just keeps getting better."

He huffed loudly and strode to the exit, pushed open the fire door and walked onto the landing. The stairs stretched downwards like the entrance to hell itself, daunting and dimly lit. Lenny swore softly then descended into the bowels of said hell. Every step he took, his hip ached and his hand throbbed with pain as he gripped the stair railing tightly.

"If Brook could see me now," he murmured as he walked gingerly down the stairs. "I'd hear more insults about my age. The only good thing about this is perhaps he can give me a massage later and ease these aching muscles."

That happy thought spurred him on, and when he reached the bottom and saw the bustling street outside, he gave a grumpy snort of relief and opened the ornate glass door to step onto the street. He'd only walked a step forward and was about to turn left towards home when someone shoved him sharply from behind.

He cried out, startled, dropping his bag and turning to face his attacker in a classic self-defence pose, knees bent, arms raised in protection. The scrawny kid who stood there, a sneer on his face and a glint of violence in his eyes, didn't look as if he was a welcoming committee of any sort.

"Give me your wallet, lady," he growled, light glinting off the knife held in his right hand.

Lenny took a deep breath. "Kid, go home," he warned quietly. "I'm not in the mood for your shit and I don't want to beat it out of you." Adrenaline rushed through his veins, and Lenny felt the familiar pull in his stomach as he readied himself for a fight. It wouldn't be his first bashing.

The look of disbelief on the kid's face—he couldn't have been more than about eighteen—at hearing a man's voice coming out of what he thought was a woman would have made Lenny laugh in less dangerous circumstances. "Look at you," the would-be thief snarled. "Call yourself a man looking like *that*?"

Lenny bristled at that comment. "This is a Vera Wang, arsehole," he snarled back. "From her Spring 2013 collection. Look at you in your Reebok tracksuit special. Are you going for the Eau de Gangsta look maybe with that dirty hoodie and sweats? Don't give me trouble," Lenny warned. "You need to know you're messing with the wrong guy."

The young man laughed loudly. "Oh yeah? A fag like you in women's clothing is going to kick my arse? I think not, pretty boy." He smirked.

Lenny rolled his eyes at that boldness. "Don't say I didn't warn you, chicken. You want my wallet, come and fucking get it."

It all went downhill from there. The kid launched himself at Lenny, who swiftly dropped his bag (again), sidestepped and struck the kid's bony shoulder with the flat of his hand, shoving the kid to the ground. Lenny's martial arts training may not have been kept up but he still remembered enough to defend himself. With a swift kick, he knocked the knife from the dazed mugger's hand. The weapon went clattering into the road.

The kid struggled to his feet, swearing viciously. He held a large piece of brick in one hand. He cried out as he launched forward again and Lenny avoided the full blow; the corner of the brick caught him a glancing blow on the side of his head. Lenny grew dizzy with a sudden rush of adrenaline. That feeling, coupled with the stabbing pain in his head, made it all too clear what he needed to do next.

The mugger's mistake was stopping to gloat over what he'd done. That split second of proud reflection when he should either have run, having accomplished what he'd set out to do, or beat Lenny senseless so that he was no threat, cost him his nose.

Lenny leapt forward, his right fist connecting, and he distinctly felt the crack beneath his knuckles. The mugger yowled in pain and fell backwards. Lenny stood there, breathing heavily as he watched the young man trying to stem the flow of blood.

"You bathdard! You broke my nothe. You mudderfucking bathdard."

The mugger mewled like a girl, and Lenny winced as he held his hands and rubbed the already swollen and scraped knuckles. He scowled when he saw the blood on his pantsuit.

"Fucker," he muttered. "You've ruined my suit." He reached into his pocket, taking out a handkerchief, holding it against the slow trickle of blood from his head. He stepped away, watching the kid who tried in vain to stop the flow of blood from his nose. "You *were* warned."

By now a small, gaping crowd had formed around them. Lenny had to admit the sight of a man in women's clothing punching another man was probably something to see. He wondered if he'd trend on YouTube. The last thing Lenny needed now was to get arrested for defending himself too vigorously. Brook would have his balls, and not in the way he liked. His breathing was slowing now, his temper lessening. He pulled out his mobile.

"Do you want me to call 999 for you?" he asked, hoping the man would refuse and feeling it was a little bizarre to be offering emergency assistance to a man you'd punched in the face.

The kid's reply was unequivocal. "Fuck you!"

At least that's what it sounded like to Lenny, although it was difficult to hear clearly through the snot and blood.

Lenny shrugged. "Suit yourself. At least I offered."

With one last expletive, the kid looked around, realised he was beaten and high-tailed it down the street as fast as he could go. Lenny watched his departure with a sense of relief. He stood nursing his already swollen and bruised hand and grimaced. He was starting to feel a little guilty about punching the man twice.

"Shall I call the police?" one of the onlookers asked anxiously. "I saw the whole thing. It was self-defence. I mean…" she flushed. "I thought it was a woman he was attacking."

Lenny grinned wryly. "I seem to get that a lot," he said drily. "No, no police on my side. They'll never find him anyway. Other than the bad guy, no one got hurt."

He took details of some of the worried onlookers, in case he needed to call on them later to back up his self-defence story then thanked them and went on his way. His knuckles hurt like hell but he felt quite frisky. He smiled widely as he walked to the tube. He might have to throw his damn pantsuit away but it looked like he'd taught that arsehole a lesson in manners. Dressed as a woman. What a turn up for the books.

***

Brook was sitting reading in the lounge when his lover walked in, and did a double take when he saw the blood-spattered suit. Lenny's wig was off, no doubt stuffed in his satchel. It was the first item he divested of when travelling up in the lift.

"Jesus, Lenny, what the hell happened to you?" He stood up and rushed to his boyfriend's side.

Lenny smiled tiredly. "A mugger tried to rob me." He chuckled. "I won, though." He rolled his shoulder. "Give me a few minutes, love, and I'll tell you all about it. I need to get out of these clothes and into the shower. I feel damn dirty." He disappeared towards the bathroom.

Brook paced the living room in agitation.

This was exactly what I'd feared might happen.

When Lenny walked in, freshly showered and wearing nothing but a pair of sweatpants, Brook pulled him closer for inspection. "Lenny, what the hell happened?"

"Just a random mugging, some little prick seeing a woman and thinking she'd be an easy target."

Brook reached up, touching the now clean wound on the side of Lenny's head. His eyes widened when he saw the scraped and bruised hand. His bones chilled.

"Did you report it to the police?"

Lenny shook his head. "No, love, I didn't. He scarpered. I got the names of the bystanders though in case it goes any further."

Brook opened his mouth to say 'I told you so' in the nicest possible way, but Lenny grinned and laid his fingers on Brook's lips. "I'm fine. And before you say anything, I didn't get mugged because I was a man dressed as a woman. He tried to mug me because he *thought* I was a woman. So the argument you may have been thinking about making holds no water. I'm just glad it happened to me, and not someone who might not have been able to fight back."

"Still, I wish I'd been there to see you kick that bastard to the curb," Brook said through gritted teeth. He admitted the thought of Lenny getting physical and all macho gave him a hard-on of note. "So how is the arsehole?"

Lenny shrugged. "I hit him. I think I broke his nose."

Brook shook his head in disbelief. "I don't believe it. Wasn't anyone around to help you?"

"It was just me and him." Lenny chuckled as he caressed Brook's cheek. "I'm fine, honestly."

Brook frowned but raised a hand to touch the injury tenderly. "It doesn't look as if it needs stitches." He lifted Lenny's hand to his lips.

"Your poor knuckles." He kissed them softly and then looked up in amusement. "Did you have to hit him? Couldn't you have done a Bruce Lee move and shoved him down to the ground?"

Lenny scowled and removed his hand. "The guy was a prick. He deserved it. He had a bloody knife."

Brook's skin chilled. "Hell, babe, it could have been bad. I'm glad you're okay. Little tosser." He heaved a breath. "Is it wrong of me to think it's quite a turn-on, thinking of you fighting like that? It must be that old primal instinct thing: Me man, you man." The relief coursing through his body at the fact Lenny could take care of himself had also lifted a burden that had still owned a little piece of his psyche.

My man is a badass motherfucker. That is so damned sexy.

Lenny regarded Brook thoughtfully. "That sounds like a fairly interesting idea for a next role play," he said. "Perhaps you can give it some thought?" He waved an airy hand. "In the meantime, I have a theory I want to test. It's called 'Using sex to relieve endorphin production in an adult male after encountering danger.' It's pretty scientific. I need a subject to fuck senseless though."

Brook laughed softly as Lenny moved towards him. He was already as hard as a rock in his chinos. It didn't take much where Lenny was concerned. "Mr One Track Mind, that's you. How would you like your 'subject' to be involved, Professor? Have you any particular scenario in mind?" He swallowed, his groin heating up at the thought of what might happen next. The fact they'd both also had their test results and no longer needed condoms was another bright spark in his life and made a real difference to their sex life.

Lenny moved over to the wall panel and pressed the button to let the blinds run across the large open picture windows of the apartment, shutting the twinkling lights of the city. The wall sconces glowed warmly.

"I don't want anyone else involved in our research project," he said huskily as he moved towards Brook. "The last thing we need is a nosy neighbour across the way with long-lens cameras filming what we're about to do." He pulled off his shirt and tossed it onto the couch.

Brook loved the sight of bare-chested Lenny. He was broad shouldered and muscled, and the thatch of blond hair on his chest leading down to what was beneath his jeans was a sight to behold. His tousled, now longer hair glinted in the dim light, his chiselled features softening as he looked at Brook. Lenny gazed into Brook's eyes with sheer despoiling intent before moving swiftly towards Brook and pulling him closer. His hardness pressed into Brook's own as both of them moaned softly. Lenny drew a deep breath as he yanked Brook's shirt out of his trousers and slid his hands into the warmth beneath.

"In answer to your question about the subject—naked, willing and right now," Lenny whispered. As Brook watched his man stalk towards him with predatory eyes, all he could do was swallow and enjoy the fact he was about to get well and truly screwed.

Chapter 18

"And so, my chickens, you all know what the wonderful Dolly Parton had to say about the matter. *'It's a good thing I was born a girl otherwise I'd be a drag queen.'*"

The audience exploded into laughter as Lenny sashayed his way across the stage, coming to stand next to the glamorous Delilah Delish, in a stunning, sequinned gold dress, topped with shoes with heels that could have been used as toothpicks. The couple did their usual bump and grind then Lenny waved out at the crowd as his eyes sought out his boyfriend sitting in the front row. He loved seeing Brook up front, watching him as he performed. It was a special occasion tonight: his and Brook's six-month anniversary, and Brook's birthday had been a few days ago. It was also only a few days to Christmas and the club was packed with holiday cheer and twinkling fairy lights.

Ryan had wanted to do a special gig with Laverne to celebrate, and the evening had been filled with glitter, exploding champagne corks and all manner of go-go boys writhing around the two of them to the beat of Adam Lambert and Lady Gaga. It had been a typical Delilah affair, camp and decadent.

"I'm heading off now, got a sexy evening planned with my man for his birthday celebration." Lenny murmured to Ryan as he licked his lips and blew a kiss at Brook. The catcalls and whistles echoed through the room and Brook stood up, took a bow then sat down again, a smile creasing his handsome face.

"Go get him, tiger," Ryan said from beyond red lipstick lips. "You're a lucky man, my friend."

Ryan's eyes were shadowed. The go-go boys took over the main stage and made another welcome appearance to the rambunctious tune of Adam Lambert's "Strut."

"Have you not heard from Mango yet?" Lenny asked quietly as he smiled at the audience. It was a great opportunity for a breather to talk. Once again Mango Munroe had done a disappearing act, leaving an unhappy Ryan behind.

Ryan waved and mimed a wanking gesture with his polished, red fingernails towards the sexy dancers to the delight of the crowd who roared in appreciation. “No. It’s been over a month and no word. I don’t even know where he bloody went, the bastard.”

Lenny’s heart went out to his suffering friend. “He’ll get in touch soon. He always does, love. Have faith.”

Ryan gave a sardonic snort. “I should forget him, right? Move on. Find someone who’ll commit? I mean, I don’t even have you anymore.”

Lenny sighed as he reached out and hugged his friend. He heard the vulnerability in Ryan’s voice. “You love the man. It’s not that easy. And I know it’s tough, us not being together anymore. You need to find someone who wants to be with you full time, honey. You deserve it.”

Ryan nodded, his eyes distant as he watched the gyrating, half-naked men on stage. “I know.” He huffed softly. “I’m being stupid. Go on, get off and be with your man. He looks lonely down there. And you have somewhere special to be.” His tone was wistful.

In full-blown Delilah Delish mode, Ryan glided to the centre of the stage and held the mike up to his painted lips. “Ladies and gentlemen, say a fond farewell to the lovely and talented Laverne Debussy-Smith. We hope to see her back soon, but for now, she has rather more pressing issues to attend to, if you know what I mean. I’m thinking a lot of press-ups are going to get done tonight.”

To the ribald and good-natured comments of the audience, Lenny waved his goodbye and stepped off stage to the wings. He was walking down the corridor with flickering overhead lights to the changing room he and Ryan shared when he heard a bray of laughter and a voice from someone he knew. He stopped, a smile forming on his face.

Well, well, well. Luck is with me tonight it would seem.

The laughter was coming from an adjacent corridor, one that led into the bowels of the building and down to the basement. Small dressing rooms lined that passage as well. Lenny made a detour and headed straight for the owner of the sound he’d heard.

Tracy Trey leaned against the wall, hair the colour of peppermint. He wore a pair of brightly coloured patchwork trousers, a filmy, silver blouse and a bright yellow military jacket studded with pearl buttons. Three young men, dancers for the show, appeared entranced by his every word as they preened and giggled, faces alight with hero worship.

Lenny thought grimly he was about to burst their bubble by kneeing their idol in the balls.

"Tracy, my darling. How lovely to see you." He strode up to the now white-faced man looking at Laverne with trepidation, and Lenny hoped his smile masked the fury he felt inside. "I think we have something to talk about, my chicken. Or would that be my little mole? Or rat?" He waved at the dancers. "You might like to get rid of the acolytes. I'm sure you wouldn't want them to see this."

Tracy positioned himself behind the three gawking youths. "Laverne, darling, we have nothing to say to each other." He actually flung his fingers out at Lenny as if warding off a bad smell. "I know you think you have an axe to grind with me, but really, can't we simply say it's in the past and put the nastiness behind us?"

Lenny shook his head. "You stole my drawings, Tracy. You should be ashamed of yourself sending that woman to do your dirty work."

Tracy giggled. "You can't prove it, darling. It's all hearsay and that woman is now in the Bahamas completely out of touch."

Lenny glared at the young men surrounding Tracy. They looked rather apprehensive. "I'd suggest you three scarper, and go and tell Ryan I'm about to kick some arse. Then he can pull me off when I get really busy."

Two of them did exactly what he'd suggested, hot-footing it down the corridor. The last one—Laverne thought his name was CoCo—glared defiantly at him.

"You cannot do that to Tracy, Laverne." His French accented voice was musical. "He is my friend and does not deserve his balls to be broken."

Lenny got closer, until he was almost chest-to-chest with Tracy's defender. CoCo's eyes went bigger and he swallowed.

Lenny prodded CoCo's chest with his finger. "Then perhaps I should start with you," he said. "How partial are you to *your* balls? This is a matter between Tracy and me, so sod off, chicken."

CoCo squeaked and scarpered, his pert arse the last thing Laverne saw as he disappeared around the corner.

Tracy looked a little paler than he had but stood his ground. "So, what, you're going to kick me in the nuts? I don't think you have the— *Oof…*"

The next sound coming out of Tracy's mouth was like the noise of a deflating balloon, high-pitched and squealing. He clutched his bruised balls, and his eyes turned up as he fell to his knees, while Lenny watched with interest. Lenny had only kneed him once, not too hard but just enough to be felt.

"That's for stealing from me, you arsehole," he snarled. Tracy's eyes watered and his mouth trembled with pain. "I should give you another one for talking crap about me on television, but I think I'll spare the effort."

Tracy launched himself upright, arms flailing as he tried to smack Lenny in the face. Lenny was taller and stronger so had no problem holding him at bay.

"Bastard," Tracy screeched. "That fucking hurt, you cross-dressing, talentless tranny."

Lenny stared at him in disbelief. "What the hell? What did you just call me, you useless shit for brains?" He grabbed Tracy's arms and wasn't able to avoid the slap to his cheek, as his waving arms found their target of Lenny's face. The sting to his flesh spurred him on and he was about to let loose on Tracy's nether regions and administer yet another soprano-making kick when strong arms pulled him away.

"Babe, leave him. He's not worth it." Brook's amused tone registered with Lenny and he swung around to stare narrowly at his boyfriend.

"Says you. I want to slap his bloody face off—"

Ryan appeared beside Brook, in full Delilah regalia, face creased in laughter as he laid his hand on Lenny's shoulder. "Laverney, enough bitch slapping. God, you two are precious. I could have sold tickets for this and made a fortune."

"Oh God, have you been speaking to Leslie?" Lenny groaned. "Please don't call me that."

He glowered at Tracy who was panting heavily and clutching his groin again. "Fine, count us even. Don't you ever try something like that again or next time I will call the police. And stop trashing me on your stupid TV show or next time I'll meet you round a dark corner and show you what it feels like to have a fist up your arse. Oh, you've probably done that before, in which case I just won't use lube."

He took a deep, righteous breath and reached up to pull off his wig, which had come loose in the fracas. Brook was laughing silently, tears rolling down his face. Lenny stared at him then grinned.

"I'm glad to see you so amused, love. Haven't you ever heard another man offer to fist someone before?"

Brook couldn't speak, simply shook his head as his body continued to shake with laughter. Lenny threw his head back like a diva. "Right, I'm off to my dressing room to clean up. Get rid of the trash please, Ryan. This is your club after all."

He flounced off down the corridor and smiled when he heard the chortles behind him. He'd kicked ass tonight. He was Laverne Debussy-Smith, and may the world quake when they heard her name.

When he entered his small dressing room, the first thing he saw was the biggest bouquet of red roses he'd ever seen sitting on his dressing table. There must have been at least thirty stems sitting in a bronze vase. He actually clasped his hands to his chest dreamily, and as he was doing it, he heard a noise behind him. He turned to see Brook standing in the dimly lit doorway, arms folded across his chest, eyes a little apprehensive. He looked more composed than he'd been, and his face still held the most beautiful smile Lenny had ever seen.

"This is beautiful." Lenny's throat was clogged with emotion. "At least, I hope they're from you."

Brook moved forward and nodded. "So do I." He grinned softly and checked the card. "Yep. They're from some soppy sap called Brook Hunter." He frowned. "Your face is marked. I should go bitch slap the bastard myself for laying a hand on you..."

Lenny reached up, forgetting for that split second he was in full Laverne costume. "Forget him, he's a dick. And thank you for the lovely flowers. Although it's supposed to be *your* birthday, not mine." He kissed Brook, trying to convey everything he felt in that one deep, heart-wrenching press of lips on lips. When they parted, Brook reached up and wiped his lips, looking at the deep pink colour on his dusky fingertips.

"Lipstick. Not a bad taste actually."

Lenny was pulled into a fiercer embrace and this time he was kissed with lips that took his in a fit of passion, in a possessiveness and desire that must have wiped every shred of lipstick he had off his lips. Brook's hands were rough and demanding as he pressed himself against Lenny's body.

He released Lenny and swatted his backside. "There, that gets rid of some of the tension. I think you need it after that catfight. Now hurry up and get changed. We have a ship to catch."

"A ship?" Lenny said, still reeling from the kiss.

Brook chuckled. "Well, a boat. I decided to give your Christmas present a few days early because I can't wait, plus it's our half-year anniversary. I've arranged a quiet romantic dinner for us on the *Princess of Persia.* You, me, our own personal chef and waiter, and a stateroom all of our own. With a hot tub." He waggled his eyebrows.

"I thought we'd agreed to have dinner at Galileo's?" Lenny managed to get out. "How long have you been planning this little excursion?"

Brook shrugged. "A little while. Ryan helped me organise it. He knows the owner of the boat."

The *Princess of Persia* was a luxurious floating restaurant that travelled up and down the Thames and was usually only available to people with too much money or good connections. Lenny supposed they fell into the latter category.

"So get your glad rags on. Make yourself even sexier." He flashed a wicked smile at Lenny and disappeared. Lenny stood, feeling a little shell-shocked. His birthday present to Brook had been a week in Venice for the two of them in a few months' time, plus a wardrobe of four specially designed suits with Brook's very own personal logo: *The Gentleman.* Brook had shown him over and over again how pleased he was with his gift, and Lenny's arse was still sore.

He showered quickly, dressed into his black Hugo Boss linen trousers and slim-fit grey shirt and shoved his feet into black double-buckle monk suede shoes. He checked himself out in the mirror and felt a sense of satisfaction that his 'glad rags' weren't half bad. Lenny picked up his Vivienne Westwood black double-breasted blazer, one of his favourite fashion accessories, and slung it over his shoulder.

"You're a walking fashion plate, baby," he murmured to himself. "That man isn't going to know what hit him."

***

The evening was as perfect as it could be. The *Princess of Persia* was as splendid as Lenny had imagined. The dinner was beyond exquisite and the slow, soft swelling of the water beneath the boat was a welcome lullaby to sitting down and enjoying a hedonistic evening of delights, the biggest of which was Brook.

Lenny's lover was attentive, loving and sexy, taking every opportunity he could to touch Lenny, kiss Lenny, brush against Lenny and drive Lenny insane with desire. When Brook stood up from the beautifully set table and gave him a come-hither grin, Lenny was rampantly ready.

"I think it's time for the hot tub," Brook whispered as his fingers trailed lightly over Lenny's collarbone, eliciting shivers and delicious tingles across his skin. His man deserved the title of King of Teasing tonight. "If you want to follow me…"

The hot tub was located along the corridor in the next section and when Lenny walked in, the room was fragranced with sandalwood, and billows of soft, white steam rose off the heated water. On the side was yet another bottle of champagne and two slim-stemmed glasses.

Without even hesitating, Brook divested himself of all his clothes and slid into the tub, his tight arse a welcome sight. Soon Lenny sat in the deep, heated water, sighing in pleasure and more than a little relief as the warmth soothed his aching cock and arse. For a long while there no sounds, except the bubbling of the water and the hiss of the generator as it powered up and down.

"So, do you want to see what your Christmas present is?" Brook asked.

Lenny opened his eyes and looked at him in amazement. "You mean there's more?"

Brook's eyes danced with anticipation. His boyfriend didn't answer, simply reached out and picked up an envelope lying on the side and handed it to Lenny.

Lenny dried his fingers on his shirt, and opened the envelope. He gasped when he saw what was inside.

"Tickets to New York next year to Fashion Week," he breathed. "And accommodation at The Gramercy Park Hotel. Oh my God, how the hell did you manage that hotel? It's, like, booked up years in advance." He was overwhelmed with love for the man sitting beaming at him.

"I knew you wanted to go, but you hadn't made any plans yet so I thought I'd do it for you. And my boss knows someone at the hotel, so it wasn't a stretch to get him to call in a favour for me." Brook's voice changed; he sounded hesitant. "This is also for you."

He reached underneath his trousers and drew out a small gold box, which he handed to Lenny. With trembling and prune wrinkled fingers, Lenny opened the box and gasped. Inside were two platinum rings. He lost his breath and looked up at Brook, who was smiling at him tremulously.

"Both of us agreed we're not ready for marriage yet, but I wondered if we could have our own promise ceremony tonight. I want to know you're mine completely and that we commit to each other without reservation." His voice thickened. "Lenny James and Laverne Debussy-Smith, will you both accept my ring?"

Lenny couldn't speak. This was so unexpected, so utterly, *fantabulously* mind blowing, that he simply couldn't find the words to express himself. He wanted to yell *yes* at the top of his voice, tell Brook how much he loved him, tell him his man wanted the same thing—yet all he could do was stare at the glinting circles of metal he held in his hand and wonder why his eyes prickled and his heart ached in a good way.

"Lenny? Are you okay? Have I assumed too much? Oh, I have, haven't I? You're not ready for this—"

The panic in Brook's voice spurred Lenny on. "Yes," he breathed out in joy. "Yes, yes, yes."

He found himself with a wet, slippery lap full of man, being kissed to oblivion, and Lenny tried valiantly to push the box he held onto the side of the hot tub before it dropped into the swirling waters.

Brook's cock pressed against his and his head swam from the sensations flooding his being. Contentment, lust, love, an overwhelming sense of well-being and relief at being accepted for who he was without conditions.

"I love you, you know that?" Brook whispered in his ear as he held Lenny's face in between wet hands and gazed at him with such tenderness Lenny almost blubbered. "Every facet of you. Every sexy, manly, wig-wearing, dress-clad facet of you. I am so proud of you, being who you want to be. One day I hope to grow up and be like you." His soft chuckle melted Lenny's bones.

"You're pretty great yourself," Lenny said gruffly, his throat aching with emotion. "I love you too. Happy birthday and anniversary, love. And happy nearly Christmas."

He reached over and picked up one of the rings and motioned to Brook to hold his hand out. Brook gave it to him and Lenny slipped the ring on his left ring finger. Brook gazed down at it, his Adam's apple bobbing then he did the same to Lenny.

They sat, Brook in Lenny's lap, water gurgling around them, and Lenny wondered if he had the same delighted smile on his face as his lover.

Brook nuzzled Lenny's neck and bit his skin softly. "Now we're promised to each other and we've finished being all mushy, it's time to enjoy ourselves." He grinned slyly. "I know you're still sore from the celebrations last night so will you make love to me please?"

Lenny swallowed, his groin uncomfortably hard, and Brook wriggled against him with a smirk. "Is that a yes I feel below me?"

Lenny smiled. "To everything," he murmured. "To you being in my life, to everything we're going to do together, to the way you make me complete. It's a big yes." He reached over and cupped Brook's face. "Thanks for accepting me in every way. I worried I'd never find anyone who'd take us both on. And then you came along and proved me wrong, even if it started out like a bad rom-com."

Brook's face creased in a slow, sweet smile. He wrapped his arms around Lenny's neck. "It's not a hardship. It's my honour to love a man like you, and to be loved back by you."

The kiss they shared went on forever and as they slid against each other's naked bodies, flesh against flesh, tongue on tongue and eager lips against lips, Lenny knew he'd come home. Home to a place where he could be himself.

And as kisses and touches became more intimate and their breathing deepened and the slickness of their skin became more urgent and needy, Lenny gave into his rising emotions and fell delightedly into the depths of Brook.

And somewhere deep inside, Laverne was cheering him on.

www.ingramcontent.com/pod-product-compliance
Lightning Source LLC
LaVergne TN
LVHW050907080826
845145LV00001B/1